A
MISS MARPLE
QUINTET

COLLINS COLLECTOR'S CHOICE

A
MISS MARPLE
QUINTET

THE MURDER AT THE VICARAGE
A MURDER IS ANNOUNCED
A POCKET FULL OF RYE
THE MIRROR CRACK'D FROM
SIDE TO SIDE
AT BERTRAM'S HOTEL

Agatha Christie

COLLINS
St James's Place, London
1978

William Collins Sons & Co Ltd
London · Glasgow · Sydney · Auckland
Toronto · Johannesburg

First published 1978
ISBN 0 00 244490 – 9
Set in Linotype Baskerville
Made and printed in Great Britain by
William Collins Sons & Co Ltd Glasgow

CONTENTS

INTRODUCTION

Miss Marple, best-known of all female sleuths, crept very quietly into the world, aged 74. Of the first novel in which she appeared, *Murder at the Vicarage*, her creator says in her delightful autobiography: 'I cannot remember where, when or how I wrote it, why I came to write it, or even what suggested to me that I should select a new character . . . Certainly at the time I had no intention of continuing her for the rest of my life. I did not know that she was to become a rival to Hercule Poirot.'

The book appeared in 1930, one of the first in a new venture by Collins, her publishers, the Crime Club, a sturdy plant now near its half-century. But Miss Marple had seen print earlier than this. She first starred, in 1928, in a series of six short stories, each based in her own home in the village of St Mary Mead, where in the sitting-room 'with broad black beams across the ceiling . . . furnished with good old furniture that belonged to it' half a dozen friends gather each Tuesday to tell turn and turn about the story of some inexplicable occurence, usually a murder, and invite the others to account for it. To our hand-clapping delight on every occasion the shrewd lawyer, the wise clergyman, the knowing novelist, the observant painter and even the former Commissioner of the Metropolitan Police fail to penetrate to the heart of the mystery but elderly Miss Marple sitting quietly knitting, very upright in her chair, does.

No wonder other stories were called for, eventually to be collected under the title *Thirteen Problems*, and no wonder, too, when Mrs Christie had begun to feel a little fed up with Hercule Poirot – she was to say in a newspaper interview a few years later 'Why – why – why did I ever invent this detestable, bombastic, tiresome little creature?' – she turned for a full-length investigation to this other figure that had sprung from her imagination.

Because Miss Marple is in many ways the direct antithesis of Hercule Poirot. Where, in the words of Mrs Christie's distinguished fellow practitioner, Christianna Brand, 'Poirot is all shine and show-off, Miss Marple is the very pink of self-deprecation.' Where Poirot is a most cunningly collected ragbag of all the odd eccentricities one would expect of a dazzlingly brilliant foreigner, Miss Marple is a single person and a real one, based indeed to some extent on her creator's own grandmother. Real, yet not so real: when it comes to detecting Miss Marple's methods are distinctly not as much of the real, logical world as are those of the Master of the Little Grey Cells. You can see this very clearly if, after reading *The Mirror Crack'd from Side to Side* in this volume, you seek out, or seek out again, a book Mrs Christie wrote almost 30 years earlier, *Lord Edgware Dies*, in which Poirot tackles essentially the same problem.

Miss Marple depends for her astonishing successes on five linked qualities that have little to do with rational deduction. First there is an extensive knowledge of people and the way they behave, springing simply from the fact of her having been around so long and from the hypothesis that the folk in quiet St Mary Mead are not so unlike the men and women of the wider, brasher world. Second comes her frank love of gossip. It is from tittle-tattle, she claims, that she has gained her knowledge of a wide variety of people and their motives, open and hidden. She admits that she may be liable to the charge of having a mind like a sink, but a sink 'is the most necessary thing in any house.'

And from her extensive knowledge of people comes her famous gift for making comparisons. On her very first appearance she recalled a housemaid from one of the bigger places in the neighbourhood, 'thoroughly to be relied upon to turn the mattresses every day – except Fridays, of course' who also proved to be her master's kept woman and thus pointed directly to the Least Likely Person in the mystery then before her. Fourthly, there is intuition. Miss Marple possesses to a high degree that gift, often at its acutest in women, of occasionally zipping straight to an answer – it may even be seen over solving a crossword – without going through the tedious business of ratiocination. And lastly she has, or at least she developed, a nose for evil. She recognises its presence. She once had an aunt, she says, who claimed she could smell when people told lies. She herself falls not far short of that.

This final quality, I say, she developed over the years, and it is a mark of the life that is in her that she did change with changing times. Not for her the fixed formula of a limited character applied over and over again to similar sets of circumstances. No, like Poirot, she knew how to shed constricting facets of herself (the black lace cap she is wearing when first described to us pretty soon quietly disappeared) and how to bring forward more useful ones, as you can see in progressing through the 35 years that separate the first book in this volume from the last. And she accepted the changes in her beloved St Mary Mead too, the changes that reflected our real world. Where in her earliest days when the call to action came she 'put Clara on board wages and sent the plate and the King Charles tankard to the bank' before going a-visiting (and a-solving), in her latter days, as described in *At Bertram's Hotel*, she is able to contemplate with calm the village's new building estate and the up-to-date shop-fronts in its High Street.

But from first to last there is always behind her, as there was behind Poirot, the hand of the all-time master trickster of the detective story. Dame Agatha, thank heavens, was never intellectual; but she was always sharply intelligent. And there are in these five novels examples in plenty brilliantly to deceive you. Her chief methods were two, the verbal and the visual. In choosing a few instances I have deliberately refrained from quoting any of the books herein. I would hate to spoil the wonderful, plain and simple pleasure that an Agatha Christie gives, though perhaps I might just hint that before reading one of the five you should polish up your spelling.

Bue let me find another illustration of the verbal trick to explain it more clearly. Take the story in which, early on, a mother expecting a child says to a newspaper interviewer 'My daughter shall grow up happy and innocent' and when that child is born she names it Evelyn. So, many years later we unsuspicious readers expect a girl called Evelyn to be that child. Yet cunningly we have never been told that the baby born was in fact a boy, a boy named Evelyn. Dame Agatha was a mistress of using our ordinary expectations, what is called the received image, for her own cunning ends.

Essentially the same process occurs with many of her pieces of visual trickery too. Take another famous example. As so often with the early Christies a butler is in play. Poirot asks him if the date on a wall calendar has been torn off since the murder took place. He walks across to the calendar, looks at it and gives his answer. At once the poor mutt of a reader begins furiously to think why that date is significant. But what Mrs Christie was telling us was that the butler was so short-sighted that he had to peer at the calendar, and that thus he is not the totally reliable witness he seems. *Hé voilà!*

So one final piece of advice before you embark on the series of delights ahead: beware of mirrors.

H. R. F. KEATING

THE MURDER
AT
THE VICARAGE

It is difficult to know quite where to begin this story, but I have fixed my choice on a certain Wednesday at luncheon at the Vicarage. The conversation, though in the main irrelevant to the matter in hand, yet contained one or two suggestive incidents which influenced later developments.

I had just finished carving some boiled beef (remarkably tough by the way) and on resuming my seat I remarked, in a spirit most unbecoming to my cloth, that anyone who murdered Colonel Protheroe would be doing the world at large a service.

My young nephew, Dennis, said instantly:

'That'll be remembered against you when the old boy is found bathed in blood. Mary will give evidence, won't you, Mary? And describe how you brandished the carving knife in a vindictive manner.'

Mary, who is in service at the Vicarage as a stepping-stone to better things and higher wages, merely said in a loud, business-like voice, 'Greens,' and thrust a cracked dish at him in a truculent manner.

My wife said in a sympathetic voice: 'Has he been *very* trying?'

I did not reply at once, for Mary, setting the greens on the table with a bang, proceeded to thrust a dish of singularly moist and unpleasant dumplings under my nose. I said, 'No, thank you,' and she deposited the dish with a clatter on the table and left the room.

'It is a pity that I am such a shocking housekeeper,' said my wife, with a tinge of genuine regret in her voice.

I was inclined to agree with her. My wife's name is Griselda – a highly suitable name for a parson's wife. But there the suitability ends. She is not in the least meek.

I have always been of the opinion that a clergyman should be unmarried. Why I should have urged Griselda to marry me at the end of twenty-four hours' acquaintance is a mystery to me. Marriage, I have always held, is a serious affair, to be entered into only after long deliberation and forethought, and suitability of tastes and inclinations is the most important consideration.

Griselda is nearly twenty years younger than myself. She is

most distractingly pretty and quite incapable of taking anything seriously. She is incompetent in every way, and extremely trying to live with. She treats the parish as a kind of huge joke arranged for her amusement. I have endeavoured to form her mind and failed. I am more than ever convinced that celibacy is desirable for the clergy. I have frequently hinted as much to Griselda, but she has only laughed.

'My dear,' I said, 'If you would only exercise a little care—'

'I do sometimes,' said Griselda. 'But, on the whole, I think things go worse when I'm trying. I'm evidently *not* a housekeeper by nature. I find it better to leave things to Mary and just make up my mind to be uncomfortable and have nasty things to eat.'

'And what about your husband, my dear?' I said reproachfully, and proceeding to follow the example of the devil in quoting Scripture for his own ends I added: 'She looketh to the ways of her household . . .'

'Think how lucky you are not to be torn to pieces by lions,' said Griselda, quickly interrupting. 'Or burnt at the stake. Bad food and lots of dust and dead wasps is really nothing to make a fuss about. Tell me more about Colonel Protheroe. At any rate the early Christians were lucky enough not to have churchwardens.'

'Pompous old brute,' said Dennis. 'No wonder his first wife ran away from him.'

'I don't see what else she could do,' said my wife.

'Griselda,' I said sharply. 'I will not have you speaking in that way.'

'Darling,' said my wife affectionately. 'Tell me about him. What was the trouble? Was it Mr Hawes's becking and nodding and crossing himself every other minute?'

Hawes is our new curate. He has been with us just over three weeks. He has High Church views and fasts on Fridays. Colonel Protheroe is a great opposer of ritual in any form.

'Not this time. He did touch on it in passing. No, the whole trouble arose out of Mrs Price Ridley's wrenched pound note.'

Mrs Price Ridley is a devout member of my congregation. Attending early service on the anniversary of her son's death, she put a pound note into the offertory bag. Later, reading the amount of the collection posted up, she was pained to observe that one ten-shilling note was the highest item mentioned.

She complained to me about it, and I pointed out, very reasonably, that she must have made a mistake.

'We're none of us so young as we were,' I said, trying to turn it off tactfully. 'And we must pay the penalty of advancing years.'

Strangely enough, my words only seemed to incense her further. She said that things had a very odd look and that she was surprised I didn't think so also. And she flounced away and, I gather, took her troubles to Colonel Protheroe. Protheroe is the kind of man who enjoys making a fuss on every conceivable occasion. He made a fuss. It is a pity he made it on a Wednesday. I teach in the Church Day School on Wednesday mornings, a proceeding that causes me acute nervousness and leaves me unsettled for the rest of the day.

'Well, I suppose he must have some fun,' said my wife, with the air of trying to sum up the position impartially. 'Nobody flutters round him and calls him the dear vicar, and embroiders awful slippers for him, and gives him bedsocks for Christmas. Both his wife and his daughter are fed up to the teeth with him. I suppose it makes him happy to feel important somewhere.'

'He needn't be offensive about it,' I said with some heat. 'I don't think he quite realized the implications of what he was saying. He wants to go over all the Church accounts – in case of defalcations – that was the word he used. Defalcations! Does he suspect me of embezzling the Church funds?'

'Nobody would suspect you of anything, darling,' said Griselda. 'You're so transparently above suspicion that really it would be a marvellous opportunity. I wish you'd embezzle the SPG funds. I hate missionaries – I always have.'

I would have reproved her for that sentiment, but Mary entered at that moment with a partially cooked rice pudding. I made a mild protest, but Griselda said that the Japanese always ate half-cooked rice and had marvellous brains in consequence.

'I dare say,' she said, 'that if you had a rice pudding like this every day till Sunday, you'd preach the most marvellous sermon.'

'Heaven forbid,' I said with a shudder.

'Protheroe's coming over tomorrow evening and we're going over the accounts together,' I went on. 'I must finish preparing my talk for the CEMS today. Looking up a reference, I became so engrossed in Canon Shirley's *Reality* that I haven't got on as well as I should. What are you doing this afternoon, Griselda?'

'My duty,' said Griselda. 'My duty as the Vicaress. Tea and scandal at four-thirty.'

'Who is coming?'

Griselda ticked them off on her fingers with a glow of virtue on her face.

'Mrs Price Ridley, Miss Wetherby, Miss Hartnell, and that terrible Miss Marple.'

'I rather like Miss Marple,' I said. 'She has, at least, a sense of humour.'

'She's the worst cat in the village,' said Griselda. 'And she always knows every single thing that happens – and draws the worst inferences from it.'

Griselda, as I have said, is much younger than I am. At my time of life, one knows that the worst is usually true.

'Well, don't expect *me* in for tea, Griselda,' said Dennis.

'Beast!' said Griselda.

'Yes, but look here, the Protheroes really *did* ask me for tennis today.'

'Beast!' said Griselda again.

Dennis beat a prudent retreat and Griselda and I went together into my study.

'I wonder what we shall have for tea,' said Griselda, seating herself on my writing-table. 'Dr Stone and Miss Cram, I suppose, and perhaps Mrs Lestrange. By the way, I called on her yesterday, but she was out. Yes, I'm sure we shall have Mrs Lestrange for tea. It's so mysterious, isn't it, her arriving like this and taking a house down here, and hardly ever going outside it? Makes one think of detective stories. You know – "*Who was she, the mysterious woman with the pale, beautiful face? What was her past history? Nobody knew. There was something faintly sinister about her.*" I believe Dr Haydock knows something about her.'

'You read too many detective stories, Griselda, I observed mildly.

'What about you?' she retorted. 'I was looking everywhere for *The Stain on the Stairs* the other day when you were in here writing a sermon. And at last I came in to ask you if you'd seen it anywhere, and what did I find?'

I had the grace to blush.

'I picked it up at random. A chance sentence caught my eye and—'

'I know those chance sentences,' said Griselda. She quoted impressively, ' "*And then a very curious thing happened – Griselda rose, crossed the room and kissed her elderly husband affectionately.*" ' She suited the action to the word.

'Is that a very curious thing?' I inquired.

'Of course it is,' said Griselda. 'Do you realize, Len, that I might have married a Cabinet Minister, a Baronet, a rich

Company Promoter, three subalterns and a ne'er-do-weel with attractive manners, and that instead I chose you? Didn't it astonish you very much?'

'At the time it did,' I replied. 'I have often wondered why you did it.'

Griselda laughed.

'It made me feel so powerful,' she murmured. 'The others thought me simply wonderful and of course it would have been very nice for *them* to have *me*. But I'm everything you most dislike and disapprove of, and yet you couldn't withstand me! My vanity couldn't hold out against that. It's so much nicer to be a secret and delightful sin to anybody than to be a feather in their cap. I make you frightfully uncomfortable and stir you up the wrong way the whole time, and yet you adore me madly. You adore me madly, don't you?'

'Naturally I am very fond of you, my dear.'

'Oh! Len, you adore me. Do you remember that day when I stayed up in town and sent you a wire you never got because the postmistress's sister was having twins and she forgot to send it round? The state you got into and you telephoned Scotland Yard and made the most frightful fuss.'

There are things one hates being reminded of. I had really been strangely foolish on the occasion in question. I said:

'If you don't mind, dear, I want to get on with the CEMS.'

Griselda gave a sigh of intense irritation, ruffled my hair up on end, smoothed it down again, said:

'You don't deserve me. You really don't. I'll have an affair with the artist. I will – really and truly. And then think of the scandal in the parish.'

'There's a good deal already,' I said mildly.

Griselda laughed, blew me a kiss, and departed through the window.

2

Griselda is a very irritating woman. On leaving the luncheon table, I had felt myself to be in a good mood for preparing a really forceful address for the Church of England Men's Society. Now I felt restless and disturbed.

Just when I was really settling down to it, Lettice Protheroe drifted in.

I use the word drifted advisedly. I have read novels in which young people are described as bursting with energy – *joie de vivre*, the magnificent vitality of youth . . . Personally, all the young people I come across have the air of animal wraiths.

Lettice was particularly wraith-like this afternoon. She is a pretty girl, very tall and fair and completely vague. She drifted through the French window, absently pulled off the yellow beret she was wearing and murmured vaguely with a kind of far-away surprise: 'Oh! it's you.'

There is a path from Old Hall through the woods which comes out by our garden gate, so that most people coming from there come in at that gate and up to the study window instead of going a long way round by the road and coming to the front door. I was not surprised at Lettice coming in this way, but I did a little resent her attitude.

If you come to a Vicarage, you ought to be prepared to find a Vicar.

She came in and collapsed in a crumpled heap in one of my big arm-chairs. She plucked aimlessly at her hair, staring at the ceiling.

'Is Dennis anywhere about?'

'I haven't seen him since lunch. I understood he was going to play tennis at your place.'

'Oh!' said Lettice. 'I hope he isn't. He won't find anybody there.'

'He said you asked him.'

'I believe I did. Only that was Friday. And today's Tuesday.'

'It's Wednesday,' I said.

'Oh! how dreadful,' said Lettice. 'That means that I've forgotten to go to lunch with some people for the third time.'

Fortunately it didn't seem to worry her much.

'Is Griselda anywhere about?'

'I expect you'll find her in the studio in the garden – sitting to Lawrence Redding.'

'There's been quite a shemozzle about him,' said Lettice. 'With father, you know. Father's dreadful.'

'What was the she— whatever it was about?' I inquired.

'About his painting me. Father found out about it. Why shouldn't I be painted in my bathing dress? If I go on a beach in it, why shouldn't I be painted in it?'

Lettice paused and then went on.

'It's really absurd – father forbidding a young man the house. Of course, Lawrence and I simply shriek about it. I shall come and be done here in your studio.'

'No, my dear,' I said. 'Not if your father forbids it.'

'Oh! dear,' said Lettice, sighing. 'How tiresome everyone is. I feel shattered. Definitely. If only I had some money I'd go away, but without it I can't. If only father would be decent and die, I should be all right.'

'You must not say things like that, Lettice.'

'Well, if he doesn't want me to want him to die, he shouldn't be so horrible over money. I don't wonder mother left him. Do you know, for years I believed she was dead. What sort of a young man did she run away with? Was he nice?'

'It was before your father came to live here.'

'I wonder what's become of her. I expect Anne will have an affair with someone soon. Anne hates me – she's quite decent to me, but she hates me. She's getting old and she doesn't like it. That's the age you break out, you know.'

I wondered if Lettice was going to spend the entire afternoon in my study.

'You haven't seen my gramophone records, have you?' she asked.

'No.'

'How tiresome. I know I've left them somewhere. And I've lost the dog. And my wrist watch is somewhere, only it doesn't much matter because it won't go. Oh! dear, I am so sleepy. I can't think why, because I didn't get up till eleven. But life's very shattering, don't you think? Oh! dear, I must go. I'm going to see Dr Stone's barrow at three o'clock.'

I glanced at the clock and remarked that it was now five-and-twenty to four.

'Oh! is it? How dreadful. I wonder if they've waited or if they've gone without me. I suppose I'd better go down and do something about it.'

She got up and drifted out again, murmuring over her shoulder:

'You'll tell Dennis, won't you?'

I said 'Yes' mechanically, only realizing too late that I had no idea what it was I was to tell Dennis. But I reflected that in all probability it did not matter. I fell to cogitating on the subject of Dr Stone, a well-known archæologist who had recently come to stay at the Blue Boar, whilst he superintended the excavation of a barrow situated on Colonel Protheroe's property. There had already been several disputes between him and the Colonel. I was amused at his appointment to take Lettice to see the operations.

It occurred to me that Lettice Protheroe was something of a minx. I wondered how she would get on with the archæologist's secretary, Miss Cram. Miss Cram is a healthy young woman of twenty-five, noisy in manner, with a high colour, fine animal spirits and a mouth that always seems to have more than its full share of teeth.

Village opinion is divided as to whether she is no better than she should be, or else a young woman of iron virtue who purposes to become Mrs Stone at an early opportunity. She is in every way a great contrast to Lettice.

I could imagine that the state of things at Old Hall might not be too happy. Colonel Protheroe had married again some five years previously. The second Mrs Protheroe was a remarkably handsome woman in a rather unusual style. I had always guessed that the relations between her and her stepdaughter were not too happy.

I had one more interruption. This time, it was my curate, Hawes. He wanted to know the details of my interview with Protheroe. I told him that the colonel had deplored his 'Romish tendencies' but that the real purpose of his visit had been on quite another matter. At the same time, I entered a protest of my own, and told him plainly that he must conform to my ruling. On the whole, he took my remarks very well.

I felt rather remorseful when he had gone for not liking him better. These irrational likes and dislikes that one takes to people are, I am sure, very unchristian.

With a sigh, I realized that the hands of the clock on my writing-table pointed to a quarter to five, a sign that it was really half-past four, and I made my way to the drawing-room.

Four of my parishioners were assembled there with teacups. Griselda sat behind the tea table trying to look natural in her environment, but only succeeded in looking more out of place than usual.

I shook hands all round and sat down between Miss Marple and Miss Wetherby.

Miss Marple is a white-haired old lady with a gentle, appealing manner – Miss Wetherby is a mixture of vinegar and gush. Of the two Miss Marple is much the more dangerous.

'We were just talking,' said Griselda in a honeysweet voice, 'about Dr Stone and Miss Cram.'

A ribald rhyme concocted by Dennis shot through my head.

'Miss Cram doesn't give a damn.'

I had a sudden yearning to say it out loud and observe the effect, but fortunately I refrained. Miss Wetherby said tersely:

'No nice girl would do it,' and shut her thin lips disapprovingly.

'Do what?' I inquired.

'Be a secretary to an unmarried man,' said Miss Wetherby in a horrified tone.

'Oh! my dear,' said Miss Marple. '*I* think married ones are the worst. Remember poor Mollie Carter.'

'Married men living apart from their wives are, of course, notorious,' said Miss Wetherby.

'And even some of the ones living with their wives,' murmured Miss Marple. 'I remember—'

I interrupted these unsavoury reminiscences.

'But surely,' I said, 'in these days a girl can take a post in just the same way as a man does.'

'To come away to the country? And stay at the same hotel?' said Mrs Price Ridley in a severe voice.

Miss Wetherby murmured to Miss Marple in a low voice. 'And all the bedrooms on the same floor . . .'

Miss Hartnell, who is weather-beaten and jolly and much dreaded by the poor, observed in a loud, hearty voice:

'The poor man will be caught before he knows where he is. He's as innocent as a babe unborn, you can see that.'

Curious what turns of phrase we employ. None of the ladies present would have dreamed of alluding to an actual baby till it was safely in the cradle, visible to all.

'Disgusting, I call it,' continued Miss Hartnell, with her usual tactlessness. 'The man must be at least twenty-five years older than she is.'

Three female voices rose at once making disconnected remarks about the Choirboys' Outing, the regrettable incident at the last Mothers' Meeting, and the draughts in the church. Miss Marple twinkled at Griselda.

'Don't you think,' said my wife, 'that Miss Cram may just like having an interesting job? And that she considers Dr Stone just as an employer?'

There was a silence. Evidently none of the four ladies agreed. Miss Marple broke the silence by patting Griselda on the arm.

'My dear,' she said, 'you are very young. The young have such innocent minds.'

Griselda said indignantly that she hadn't got at all an innocent mind.

'Naturally,' said Miss Marple, unheeding of the protest, 'you think the best of everyone.'

'Do you really think she wants to marry that bald-headed dull man?'

'I understand he is quite well off,' said Miss Marple. 'Rather a violent temper, I'm afraid. He had quite a serious quarrel with Colonel Protheroe the other day.'

Everyone leaned forward interestedly.

'Colonel Protheroe accused him of being an ignoramus.'

'How like Colonel Protheroe, and how absurd,' said Mrs Price Ridley.

'Very like Colonel Protheroe, but I don't know about it being absurd,' said Miss Marple. 'You remember the woman who came down here and said she represented Welfare, and after taking subscriptions she was never heard of again and proved to have nothing whatever to do with Welfare. One is so inclined to be trusting and take people at their own valuation.'

I should never have dreamed of describing Miss Marple as trusting.

'There's been some fuss about that young artist, Mr Redding, hasn't there?' asked Miss Wetherby.

Miss Marple nodded.

'Colonel Protheroe turned him out of the house. It appears he was painting Lettice in her bathing dress.'

'I always *thought* there was something between them,' said Mrs Price Ridley. 'That young fellow is always mouching off up there. Pity the girl hasn't got a mother. A stepmother is never the same thing.'

'I dare say Mrs Protheroe does her best,' said Miss Hartnell.

'Girls are so sly,' deplored Mrs Price Ridley.

'Quite a romance, isn't it?' said the softer-hearted Miss Wetherby. 'He's a very good-looking young fellow.'

'But loose,' said Miss Hartnell. 'Bound to be. An artist! Paris! Models! The Altogether!'

'Painting her in her bathing dress,' said Mrs Price Ridley. 'Not quite nice.'

'He's painting me too,' said Griselda.

'But not in your bathing dress, dear,' said Miss Marple.

'It might be worse,' said Griselda solemnly.

'Naughty girl,' said Miss Hartnell, taking the joke broad-mindedly. Everybody else looked slightly shocked.

'Did dear Lettice tell you of the trouble?' asked Miss Marple of me.

'Tell me?'

'Yes. I saw her pass through the garden and go round to the study window.'

Miss Marple always sees everything. Gardening is as good as a smoke screen, and the habit of observing birds through powerful glasses can always be turned to account.

'She mentioned it, yes,' I admitted.

'Mr Hawes looked worried,' said Miss Marple. 'I hope he hasn't been working too hard.'

'Oh!' cried Miss Wetherby excitedly. 'I quite forgot. I knew I had some news for you. I saw Dr Haydock coming out of Mrs Lestrange's cottage.'

Everyone looked at each other.

'Perhaps she's ill,' suggested Mrs Price Ridley.

'It must have been very sudden, if so,' said Miss Hartnell. 'For I saw her walking round her garden at three o'clock this afternoon, and she seemed in perfect health.'

'She and Dr Haydock must be old acquaintances,' said Mrs Price Ridley. 'He's been very quiet about it.'

'It's curious,' said Miss Wetherby, 'that he's never *mentioned* it.'

'As a matter of fact—' said Griselda in a low, mysterious voice, and stopped. Everyone leaned forward excitedly.

'I happen to *know*,' said Griselda impressively. 'Her husband was a missionary. Terrible story. *He was eaten*, you know. Actually eaten. And she was forced to become the chief's head wife. Dr Haydock was with an expedition and rescued her.'

For a moment excitement was rife, then Miss Marple said reproachfully, but with a smile: 'Naughty girl!'

She tapped Griselda reprovingly on the arm.

'Very unwise thing to do, my dear. If you make up these things, people are quite likely to believe them. And sometimes that leads to complications.'

A distinct frost had come over the assembly. Two of the ladies rose to take their departure.

'I wonder if there *is* anything between young Lawrence Redding and Lettice Protheroe,' said Miss Wetherby. 'It certainly looks like it. What do you think, Miss Marple?'

Miss Marple seemed thoughtful.

'I shouldn't have said so myself. Not *Lettice*. *Quite* another person I should have said.'

'But Colonel Protheroe must have thought—'

'He has always struck me as rather a stupid man,' said Miss Marple. 'The kind of man who gets the wrong idea into his head and is obstinate about it. Do you remember Joe Bucknell who used to keep the Blue Boar? Such a to-do about his daughter carrying on with young Bailey. And all the time it was that minx of a wife of his.'

She was looking full at Griselda as she spoke, and I suddenly felt a wild surge of anger.

'Don't you think, Miss Marple,' I said, 'that we're all inclined to let our tongues run away with us too much. Charity thinketh no evil, you know. Inestimable harm may be done by foolish wagging of tongues in ill-natured gossip.'

'Dear vicar, said Miss Marple, 'you are so unworldly. I'm afraid that observing human nature for as long as I have done, one gets not to expect very much from it. I dare say the idle tittle-tattle is very wrong and unkind, but it is so often true, isn't it?'

That last Parthian shot went home.

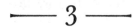

3

'Nasty old cat,' said Griselda, as soon as the door was closed.

She made a face in the direction of the departing visitors and then looked at me and laughed.

'Len, do you really suspect me of having an affair with Lawrence Redding?'

'My dear, of course not.'

'But you thought Miss Marple was hinting at it. And you rose to my defence simply beautifully. Like – like an angry tiger.'

A momentary uneasiness assailed me. A clergyman of the Church of England ought never to put himself in the position of being described as an angry tiger.

'I felt the occasion could not pass without a protest,' I said. 'But Griselda, I wish you would be a little more careful in what you say.'

'Do you mean the cannibal story?' she asked. 'Or the suggestion that Lawrence was painting me in the nude! If they only knew that he was painting me in a thick cloak with a very high fur collar – the sort of thing that you could go quite purely to see the Pope in – not a bit of sinful flesh showing anywhere! In fact, it's all marvellously pure. Lawrence never even attempts to make love to me – I can't think why.'

'Surely, knowing that you're a married woman—'

'Don't pretend to come out of the ark, Len. You know very well that an attractive young woman with an elderly husband is a kind of gift from heaven to a young man. There must be some other reason – it's not that I'm unattractive – I'm not.'

'Surely you don't want him to make love to you?'

'N-n-o,' said Griselda, with more hesitation than I thought becoming.

'If he's in love with Lettice Protheroe—'

'Miss Marple didn't seem to think he was.'

'Miss Marple may be mistaken.

'She never is. That kind of old cat is always right.' She paused a minute and then said, with a quick sidelong glance at me: 'You do believe me, don't you? I mean, that there's nothing between Lawrence and me.'

'My dear Griselda,' I said, surprised. 'Of course.'

My wife came across and kissed me.

'I wish you weren't so terribly easy to deceive, Len. You'd believe me whatever I said.'

'I should hope so. But, my dear, I do beg of you to guard your tongue and be careful what you say. These women are singularly deficient in humour, remember, and take everything seriously.'

'What they need,' said Griselda, 'is a little immorality in their lives. Then they wouldn't be so busy looking for it in other people's.'

And on this she left the room, and glancing at my watch I hurried out to pay some visits that ought to have been made earlier in the day.

The Wednesday evening service was sparsely attended as usual, but when I came out through the church, after disrobing in the vestry, it was empty save for a woman who stood staring up at one of our windows. We have some rather fine old stained glass, and indeed the church itself is well worth looking at. She turned at my footsteps, and I saw that it was Mrs Lestrange.

We both hesitated a moment, and then I said:

'I hope you like our little church.'

'I've been admiring the screen,' she said.

Her voice was pleasant, low, yet very distinct, with a clear-cut enunciation. She added:

'I'm so sorry to have missed your wife yesterday.'

We talked a few minutes longer about the church. She was evidently a cultured woman who knew something of Church history and architecture. We left the building together and walked down the road, since one way to the Vicarage led past her house. As we arrived at the gate, she said pleasantly:

'Come in, won't you? And tell me what you think of what I have done.'

I accepted the invitation. Little Gates had formerly belonged to an Anglo-Indian colonel, and I could not help feeling relieved by the disappearance of the brass tables and Burmese idols. It was furnished now very simply, but in exquisite taste. There was a sense of harmony and rest about it.

Yet I wondered more and more what had brought such a woman as Mrs Lestrange to St Mary Mead. She was so very clearly a woman of the world that it seemed a strange taste to bury herself in a country village.

In the clear light of her drawing-room I had an opportunity of observing her closely for the first time.

She was a very tall woman. Her hair was gold with a tinge of red in it. Her eyebrows and eyelashes were dark, whether by art or by nature I could not decide. If she was, as I thought, made up, it was done very artistically. There was something Sphinxlike about her face when it was in repose and she had the most curious eyes I have ever seen – they were almost golden in shade.

Her clothes were perfect and she had all the ease of manner of a well-bred woman, and yet there was something about her that was incongruous and baffling. You felt that she was a mystery. The word Griselda had used occurred to me – *sinister*. Absurd, of course, and yet – was it so absurd? The thought sprang unbidden into my mind: 'This woman would stick at nothing.'

Our talk was on most normal lines – pictures, books, old churches. Yet somehow I got very strongly the impression that there was something else – something of quite a different nature that Mrs Lestrange wanted to say to me.

I caught her eyes on me once or twice, looking at me with a curious hesitancy, as though she were unable to make up her mind. She kept the talk, I noticed, strictly to impersonal subjects. She made no mention of a husband or of friends or relations.

But all the time there was that strange urgent appeal in her glance. It seemed to say: 'Shall I tell you? I want to. Can't you help me?'

Yet in the end it died away – or perhaps it had all been my fancy. I had the feeling that I was being dismissed. I rose and took my leave. As I went out of the room, I glanced back and saw her staring after me with a puzzled, doubtful expression. On an impulse I came back:

'If there is anything I can do—'

She said doubtfully: 'It's very kind of you—'

We were both silent. Then she said:

'I wish I knew. It's very difficult. No, I don't think anyone can help me. But thank you for offering to do so.'

That seemed final, so I went. But as I did so, I wondered. We are not used to mysteries in St Mary Mead.

So much is this the case that as I emerged from the gate I was pounced upon. Miss Hartnell is very good at pouncing in a heavy and cumbrous way.

'I saw you!' she exclaimed with ponderous humour. 'And I *was* so excited. Now can you tell us all about it.'

'About what?'

'The mysterious lady! Is she a widow or has she a husband somewhere?'

'I really couldn't say. She didn't tell me.'

'How very peculiar. One would think she would be certain to mention something casually. It almost looks, doesn't it, as though she had a reason for not speaking?'

'I really don't see that.'

'Ah! but as dear Miss Marple says, you are so unworldly, dear vicar. Tell me, has she known Dr Haydock long?'

'She didn't mention him, so I don't know.'

'Really? But what did you talk about then?'

'Pictures, music, books,' I said truthfully.

Miss Hartnell, whose only topics of conversation are the purely personal, looked suspicious and unbelieving. Taking advantage of a momentary hesitation on her part as to how to proceed next, I bade her good night and walked rapidly away.

I called in at a house farther down the village and returned to the Vicarage by the garden gate, passing, as I did so, the danger point of Miss Marple's garden. However, I did not see how it was humanly possible for the news of my visit to Mrs Lestrange to have yet reached her ears, so I felt reasonably safe.

As I latched the gate, it occurred to me that I would just step down to the shed in the garden which young Lawrence Redding

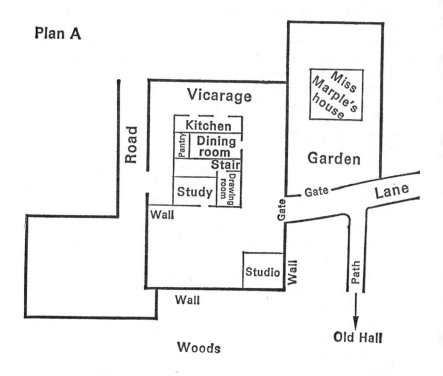

Plan A

was using as a studio, and see for myself how Griselda's portrait was progressing.

I append a rough sketch here which will be useful in the light of after happenings, only sketching in such details as are necessary.

I had no idea there was anyone in the studio. There had been no voices from within to warn me, and I suppose that my own footsteps made no noise upon the grass.

I opened the door and then stopped awkwardly on the threshold. For there were two people in the studio, and the man's arms were round the woman and he was kissing her passionately.

The two people were the artist, Lawrence Redding, and Mrs Protheroe.

I backed out precipitately and beat a retreat to my study. There I sat down in a chair, took out my pipe, and thought things over. The discovery had come as a great shock to me. Especially since my conversation with Lettice that afternoon, I had felt fairly certain that there was some kind of understanding growing up between her and the young man. Moreover, I was convinced that she herself thought so. I felt positive that she had no idea of the artist's feelings for her stepmother.

A nasty tangle. I paid a grudging tribute to Miss Marple. She had not been deceived but had evidently suspected the true state of things with a fair amount of accuracy. I had entirely misread her meaning glance at Griselda.

I had never dreamed of considering Mrs Protheroe in the matter. There has always been rather a suggestion of Cæsar's wife about Mrs Protheroe – a quiet, self-contained woman whom one would not suspect of any great depths of feeling.

I had got to this point in my meditations when a tap on my study window aroused me. I got up and went to it. Mrs Protheroe was standing outside. I opened the window and she came in, not waiting for an invitation on my part. She crossed the room in a breathless sort of way and dropped down on the sofa.

I had the feeling that I had never really seen her before. The quiet self-contained woman that I knew had vanished. In her place was a quick-breathing, desperate creature. For the first time I realized that Anne Protheroe was beautiful.

She was a brown-haired woman with a pale face and very deep set grey eyes. She was flushed now and her breast heaved. It was as though a statue had suddenly come to life. I blinked my eyes at the transformation.

'I thought it best to come,' she said. 'You – you saw just now?' I bowed my head.

She said very quietly: 'We love each other . . .'

And even in the middle of her evident distress and agitation she could not keep a little smile from her lips. The smile of a woman who sees something very beautiful and wonderful.

I still said nothing, and she added presently:

'I suppose to you that seems very wrong?'

'Can you expect me to say anything else, Mrs Protheroe?'

'No – no, I suppose not.'

I went on, trying to make my voice as gentle as possible:

'You are a married woman—'

She interrupted me.

'Oh! I know – I know. Do you think I haven't gone over all that again and again? I'm not a bad woman really – I'm not. And things aren't – aren't – as you might think they are.'

I said gravely: 'I'm glad of that.'

She asked rather timorously:

'Are you going to tell my husband?'

I said rather dryly:

'There seems to be a general idea that a clergyman is incapable of behaving like a gentleman. That is not true.'

She threw me a grateful glance.

'I'm so unhappy. Oh! I'm so dreadfully unhappy. I can't go on. I simply can't go on. And I dont know what to do.' Her voice rose with a slightly hysterical note in it. 'You don't know what my life is like. I've been miserable with Lucius from the beginning. No woman could be happy with him. I wish he were dead . . . It's awful, but I do . . . I'm desperate. I tell you, I'm desperate.' She started and looked over at the window.

'What was that? I thought I heard someone? Perhaps it's Lawrence.'

I went over to the window which I had not closed as I had thought. I stepped out and looked down the garden, but there was no one in sight. Yet I was almost convinced that I, too, had heard someone. Or perhaps it was her certainty that had convinced me.

When I re-entered the room she was leaning forward, drooping her head down. She looked the picture of despair. She said again:

'I don't know what to do. I don't know what to do.'

I came and sat down beside her. I said the things I thought it was my duty to say, and tried to say them with the necessary conviction, uneasily conscious all the time that that same morning I had given voice to the sentiment that a world without Colonel Protheroe in it would be improved for the better.

Above all, I begged her to do nothing rash. To leave her home and her husband was a very serious step.

I don't suppose I convinced her. I have lived long enough in the world to know that arguing with anyone in love is next door to useless, but I do think my words brought to her some measure of comfort.

When she rose to go, she thanked me, and promised to think over what I had said.

Nevertheless, when she had gone, I felt very uneasy. I felt that hitherto I had misjudged Anne Protheroe's character. She impressed me now as a very desperate woman, the kind of woman who would stick at nothing once her emotions were aroused. And she was desperately, wildly, madly in love with Lawrence Redding, a man several years younger than herself. I didn't like it.

—— 4 ——

I had entirely forgotten that we had asked Lawrence Redding to dinner that night. When Griselda burst in and scolded me, pointing out that it lacked two minutes to dinner time, I was quite taken aback.

'I hope everything will be all right,' Griselda called up the stairs after me. 'I've thought over what you said at lunch, and I've really thought of some quite good things to eat.'

I may say, in passing, that our evening meal amply bore out Griselda's assertion that things went much worse when she tried than when she didn't. The menu was ambitious in conception, and Mary seemed to have taken a perverse pleasure in seeing how best she could alternate undercooking and overcooking. Some oysters which Griselda had ordered, and which would seem to be beyond the reach of incompetence, we were, unfortunately, not able to sample as we had nothing in the house to open them with – an omission which was discovered only when the moment for eating them arrived.

I had rather doubted whether Lawrence Redding would put in an appearance. He might very easily have sent an excuse.

However, he arrived punctually enough, and the four of us went in to dinner.

Lawrence Redding has an undeniably attractive personality. He is, I suppose, about thirty years of age. He has dark hair, but his eyes are of a brilliant, almost startling blue. He is the kind of young man who does everything well. He is good at games, an excellent shot, a good amateur actor, and can tell a first-rate story. He is capable of making any party go. He has, I think, Irish blood in his viens. He is not, at all, one's idea of the typical artist. Yet I believe he is a clever painter in the modern style. I know very little of painting myself.

It was only natural that on this particular evening he should appear a shade *distrait*. On the whole, he carried off things very well. I don't think Griselda or Dennis noticed anything wrong. Probably I should not have noticed anything myself if I had not known beforehand.

Griselda and Dennis were particularly gay – full of jokes about Dr Stone and Miss Cram – the Local Scandal! It suddenly came home to me with something of a pang that Dennis

29

is nearer Griselda's age than I am. He calls me Uncle Len, but her Griselda. It gave me, somehow, a lonely feeling.

I must, I think, have been upset by Mrs Protheroe. I'm not usually given to such unprofitable reflections.

Griselda and Dennis went rather far now and then, but I hadn't the heart to check them. I have always thought it a pity that the mere presence of a clergyman should have a damping effect.

Lawrence took a gay part in the conversation. Nevertheless I was aware of his eyes continually straying to where I sat, and I was not surprised when after dinner he manœuvred to get me into the study.

As soon as we were alone his manner changed.

'You've surprised our secret, sir,' he said. 'What are you going to do about it?'

I could speak far more plainly to Redding than I could to Mrs Protheroe, and I did so. He took it very well.

'Of course,' he said, when I had finished, 'you're bound to say all this. You're a parson. I don't mean that in any way offensively. As a matter of fact I think you're probably right. But this isn't the usual sort of thing between Anne and me.'

I told him that people had been saying that particular phrase since the dawn of time, and a queer little smile creased his lips.

'You mean everyone thinks their case is unique? Perhaps so. But one thing you must believe.'

He assured me that so far – 'there was nothing wrong in it.' Anne, he said, was one of the truest and most loyal women that ever lived. What was going to happen he didn't know.

'If this were only a book,' he said gloomily, 'the old man would die – and a good riddance to everybody.'

I reproved him.

'Oh! I didn't mean I was going to stick him in the back with a knife, though I'd offer my best thanks to anyone else who did so. There's not a soul in the world who's got a good word to say for him. I rather wonder the first Mrs Protheroe didn't do him in. I met her once, years ago, and she looked quite capable of it. One of those calm dangerous women. He goes blustering along, stirring up trouble everywhere, mean as the devil, and with a particularly nasty temper. You don't know what Anne has had to stand from him. If I had a penny in the world I'd take her away without any more ado.'

Then I spoke to him very earnestly. I begged him to leave St Mary Mead. By remaining there, he could only bring greater unhappiness on Anne Protheroe than was already her lot. People would talk, the matter would get to Colonel Protheroe's ears – and things would be made infinitely worse for her.

Lawrence protested.

'Nobody knows a thing about it except you, padre.'

'My dear young man, you underestimate the detective instinct of village life. In St Mary Mead everyone knows your most intimate affairs. There is no detective in England equal to a spinster lady of uncertain age with plenty of time on her hands.'

He said easily that that was all right. Everyone thought it was Lettice.

'Has it occurred to you,' I asked, 'that possibly Lettice might think so herself?'

He seemed quite surprised by the idea. Lettice, he said, didn't care a hang about him. He was sure of that.

'She's a queer sort of girl,' he said. 'Always seems in a kind of dream, and yet underneath I believe she's really rather practical. I believe all that vague stuff is a pose. Lettice knows jolly well what she's doing. And there's a funny vindictive streak in her. The queer thing is that she hates Anne. Simply loathes her. And yet Anne's been a perfect angel to her always.'

I did not, of course, take his word for this last. To infatuated young men, their inamorata always behaves like an angel. Still, to the best of my observation, Anne had always behaved to her stepdaughter with kindness and fairness. I had been surprised myself that afternoon at the bitterness of Lettice's tone.

We had to leave the conversation there, because Griselda and Dennis burst in upon us and said I was not to make Lawrence behave like an old fogy.

'Oh! dear,' said Griselda, throwing herself into an arm-chair. 'How I would like a thrill of some kind. A murder – or even a burglary.'

'I don't suppose there's anyone much worth burgling,' said Lawrence, trying to enter into her mood. 'Unless we stole Miss Hartnell's false teeth.'

'They do click horribly,' said Griselda. 'But you're wrong about there being no one worth while. There's some marvellous old silver at Old Hall. Trencher salts and a Charles II Tazza – all kinds of things like that. Worth thousands of pounds, I believe.'

'The old man would probably shoot you with an army revolver,' said Dennis. 'Just the sort of thing he'd enjoy doing.'

'Oh! we'd get in first and hold him up, said Griselda. 'Who's got a revolver?'

'I've got a Mauser pistol,' said Lawrence.

'Have you? How exciting. Why do you have it?'

'Souvenir of the war,' said Lawrence briefly.

'Old Protheroe was showing the silver to Stone today,' volunteered Dennis. 'Old Stone was pretending to be no end interested in it.'

'I thought they'd quarrelled about the barrow,' said Griselda.

'Oh! they've made that up,' said Dennis. 'I can't think what people want to grub about in barrows for, anyway.'

'That man Stone puzzles me,' said Lawrence. 'I think he must be very absent-minded. You'd swear sometimes he knew nothing about his own subject.'

'That's love,' said Dennis. 'Sweet Gladys Cram, you are no sham. Your teeth are white and fill me with delight. Come, fly with me, my bride to be. And at the Blue Boar, on the bedroom floor—'

'That's enough, Dennis,' I said.

'Well,' said Lawrence Redding, 'I must be off. Thank you very much, Mrs Clement, for a very pleasant evening.'

Griselda and Dennis saw him off. Dennis returned to the study alone. Something had happened to ruffle the boy. He wandered about the room aimlessly, frowning and kicking the furniture.

Our furniture is so shabby already that it can hardly be damaged further, but I felt impelled to utter a mild protest.

'Sorry,' said Dennis.

He was silent for a moment and then burst out:

'What an absolutely rotten thing gossip is!'

I was a little surprised. 'What's the matter?' I asked.

'I don't know whether I ought to tell you.'

I was more and more surprised.

'It's such an absolutely rotten thing,' Dennis said again. 'Going round and saying things. Not even saying them. Hinting them. No, I'm damned – sorry – if I tell you! It's too absolutely rotten.'

I looked at him curiously, but I did not press him further. I wondered very much, though. It is very unlike Dennis to take anything to heart.

Griselda came in at that moment.

'Miss Wetherby's just rung up,' she said. 'Mrs Lestrange went out at a quarter-past eight and hasn't come in yet. Nobody knows where she's gone.'

'Why should they know?'

'But it isn't to Dr Haydock's. Miss Wetherby does know that, because she telephoned to Miss Hartnell who lives next door to him and who would have been sure to see her.'

'It is a mystery to me,' I said, 'how anyone ever gets any nourishment in this place. They must eat their meals standing up by the window so as to be sure of not missing anything.'

'And that's not all,' said Griselda, bubbling with pleasure. 'They've found out about the Blue Boar. Dr Stone and Miss Cram have got rooms next door to each other, BUT' – she waved an impressive forefinger – '*no communicating door!*'

'That,' I said, 'must be very disappointing to everybody.'

At which Griselda laughed.

Thursday started badly. Two of the ladies of my parish elected to quarrel about the church decorations. I was called in to adjudicate between two middle-aged ladies, each of whom was literally trembling with rage. If it had not been so painful, it would have been quite an interesting physical phenomenon.

Then I had to reprove two of our choirboys for persistent sweet-sucking during the hours of divine service, and I had an uneasy feeling that I was not doing the job as wholeheartedly as I should have done.

Then our organist, who is distinctly 'touchy', had taken offence and had to be smoothed down.

And four of my poorer parishioners declared open rebellion against Miss Hartnell, who came to me bursting with rage about it.

I was just going home when I met Colonel Protheroe. He was in high good-humour, having sentenced three poachers, in his capacity as magistrate.

'Firmness,' he shouted in his stentorian voice. He is slightly deaf and raises his voice accordingly as deaf people often do. 'That's what's needed nowadays – firmness! Make an example. That rogue Archer came out yesterday and is vowing vengeance against me, I hear. Impudent scoundrel. Threatened men live long, as the saying goes. I'll show him what his vengeance is worth next time I catch him taking my pheasants. Lax! We're too lax nowadays! I believe in showing a man up for what he is. You're always being asked to consider a man's wife and children. Damned nonsense. Fiddlesticks. Why should a man escape the consequences of his acts just because he whines about his wife and children? It's all the same to me – no matter what a man is – doctor, lawyer, clergyman, poacher, drunken wastrel

33

– if you catch him on the wrong side of the law, let the law punish him. You agree with me, I'm sure.'

'You forget,' I said. 'My calling obliges me to respect one quality above all others – the quality of mercy.'

'Well, I'm a just man. No one can deny that.'

I did not speak, and he said sharply:

'Why don't you answer? A penny for your thoughts, man.'

I hesitated, then I decided to speak.

'I was thinking,' I said, 'that when my time comes, I should be sorry if the only plea I had to offer was that of justice. Because it might mean that only justice would be meted out to me ...'

'Pah! What we need is a little militant Christianity. I've always done my duty, I hope. Well, no more of that. I'll be along this evening, as I said. We'll make it a quarter-past six instead of six, if you don't mind. I've got to see a man in the village.'

'That will suit me quite well.'

He flourished his stick and strode away. Turning, I ran into Hawes. I thought he looked distinctly ill this morning. I had meant to upbraid him mildly for various matters in his province which had been muddled or shelved, but seeing his white strained face, I felt that the man was ill.

I said as much, and he denied it, but not very vehemently. Finally he confessed that he was not feeling too fit, and appeared ready to accept my advice of going home to bed.

I had a hurried lunch and went out to do some visits. Griselda had gone to London by the cheap Thursday train.

I came in about a quarter to four with the intention of sketching the outline of my Sunday sermon, but Mary told me that Mr Redding was waiting for me in the study.

I found him pacing up and down with a worried face. He looked white and haggard.

He turned abruptly at my entrance.

'Look here, sir. I've been thinking over what you said yesterday. I've had a sleepless night thinking about it. You're right. I've got to cut and run?'

'My dear boy, I said.

'You were right in what you said about Anne. I'll only bring trouble on her by staying here. She's – she's too good for anything else. I see I've got to go. I've made things hard enough for her as it is, Heaven help me.'

'I think you have made the only decision possible,' I said. 'I know that it is a hard one, but believe me, it will be for the best in the end.'

'I could see that he thought that that was the kind of thing easily said by someone who didn't know what he was talking about.

'You'll look after Anne? She needs a friend.'

'You can rest assured that I will do everything in my power.'

'Thank you, sir.' He wrung my hand. 'You're a good sort, padre. I shall see her to say goodbye this evening, and I shall probably pack up and go tomorrow. No good prolonging the agony. Thanks for letting me have the shed to paint in. I'm sorry not to have finished Mrs Clement's portrait.'

'Don't worry about that, my dear boy. Goodbye, and God bless you.'

When he had gone I tried to settle down to my sermon, but with very poor success. I kept thinking of Lawrence and Anne Protheroe.

I had rather an unpalatable cup of tea, cold and black, and at half-past five the telephone rang. I was informed that Mr Abbott of Lower Farm was dying and would I please come at once.

I rang up Old Hall immediately, for Lower Farm was nearly two miles away and I could not possibly get back by six-fifteen. I have never succeded in learning to ride a bicycle.

I was told, however, that Colonel Protheroe had just started out in the car, so I departed, leaving word with Mary that I had been called away, but would try to be back by six-thirty or soon after.

—— 5 ——

It was nearer seven than half-past six when I approached the Vicarage gate on my return. Before I reached it, it swung open and Lawrence Redding came out. He stopped dead on seeing me, and I was immediately struck by his appearance. He looked like a man who was on the point of going mad. His eyes stared in a peculiar manner, he was deathly white, and he was shaking and twitching all over.

I wondered for a moment whether he could have been drinking, but repudiated the idea immediately.

'Hullo,' I said, 'have you been to see me again? Sorry I was

out. Come back now. I've got to see Protheroe about some accounts – but I dare say we shan't be long.'

'Protheroe,' he said. He began to laugh. 'Protheroe? You're
going to see Protheroe? Oh! you'll see Protheroe all right. Oh!
my God – yes.'

I stared. Instinctively I stretched out a hand towards him. He
drew sharply aside.

'No,' he almost cried out. 'I've got to get away – to think. I've
got to think. I must think.'

He broke into a run and vanished rapidly down the road towards the village, leaving me staring after him, my first idea of
drunkenness recurring.

Finally I shook my head, and went on to the Vicarage. The
front door is always left open, but nevertheless I rang the bell.
Mary came, wiping her hands on her apron.

'So you're back at last,' she observed.

'Is Colonel Protheroe here?' I asked.

'In the study. Been here since a quarter past six.'

'And Mr Redding's been here?'

'Come a few minutes ago. Asked for you. I told him you'd be
back any minute and that Colonel Protheroe was waiting in the
study, and he said he'd wait too, and went there. He's there
now.'

'No, he isn't,' I said. 'I've just met him going down the road.'

'Well, I didn't hear him leave. He can't have stayed more than
a couple of minutes. The mistress isn't back from town yet.'

I nodded absent-mindedly. Mary beat a retreat to the kitchen
quarters and I went down the passage and opened the study
door.

After the dusk of the passage, the evening sunshine that was
pouring into the room made my eyes blink. I took a step or two
across the floor and then stopped dead.

For a moment I could hardly take in the meaning of the scene
before me.

Colonel Protheroe was lying sprawled across my writing-table
in a horrible unnatural position. There was a pool of some dark
fluid on the desk by his head, and it was slowly dripping on to
the floor with a horrible drip, drip, drip.

I pulled myself together and went across to him. His skin was
cold to the touch. The hand that I raised fell back lifeless. The
man was dead – shot through the head.

I went to the door and called Mary. When she came I ordered
her to run as fast as she could and fetch Dr Haydock, who lives

just at the corner of the road. I told her there had been an accident.

Then I went back and closed the door to await the doctor's coming.

Fortunately, Mary found him at home. Haydock is a good fellow, a big, fine, strapping man with an honest, rugged face.

His eyebrows went up when I pointed silently across the room. But, like a true doctor, he showed no signs of emotion. He bent over the dead man, examining him rapidly. Then he straightened himself and looked across at me.

'Well?' I asked.

'He's dead right enough – been dead half an hour, I should say.'

'Suicide?'

'Out of the question, man. Look at the position of the wound. Besides, if he shot himself, where's the weapon?'

True enough, there was no sign of any such thing.

'We'd better not mess around with anything,' said Haydock. 'I'd better ring up the police.'

He picked up the receiver and spoke into it. He gave the facts as curtly as possible and then replaced the telephone and came across to where I was sitting.

'This is a rotten business. How did you come to find him?'

I explained. 'Is – is it murder?' I asked rather faintly.

'Looks like it. Mean to say, what else can it be? Extraordinary business. Wonder who had a down on the poor old fellow. Of course I know he wasn't popular, but one isn't often murdered for that reason – worse luck.'

'There's one rather curious thing,' I said. 'I was telephoned for this afternoon to go to a dying parishioner. When I got there everyone was very surprised to see me. The sick man was very much better than he had been for some days, and his wife flatly denied telephoning for me at all.'

'Haydock drew his brows together.

'That's suggestive – very. You were being got out of the way. Where's your wife?'

'Gone up to London for the day.'

'And the maid?'

'In the kitchen – right at the other side of the house.'

'Where she wouldn't be likely to hear anything that went on in here. It's a nasty business. Who knew that Protheroe was coming here this evening?'

'He referred to the fact this morning in the village street at the top of his voice as usual.'

'Meaning that the whole village knew it? Which they always do in any case. Know of anyone who had a grudge against him?'

The thought of Lawrence Redding's white face and staring eyes came to my mind. I was spared answering by a noise of shuffling feet in the passage outside.

'The police,' said my friend, and rose to his feet.

Our police force was represented by Constable Hurst, looking very important but slightly worried.

'Good evening, gentlemen,' he greeted us. 'The Inspector will be here any minute. In the meantime I'll follow out his instructions. I understand Colonel Protheroe's been found shot – in the Vicarage.'

He paused and directed a look of cold suspicion at me, which I tried to meet with a suitable bearing of conscious innocence.

He moved over to the writing-table and announced:

'Nothing to be touched until the Inspector comes.'

For the convenience of my readers I append a sketch plan of the room.

He got out his notebook, moistened his pencil and looked expectantly at both of us.

I repeated my story of discovering the body. When he had got it all down, which took some time, he turned to the doctor.

'In your opinion, Dr Haydock, what was the cause of death?'

'Shot through the head at close quarters.'

'And the weapon?'

'I can't say with certainty until we get the bullet out. But I should say in all probability the bullet was fired from a pistol of small calibre – say a Mauser .25.'

I started, remembering our conversation of the night before, and Lawrence Redding's admission. The police constable brought his cold, fish-like eye round on me.

'Did you speak, sir?'

I shook my head. Whatever suspicions I might have, they were no more than suspicions, and as such to be kept to myself.

'When, in your opinion, did the tragedy occur?'

The doctor hesitated for a minute before he answered. Then he said:

'The man has been dead just over half an hour, I should say. Certainly no longer.'

Hurst turned to me. 'Did the girl hear anything?'

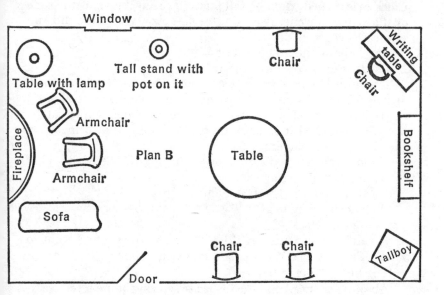

Plan B

'As far as I know she heard nothing,' I said. 'But you had better ask her.'

But at this moment Inspector Slack arrived, having come by car from Much Benham, two miles away.

All that I can say of Insepector Slack is that never did a man more determinedly strive to contradict his name. He was a dark man, restless and energetic in manner, with black eyes that snapped ceaselessly. His manner was rude and overbearing in the extreme.

He acknowledged our greetings with a curt nod, seized his subordinate's note-book, perused it, exchanged a few curt words with him in an undertone, then strode over to the body.

'Everything's been messed up and pulled down, I suppose,' he said.

'I've touched nothing,' said Haydock.

'No more have I,' I said.

The Inspector busied himself for some time peering at the things on the table and examining the pool of blood.

'Ah!' he said in a tone of triumph. 'Here's what we want. Clock overturned when he fell forward. That'll give us the time of the crime. Twenty-two minutes past six. What time did you say death occurred, doctor?'

'I said about half an hour, but—'

The inspector consulted his watch.

'Five minutes past seven. I got word about ten minutes ago, at five minutes to seven. Discovery of the body was at about a quarter to seven. I understand you were fetched immediately. Say you examined it at ten minutes to— Why, that brings it to the identical second almost!'

'I don't guarantee the time absolutely,' said Haydock. 'That is an approximate estimate.'

' Good enough, sir, good enough.'

I had been trying to get a word in.

'About that clock—'

'If you'll excuse me, sir, I'll ask you any questions I want to know. Time's short. What I want is absolute silence.'

'Yes, but I'd like to tell you—'

'Absolute silence,' said the inspector, glaring at me ferociously. I gave him what he asked for.

He was still peering about the writing-table.

'What was he sitting here for,' he grunted. 'Did he want to write a note – Hallo – what's this?'

He held up a piece of note-paper triumphantly. So pleased was he with his find that he permitted us to come to his side and examine it with him.

It was a piece of Vicarage note-paper, and it was headed at the top 6.20.

DEAR CLEMENT – it began – Sorry I cannot wait any longer, but I must . . .

Here the writing tailed off in a scrawl.

'Plain as a pikestaff,' said Inspector Slack triumphantly. 'He sits down here to write this, an enemy comes softly in through the window and shoots him as he writes. What more do you want?'

'I'd just like to say—' I began.

'Out of the way, if you please, sir. I want to see if there are footprints.'

He went down on his hands and knees, moving towards the open window.

'I think you ought to know—' I said obstinately.

The Inspector rose. He spoke without heat, but firmly.

'We'll go into all that later. I'd be obliged if you gentlemen will clear out of here. Right out, if you please.'

We permitted ourselves to be shooed out like children.

Hours seemed to have passed – yet it was only a quarter-past seven.

'Well,' said Haydock. 'That's that. When the conceited ass wants me, you can send him over to the surgery. So long.'

'The mistress is back,' said Mary, making a brief appearance from the kitchen. Her eyes were round and agog with excitement. 'Come in about five minutes ago.'

I found Griselda in the drawing-room. She looked frightened, but excited.

I told her everything and she listened attentively.

'The letter is headed 6.20,' I ended. 'And the clock fell over and has stopped at 6.22.'

'Yes,' said Griselda. 'But that clock, didn't you tell him that it was always kept a quarter of an hour fast?'

'No,' I said. 'I didn't. He wouldn't let me. I tried my best.'

Griselda was frowning in a puzzled manner.

'But, Len,' she said, 'that makes the whole thing perfectly extraordinary. Because when that clock said twenty past six it was really only five minutes past, and at five minutes past I don't suppose Colonel Protheroe had even arrived at the house.'

—— 6 ——

We puzzled over the business of the clock for some time, but we could make nothing of it. Griselda said I ought to make another effort to tell Inspector Slack about it, but on that point I was feeling what I can only describe as 'mulish'.

Inspector Slack had been abominably and most unnecessarily rude. I was looking forward to a moment when I could produce my valuable contribution and effect his discomfort. I would then say in a tone of mild reproach:

'If you had only listened to me, Inspector Slack—'

I expected that he would at least speak to me before he left the house, but to our surprise we learned from Mary that he had departed, having locked up the study door and issued orders that no one was to attempt to enter the room.

Griselda suggested going up to Old Hall.

'It will be so awful for Anne Protheroe – with the police and everything,' she said. 'Perhaps I might be able to do something for her.'

I cordially approved of this plan, and Griselda set off with instructions that she was to telephone to me if she thought that I could be of any use or comfort to either of the ladies.

I now proceeded to ring up the Sunday School teachers, who were coming at 7.45 for their weekly preparation class. I thought that under the circumstances it would be better to put them off.

Dennis was the next person to arrive on the scene, having just returned from a tennis party. The fact that murder had taken place at the Vicarage seemed to afford him acute satisfaction.

'Fancy being right on the spot in a murder case,' he exclaimed. 'I've always wanted to be right in the midst of one. Why have the police locked up the study? Wouldn't one of the other door keys fit it?'

I refused to allow anything of the sort to be attempted. Dennis gave in with a bad grace. After extracting every possible detail from me he went out into the garden to look for footprints, remarking cheerfully that it was lucky it was only old Protheroe, whom everyone disliked.

His cheerful callousness rather grated on me, but I reflected that I was perhaps being hard on the boy. At Dennis's age a detective story is one of the best things in life, and to find a real detective story, complete with corpse, waiting on one's own front doorstep, so to speak, is bound to send a healthy-minded boy into the seventh heaven of enjoyment. Death means very little to a boy of sixteen.

Griselda came back in about an hour's time. She had seen Anne Protheroe, having arrived just after the Inspector had broken the news to her.

On hearing that Mrs Protheroe had last seen her husband in the village about a quarter to six, and that she had no light of any kind to throw upon the matter, he had taken his departure, explaining that he would return on the morrow for a fuller interview.

'He was quite decent in his way,' said Griselda grudgingly.

'How did Mrs Protheroe take it?' I asked.

'Well – she was very quiet – but then she always is.'

'Yes,' I said. 'I can't imagine Anne Protheroe going into hysterics.'

'Of course it was a great shock. You could see that. She thanked me for coming and said she was very grateful but that there was nothing I could do.'

'What about Lettice?'

'She was out playing tennis somewhere. She hadn't got home yet.' There was a pause, and then Griselda said:

'You know, Len, she was really very queer – very queer indeed.'

'The shock,' I suggested.

'Yes – I suppose so. And yet—' Griselda furrowed her brows perplexedly. 'It wasn't like that, somehow. She didn't seem so much bowled over as – well – terrified.'

'Terrified?'

'Yes – not showing it, you know. At least not meaning to show it. But a queer watchful look in her eyes. I wonder if she has a sort of idea who did kill him. She asked again and again if anyone were suspected.'

'Did she?' I said thoughtfully.

'Yes. Of course Anne's got marvellous self-control, but one could see that she was terribly upset. More so than I would have thought, for after all it wasn't as though she were so devoted to him. I should have said she rather disliked him, if anything.'

'Death alters one's feelings sometimes,' I said.

'Yes, I suppose so.'

Dennis came in and was full of excitement over a footprint he had found in one of the flower beds. He was sure that the police had overlooked it and that it would turn out to be the turning point of the mystery.

I spent a troubled night. Dennis was up and about and out of the house long before breakfast to 'study the latest developments', as he said.

Nevertheless it was not he, but Mary, who brought us the morning's sensational bit of news.

We had just sat down to breakfast when she burst into the room, her cheeks red and her eyes shining, and addressed us with her customary lack of ceremony.

'Would you believe it? The baker's just told me. They've arrested young Mr Redding.'

'Arrested Lawrence,' cried Griselda incredulously. 'Imposs-ible. It must be some stupid mistake.'

'No mistake about it, mum,' said Mary with a kind of gloating exultation. 'Mr Redding, he went there himself and gave himself up. Last night, last thing. Went right in, threw down the pistol on the table, and "I did it", he says. Just like that.'

She looked at us both, nodded her head vigorously, and withdrew, satisfied with the effect she had produced. Griselda and I stared at each other.

'Oh! it isn't true,' said Griselda. 'It *can't* be true.'

She noticed my silence, and said: 'Len, *you* don't think it's true?'

I found it hard to answer her. I sat silent, thoughts whirling through my head.

'He must be mad,' said Griselda. 'Absolutely mad. Or do you think they were looking at the pistol together and it suddenly went off?'

'That doesn't sound at all a likely thing to happen.'

'But it must have been an accident of some kind. Because there's not a shadow of a motive. What earthly reason could Lawrence have for killing Colonel Protheroe?'

I could have answered that question very decidedly, but I wished to spare Anne Protheroe as far as possible. There might still be a chance of keeping her name out of it.

'Remember they had had a quarrel,' I said.

'About Lettice and her bathing dress. Yes, but that's absurd; and even if he and Lettice were engaged secretly – well, that's not a reason for killing her father.'

'We don't know what the true facts of the case may be, Griselda.'

'You *do* believe it, Len! Oh! how can you! I tell you, I'm *sure* Lawrence never touched a hair of his head.'

'Remember, I met him just outside the gate. He looked like a madman.'

'Yes, but – oh! it's impossible.'

'There's the clock, too,' I said. This explains the clock. Lawrence must have put it back to 6.20 with the idea of making an alibi for himself. Look how Inspector Slack fell into the trap.'

'You're wrong, Len. Lawrence knew about that clock being fast. "Keeping the vicar up to time!" he used to say. Lawrence would never have made the mistake of putting it back to 6.22. He'd have put the hands somewhere possible – like a quarter to seven.'

'He mayn't have know what time Protheroe got here. Or he may have simply forgotten about the clock being fast.'

Griselda disagreed.

'No, if you were committing a murder, you'd be awfully careful about things like that.'

'You don't know, my dear,' I said mildly. 'You've never done one.'

Before Griselda could reply, a shadow fell across the breakfast table, and a very gentle voice said:

'I hope I am not intruding. You must forgive me. But in the sad circumstances – the very sad circumstances—'

It was our neighbour, Miss Marple. Accepting our polite disclaimers, she stepped in through the window, and I drew up a chair for her. She looked faintly flushed and quite excited.

'Very terrible, is it not? Poor Colonel Protheroe. Not a very pleasant man, perhaps, and not exactly popular, but it's none the less sad for that. And actually shot in the Vicarage study, I understand?'

I said that that had indeed been the case.

'But the dear vicar was not here at the time?' Miss Marple questioned of Griselda. I explained where I had been.

'Mr Dennis is not with you this morning?' said Miss Marple, glancing round.

'Dennis,' said Griselda, 'fancies himself as an amateur detective. He is very excited about a footprint he found in one of the flower beds, and I fancy has gone off to tell the police about it.'

'Dear, dear,' said Miss Marple. 'Such a to-do, is it not? And Mr Dennis thinks he knows who committed the crime. Well, I suppose we all think we know.'

'You mean it is obvious?' said Griselda.

'No, dear, I didn't mean that at all. I dare say everyone thinks it is somebody different. That is why it is so important to have *proofs*. I, for instance, am quite *convinced* I know who did it. But I must admit I haven't one shadow of proof. One must, I know, be very careful of what one says at a time like this – criminal libel, don't they call it? I had made up my mind to be *most* careful with Inspector Slack. He sent word he would come and see me this morning, but now he has just phoned up to say it won't be necessary after all.'

'I suppose, since the arrest, it isn't necessary,' I said.

'The arrest?' Miss Marple leaned forward, her cheeks pink with excitement. 'I didn't know there had been an arrest.'

It is so seldom that Miss Marple is worse informed than we are that I had taken it for granted that she would know the latest developments.

'It seems we have been talking at cross purposes,' I said. 'Yes, there has been an arrest – Lawrence Redding.'

'Lawrence Redding?' Miss Marple seemed very surprised. 'Now I should not have thought—'

Griselda interrupted vehemently.

'I can't believe it even now. No, not though he has actually confessed.'

'Confessed?' said Miss Marple. 'You say he has confessed? Oh! dear, I see I have been sadly at sea – yes, sadly at sea.'

'I can't help feeling it must have been some kind of an accident,' said Griselda. 'Don't you thing so, Len? I mean his coming forward to give himself up looks like that.'

Miss Marple leant forward eagerly.

'He gave himself up, you say?

'Yes.'

'Oh!' said Miss Marple, with a deep sigh. 'I am so glad – so very glad.'

I looked at her in some surprise.

'It shows a true state of remorse, I suppose,' I said.

'Remorse?' Miss Marple looked very surprised. 'Oh! but surely, dear, dear vicar, you don't think that he is guilty?'

It was my turn to stare.

'But since he has confessed—'

'Yes, but that just proves it, doesn't it? I mean that he had nothing to do with it.'

'No,' I said. 'I may be dense, but I can't see that it does. If you have not committed a murder, I cannot see the object of pretending you have.'

'Oh! of course, there's a reason,' said Miss Marple. 'Naturally. Theres always a reason, isn't there? And young men are so hot-headed and often prone to believe the worst.'

She turned to Griselda.

'Don't you agree with me, my dear?'

'I – I don't know, said Griselda. 'It's difficult to know what to think. I can't see any reason for Lawrence behaving like a perfect idiot.'

'If you had seen his face last night—' I began.

'Tell me,' said Miss Marple.

I described my homecoming while she listened attentively. When I had finished she said:

'I know that I am very often rather foolish and don't take in things as I should, but I really do not see your point.

'It seems to me that if a young man had made up his mind

46

to the great wickedness of taking a fellow creature's life, he would not appear distraught about it afterwards. It would be a premeditated and cold-blooded action and though the murderer might be a little flurried and possibly might make some small mistake, I do not think it likely he would fall into a state of agitation such as you describe. It is difficult to put onself in such a position, but I cannot imagine getting into a state like that myself.

'We don't know the circumstances,' I argued. 'If there was a quarrel, the shot may have been fired in a sudden burst of passion, and Lawrence might afterwards have been appalled at what he had done. Indeed, I prefer to think that that is what did actually occur.'

'I know, dear Mr Clement, that there are many ways we prefer to look at things. But one must actually take facts as they are, must one not? And it does not seem to me that the facts bear the interpretation you put upon them. Your maid distinctly stated that Mr Redding was only in the house a couple of minutes, not long enough, surely, for a quarrel such as you describe. And then again, I understand the colonel was shot through the back of the head while he was writing a letter – at least that is what my maid told me.'

'Quite true,' said Griselda. 'He seems to have been writing a note to say he couldn't wait any longer. The note was dated 6.20, and the clock on the table was overturned and had stopped at 6.22, and that's just what has been puzzling Len and myself so frightfully.'

She explained our custom of keeping the clock a quarter of an hour fast.

'Very curious,' said Miss Marple. 'Very curious indeed. But the note seems to me even more curious still. I mean—'

She stopped and looked round. Lettice Protheroe was standing outside the window. She came in, nodding to us and murmuring 'Morning'.

She dropped into a chair and said, with rather more animation than usual:

'They've arrested Lawrence, I hear.'

'Yes,' said Griselda. 'It's been a great shock to us.'

'I never really thought anyone would murder father,' said Lettice. She was obviously taking a pride in letting no hint of distress or emotion escape her. 'Lots of people wanted to, I'm sure. There are times when I'd have liked to do it myself.'

'Won't you have something to eat or drink, Lettice?' asked Griselda.

'No, thank you. I just drifted round to see if you'd got my beret here – a queer little yellow one. I think I left it in the study the other day.'

'If you did, it's there still,' said Griselda. 'Mary never tidies anything.'

'I'll go and see, said Lettice, rising. 'Sorry to be such a bother, but I seem to have lost everything else in the hat line.'

'I'm afraid you can't get it now,' I said. 'Inspector Slack has locked the room up.'

'Oh! what a bore. Can't we get in through the window?'

'I'm afraid not. It is latched on the inside. Surely, Lettice, a yellow beret won't be much good to you at present?'

'You mean mourning and all that? I shan't bother about mourning. I think it's an awfully archaic idea. It's a nuisance about Lawrence – yes, it's a nuisance.'

She got up and stood frowning abstractedly.

'I suppose its all on account of me and my bathing dress. So silly, the whole thing . . .'

Griselda opened her mouth to say something, but for some unexplained reason shut it again.

A curious smile came to Lettice's lips.

'I think,' she said softly, 'I'll go home and tell Anne about Lawrence being arrested.'

She went out of the window again. Giselda turned to Miss Marple. 'Why did you step on my foot?'

The old lady was smiling.

'I thought you were going to say something, my dear. And it is often so much better to let things develop on their own lines. I don't think, you know, that that child is half so vague as she pretends to be. She's got a very definite idea in her head and she's acting upon it.'

Mary gave a loud knock on the dining-room door and entered hard upon it.

'What is it? said Griselda. 'And Mary, you must remember not to knock on doors. I've told you about it before.'

'Thought you might be busy,' said Mary. 'Colonel Melchett's here. Wants to see the master.'

Colonel Melchett is Chief Constable of the county. I rose at once.

'I thought you wouldn't like my leaving him in the hall, so I put him in the drawing-room,' went on Mary. 'Shall I clear?'

'Not yet,' said Griselda. 'I'll ring.'

She turned to Miss Marple and I left the room.

—— 7 ——

Colonel Melchett is a dapper little man with a habit of snorting suddenly and unexpectedly. He has red hair and rather keen bright blue eyes.

'Good morning, vicar, he said. 'Nasty business, eh? Poor old Protheroe. Not that I liked him. I didn't. Nobody did, for that matter. Nasty bit of work for you, too. Hope it hasn't upset your missus?'

I said Griselda had taken it very well.

'That's lucky. Rotten thing to happen in one's house. I must say I'm surprised at young Redding – doing it the way he did. No sort of consideration for anyone's feelings.'

A wild desire to laugh came over me, but Colonel Melchett evidently saw nothing odd in the idea of a murderer being considerate, so I held my peace.

'I must say I was rather taken aback when I heard the fellow had marched in and given himself up,' continued Colonel Melchett, dropping on to a chair.

'How did it happen exactly?'

'Last night. About ten o'clock. Fellow rolls in, throws down a pistol, and says: "Here I am. I did it." Just like that.'

'What account does he give of the business?'

'Precious little. He was warned, of course, about making a statement. But he merely laughed. Said he came here to see you – found Protheroe here. They had words and he shot him. Won't say what the quarrel was about. Look here, Clement – just between you and me, do you know anything about it? I've heard rumours – about his being forbidden the house and all that. What was it – did he seduce the daughter, or what? We don't want to bring the girl into it more than we can help for everybody's sake. Was that the trouble?'

'No,' I said. 'You can take it from me that it was something quite different, but I can't say more at the present juncture.'

He nodded and rose.

'I'm glad to know. There's a lot of talk. Too many women in this part of the world. Well, I must get along. I've got to see

Haydock. He was called out to some case or other, but he ought to be back by now. I don't mind telling you I'm sorry about Redding. He always struck me as a decent young chap. Perhaps they'll think out some kind of defence for him. After-effects of war, shell shock, or something. Especially if no very adequate motive turns up. I must be off. Like to come along?'

I said I would like to very much, and we went out together.

Haydock's house is next door to mine. His servant said the doctor had just come in and showed us into the dining-room, where Haydock was sitting down to a steaming plate of eggs and bacon. He greeted me with an amiable nod.

'Sorry I had to go out. Confinement case. I've been up most of the night, over your business. I've got the bullet for you.'

He shoved a little box along the table. Melchett examined it.

'Point two five?'

Haydock nodded.

'I'll keep the technical details for the inquest,' he said. 'All you want to know is that death was practically instantaneous. Silly young fool, what did he want to do it for? Amazing, by the way, that nobody heard the shot.'

'Yes,' said Melchett, 'that surprises me.'

'The kitchen window gives on the other side of the house,' I said. 'With the study door, the pantry door, and the kitchen door all shut, I doubt if you would hear anything, and there was no one but the maid in the house.'

'H'm,' said Melchett. 'It's odd, all the same. I wonder the old lady – what's her name – Marple, didn't hear it. The study window was open.'

'Perhaps she did,' said Haydock.

'I don't think she did,' said I. 'She was over at the Vicarage just now and she didn't mention anything of the kind which I'm certain she would have done if there had been anything to tell.'

'May have heard it and paid no attention to it – thought it was a car back-firing.'

It struck me that Haydock was look much more jovial and good-humoured this morning. He seemed like a man who was decorously trying to subdue unusually good spirits.

'Or what about a silencer?' he added. 'That's quite likely. Nobody would hear anything then.'

Melchett shook his head.

'Slack didn't find anything of the kind, and he asked Redding, and Redding didn't seem to know what he was talking about at first and then denied point blank using anything of the kind. And I suppose one can take his word for it.'

'Yes, indeed, poor devil.'

'Damned young fool,' said Colonel Melchett. 'Sorry, Clement. But he really is! Somehow one can't get used to thinking of him as a murderer.'

'Any motive?' asked Haydock, taking a final draught of coffee and pushing back his chair.

'He says they quarrelled and he lost his temper and shot him.'

'Hoping for manslaughter, eh?' The doctor shook his head. 'That story doesn't hold water. He stole up behind him as he was writing and shot him through the head. Precious little "quarrel" about that.'

'Anyway, there wouldn't have been time for a quarrel,' I said, remembering Miss Marple's words. 'To creep up, shoot him, alter the clock hands back to 6,20, and leave again would have taken him all his time. I shall never forget his face when I met him outside the gate or the way he said, "You want to see Protheroe – oh, you'll see him all right!' That in itself ought to have made me suspicious of what had just taken place a few minutes before.'

Haydock stared at me.

'What do you mean – what had just taken place? When do you think Redding shot him?'

'A few minutes before I got to the house.'

The doctor shook his head.

'Impossible. Plumb impossible. He'd been dead much longer than that.'

'But, my dear man,' cried Colonel Melchett, 'you said yourself that half an hour was only an approximate estimate.'

'Half an hour, thirty-five minutes, twenty-five minutes, twenty minutes – possibly, but less no. Why, the body would have been warm when I got to it.'

We stared at each other. Haydock's face had changed. It had gone suddenly grey and old. I wondered at the change in him.

'But, look here, Haydock.' The colonel found his voice. 'If Redding admits shooting him at a quarter to seven—'

Haydock sprang to his feet.

'I tell you it's impossible,' he roared. 'If Redding says he killed Protheroe at a quarter to seven, then Redding lies. Hang it all, I tell you I'm a doctor, and I know. The blood had begun to congeal.'

'If Redding is lying,' began Melchett. He stopped, shook his head.

'We'd better go down to the police station and see him,' he said.

—— 8 ——

We were rather silent on our way down to the police station. Haydock drew behind a little and murmured to me:

'You know I don't like the look of this. I don't like it. There's something here we don't understand.'

He looked thoroughly worried and upset.

Inspector Slack was at the police station and presently we found ourselves face to face with Lawrence Redding.

He looked pale and strained but quite composed – marvellously so, I thought, considering the circumstances. Melchett snorted and hummed, obviously nervous.

'Look here, Redding, he said, 'I understand you made a statement to Inspector Slack here. You state you went to the Vicarage at approximately a quarter to seven, found Protheroe there, quarrelled with him, shot him, and came away. I'm not reading it over to you, but that's the gist of it.'

'Yes.'

'I'm going to ask a few questions. You've already been told that you needn't answer them unless you choose. Your solicitor—'

Lawrence interrupted.

'I've nothing to hide. I killed Protheroe.'

'Ah! well—' Melchett snorted. 'How did you happen to have a pistol with you?'

Lawrence hesitated. 'It was in my pocket.'

'You took it with you to the Vicarage?'

'Yes.'

'Why?'

'I always take it.'

He had hesitated again before answering, and I was absolutely sure that he was not speaking the truth.

'Why did you put the clock back?'

'The clock?' He seemed puzzled.

'Yes, the hands pointed to 6.22.'

A look of fear sprang up in his face.

'Oh! that – yes. I – I altered it.'

Haydock spoke suddenly.

'Where did you shoot Colonel Protheroe?'

'In the study at the Vicarage.'

'I mean in what part of the body?'

'Oh! – I – through the head, I think. Yes, through the head.'

'Aren't you sure?'

'Since you know, I can't see why it is necessary to ask me.'

It was a feeble kind of bluster. There was some commotion outside. A constable without a helmet brought in a note.

'For the vicar. It says very urgent on it.'

I tore it open and read:

> Please – please – come to me. I don't know what to do. It is all too awful. I want to tell someone. Please come immediately, and bring anyone you like with you – ANNE PROTHEROE.

I gave Melchett a meaning glance. He took the hint. We all went out together. Glancing over my shoulder, I had a glimpse of Lawrence Redding's face. His eyes were riveted on the paper in my hand, and I have hardly ever seen such a terrible look of anguish and despair in any human being's face.

I remembered Anne Protheroe sitting on my sofa and saying: 'I'm a desperate woman,' and my heart grew heavy within me. I saw now the possible reason for Lawrence Redding's heroic self-accusation. Melchett was speaking to Slack.

'Have you got any line on Redding's movements earlier in the day? There's some reason to think he shot Protheroe earlier than he says. Get on to it, will you?'

He turned to me and without a word I handed him Anne Protheroe's letter. He read it and pursed up his lips in astonishment. Then he looked at me inquiringly.

'Is this what you were hinting at this morning?'

'Yes. I was not sure then if it was my duty to speak. I am quite sure now.' And I told him of what I had seen that night in the studio.

The colonel had a few words with the inspector and then we set off for Old Hall. Dr Haydock came with us.

A very correct butler opened the door, with just the right amount of gloom in his bearing.

'Good morning,' said Melchett. 'Will you ask Mrs Protheroe's maid to tell her we are here and would like to see her, and then return here and answer a few questions.'

The butler hurried away and presently returned with the news that he had despatched the message.

'Now let's hear something about yesterday,' said Colonel Melchett. 'Your master was in to lunch?'

'Yes, sir.'

'And in his usual spirits?'

'As far as I could see, yes, sir.'

'What happened after that?'

'After luncheon Mrs Protheroe went to lie down and the colonel went to his study. Miss Lettice went out to a tennis party in the two-seater. Colonel and Mrs Protheroe had tea at four-thirty, in the drawing-room. The car was ordered for five-thirty to take them to the village. Immediately after they had left Mr Clement rang up' – he bowed to me – 'I told him they had started.'

'H'm,' said Colonel Melchett. 'When was Mr Redding last here?'

'On Tuesday afternoon, sir.'

'I understand that there was a disagreement between them?'

'I believe so, sir. The colonel gave me orders that Mr Redding was not to be admitted in future.'

'Did you overhear the quarrel at all?' asked Colonel Melchett bluntly.

'Colonel Protheroe, sir, had a very loud voice, especially when it was raised in anger. I was unable to help overhearing a few words here and there.'

'Enough to tell you the cause of the dispute?'

'I understood, sir, that it had to do with a portrait Mr Redding had been painting – a portrait of Miss Lettice.'

Melchett grunted.

'Did you see Mr Redding when he left?'

'Yes, sir, I let him out.'

'Did he seem angry?'

'No, sir; if I may say so, he seemed rather amused.'

'Ah! He didn't come to the house yesterday?'

'No, sir.'

'Anyone else come?'

'Not yesterday, sir.'

'Well, the day before?'

'Mr Dennis Clement came in the afternoon. And Dr Stone was here for some time. And there was a lady in the evening.'

'A lady?' Melchett was surprised. 'Who was she?'

The butler couldn't remember her name. It was a lady he

had not seen before. Yes, she had given her name, and when he told her that the family were at dinner, she had said that she would wait. So he had shown her into the little morning-room.

She had asked for Colonel Protheroe, not Mrs Protheroe. He had told the colonel and the colonel had gone to the morning-room directly dinner was over.

How long had the lady stayed? He thought about half an hour. The colonel himself had let her out. Ah! yes, he remembered her name now. The lady had been a Mrs Lestrange.

This was a surprise.

'Curious,' said Melchett. 'Really very curious.'

But we pursued the matter no further, for at that moment a message came that Mrs Protheroe would see us.

Anne was in bed. Her face was pale and her eyes very bright. There was a look on her face that puzzled me – a kind of grim determination. She spoke to me.

'Thank you for coming so promptly,' she said. 'I see you've understood what I meant by bringing anyone you liked with you.' She paused.

'It's best to get it over quickly, isn't it?' she said. She gave a queer, half-pathetic little smile. 'I suppose you're the person I ought to say it to, Colonel Melchett. You see, it was I who killed my husband.'

Colonel Melchett said gently:

'My dear Mrs Protheroe—'

'Oh! it's quite true. I suppose I've said it rather bluntly but I never can go into hysterics over anything. I've hated him for a long time, and yesterday I shot him.'

She lay back on the pillows and closed her eyes.

'That's all. I suppose you'll arrest me and take me away. I'll get up and dress as soon as I can. At the moment I am feeling rather sick.'

'Are you aware, Mrs Protheroe, that Mr Lawrence Redding has already accused himself of committing the crime?'

Anne opened her eyes and nodded brightly.

'I know. Silly boy. He's very much in love with me, you know. It was frightfully noble of him – but very silly.'

'He knew that it was you who had committed the crime?'

'Yes.'

'How did he know?'

She hesitated.

'Did you tell him?'

Still she hesitated. Then at last she seemed to make up her mind.

'Yes – I told him . . .'

She twitched her shoulders with a movement of irritation.

'Can't you go away now? I've told you. I don't want to talk about it any more.'

'Where did you get the pistol, Mrs Protheroe?'

'The pistol! Oh! it was my husband's. I got it out of the drawer of his dressing-table.'

'I see. And you took it with you to the Vicarage?'

'Yes. I knew he would be there—'

'What time was this?'

'It must have been after six – quarter – twenty past – something like that.'

'You took the pistol meaning to shoot your husband?'

'No – I – I meant it for myself.'

'I see. But you went to the Vicarage?'

'Yes. I went along to the window. There were no voices. I looked in. I saw my husband. Something came over me – and I fired.'

'And then?'

'Then? Oh! then I went away.'

'And told Mr Redding what you had done?'

Again I noticed the hesitation in her voice before she said 'Yes.'

'Did anybody see you entering or leaving the Vicarage?'

'No – at least, yes. Old Miss Marple. I talked to her a few minutes. She was in her garden.'

She moved restlessly on the pillows.

'Isn't that enough? I've told you. Why do you want to go on bothering me?'

Dr Haydock moved to her side and felt her pulse.

He beckoned to Melchett.

'I'll stay with her,' he said in a whisper, 'whilst you make the necessary arrangements. She oughtn't to be left. Might do herself a mischief.'

Melchett nodded.

We left the room and descended the stairs. I saw a thin, cadaverous-looking man come out of the adjoining room and on impulse I remounted the stairs.

'Are you Colonel Protheroe's valet?'

The man looked surprised. 'Yes, sir.'

'Do you know whther your late master kept a pistol any-where?'

'Not that I know of, sir.'

'Not in one of the drawers of his dressing-table? Think, man.'

The vallet shook his head decisively.

'I'm quite sure he didn't, sir. I'd have seen it if so. Bound to.'

I hurried down the stairs after the others.

Mrs Protheroe had lied about the pistol.

Why?

9

After leaving a message at the police station, the Chief Constable announced his intention of paying a visit to Miss Marple.

'You'd better come with me, vicar,' he said. 'I don't want to give a member of your flock hysterics. So lend the weight of your soothing presence.'

I smiled. For all her fragile appearance, Miss Marple is cap-able of holding her own with any policeman or Chief Con-stable in existence.

'What's she like?' asked the colonel, as we rang the bell. 'Any-thing she says to be depended upon or otherwise?'

I considered the matter.

'I think she is quite dependable,' I said cautiously. 'That is, in so far as she is talking of what she has actually seen. Beyond that, of course, when you get on to what she thinks – well, that is another matter. She has a powerful imagination and system-atically thinks the worst of everyone.'

'The typical elderly spinster, in fact,' said Melchett with a laugh. 'Well, I ought to know the breed by now. Gad, the tea parties down here!'

We were admitted by a very diminutive maid and shown into a small drawing-room.

'A bit crowded,' said Colonel Melchett, looking round. 'But plenty of good stuff. A lady's room, eh, Clement?'

I agreed, and at that moment the door opened and Miss Marple made her appearance.

'Very sorry to bother you, Miss Marple,' said the colonel, when I had introduced him, putting on his bluff military manner which he had an idea was attractive to elderly ladies. 'Got to do my duty, you know.'

'Of course, of course,' said Miss Marple. 'I quite understand. Won't you sit down? And might I offer you a little glass of cherry brandy? My own making. A recipe of my grandmother's.'

'Thank you very much, Miss Marple. Very kind of you. But I think I won't. Nothing till lunch time, that's my motto. Now, I want to talk to you about this sad business – very sad business indeed. Upset us all, I'm sure. Well, it seems possible that owing to the position of your house and garden, you may have been able to tell us something we want to know about yesterday evening.'

'As a matter of fact I *was* in my little garden from five o'clock onwards yesterday, and, of course, from there – well, one simply cannot help seeing anything that is going on next door.'

'I understand, Miss Marple, that Mrs Protheroe passed this way yesterday evening?'

'Yes, she did. I called out to her, and she admired my roses.'

'Could you tell us about what time that was?'

'I should say it was just a minute or two after a quarter past six. Yes, that's right. The church clock had just chimed the quarter.'

'Very good. What happened next?'

'Well, Mrs Protheroe said she was calling for her husband at the Vicarage so that they could go home together. She had come along the lane, you understand, and she went into the Vicarage by the back gate and across the garden.'

'She came from the lane?'

'Yes, I'll show you.'

Full of eagerness, Miss Marple led us out into the garden and pointed out the lane that ran along by the bottom of the garden.

'The path opposite with the stile leads to the Hall,' she explained. 'That was the way they were going home together. Mrs Protheroe came from the village.'

'Perfectly, perfectly,' said Colonel Melchett. 'And she went across to the Vicarage, you say?'

'Yes. I saw her turn the corner of the house. I suppose the colonel wasn't there yet, because she came back almost immediately, and went down the lawn to the studio – that building there. The one the vicar lets Mr Redding use as a studio.'

'I see. And – you didn't happen to hear a shot, Miss Marple?'

'I didn't hear a shot then,' said Miss Marple.

'But did you hear one sometime?'

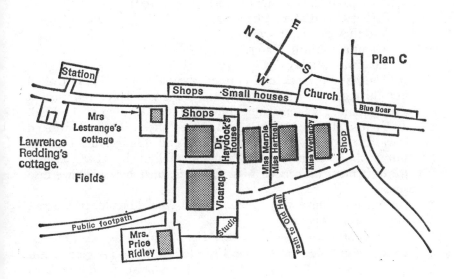

'Yes, I think there was a shot somewhere in the woods. But quite five or ten minutes afterwards – and, as I say, out in the woods. At least I think so. It couldn't have been – surely it couldn't have been—'

She stopped, pale with excitement.

'Yes, yes, we'll come to all that presently,' said Colonel Melchett. 'Please go on with your story. Mrs Protheroe went down to the studio?'

'Yes, she went inside and waited. Presently Mr Redding came along the lane from the village. He came to the Vicarage gate, looked all round—'

'And saw you, Miss Marple.'

'As a matter of fact, he didn't see me,' said Miss Marple, flushing slightly. 'Because, you see, just at that minute I was bending right over – trying to get up one of those nasty dandelions, you know. So difficult. And then he went through the gate and down to the studio.'

He didn't go near the house?'

'Oh, no! he went straight to the studio. Mrs Protheroe came to the door to meet him, and then they both went inside.'

Here Miss Marple contributed a singularly eloquent pause.

'Perhaps she was sitting to him?' I suggested.

'Perhaps,' said Miss Marple.

'And they came out – when?'

'About ten minutes later.'

'That was roughly?'

'The church clock had chimed the half-hour. They strolled out through the garden gate and along the lane, and just at that minute, Dr Stone came down the path leading to the Hall, and climbed over the stile and joined them. They all walked towards the village together. At the end of the lane, I think, but I can't be quite sure, they were joined by Miss Cram. I think it must have been Miss Cram because her skirts were so short.'

'You must have very good eyesight Miss Marple, if you can observe as far as that.'

'I was observing a bird,' said Miss Marple. 'A golden crested wren, I think he was. A sweet little fellow. I had my glasses out, and that's how I happened to see Miss Cram (if it was Miss Cram, and I think so), join them.'

'Ah! well, that may be so,' said Colonel Melchett. 'Now, since you seem very good at observing, did you happen to notice, Miss Marple, what sort of expression Mrs Protheroe and Mr Redding had as they passed along the lane?'

'They were smiling and talking,' said Miss Marple. 'They seemed very happy to be together, if you know what I mean.'

'They didn't seem upset or disturbed in any way?'

'Oh, no! Just the opposite.'

'Deuced odd,' said the colonel. 'There's something deuced odd about the whole thing.'

Miss Marple suddenly took our breath away by remarking in a placid voice:

'Has Mrs Protheroe been saying that she committed the crime now?'

'Upon my soul,' said the colonel, 'how did you come to guess that, Miss Marple?'

'Well, I rather thought it might happen,' said Miss Marple. 'I think dear Lettice thought so, too. She's really a very sharp girl. Not always very scrupulous, I'm afraid. So Anne Protheroe says she killed her husband. Well, well. I don't think it's true.

No, I'm almost sure it isn't true. Not with a woman like Anne Protheroe. Although one never can be quite sure about anyone, can one? At least that's what I've found. When does she say she shot him?'

'At twenty minutes past six. Just after speaking to you.'

Miss Marple shook her head slowly and pityingly. The pity was, I think, for two full-grown men being so foolish as to believe such a story. At least that is what we felt like.

'What did she shoot him with?'

'A pistol.'

'Where did she find it?'

'She brought it with her.'

'Well, that she didn't do,' said Miss Marple, with unexpected decision. 'I can swear to that. She'd no such thing with her.'

'You mightn't have seen it.'

'Of course I should have seen it.'

'If it had been in her handbag.'

'She wasn't carrying a handbag.'

'Well it might have been concealed – er – upon her person.'

Miss Marple directed a glance of sorrow and scorn upon him.

'My dear Colonel Melchett, you know what young women are nowadays. Not ashamed to show exactly how the Creator made them. She hadn't so much as a handkerchief in the top of her stocking.'

Melchett was obstinate.

'You must admit that it all fits in,' he said. 'The time, the overturned clock pointing to 6.22—'

Miss Marple turned on me.

'Do you mean you haven't told him about that clock yet?'

'What about the clock, Clement?'

I told him. He showed a good deal of annoyance.

'Why on earth didn't you tell Slack this last night?'

'Because,' I said, 'he wouldn't let me.'

'Nonsense, you ought to have insisted.'

'Probably,' I said, 'Inspector Slack behaves quite differently to you than he does to me. I had no earthly chance of insisting.'

'It's an extraordinary business altogether,' said Melchett. 'If a third person comes along and claims to have done this murder, I shall go into a lunatic asylum.'

'If I might be allowed to suggest—' murmured Miss Marple.

'Well?'

'If you were to tell Mr Redding what Mrs Protheroe has done and then explain that you don't really believe it is her. And

61

then if you were to go to Mrs Protheroe and tell her that Mr Redding is all right – why then, they might each of them tell you the truth. And the truth *is* helpful, though I dare say they don't know very much themselves, poor things.'

'It's all very well, but they are the only two people who had a motive for making away with Protheroe.'

'Oh, I wouldn't say that, Colonel Melchett,' said Miss Marple.

'Why, can you think of anyone else?'

'Oh! yes, indeed. Why,' she counted on her fingers, 'one, two, three, four, five, six – yes, and a possible seven. I can think of at least seven people who might be very glad to have Colonel Protheroe out of the way.'

The colonel looked at her feebly.

'Seven people? In St Mary Mead?'

Miss Marple nodded brightly.

'Mind you I name no names,' she said. 'That wouldn't be right. But I'm afraid there's a lot of wickedness in the world. A nice honourable upright soldier like you doesn't know about these things, Colonel Melchett.'

I thought the Chief Constable was going to have apoplexy.

—— 10 ——

His remarks on the subject of Miss Marple as we left the house were far from complimentary.

'I really believe that wizened-up old maid thinks she knows everything there is to know. And hardly been out of this village all her life. Preposterous. What can she know of life?'

I said mildly that though doubtless Miss Marple knew next to nothing of Life with a capital L, she knew practically everything that went on in St Mary Mead.

Melchett admitted that grudgingly. She was a valuable witness – particularly valuable from Mrs Protheroe's point of view.

'I suppose there's no doubt about what she says, eh?'

'If Miss Marple says she had no pistol with her, you can take it for granted that it is so,' I said. 'If there was the least possibility of such a thing, Miss Marple would have been on to it like a knife.'

'That's true enough. We'd better go and have a look at the studio.'

4

The so-called studio was a mere rough shed with a skylight. There were no windows and the door was the only means of entrance or egress. Satisfied on this score, Melchett announced his intention of visiting the Vicarage with the inspector.

'I'm going to the police station now.'

As I entered through the front door, a murmur of voices caught my ear. I opened the drawing-room door.

On the sofa beside Griselda, conversing animatedly, sat Miss Gladys Cram. Her legs, which were encased in particularly shiny pink stockings, were crossed, and I had every opportunity of observing that she wore pink striped silk knickers.

'Hullo, Len,' said Griselda.

'Good morning, Mr Clement,' said Miss Cram. 'Isn't the news about the colonel really too awful? Poor old gentleman.'

'Miss Cram,' said my wife, 'very kindly came in to offer to help us with the Guides. We asked for helpers last Sunday, you remember.'

I did remember, and I was convinced, and so, I knew from her tone, was Griselda, that the idea of enrolling herself among them would never have occurred to Miss Cram but for the exciting incident which had taken place at the Vicarage.

'I was only just saying to Mrs Clement,' went on Miss Cram, 'you could have struck me all of a heap when I heard the news. A murder? I said. In this quiet one-horse village – for quiet it is, you must admit – not so much as a picture house, and as for Talkies! And then when I heard it was Colonel Protheroe – why, I simply couldn't believe it. He didn't seem the kind, somehow, to get murdered.'

'And so,' said Griselda, 'Miss Cram came round to find out all about it.'

I feared this plain speaking might offend the lady, but she merely flung her head back and laughed uproariously, showing every tooth she possessed.

'That's too bad. You're a sharp one, aren't you, Mrs Clement? But it's only natural, isnt it, to want to hear the ins and outs of a case like this? And I'm sure I'm willing enough to help with the Guides in any way you like. Exciting, that's what it is. I've been stagnating for a bit of fun. I have, really I have. Not that my job isn't a very good one, well paid, and Dr Stone quite the gentleman in every way. But a girl wants a bit of life out of office hours, and except for you, Mrs Clement, who is there in the place to talk to except a lot of old cats?'

'There's Lettice Protheroe,' I said.

Gladys Cram tossed her head.

'She's too high and mighty for the likes of me. Fancies herself the county, and wouldn't demean herself by noticing a girl who had to work for her living. Not but what I *did* hear her talking of earning her living herself. And who'd employ her, I should like to know? Why, she'd be fired in less than a week. Unless she went as one of those mannequins, all dressed up and sidling about. She could do that, I expect.'

'She'd make a very good mannequin,' said Griselda. 'She's got such a lovely figure.' There's nothing of the cat about Griselda. 'When was she talking of earning her own living?'

Miss Cram seemed momentarily discomfited, but recovered herself with her usual archness.

'That would be telling, wouldn't it?' she said. 'But she did say so. Things not very happy at home, I fancy. Catch me living at home with a stepmother. I wouldn't sit down under it for a minute.'

'Ah! but you're so high spirited and independent,' said Griselda gravely, and I looked at her with suspicion.

Miss Cram was clearly pleased.

'That's right. That's me all over. Can be led, not driven. A palmist told me that not so very long ago. No. I'm not one to sit down and be bullied. And I've made it clear all along to Dr Stone that I must have my regular times off. These scientific gentlemen, they think a girl's a kind of machine – half the time they just don't notice her or remember she's there.'

'Do you find Dr Stone pleasant to work with? It must be an interesting job if you are interested in archæology.'

'Of course, I don't know much about it,' confessed the girl. 'It still seems to me that digging up people that are dead and have been dead for hundreds of years isn't – well, it seems a bit nosey, doesn't it? And there's Dr Stone so wrapped up in it all that half the time he'd forget his meals if it wasn't for me.'

'Is he at the barrow this morning?' asked Griselda.

Miss Cram shook her head.

'A bit under the weather this morning, she explained. 'Not up to doing any work. That means a holiday for little Gladys.'

'I'm sorry,' I said.

'Oh! it's nothing much. There's not going to be a second death. But do tell me, Mr Clement, I hear you've been with the police all morning. What do they think?'

'Well,' I said slowly, 'there is still a little – uncertainty.'

'Ah!' cried Miss Cram. 'Then they don't think it is Mr

Lawrence Redding after all. So handsome, isn't he? Just like a movie star. And such a nice smile when he says good morning to you. I really couldn't believe my ears when I heard the police had arrested him. Still, one has always heard they're very stupid – the county police.'

'You can hardly blame them in this instance,' I said. 'Mr Redding came in and gave himself up.'

'What?' the girl was clearly dumbfounded. 'Well – of all the poor fish! If I'd committed a murder, I wouldn't go straight off and give myself up. I should have thought Lawrence Redding would have had more sense. To give in like that! What did he kill Protheroe for? Did he say? Was it just a quarrel?'

'It's not absolutely certain that he did kill him,' I said.

'But surely – if he says he has – why really, Mr Clement, he ought to know.'

'He ought to, certainly,' I agreed. 'But the police are not satisfied with his story.'

'But why should he say he'd done it if he hasn't?'

That was a point on which I had no intention of enlightening Miss Cram. Instead I said rather vaguely:

'I believe that in all prominent murder cases, the police receive numerous letters from people accusing themselves of the crime.'

Miss Cram's reception of this piece of information was:

'They must be chumps!' in a tone of wonder and scorn.

'Well,' she said with a sigh, 'I suppose I must be trotting along.' She rose. 'Mr Redding accusing himself of the murder will be a bit of news for Dr Stone.'

'Is he inteesrted? asked Griselda.

Miss Cram furrowed her brows perplexedly.

'He's a queer one. You never can tell with him. All wrapped up in the past. He'd a hundred times rather look at a nasty old bronze knife out of one of those humps of ground than he would see the knife Crippen cut up his wife with, supposing he had a chance to.'

'Well,' I said, 'I must confess I agree with him.'

Miss Cram's eyes expressed incomprehension and slight contempt. Then with reiterated goodbyes, she took her departure.

'Not such a bad sort, really,' said Griselda, as the door closed behind her. 'Terribly common, of course, but one of those big, bouncing, good-humoured girls that you can't dislike. I wonder what really brought her here?'

'Curiosity.'

'Yes, I suppose so. Now, Len, tell me all about it. I'm simply dying to hear.'

I sat down and recited faithfully all the happenings of the morning, Griselda interpolating the narrative with little exclamations of surprise and interest.

'So it was Anne Lawrence was after all along! Not Lettice. How blind we've all been! That must have been what old Miss Marple was hinting at yesterday. Don't you think so?'

'Yes,' I said, averting my eyes.

Mary entered.

'There's a couple of men here – come from a newspaper, so they say. Do you want to see them?'

'No,' I said, 'certainly not. Refer them to Inspector Slack at the police station.'

Mary nodded and turned away.

'And when you've got rid of them,' I said, 'come back here. There's something I want to ask you.'

Mary nodded again.

It was some few minutes before she returned.

'Had a job getting rid of them, she said. 'Persistent. You never saw anything like it. Wouldn't take no for an answer.'

'I expect we shall be a good deal troubled with them,' I said. 'Now, Mary, what I want to ask you is this: Are you quite certain you didn't hear the shot yesterday evening?'

'The shot what killed him? No, of course I didn't. If I had of done, I should have gone in to see what had happened.'

'Yes, but—' I was remembering Miss Marple's statement that she had heard a shot 'in the wood'. I changed the form of my question. 'Did you hear any other shot – one down in the wood, for instance?'

'Oh! that.' The girl paused. 'Yes, now I come to think of it, I believe I did. Not a lot of shots, just one. Queer sort of bang it was.'

'Exactly,' I said. 'Now what time was that?'

'Time?'

'Yes, time.'

'I couldn't say, I'm sure. Well after tea-time. I do know that.'

'Can't you get a little nearer than that?'

'No, I can't. I've got my work to do, haven't I? I can't go on looking at clocks the whole time – and it wouldn't be much good anyway – the alarm loses a good three-quarters every day, and what with putting it on and one thing and another, I'm never exactly sure what time it is.'

This perhaps explains why our meals are never punctual. They are sometimes too late and sometimes bewilderingly early.

'Was it long before Mr Redding came?'

'No, it wasn't long. Ten minutes – a quarter of an hour – not longer than that.'

I nodded my head, satisfied.

'Is that all?' said Mary. 'Because what I mean to say is, I've got the joint in the oven and the pudding boiling over as likely as not.'

'That's all right. You can go.'

She left the room, and I turned to Griselda.

'Is it quite out of the question to induce Mary to say sir or ma'am?'

'I have told her. She doesn't remember. She's just a raw girl, remember?'

'I am perfectly aware of that,' I said. 'But raw things do not necessarily remain raw for ever. I feel a tinge of cooking might be induced in Mary.'

'Well, I don't agree with you,' said Griselda. 'You know how little we can afford to pay a servant. If once we got her smartened up at all, she'd leave. Naturally. And get higher wages. But as long as Mary can't cook and has those awful manners – well, we're safe, nobody else would have her.'

I perceived that my wife's methods of housekeeping were not so entirely haphazard as I had imagined. A certain amount of reasoning underlay them. Whether it was worth while having a maid at the price of her not being able to cook, and having a habit of throwing dishes and remarks at one with the same disconcerting abruptness, was a debatable matter.

'And anyway,' continued Griselda, 'you must make allowances for her manner being worse than usual just now. You can't expect her to feel exactly sympathetic about Colonel Protheroe's death when he jailed her young man.'

'Did he jail her young man?'

'Yes, for poaching. You know, that man, Archer. Mary has been walking out with him for two years.'

'I didn't know that.'

'Darling Len, you never know anything.'

'It's queer,' I said, 'that everyone says the shot came from the wood.'

'I don't think it's queer at all,' said Griselda. 'You see, one so often does hear shots in the wood. So naturally, when you do hear a shot, you just assume as a matter of course that it *is* in the wood. It probably just sounds a bit louder than usual. Of course, if one were in the next room, you'd realize that it was in the house, but from Mary's kitchen with the window right the other side of the house, I don't believe you'd ever think of such a thing.'

The door opened again.

'Colonel Melchett's back,' said Mary. 'And that police inspector with him, and they say they'd be glad if you'd join them. They're in the study.'

—— I I ——

I saw at a glance that Colonel Melchett and Inspector Slack had not been seeing eye to eye about the case. Melchett looked flushed and annoyed and the inspector looked sulky.

'I'm sorry to say,' said Melchett, 'that Inspector Slack doesn't agree with me in considering young Redding innocent.'

'If he didn't do it, what does he go and say he did it for?' asked Slack sceptically.

'Mrs Protheroe acted in an exactly similar fashion, remember, Slack.'

'That's different. She's a woman, and women act in that silly way. I'm not saying she did it for a moment. She heard he was accused and she trumped up a story. I'm used to that sort of game. You wouldn't believe the fool things I've known women do. But Redding's different. He's got his head screwed on all right. And if he admits he did it, well, I say he did do it. It's his pistol – you can't get away from that. And thanks to this business of Mrs Protheroe, we know the motive. That was the weak point before, but now we know it – why, the whole thing's plain sailing.'

'You think he can have shot him earlier? At six-thirty, say?'

'He can't have done that.'

'You've checked up his movements?'

The inspector nodded.

'He was in the village near the Blue Boar at ten past six. From there he came along the back lane where you say the old lady next door saw him – she doesn't miss much, I should say – and kept his appointment with Mrs Protheroe in the studio in the garden. They left there together just after six-thirty, and went along the lane to the village, being joined by Dr Stone. He corroborates that all right – I've seen him. They all stood talking just by the post office for a few minutes, then Mrs Protheroe went into Miss Hartnell's to borrow a gardening magazine. That's all right too. I've seen Miss Hartnell. Mrs Protheroe remained there talking to her till just on seven o'clock, when she exclaimed at the lateness of the hour and said she must get home.'

'What was her manner?'

'Very easy and pleasant, Miss Hartnell said. She seemed in good spirits – Miss Hartnell is quite sure there was nothing on her mind.'

'Well, go on.'

'Redding, he went with Dr Stone to the Blue Boar and they had a drink together. He left there at twenty minutes to seven, went rapidly along the village street and down the road to the Vicarage. Lots of people saw him.'

'Not down the back lane this time?' commented the colonel.

'No – he came to the front, asked for the vicar, heard Colonel Protheroe was there, went in – and shot him – just as he said he did! That's the truth of it, and we needn't look further.'

Melchett shook his head.

'There's the doctor's evidence. You can't get away from that. Protheroe was shot not later than six-thirty.'

'Oh! doctors!' Inspector Slack looked contemptuous. 'If you're going to believe doctors. Take out all your teeth – that's what they do nowadays – and then say they're very sorry, but all the time it was appendicitis. Doctors!'

'This isn't a question of diagnosis. Dr Haydock was absolutely positive on the point. You can't go against the medical evidence, Slack.'

'And there's my evidence for what it is worth,' I said, suddenly recalling a forgotten incident. 'I touched the body and it was cold. That I can swear to.'

'You see, Slack?' said Melchett.

'Well, of course, if that's so. But there it was – a beautiful case. Mr Redding only too anxious to be hanged, so to speak.'

'That, in itself, strikes me as a little unnatural,' observed Colonel Melchett.

'Well, there's no accounting for tastes,' said the inspector. 'There's a lot of gentlemen went a bit balmy after the war. Now, I suppose, it means starting again at the beginning.' He turned on me. 'Why you went out of your way to mislead me about the clock, sir, I can't think. Obstructing the ends of justice, that's what that was.'

'I tried to tell you on three separate occasions,' I said. 'And each time you shut me up and refused to listen.'

'That's just a way of speaking, sir. You could have told me perfectly well if you had had a mind to. The clock and the note seemed to tally perfectly. Now, according to you, the clock was all wrong. I never knew such a case. What's the sense of keeping a clock a quarter of an hour fast anyway?'

'It is supposed,' I said, 'to induce punctuality.'

'I don't think we need go further into that now, Inspector,' said Colonel Melchett tactfully. 'What we want now is the true story from both Mrs Protheroe and young Redding. I telephoned to Haydock and asked him to bring Mrs Protheroe over here with him. They ought to be here in about a quarter of an hour. I think it would be as well to have Redding here first.'

'I'll get on to the station,' said Inspector Slack, and took up the telephone.

'And now,' he said, replacing the receiver, 'we'll get to work on this room.' He looked at me in a meaning fashion.

'Perhaps,' I said, 'you'd like me out of the way.'

The inspector immediately opened the door for me. Melchett called out:

'Come back when young Redding arrives, will you, vicar? You're a friend of his and you may have sufficient influence to persuade him to speak the truth.'

I found my wife and Miss Marple with their heads together.

'We've been discussing all sorts of possibilities,' said Griselda. 'I wish you'd solve the case, Miss Marple, like you did the way Miss Wetherby's gill of picked shrimps disappeared. And all because it reminded you of something quite different about a sack of coals.'

'You're laughing, my dear,' said Miss Marple, 'but after all, that is a very sound way of arriving at the truth. It's really what people call intuition and make such a fuss about. Intuition is like reading a word without having to spell it out. A child can't do that because it has had so little experience. But a grown-up person knows the word because they've seen if often before. You catch my meaning, vicar?'

'Yes,' I said slowly, 'I think I do. You mean that if a thing reminds you of something else – well, its probably the same kind of thing.'

'Exactly.'

'And what precisely does the murder of Colonel Protheroe remind you of?'

Miss Marple sighed.

'That is just the difficulty. So many parallels come to the mind. For instance, there was Major Hargraves, a churchwarden and a man highly respected in every way. And all the time he was keeping a separate second establishment – a former house-maid, just think of it! And five children – actually five childen – a terrible shock to his wife and daughter.'

I tried hard to visualize Colonel Protheroe in the role of secret sinner and failed.

'And then there was that laundry business,' went on Miss Marple. 'Miss Hartnell's opal pin – left most imprudently in a frilled blouse and sent to the laundry. And the woman who took it didn't want it in the least and wasn't by any means a thief. She simply hid it in another woman's house and told the police she'd seen this other woman take it. Spite, you know, sheer spite. It's an astonishing motive – spite. A man in it, of course. There always is.'

This time I failed to see any parallel, however remote.

'And then there was poor Elwell's daughter – such a pretty ethereal girl – tried to stifle her little brother. And there was the money for the Choirboys' Outing (before your time, vicar) actually taken by the organist. His wife was sadly in debt. Yes, this case makes one think so many things – too many. It's very hard to arrive at the truth.'

'I wish you would tell me,' I said, 'who were the seven suspects?'

'The seven suspects?'

'You said you could think of seven people who would – well, be glad of Colonel Protheroe's death.'

'Did I? Yes, I remember I did.'

Was that true?'

'Oh! certainly it was true. But I mustn't mention names. You can think of them quite easily yourself, I am sure.'

'Indeed I can't. There is Lettice Protheroe, I suppose, since she probably comes into money on her father's death. But it is absurd to think of her in such a connection, and outside her I can think of nobody.'

'And you, my dear?' said Miss Marple, turning to Griselda.

Rather to my surprise Griselda coloured up. Something very like tears started into her eyes. She clenched both her small hands.

'Oh!' she cried indignantly. 'People are hateful – hateful. The things they say! The beastly things they say . . .'

I looked at her curiously. It is very unlike Griselda to be so upset. She noticed my glance and tried to smile.

'Don't look at me as though I were an interesting specimen you didn't understand, Len. Don't let's get heated and wander from the point. I don't believe that it was Lawrence or Anne, and Lettice is out of the question. There must be some clue or other that would help us.'

'There is the note, of course,' said Miss Marple. 'You will remember my saying this morning that that struck me as exceedingly peculiar.'

'It seems to fix the time of death with remarkable accuracy,' I said. 'And yet, is that possible? Mrs Protheroe would only have just left the study. She would hardly have had time to reach the studio. The only way in which I can account for it is that he consulted his own watch and that his watch was slow. That seems to me a feasible solution.'

'I have another idea,' said Griselda. 'Suppose, Len, that the clock had already been put back – no, that comes to the same thing – how stupid of me!'

'It hadn't been altered when I left,' I said. 'I remember comparing it with my watch. Still, as you say, that has no bearing on the present matter.'

'What do you think, Miss Marple?' asked Griselda.

'My dear, I confess I wasn't thinking about it from that point of view at all. What strikes me as so curious, and has done from the first, is the subject matter of that letter.'

'I don't see that,' I said. 'Colonel Protheroe merely wrote that he couldn't wait any longer—'

'*At twenty minutes past six?*' said Miss Marple. 'Your maid, Mary, had already told him that you wouldn't be in till half-past six at the earliest, and he had appeared to be quite willing to wait until then. And yet at twenty past six he sits down and says he "can't wait any longer".'

I stared at the old lady, feeling an increased respect for her mental powers. Her keen wits had seen what we had failed to perceive. It *was* an odd thing – a very odd thing.

'If only,' I said, 'the letter hadn't been dated—'

Miss Marple nodded her head.

'Exactly,' she said. 'If it *hadn't* been dated!'

I cast my mind back, trying to recall that sheet of notepaper and the blurred scrawl, and at the top that neatly printed 6.20.

Surely these figures were on a different scale to the rest of the letter. I gave a gasp.

'Supposing,' I said, 'it wasn't dated. Supposing that round about 6.30 Colonel Protheroe got impatient and sat down to say he couldn't wait any longer. And as he was sitting there writing, someone came in through the window—'

'Or through the door,' suggested Griselda.

'He'd hear the door and look up.'

'Colonel Protheroe was rather deaf, you remember,' said Miss Marple.

'Yes, that's true. He wouldn't hear it. Whichever way the murderer came, he stole up behind the colonel and shot him. Then he saw the note and the clock and the idea came to him. He put 6.20 at the top of the letter and he altered the clock to 6.22. It was a clever idea. It gave him, or so he would think, a perfect alibi.'

'And what we want to find,' said Griselda, 'is someone who has a cast iron alibi for 6.20, but no alibi at all for – well, that isn't so easy. One can't fix the time.'

'We can fix it within very narrow limits,' I said. 'Haydock places 6.30 as the outside limit of time. I suppose one could perhaps shift it to 6.35: from the reasoning we have just been following out, it seems clear that Protheroe would not have got impatient before 6.30. I think we can say we do know pretty well.'

'Then that shot I heard – yes, I suppose it is quite possible. And I thought nothing about it – nothing at all. Most vexing. And yet, now I try to recollect, it does seem to me that it was different from the usual sort of shot one hears. Yes, there was a difference.'

'Louder?' I suggested.

No, Miss Marple didn't think it had been louder. In fact, she found it hard to say in what way it had been different, but she still insisted that it was.

I thought she was probably persuading herself of the fact rather than actually remembering it, but she had just contributed such a valuable new outlook to the problem that I felt highly respectful towards her.

She rose, murmuring that she must really get back – it had been so tempting just to run over and discuss the case with dear Griselda. I escorted her to the boundary wall and the back gate and returned to find Griselda wrapped in thought.

'Still puzzling over that note?'

'No.'

She gave a sudden shiver and shook her shoulders impatiently.

'Len, I've been thinking. How badly someone must have hated Anne Protheroe!'

'Hated her?'

'Yes. Don't you see? There's no real evidence against Lawrence – all the evidence against him is what you might call accidental. He just happens to take it into his head to come here. If he hadn't – well, no one would have thought of connecting him with the crime. But Anne is different. Suppose someone knew that she was here at exactly 6.20 – the clock and the time on the letter – everything pointing to her. I don't think it was only because of an alibi it was moved to that exact time – I think there was more in it than that – a direct attempt to fasten the business on her. If it hadn't been for Miss Marple saying she hadn't got the pistol with her and noticing that she was only a moment before going down to the studio – Yes, if it hadn't been for that . . .' She shivered again. 'Len, I feel that someone hated Anne Protheroe very much. I – I don't like it.'

12

I was summoned to the study when Lawrence Redding arrived. He looked haggard, and, I thought, suspicious. Colonel Melchett greeted him with something approaching cordiality.

'We want to ask you a few questions – here, on the spot,' he said.

Lawrence sneered slightly.

'Isn't that a French idea? Reconstruction of the crime?'

'My dear boy,' said Colonel Melchett, 'don't take that tone with us. Are you aware that someone else has also confessed to committing the crime which you pretend to have committed?'

The effect of these words on Lawrence was painful and immediate.

'S-s-omeone else?' he stammered. 'Who – who?'

'Mrs Protheroe,' said Colonel Melchett, watching him.

'Absurd. She never did it. She couldn't have. It's impossible.'

Melchett interrupted him.

'Strangely enough, we did not believe her story. Neither, I may say, do we believe yours. Dr Haydock says positively that the murder could not have been committed at the time you say it was.'

'Dr Haydock says that?'

'Yes, so, you see, you are cleared whether you like it or not. And now we want you to help us, to tell us exactly what occurred.

Lawrence still hesitated.

'You're not deceiving me about – about Mrs Protheroe? You really don't suspect her?'

'On my word of honour,' said Colonel Melchett.

Lawrence drew a deep breath.

'I've been a fool,' he said. 'An absolute fool. How could I have thought for one minute that she did it—'

'Suppose you tell us all about it?' suggested the Chief Constable.

'There's not much to tell. I – I met Mrs Protheroe that afternoon –' He paused.

'We know all about that,' said Melchett. 'You may think that your feeling for Mrs Protheroe and hers for you was a dead secret, but in reality it was known and commented upon. In any case, everything is bound to come out now.'

'Very well, then. I expect you are right. I had promised the vicar here' (he glanced at me) 'to – to go right away. I met Mrs Protheroe that evening in the studio at a quarter past six. I told her of what I had decided. She, too, agreed that it was the only thing to do. We – we said goodbye to each other.

'We left the studio, and almost at once Dr Stone joined us. Anne managed to seem marvellously natural. I couldn't do it. I went off with Stone to the Blue Boar and had a drink. Then I thought I'd go home, but when I got to the corner of this road, I changed my mind and decided to come along and see the vicar. I felt I wanted someone to talk to about the matter.

'At the door, the maid told me the vicar was out, but would be in shortly, but that Colonel Protheroe was in the study waiting for him. Well, I didn't like to go away again – looked as though I were shirking meeting him. So I said I'd wait too, and I went into the study.'

He stopped.

'Well?' said Colonel Melchett.

'Protheroe was sitting at the writing-table – just as you found him. I went up to him – touched him. He was dead. Then I looked down and saw the pistol lying on the floor beside him. I picked it up – *and at once saw that it was my pistol.*

'That gave me a turn. My pistol! And then, straightaway I leaped to one conclusion. Anne must have bagged my pistol some time or other – meaning it for herself if she couldn't bear things any longer. Perhaps she had had it with her today. After we parted in the village she must have come back here and – and – oh! I suppose I was mad to think of it. But that's what I thought. I slipped the pistol in my pocket and came away. Just outside the Vicarage gate, I met the vicar. He said something nice and normal about seeing Protheroe – suddenly I had a wild desire to laugh. His manner was so ordinary and everyday and there was I all strung up. I remember shouting out something absurd and seeing his face change. I was nearly off my head, I believe. I went walking – walking – at last I couldn't bear it any longer. If Anne had done this ghastly thing, I was, at least, morally responsible. I went and gave myself up.'

There was a silence when he had finished. Then the colonel said in a businesslike voice:

'I would like to ask just one or two questions. First, did you touch or move the body in any way?'

'No, I didn't touch it at all. One could see he was dead without touching him.'

'Did you notice a note lying on the blotter half concealed by his body?'

'No.'

'Did you interfere in any way with the clock?'

'I never touched the clock. I seem to remember a clock lying overturned on the table, but I never touched it.'

'Now as to this pistol of yours, when did you last see it?'

Lawrence Redding reflected. 'It's hard to say exactly.'

'Where do you keep it?'

'Oh! in a litter of odds and ends in the sitting-room in my cottage. On one of the shelves of the bookcase.'

'You left it lying about carelessly?'

'Yes. I really didn't think about it. It was just there.'

'So that anyone who came to your cottage could have seen it?'

'Yes.'

'And you don't remember when you last saw it?'

Lawrence drew his brows together in a frown of recollection.

'I'm almost sure it was there the day before yesterday. I remember pushing it aside to get an old pipe. I think it was the day before yesterday – but it may have been the day before that.'

'Who has been to your cottage lately?'

'Oh! crowds of people. Someone is always drifting in and out.

I had a sort of tea party the day before yesterday. Lettice Protheroe, Dennis, and all their crowd. And then one or other of the
old Pussies comes in now and again.'

'Do you lock the cottage up when you go out?'

'No; why on earth should I? I've nothing to steal. And no one
does lock their houses up round here.'

'Who looks after your wants there?'

'An old Mrs Archer comes in every morning to "do for me"
as it's called.'

'Do you think she would remember when the pistol was there
last?

'I don't know. She might. But I don't fancy conscientious
dusting is her strong point.'

'It comes to this – that almost anyone might have taken that
pistol?'

'It seems so – yes.'

The door opened and Dr Haydock came in with Anne Protheroe.

She started at seeing Lawrence. He, on his part, made a tentative step towards her.

'Forgive me, Anne,' he said. 'It was abominable of me to think
what I did.'

'I—' She faltered, then looked appealingly at Colonel Melchett. 'It is true, what Dr Haydock told me?'

'That Mr Redding is cleared of suspicion? Yes. And now what
about this story of yours, Mrs Protheroe? Eh, what about it?'

She smiled rather shamefacedly.

'I suppose you think it dreadful of me?'

'Well, shall we say – very foolish? But that's all over. What I
want now, Mrs Protheroe, is the truth – the absolute truth.'

She nodded gravely.

'I will tell you. I suppose you know about – about everything.'

'Yes.'

'I was to meet Lawrence – Mr Redding – that evening at the
studio. At a quarter past six. My husband and I drove into the
village together. I had some shopping to do. As we parted he
mentioned casually that he was going to see the vicar. I couldn't
get word to Lawrence, and I was rather uneasy. I – well, it was
awkward meeting him in the Vicarage garden whilst my husband
was at the Vicarage.'

Her cheeks burned as she said this. It was not a pleasant moment for her.

'I reflected that perhaps my husband would not stay very

long. To find this out, I came along the back lane and into the garden. I hoped no one would see me, but of course old Miss Marple had to be in her garden! She stopped me and we said a few words, and I explained I was going to call for my husband. I felt I had to say something. I don't know whether she believed me or not. She looked rather – funny.

'When I left her, I went straight across to the Vicarage and round the corner of the house to the study window. I crept up to it very softly, expecting to hear the sound of voices. But to my surprise there were none. I just glanced in, saw the room was empty, and hurried across the lawn and down to the studio where Lawrence joined me almost at once.'

'You say the room was empty, Mrs Protheroe?'

'Yes, my husband was not there.'

'Extraordinary.'

'You mean, ma'am, that you didn't see him?' said the inspector.

'No, I didn't see him.'

Inspector Slack whispered to the Chief Constable, who nodded.

'Do you mind, Mrs Protheroe, just showing us exactly what you did?'

'Not at all.'

She rose, Inspector Slack pushed open the window for her, and she stepped out on the terrace and round the house to the left.

Inspector Slack beckoned me imperiously to go and sit at the writing-table.

Somehow I didn't much like doing it. It gave me an uncomfortable feeling. But, of course, I complied.

Presently I heard footsteps outside, they paused for a minute, then retreated. Inspector Slack indicated to me that I could return to the other side of the room. Mrs Protheroe re-entered through the window.

'Is that exactly how it was?' asked Colonel Melchett.

'I think exactly.'

'Then can you tell us, Mrs Protheroe, just exactly where the vicar was in the room when you looked in?' asked Inspector Slack.

'The vicar? I – no, I'm afraid I can't. I didn't see him.'

Inspector Slack nodded.

'That's how you didn't see your husband. He was round the corner at the writing-desk.'

'Oh!' she paused. Suddenly her eyes grew round with horror.
'It wasn't there that – that—'

'Yes, Mrs Protheroe. It was while he was sitting there.'

'Oh!' She quivered.

He went on with his questions.

'Did you know, Mrs Protheroe, that Mr Redding had a pistol?'

'Yes. He told me so once.'

'Did you ever have that pistol in your possession?'

She shook her head. 'No.'

'Did you know where he kept it?'

'I'm not sure. I think – yes, I think I've seen it on a shelf in
his cottage. Didn't you keep it there, Lawrence?'

'When was the last time you were at the cottage, Mrs Protheroe?'

'Oh! about three weeks ago. My husband and I had tea there
with him.'

'And you have not been there since?'

'No. I never went there. You see, it would probably cause a
lot of talk in the village.'

'Doubtless,' said Colonel Melchett dryly. 'Where were you in
the habit of seeing Mr Redding, if I may ask?'

'He used to come up to the Hall. He was painting Lettice.
We – we often met in the woods afterwards.'

Colonel Melchett nodded.

'Isn't that enough?' Her voice was suddenly broken. 'It's so
awful – having to tell you all these things. And – and there
wasn't anything wrong about it. There wasn't – indeed, there
wasn't. We were just friends. We – we couldn't help caring for
each other.'

She looked pleadingly at Dr Haydock, and that soft-hearted
man stepped forward.

'I really think, Melchett,' he said, 'that Mrs Protheroe has had
enough. She's had a great shock – in more ways than one.'

The Chief Constable nodded.

'There is really nothing more I want to ask you, Mrs Protheroe,' he said. 'Thank you for answering my questions so frankly.'

'Then – then I may go?'

'Is your wife in?' asked Haydock. 'I think Mrs Protheroe
would like to see her.'

'Yes,' I said, 'Griselda is in. You'll find her in the drawing-
room.'

She and Haydock left the room together and Lawrence Redding with them.

Colonel Melchett had pursed up his lips and was playing with a paper-knife. Slack was looking at the note. It was then that I mentioned Miss Marple's theory. Slack looked closely at it.

'My word,' he said, 'I believe the old lady's right. Look here, sir, don't you see? – these figures are written in different ink. That date was written with a fountain pen or I'll eat my boots!'

We were all rather excited.

'You've examined the note for fingerprints, of course,' said the Chief Constable.

'What do you think, Colonel? No fingerprints on the note at all. Fingerprints on the pistol those of Mr Lawrence Redding. May have been some others once, before he went fooling round with it and carrying it around in his pocket, but there's nothing clear enough to get hold of now.'

'At first the case looked very black against Mrs Protheroe,' said the colonel thoughtfully. 'Much blacker than against young Redding. There was that old woman Marple's evidence that she didn't have the pistol with her, but these elderly ladies are often mistaken.'

I was silent, but I did not agree with him. I was quite sure that Anne Protheroe had had no pistol with her since Miss Marple had said so. Miss Marple is not the type of elderly lady who makes mistakes. She has got an uncanny knack of being always right.

'What did get me was that nobody heard the shot. If it was fired then – somebody *must* have heard it – wherever they thought it came from. Slack, you'd better have a word with the maid.'

Inspector Slack moved with alacrity towards the door.

'I shouldn't ask her if she heard a shot in the house,' I said. 'Because if you do, she'll deny it. Call it a shot in the wood. That's the only kind of shot she'll admit to hearing.'

'I know how to manage them, said Inspector Slack, and disappeared.

'Miss Marple says she heard a shot later,' said Colonel Melchette thoughtfully. 'We must see if she can fix the time at all precisely. Of course it may be a stray shot that had nothing to do with the case.'

'It may be, of course,' I agreed.

The colonel took a turn or two up and down the room.

'Do you know, Clement,' he said suddenly, 'I've a feeling that this is going to turn out a much more intricate and difficult business than any of us think. Dash it all, there's something behind it.' He snorted. 'Something we don't know about. We're only beginning, Clement. Mark my words, we're only beginning. All these things, the clock, the note, the pistol – they don't make sense as they stand.'

I shook my head. They certainly didn't.

'But I'm going to get to the bottom of it. No calling in of Scotland Yard. Slack's a smart man. He's a very smart man. He's a kind of ferret. He'll nose his way through to the truth. He's done several very good things already, and this case will be his *chef d'œuvre*. Some men would call in Scotland Yard. I shan't. We'll get to the bottom of this here in Downshire.'

'I hope so, I'm sure,' I said.

I tried to make my voice enthusiastic, but I had already taken such a dislike to Inspector Slack that the prospect of his success failed to appeal to me. A successful Slack would, I thought, be even more odious than a baffled one.

'Who has the house next door? asked the colonel suddenly.

'You mean at the end of the road?' Mrs Price Ridley.'

'We'll go along to her after Slack has finished with your maid. She might just possibly have heard something. She isn't deaf or anything, is she?'

'I should say her hearing was remarkably keen. I'm going by the amount of scandal she has started by "just happening to overhear accidentally".'

'That's the kind of woman we want. Oh! here's Slack.'

The inspector had the air of one emerging from a severe tussle.

'Phew!' he said. 'That's a tartar you've got, sir.'

'Mary is essentially a girl of strong character,' I replied.

'Doesn't like the police,' he said. 'I cautioned her – did what I could to put the fear of the law into her, but no good. She stood right up to me.'

'Spirited,' I said, feeling more kindly towards Mary.

'But I pinned her down all right. She heard one shot – and one shot only. And it was a good long time after Colonel Protheroe came. I couldn't get her to name a time, but we fixed it at last by means of the fish. The fish was late, and she blew the boy up when he came, and he said it was barely half-past six anyway, and it was just after that she heard the shot. Of course, that's not accurate, so to speak, but it gives us an idea.'

'H'm,' said Melchett.

'I don't think Mrs Protheroe's in this after all,' said Slack, with a note of regret in his voice. 'She wouldn't have had time, to begin with, and then women never like fiddling with fire-arms. Arsenic's more in their line. No, I don't think she did it. It's a pity!' He sighed.

Melchett explained that he was going round to Mrs Price Ridley's, and Slack approved.

'May I come with you?' I asked. 'I'm getting interested.'

I was given permission, and we set forth. A loud 'Hie' greeted us as we emerged from the Vicarage gate, and my nephew, Dennis, came running up the road from the village to join us.

'Look here,' he said to the inspector, 'what about that foot-print I told you about?'

'Gardener's,' said Inspector Slack laconically.

'You don't think it might be someone else wearing the gar-dener's boots?'

'No, I don't!' said Inspector Slack in a discouraging way.

It would take more than that to discourage Dennis, however. He held out a couple of burnt matches.

'I found these by the Vicarage gate.'

'Thank you,' said Slack, and put them in his pocket.

Matters appeared now to have reached a deadlock.

'You're not arresting Uncle Len, are you?' inquired Dennis facetiously.

'Why should I?' inquired Slack.

'There's a lot of evidence against him,' declared Dennis. 'You ask Mary. Only the day before the murder he was wishing Colonel Protheroe out of the world. Weren't you, Uncle Len?'

'Er—' I began.

Inspector Slack turned a slow suspicious stare upon me, and I felt hot all over. Dennis is exceedingly tiresome. He ought to realize that a policeman seldom has a sense of humour.

'Don't be absurd, Dennis,' I said irritably.

The innocent child opened his eyes in a stare of surprise.

'I say, it's only a joke,' he said. 'Uncle Len just said that any-one who murdered Colonel Protheroe would be doing the world a service.'

'Ah!' said Inspector Slack, 'that explains something the maid said.'

Servants very seldom have any sense of humour either. I cursed Dennis heartily in my mind for bringing the matter up. That and the clock together will make the inspector suspicious of me for life.

'Come on, Clement,' said Colonel Melchett.

'Where are you going? Can I come, too?' asked Dennis.

'No, you can't,' I snapped.

We left him looking after us with a hurt expression. We went up to the neat front door of Mrs Price Ridley's house and the inspector knocked and rang in what I can only describe as an official manner. A pretty parlourmaid answered the bell.

'Mrs Price Ridley in?' inquired Melchett.

'No, sir.' The maid paused and added: 'She's just gone down to the police station.'

This was a totally unexpected development. As we retraced our steps Melchett caught me by the arm and murmured:

'If she's gone to confess to the crime, too, I really shall go off my head.'

13

I hardly thought it likely that Mrs Price Ridley had anything so dramatic in view, but I did wonder what had taken her to the police station. Had she really got evidence of importance, or that she thought of importance, to offer? At any rate, we should soon know.

We found Mrs Price Ridley talking at a high rate of speed to a somewhat bewildered-looking police constable. That she was extremely indignant I knew from the way the bow in her hat was trembling. Mrs Price Ridley wears what, I believe, are known as 'Hats for Matrons' – they make a speciality of them in our adjacent town of Much Benham. They perch easily on a superstructure of hair and are somewhat overweighted with large bows of ribbon. Griselda is always threatening to get a matron's hat.

Mrs Price Ridley paused in her flow of words upon our entrance.

'Mrs Price Ridley?' inquired Colonel Melchett, lifting his hat.

'Let me introduce Colonel Melchett to you, Mrs Price Ridley,' I said. 'Colonel Melchett is our Chief Constable.'

Mrs Price Ridley looked at me coldly, but produced the semblance of a gracious smile for the colonel.

'We've just been round to your house, Mrs Price Ridley,' explained the colonel, 'and heard you had come down here.'

Mrs Price Ridley thawed altogether.

'Ah!' she said, 'I'm glad *some* notice is being taken of the occurrence. Disgraceful, I call it. Simply disgraceful.'

There is no doubt that murder is disgraceful, but it is not the word I should use to describe it myself. It surprised Melchett too, I could see.

'Have you any light to throw upon the matter?' he asked.

'That's your business. It's the business of the police. What do we pay rates and taxes for, I should like to know?'

One wonders how many times that query is uttered in a year!

'We're doing our best, Mrs Price Ridley,' said the Chief Constable.

'But the man here hadn't even heard of it till I told him about it!' cried the lady.

We all looked at the constable.

'Lady been rung up on the telephone,' he said. 'Annoyed. Matter of obscene language, I understand.'

'Oh! I see.' The colonel's brow cleared. 'We've been talking at cross purposes. You came down here to make a complaint, did you?'

Melchett is a wise man. He knows that when it is a question of an irate middle-aged lady, there is only one thing to be done – to listen to her. When she has said all that she wants to say, there is a chance that she will listen to you.

Mrs Price Ridley surged into speech.

'Such disgraceful occurrences ought to be prevented. They ought not to occur. To be rung up in one's own house and insulted – yes, insulted. I'm not accustomed to such things happening. Ever since the war there has been a loosening of moral fibre. Nobody minds what they say, and as to the clothes they wear—'

'Quite,' said Colonel Melchett hastily. 'What happened exactly?'

Mrs Price Ridley took breath and started again.

'I was rung up—'

'When?'

'Yesterday afternoon – evening to be exact. About half-past six. I went to the telephone, suspecting nothing. Immediately I was foully attacked, threatened—'

'What actually was said?'

Mrs Price Ridley got slightly pink.

'That I decline to state.'

'Obscene language,' murmured the constable in a ruminative bass.

'Was bad language used?' asked Colonel Melchett.

'It depends on what you call bad language.'

'Could you understand it?' I asked.

'Of course I could understand it.'

'Then it couldn't have been bad language,' I said.

Mrs Price Ridley looked at me suspiciously.

'A refined lady,' I explained, 'is naturally unacquainted with bad language.'

'It wasn't that kind of thing,' said Mrs Price Ridley. 'At first, I must admit, I was quite taken in. I thought it was a genuine message. Then the – er – person became abusive.'

'Abusive?'

'Most abusive. I was quite alarmed.'

'Used threatening language, eh?'

'Yes. I am not accustomed to being threatened.'

'What did they threaten you with? Bodily damage?'

'Not exactly.'

'I'm afraid, Mrs Price Ridley, you must be more explicit. In what way were you threatened?'

This Mrs Price Ridley seemed singularly reluctant to answer.

'I can't remember exactly. It was all so upsetting. But right at the end – when I was really *very* upset, this – this – *wretch* laughed.'

'Was it a man's voice or a woman's?'

'It was a degenerate voice,' said Mrs Price Ridley, with dignity. 'I can only describe it as a kind of perverted voice. Now gruff, now squeaky. Really a very *peculiar* voice.'

'Probably a practical joke,' said the colonel soothingly.

'A most wicked thing to do, if so. I might have had a heart attack.'

'We'll look into it,' said the colonel: 'eh, inspector? Trace the telephone call. You can't tell me more definitely exactly what was said, Mrs Price Ridley?'

A struggle began in Mrs Price Ridley's ample black bosom. The desire for reticence fought against a desire for vengeance. Vengeance triumphed.

'This, of course, will go no further,' she began.

'Of course not.'

'This creature began by saying – I can hardly bring myself to repeat it—'

'Yes, yes,' said Melchett encouragingly.

' *"You are a wicked scandal-mongering old woman!"* Me, Colonel Melchett – a scandal-mongering old woman. *"But this* *time you've gone too far. Scotland Yard are after you for libel." '

'Naturally, you were alarmed,' said Melchett, biting his moustache to conceal a smile.

' *"Unless you hold your tongue in future, it will be the worse for you – in more ways than one."* I can't describe to you the menacing way *that* was said. I gasped, "Who are you?' faintly – like that, and the voice answered, *"The Avenger."* I gave a little shriek. It sounded so awful, and then – the person laughed. Laughed! Distinctly. And that was all. I heard them hang up the receiver. Of course I asked the exchange what number had been ringing me up, but they said thy didn't know. You know what exchanges are. Thoroughly rude and unsympathetic.'

'Quite,' I said.

'I felt quite faint,' continued Mrs Price Ridley. 'All on edge and so nervous that when I heard a shot in the woods, I do declare I jumped almost out of my skin. That will show you.'

'A shot in the woods?' said Inspector Slack alertly.

'In my excited state, it simply sounded to me like a cannon going off. "Oh!" I said, and sank down on the sofa in a state of prostration. Clara had to bring me a glass of damson gin.'

'Shocking,' said Melchett. 'Shocking. All very trying for you. And the shot sounded very loud, you say? As though it were near at hand?'

'That was simply the state of my nerves,'

'Of course. Of course. And what time was all this? To help us in tracing the telephone call, you know.'

'About half-past six.'

'You can't give it us more exactly than that?'

'Well, you see, the little clock on my mantlepiece had just chimed the half-hour, and I said, "Surely that clock is fast." (It does gain, that clock.) And I compared it with the watch I was wearing and that only said ten minutes past, but then I put it to my ear and found it had stopped. So I thought: "Well, if that clock *is* fast, I shall hear the church tower in a moment or two." And then, of course, the telephone bell rang, and I forgot all about it.' She paused breathless.

'Well, that's near enough,' said Colonel Melchett. 'We'll have it looked into for you, Mrs Price Ridley.'

'Just think of it as a silly joke, and don't worry, Mrs Price Ridley,' I said.

She looked at me coldly. Evidently the incident of the pound note still rankled.

'Very strange things have been happening in this village

lately,' she said, addressing herself to Melchett. 'Very strange things indeed. Colonel Protheroe was going to look into them, and what happened to him, poor man? Perhaps I shall be the next?'

And on that she took her departure, shaking her head with a kind of ominous melancholy. Melchett muttered under his breath: 'No such luck.' Then his face grew grave, and he looked inquiringly at Inspector Slack.

That worthy nodded his head slowly.

'This about settles it, sir. That's three people who heard the shot. We've got to find out now who fired it. This business of Mr Redding's has delayed us. But we've got several starting points. Thinking Mr Redding was guilty, I didn't bother to look into them. But that's all changed now. And now one of the first things to do is to look up that telephone call.'

'Mrs Price Ridley's?'

The inspector grinned.

'No – though I suppose we'd better make a note of that or else we shall have the old girl bothering in here again. No, I meant that fake call that got the vicar out of the way.'

'Yes,' said Melchett, 'that's important.'

'And the next thing is to find out what everyone was doing that evening between six and seven. Everyone at Old Hall, I mean, and pretty well everyone in the village as well.'

I gave a sigh.

'What wonderful energy you have, Inspector Slack.'

'I believe in hard work. We'll begin by just noting down your own movements, Mr Clement.'

'Willingly. The telephone call came through about half-past five.'

'A man's voice, or a woman's?'

'A woman's. At least it sounded like a woman's. But of course I took it for granted it was Mrs Abbott speaking.'

'You didn't recognize it as being Mrs Abbott's?'

'No, I can't say I did. I didn't notice the voice particularly or think about it.'

'And you started right away? Walked? Haven't you got a bicycle?'

'No.'

'I see. So it took you – how long?'

'It's nearly two miles, which ever way you go.'

'Through Old Hall woods is the shortest way, isn't it?'

'Actually, yes. But it's not particularly good going. I went and came back by the footpath across the fields.'

'The one that comes out opposite the Vicarage gate?'

'Yes.'

'And Mrs Clement?'

'My wife was in London. She arrived back by the 6.50 train.'

'Right. The maid I've seen. That finishes with the Vicarage. I'll be off to Old Hall next. And then I want an interview with Mrs Lestrange. Queer, her going to see Protheroe the night before he was killed. A lot of queer things about this case.'

I agreed.

Glancing at the clock, I realized that it was nearly lunch time. I invited Melchett to partake of pot luck with us, but he excused himself on the plea of having to go to the Blue Boar. The Blue Boar gives you a first-rate meal of the joint and two-vegetable type. I thought his choice was a wise one. After her interview with the police, Mary would probably be feeling more temperamental than usual.

—— 14 ——

On my way home, I ran into Miss Hartnell and she detained me at least ten minutes, declaiming in her deep bass voice against the improvidence and ungratefulness of the lower classes. The crux of the matter seemed to be that The Poor did not want Miss Hartnell in their houses. My sympathies were entirely on their side. I am debarred by my social standing from expressing my prepudices in the forceful manner they do.

I soothed her as best I could and made my escape.

Haydock overtook me in his car at the corner of the Vicarage road. 'I've just taken Mrs Protheroe home,' he called.

He waited for me at the gate of his house.

'Come in a minute,' he said. I complied.

'This is an extraordinary business,' he said, as he threw his hat on a chair and opened the door into his surgery.

He sank down on a shabby leather chair and stared across the room. He looked harried and perplexed.

I told him that we had succeeded in fixing the time of the shot. He listened with an almost abstracted air.

'That lets Anne Protheroe out,' he said. 'Well, well, I'm glad it's neither of those two. I like 'em both.'

I believed him, and yet it occurred to me to wonder why, since, as he said, he liked them both, their freedom from complicity seemed to have had the result of plunging him in gloom. This morning he had looked like a man with a weight lifted from his mind, now he looked thoroughly rattled and upset.

And yet I was convinced that he meant what he said. He was fond of both Anne Protheroe and Lawrence Redding. Why, then, this gloomy absorption? He roused himself with an effort.

'I meant to tell you about Hawes. All this business has driven him out of my mind.

'Is he really ill?'

'There's nothing radically wrong with him. You know, of course, that he's had Encephalitis Lethargica, sleepy sickness, as it's commonly called?'

'No,' I said, very much surprised. 'I didn't know anything of the kind. He never told me anything about it. When did he have it?'

'About a year ago. He recovered all right – as far as one ever recovers. It's a strange disease – has a queer moral effect. The whole character may change after it.'

He was silent for a moment or two, and then said:

'We think with horror now of the days when we burnt witches. I believe the day will come when we will shudder to think that we ever hanged criminals.'

'You don't believe in capital punishment?'

'It's not so much that.' He paused. 'You know, 'he said slowly, 'I'd rather have my job than yours.'

'Why?'

'Because your job deals very largely with what we call right and wrong – and I'm not at all sure that there's any such thing. Suppose it's all a question of glandular secretion. Too much of one gland, too little of another – and you get your murderer, your thief, your habitual criminal. Clement, I believe the time will come when we'll be horrified to think of the long centuries in which we've indulged in what you may call moral reprobation, to think how we've punished people for disease – which they can't help, poor devils. You don't hang a man for having tuberculosis.'

'He isn't dangerous to the community.'

'In a sense he is. He infects other people. Or take a man who fancies he's the Emperor of China. You don't say how wicked of him. I take your point about the community. The community must be protected. Shut up these people where they can't do any harm – even put them peacefully out of the way – yes, I'd go as far as that. But don't call it punishment. Don't bring shame on them and their innocent families.'

I looked at him curiously.

'I've never heard you speak like this before.'

'I don't usually air my theories abroad. Today I'm riding my hobby. You're an intelligent man, Clement, which is more than some parsons are. You won't admit, I dare say, that there's no such thing as what is technically termed "Sin", but you're broadminded enough to consider the possibility of such a thing.'

'It strikes at the root of all accepted ideas,' I said.

'Yes, we're a narrow-minded, self-righteous lot, only too keen to judge matters we know nothing about. I honestly believe crime is a case for the doctor, not the policeman and not the parson. In the future, perhaps, there won't be any such thing.'

'You'll have cured it?'

'We'll have cured it. Rather a wonderful thought. Have you ever studied the statistics of crime? No – very few people have. I have, though. You'd be amazed at the amount there is of adolescent crime, glands again, you see. Young Neil, the Oxford-shire murderer – killed five little girls before he was suspected. Nice lad – never given any trouble of any kind. Lily Rose, the little Cornish girl – killed her uncle because he docked her of sweets. Hit him when he was asleep with a coal hammer. Went home and a fortnight later killed her elder sister who had annoyed her about some trifling matter. Neither of them hanged, of course. Sent to a home. May be all right later – may not. Doubt if the girl will. The only thing she cares about is seeing the pigs killed. Do you know when suicide is commonest? Fifteen to sixteen years of age. From self-murder to murder of someone else isn't a very long step. But it's not a moral lack – it's a physical one.'

'What you say is terrible!'

'No – it's only new to you. New truths have to be faced. One's ideas adjusted. But sometimes – it makes life difficult.'

He sat there frowning, yet with a strange look of weariness.

'Haydock,' I said, 'if you suspected – if you knew – that a certain person was a murderer, would you give that person up to the law, or would you be tempted to shield them?'

I was quite unprepared for the effect of my question. He turned on me angrily and suspiciously.

'What makes you say that, Clement? What's in your mind? Out with it, man.'

'Why, nothing particular,' I said, rather taken aback. 'Only – well, murder is in our minds just now. If by any chance you happened to discover the truth – I wondered how you would feel about it, that was all.'

His anger died down. He stared once more straight ahead of him like a man trying to read the answer to a riddle that perplexes him, yet which exists only in his own brain.

'If I suspected – if I knew – I should do my duty, Clement. At least, I hope so.'

'The question is – which way would you consider your duty lay?'

He looked at me with inscrutable eyes.

'That question comes to every man some time in his life, I suppose, Clement. And every man has to decide it in his own way.'

'You don't know?'

'No, I don't know ...'

I felt the best thing was to change the subject.

'That nephew of mine is enjoying this case thoroughly,' I said. 'Spends his entire time looking for footprints and cigarette ash.'

Haydock smiled. 'What age is he?'

'Just sixteen. You don't take tragedies seriously at that age. It's all Sherlock Holmes and Arsene Lupin to you.'

Haydock said thoughtfully:

'He's a fine-looking boy. What are you going to do with him?'

'I can't afford a University education, I'm afraid. The boy himself wants to go into the Merchant Service. He failed for the Navy.'

'Well – it's a hard life – but he might do worse. Yes, he might do worse.'

'I must be going,' I exclaimed, catching sight of the clock. 'I'm nearly half an hour late for lunch.'

My family were just sitting down when I arrived. They demanded a full account of the morning's activities, which I gave them, feeling, as I did so, that most of it was in the nature of an anticlimax.

Dennis, however, was highly entertained by the history of Mrs Price Ridley's telephone call, and went into fits of laughter as I enlarged upon the nervous shock her system had sustained and the necessity for reviving her with damson gin.

'Serve the old cat right,' he exclaimed. 'She's got the worst tongue in the place. I wish I'd thought of ringing her up and giving her a fright. I say, Uncle Len, what about giving her a second dose?'

I hastily begged him to do nothing of the sort. Nothing is more dangerous than the well-meant efforts of the younger generation to assist you and show their sympathy.

Dennis's mood changed suddenly. He frowned and put on his man-of-the-world air.

'I've been with Lettice most of the morning,' he said. 'You know, Giselda, she's really *very* worried. She doesn't want to show it, but she is. Very worried indeed.'

'I should hope so,' said Griselda, with a toss of her head. Griselda is not too fond of Lettice Protheroe.

'I don't think you're ever quite fair to Lettice.'

'Don't you?' said Griselda.

'Lot's of people don't wear mourning.'

Griselda was silent and so was I. Dennis continued:

'She doesn't talk to most people, but she *does* talk to me. She's awfully worried about the whole thing, and she thinks something ought to be done about it.'

'She will find,' I said, 'that Inspector Slack shares her opinion. He is going up to Old Hall this afternoon, and will probably make the life of everybody there quite unbearable to them in his efforts to get at the truth.'

'What do you think *is* the truth, Len?' asked my wife suddenly.

'It's hard to say, my dear. I can't say that at the moment I've any idea at all.'

'Did you say that Inspector Slack was going to trace that telephone call – the one that took you to the Abbotts'?'

'Yes.'

'But can he do it? Isn't it a very difficult thing to do?'

'I should not imagine so. The exchange will have a record of the calls.'

'Oh!' My wife relapsed into thought.

'Uncle Len,' said my nephew, 'why were you so ratty with me this morning for joking about your wishing Colonel Protheroe to be murdered?'

'Because,' I said, 'there is a time for everything. Inspector Slack has no sense of humour. He took your words quite seriously, will probably cross-examine Mary, and will get out a warrant for my arrest.'

'Doesn't he know when a fellow's ragging?'

'No,' I said, 'he does not. He has attained to his present position through hard work and zealous attention to duty. That has left him no time for the minor recreations of life.'

'Do you like him, Uncle Len?'

'No,' I said, 'I do not. From the first moment I saw him I disliked him intensely. But I have no doubt that he is a highly successful man in his profession.'

'You think he'll find out who shot old Protheroe?'

'If he doesn't,' I said, 'it will not be for the want of trying.'

Mary appeared and said:

'Mr Hawes wants to see you. I've put him in the drawing-room, and here's a note. Waiting for an answer. Verbal will do.'

I tore open the note and read it.

DEAR MR CLEMENT– I should be so very grateful if you could come and see me this afternoon as early as possible. I am in great trouble and would like your advice,

Sincerely yours,

ESTELLE LESTRANGE.

'Say I will come round in about half an hour,' I said to Mary. Then I went into the drawing-room to see Hawes.

—— 15 ——

Hawes's appearance distressed me very much. His hands were shaking and his face kept twitching nervously. In my opinion he should have been in bed, and I told him so. He insisted that he was perfectly well.

'I assure you, sir, I never felt better. Never in my life.'

This was obviously so wide of the truth that I hardly knew how to answer. I have a certain admiration for a man who will not give in to illness, but Hawes was carrying the thing rather too far.

'I called to tell you how sorry I was – that such a thing should happen in the Vicarage.'

'Yes,' I said, 'it's not very pleasant.'

'It's terrible – quite terrible. It seems they haven't arrested Mr Redding after all?'

'No. That was a mistake. He made – er – rather a foolish statement.'

'And the police are now quite convinced that he is innocent?'

'Perfectly.'

'Why is that, may I ask? Is it – I mean, do they suspect anyone else?'

I should never have suspected that Hawes would take such a keen interest in the details of a murder case. Perhaps it is because it happened in the Vicarage. He appeared as eager as a reporter.

'I don't know that I am completely in Inspector Slack's confidence. So far as I know, he does not suspect anyone in particular. He is at present engaged in making inquiries.'

'Yes. Yes – of course. But who can one imagine doing such a dreadful thing?'

I shook my head.

'Colonel Protheroe was not a popular man, I know that. But murder! For murder – one would need a very strong motive.'

'So I should imagine,' I said.

'Who could have such a motive? Have the police any idea?'

'I couldn't say.'

'He might have made enemies, you know. The more I think about it, the more I am convinced that he was the kind of man to have enemies. He had a reputation on the Bench for being very severe.'

'I suppose he had.'

'Why, don't you remember, sir? He was telling you yesterday morning about having been threatened by that man Archer.'

'Now I come to think of it, so he did,' I said. 'Of course, I remember. You were quite near us at the time.'

'Yes, I overheard what he was saying. Almost impossible to help it with Colonel Protheroe. He had such a very loud voice, hadn't he? I remember being impressed by your own words. That when his time came, he might have justice meted out to him instead of mercy.'

'Did I say that?' I asked, frowning. My remembrance of my own words was slightly different.

'You said it very impressively, sir. I was struck by your words. Justice is a terrible thing. And to think the poor man was struck down shortly afterwards. It's almost as though you had a premonition.'

'I had nothing of the sort,' I said shortly. I rather dislike

Hawes's tendency to mysticism. There is a touch of the visionary about him.

'Have you told the police about this man Archer, sir?'

'I know nothing about him.'

'I mean, have you repeated to them what Colonel Protheroe said – about Archer having threatened him?'

'No,' I said slowly. 'I have not.'

'But you are going to do so?'

I was silent. I dislike hounding a man down who has already got the forces of law and order against him. I held no brief for Archer. He is an inveterate poacher – one of those cheerful ne'er-do-weels that are to be found in any parish. Whatever he may have said in the heat of anger when he was sentenced I had no definite knowledge that he felt the same when he came out of prison.

'You heard the conversation,' I said at last. 'If you feel it your duty to go to the police with it, you must do so.'

'It would come better from you, sir.'

'Perhaps – but to tell the truth – well, I've no fancy for doing it. I might be helping to put the rope round the neck of an innocent man.'

'But if he shot Colonel Protheroe—'

'Oh, if! There's no evidence of any kind that he did.'

'His threats.'

'Strictly speaking, the threats were not his, but Colonel Protheroe's. Colonel Protheroe was threatening to show Archer what vengeance was worth next time he caught him.'

'I don't understand your attitude, sir.'

'Don't you,' I said wearily. 'You're a young man. You're zealous in the cause of right. When you get to my age, you'll find that you like to give people the benefit of the doubt.'

'It's not – I mean—'

He paused, and I looked at him in surprise.

'You haven't any – any idea of your own – as to the identity of the murderer, I mean?'

'Good heavens, no.'

Hawes persisted. 'Or as to the – the motive?'

'No. Have you?'

'I? No, indeed. I just wondered. If Colonel Protheroe had – had confided in you in any way – mentioned anything . . .'

'His confidence, such as they were, were heard by the whole village street yesterday morning,' I said dryly.

'Yes. Yes, of course. And you don't think – about Archer?'

'The police will know all about Archer soon enough,' I said. 'If I'd heard him threaten Colonel Protheroe myself, that would be a different matter. But you may be sure that if he actually has threatened him, half the people in the village will have heard him, and the news will get to the police all right. You, of course, must do as you like about the matter.'

But Hawes seemed curiously unwilling to do anything himself.

The man's whole attitude was nervous and queer. I recalled what Haydock had said about his illness. There, I supposed, lay the explanation.

He took his leave unwillingly, as though he had more to say, and didn't know how to say it.

Before he left, I arranged with him to take the service for the Mothers' Union, followed by the meeting of District Visitors. I had several projects of my own for the afternoon.

Dismissing Hawes and his troubles from my mind I started off for Mrs Lestrange.

On the table in the hall lay the *Guardian* and the *Church Times* unopened.

As I walked, I remembered that Mrs Lestrange had had an interview with Colonel Protheroe the night before his death. It was possible that something had transpired in that interview which would throw light upon the problem of his murder.

I was shown straight into the little drawing-room, and Mrs Lestrange rose to meet me. I was struck anew by the marvellous atmosphere that this woman could create. She wore a dress of some dead black material that showed off the extraordinary fairness of her skin. There was something curiously dead about her face. Only the eyes were burningly alive. There was a watchful look in them today. Otherwise she showed no signs of animation.

'It was very good of you to come, Mr Clement,' she said, as she shook hands. 'I wanted to speak to you the other day. Then I decided not to do so. I was wrong.'

'As I told you then, I shall be glad to do anything that can help you.'

'Yes, you said that. And you said it as though you meant it. Very few people, Mr Clement, in this world have ever sincerely wished to help me.'

'I can hardly believe that, Mrs Lestrange.'

'It is true. Most people – most men, at any rate, are out for their own hand.' There was a bitterness in her voice.

I did not answer, and she went on:

'Sit down, won't you?'

I obeyed, and she took a chair facing me. She hesitated a moment and then began to speak very slowly and thoughtfully, seeming to weigh each word as she uttered it.

'I am in a very peculiar position, Mr Clement, and I want to ask your advice. That is, I want to ask your advice as to what I should do next. What is past is past and cannot be undone. You understand?'

Before I could reply, the maid who had admitted me opened the door and said with a scared face:

'Oh! please, ma'am, there is a police inspector here, and he says he must speak to you, please.'

There was a pause. Mrs Lestrange's face did not change. Only her eyes very slowly closed and opened again. She seemed to swallow once or twice, then she said in exactly the same clear, calm voice: 'Show him in, Hilda.'

I was about to rise, but she motioned me back again with an imperious hand.

'If you do not mind – I should be much obliged if you would stay.'

I resumed my seat.

'Certainly, if you wish it,' I murmured, as Slack entered with a brisk regulation tread.

'Good afternoon, madam,' he began.

'Good afternoon, Inspector.'

At this moment, he caught sight of me and scowled. There is no doubt about it, Slack does not like me.

'You have no objection to the vicar's presence, I hope?'

I suppose that Slack could not very well say he had.

'No-o,' he said grudgingly. 'Though, perhaps, it might be better—'

Mrs Lestrange paid no attention to the hint.

'What can I do for you, Inspector?' she asked.

'It's this way, madam. Murder of Colonel Protheroe. I'm in charge of the case and making inquiries.'

Mrs Lestrange nodded.

'Just as a matter of form, I'm asking everyone just where they were yesterday evening between the hours of 6 and 7 p.m. Just as a matter of form, you understand.'

Mrs Lestrange did not seem in the least discomposed.

'You want to know where I was yesterday evening between six and seven?'

'If you please, madam.'

'Let me see.' She reflected a moment. 'I was here. In this house.'

'Oh!' I saw the inspector's eyes flash. 'And your maid – you have only one maid, I think – can confirm that statement?'

'No, it was Hilda's afternoon out.'

'I see.'

'So, unfortunately, you will have to take my word for it,' said Mrs Lestrange pleasantly.

'You seriously declare that you were at home all the afternoon?'

'You said between six and seven, Inspector. I was out for a walk early in the afternoon. I returned some time before five o'clock.'

'Then if a lady – Miss Hartnell, for instance – were to declare that she came here about six o'clock, rang the bell, but could make no one hear and was compelled to go away again – you'd say she was mistaken, eh?'

'Oh! no,' Mrs Lestrange shook her head.

'But—'

'If your maid is in, she can say not at home. If one is alone and does not happen to want to see callers – well, the only thing to do it to let them ring.'

Inspector Slack looked slightly baffled.

'Elderly women bore me dreadfully,' said Mrs Lestrange. 'And Miss Hartnell is particularly boring. She must have rung at least half a dozen times before she went away.'

She smiled sweetly at Inspector Slack.

The inspector shifted his ground.

'Then if anyone were to say they'd seen you out and about then—'

'Oh! but they didn't, did they?' She was quick to sense his weak point. 'No one saw me out, because I was in, you see.'

'Quite so, madam.'

The inspector hitched his chair a little nearer.

'Now I understand, Mrs Lestrange, that you paid a visit to Colonel Protheroe at Old Hall the night before his death.'

Mrs Lestrange said calmly: 'That is so.'

'Can you indicate to me the nature of that interview?'

'It concerned a private matter, Inspector.'

'I'm afraid I must ask you to tell me the nature of that private matter.'

'I shall not tell you anything of the kind. I will only assure you that nothing which was said at that interview could possibly have any bearing upon the crime.'

'I don't think you are the best judge of that.'

'At any rate, you will have to take my word for it, Inspector.'

'In fact, I have to take your word about everything.'

'It does seem rather like it,' she agreed, still with the same smiling calm.

Inspector Slack grew very red.

'This is a serious matter, Mrs Lestrange. I want the truth—' He banged his fist down on a table. 'And I mean to get it.'

Mrs Lestrange said nothing at all.

'Don't you see, madam, that you're putting yourself in a very fishy position?'

Still Mrs Lestrange said nothing.

'You'll be required to give evidence at the inquest.'

'Yes.'

Just the monosyllable. Unemphatic, uninterested. The inspector altered his tactics.

'You were acquainted with Colonel Protheroe?'

'Yes, I was acquainted with him.'

'Well acquainted?'

There was a pause before she said:

'I had not seen him for several years.'

'You were acquainted with Mrs Protheroe?'

'No.'

'You'll excuse me, but it was a very unusual time to make a call.'

'Not from my point of view.'

'What do you mean by that?'

'I wanted to see Colonel Protheroe alone. I did not want to see Mrs Protheroe or Miss Protheroe. I considered this the best way of accomplishing my object.'

'Why didn't you want to see Mrs or Miss Protheroe?'

'That, Inspector, is my business.'

'Then you refuse to say more?'

'Absolutely.'

Inspector Slack rose.

'You'll be putting yourself in a nasty position, madam, if you're not careful. All this looks bad – it looks very bad.'

She laughed. I could have told Inspector Slack that this was not the kind of woman who is easily frightened.

'Well,' he said, extricating himself with dignity, 'don't say I haven't warned you, that's all. Good afternoon, madam, and mind you we're going to get at the truth.'

He departed. Mrs Lestrange rose and held out her hand.

'I am going to send you away – yes, it is better so. You see, it is too late for advice now. I have chosen my part.'

She repeated in a rather forlorn voice:

'I have chosen my part.'

—— 16 ——

As I went out I ran into Haydock on the doorstep. He glanced sharply after Slack, who was just passing through the gate, and demanded: 'Has he been questioning her?'

'Yes.'

'He's been civil, I hope?'

Civility, to my mind, is an art which Inspector Slack has never learnt, but I presumed that according to his own lights, civil he had been, and anyway, I didn't want to upset Haydock any further. He was looking worried and upset as it was. So I said he had been quite civil.

Haydock nodded and passed on into the house, and I went on down the village street, where I soon caught up the inspector. I fancy that he was walking slowly on purpose. Much as he dislikes me, he is not the man to let dislike stand in the way of acquiring any useful information.

'Do you know anything about the lady?' he asked me point blank.

I said I knew nothing whatever.

'She's never said anything about why she came here to live?'

'No.'

'Yet you go and see her?'

It is one of my duties to call on my parishioners,' I replied, evading the remark that I had been sent for.

'H'm, I suppose it is.' He was silent for a minute or two and then, unable to resist discussing his recent failure, he went on: 'Fishy business, it looks to me.'

'You think so?'

'If you ask me, I say "blackmail". Seems funny, when you think of what Colonel Protheroe was always supposed to be. But there, you never can tell. He wouldn't be the first churchwarden who'd led a double life.'

Faint remembrances of Miss Marple's remarks on the same subject floated through my mind.

'You really think that's likely?'

'Well, it fits the facts, sir. Why did a smart, well-dressed lady come down to this quiet little hole? Why did she go and see him at that funny time of day? Why did she avoid seeing Mrs and Miss Protheroe? Yes, it all hangs together. Awkward for her to admit – blackmail's a punishable offence. But we'll get the truth out of her. For all we know it may have a very important bearing on the case. If Colonel Protheroe had some guilty secret in his life – something disgraceful – well, you can see for yourself what a field it opens up.'

I suppose it did.

'I've been trying to get the butler to talk. He might have over-heard some of the conversation between Colonel Protheroe and Lestrange. Butlers do sometimes. But he swears he hasn't the least idea of what the conversation was about. By the way, he got the sack through it. The colonel went for him, being angry at his having let her in. The butler retorted by giving notice. Says he didn't like the place anyway and had been thinking of leaving for some time.'

'Really.'

'So that gives us another person who had a grudge against the colonel.'

'You don't seriously suspect the man – what's his name, by the way?'

'His name's Reeves, and I don't say I do suspect him. What I say is, you never know. I don't like that soapy, oily manner of his.'

I wonder what Reeves would say of Inspector's Slack's manner.

'I'm going to question the chauffeur now.'

'Perhaps, then,' I said, 'you'll give me a lift in your car. I want a short interview with Mrs Protheroe.'

'What about?'

'The funeral arrangements.'

'Oh!' Inspector Slack was slightly aback. 'The inquest's to-morrow, Saturday.'

'Just so. The funeral will probably be arranged for Tuesday.'

Inspector Slack seemed to be a little ashamed of himself for his brusqueness. He held out an olive branch in the shape of an invitation to be present at the interview with the chauffeur, Manning.

Manning was a nice lad, not more than twenty-five or -six years of age. He was inclined to be awed by the inspector.

'Now, then, my lad,' said Slack, 'I want a little information from you.'

'Yes, sir,' stammered the chaffeur. 'Certainly, sir.'

If he had committed the murder himself he could not have been more alarmed.

'You took your master to the village yesterday?'

'Yes, sir.'

'What time was that?'

'Five-thirty.'

'Mrs Protheroe went too?'

'Yes, sir.'

'You went straight to the village?'

'Yes, sir.'

'You didn't stop anywhere on the way?'

'No, sir.'

'What did you do when you got there?'

'The colonel got out and told me he wouldn't want the car again. He'd walk home. Mrs Protheroe had some shopping to do. The parcels were put in the car. Then she said that was all, and I drove home.'

'Leaving her in the village?'

'Yes, sir.'

'What time was that?'

'A quarter past six, sir. A quarter past exactly.'

'Where did you leave her?'

'By the church, sir.'

'Had the colonel mentioned at all where he was going?'

'He said something about having to see the vet . . . something to do with one of the horses.'

'I see. And you drove straight back here?'

'Yes, sir.'

'There are two entrances to Old Hall, by the South Lodge and by the North Lodge. I take it that going to the village you would go by the South Lodge?'

'Yes, sir, always.'

'And you came back the same way?'

'Yes, sir.'

'H'm. I think that's all. Ah! here's Miss Protheroe.'

Lettice drifted towards us.

'I want the Fiat, Manning,' she said. 'Start her for me, will you?'

'Very good, miss.'

He went towards a two-seater and lifted the bonnet.

'Just a minute, Miss Protheroe,' said Slack. 'It's necessary that I should have a record of everybody's movements yesterday afternoon. No offence meant.'

Lettice stared at him.

'I never know the time of anything,' she said.

'I understand you went out soon after lunch yesterday?'

She nodded.

'Where to, please?'

'To play tennis.'

'Who with?'

'The Hartley Napiers.'

'At Much Benham?'

'Yes.'

'And you returned?'

'I don't know. I tell you I never know these things.'

'You returned,' I said, 'about seven-thirty.'

'That's right,' said Lettice. 'In the middle of the shemozzle. Anne having fits and Griselda supporting her.'

'Thank you, miss,' said the inspector. 'That's all I want to know.'

'How queer,' said Lettice. 'It seems so uninteresting.'

She moved towards the Fiat.

The inspector touched his forehead in a surreptitious manner.

'A bit wanting?' he suggested.

'Not in the least,' I said. 'But she likes to be thought so.'

'Well, I'm off to question the maids now.'

One cannot really like Slack, but one can admire his energy.

We parted company and I inquired of Reeves if I could see Mrs Protheroe. 'She is lying down, sir, at the moment.'

'Then I'd better not disturb her.'

'Perhaps if you would wait, sir; I know that Mrs Protheroe is anxious to see you. She was saying as much at luncheon.'

He showed me into the drawing-room, switching on the electric lights since the blinds were down.

'A very sad business all this,' I said.

'Yes, sir.' His voice was cold and respectful.

I looked at him. What feelings were at work under that impassive demeanour? Were there things that he knew and could have told us? There is nothing so inhuman as the mask of the good servant.

'Is there anything more, sir?'

Was there just a hint of anxiety to be gone behind that correct expression?

'There's nothing more,' I said.

I had a very short time to wait before Anne Protheroe came to me. We discussed and settled a few arrangements and then:

'What a wonderfully kind man Dr Haydock is!' she exclaimed.

'Haydock is the best fellow I know.'

'He has been amazingly kind to me. But he looks very sad, doesn't he?'

It had never occurred to me to think of Haydock as sad. I turned the idea over in my mind.

'I don't think I've ever noticed it,' I said at last.

'I never have, until today.'

'One's own troubles sharpen one's eyes sometimes,' I said.

'That's very true. She paused and then said:

'Mr Clement, there's one thing I absolutely *cannot* make out. If my husband were shot immediately after I left him, how was it that I didn't hear the shot?'

'They have reason to believe that the shot was fired later.'

'But the 6.20 on the note?'

'Was possibly added by a different hand – the murderer's.'

Her cheek paled.

'How horrible!'

'It didn't strike you that the date was not in his handwriting?'

'None of it looked like his handwriting.'

There was some truth in this observation. It was a somewhat illegible scrawl, not so precise as Protheroe's writing usually was.

'You are sure they don't still suspect Lawrence?'

'I think he is definitely cleared.'

'But, Mr Clement, who can it be? Lucius was not popular, I know, but I don't think he had any real enemies. Not – not that kind of enemy.'

I shook my head. 'It's a mystery.'

I thought wonderingly of Miss Marple's seven suspects. Who could they be?

After I took leave of Anne, I proceeded to put a certain plan of mine into action.

I returned from Old Hall by way of the private path. When I reached the stile, I retraced my steps and, choosing a place where

I fancied the undergrowth showed signs of being disturbed. I turned aside from the path and forced my way through the bushes. The wood was a thick one, with a good deal of tangled undergrowth. My progress was not very fast, and I suddenly became aware that someone else was moving amongst the bushes not very far from me. As I paused irresolutely, Lawrence Redding came into sight. He was carrying a large stone.

I suppose I must have looked surprised, for he suddenly burst out laughing.

'No,' he said, 'it's not a clue, it's a peace offering.'

'A peace offering?'

'Well, a basis for negotiations, shall we say? I want an excuse for calling on your neighbour, Miss Marple, and I have been told there is nothing she likes so much as a nice bit of rock or stone for the Japanese gardens she makes.'

'Quite true,' I said. 'But what do you want with the old lady?'

'Just this. If there was anything to be seen yesterday evening Miss Marple saw it. I don't mean anything necessarily connected with the crime – that she would think connected with the crime. I mean some outré or bizarre incident, some simple little haping that might give us a clue to the truth. Something that she wouldn't think worth while mentioning to the police.'

'It's possible, I suppose.'

'It's worth trying anyhow. Clement, I'm going to get to the bottom of this business. For Anne's sake, if nobody else's. And I haven't any too much confidence in Slack – he's a zealous fellow, but zeal can't really take the place of brains.'

'I see,' I said, 'that you are that favourite character of fiction, the amateur detective. I don't know that they really hold their own with the professional in real life.'

He looked at me shrewdly and suddenly laughed.

'What are you doing in the wood, padre?'

I had the grace to blush.

'Just the same as I am doing, I dare swear. We've got the same idea, haven't we? *How did the murderer come to the study?* First way, along the lane and through the gate, second way, by the front door, third way – is there a third way? My idea was to see if there was any signs of the bushes being disturbed or broken anywhere near the wall of the Vicarage garden.'

'That was just my idea,' I admitted.

'I hadn't really got down to the job, though,' continued Lawrence. 'Because it occurred to me that I'd like to see Miss

Marple first, to make quite sure that no one did pass along the lane yesterday evening whilst we were in the studio.'

I shook my head.

'She was quite positive that nobody did.'

'Yes, nobody whom she would call anybody – sounds mad, but you see what I mean. But there might have been someone like a postman or a milkman or a butcher's boy – someone whose presence would be so natural that you wouldn't think of mentioning it.'

'You've been reading G. K. Chesterton,' I said, and Lawrence did not deny it.

'But don't you think there's just possibly something in the idea?'

'Well, I suppose there might be,' I admitted.

Without further ado, we made our way to Miss Marple's. She was working in the garden, and called out to us as we climbed over the stile.

You see,' murmured Lawrence, 'she sees everybody.'

She received us very graciously and was much pleased with Lawrence's immense rock, which he presented with all due solemnity.

'It's very thoughtful of you, Mr Redding. Very thoughtful indeed.'

Emboldened by this, Lawrence embarked on his questions. Miss Marple listened attentively.

'Yes, I see what you mean, and I quite agree, it is the sort of thing no one mentions or bothers to mention. But I can assure you that there was nothing of the kind. Nothing whatever.'

'You are sure, Miss Maple?'

'Quite sure.'

'Did you see anyone go by the path into the wood that afternoon?' I asked. 'Or come from it?'

'Oh! yes, quite a number of people. Dr Stone and Miss Cram went that way – it's the nearest way to the Barrow for them. That was a little after two o'clock. And Dr Stone returned that way – as you know, Mr Redding, since he joined you and Mrs Protheroe.'

'By the way,' I said. 'That shot – the one you heard, Miss Marple. Mr Redding and Mrs Protheroe must have heard it too.'

I looked inquiringly at Lawrence.

'Yes,' he said, frowning. 'I believe I did hear some shots. Weren't there one or two shots?'

'I only heard one,' said Miss Marple.

'It's only the vaguest impression in my mind,' said Lawrence. 'Curse it all, I wish I could remember. If only I'd known. You see, I was so completely taken up with – with—'

He paused, embarrassed.

I gave a tactful cough. Miss Marple, with a touch of prudishness, changed the subject.

'Inspector Slack has been trying to get me to say whether I heard the shot after Mr Redding and Mrs Protheroe had left the studio or before. I've had to confess that I really could not say definitely, but I have the impression – which is growing stronger the more I think about it – that it was after.'

'Then that lets the celebrated Dr Stone out anyway,' said Lawrence, with a sigh. 'Not that there has ever been the slightest reason why he should be suspected of shooting poor old Protheroe.'

'Ah!' said Miss Marple. 'But I always find it prudent to suspect everybody just a little. What I say is, you really never *know*, do you?'

This was typical of Miss Marple. I asked Lawrence if he agreed with her about the shot.

'I really can't say. You see, it was such an ordinary sound. I should be inclined to think it had been fired when we were in the studio. The sound would have been deadened and – and one would have noticed it less there.'

For other reasons than the sound being deadened, I thought to myself!'

'I must ask Anne,' said Lawrence. 'She may remember. By the way, there seems to me to be one curious fact that needs explanation. Mrs Lestrange, the Mystery Lady of St Mary Mead, paid a visit to old Protheroe after dinner on Wednesday night. And nobody seems to have any idea what it was all about. Old Protheroe said nothing to either his wife or Lettice.'

'Perhaps the vicar knows,' said Miss Marple.

Now how did the woman know that I had been to visit Mrs Lestrange that afternoon? The way she always knows things is uncanny.

I shook my head and said I could throw no light upon the matter.

'What does Inspector Slack think?' asked Miss Marple.

'He's done his best to bully the butler – but apparently the butler wasn't curious enough to listen at the door. So there it is – no one knows.'

'I expect someone overheard something, though, don't you?'

said Miss Marple. 'I mean, somebody always *does*. I think that is where Mr Redding might find out something.'

'But Mrs Protheroe knows nothing.'

'I didn't mean Anne Protheroe,' said Miss Marple. 'I meant the women servants. They do so hate telling anything to the police. But a nice-looking young man – you'll excuse me, Mr Redding – and one who has been unjustly suspected – oh! I'm sure they'd tell him at once.'

'I'll go and have a try this evening,' said Lawrence with vigour. 'Thanks for the hint, Miss Marple. I'll go after – well, after a little job the vicar and I are going to do.'

It occurred to me that we had better be getting on with it. I said goodbye to Miss Marple and we entered the woods once more.

First we went up the path till we came to a new spot where it certainly looked as though someone had left the path on the right-hand side. Lawrence explained that he had already followed this particular trail and found it led nowhere, but he added that we might as well try again. He might have been wrong.

It was, however, as he had said. After about ten or twelve yards any sign of broken and trampled leaves petered out. It was from this spot that Lawrence had broken back towards the path to meet me earlier in the afternoon.

We emerged on the path again and walked a little farther along it. Again we came to a place where the bushes seemed disturbed. The signs were very slight but, I thought, unmistakable. This time the trail was more promising. By a devious course, it wound steadily nearer to the Vicarage. Presently we arrived at where the bushes grew thickly up to the wall. The wall is a high one and ornamented with fragments of broken bottles on the top. If anyone had placed a ladder against it, we ought to find traces of their passage.

We were working our way slowly along the wall when a sound came to our ears of a breaking twig. I pressed forward, forcing my way through a thick tangle of shrubs – and came face to face with Inspector Slack.

'So it's you,' he said. 'And Mr Redding. Now what do you think you two gentlemen are doing?'

Slightly crestfallen, we explained.

'Quite so,' said the inspector. 'Not being the fools we're usually thought to be, I had the same idea myself. I've been here over an hour. Would you like to know something?'

'Yes,' I said meekly.

'Whoever murdered Colonel Protheroe didn't come this way to do it! There's not a sign either on this side of the wall, or the other. Whoever murdered Colonel Protheroe came through the front door. There's no other way he could have come.'

'Impossible,' I cried.

'Why impossible? Your door stands open. Anyone's only got to walk in. They can't be seen from the kitchen. They know you're safely out of the way, they know Mrs Clement is in London, they know Mr Dennis is at a tennis party. Simple as ABC. And they don't need to go or come through the village. Just opposite the Vicarage gate is a public footpath, and from it you can turn into these same woods and come out whichever way you choose. Unless Mrs Price Ridley were to come out of her front gate at that particular minute, it's all clear sailing. A great deal more so than climbing over walls. The side windows of the upper story of Mrs Price Ridley's house do overlook most of that wall. No, depend upon it, that's the way he came.'

It really seemed as though he must be right.

—— 17 ——

Inspector Slack came round to see me the following morning. He is, I think, thawing towards me. In time, he may forget the incident of the clock.

'Well, sir,' he greeted me. 'I've traced that telephone call that you received.'

'Indeed?' I said eagerly.

'It's rather odd. It was put through from the North Lodge of Old Hall. Now that lodge is empty, the lodge-keepers have been pensioned off and the new lodge-keepers aren't in yet. The place was empty and convenient – a window at the back was open. No fingerprints on the instrument itself – it had been wiped clear. That's suggestive.'

'How do you mean?'

'I mean that it shows that call was put through deliberately to get you out of the way. Therefore the murder was carefully planned in advance. If it had been just a harmless practical joke, the fingerprints wouldn't have been wiped off so carefully.'

'No. I see that.'

'It also shows that the murderer was well acquainted with Old Hall and its surroundings. It wasn't Mrs Protheroe who put that call through. I've accounted for every moment of her time that afternoon. There are half a dozen servants who can swear that she was at home up till five-thirty. Then the car came round and drove Colonel Protheroe and her to the village. The colonel went to see Quinton, the vet, about one of the horses. Mrs Protheroe did some ordering at the grocer's and at the fish shop, and from there came straight down the back lane where Miss Marple saw her. All the shops agree she carried no handbag with her. The old lady was right.'

'She usually is,' I said mildly.

'And Miss Protheroe was over at Much Benham at 5.30.'

'Quite so,' I said. 'My nephew was there too.'

'That disposes of her. The maids seem all right – a bit hysterical and upset, but what can you expect? Of course, I've got my eye on the butler – what with giving notice and all. But I don't think he knows anything about it.'

'Your inquiries seem to have had rather a negative result, Inspector.'

'They do and they do not, sir. There's one very queer thing has turned up – quite unexpectedly, I may say.'

'Yes?'

'You remember the fuss that Mrs Price Ridley, who lives next door to you, was kicking up yesterday morning? About being rung up on the telephone?'

'Yes?' I said.

'Well, we traced the call just to calm her – and where on this earth do you think it was put through from?'

'A call office?' I hazarded.

'No, Mr Clement. That call was put through from Mr Lawrence Redding's cottage.'

'What?' I exclaimed, surprised.

'Yes. A bit odd, isn't it? Mr Redding had nothing to do with it. At that time, 6.30, he was on his way to the Blue Boar with Dr Stone in full view of the village. But there it is. Suggestive, eh? Someone walked into that empty cottage and used the telephone; who was it? That's two queer telephone calls in one day. Makes you think there's some connection between them. I'll eat my hat if they weren't both put through by the same person.'

'But with what object?'

'Well, that's what we've got to find out. There seems no particular point in the second one, but there must be a point somewhere. And you see the significance? Mr Redding's house used to telephone from. Mr Redding's pistol. All throwing suspicion on Mr Redding.'

'It would be more to the point to have put through the *first* call from his house,' I objected.

'Ah! but I've been thinking that out. What did Mr Redding do most afternoons? He went up to Old Hall and painted Miss Protheroe. And from his cottage he'd go on his motor bicycle, passing through the North Gate. Now you see the point of the call being put through from there. *The murderer is someone who didn't know about the quarrel and that Mr Redding wasn't going up to Old Hall any more.*'

I reflected a moment to let the inspector's point sink into my brain. They seemed to me logical and unavoidable.

'Were there any fingerprints on the receiver in Mr Redding's cottage?' I asked.

'There were not,' said the inspector bitterly. 'That dratted old woman who goes and does for him had been and dusted them off yesterday morning.' He reflected wrathfully for a few minutes. 'She's a stupid old fool, anyway. Can't remember when she saw the pistol last. It might have been there on the morning of the crime, or it might not. 'She couldn't say, she's sure.' They're all alike!

'Just as a matter of form, I went round and saw Dr Stone,' he went on. 'I must say he was pleasant as could be about it. He and Miss Cram went up to that mound – or barrow – or whatever you call it, about half-past two yesterday, and stayed there all the afternoon. Dr Stone came back alone, and she came later. He says he didn't hear any shot, but admits he's absent-minded. But it all bears out what we think.'

'Only,' I said, 'you haven't caught the murderer.'

'Hm,' said the inspector. 'It was a woman's voice you heard through the telephone. It was in all probability a woman's voice Mrs Price Ridley heard. If only that shot hadn't come hard on the close of the telephone call – well, I'd know where to look.'

'Where?'

'Ah! that's just what it's best not to say, sir.'

Unblushingly, I suggested a glass of old port. I have some very fine old vintage port. Eleven o'clock in the morning is not the usual time for drinking port, but I did not think that mattered with Inspector Slack. It was, of course, cruel abuse of the vintage port, but one must not be squeamish about such things.

When Inspector Slack had polished off the second glass, he

began to unbend and become genial. Such is the effect of that particular port.

'I don't suppose it matters with you, sir,' he said. 'You'll keep it to yourself? No letting it get round the parish.'

I reassured him.

'Seeing as the whole thing happened in your house, it almost seems as though you had a right to know.'

'Just what I feel myself,' I said.

'Well, then, sir, what about the lady who called on Colonel Protheroe the night before the murder?'

'Mrs Lestrange,' I cried, speaking rather loud in my astonishment.

The inspector threw me a reproachful glance.

'Not so loud, sir. Mrs Lestrange is the lady I've got my eye on. You remember what I told you – blackmail.'

'Hardly a reason for murder. Wouldn't it be a case of killing the goose that laid the golden eggs? That is, assuming that your hypothesis is true, which I don't for a minute admit.'

The inspector winked at me in a common manner.

'Ah! she's the kind the gentlemen will always stand up for. Now look here, sir. Suppose she's successfully blackmailed the old gentleman in the past. After a lapse of years, she gets wind of him, comes down here and tries it on again. *But*, in the meantime, things have changed. The law has taken up a very different stand. Every facility is given nowadays to people prosecuting for blackmail – names are not allowed to be reported in the press. Suppose Colonel Protheroe turns round and says he'll have the law on her. She's in a nasty position. They give a very severe sentence for blackmail. The boot's on the other leg. The only thing to do to save herself is to put him out good and quick.'

I was silent. I had to admit that the case the inspector had built up was plausible. Only one thing to my mind made it inadmissible – the personality of Mrs Lestrange.

'I don't agree with you, Inspector,' I said, 'Mrs Lestrange doesn't seem to me to be a potential blackmailer. She's – well, it's an old-fashioned word, but she's a – lady.'

He threw me a pitying glance.

'Ah! well, sir, he said tolerantly, 'you're a clergyman. You don't know half of what goes on. Lady indeed! You'd be surprised if you knew some of the things I know.'

'I'm not referring to mere social position. Anyway, I should imagine Mrs Lestrange to be a *déclassée*. What I mean is a question of – personal refinement.'

'You don't see her with the same eyes as I do, sir. I may be a man – but I'm a police officer, too. They can't get over me with their personal refinement. Why, that woman is the kind who could stick a knife into you without turning a hair.'

Curiously enough, I could believe Mrs Lestrange guilty of murder much more easily than I could believe her capable of blackmail.

'But, of course, she can't have been telephoning to the old lady next door and shooting Colonel Protheroe at one and the same time,' continued the inspector.

The words were hardly out of his mouth when he slapped his leg ferociously.

'Got it,' he exclaimed. 'That's the point of the telephone call. Kind of *alibi*. Knew we'd connect it with the first one. I'm going to look into this. She may have bribed some village lad to do the phoning for her. *He'd* never think of connecting it with the murder.'

The inspector hurried off.

'Miss Marple wants to see you,' said Griselda, putting her head in. 'She sent over a very incoherent note – all spidery and underlined. I couldn't read most of it. Apparently she can't leave home herself. Hurry up and go across and see her and find out what it is. I've got my old women coming in two minutes or I'd come myself. I do hate old women – they tell you about their bad legs and sometimes insist on showing them to you. What luck that the inquest is this afternoon! You won't have to go and watch the Boys' Club Cricket Match.'

I hurried off, considerably exercised in my mind as to the reason for this summons.

I found Miss Marple in what, I believe, is described as a fluster. She was very pink and slightly incoherent.

'My nephew,' she explained. 'My nephew, Raymond West, the author. He is coming down today. Such a to-do. I have to see to everything myself. You cannot trust a maid to air a bed properly, and we must, of course, have a meat meal tonight. Gentlemen require such a lot of meat, do they not? And drink. They certainly should be some drink in the house – and a siphon.'

'If I can do anything—' I began.

'Oh! how very kind. But I did not mean that. There is plenty of time really. He brings his own pipe and tobacco, I am glad to say. Glad because it saves me from knowing which kind of cigarettes are right to buy. But rather sorry, too, because it takes so long for the smell to get out of the curtains. Of course, I open the window and shake them well very early every morning. Raymond gets up very late – I think writers often do. He writes very clever books, I believe, though people are not really nearly so unpleasant as he makes out. Clever young men know so little of life, don't you think?'

'Would you like to bring him to dinner at the Vicarage?' I asked, still unable to gather why I had been summoned.

'Oh! no, thank you,' said Miss Marple. 'It's very kind of you,' she added.

'There was – er – stomething you wanted to see me about, I think,' I suggested desperately.

'Oh! of course. In all the excitement it had gone right out of my head.' She broke off and called to her maid. 'Emily – Emily. Not those sheets. The frilled ones with the monogram, and don't put them too near the fire.'

She closed the door and returned to me on tiptoe.'

'It's just rather a curious thing that happened last night,' she explained. 'I thought you would like to hear about it, though at the moment it doesn't seem to make sense. I felt very wakeful last night – wondering about all this sad business. And I got up and looked out of my window. And what do you think I saw?'

I looked, inquiring.

'Gladys Cram,' said Miss Marple, with great emphasis. 'As I live, going into the wood with a suit-case.'

'A suit-case?'

'Isn't it extraordinary? What should she want with a suit-case in the wood at twelve o'clock at night?'

'You see,' said Miss Marple. 'I daresay it has nothing to do with the murder. But it is a Peculiar Thing. And just at present we all feel we must take notice of Peculiar Things.'

'Perfectly amazing,' I said. 'Was she going to – er – sleep in the barrow by any chance?'

'She didn't, at any rate,' said Miss Marple. 'Because quite a short time afterwards she came back, and she hadn't got the suit-case with her.'

18

The inquest was held that afternoon (Saturday) at two o'clock at the Blue Boar. The local excitement was, I need hardly say, tremendous. There had been no murder in St Mary Mead for at least fifteen years. And to have someone like Colonel Protheroe murdered actually in the Vicarage study is such a feast of sensation as rarely falls to the lot of a village population.

Various comments floated to my ears which I was probably not meant to hear.

'There's vicar. Looks pale, don't he? I wonder if he had a hand in it. 'Twas done at Vicarage, after all.' 'How can you, Mary Adams? And him visiting Henry Abbott at the time.' 'Oh! but they do say him and the colonel had words. There's Mary Hill. Giving herself airs, she is, on account of being in service there. Hush, here's coroner.'

The coroner was Dr Roberts of our adjoining town of Much Benham. He cleared his throat, adjusted his eye-glasses, and looked important.

To recapitulate all the evidence would be merely tiresome. Lawrence Redding gave evidence of finding the body, and identified the pistol as belonging to him. To the best of his belief he had seen it on the Tuesday, two days previously. It was kept on a shelf in his cottage, and the door of the cottage was habitually unlocked.

Mrs Protheroe gave evidence that she had last seen her husband at about a quarter to six when they separated in the village street. She agreed to call for him at the Vicarage later. She had gone to the Vicarage about a quarter past six, by way of the back lane and the garden gate. She had heard no voices in the study and had imagined that the room was empty, but her husband might have been sitting at the writing-table, in which case she would not have seen him. As far as she knew, he had been in his usual health and spirits. She knew of no enemy who might have had a grudge against him.

I gave evidence next, told of my appointment with Protheroe and my summons to the Abbotts'. I described how I had found the body and my summoning of Dr Haydock.

'How many people, Mr Clement, were aware that Colonel Protheroe was coming to see you that evening?'

'A good many, I should imagine. My wife knew, and my

nephew, and Colonel Protheroe himself alluded to the fact that morning when I met him in the village. I should think several people might have overheard him, as, being slightly deaf, he spoke in a loud voice.'

'It was, then, a matter of common knowledge? Anyone might know?'

I agreed.

Haydock followed. He was an important witness. He described carefully and technically the appearance of the body and the exact injuries. It was his opinion that deceased had been shot whilst actually in the act of writing. He placed the time of death at approximately 6.20 to 6.30 – certainly not later than 6.35. That was the outside limit. He was positive and emphatic on that point. There was no question of suicide, the wound could not have been self-inflicted.

Inspector Slack's evidence was discreet and abridged. He described his summons and the circumstances under which he had found the body. The unfinished letter was produced and the time on it – 6.20 – noted. Also the clock. It was tacitly assumed that the time of death was 6.22. The police were giving nothing away. Anne Protheroe told me afterwards that she had been told to suggest a slightly earlier period of time than 6.20 for her visit.

Our maid, Mary, was the next witness, and proved a somewhat truculent one. She hadn't heard anything, and didn't want to hear anything. It wasn't as though gentlemen who came to see the vicar usually got shot. They didn't. She'd got her own jobs to look after. Colonel Protheroe had arrived at a quarter past six exactly. No, she didn't look at the clock. She heard the church chime after she had shown him into the study. She didn't hear any shot. If there had been a shot she'd have heard it. Well, of course, she knew there must have been a shot, since the gentleman was found shot – but there it was. She hadn't heard it.

The coroner did not press the point. I realized that he and Colonel Melchett were working in agreement.

Mrs Lestrange had been subpœnaed to give evidence, but a medical certificate, signed by Dr Haydock, was produced saying she was too ill to attend.

There was only one other witness, a somewhat doddering old woman. The one who, in Slack's phrase, 'did for' Lawrence Redding.

Mrs Archer was shown the pistol and recognised it as the one she had seen in Mr Redding's sitting-room 'over against the bookcase, he kept it, lying about.' She had last seen it on the day of the murder. Yes – in answer to a further question – she was quite sure it was there at lunch time on Thursday – quarter to one when she left.

I remembered what the inspector had told me, and I was mildly surprised. However vague she might have been when he questioned her, she was quite positive about it now.

The coroner summed up in a negative manner, but with a good deal of firmness. The verdict was given almost immediately:

Murder by Person or Persons unknown.

As I left the room I was aware of a small army of young men with bright, alert faces and a kind of superficial resemblance to each other. Several of them were already known to me by sight as having haunted the Vicarage the last few days. Seeking to escape, I plunged back into the Blue Boar and was lucky enough to run straight into the archæologist, Dr Stone. I clutched at him without ceremony.

'Journalists,' I said briefly and expressively. 'If you could deliver me from their clutches?'

'Why, certainly, Mr Clement. Come upstairs with me.'

He led the way up the narrow staircase and into his sitting-room, where Miss Cram was sitting rattling the keys of a typewriter with a practised touch. She greeted me with a broad smile of welcome and seized the opportunity to stop work.

'Awful, isn't it?' she said. 'Not knowing who did it, I mean. Not but that I'm disappointed in an inquest. Tame, that's what I call it. Nothing what you might call spicy from beginning to end.'

'You were there, then, Miss Cram?'

'I was there all right. Fancy your not seeing me. Didn't you see me? I feel a bit hurt about that. Yes, I do. A gentleman, even if he is a clergyman, ought to have eyes in his head.'

'Were you present also?' I asked Dr Stone, in an effort to escape from this playful badinage. Young women like Miss Cram always make me feel awkward.

'No, I'm afraid I feel very little interest in such things. I am a man very wrapped up in his own hobby.'

'It must be a very interesting hobby,' I said.

'You know something of it, perhaps?'

I was obliged to confess that I knew next to nothing.

Dr Stone was not the kind of man whom a confession of ignorance daunts. The result was exactly the same as though I had said that the excavation of barrows was my only relaxation. He surged and eddied into speech. Long barrows, round barrows, stone age, bronze age, paleolithic, neolithic kistvæns and cromlechs – it burst forth in a torrent. I had little to do save nod my head and look intelligent – and that last is perhaps over optimistic. Dr Stone boomed on. He was a little man. His head was round and bald, his face was round and rosy, and he beamed at you through very strong glasses. I have never know a man so enthusiastic on so little encouragement. He went into every argument for and against his own pet theory – which, by the way, I quite failed to grasp!

He detailed at great length his difference of opinion with Colonel Protheroe.

'An opinionated boor,' he said with heat. 'Yes, yes, I know he is dead, and one should speak no ill of the dead. But death does not alter facts. An opinionated boor describes him exactly. Because he had read a few books, he set himself up as an authority – against a man who has made a lifelong study of the subject. My whole life, Mr Clement, has been given up to this work. My whole life—'

He was spluttering with excitement. Gladys Cram brought him back to earth with a terse sentence.

'You'll miss your train if you don't look out,' she observed.

'Oh!' The little man stopped in mid speech and dragged a watch from his pocket. 'Bless my soul. Quarter to? Impossible.'

'Once you start talking you never remember the time. What you'd do without me to look after you, I really don't know.'

'Quite right, my dear, quite right.' He patted her affectionately on the shoulder. 'This is a wonderful girl, Mr Clement. Never forgets anything. I consider myself extremely lucky to have found her.'

'Oh! go on, Dr Stone,' said the lady. 'You spoil me, you do.'

'I could not help feeling that I should be in a material position to add my support to the second school of thought – that which forsees lawful matrimony as the future of Dr Stone and Miss Cram. I imagined that in her own way Miss Cram was rather a clever young woman.

'You'd better be getting along,' said Miss Cram.

'Yes, yes, so I must.'

He vanished into the room next door and returned carrying a suit-case.

'You are leaving?' I asked in some surprise.

'Just running up to town for a couple of days,' he explained. 'My old mother to see tomorrow, some business with my lawyers on Monday. On Tuesday I shall return. By the way, I suppose that Colonel Protheroe's death will make no difference to our arrangements. As regards the barrow, I mean. Mrs Protheroe will have no objection to our continuing the work?'

'I should not think so.'

As he spoke, I wondered who actually would be in authority at Old Hall. It was just possible that Protheroe might have left it to Lettice. I felt that it would be interesting to know the contents of Protheroe's will.

'Causes a lot of trouble in a family, a death does,' remarked Miss Cram, with a kind of gloomy relish. 'You wouldn't believe what a nasty spirit there sometimes is.'

'Well, I must really be going.' Dr Stone made ineffectual attempts to control the suit-case, a large rug and an unwieldy umbrella. I came to his rescue. He protested.

'Don't trouble – don't trouble. I can manage perfectly. Doubtless there will be somebody downstairs.'

But down below there was no trace of a boots or anyone else. I suspect that they were being regaled at the expense of the press. Time was getting on, so we set out together to the station, Dr Stone carrying the suit-case, and I holding the rug and umbrella.

Dr Stone ejaculated remarks in between panting breaths as we hurried along.

'Really too good of you – didn't mean – to trouble you . . . Hope we shan't miss – the train – Gladys is a good girl – really a wonderful girl – a very sweet nature – not too happy at home, I'm afraid – absolutely – the heart of a child – heart of a child, I do assure you, in spite of – difference in our ages – find a lot in common . . .'

We saw Lawrence Redding's cottage just as we turned off to the station. It stands in an isolated position with no other house near it. I observed two young men of smart appearance standing on the doorstep and a couple more peering in at the windows. It was a busy day for the press.

'Nice fellow, young Redding,' I remarked, to see what my companion would say.

He was so out of breath by this time that he found it difficult to say anything, but he puffed out a word which I did not at first quite catch.

'Dangerous,' he gasped, when I asked him to repeat his remark.

'Dangerous?'

'Most dangerous. Innocent girls – know no better – taken in by a fellow like that – always hanging round women . . . No good.'

From which I deduced that the only young man in the village had not passed unnoticed by the fair Gladys.

'Goodness,' ejaculated Dr Stone. 'The train!'

We were close to the station by this time and we broke into a fast sprint. A down train was standing in the station and the up London train was just coming in.

At the door of the booking office we collided with a rather exquisite young man, and I recognized Miss Marple's nephew just arriving. He is, I think, a young man who does not like to be collided with. He prides himself on his poise and general air of detachment, and there is no doubt that vulgar contact is detrimental to poise of any kind. He staggered back. I apologized hastily and we passed in. Dr Stone climbed on the train and I handed up his baggage just as the train gave an unwilling jerk and started.

I waved to him and then turned away. Raymond West had departed, but our local chemist, who rejoices in the name of Cherubim, was just setting out for the village. I walked beside him.

'Close shave that,' he observed. 'Well, how did the inquest go, Mr Clement?'

I gave him the verdict.

'Oh! so that's what happened. I rather thought that would be the verdict. Where's Dr Stone off to?'

I repeated what he had told me.

'Lucky not to miss the train. Not that you ever know on this line. I tell you, Mr Clement, it's a crying shame. Disgraceful, that's what I call it. Train I came down by was ten minutes late. And that on a Saturday with no traffic to speak of. And on Wednesday – no, Thursday – yes, Thursday it was – I remember it was the day of the murder because I meant to write a strongly-worded complaint to the company – and the murder put it out of my head – yes, last Thursday. I had been to a meeting of the Pharmaceutical Society. How late do you think the 6.50 was? *Half an hour.* Half an hour exactly! What do you think of that? Ten minutes I don't mind. But if the train doesn't get in till twenty past seven, well, you can't get home before half-past. What I say is, why call it the 6.50?'

'Quite so,' I said, and wishing to escape from the monologue I broke away with the excuse that I had something to say to Lawrence Redding whom I saw approaching us on the other side of the road.

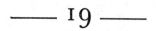

19

'Very glad to have met you,' said Lawrence. 'Come to my place.'

We turned in at the little rustic gate, went up the path, and he drew a key from his pocket and inserted it in the lock.

'You keep the door locked now,' I observed.

'Yes.' He laughed rather bitterly. 'Case of stable door when the steed is gone, eh? It is rather like that. You know, padre,' he held the door open and I passed inside, 'there's something about all this businss that I don't like. It's too much of – how shall I put it – an inside job. Someone knew about that pistol of mine. That means that the murderer, whoever he was, must have actually been in this house – perhaps even had a drink with me.'

'Not necessarily,' I objected. 'The whole village of St Mary Mead probably knows exactly where you keep your toothbrush and what kind of tooth powder you use.'

'But why should it interest them?'

'I don't know,' I said, 'but it does. If you change your shaving cream it will be a topic of conversation.'

'They must be very hard up for news.'

'They are. Nothing exciting ever happens here.'

'Well, it has now – with a vengeance.'

I agreed.

'And who tells them all these things anyway? Shaving cream and things like that?'

'Probably old Mrs Archer.'

'That old crone? She's practically a half-wit, as far as I can make out.'

'That's merely the camouflage of the poor,' I explained. 'They take refuge behind a mask of stupidity. You'll probably find that the old lady has all her wits about her. By the way, she

seems very certain now that the pistol was in its proper place
midday Thursday. What's made her so positive all of a sudden?'

'I haven't the least idea.'

'Do you think she's right?'

'There again I haven't the least idea. I don't go round taking
an inventory of my possessions every day.'

I looked round the small living-room. Every shelf and table
was littered with miscellaneous articles. Lawrence lived in the
midst of an artistic disarray that would have driven me quite
mad.

'It's a bit of a job finding things sometimes,' he said, observing
my glance. 'On the other hand, everything is handy – not tucked
away.'

'Nothing is tucked away, certainly,' I agreed. 'It might perhaps have been better if the pistol had been.'

'Do you know I rather expected the coroner to say something
of the sort. Coroners are such asses. I expected to be censured
or whatever they call it.'

'By the way,' I asked, 'was it loaded?'

Lawrence shook his head.

'I'm not quite so careless as that. It was unloaded, but there
was a box of cartridges beside it.'

'It was apparently loaded in all six chambers and one shot
had been fired.'

Lawrence nodded.

'And whose hand fired it? It's all very well, sir, but unless
the real murderer is discovered I shall be suspected of the crime
to the day of my death.'

'Don't say that, my boy.'

'But I do say it.'

He became silent, frowning to himself. He roused himself
at last and said:

'But let me tell you how I got on last night. You know, old
Miss Marple knows a thing or two.'

'She is, I believe, rather unpopular on that account.'

Lawrence proceeded to recount his story.

He had, following Miss Marple's advice, gone up to Old Hall.
There, with Anne's assistance, he had had an interview with
the parlourmaid. Anne had said simply:

'Mr Redding wants to ask you a few questions, Rose.'

Then she had left the room.

Lawrence had felt somewhat nervous. Rose, a pretty girl of

twenty-five, gazed at him with a limpid gaze which he found rather disconcerting.

'It's – it's about Colonel Protheroe's death.'

'Yes, sir.'

'I'm very anxious, you see, to get at the truth.'

'Yes, sir.'

'I feel that there may be – that someone might – that – that there might be some incident—'

At this point Lawrence felt that he was not covering himself with glory, and heartily cursed Miss Marple and her suggestions.

'I wondered if you could help me?'

'Yes, sir?'

Rose's demeanour was still that of the perfect servant, polite, anxious to assist, and completely uninterested.

'Dash it all,' said Lawrence, 'haven't you talked the thing over in the servants' hall?'

This method of attack flustered Rose slightly. Her perfect poise was shaken.

'In the servants' hall, sir?'

'Or the housekeeper's room, or the bootboy's dugout, or wherever you do talk? There must be *some* place.'

Rose displayed a very faint disposition to giggle, and Lawrence felt encouraged.

'Look here, Rose, you're an awfully nice girl. I'm sure you must understand what I'm feeling like. I don't want to be hanged. I didn't murder your master, but a lot of people think I did. Can't you help me in any way?'

I can imagine at this point that Lawrence must have looked extremely appealing. His handsome head thrown back, his Irish blue eyes appealing. Rose softened and capitulated.

'Oh! sir, I'm sure – if any of us could help in any way. None of us think you did it, sir. Indeed we don't.'

'I know, my dear girl, but that's not going to help me with the police.'

'The police!' Rose tossed her head. 'I can tell you, sir, we don't think much of that inspector. Slack, he calls himself. The police indeed.'

'All the same, the police are very powerful. Now, Rose, you say you'll do your best to help me. I can't help feeling that there's a lot we haven't got at yet. The lady, for instance, who called to see Colonel Protheroe the night before he died.'

'Mrs Lestrange?'

'Yes, Mrs Lestrange. I can't help feeling there's something rather odd about that visit of hers.'

'Yes, indeed, sir, that's what we all said.'

'You did?'

'Coming the way she did. And asking for the colonel. And of course there's been a lot of talk – nobody knowing anything about her down here. And Mrs Simmons, she's the housekeeper, sir, she gave it as her opinion that she was a regular bad lot. But after hearing what Gladdie said, well, I didn't know what to think.'

'What did Gladdie say?'

'Oh! nothing, sir. It was just – we were talking, you know.'

Lawrence looked at her. He had the feeling of something kept back.

'I wonder very much what her interview with Colonel Protheroe was about.'

'Yes, sir.'

'I believe you know, Rose?'

'Me? Oh! no, sir. Indeed I don't. How could I?'

'Look here, Rose. You said you'd help me. If you overheard anything, anything at all – it mightn't seem important, but anything . . . I'd be so awfully grateful to you. After all, anyone might – might chance – just *chance* to overhear something.'

'But I didn't, sir, really I didn't.'

'Then somebody else did,' said Lawrence acutely.

'Well, sir—'

'Do tell me, Rose.'

'I don't know what Gladdie would say, I'm sure.'

'She'd want you to tell me. Who *is* Gladdie, by the way?'

'She's the kitchenmaid, sir. And you see, she'd just stepped out to speak to a friend, and she was passing the window – the study window – and the master was there with the lady. And of course he did speak very loud, the master did, always. And naturally, feeling a little curious – I mean—'

'Awfully natural,' said Lawrence, 'I mean one would simply have to listen.'

'But of course she didn't tell anyone – except me. And we both thought it very odd. But Gladdie couldn't say anything, you see, because if it was known she'd gone out to meet a – a friend – well, it would have meant a lot of unpleasantness with Mrs Pratt, that's the cook, sir. But I'm sure she'd tell you anything, sir, willing.'

'Well, can I go to the kitchen and speak to her?'

Rose was horrified by the suggestion.

'Oh! no, sir, that would never do. And Gladdie's a very nervous girl anyway.'

At last the matter was settled, after a lot of discussion over difficult points. A clandestine meeting was arranged in the shrubbery.

Here, in due course, Lawrence was confronted by the nervous Gladdie whom he described as more like a shivering rabbit than anything human. Ten minutes were spent in trying to put the girl at ease, the shivering Gladys explaining that she couldn't ever – that she didn't ought, that she didn't think Rose would have given her away, that anyway she hadn't meant no harm, indeed she hadn't, and that she'd catch it badly if Mrs Pratt ever came to hear of it.

Lawrence reassured, cajoled, persuaded – at last Gladys consented to speak. 'If you'll be sure it'll go no further sir.'

'Of course it won't.'

'And it won't be brought up against me in a court of law?'

'Never.'

'And you won't tell the mistress?'

'Not on any account.'

'If it were to get to Mrs Pratt's ears—'

'It won't. Now tell me, Gladys.'

'If you're sure it's all right?'

'Of course it is. You'll be glad some day you've saved me from being hanged.'

Gladys gave a little shriek.

'Oh! indeed, I wouldn't like that, sir. Well, it's very little I heard – and that entirely by accident as you might say—'

'I quite understand.'

'But the master, he was evidently very angry. "After all these years" – that's what he was saying – "you dare to come here—" "It's an outrage—" I couldn't hear what the lady said – but after a bit he said, "I utterly refuse – utterly—" I can't remember everything – seemed as though they were at it hammer and tongs, she wanting him to do something and he refusing. "It's a disgrace that you should have come down here," that's one thing he said. And "You shall not see her – I forbid it—" and that made me prick up my ears. Looked as though the lady wanted to tell Mrs Protheroe a thing or two, and he was afraid about it. And I thought to myself, "Well, now, fancy the master. Him so particular. And maybe no beauty himself when all's said and done. Fancy!" I said. And "Men are all alike," I said to my friend later. Not that he'd agree. Argued, he did. But he did admit he was surprised at Colonel Protheroe – him being a churchwarden and handing round the plate and reading the lessons on Sundays. "But there," I said, "that's very often the worst." For that's what I've heard my mother say, many a time.'

Gladdie paused, out of breath, and Lawrence tried tactfully to get back to where the conversation had started.

'Did you hear anything else?

'Well, it's difficult to remember exactly, sir. It was all much the same. He said once or twice, "I don't believe it." Just like that. "Whatever Haydock says, I don't believe it." '

'He said that, did he? "Whatever Haydock says"?'

'Yes. And he said it was all a plot.'

'You didn't hear the lady speak at all?'

'Only just at the end. She must have got up to go and come nearer the window. And I heard what she said. Made my blood run cold, it did. I'll never forget it. *"By this time tomorrow night, you may be dead,"* she said. Wicked the way she said it. As soon as I heard the news. "There," I said to Rose. "There!" '

Lawrence wondered. Principally he wondered how much of Gladys's story was to be depended upon. True in the main, he suspected that it had been embellished and polished since the murder. In especial he doubted the accuracy of the last remark. He thought it highly possible that it owed its being to the fact of the murder.

He thanked Gladys, rewarded her suitably, reassured her as to her misdoings being made known to Mrs Pratt, and left Old Hall with a good deal to think over.

One thing was clear, Mrs Lestrange's interview with Colonel Protheroe had certainly not been a peaceful one, and it was one which he was anxious to keep from the knowledge of his wife.

I thought of Miss Marple's churchwarden with his separate establishment. Was this a case resembling that?

I wondered more than ever where Haydock came in? He had saved Mrs Lestrange from having to give evidence at the inquest. He had done his best to protect her from the police.

How far would he carry that protection?

Supposing he suspected her of crime – would he still try and shield her?

She was a curious woman – a woman of very strong magnetic charm. I myself hated the thought of connecting her with the crime in any way.

Something in me said, 'It can't be her!' Why?

And an imp in my brain replied: 'Because she's a very beautiful and attractive woman. That's why!'

There is, as Miss Marple would say, a lot of human nature in all of us.

——— 20 ———

When I got back to the Vicarage I found that we were in the middle of a domestic crisis.

Griselda met me in the hall and with tears in her eyes dragged me into the drawing-room. 'She's going.'

'Who's going?'

'Mary. She's given notice.'

I really could not take the announcement in a tragic spirit.

'Well,' I said, 'we'll have to get another servant.'

It seemed to me a perfectly reasonable thing to say. When one servant goes, you get another. I was at a loss to understand Griselda's look of reproach.

'Len – you are absolutely heartless. You don't *care*.'

I didn't. In fact, I felt almost light-hearted at the prospect of no more burnt puddings and undercooked vegetables.

'I'll have to look for a girl, and find one, and train her,' continued Griselda in a voice of acute self-pity.

'Is Mary trained?' I said.

'Of course she is.'

'I suppose,' I said, 'that somebody has heard her address us as sir or ma'am and has immediately wrested her from us as a paragon. All I can say is, they'll be disappointed.'

'It isn't that,' said Griselda. 'Nobody else wants her. I don't see how they could. It's her feelings. They're upset because Lettice Protheroe said she didn't dust properly.'

Griselda often comes out with surprising statements, but this seemed to me so surprising that I questioned it. It seemed to me the most unlikely thing in the world that Lettice Protheroe should go out of her way to interfere in our domestic affairs and reprove our maid for slovenly housework. It was completely un-Lettice-like, and I said so.

'I don't see,' I said, 'what our dust has to do with Lettice Protheroe.'

'Nothing at all,' said my wife. 'That's why it's so unreasonable. I wish you'd go and talk to Mary yourself. She's in the kitchen.'

I had no wish to talk to Mary on the subject, but Griselda, who is very energetic and quick, fairly pushed me through the baize door into the kitchen before I had time to rebel.

Mary was peeling potatoes at the sink.

'Er – good afternoon,' I said nervously.

Mary looked up and snorted, but made no other response.

'Mrs Clement tells me that you wish to leave us,' I said.

Mary condescended to reply to this.

'There's some things,' she said darkly, 'as no girl can be asked to put up with.'

'Will you tell me exactly what it is that has upset you?'

'Tell you that in two words, I can.' (Here, I may say, she vastly underestimated.) 'People coming snooping round here when my back's turned. Poking round. And what business of hers is it, how often the study is dusted or turned out? If you and the missus don't complain, it's nobody else's business. If I give satisfaction to you that's all that matters, I say.'

Mary has never given satisfaction to me. I confess that I have a hankering after a room thoroughly dusted and tidied every morning. Mary's practice of flicking off the more obvious deposit on the surface of low tables is to my thinking grossly inadequate. However, I realized that at the moment it was no good to go into side issues.

'Had to go to that inquest, didn't I? Standing up before twelve men, a respectable girl like me! And who knows what questions you may be asked. I'll tell you this. I've never before been in a place where they had a murder in the house, and I never want to be again.'

'I hope you won't,' I said. 'On the law of averages, I should say it was very unlikely.'

'I don't hold with the law. *He* was a magistrate. Many a poor fellow sent to jail for potting at a rabbit – and him with his pheasants and what not. And then, before he's so much as decently buried, that daughter of his comes round and says I don't do my work properly.'

'Do you mean that Miss Protheroe has been here?'

'Found her here when I come back from the Blue Boar. In the study she was. And "Oh!" she says. "I'm looking for my little yellow beret – a little yellow hat. I left it here the other day." "Well," I says, "I haven't seen no hat. It wasn't here when I done the room on Thursday morning," I says. And "Oh!" she

says, "but I dare say you wouldn't see it. You don't spend much
time doing a room, do you?" And with that she draws her finger
along the mantelshelf and looks at it. As though I had time on
a morning like this to take off all them ornaments and put them
back, with the police only unlocking the room the night before.
"If the vicar and his lady are satisfied that's all that matters,
I think, miss," I said. And she laughs and goes out of the window and says, "Oh! but are you sure they are?" '

'I see,' I said.

'And there it is! A girl has her feelings! I'm sure I'd work
my fingers to the bone for you and the missus. And if she wants
a new-fangled dish tried, I'm always ready to try it.'

'I'm sure you are,' I said soothingly.

'But she must have heard something or she wouldn't have
said what she did. And if I don't give satisfaction I'd rather go.
Not that I take any notice of what Miss Protheroe says. She's
not loved up at the Hall, I can tell you. Never a please or a
thank you, and everything scattered right and left. I wouldn't
set any store by Miss Lettice Protheroe myself for all that Mr
Dennis is so set upon her. But she's the kind that can always
twist a young gentleman round her little finger.'

During all this, Mary had been extracting eyes from potatoes
with such energy that they had been flying round the kitchen
like hailstones. At this moment one hit me in the eye and caused
a momentary pause in the conversation.

'Don't you think,' I said, as I dabbed my eye with my handkerchief, 'that you have been rather too inclined to take offence
where none is meant? You know, Mary, your mistress will be
very sorry to lose you.'

'I've nothing against the mistress – or against you, sir, for that
matter.'

'Well, then, don't you think you're being rather silly?'

Mary sniffed.

'I was a bit upset like – after the inquest and all. And a girl
has her feelings. But I wouldn't like to cause the mistress inconvenience.'

'Then that's all right,' I said.

I left the kitchen to find Griselda and Dennis waiting for me
in the hall. 'Well?' exclaimed Griselda.

'She's staying,' I said, and sighed.

'Len,' said my wife, 'you *have* been clever.'

I felt rather inclined to disagree with her. I did not think I
had been clever. It is my firm opinion that no servant could be

a worse one than Mary. Any change, I consider, would have been a change for the better.

But I like to please Griselda. I detailed the heads of Mary's grievance.

'How like Lettice,' said Dennis. 'She couldn't have left that yellow beret of hers here on Wednesday. She was wearing it for tennis on Thursday.'

'That seems to me highly probable,' I said.

'She never knows where she's left anything,' said Dennis, with a kind of affectionate pride and admiration that I felt was entirely uncalled for. 'She loses about a dozen things every day.'

'A remarkably attractive trait,' I observed.

Any sarcasm missed Dennis.

'She *is* attractive,' he said, with a deep sigh. 'People are always proposing to her – she told me so.'

'They must be illicit proposals if they're made to her down here,' I remarked. 'We haven't got a bachelor in the place.'

'There's Dr Stone,' said Griselda, her eyes dancing.

'He asked her to come and see the barrow the other day,' I admitted.

'Of course he did,' said Griselda. 'She *is* attractive, Len. Even bald-headed archæologists feel it.'

'Lots of SA,' said Dennis sapiently.

And yet Lawrence Redding is completely untouched by Lettice's charm. Griselda, however, explained that with the air of one who knew she was right.

'Lawrence has got lots of SA himself. That kind always likes the – how shall I put it – the Quaker type. Very restrained and diffident. The kind of women whom everybody calls cold. I think Anne is the only woman who could ever hold Lawrence. I don't think they'll ever tire of each other. All the same, I think he's been rather stupid in one way. He's rather made use of Lettice, you know. I don't think he ever dreamed she cared – he's awfully modest in some ways – but I have a feeling she does.'

'She can't bear him,' said Dennis positively. 'She told me so.'

I have never seen anything like the pitying silence with which Griselda received this remark.

I went into my study. There was, to my fancy, still a rather eerie feeling in the room. I knew that I must get over this. Once give in to that feeling, and I should probably never use the study again. I walked thoughtfully over to the writing-table. Here Protheroe had sat, red-faced, hearty, self-righteous, and here, in a moment of time, he had been struck down. Here, where I was standing, an enemy had stood ...

And so – no more Protheroe ...

Here was the pen his fingers had held.

On the floor was a faint dark stain – the rug had been sent to the cleaners, but the blood had soaked through.

I shivered.

'I can't use this room,' I said aloud. 'I can't use it.'

Then my eye was caught by something – a mere speck of bright blue. I bent down. Between the floor and the desk I saw a small object. I picked it up.

I was standing staring at it in the palm of my hand when Griselda came in.

'I forgot to tell you, Len. Miss Marple wants us to go over tonight after dinner. To amuse the nephew. She's afraid of his being dull. I said we'd go.'

'Very well, my dear.'

'What are you looking at?'

'Nothing.'

I closed my hand, and looking at my wife, observed:

'If you don't amuse Master Raymond West, my dear, he must be very hard to please.'

My wife said: 'Don't be ridiculous, Len,' and turned pink. She went out again, and I unclosed my hand.

In the palm of my hand was a blue lapis lazuli ear-ring set in seed pearls.

It was rather an unusual jewel, and I knew very well where I had seen it last.

21

I cannot say that I have at any time a great admiration for Mr Raymond West. He is, I know, supposed to be a brilliant novelist and has made quite a name as a poet. His poems have no capital letters in them, which is, I believe, the essence of modernity. His books are about unpleasant people leading lives of surpassing dullness.

He has a tolerant affection for 'Aunt Jane,' whom he alludes to in her presence as a 'survival.'

She listens to his talk with a flattering interest, and if there is sometimes an amused twinkle in her eye I am sure he never notices it.

He fastened on Griselda at once with flattering abruptness. They discussed modern plays and from there went on to modern schemes of decoration. Griselda affects to laugh at Raymond West, but she is, I think, susceptible to his conversation.

During my (dull) conversation with Miss Marple, I heard at intervals the reiteration 'buried as you are down here'.

It began at last to irritate me. I said suddenly:

'I suppose you consider us very much out of things down here?'

Raymond West waved his cigarette.

'I regard St Mary Mead,' he said authoriatively, 'as a stagnant pool.'

He looked at us, prepared for resentment at his statement, but somewhat, I think, to his chagrin, no one displayed annoyance.

'That is really not a very good simile, dear Raymond,' said Miss Marple briskly. 'Nothing, I believe, is so full of life under the microscope as a drop of water from a stagnant pool.'

'Life – of a kind,' admitted the novelist.

'It's all much the same kind, really, isn't it?' said Miss Marple.

'You compare yourself to a denizen of a stagnant pond, Aunt Jane?'

'My dear, you said something of the sort in your last book, I remember.'

No clever young man likes having his works quoted against himself. Raymond West was no exception.

'That was entirely different,' he snapped.

'Life is, after all, very much the same everywhere,' said Miss Marple in her placid voice. 'Getting born, you know, and growing up – and coming into contact with other people – getting jostled – and then marriage and more babies—'

'And finally death,' said Raymond West. 'And not death with a death certificate always. Death in life.'

'Talking of death,' said Griselda, 'you know we've had a murder here?'

Raymond West waved murder away with his cigarette.

'Murder is so crude,' he said. 'I take no interest in it.'

That statement did not take me in for a moment. They say all the world loves a lover – apply that saying to murder and you have an even more infallible truth. No one can fail to be interested in a murder. Simple people like Griselda and myself can admit the fact, but anyone like Raymond West has to pretend to be bored – at any rate for the first five minutes.

Miss Marple, however, gave her nephew away by remarking:
'Raymond and I have been discussing nothing else all through dinner.'

'I take a great interest in all the local news,' said Raymond hastily. He smiled benignly and tolerantly at Miss Marple.

'Have you a theory, Mr West?' asked Griselda.

'Logically, said Raymond West, again flourishing his cigarette, 'only one person could have killed Protheroe.'

'Yes?' said Griselda.

We hung upon his words with flattering attention.

'The vicar,' said Raymond, and pointed an accusing finger at me.

I gasped.

'Of course,' he reassured me, 'I know you didn't do it. Life is never what it should be. But think of the drama – the fitness – churchwarden murdered in the vicar's study by the vicar. Delicious!'

'And the motive?' I inquired.

'Oh! that's interesting.' He sat up – allowed his cigarette to go out. 'Inferiority complex, I think. Possibly too many inhibitions. I should like to write the story of the affair. Amazingly complex. Week after week, year after year, he's seen the man – at vestry meetings – at choirboys' outings – handing round the bag in church – bringing it to the altar. Always he dislikes the man – always he chokes down his dislike. It's unchristian, he won't encourage it. And so it festers underneath, and one day—'

He made a graphic gesture.

Griselda turned to me.

'Have you ever felt like that, Len?'

'Never,' I said truthfully.

'Yet I hear you were wishing him out of the world not so long ago,' remarked Miss Marple.

(That miserable Dennis! But my fault, of course, for ever making the remark.)

'I'm afraid I was,' I said. 'It was a stupid remark to make, but really I'd had a very trying morning with him.'

'That's disappointing,' said Raymond West. 'Because, of course, if your subconscious were really planning to do him in, it would never have allowed you to make that remark.'

He sighed.

'My theory falls to the ground. This is probably a very

ordinary murder – a revengeful poacher or something of that sort.'

'Miss Cram came to see me this afternoon,' said Miss Marple. 'I met her in the village and I asked her if she would like to see my garden.'

'Is she fond of gardens?' asked Griselda.

'I don't think so,' said Miss Marple, with a faint twinkle. 'But it makes a very useful excuse for talk, don't you think?'

'What did you make of her?' asked Griselda. 'I don't believe she's really so bad.'

'She volunteered a lot of information – really a lot of information,' said Miss Marple. 'About herself, you know, and her people. They all seem to be dead or in India. Very sad. By the way, she has gone to Old Hall for the weekend.'

'What?'

'Yes, it seems Mrs Protheroe asked her – or she suggested it to Mrs Protheroe – I don't quite know which way about it was. To do some secretarial work for her – there are so many letters to cope with. It turned out rather fortunately. Dr Stone being away, she has nothing to do. What an excitement this barrow has been.'

'Stone?' said Raymond. 'Is that the archæologist fellow?'

'Yes, he is excavating a barrow. On the Protheroe property.'

'He's a good man,' said Raymond. 'Wonderfully keen on his job. I met him at a dinner not long ago and we had a most interesting talk. I must look him up.'

'Unfortunately,' I said, 'he's just gone to London for the weekend. Why, you actually ran into him at the station this afternoon.'

'I ran into you. You had a little fat man with you – with glasses on.'

'Yes – Dr Stone.'

'But, my dear fellow – that wasn't Stone.'

'Not Stone?'

'Not the archæologist. I know him quite well. The man wasn't Stone – not the faintest resemblance.'

We stared at each other. In particular I stared at Miss Marple.

'Extraordinary,' I said.

'The suit-case,' said Miss Marple.

'But why?' said Griselda.

'It reminds me of the time the man went round pretending to be the gas inspector,' murmured Miss Marple. 'Quite a little haul, he got.'

'An imposter,' said Raymond West. 'Now this is really interesting.'

'The question is, has it anything to do with the murder?' said Griselda.

'Not necessarily,' I said. 'But—' I looked at Miss Marple.

'It is,' she said, 'a Peculiar Thing. Another Peculiar Thing.'

'Yes,' I said, rising. 'I rather feel the inspector ought to be told about this at once.'

22

Inspector Slack's orders, once I had got him on the telephone, were brief and emphatic. Nothing was to 'get about'. In particular, Miss Cram was not to be alarmed. In the meantime, a search was to be instituted for the suit-case in the neighbourhood of the barrow.

Griselda and I returned home very excited over this new development. We could not say much with Dennis present, as we had faithfully promised Inspector Slack to breathe no word to anybody.

In any case, Dennis was full of his own troubles. He came into my study and began fingering things and shuffling his feet and looking thoroughly embarrassed.

'What is it, Dennis?' I said at last.

'Uncle Len, I don't want to go to sea.'

I was astonished. The boy had been so very decided about his career up to now.

'But you were so keen on it.'

'Yes, but I've changed my mind.'

'What do you want to do?'

'I want to go into finance.'

I was even more surprised.

'What do you mean – finance?'

'Just that. I want to go into the city.'

'But, my dear boy, I am sure you would not like the life. Even if I obtained a post for you in a bank—'

Dennis said that wasn't what he meant. He didn't want to go into a bank. I asked him what exactly he did mean, and of course, as I suspected, the boy didn't really know.

By 'going into finance', he simply meant getting rich quickly, which with the optimism of youth he imagined was a certainty if one 'went into the city'. I disabused him of this notion as gently as I could.

'What's put it into your head?' I asked. 'You were so satisfied with the idea of going to sea.'

'I know, Uncle Len, but I've been thinking. I shall want to marry some day – and, I mean, you've got to be rich to marry a girl.'

'Facts disprove your theory,' I said.

'I know – but a real girl. I mean, a girl who's used to things.'

It was very vague, but I thought I knew what he meant.

'You know,' I said gently, 'all girls aren't like Lettice Protheroe.'

He fired up at once.

'You're awfully unfair to her. You don't like her. Griselda doesn't either. She says she's tiresome.'

From the feminine point of view Griselda is quite right. Lettice *is* tiresome. I could quite realize, however, that a boy would resent the adjective.

'If only people made a few allowances. Why even the Hartley Napiers are going about grousing about her at a time like this! Just because she left their old tennis party a bit early. Why should she stay if she was bored? Jolly decent of her to go at all, I think.

'Quite a favour,' I said, but Dennis suspected no malice. He was full of his own grievance on Lettice's behalf.

'She's awfully unselfish really. Just to show you, she made me stay. Naturally I wanted to go too. But she wouldn't hear of it. Said it was too bad on the Napiers. So, just to please her, I stopped on a quarter of an hour.'

The young have very curious views on unselfishness.

'And now I hear Susan Hartley Napier is going about everywhere saying Lettice has rotten manners.'

'If I were you,' I said, 'I shouldn't worry.'

'It's all very well, but—'

He broke off.

'I'd – I'd do anything for Lettice.'

'Very few of us can do anything for anyone else,' I said. 'However much we wish it, we are powerless.'

'I wish I were dead,' said Dennis.

Poor lad. Calf love is a virulent disease. I forebore to say any of the obvious and probably irritating things which come so easily to one's lips. Instead, I said good night, and went up to bed.

I took the eight o'clock service the following morning and when I returned found Griselda sitting at the breakfast table with an open note in her hand. It was from Anne Protheroe.

DEAR GRISELDA – If you and the vicar could come up and lunch here quietly today, I should be so very grateful. Something very strange has occurred, and I should like Mr Clement's advice.
Please don't mention this when you come, as I have said nothing to anyone.
With love,
Yours affectionately,
ANNE PROTHEROE.

'We must go, of course,' said Griselda.
I agreed.
'I wonder what can have happened?'
I wondered too.
'You know,' I said to Griselda, 'I don't feel we are really at the end of this case yet.'
'You mean not till someone has really been arrested?'
'No,' I said, 'I didn't mean that. I mean that there are ramifications, undercurrents, that we know nothing about. There are a whole lot of things to clear up before we get at the truth.'
'You mean things that don't really matter, but that get in the way?'
'Yes, I think that expresses my meaning very well.'
'I think we're all making a great fuss,' said Dennis, helping himself to marmalade. 'It's a jolly good thing old Protheroe is dead. Nobody liked him. Oh! I know the police have got to worry – it's their job. But I rather hope myself they'll never find out. I should hate to see Slack promoted going about swelling with importance over his cleverness.'
I am human enough to feel that I agree over the matter of Slack's promotion. A man who goes about systematically rubbing people up the wrong way cannot hope to be popular.
'Dr Haydock thinks rather like I do,' went on Dennis. 'He'd never give a murderer up to justice. He said so.'
I think that that is the danger of Haydock's views. They may be sound in themselves – it is not for me to say – but they produce an impression on the young, careless mind which I am sure Haydock himself never meant to convey.
Griselda looked out of the window and remarked that there were reporters in the garden.

'I suppose they're photographing the study windows again,' she said, with a sigh.

We had suffered a good deal in this way. There was first the idle curiosity of the village – everyone had come to gape and stare. There were next the reporters armed with cameras, and the village again to watch the reporters. In the end we had to have a constable from Much Benham on duty outside the window.

'Well,' I said, 'the funeral is tomorrow morning. After that, surely, the excitement will die down.'

I noticed a few reporters hanging about Old Hall when we arrived there. They accosted me with various queries to which I gave the invariable answer (we had found it the best), that, 'I had nothing to say.'

We were shown by the butler into the drawing-room, the sole occupant of which turned out to be Miss Cram – apparently in a state of high enjoyment.

'This is a surprise, isn't it?' she said, as she shook hands. 'I never should have thought such a thing, but Mrs Protheroe is kind, isn't she? And, of course, it isn't what you might call nice for a young girl to be staying alone at a place like the Blue Boar, reporters about and all. And, of course, it's not as though I haven't been able to make myself useful – you really need a secretary at a time like this, and Miss Protheroe doesn't do anything to help, does she?'

I was amused to notice that the old animosity against Lettice persisted, but that the girl had apparently become a warm partisan of Anne's. At the same time I wondered if the story of her coming here was strictly accurate. In her account the initiative had come from Anne, but I wondered if that were really so. The first mention of disliking to be at the Blue Boar alone might have easily come from the girl herself. Whilst keeping an open mind on the subject, I did not fancy that Miss Cram was strictly truthful.

At that moment Anne Protheroe entered the room.

She was dressed very quietly in black. She carried in her hand a Sunday paper which she held out to me with a rueful glance.

'I've never had any experience of this sort of thing. It's pretty ghastly, isn't it? I saw a reporter at the inquest. I just said that I was terribly upset and had nothing to say, and then he asked me if I wasn't very anxious to find my husband's murderer, and I said "Yes". And then whether I had any suspicions, and I said "No". And whether I didn't think the crime showed local knowledge, and I said it seemed to certainly. And that was all. And now look at this!'

In the middle of the page was a photograph, evidently taken at least ten years ago – Heaven knows where they had dug it out. There were large headlines:

WIDOW DECLARES SHE WILL NEVER REST TILL SHE HAS HUNTED DOWN HUSBAND'S MURDERER.

Mrs Protheroe, the widow of the murdered man, is certain that the murderer must be looked for locally. She has suspicions, but no certainty. She declared herself prostrate with grief, but re-iterated her determination to hunt down the murderer.

'It doesn't sound like me, does it?' said Anne.

'I dare say it might have been worse,' I said, handing back the paper.

'Impudent, aren't they?' said Miss Cram. 'I'd like to see one of those fellows trying to get something out of me.'

By the twinkle in Griselda's eye, I was convinced that she regarded this statement as being more literally true than Miss Cram intended it to appear.

Luncheon was announced, and we went in. Lettice did not come in till half-way through the meal, when she drifted into the empty place with a smile for Griselda and a nod for me. I watched her with some attention, for reasons of my own, but she seemed much the same vague creature as usual. Extremely pretty – that in fairness I had to admit. She was still not wearing mourning, but was dressed in a shade of pale green that brought out all the delicacy of her fair colouring.

After we had had coffee, Anne said quietly:'

'I want to have a little talk with the vicar. I will take him up to my sitting-room.'

At last I was to learn the reason of our summons. I rose and followed her up the stairs. She paused at the door of the room. As I was about to speak, she stretched out a hand to stop me. She remained listening, looking down towards the hall.

'Good. They are going out into the garden. No – don't go in there. We can go straight up.'

Much to my surprise she led the way along the corridor to the extremity of the wing. Here a narrow ladder-like staircase rose to the floor above, and she mounted it, I following. We found ourselves in a dusty boarded passage. Anne opened a door and led me into a large dim attic which was evidently used as a lumber room. There were trunks there, old broken furniture, a few stacked pictures, and the many countless odds and ends which a lumber room collects.

My surprise was so evident that she smiled faintly.

'First of all, I must explain. I am sleeping very lightly just now. Last night – or rather this morning about three o'clock, I was convinced that I heard someone moving about the house. I listened for some time, and at last got up and came out to see. Out on the landing I realized that the sounds came, not from down below, but from up above. I came along to the foot of these stairs. Again I thought I heard a sound. I called up, "Is anybody there?" But there was no answer, and I heard nothing more, so I assumed that my nerves had been playing tricks on me, and went back to bed.

'However, early this morning, I came up here – simply out of curiosity. And I found *this!*'

She stooped down and turned round a picture that was leaning against the wall with the back of the canvas towards us.

I gave a gasp of surprise. The picture was evidently a portrait in oils, but the face had been hacked and cut in such a savage way as to render it unrecognizable. Moreover, the cuts were clearly quite fresh.

'What an extraordinary thing,' I said.

'Isn't it? Tell me, can you think of any explanation?'

I shook my head.

'There's a kind of savagery about it,' I said, 'that I don't like. It looks as though it had been done in a fit of maniacal rage.'

'Yes, that's what I thought.'

'What is the portrait?'

'I haven't the least idea. I have never seen it before. All these things were in the attic when I married Lucius and came here to live. I have never been through them or bothered about them.'

'Extraordinary,' I commented.

I stooped down and examined the other pictures. They were very much what you would expect to find – some very mediocre landscapes, some oleographs and a few cheaply-framed reproductions.

There was nothing else helpful. A large old-fashioned trunk, of the kind that used to be called an 'ark', had the initials E.P. upon it. I raised the lid. It was empty. Nothing else in the attic was the least suggestive.

'It really is a most amazing occurrence,' I said. 'It's so – sense-
less.'

'Yes,' said Anne. 'That frightens me a little.'

There was nothing more to see. I accompanied her down to
her sitting-room where she closed the door.

'Do you think I ought to do anything about it? Tell the
police?'

I hesitated.

'It's hard to say on the face of it whether—'

'It has anything to do with the murder or not,' finished Anne.

'I know. That's what is so difficult. On the face of it, there seems
no connection whatever.'

'No,' I said, 'but it is another Peculiar Thing.'

We both sat silent with puzzled brows.

'What are your plans, if I may ask?' I said presently.

She lifted her head.

'I'm going to live here for at least another six months!' She
said it defiantly. 'I don't want to. I hate the idea of living here.
But I think it's the only thing to be done. Otherwise people will
say that I ran away – that I had a guilty conscience.'

'Surely not.'

'Oh! yes, they will. Especially when –' She paused and then
said: 'When the six months are up – I am going to marry
Lawrence.' Her eyes met mine. 'We're neither of us going to
wait any longer.'

'I supposed,' I said, 'that that would happen.'

Suddenly she broke down, burying her head in her hands.

'You don't know how grateful I am to you – you don't know.
We'd said goodbye to each other – he was going away. I feel –
I feel not so awful about Lucius's death. If we'd been planning
to go away together, and he'd died then – it would be so awful
now. But you made us both see how wrong it would be. That's
why I'm grateful.'

'I, too, am thankful,' I said gravely.

'All the same, you know,' she sat up. 'Unless the real murderer is found they'll always think it was Lawrence – oh! yes,
they will. And especially when he marries me.'

'My dear, Dr Haydock's evidence made it perfectly clear—'

'What do people care about evidence? They don't even know
about it. And medical evidence never means anything to out-
siders anyway. That's another reason why I'm staying on here.
Mr Clement, *I'm going to find out the truth.*'

Her eyes flashed as she spoke. She added:

'That's why I asked that girl here.'

'Miss Cram?'

'Yes.'

'You did ask her, then. I mean, it was your idea?'

'Entirely. Oh! as a matter of fact, she whined a bit. At the inquest – she was there when I arrived. No, I asked her here deliberately.'

'But surely,' I cried, 'you don't think that that silly young woman could have anything to do with the crime?'

'It's awfully easy to appear silly, Mr Clement. It's one of the easiest things in the world.'

'Then you really think—?'

'No, I don't. Honestly, I don't. What I do think is that that girl knows something – or might know something. I wanted to study her at close quarters.'

'And the very night she arrives, that picture is slashed,' I said thoughtfully.

'You think she did it? But why? It seems so utterly absurd and impossible.'

'It seems to me utterly impossible and absurd that your husband should have been murdered in my study,' I said bitterly. 'But he was.'

'I know.' She laid her hand on my arm. 'It's dreadful for you. I do realize that, though I haven't said very much about it.'

I took the blue lapis lazuli ear-ring from my pocket and held it out to her.

'This is yours, I think?'

'Oh! yes.' She held out her hand for it with a pleased smile. 'Where did you find it?'

But I did not put the jewel into her outstretched hand.

'Would you mind,' I said. 'if I kept it a little longer?'

'Why, certainly.' She looked puzzled and a little inquiring. I did not satisfy her curiosity.

Instead I asked her how she was situated financially.

'It is an impertinent question,' I said, 'but I really do not mean it as such.'

'I don't think it's impertinent at all. You and Griselda are the best friends I have here. And I like that funny old Miss Marple. Lucius was very well off, you know. He left things pretty equally divided between me and Lettice. Old Hall goes to me, but Lettice is to be allowed to choose enough furniture to furnish a small house, and she is left a separate sum for the purpose of buying one, so as to even things up.'

'What are her plans, do you know?'

Anne made a comical grimace.

'She doesn't tell them to me. I imagine she will leave here as soon as possible. She doesn't like me – she never has. I dare say it's my fault, though I've really always tried to be decent. But I suppose any girl resents a young stepmother.'

'Are you fond of her?' I asked bluntly.

She did not reply at once, which convinced me that Anne Protheroe is a very honest woman.

'I was at first,' she said. 'She was such a pretty little girl. I don't think I am now. I don't know why. Perhaps it's because she doesn't like me. I like being liked, you know.'

'We all do,' I said, and Anne Protheroe smiled.

I had one more task to perform. That was to get a word alone with Lettice Protheroe. I managed that easily enough, catching sight of her in the deserted drawing-room. Griselda and Gladys Cram were out in the garden.

I went in and shut the door.

'Lettice,' I said, 'I want to speak to you about something.'

She looked up indifferently.

'Yes?'

I had thought beforehand what to say. I held out the lapis ear-ring and said quietly:

'Why did you drop that in my study?'

I saw her stiffen for a moment – it was almost instantaneous. Her recovery was so quick that I myself could hardly have sworn to the movement. Then she said carelessly:

'I never dropped anything in your study. That's not mine. That's Anne's.'

'I know that,' I said.

'Well, why ask me, then? Anne must have dropped it.'

'Mrs Protheroe has only been in my study once since the murder, and then she was wearing black and so would not have been likely to have had on a blue ear-ring.'

'In that case,' said Lettice, 'I suppose she must have dropped it before.' She added: 'That's only logical.'

'It's very logical,' I said. 'I suppose you don't happen to remember when your stepmother was wearing these ear-rings last?'

'Oh!' She looked at me with a puzzled, truthful gaze. 'Is it very important?'

'It might be,' I said.

'I'll try and think. She sat there knitting her brows. I have never seen Lettice Protheroe look more charming than she did at that moment. 'Oh! yes,' she said suddenly. 'She had them on – on Thursday. I remember now.'

'Thursday,' I said slowly, 'was the day of the murder. Mrs Protheroe came to the study in the garden that day, but if you remember, in her evidence, she only came as far as the study window, not inside the room.'

'Where did you find this?'

'Rolled underneath the desk.'

'Then it looks, doesn't it,' said Lettice coolly, 'as though she hadn't spoken the truth?'

'You mean that she came right in and stood by the desk?'

'Well, it looks like it, doesn't it?'

Her eyes met mine serenely.

'If you want to know,' she said calmly, 'I never have thought she was speaking the truth.'

'And I *know you* are not, Lettice.'

'What do you mean?'

She was startled.

'I mean,' I said, 'that the last time I saw this ear-ring was on Friday morning when I came up here with Colonel Melchett. It was lying with its fellow on your stepmother's dressing-table. I actually handled them both.'

'Oh –!' She wavered, then suddenly flung herself sideways over the arm of her chair and burst into tears. Her short fair hair hung down almost touching the floor. It was a strange attitude – beautiful and unrestrained.

I let her sob for some moments in silence and then I said very gently:

'Lettice, why did you do it?'

'What?'

She sprang up, flinging her hair wildly back. She looked wild – almost terrified.

'What do you mean?'

'What made you do it? Was it jealousy? Dislike of Anne?'

'Oh! – oh! yes.' She pushed the hair back from her face and seemed suddenly to regain complete self-possession. 'Yes, you can call it jealousy. I've always disliked Anne – ever since she came queening it here. I put the damned thing under the desk. I hoped it would get her into trouble. It would have done if you hadn't been such a Nosey Parker, fingering things on dressing-tables. Anyway, it isn't a clergyman's business to go about helping the police.'

It was a spiteful, childish outburst. I took no notice of it.

Indeed, at that moment, she seemed a very pathetic child indeed. Her childish attempt at vengeance against Anne seemed hardly to be taken seriously. I told her so, and added that I should return the ear-ring to her and say nothing of the circumstances in which I had found it. She seemed rather touched by that.

'That's nice of you,' she said.

She paused a minute and then said, keeping her face averted and evidently choosing her words with care.

'You know, Mr Clement, I should – I should get Dennis away from here soon, if I were you. I – I think it would be better.'

'Dennis?' I raised my eyebrows in slight surprise but with a trace of amusement too.

'I think it would be better.' She added, still in the same awkward manner: 'I'm sorry, about Dennis. I didn't think he – anyway, I'm sorry.'

We left it at that.

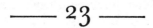

—— 23 ——

On the way back, I proposed to Griselda that we should make a detour and go round by the barrow. I was anxious to see if the police were at work and if so, what they had found. Griselda, however, had things to do at home, so I was left to make the expedition on my own.

I found Constable Hurst in charge of operations.

'No sign so far, sir,' he reported. 'And yet it stands to reason that this is the only place for a *cache*.'

His use of the word cache puzzled me for a moment, as he pronounced it catch, but his real meaning occurred to me almost at once.

'Whatimeantersay is, sir, where else could the young woman be going starting into the wood by that path? It leads to Old Hall, and it leads here, and that's about all.'

'I suppose,' I said, 'that Inspector Slack would disdain such a simple course as asking the young lady straight out.'

'Anxious not to put the wind up her,' said Hurst. 'Anything she writes to Stone or he writes to her may throw light on things – once she knows we're on to her, she'd shut up like *that*.'

Like *what* exactly was left in doubt, but I personally doubted

Miss Gladys Cram ever being shut up in the way described. It was impossible to imagine her as other than overflowing with conversation.

'When a man's an h'impostor, you want to know *why* he's an h'impostor, said Constable Hurst didactically.

'Naturally, I said.

'And the answer is to be found in this here barrow – or else why was he for ever messing about with it?'

'A *raison d'être* for prowling about,' I suggested, but this bit of French was too much for the constable. He revenged himself for not understanding it by saying coldly:

'That's the h'amateur's point of view.'

'Anyway, you haven't found the suit-case,' I said.

'We shall do, sir. Not a doubt of it.'

'I'm not so sure,' I said. 'I've been thinking. Miss Marple said it was quite a short time before the girl reappeared empty-handed. In that case, she wouldn't have had time to get up here and back.'

'You can't take any notice of what old ladies say. When they've seen something curious, and are waiting all eager like, why, time simply flies for them. And anyway, no lady knows anything about time.'

I often wonder why the whole world is so prone to generalize. Generalizations are seldom or never true and are usually inaccurate. I have a poor sense of time myself (hence the keeping of my clock fast) and Miss Marple, I should say, has a very acute one. Her clocks keep time to the minute and she herself is rigidly punctual on every occasion.

However, I had no intention of arguing with Constable Hurst on the point. I wished him good afternoon and good luck and went on my way.

It was just as I was nearing home that the idea came to me. There was nothing to lead up to it. It just flashed into my brain as a possible solution.

You will remember that on my first search of the path, the day after the murder, I had found the bushes disturbed in a certain place. They proved, or so I thought at the time, to have been disturbed by Lawrence, bent on the same errand as myself.

But I remembered that afterwards he and I together had come upon another faintly marked trail which proved to be that of the inspector. On thinking it over, I distinctly remembered that the first trail (Lawrence's) had been much more noticeable than the second, as though more than one person had been passing that way. And I reflected that that was probably what had drawn Lawrence's attention to it in the first instance. Supposing that it had originally been made by either Dr Stone or else Miss Cram?

I remembered, or else I imagined remembering, that there had been several withered leaves on broken twigs. If so, the trail could not have been made the afternoon of our search.

I was just approaching the spot in question. I recognized it easily enough and once more forced my way through the bushes. This time I noticed fresh twigs broken. Someone *had* passed this way since Lawrence and myself.

I soon came to the place where I had encountered Lawrence. The faint trail, however, persisted farther, and I continued to follow it. Suddenly it widened out into a little clearing which showed signs of recent upheaval. I say a clearing, because the denseness of the undergrowth was thinned out there, but the branches of the trees met overhead and the whole place was not more than a few feet across.

On the other side, the undergrowth grew densely again, and it seemed quite clear that no one had forced a way through it recently. Nevertheless, it seemed to have been disturbed in one place.

I went across and kneeled down, thrusting the bushes aside with both hands. A glint of a shiny brown surface rewarded me. Full of excitement. I thrust my arm in and with a good deal of difficulty I extracted a small brown suit-case.

I uttered an ejaculation of triumph. I had been successful. Coldly snubbed by Constable Hurst, I had yet proved right in my reasoning. Here without doubt was the suit-case carried by Miss Cram. I tried the hasp, but it was locked.

As I rose to my feet I noticed a small brownish crystal lying on the ground. Almost automatically, I picked it up and slipped it into my pocket.

Then grasping my find by the handle, I retraced my steps to the path.

As I climbed over the stile into the lane, an agitated voice near at hand called out:

'Oh! Mr Clement. You've found it! How clever of you!'

Mentally registering the fact that in the art of seeing without being seen, Miss Marple had no rival, I balanced my find on the palings between us.

'That's the one,' said Miss Marple. 'I'd know it anywhere.'

This, I thought, was a slight exaggeration. There are thousands of cheap shiny suit-cases all exactly alike. No one could recognize one particularly one seen from such a distance away by moonlight, but I realized that the whole business of the suit-case was Miss Marple's particular triumph and, as such, she was entitled to a little pardonable exaggeration.

'It's locked, I suppose, Mr Clement?'

'Yes. I'm just going to take it down to the police station.'

'You don't think it would be better to telephone?'

Of course unquestionably it would be better to telephone. To stride through the village, suit-case in hand, would be to court a probably undesirable publicity.

So I unlatched Miss Marple's garden gate and entered the house by the French window, and from the sanctity of the drawing-room with the door shut, I telephoned my news.

The result was that Inspector Slack announced he would be up himself in a couple of jiffies.

When he arrived it was in his most cantankerous mood.

'So we've got it, have we?' he said. 'You know, sir, you shouldn't keep things to yourself. If you've any reason to believe you know where the article in question was hidden, you ought to have reported it to the proper authorities.'

'It was a pure accident,' I said. 'The idea just happened to occur to me.'

'And that's a likely tale. Nearly three-quarters of a mile of woodland, and you go right to the proper spot and lay your hand upon it.'

I would have given Inspector Slack the steps in reasoning which led me to this particular spot, but he had achieved his usual result of putting my back up. I said nothing.

'Well?' said Inspector Slack, eyeing the suit-case with dislike and would-be indifference, 'I suppose we might as well have a look at what's inside.'

He had brought an assortment of keys and wire with him. The lock was a cheap affair. In a couple of seconds the case was open.

I don't know what we had expected to find – something sternly sensational, I imagine. But the first thing that met our eyes was a greasy plaid scarf. The Inspector lifted it out. Next came a faded dark blue overcoat, very much the worse for wear. A checked cap followed.

'A shoddy lot,' said the inspector.

A pair of boots very down at heel and battered came next. At the bottom of the suit-case was a parcel done up in newspaper.

'Fancy shirt, I suppose,' said the inspector bitterly, as he tore it open.

A moment later he had caught his breath in surprise.

For inside the parcel were some demure little silver objects and a round platter of the same metal.

Miss Marple gave a shrill exclamation of recognition.

'The trencher salts,' she exclaimed. 'Colonel Protheroe's trencher salts, and the Charles II tazza. Did you ever hear of such a thing!'

The inspector had got very red.

'So that was the game,' he muttered. 'Robbery. But I can't make it out. There's been no mention of these things being missing.'

'Perhaps they haven't discovered the loss,' I suggested. 'I presume these valuable things would not have been kept out in common use. Colonel Protheroe probably kept them locked away in a safe.'

'I must investigate this,' said the inspector. 'I'll go right up to Old Hall now. So that's why our Dr Stone made himself scarce. What with the murder and one thing and another, he was afraid we'd get wind of his activities. As likely as not his belongings might have been searched. He got the girl to hide them in the wood with a suitable change of clothing. He meant to come back by a roundabout route and go off with them one night whilst she stayed here to disarm suspicion. Well, there's one thing to the good. This lets him out over the murder. He'd nothing to do with that. Quite a different game.'

He repacked the suit-case and took his departure, refusing Miss Marple's offer of a glass of sherry.

'Well, that's one mystery cleared up,' I said with a sigh. 'What Slack says is quite true; there are no grounds for suspecting him of the murder. Everything's accounted for quite satisfactorily.'

'It really would seem so,' said Miss Marple. 'Although one never can be quite certain, can one?'

'There's a complete lack of motive.' I pointed out. 'He'd got what he came for and was clearing out.'

'Y – es.'

She was clearly not quite satisfied, and I looked at her in some curiosity. She hastened to answer my inquiring gaze with a kind of apologetic eagerness.

'I've no doubt I am *quite* wrong. I'm so stupid about these things. But I just wondered – I mean this silver is very valuable, is it not?'

'A tazza sold the other day for over a thousand pounds, I believe.'

'I mean – it's not the value of the metal.'

'No, it's what one might call a connoisseur's value.'

'That's what I mean. The sale of such things would take a little time to arrange, or even if it was arranged, it couldn't be carried through without secrecy. I mean – if the robbery were reported and a hue and cry were raised, well, the things couldn't be marketed at all.'

'I don't quite see what you mean,' I said.

'I know I'm putting it badly.' She became more flustered and apologetic. 'But it seems to me that – that the things couldn't just have been abstracted, so to speak. The only satisfactory thing to do would be to replace these things with copies. Then, perhaps, the robbery wouldn't be discovered for some time.'

'That's a very ingenious idea,' I said.

'It would be the only way to do it, wouldn't it? And if so, of course, as you say, once the substitution had been accomplished there wouldn't have been any reason for murdering Colonel Protheroe – quite the reverse.'

'Exactly,' I said. 'That's what I said.'

'Yes, but I just wondered – I don't know, of course – and Colonel Protheroe always talked a lot about doing things before he actually did do them, and, of course, sometimes never did them at all, but he did say—'

'Yes?'

'That he was going to have all his things valued – a man down from London. For probate – no, that's when you're dead – for insurance. Someone told him that was the thing to do. He talked about it a great deal, and the importance of having it done. Of course, I don't know if he had made any actual arrangements, but if he had . . .'

'I see,' I said slowly.

'Of course, the moment the expert saw the silver, he'd know, and then Colonel Protheroe would remember having shown the things to Dr Stone – I wonder if it was done then – legerdemain, don't they call it? So clever – and then, well, the fat would be in the fire, to use an old-fashioned expression.'

'I see your idea,' I said. 'I think we ought to find out for certain.'

I went once more to the telephone. In a few minutes I was through to Old Hall and speaking to Anne Protheroe.

'No, it's nothing very important. Has the inspector arrived

yet? Oh! well, he's on his way. Mrs Protheroe, can you tell me
if the contents of Old Hall were ever valued? What's that you
say?'

Her answer came clear and prompt. I thanked her, replaced
the receiver, and turned to Miss Marple.

'That's very definite. Colonel Protheroe had made arrangements for a man to come down from London on Monday – tomorrow – to make a full valuation. Owing to the colonel's death,
the matter has been put off.'

'Then there *was* a motive,' said Miss Marple softly.

'A motive, yes. But that's all. You forget. When the shot was
fired, Dr Stone had just joined the others, or was climbing over
the stile in order to do so.'

'Yes,' said Miss Marple thoughtfully. 'So that rules him out.'

—— 24 ——

I returned to the Vicarage to find Hawes waiting for me in my
study. He was pacing up and down nervously, and when I
entered the room he started as though he had been shot.

'You must excuse me,' he said, wiping his forehead. 'My nerves
are all to pieces lately.'

'My dear fellow,' I said, 'you positively must get away for a
change. We shall have you breaking down altogether, and that
will never do.'

'I can't desert my post. No, that is a thing I will never do.'

'It's not a case of desertion. You are ill. I'm sure Haydock
would agree with me.'

'Haydock – Haydock. What kind of a doctor is he? An ignorant country practitioner.'

'I think you're unfair to him. He has always been considered
a very able man in his profession.'

'Oh! perhaps. Yes, I dare say. But I don't like him. However,
that's not what I came to say. I came to ask you if you would be
kind enough to preach tonight instead of me. I – I really do not
feel equal to it.'

'Why, certainly. I will take the service for you.'

'No, no. I wish to take the service. I am perfectly fit. It is only
the idea of getting up in the pulpit, of all those eyes staring at
me ...'

He shut his eyes and swallowed convulsively.

It is clear to me that there is something very wrong indeed the matter with Hawes. He seemed aware of my thoughts, for he opened his eyes and said quickly:

'There is nothing really wrong with me. It is just these headaches – these awful racking headaches. I wonder if you could let me have a glass of water.'

'Certainly,' I said.

I went and fetched it myself from the tap. Ringing bells is a profitless form of exercise in our house.

I brought the water to him and he thanked me. He took from his pocket a small cardboard box, and opening it, extracted a rice-paper capsule, which he swallowed with the aid of the water.

'A headache powder,' he explained.

I suddenly wondered whether Hawes might have become addicted to drugs. It would explain a great many of his peculiarities.

'You don't take too many, I hope,' I said.

'No – oh, no. Dr Haydock warned me against that. But it is really wonderful. They bring instant relief.'

Indeed he already seemed calmer and more composed.

He stood up.

'Then you will preach tonight? It's very good of you, sir.'

'Not at all. And I insist on taking the service too. Get along home and rest. No, I won't have any argument. Not another word.'

He thanked me again. Then he said, his eyes sliding past me to the window:

'You – you have been up at Old Hall today, haven't you, sir?'

'Yes.'

'Excuse me – but were you sent for?'

I looked at him in surprise, and he flushed.

'I'm sorry, sir. I – I just thought some new development might have arisen and that that was why Mrs Protheroe had sent for you.'

I had not the faintest intention of satisfying Hawes's curiosity.

'She wanted to discuss the funeral arrangements and one or two other small matters with me,' I said.

'Oh! that was all. I see.'

I did not speak. He fidgeted from foot to foot, and finally said:

'Mr Redding came to see me last night. I – I can't imagine why.'

'Didn't he tell you?'

'He – he just said he thought he'd look me up. Said it was a bit lonely in the evenings. He's never done such a thing before.'

'Well, he's supposed to be pleasant company,' I said, smiling.

'What does he want to come and see me for? I don't like it.' His voice rose shrilly. 'He spoke of dropping in again. What does it all mean? What idea do you think he has got into his head?'

'Why should you suppose he has any ulterior motive?' I asked.

'I don't like it, repeated Hawes obstinately. 'I've never gone against *him* in any way. I never suggested that *he* was guilty – even when he accused himself I said it seemed most incomprehensible. If I've had suspicions of anybody it's been of Archer –never of him. Archer is a totally different proposition – a godless irreligious ruffian. A drunken blackguard.'

'Don't you think you're being a little harsh?' I said. 'After all, we really know very little about the man.'

'A poacher, in and out of prison, capable of anything.'

'Do you really think he shot Colonel Protheroe?' I asked curiously.

Hawes has an inveterate dislike of answering yes or no. I have noticed it several times lately.

'Don't you think yourself, sir, that it's the only possible solution?'

'As far as we know,' I said, 'there's no evidence of any kind against him.'

'His threats,' said Hawes eagerly. 'You forget about his threats.'

I am sick and tired of hearing about Archer's threats. As far as I can make out, there is no direct evidence that he ever made any.

'He was determined to be revenged on Colonel Protheroe. He primed himself with drink and then shot him.'

'That's pure supposition.'

'But you will admit that it's perfectly probable?'

'No, I don't.'

'Possible, then?'

'Possible, yes.'

Hawes glanced at me sideways.

'Why don't you think it's probable?'

'Because,' I said, 'a man like Archer wouldn't think of shooting a man with a pistol. It's the wrong weapon.'

Hawes seemed taken aback by my argument. Evidently it wasn't the objection he had expected.

'Do you really think the objection is feasible?' he asked doubtingly.

'To my mind it is a complete stumbling block to Archer's having committed the crime,' I said.

In face of my positive assertion, Hawes said no more. He thanked me again and left.

I had gone as far as the front door with him, and on the hall table I saw four notes. They had certain characteristics in common. The handwriting was almost unmistakably feminine, they all bore the words, 'By hand, Urgent,' and the only difference I could see was that one was noticeably dirtier than the rest.

Their similarity gave me a curious feeling of seeing – not double, but quadruple.

Mary came out of the kitchen and caught me staring at them.

'Come by hand since lunch time,' she volunteered. 'All but one. I found that in the box.'

I nodded, gathered them up, and took them into the study. The first one ran thus:

DEAR MR CLEMENT – Something has come to my knowledge which I feel you ought to know. It concerns the death of poor Colonel Protheroe. I should much appreciate your advice on the matter – whether to go to the police or not. Since my dear husband's death, I have such a shrinking from every kind of publicity. Perhaps you could run in and see me for a few minutes this afternoon.

Yours sincerely,

MARTHA PRICE RIDLEY.

I opened the second:

DEAR MR CLEMENT – I am so troubled – so *exercised* in my mind – to know what I ought to do. Something has come to my ears that I feel may be important. I have such a *horror* of being mixed up with the police in any way. I am so disturbed and distressed. Would it be asking too much of you, dear vicar, to drop in for a few minutes and solve my doubts and perplexities for me in the wonderful way you always do?

Forgive my troubling you,
Yours very sincerely,

CAROLINE WETHERBY.

The third, I felt, I could almost have recited beforehand.

DEAR MR CLEMENT – Something most important has come to my ears. I feel you should be the first to know about it. Will you call in and see me this afternoon some time. I will wait in for you.

This militant epistle was signed 'AMANDA HARTNELL.' I opened the fourth missive. It has been my good fortune to be troubled with very few anonymous letters. An anonymous letter is, I think, the meanest and cruellest weapon there is. This one was no exception. It purported to be written by an illiterate person, but several things inclined me to disbelieve that assumption.

DEAR VICAR – I think you ought to know what is Going On. Your lady has been seen coming out of Mr Redding's cottage in a surreptitious manner. You know wot i mean. The two are Carrying On together. i think you ought to know.
A FRIEND.

I made a faint exclamation of disgust and crumpling up the paper tossed it into the open grate just as Griselda entered the room.

'What's that you're throwing down so contemptuously?' she asked.

'Filth,' I said.

Taking a match from my pocket, I struck it and bent down. Griselda, however, was too quick for me. She had stooped down and caught up the crumpled ball of paper and smoothed it out before I could stop her.

She read it, gave a little exclamation of disgust, and tossed it back to me, turning away as she did so. I lighted it and watched it burn.

Griselda had moved away. She was standing by the window looking out into the garden.

'Len,' she said, without turning round.

'Yes, my dear.'

'I'd like to tell you something. Yes, don't stop me. I want to, please. When – when Lawrence Redding came here, I let you think that I had only known him slightly before. That wasn't true. I – had known him rather well. In fact, before I met you, I had been rather in love with him. I think most people are with Lawrence. I was – well, absolutely silly about him at one time. I don't mean I wrote him compromising letters or anything idiotic like they do in books. But I was rather keen on him once.'

'Why didn't you tell me?' I asked.

'Oh! because! I don't know exactly except that – well, you're foolish in some ways. Just because you're so much older than I am, you think that I – well, that I'm likely to like other people. I thought you'd be tiresome, perhaps, about me and Lawrence being friends.'

'You're very clever at concealing things, I said, remembering what she had told me in that room less than a week ago, and the ingenuous natural way she had talked.

'Yes, I've always been able to hide things. In a way, I like doing it.'

Her voice held a childlike ring of pleasure in it.

'But it's quite true what I said. I didn't know about Anne, and I wondered why Lawrence was so different, not – well, really not noticing me. I'm not used to it.'

There was a pause.

'You do understand, Len?' said Griselda anxiously.

'Yes,' I said, 'I understand.'

But did I?

—— 25 ——

I found it hard to shake off the impression left by the anonymous letter. Pitch soils.

However, I gathered up the other three letters, glanced at my watch, and started out.

I wondered very much what this might be that had 'come to the knowledge' of three ladies simultaneously. I took it to be the same piece of news. In this, I was to realize that my psychology was at fault.

I cannot pretend that my calls took me past the police station. My feet gravitated there of their own accord. I was anxious to know whether Inspector Slack had returned from Old Hall.

I found that he had, and further, that Miss Cram had returned with him. The fair Gladys was seated in the police station carrying off matters with a high hand. She denied absolutely having taken the suit-case to the woods.

'Just because one of these gossiping old cats has nothing better to do than look out of her window all night you go and pitch upon me. She's been mistaken once, remember, when she said she saw me at the end of the lane on the afternoon of the murder, and if she was mistaken then, in daylight, how can she possibly have recognised me by moonlight?

'Wicked it is, the way these old ladies go on down here. Say anything, they will. And me asleep in my bed as innocent as can be. You ought to be ashamed of yourselves, the lot of you.'

'And supposing the landlady of the Blue Boar identifies the suit-case as yours, Miss Cram?'

'If she says anything of the kind, she's wrong. There's no name on it. Nearly everybody's got a suit-case like that. As for poor Dr Stone, accusing him of being a common burglar! And he has a lot of letters after his name.'

'You refuse to give us any explanation, then, Miss Cram?'

'No refusing about it. You've made a mistake, that's all. You and your meddlesome Marples. I won't say a word more – not without my solicitor present. I'm going this minute – unless you're going to arrest me.'

For answer, the inspector rose and opened the door for her, and with a toss of the head, Miss Cram walked out.

'That's the line she takes,' said Slack, coming back to his chair. 'Absolute denial. And, of course, the old lady *may* have been mistaken. No jury would believe you could recognise anyone from that distance on a moonlit night. And, of course, as I say, the old lady may have made a mistake.'

'She may,' I said, 'but I don't think she did. Miss Marple is usually right. That's what makes her unpopular.

The inspector grinned.

'That's what Hurst says. Lord, these villages!'

'What about the silver, Inspector?'

'Seemed to be perfectly in order. Of course, that meant one lot or the other must be a fake. There's a very good man in Much Benham, an authority on old silver. I've phoned over to him and sent a car to fetch him. We'll soon know which is which. Either the burglary was an accomplished fact, or else it was only planned. Doesn't make a frightful lot of difference either way – I mean as far as we're concerned. Robbery's a small business compared with murder. These two aren't concerned with the murder. We'll maybe get a line on him through the girl – that's why I let her go without any more fuss.'

'I wondered, I said.

'A pity about Mr Redding. It's not often you find a man who goes out of his way to oblige you.'

'I suppose not,' I said, smiling slightly.

'Women cause a lot of trouble,' moralized the inspector. He sighed and then went on, somewhat to my surprise: 'Of course there's Archer.'

'Oh!' I said. 'You've thought of him?'

'Why, naturally, sir, first thing. It didn't need any anonymous letters to put me on his track.

'Anonymous letters,' I said sharply. 'Did you get one, then?'

'That's nothing new, sir. We get a dozen a day, at least. Oh! yes, we were put wise to Archer. As though the police couldn't look out for themselves! Archer's been under suspicion from the first. The trouble of it is, he's got an alibi. Not that it amounts to anything, but it's awkward to get over.'

'What do you mean by its not amounting to anything?' I asked.

'Well, it appears he was with a couple of pals all the afternoon. Not, as I say, that that counts much. Men like Archer and his pals would swear to anything. There's no believing a word they say. *We* know that. But the public doesn't, and the jury's taken from the public, more's the pity. They know nothing, and ten to one believe everything that's said in the witness box, no matter who it is that says it. And of course Archer himself will swear till he's black in the face that he didn't do it.'

'Not so obliging as Mr Redding,' I said with a smile.

'Not he,' said the inspector, making the remark as a plain statement of fact.

'It is natural, I suppose, to cling to life,' I mused.

'You'd be surprised if you knew the murderers that have got off through the soft-heartedness of the jury,' said the inspector gloomily.

'But do you really think that Archer did it?' I asked.

It has struck me as curious all along that Inspector Slack never seems to have any personal views of his own on the murder. The easiness or difficulty of getting a conviction are the only points that seem to appeal to him.

'I'd like to be a bit surer,' he admitted. 'A fingerprint now, or a footprint, or seen in the vicinity about the time of the crime. Can't risk arresting him without something of that kind. He's been seen round Mr Redding's house once or twice, but he'd say that was to speak to his mother. A decent body, she is. No, on the whole, I'm for the lady. If I could only get definite proof of blackmail – but you can't get definite proof of anything in this crime! It's theory, theory, theory. It's a sad pity that there's not a single spinster lady living along your road, Mr Clement. I bet she'd have seen something if there had been.'

His words reminded me of my calls, and I took leave of him. It was about the solitary instance when I had seen him in a genial mood.

My first call was on Miss Hartnell. She must have been watching for me from the window, for before I had time to ring she had opened the front door, and clasping my hand firmly in hers, had led me over the threshold.

'So good of you to come. In here. More private.'

We entered a microscopic room, about the size of a hen-coop. Miss Hartnell shut the door and with an air of deep secrecy waved me to a seat (there were only three). I perceived that she was enjoying herslf.

'I'm never one to beat about the bush,' she said in her jolly voice, the latter slightly toned down to meet the requirements of the situation. 'You know how things go the round in a village like this.'

'Unfortunately,' I said, 'I do.'

'I agree with you. Nobody dislikes gossip more than I do. But there it is. I thought it my duty to tell the police inspector that I'd called on Mrs Lestrange the afternoon of the murder and that she was out. I don't expect to be thanked for doing my duty, I just do it. Ingratitude is what you meet with first and last in this life. Why, only yesterday that impudent Mrs Baker—'

'Yes, yes,' I said, hoping to avert the usual tirade. 'Very sad, very sad. But you were saying.'

'The lower classes don't know who are their best friends,' said Miss Hartnell. 'I always say a word in season when I'm visiting. Not that I'm ever thanked for it.'

'You were telling the inspector about your call upon Mrs Lestrange,' I prompted.

'Exactly – and by the way, he didn't thank me. Said he'd ask for information when he wanted it – not those words exactly, but that was the spirit. There's a different class of men in the police force nowadays.'

'Very probably,' I said. 'But you were going to say something?'

'I decided that this time I wouldn't go near any wretched inspector. After all, a clergyman is a gentleman – at least some are,' she added.

I gathered that the qualification was intended to include me. 'If I can help you in any way,' I began.

'It's a matter of duty,' said Miss Hartnell, and closed her mouth with a snap. 'I don't want to have to say these things. No one likes it less. But duty is duty.'

I waited.

'I've been given to understand,' went on Miss Hartnell, turning rather red, 'that Mrs Lestrange gives out that she was at home all the time – that she didn't answer the door because – well, because she didn't choose. Such airs and graces. I only called as a matter of duty, and to be treated like that!'

'She has been ill,' I said mildly.

'Ill? Fiddlesticks. You're too unworldly, Mr Clement. There's nothing the matter with that woman. Too ill to attend the inquest indeed! Medical certificate from Dr Haydock! She can wind him round her little finger, everyone knows that. Well, where was I?'

I didn't quite know. It is difficult with Miss Hartnell to know where narrative ends and vituperation begins.

'Oh! about calling on her that afternoon. Well, it's fiddlesticks to say she was in the house. She wasn't. I know.'

'How can you possibly know?'

Miss Hartnell's face turned a little redder. In someone less truculent, her demeanour might have been called embarrassed.

'I'd knocked and rung,' she explained. 'Twice. If not three times. And it occurred to me suddenly that the bell might be out of order.'

She was, I was glad to note, unable to look me in the face when saying this. The same builder builds all our houses and the bells he installs are always clearly audible when standing on the mat outside the front door. Both Miss Hartnell and I knew this perfectly well, but I supposed decencies have to be preserved.

'Yes?' I murmured.

'I didn't want to push my card through the letter box. That would seem so rude, and whatever I am, I am never rude.'

She made this amazing statement without a tremor.

'So I thought I would just go round the house and – and tap on the window pane,' she continued unblushingly. 'I went all round the house and looked in at all the windows, but there was no one in the house at all.'

I understood her perfectly. Taking advantage of the fact that the house was empty, Miss Hartnell had given unbridled rein to her curiosity and had gone round the house, examining the garden and peering in at all the windows to see as much as she could of the interior. She had chosen to tell her story to me, believing that I should be a more sympathetic and lenient audience than the police. The clergy are supposed to give the benefit of the doubt to their parishioners.

I made no comment on the situation. I merely asked a question.

'What time was this, Miss Hartnell?'

'As far as I can remember,' said Miss Hartnell, 'it must have been close on six o'clock. I went straight home afterwards, and I got in about ten past six, and Mrs Protheroe came in somewhere round about the half-hour, leaving Dr Stone and Mr Redding outside, and we talked about bulbs. And all the time the poor colonel lying murdered. It's a sad world.'

'It is sometimes a rather unpleasant one,' I said.

I rose.

'And that is all you have to tell me?'

'I just thought it might be important.'

'It might,' I agreed.

And refusing to be drawn further, much to Miss Hartnell's disappointment, I took my leave.

Miss Wetherby, whom I visited next, received me in a kind of flutter.

'Dear vicar, how truly kind. You've had tea? Really, you won't? A cushion for your back? It is so kind of you to come round so promptly. Always willing to put yourself out for others.'

There was a good deal of this before we came to the point, and even then it was approached with a good deal of circumlocution.

'You must understand that I heard this on the best authority.'

In St Mary Mead the best authority is always somebody else's servant.

'You can't tell me who told you?'

'I promised, dear Mr Clement. And I always think a promise should be a sacred thing.'

She looked very solemn.

'Shall we say a little bird told me? That is safe, isn't it?'

I longed to say, 'It's damned silly.' I rather wish I had. I should have liked to observe the effect on Miss Wetherby.

'Well, this little bird told that she saw a certain lady, who shall be nameless.'

'Another kind of bird?' I inquired.

To my great surprise Miss Wetherby went off into paroxysms of laughter and tapped me playfully on the arm, saying:

'Oh! vicar, you must not be so naughty.'

When she had recovered, she went on.

'A certain lady, and where do you think this certain lady was going? She turned into the Vicarage road, but before she did so, she looked up and down the road in a most peculiar way – to see if anyone she knew were noticing her, I imagine.'

'And the little bird—' I inquired.

'Paying a visit to the fishmonger's – in the room over the shop.'

I now know where maids go on their days out. I know there is one place they never go if they can help – anywhere in the open air.

'And the time,' continued Miss Wetherby, leaning forward mysteriously, 'was just before six o'clock.'

'On which day?'

Miss Wetherby gave a little scream.

'The day of the murder, of course, didn't I say so?'

'I inferred it,' I replied. 'And the name of the lady?'

'Begins with an L,' said Miss Wetherby, nodding her head several times.

Feeling that I had got to the end of the information Miss Wetherby had to import, I rose to my feet.

'You won't let the police cross-question me, will you?' said Miss Wetherby, pathetically, as she clasped my hand in both of hers. 'I do shrink from publicity. And to stand up in court!'

'In special cases,' I said, 'they let witnesses sit down.'

And I escaped.

There was still Mrs Price Ridley to see. That lady put me in my place at once.

'I will not be mixed up in any police court business,' she said firmly, after shaking my hand coldly. 'You understand that, on the other hand, having come across a circumstance which needs explaining, I think it should be brought to the notice of the authorities.'

'Does it concern Mrs Lestrange?' I asked.

'Why should it?' demanded Mrs Price Ridley coldly.

She had me at a disadvantage there.

'It's a very simple matter,' she continued. 'My maid, Clara, was standing at the front gate, she went down there for a minute or two – *she* says to get a breath of fresh air. Most unlikely, I should say. Much more probable that she was looking out for the fishmonger's boy – if he calls himself a boy – impudent young jackanapes, thinks because he's seventeen he can joke with all the girls. Anyway, as I say, she was standing at the gate and she heard a sneeze.'

'Yes,' I said, waiting for more.

'That's all. I tell you she heard a sneeze. And don't start telling me I'm not so young as I once was and may have made a mistake, because it was Clara who heard it and she's only nineteen.'

'But,' I said, 'why shouldn't she have heard a sneeze?'

Mrs Price Ridley looked at me in obvious pity for my poorness of intellect.

'She heard a sneeze on the day of the murder at a time when there was no one in your house. Doubtless the murderer was concealed in the bushes waiting his opportunity. What you have to look for is a man with a cold in his head.'

'Or a sufferer from hay fever.' I suggested. 'But as a matter of fact, Mrs Price Ridley, I think that mystery has a very easy solution. Our maid, Mary, has been suffering from a severe cold in the head. In fact, her sniffing has tried us very much lately. It must have been her sneeze your maid heard.'

'It was a man's sneeze,' said Mrs Price Ridley firmly. 'And you couldn't hear your maid sneeze in your kitchen from our gate.'

'You couldn't hear anyone sneezing in the study from your gate,' I said. 'Or at least, I very much doubt it.'

'I said the man might have been concealed in the shrubbery,' said Mrs Price Ridley. 'Doubtless when Clara had gone in, he effected an entrance by the front door.'

'Well, of course, that's possible,' I said.

I tried not to make my voice consciously soothing, but I must have failed, for Mrs Price Ridley glared at me suddenly.

'I am accustomed not to be listened to, but I might mention also that to leave a tennis racquet carelessly flung down on the grass without a press completely ruins it. And tennis racquets are very expensive nowadays.'

There did not seem to be rhyme or reason in this flank attack. It bewildered me utterly.

'But perhaps you don't agree,' said Mrs Price Ridley.

'Oh! I do – certainly.'

'I am glad. Well, that is all I have to say. I wash my hands of the whole affair.'

She leaned back and closed her eyes like one weary of this world. I thanked her and said goodbye.

On the doorstep, I ventured to ask Clara about her mistress's statement.

'It's quite true, sir, I heard a sneeze. And it wasn't an ordinary sneeze – not by any means.'

Nothing about a crime is ever ordinary. The shot was not an ordinary kind of shot. The sneeze was not a usual kind of sneeze. It was, I presume, a special murderer's sneeze. I asked the girl what time this had been, but she was very vague, some time between a quarter and half-past six she thought. Anyway, 'it was before the mistress had the telephone call and was took bad.'

I asked her if she had heard a shot of any kind. And she said the shots had been something awful. After that, I placed very little credence in her statements.

I was just turning in at my own gate when I decided to pay a friend a visit.

Glancing at my watch, I saw that I had just time for it before taking Evensong. I went down the road to Haydock's house. He came out on the doorstep to meet me.

I noticed afresh how worried and haggard he looked. This business seemed to have aged him out of all knowledge.

'I'm glad to see you,' he said. 'What's the news?'

I told him the latest Stone development.

'A high-class thief,' he commented. 'Well, that explains a lot of things. He'd read up his subject, but he made slips from time to time to me. Protheroe must have caught him out once. You remember the row they had. What do you think about the girl? Is she in it too?'

'Opinion as to that is undecided,' I said. 'For my own part, I think the girl is all right.

'She's such a prize idiot,' I added.

'Oh! I wouldn't say that. She's rather shrewd, is Miss Gladys Cram. A remarkably healthy specimen. Not likely to trouble members of my profession.

I told him that I was worried about Hawes, and that I was anxious that he should get away for a real rest and change.

Something evasive came into his manner when I said this. His answer did not ring quite true.

'Yes,' he said slowly. 'I suppose that would be the best thing. Poor chap. Poor chap.'

'I thought you didn't like him.'

'I don't – not much. But I'm sorry for a lot of people I don't like.' He added after a minute or two: 'I'm even sorry for

Protheroe. Poor fellow – nobody ever liked him much. Too full of his own rectitude and too self-assertive. It's an unlovable mixture. He was always the same – even as a young man.'

'I didn't know you knew him then?'

'Oh, yes! When he lived in Westmorland, I had a practice not far away. That's a long time ago now. Nearly twenty years.'

I sighed. Twenty years ago Griselda was five years old. Time is an odd thing . . .

'Is that all you came to say to me, Clement?'

I looked up with a start. Haydock was watching me with keen eyes.

'There's something else, isn't there?' he said.

I nodded.

I had been uncertain whether to speak or not when I came in but now I decided to do so. I like Haydock as well as any man I know. He is a splendid fellow in every way. I felt that what I had to tell might be useful to him.

I recited my interviews with Miss Hartnell and Miss Wetherby.

He was silent for a long time after I'd spoken.

'It's quite true, Clement,' he said at last. 'I've been trying to shield Mrs Lestrange from any inconvenience that I could. As a matter of fact, she's an old friend. But that's not my only reason. That medical certificate of mine isn't the put-up job you all think it was.'

He paused, and then said gravely:

'This is between you and me, Clement. Mrs Lestrange is doomed.'

'What?'

'She's a dying woman. I give her a month at longest. Do you wonder that I want to keep her from being badgered and questioned?'

He went on:

'When she turned into this road that evening it was here she came – to this house.'

'You haven't said so before.'

'I didn't want to create talk. Six to seven isn't my time for seeing patients, and everyone knows that. But you can take my word for it that she was here.'

'She wasn't here when I came for you, though. I mean, when we discovered the body.'

'No,' he seemed perturbed. 'She'd left – to keep an appointment.'

'In what direction was the appointment? In her own house?'
'I don't know, Clement. On my honour, I don't know.'
I believed him, but—
'And supposing an innocent man is hanged?' I said.
He shook his head.
'No,' he said. 'No one will be hanged for the murder of
Colonel Protheroe. You can take my word for that.'
But that is just what I could not do. And yet the certainty in
his voice was very great.
'No one will be hanged,' he repeated.
'This man, Archer—'
He made an impatient movement.
'Hasn't got brains enough to wipe his fingerprints off the
pistol.'
'Perhaps not,' I said dubiously.
Then I remembered something, and taking the little brown-
ish crystal I had found in the wood from my pocket, I held it
out to him and asked him what it was.
'H'm,' he hesitated. 'Looks like picric acid. Where did you
find it?'
'That,' I replied, 'is Sherlock Holmes's secret.'
He smiled.
'What is picric acid?'
'Well, it's an explosive.'
'Yes, I know that, but it's got another use, hasn't it?'
He nodded.
'It's used medically – in solution for burns. Wonderful stuff.'
I held out my hand, and rather reluctantly he handed it back
to me.
'It's of no consequence probably,' I said. 'But I found it in
rather an unusual place.'
'You won't tell me where?'
Rather childishly, I wouldn't.
He had his secrets. Well, I would have mine.
I was a little hurt that he had not confided in me more fully.

—— 26 ——

I was in a strange mood when I mounted the pulpit that night.
The church was unusually full. I cannot believe that it was

the prospect of Hawes preaching which had attracted so many. Hawes's sermons are dull and dogmatic. And if the news had got round that I was preaching instead, that would not have attracted them either. For my sermons are dull and scholarly. Neither, I am afraid, can I attribute it to devotion.

Everybody had come, I concluded, to see who else was there, and possibly to exchange a little gossip in the church porch afterwards.

Haydock was in church, which is unusual, and also Lawrence Redding. And to my surprise, beside Lawrence I saw the white, strained face of Hawes. Anne Protheroe was there, but she usually attends Evensong on Sundays, though I had hardly thought she would today. I was far more surprised to see Lettice. Church-going was compulsory on Sunday morning – Colonel Protheroe was adamant on that point, but I had never seen Lettice at evening service before.

Gladys Cram was there, looking rather blatantly young and healthy against a background of wizened spinsters, and I fancied that a dim figure at the end of the church who had slipped in late, was Mrs Lestrange.

I need hardly say that Mrs Price Ridley, Miss Hartnell, Miss Wetherby, and Miss Marple were there in full force. All the village people were there, with hardly a single exception. I don't know when we have had such a crowded congregation.

Crowds are queer things. There was a magnetic atmosphere that night, and the first person to feel its influence was myself.

As a rule, I prepare my sermons beforehand. I am careful and conscientious over them, but no one is better aware than myself of their deficiencies.

Tonight I was of necessity preaching *extempore*, and as I looked down on the sea of upturned faces, a sudden madness entered my brain. I ceased to be in any sense a Minister of God. I became an actor. I had an audience before me and I wanted to move that audience – and more, I felt the power to move it.

I am not proud of what I did that night. I am an utter disbeliever in the emotional Revivalist spirit. Yet that night I acted the part of a raving, ranting evangelist.

I gave out my text slowly.

I came not to call the righteous, but sinners to repentance.

I repeated it twice, and I heard my own voice, a resonant, ringing voice unlike the voice of the everyday Leonard Clement.

I saw Griselda from her front pew look up in surprise and Dennis follow her example.

I held my breath for a moment or two, and then I let myself rip.

The congregation in that church were in a state of pent-up emotion, ripe to be played upon. I played upon them. I exhorted sinners to repentance. I lashed myself into a kind of emotional frenzy. Again and again I threw out a denouncing hand and reiterated the phrase.

'I am speaking to *you* . . .'

And each time, from different parts of the church, a kind of sighing gasp went up.

Mass emotion is a strange and terrible thing.

'I finished up with those beautiful and poignant words – perhaps the most poignant words in the whole Bible:

'*This night thy soul shall be required of thee* . . .'

It was a strange, brief possession. When I got back to the Vicarage I was my usual faded, indeterminate self. I found Griselda rather pale. She slipped her arm through mine.

'Len,' she said, 'you were rather terrible tonight. I – I didn't like it. I've never heard you preach like that before.'

'I don't suppose you ever will again,' I said, sinking down wearily on the sofa. I was tired.

'What made you do it?'

'A sudden madness came over me.'

'Oh! it – it wasn't something special?'

'What do you mean – something special?'

'I wondered – that was all. You're very unexpected, Len. I never feel I really know you.'

We sat down to cold supper, Mary being out.

'There's a note for you in the hall,' said Griselda. 'Get it, will you, Dennis?'

Dennis, who had been very silent, obeyed.

I took it and groaned. Across the top left-hand corner was written: *By hand – Urgent.*

'This,' I said, 'must be from Miss Marple. There's no one else left.'

I had been perfectly correct in my assumption.

DEAR MR CLEMENT – I should so much like to have a little chat with you about one or two things that have occurred to me. I feel we should all try and help in elucidating this sad mystery. I will come over about half-past nine, if I may, and tap on your study window. Perhaps dear Griselda would be so very kind as to run over here and cheer up my nephew.

And Mr Dennis too, of course, if he cares to come. If I do not hear, I will expect them and will come over myself at the time I have stated.

Yours very sincerely,

JANE MARPLE.

I handed the note to Griselda.

'Oh! we'll go,' she said cheerfully. 'A glass or two of home-made liqueur is just what one needs on Sunday evening. I think it's Mary's blancmange that is so frightfully depressing. It's like something out of a mortuary.'

Dennis seemed less charmed at the prospect.

'It's all very well for you,' he grumbled. 'You can talk all this highbrow stuff about art and books. I always feel a perfect fool sitting and listening to you.'

'That's good for you,' said Griselda serenely. 'It puts you in your place. Anyway, I don't think Mr Raymond West is so frightfully clever as he pretends to be.'

'Very few of us are,' I said.

I wondered very much what exactly it was that Miss Marple wished to talk over. Of all the ladies in my congregation, I consider her by far the shrewdest. Not only does she see and hear practically everything that goes on, but she draws amazingly neat and apposite deductions from the facts that come under her notice.

If I were at any time to set out on a career of deceit, it would be of Miss Marple that I should be afraid.

What Griselda called the Nephew Amusing Party stared off at a little after nine, and whilst I was waiting for Miss Marple to arrive I amused myself by drawing up a kind of schedule of the facts connected with the crime. I arranged them so far as possible in chronological order. I am not a punctual person, but I am a neat one, and I like things jotted down in a methodical fashion.

At half-past nine punctually, there was a little tap on the window, and I rose and admitted Miss Marple.

She had a very fine Shetland shawl thrown over her head and shoulders and was looking rather old and frail. She came in full of little fluttering remarks.

'So good of you to let me come – and so good of dear Griselda – Raymond admires her so much – the perfect Greuze he always calls her . . . Shall I sit here? I am not taking your chair? Oh! thank you . . . No, I won't have a footstool.'

I deposited the Shetland shawl on a chair and returned to take a chair facing my guest. We looked at each other, and a little deprecating smile broke out on her face.

'I feel that you must be wondering why – why I am so interested in all this. You may possibly think it's very unwomanly. No – please – I should like to explain if I may.'

She paused a moment, a pink colour suffusing her cheeks.

'You see,' she began at last, 'living alone, as I do, in a rather out-of-the-way part of the world one has to have a hobby. There is, of course, woolwork, and Guides, and Welfare, and sketching, but my hobby is – and always has been – Human Nature. So varied – and so very fascinating. And, of course, in a small village, with nothing to distract one, one has such ample opportunity for becoming what I might call proficient in one's study. One begins to class people, quite definitely, just as though they were birds or flowers, group so-and-so, genus this, species that. Sometimes, of course, one makes mistakes, but less and less as time goes on. And then, too, one tests on oneself. One takes a little problem – for instance, the gill of picked shrimps that amused dear Griselda so much – a quite unimportant mystery but absolutely incomprehensible unless one solves it right. And then there was that matter of the changed cough drops, and the butcher's wife's umbrella – the last absolutely meaningless unless on the assumption that the greengrocer was not behaving at all nicely with the chemist's wife – which, of course, turned out to be the case. It is so fascinating, you know, to apply one's judgment and find that one is right.'

'You usually are, I believe,' I said, smiling.

'That, I am afraid, is what has made me a little conceited,' confessed Miss Marple. 'But I have always wondered whether, if some day a really big mystery came along, I should be able to do the same thing. I mean – just solve it correctly. Logically, it ought to be exactly the same thing. After all, a tiny working model of a torpedo is just the same as a real torpedo.'

'You mean it's all a question of relativity,' I said slowly. 'It should be – logically, I admit. But I don't know whether it really is.'

'Surely it must be the same,' said Miss Marple. 'The – what one used to call the factors at school – are the same. There's money, and mutual attraction between people of an – er – opposite sex – and there's queerness, of course – so many people are a little queer, aren't they? – in fact, most people are when you know them well. And normal people do such astonishing things sometimes, and abnormal people are sometimes so very sane and ordinary. In fact, the only way is to compare people with other people you have known or come across. You'd be surprised if you knew how very few distinct types there are in all.'

'You frighten me,' I said. 'I feel I'm being put under the microscope.'

'Of course, I wouldn't dream of saying any of this to Colonel Melchett – such an autocratic man, isn't he? – and poor Inspector Slack – well, he's exactly like the young lady in the boot shop who wants to sell you patent leather because she's got it in your size, and doesn't take any notice of the fact that you want brown calf.'

That, really, is a very good description of Slack.

'But you, Mr Clement, know, I'm sure, quite as much about the crime as Inspector Slack. I thought, if we could work together—'

'I wonder,' I said. 'I think each one of us in his secret heart fancies himself as Sherlock Holmes.'

Then I told her of the three summonses I had received that afternoon. I told her of Anne's discovery of the picture with the slashed face. I also told her of Miss Cram's attitude at the police station, and I described Haydock's identification of the crystal I had picked up.

'Having found that myself,' I finished up, 'I should like it to be important. But it's probably got nothing to do with the case.'

'I have been reading a lot of American detective stories from the library lately,' said Miss Marple, 'hoping to find them helpful.'

'Was there anything in them about picric acid?'

'I'm afraid not. I do remember reading a story once, though, in which a man was poisoned by picric acid and lanoline being rubbed on him as an ointment.'

'But as nobody has been poisoned here, that doesn't seem to enter into the question,' I said.

Then I took up my schedule and handed it to her.

'I've tried,' I said, 'to recapitulate the facts of the case as clearly as possible.'

MY SCHEDULE

Thursday, 21st inst.

12.30 a.m. – Colonel Protheroe alters his appointment from six to six-fifteen. Overheard by half village very probably.

12.45 – Pistol last seen in its proper place. (But this is doubtful, as Mrs Archer had previously said she could not remember.)

5.30 (approx.) – Colonel and Mrs Protheroe leave Old Hall for village in car.

5.30 – Fake call put through to me from the North Lodge, Old Hall.

6.15 (or a minute or two earlier) – Colonel Protheroe arrives at Vicarage. Is shown into study by Mary.

6.20 – Mrs Protheroe comes along back lane and across garden to study window. Colonel Protheroe not visible.

6.29 – Call from Lawrence Redding's cottage put through to Mrs Price Ridley (according to Exchange).

6.30–6.35 – Shot heard. (Accepting telephone call time as correct.) Lawrence Redding, Anne Protheroe and Dr Stone's evidence seem to point to its being earlier, but Mrs P. R. probably right.

6.45 – Lawrence Redding arrives Vicarage and finds the body.

6.48 – I meet Lawrence Redding.

6.49 – Body discovered by me.

6.55 – Haydock examines body.

NOTE – The only two people who have no kind of alibi for 6.30–6.35 are Miss Cram and Mrs Lestrange. Miss Cram says she was at the barrow, but no confirmation. It seems reasonable, however, to dismiss her from case as there seems nothing to connect her with it. Mrs Lestrange left Dr Haydock's house some time after six to keep an appointment. Where was the appointment, and with whom? It could hardly have been with Colonel Protheroe, as he expected to be engaged with me. It is true that Mrs Lestrange was near the spot at the time the crime was committed, but it seems doubtful what motive she could have had for murdering him. She did not gain by his death, and the inspector's theory of blackmail I cannot accept. Mrs Lestrange is not the kind of woman. Also it seems unlikely that she should have got hold of Lawrence Redding's pistol.

'Very clear,' said Miss Marple, nodding her head in approval. 'Very clear indeed. Gentlemen always make such excellent memoranda.'

'You agree with what I have written?' I asked.

'Oh, yes – you have put it all beautifully.'

I asked her the question then that I had been meaning to put all along.

'Miss Marple,' I said. 'Who do you suspect? You once said that there were seven people.'

'Quite that, I should think,' said Miss Marple absently. 'I expect every one of us suspects someone different. In fact, one can see they do.'

She didn't ask me who I suspected.

'The point is,' she said, 'that one must provide an explanation for everything. Each thing has got to be explained away satisfactorily. If you have a theory that fits every fact – well, then, it must be the right one. But that's extremely difficult. If it wasn't for that note—'

'The note?' I said, surprised.

'Yes, you remember, I told you. That note has worried me all along. It's wrong, somehow.'

'Surely,' I said, 'that is explained now. It was written at six thirty-five and another hand – the murderer's – put the misleading 6.20 at the top. I think that is clearly established.'

'But even then,' said Miss Marple, 'it's all wrong.'

'But why?'

'Listen.' Miss Marple leant forward eagerly. 'Mrs Protheroe passed my garden, as I told you, and she went as far as the study window and she looked in and she didn't see Colonel Protheroe.'

'Because he was writing at the desk,' I said.

'And that's what's all wrong. That was at twenty past six. We agreed that he wouldn't sit down to say he couldn't wait any longer until after half-past six – so, why was he sitting at the writing-table then?'

'I never thought of that,' I said slowly.

'Let us, dear Mr Clement, just go over it again. Mrs Protheroe comes to the window and she thinks the room is empty – she must have thought so, because otherwise she would never have gone down to the studio to meet Mr Redding. It wouldn't have been safe. The room must have been absolutely silent if she thought it was empty. And that leaves us three alternatives, doesn't it?'

'You mean—'

'Well, the first alternative would be that Colonel Protheroe was dead already – but I don't think that's the most likely one. To begin with he'd only been there about five minutes and she or I would have heard the shot, and secondly, the same difficulty remains about his being at the writing-table. The second alternative is, of course, that he was sitting at the writing-table writing a note, but in that case it must have been a different note altogether. It can't have been to say he couldn't wait. And the third—'

'Yes?' I said.

'Well, the third is, of course, that Mrs Protheroe was right, and that the room was actually empty.'

'You mean that, after he had been shown in, he went out again and came back later?'

'Yes.'

'But why should he have done that?'

Miss Marple spread out her hands in a little gesture of bewilderment.

'That would mean looking at the case from an entirely different angle,' I said.

'One so often has to do that – about everything. Don't you think so?'

I did not reply. I was going over carefully in my mind the three alternatives that Miss Marple had suggested.

With a slight sigh the old lady rose to her feet.

'I must be getting back. I am very glad to have had this little chat – though we haven't got very far, have we?'

'To tell you the truth,' I said, as I fetched her shawl, 'the whole thing seems to me a bewildering maze.'

'Oh! I wouldn't say that. I think, on the whole, one theory fits nearly everything. That is, if you admit one coincidence – and I think one coincidence is allowable. More than one, of course, is unlikely.'

'Do you really think that? About the theory, I mean?' I asked looking at her.

'I admit that there is one flaw in my theory – one fact that I can't get over. Oh! if only that note had been something quite different—'

She sighed and shook her head. She moved towards the window and absent-mindedly reached up her hand and felt the rather depressed-looking plant that stood in a stand.

'You know, dear Mr Clement, this should be watered oftener. Poor thing, it needs it badly. Your maid should water it every day. I suppose it is she who attends to it?'

'As much,' I said, 'as she attends to anything.'

'A little raw at present,' suggested Miss Marple.

'Yes,' I said. 'And Griselda steadily refuses to attempt to cook. Her idea is that only a thoroughly undesirable maid will remain with us. However, Mary herself gave us notice the other day.'

'Indeed. I always imagined she was very fond of you both.'

'I haven't noticed it,' I said. 'But, as a matter of fact, it was Lettice Protheroe who upset her. Mary came back from the inquest in rather a temperamental state and found Lettice here and – well, they had words.'

'Oh!' said Miss Marple. She was just about to step through the window when she stopped suddenly, and a bewildering series of changes passed over her face.

'Oh! dear,' she muttered to herself. 'I *have* been stupid. So that was it. Perfectly possible all the time.'

'I beg your pardon?'

She turned a worried face upon me.

'Nothing. An idea that has just occurred to me. I must go home and think things out thoroughly. Do you know, I believe I have been extremely stupid – almost incredibly so.'

'I find that hard to believe,' I said gallantly.

I escorted her through the window and across the lawn.

'Can you tell me what it is that has occurred to you so suddenly?' I asked.

'I would rather not – just at present. You see, there is still a possibility that I may be mistaken. But I do not think so. Here we are at my garden gate. Thank you so much. Please do not come any further.'

'Is the note still a stumbling block?' I asked, as she passed through the gate and latched it behind her.

She looked at me abstractedly.

'The note? Oh! of course that wasn't the real note. I never thought it was. Good night, Mr Clement.'

She went rapidly up the path to the house, leaving me staring after her.

I didn't know what to think.

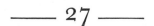

27

Griselda and Dennis had not yet returned. I realized that the most natural thing would have been for me to go up to the house with Miss Marple and fetch them home. Both she and I had been so entirely taken up with out preoccupation over the mystery that we had forgotten anybody existed in the world except ourselves.

I was just standing in the hall, wondering whether I would not even now go over and join them, when the door bell rang.

I crossed over to it. I saw there was a letter in the box, and presuming that this was the cause of the ring, I took it out. As I did so, however, the bell rang again, and I shoved the letter hastily into my pocket and opened the front door. It was Colonel Melchett.

'Hallo, Clement. I'm on my way home from town in the car. Thought I'd just look in and see if you could give me a drink.'

'Delighted,' I said. 'Come into the study.'

He pulled off the leather coat that he was wearing and followed me into the study. I fetched the whisky and soda and two glasses. Melchett was standing in front of the fireplace, legs wide apart, stroking his closely-cropped moustache.

'I've got one bit of news for you, Clement. Most astounding thing you've ever heard. But let that go for the minute. How are things going down here? Any more old ladies hot on the scent?'

'They're not doing so badly,' I said. 'One of them, at all events, thinks she's got there.'

'Our friend, Miss Marple, eh?'

'Our friend, Miss Marple.'

'Women like that always think they know everything,' said Colonel Melchett.

He sipped his whisky and soda appreciatively.

'It's probably unnecessary interference on my part, asking,' I said. 'But I suppose somebody has questioned the fish boy. I mean, if the murderer left by the front door, there's a chance the boy may have seen him.'

'Slack questioned him right enough,' said Melchett. 'But the boy says he didn't meet anybody. Hardly likely he would. The murderer wouldn't be exactly courting observation. Lots of cover by your front gate. He would have taken a look to see if the road was clear. The boy had to call at the Vicarage, at Haydock's, and at Mrs Price Ridley's. Easy enough to dodge him.'

'Yes,' I said, 'I suppose it would be.'

'On the other hand,' went on Melchett, 'if by any chance that rascal Archer did the job, and young Fred Jackson saw him about the place, I doubt very much whether he'd let on. Archer is a cousin of his.'

'Do you seriously suspect Archer?'

'Well, you know, old Protheroe had his knife into Archer

pretty badly. Lots of bad blood between them. Leniency wasn't Protheroe's strong point.'

'No,' I said. 'He was a very ruthless man.'

'What I say is,' said Melchett, 'Live and let live. Of course, the law's the law, but it never hurts to give a man the benefit of the doubt. That's what Protheroe never did.'

'He prided himself on it,' I said.

There was a pause, and then I asked:

'What is this "astounding bit of news" you promised me?'

'Well, it *is* astounding. You know that unfinished letter that Protheroe was writing when he was killed?'

'Yes.'

'We got an expert on it – to say whether the 6.20 was added by a different hand. Naturally we sent up samples of Protheroe's handwriting. And do you know the verdict?' *That letter was never written by Protheroe at all.*'

'You mean a forgery?'

'It's a forgery. The 6.20 they think is written in a different hand again – but they're not sure about that. The heading is in a different ink, but the letter itself is a forgery. Protheroe never wrote it.'

'Are you certain?'

'Well, they're as certain as experts ever are. You know what an expert is! Oh! but they're sure enough.'

'Amazing,' I said. Then a memory assailed me.

'Why,' I said, 'I remember at the time Mrs Protheroe said it wasn't like her husband's handwriting at all, and I took no notice.'

'Really?'

'I thought it one of those silly remarks women will make. If there seemed one thing sure on earth it was that Protheroe had written that note.'

We looked at each other.

'It's curious,' I said slowly. 'Miss Marple was saying this evening that that note was all wrong.'

'Confound the woman, she couldn't know more about it if she had committed the murder herself.'

At that moment the telephone bell rang. There is a queer kind of psychology about a telephone bell. It rang now persistently and with a kind of sinister significance.

I went over and took up the receiver.

'This is the Vicarage,' I said. 'Who's speaking?'

A strange, high-pitched hysterical voice came over the wire:]

'*I want to confess,*' it said. '*My God, I want to confess.*'

'Hallo,' I said, 'hallo. Look here, you've cut me off. What number was that?'

A languid voice said it didn't know. It added that it was sorry I had been troubled.

I put down the receiver, and turned to Melchett.

'You once said,' I remarked, 'that you would go mad if anyone else accused themselves of the crime.'

'What about it?'

'That was someone who wanted to confess . . . And the exchange has cut us off.'

Melchett dashed over and took up the receiver.

'I'll speak to them.'

'Do,' I said. 'You may have some effect. I'll leave you to it. I'm going out. I've a fancy I recognized that voice.'

—— 28 ——

I hurried down the village street. It was eleven o'clock, and at eleven o'clock on a Sunday night the whole village of St Mary Mead might be dead. I saw, however, a light in a first floor window as I passed, and, realizing that Hawes was still up, I stopped and rang the door bell.

After what seemed a long time, Hawes's landlady, Mrs Sadler, laboriously unfastened two bolts, a chain, and turned a key and peered out at me suspiciously.

'Why, it's Vicar!' she exclaimed.

'Good evening,' I said. 'I want to see Mr Hawes. I see there's a light in the window, so he's up still.'

'That may be. I've not seen him since I took up his supper. He's had a quiet evening – no one to see him, and he's not been out.'

I nodded, and passing her, went quickly up the stairs. Hawes has a bedroom and sitting-room on the first floor.

I passed into the latter. Hawes was lying back in a long chair asleep. My entrance did not wake him. An empty cachet box and a glass of water, half-full, stood beside him.

On the floor, by his left foot, was a crumpled sheet of paper with writing on it. I picked it up and straightened it out.

'It began: '*My dear Clement—*'

I read it through, uttered an exclamation and shoved it into my pocket. Then I bent over Hawes and studied him attentively. Next, reaching for the telephone which stood by his elbow, I gave the number of the Vicarage. Melchett must have been still trying to trace the call, for I was told that the number was engaged. Asking them to call me, I put the instrument down again.

I put my hand into my pocket to look at the paper I had picked up once more. With it, I drew out the note that I had found in the letter box and which was still unopened.

Its appearance was horribly familiar. It was the same handwriting as the anonymous letter that had come that afternoon.

I tore it open.

I read it once – twice – unable to realize its contents.

I was beginning to read it a third time when the telephone rang. Like a man in a dream I picked up the receiver and spoke.

'Hallo?'

'Hallo.'

'Is that you, Melchett?'

'Yes, where are you? I've traced that call. The number is—'

'I know the number.'

'Oh! good. Is that where you are speaking from?'

'Yes.'

'What about that confession?'

'I've got the confession all right.'

'You mean you've got the murderer?'

I had then the strongest temptation of my life. I looked at Hawes. I looked at the crumpled letter. I looked at the anonymous scrawl. I looked at the empty-cachet box with the name of Cherubim on it. I remembered a certain casual conversation.

I made an immense effort.

'I – don't know,' I said. 'You'd better come round.'

And I gave him the address.

Then I sat down in the chair opposite Hawes to think.

I had two clear minutes in which to do so.

In two minutes' time, Melchett would have arrived.

I took up the anonymous letter and read it through again for the third time.

Then I closed my eyes and thought . . .

I don't know how long I sat there –only a few minutes in reality, I suppose. Yet it seemed as though an eternity had passed when I heard the door open and, turning my head, looked up to see Melchett entering the room.

He stared at Hawes asleep in his chair, then turned to me.

'What's this, Clement? What does it all mean?'

Of the two letters in my hand I selected one and passed it to him. He read it aloud in a low voice.

My dear Clement – It is a peculiarly unpleasant thing that I have to say. After all, I think I prefer writing it. We can discuss it at a later date. It concerns the recent peculations. I am sorry to say that I have satisfied myself beyond any possible doubt as to the identity of the culprit. Painful as it is for me to have to accuse an ordained priest of the church, my duty is only too painfully clear. An example must be made and—

He looked at me questioningly. At this point the writing tailed off in an undistinguishable scrawl where death had overtaken the writer's hand.

Melchett drew a deep breath, then looked at Hawes.

'So that's the solution! The one man we never even considered. And remorse drove him to confess!'

'He's been very queer lately,' I said.

Suddenly Melchett strode across to the sleeping man with a sharp exclamation. He seized him by the shoulder and shook him, at first gently, then with increasing violence.

'He's not asleep! He's drugged! What's the meaning of this?'

His eyes went to the empty cachet box. He picked it up.

'Has he—'

'I think so,' I said. 'He showed me these the other day. Told me he'd been warned against an overdose. It's his way out, poor chap. Perhaps the best way. It's not for us to judge him.'

But Melchett was Chief Constable of the County before anything else. The arguments that appealed to me had no weight with him. He had caught a murderer and he wanted his murderer hanged.

In one second he was at the telephone, jerking the receiver up and down impatiently until he got a reply. He asked for Haydock's number. Then there was a further pause during which he stood, his ear to the telephone and his eyes on the limp figure in the chair.

'Hallo – hallo – hallo – is that Dr Haydock's? Will the doctor come round at once to High Street? Mr Hawes's. It's urgent . . . what's that? . . . Well, what number is it then? . . . Oh, sorry.'

He rang off, fuming.

'Wrong number, wrong number – always wrong numbers!' And a man's life hanging on it. HALLO – you gave me the wrong number . . . Yes – don't waste time – give me three nine – *nine*, not five.'

Another period of impatience – shorter this time.

'Hallo – is that you, Haydock? Melchett speaking. Come to 19 High Street at once, will you? Hawes has taken some kind of overdose. At once, man, it's vital.'

He rang off, strode impatiently up and down the room.

'Why on earth you didn't get hold of the doctor at once, Clement, I cannot think. Your wits must have all gone wool gathering.'

Fortunately it never occurs to Melchett that anyone can possibly have any different ideas on conduct to those he holds himself. I said nothing, and he went on:

'Where did you find this letter?'

'Crumpled on the floor – where it had fallen from his hand.'

'Extraordinary business – that old maid was right about its being the wrong note we found. Wonder how she tumbled to that. But what an ass the fellow was not to destroy this one. Fancy keeping it – the most damaging evidence you can imagine!'

'Human nature is full of inconsistencies.'

'If it weren't, I doubt if we should ever catch a murderer!' Sooner or later they always do some fool thing. You're looking very under the weather, Clement. I suppose this has been the most awful shock to you?'

'It has. As I say, Hawes has been queer in his manner for some time, but I never dreamed—'

'Who would? Hallo, that sounds like a car.' He went across to the window, pushing up the sash and leaning out. 'Yes, it's Haydock all right.'

A moment later the doctor entered the room.

In a few succinct words, Melchett explained the situation.

Haydock is not a man who ever shows his feelings. He merely raised his eyebrows, nodded, and strode across to his patient. He felt his pulse, raised the eyelid and looked intently at the eye.

Then he turned to Melchett.

'Want to save him for the gallows?' he asked. 'He's pretty far gone, you know. It will be touch and go, anyway. I doubt if I can bring him round.'

'Do everything possible.'

'Right.'

He busied himself with the case he had brought with him, preparing a hypodermic injection which he injected into Hawes's arm. Then he stood up.

'Best thing is to run him into Much Benham – to the hospital there. Give me a hand to get him down to the car.'

We both lent our assistance. As Haydock climbed into the driving seat, he threw a parting remark over his shoulder.

'You won't be able to hang him, you know, Melchett.'

'You mean he won't recover?'

'May or may not. I didn't mean that. I meant that even if he does recover – well, the poor devil wasn't responsible for his actions. I shall give evidence to that effect.'

'What did he mean by that?' asked Melchett as we went up-stairs again.

I explained that Hawes had been a victim of encephalitis lethargica.

'Sleepy sickness, eh? Always some good reason nowadays for every dirty action that's done. Don't you agree?'

'Science is teaching us a lot.'

'Science be damned – I beg your pardon, Clement; but all this namby pambyism annoys me. I'm a plain man. Well, I suppose we'd better have a look round here.'

But at this moment there was an interruption – and a most amazing one. The door opened and Miss Marple walked into the room.

She was pink and somewhat flustered, and seemed to realize our condition of bewilderment.

'So sorry – so very sorry – to intrude – good-evening, Colonel Melchett. As I say, I am so sorry, but hearing that Mr Hawes was taken ill, I felt I must come round and see if I couldn't do something.'

She paused. Colonel Melchett was regarding her in a some-what disgusted fashion.

'Very kind of you, Miss Marple,' he said dryly. 'But no need to trouble. How did you know, by the way?'

It was the question I had been yearning to ask!

'The telephone,' explained Miss Marple. 'So careless with

their wrong numbers, aren't they? You spoke to me first, thinking I was Dr Haydock. My number is three five.'

'So that was it!' I exclaimed.

There is always some perfectly good and reasonable explanation for Miss Marple's omniscience.

'And so,' she continued. 'I just came round to see if I could
be of any use.'

'Very kind of you,' said Melchett again, even more dryly this
time. 'But nothing to be done. Haydock's taken him off to
hospital.'

'Actually to hospital? Oh, that's a great relief! I am so very
glad to hear it. He'll be quite safe there. When you say "nothing
to be done", you don't mean that there's nothing to be done for
him, do you? You don't mean that he won't recover?'

'It's very doubtful,' I said.

Miss Marple's eyes had gone to the cachet box.

'I suppose he took an overdose?' she said.

Melchett, I think, was in favour of being reticent. Perhaps I
might have been under other circumstances. But my discussion
of the case with Miss Marple was too fresh in my mind for me
to have the same view, though I must admit that her rapid appearance on the scene and eager curiosity repelled me slightly.

'You had better look at this,' I said, and handed her Protheroe's unfinished letter.

She took it and read it without any appearance of surprise.

'You had already deduced something of the kind, had you
not?' I asked.

'Yes – yes, indeed. May I ask you, Mr Clement, what made
you come here this evening? That is a point which puzzles me.
You and Colonel Melchett – not at all what I should have expected.

I explained the telephone call and that I believed I had recognized Hawes's voice. Miss Marple nodded thoughtfully.

'Very interesting. Very providential – if I may use the term.
Yes, it brought you here in the nick of time.'

'In the nick of time for what?' I said bitterly.

Miss Marple looked surprised.

'To save Mr Hawes's life, of course.'

'Don't you think,' I said, 'that it might be better if Hawes
didn't recover? Better for him – better for everyone. We know
the truth now and—'

I stopped – for Miss Marple was nodding her head with such

a peculiar vehemence that it made me lose the thread of what I was saying.

'Of course,' she said. 'Of course! That's what he wants you to think! That you know the truth – and that it's best for everyone as it is. Oh, yes, it all fits in – the letter, and the overdose, and poor Mr Hawes's state of mind and his confession. It all fits in – *but it's wrong ...*'

We stared at her.

'That's why I am so glad Mr Hawes is safe – in hospital – where no one can get at him. If he recovers, he'll tell you the truth.'

'The truth?'

'Yes – that he never touched a hair of Colonel Protheroe's head.'

'But the telephone call,' I said. 'The letter – the overdose. It's all so clear.'

'That's what he wants you to think. Oh, he's very clever! Keeping the letter and using it this way was very clever indeed.'

'Who do you mean,' I said 'by "he"?'

'I mean the murderer,' said Miss Marple.

She added very quietly:

'I mean Mr Lawrence Redding ...'

—— 30 ——

We stared at her. I really think that for a moment or two we really believed she was out of her mind. The accusation seemed so utterly preposterous.

Colonel Melchett was the first to speak. He spoke kindly and with a kind of pitying tolerance.

'That is absurd, Miss Marple,' he said. 'Young Redding has been completely cleared.'

'Naturally,' said Miss Marple. 'He saw to that.'

'On the contrary,' said Colonel Melchett dryly. 'He did his best to get himself accused of the murder.'

'Yes,' said Miss Marple. 'He took us all in that way – myself as much as anyone else. You will remember, dear Mr Clement, that I was quite taken aback when I heard Mr Redding had confessed to the crime. It upset all my ideas and made me think him innocent – when up to then I had felt convinced that he was guilty.'

'Then it was Lawrence Redding you suspected?'

'I know that in books it is always the most unlikely person. But I never find that rule applies in real life. There it is so often the obvious that is true. Much as I have always liked Mrs Protheroe, I could not avoid coming to the conclusion that she was completely under Mr Redding's thumb and would do anything he told her, and, of course, he is not the kind of young man who would dream of running away with a penniless woman. From his point of view it was necessary that Colonel Protheroe should be removed – and so he removed him. One of those charming young men who have *no* moral sense.'

Colonel Melchett had been snorting impatiently for some time. Now he broke out.

'Absolute nonsense – the whole thing! Redding's time is fully accounted for up to 6.45 and Haydock says positively Protheroe couldn't have been shot then. I suppose you think you know better than a doctor. Or do you suggest that Haydock is deliberately lying – the Lord knows why?'

'I think Dr Haydock's evidence was absolutely truthful. He is a very upright man. And, of course, it was Mrs Protheroe who actually shot Colonel Protheroe – not Mr Redding.'

Again we stared at her. Miss Marple arranged her lace fichu, pushed back the fleecy shawl that draped her shoulders, and began to deliver a gentle old-maidish lecture comprising the most astounding statements in the most natural way in the world.

'I have not thought it right to speak until now. One's own belief – even so strong as to amount to knowledge – is not the same as proof. And unless one has an explanation that will fit all the facts (as I was saying to dear Mr Clement this evening) one cannot advance it with any real conviction. And my own explanation was not quite complete – it lacked just one thing – but suddenly, just as I was leaving Mr Clement's study, I noticed the palm in the pot by the window – and – well, there the whole thing was! Clear as daylight!'

'Mad – quite mad,' muttered Melchett to me.

But Miss Marple beamed on us serenely and went on in her gentle ladylike voice.

'I was very sorry to believe what I did – very sorry. Because I liked them both. But you know what human nature is. And to begin with, when first he and then she both confessed in the most foolish way – well, I was more relieved than I could say. I had been wrong. And I began to think of other people who had a possible motive for wishing Colonel Protheroe out of the way.'

'The seven suspects!' I murmured.

She smiled at me.

'Yes, indeed. There was that man Archer – not likely, but primed with drink (so inflaming) you never know. And, of course, there was your Mary. She's been walking out with Archer a long time, and she's a queer-tempered girl. Motive *and* opportunity – why, she was alone in the house! Old Mrs Archer could easily have got the pistol from Mr Redding's house for either of those two. And then, of course, there was Lettice – wanting freedom and money to do as she liked. I've known many cases where the most beautiful and ethereal girls have shown next to no moral scruple – though, of course, gentlemen never wish to believe it of them.'

I winced.

'And then there was the tennis racquet,' continued Miss Marple.

'The tennis racquet?'

'Yes, the one Mrs Price Ridley's Clara saw lying on the grass by the Vicarage gate. That looked as though Mr Dennis had got back earlier from his tennis party than he said. Boys of sixteen are so very susceptible and so very unbalanced. Whatever the motive – for Lettice's sake or for yours, it was a possibility. And then, of course, there was poor Mr Hawes and you – not both of you naturally – but alternatively, as the lawyers say.'

'Me?' I exclaimed in lively astonishment.

'Well, yes. I do apologize – and indeed I never really thought – but there was the question of these disappearing sums of money. Either you or Mr Hawes must be guilty, and Mrs Price Ridley was going about everywhere hinting that you were the person at fault – principally because you objected so vigorously to any kind of inquiry into the matter. Of course, I myself was always convinced it was Mr Hawes – he reminded me so much of that unfortunate organist I mentioned; but all the same one couldn't be absolutely *sure*—'

'Human nature being what it is,' I ended grimly.

'Exactly. And then, of course, there was dear Griselda.'

'But Mrs Clements was completely out of it,' interrupted Melchett. 'She returned by the 6.50 train.'

'That's what she *said*,' retorted Miss Marple. 'One should never go by what people say. The 6.50 was half an hour late that night. But at a quarter-past seven I saw her with my own eyes starting for Old Hall. So it followed that she must have come by the earlier train. Indeed she was seen; but perhaps you know that?'

She looked at me inquiringly.

Some magnetism in her glance impelled me to hold out the last anonymous letter, the one I had opened so short a time ago. It set out in detail that Griselda had been seen leaving Lawrence Redding's cottage by the back window at twenty past six on the fatal day.

I said nothing then or at any time of the dreadful suspicion that had for one moment assailed my mind. I had seen it in nightmare terms – a past intrigue between Lawrence and Griselda, the knowledge of it coming to Protheroe's ears, his decision to make me acquainted with the facts – and Griselda, desperate, stealing the pistol and silencing Protheroe. As I say – a nightmare only – but invested for a few long minutes with a dreadful appearance of reality.

I don't know whether Miss Marple had any inkling of all this. Very probably she had. Few things are hidden from her. She handed me back the note with a little nod.

'That's been all over the village,' she said. 'And it did look rather suspicious, didn't it? Especially with Mrs Archer swearing at the inquest that the pistol was still in the cottage when she left at midday.'

She paused a minute and then went on.

'But I'm wandering terribly from the point. What I want to say – and I believe it my duty – is to put my own explanation of the mystery before you. If you don't believe it – well, I shall have done my best. Even as it is, my wish to be quite sure before I spoke may have cost poor Mr Hawes his life.'

Again she paused, and when she resumed, her voice held a different note. It was less apologetic, more decided.

'That is my own explanation of the facts. By Thursday afternoon the crime had been fully planned down to the smallest detail. Lawrence Redding first called on the vicar, knowing him to be out. He had with him the pistol which he concealed in that pot in the stand by the window. When the vicar came in, Lawrence explained his visit by a statement that he had made up his mind to go away. At five-thirty, Lawrence Redding telephoned from the North Lodge to the vicar, adopting a woman's voice (you remember what a good amateur actor he was).

'Mrs Protheroe and her husband had just started for the

village. And – a very curious thing (though no one happened to think of it that way) – Mrs Protheroe took no hand-bag with her. Really a *most* unusual thing for a woman to do. Just before twenty past six she passes my garden and stops and speaks, so as to give me every opportunity of noticing that she has no weapon with her and also that she is quite her normal self. They realized, you see, that I am a noticing kind of person. She disappears round the corner of the house to the study window. The poor colonel is sitting at the desk writing his letter to you. He is deaf, as we all know. She takes the pistol from the bowl where it is waiting for her, comes up behind him and shoots him through the head, throws down the pistol and is out again like a flash, and going down the garden to the studio. Nearly anyone would swear that there couldn't have been time!'

'But the shot?' objected the colonel. 'You didn't hear the shot?'

'There is, I believe, an invention called a Maxim silencer. So I gather from detective stories. I wonder if, possibly, the sneeze that the maid, Clara, heard might have actually been the shot? But no matter. Mrs Protheroe is met at the studio by Mr Redding. They go in together – and, human nature being what it is, I'm afraid they realize that I shan't leave the garden till they come out again!'

I had never liked Miss Marple better than at this moment, with her humorous perception of her own weakness.

'When they do come out, their demeanour is gay and natural. And there, in reality, they made a mistake. Because if they had really said goodbye to each other, as they pretended, they would have looked very different. But you see, that was their weak point. They simply *dare* not appear upset in any way. For the next ten minutes they are careful to provide themselves with what is called an alibi, I believe. Finally Mr Redding goes to the Vicarage, leaving it as late as he dares. He probably saw you on the footpath from far away and was able to time matters nicely. He picks up the pistol and the silencer, leaves the forged letter with the time on it written in a different ink and apparently in a different handwriting. When the forgery is discovered it will look like a clumsy attempt to incriminate Anne Protheroe.

'But when he leaves the letter, he finds the one actually written by Colonel Protheroe – something quite unexpected. And being a very intelligent young man, and seeing that this letter may come in very useful to him, he takes it away with him. He alters the hands of the clock to the same time as the letter – knowing that it is always kept a quarter of an hour fast. The same idea – attempting to throw suspicion on Mrs Protheroe. Then he leaves, meeting you outside the gate, and acting the part of someone nearly distraught. As I say, he is really most intelligent. What would a murderer who had committed a crime try to do? Behave naturally, of course. So that is just what Mr Redding does not do. He gets rid of the silencer, but marches into the police station with the pistol and makes a perfectly ridiculous self-accusation which takes everybody in.'

There was something fascinating in Miss Marple's résumé of the case. She spoke with such certainty that we both felt that in this way and in no other could the crime have been committed.

'What about the shot heard in the wood?' I asked. 'Was that the coincidence to which you were referring earlier this evening?'

'Oh! dear, no.' Miss Marple shook her head briskly. '*That* wasn't a coincidence – very far from it. It was absolutely necessary that a shot should be heard – otherwise suspicion of Mrs Protheroe might have continued. How Mr Redding arranged it, I don't quite know. But I understand that picric acid explodes if you drop a weight on it, and you will remember, dear vicar, that you met Mr Redding carrying a large stone just in the part of the wood where you picked up that crystal later. Gentlemen are so clever at arranging things – the stone suspended above the crystals and then a time fuse – or do I mean a slow match? Sometimes that would take about twenty minutes to burn through – so that the explosion would come about 6.30 when he and Mrs Protheroe had come out of the studio and were in full view. A very safe device because what would there be to find afterwards – only a big stone! But even that he tried to remove – when you came upon him.'

'I believe you are right,' I exclaimed, remembering the start of surprise Lawrence had given on seeing me that day. It had seemed natural enough at the time, but now . . .

Miss Marple seemed to read my thoughts, for she nodded her head shrewdly.

'Yes,' she said, 'it must have been a very nasty shock for him to come across you just then. But he turned it off very well – pretending he was bringing it to me for my rock gardens. Only—' Miss Marple became suddenly very emphatic – '*It was the wrong sort of stone for my rock gardens!* And that put me on the right track!'

All this time Colonel Melchett had sat like a man in a trance. Now he showed signs of coming too. He snorted once or twice, blew his nose in a bewildered fashion, and said:

'Upon my word! Well, upon my word!'

Beyond that, he did not commit himself. I think that he, like myself, was impressed with the logical certainty of Miss Marple's conclusions. But for the moment he was not willing to admit it.

Instead, he stretched out a hand, picked up the crumpled letter and barked out:

'All very well. But how do you account for this fellow Hawes! Why, he actually rang up and confessed.'

'Yes, that was what was so providential. The vicar's sermon, doubtless. You know, dear Mr Clement, you really preached a most remarkable sermon. It must have affected Mr Hawes deeply. He could bear it no longer, and felt he must confess – about the misappropriations of the church funds.'

'What?'

'Yes – and that, under Providence, is what has saved his life. (For I hope and trust it *is* saved. Dr Haydock is so clever.) As I see the matter, Mr Redding kept this letter (a risky thing to do, but I expect he hid it in some safe place) and waited till he found out for certain to whom it referred. He soon made quite sure that it was Mr Hawes. I understand he came back here with Mr Hawes last night and spent a long time with him. I suspect that he then substituted a cachet of his own for one of Mr Hawes's, and slipped this letter in the pocket of Mr Hawes's dressing-gown. The poor young man would swallow the fatal cachet in all innocence – after his death his things would be gone through and the letter found and everyone would jump to the conclusion that he had shot Colonel Protheroe and taken his own life out of remorse. I rather fancy Mr Hawes must have found that letter tonight just after taking the fatal cachet. In his disordered state, it must have seemed like something supernatural, and, coming on top of the vicar's sermon, it must have impelled him to confess the whole thing.'

'Upon my word,' said Colonel Melchett. 'Upon my word! *Most* extraordinary! I – I – don't believe a word of it.'

He had never made a statement that sounded more unconvincing. It must have sounded so in his own ears, for he went on:

'And can you explain the other telephone call – the one from Mr Redding's cottage to Mrs Price Ridley?'

'Ah!' said Miss Marple. 'That is what I call the coincidence. Dear Griselda sent that call – she and Mr Dennis between them, I fancy. They had heard the rumours Mrs Price Ridley was circulating about the vicar, and they thought of this (perhaps rather childish) way of silencing her. The coincidence lies in the fact that the call should have been put through at exactly the same time as the fake shot from the wood. It led one to believe that the two must be connected.'

I suddenly remembered how everyone who spoke of that shot had described it as 'different' from the usual shot. They had been right. Yet how hard to explain just in what way the 'difference' of the shot consisted.

Colonel Melchett cleared his throat.

'Your solution is a very plausible one, Miss Marple,' he said. 'But you will allow me to point out that there is not a shadow of proof.'

'I know,' said Miss Marple. 'But you believe it to be true, don't you?'

There was a pause, then the colonel said almost reluctantly: 'Yes, I do. Dash it all, it's the only way the thing could have happened. But there's no proof – not an atom.'

Miss Marple coughed.

'That is why I thought perhaps – under the circumstances—'

'Yes?'

'A little trap might be permissible.'

——— 3 I ———

Colonel Melchett and I both stared at her.

'A trap? What kind of a trap?'

Miss Marple was a little diffident, but it was clear that she had a plan fully outlined.

'Supposing Mr Redding were to be rung up on the telephone and warned.'

Colonel Melchett smiled.

' "All is discovered. Fly!" That's an old wheeze, Miss Marple. Not that it isn't often successful! But I think in this case young Redding is too downy a bird to be caught that way.'

'It would have to be something specific. I quite realize that,' said Miss Marple. 'I would suggest – this is just a mere suggestion – that the warning should come from somebody who is known to have rather unusual views on these matters. Dr Haydock's conversation would lead anyone to suppose that he might view such a thing as murder from an unusual angle. If he were to hint that somebody – Mrs Sadler – or one of her children – had actually happened to see the transposing of the cachets – well, of course, if Mr Redding is an innocent man, that statement will mean nothing to him, but if he isn't—'

'If he isn't?'

'Well, he might just possibly do something foolish.'

'And deliver himself into our hands. It's possible. Very ingenious, Miss Marple. But will Haydock stand for it? As you say, his views—'

Miss Marple interrupted him brightly.

'Oh! but that's theory! So very different from practice, isn't it? But anyway, here he is, so we can ask him.'

Haydock was, I think, rather astonished to find Miss Marple with us. He looked tired and haggard.

'It's been a near thing,' he said. 'A very near thing. But he's going to pull through. It's a doctor's business to save his patient and I saved him, but I'd have been just as glad if I hadn't pulled it off.'

'You may think differently,' said Melchett, 'when you have heard what we have to tell you.'

And briefly and succinctly, he put Miss Marple's theory of the crime before the doctor, ending up with her final suggestion.

We were then privileged to see exactly what Miss Marple meant by the difference between theory and practice.

Haydock's views appeared to have undergone complete transformation. He would, I think, have liked Lawrence Redding's head on a charger. It was not, I imagine, the murder of Colonel Protheroe that so stirred his rancour. It was the assault on the unlucky Hawes.

'The damned scoundrel,' said Haydock. 'The damned scoundrel! That poor devil Hawes. He's got a mother and a sister too. The stigma of being the mother and sister of a murderer would have rested on them for life, and think of their mental anguish. Of all the cowardly dastardly tricks!'

For sheer primitive rage, commend me to a thorough-going humanitarian when you get him well roused.

'If this thing's true,' he said, 'you can count on me. The fellow's not fit to live. A defenceless chap like Hawes.'

A lame dog of any kind can always count on Haydock's sympathy.

He was eagerly arranging details with Melchett when Miss Marple rose and I insisted on seeing her home.

'It is most kind of you, Mr Clement,' said Miss Marple, as we walked down the deserted street. 'Dear me, past twelve o'clock. I hope Raymond has gone to bed and not waited up.'

'He should have accompanied you,' I said.

'I didn't let him know I was going,' said Miss Marple.

I smiled suddenly as I remembered Raymond West's subtle psychological analysis of the crime.

'If your theory turns out to be the truth – which I for one do not doubt for a minute,' I said, 'you will have a very good score over your nephew.'

Miss Marple smiled also – an indulgent smile.

'I remember a saying of my Great Aunt Fanny's. I was sixteen at the time and thought it particularly foolish.'

'Yes?' I inquired.

'She used to say: "The young people think the old people are fools; but the old people *know* the young people are fools!" '

—— 32 ——

There is little more to be told. Miss Marple's plan succeeded. Lawrence Redding was not an innocent man, and the hint of a witness of the change of capsule did indeed cause him to do 'something foolish'. Such is the power of an evil conscience.

He was, of course, peculiarly placed. His first impulse, I imagine, must have been to cut and run. But there was his accomplice to consider. He could not leave without getting word to her, and he dared not wait till morning. So he went up to Old Hall that night – and two of Colonel Melchett's most efficient officers followed him. He threw gravel at Anne Protheroe's window, aroused her, and an urgent whisper brought her down to speak with him. Doubtless they felt safer outside than in – with the possibility of Lettice waking. But as it happened, the two police officers were able to overhear their conversation in full. It left the matter in no doubt. Miss Marple had been right on every count.

The trial of Lawrence Redding and Anne Protheroe is a

THE MURDER AT THE VICARAGE

matter of public knowledge. I do not propose to go into it. I will only mention that great credit was reflected upon Inspector Slack, whose zeal and intelligence had resulted in the criminals being brought to justice. Naturally, nothing was said of Miss Marple's share in the business. She herself would have been horrified at the thought of such a thing.

Lettice came to see me just before the trial took place. She drifted through my study window, wraith-like as ever. She told me then that she had all along been convinced of her step-mother's complicity. The loss of the yellow beret had been a mere excuse for searching the study. She hoped against hope that she might find something the police had overlooked.

'You see,' she said in her dreamy voice, 'they didn't hate her like I did. And hate makes things easier for you.'

Disappointed in the result of her search, she had deliberately dropped Anne's ear-ring by the desk.

'Since I *knew* she had done it, what did it matter? One way was as good as another. She *had* killed him.'

I sighed a little. There was always some things that Lettice will never see. In some respects she is morally colour blind.

'What are you going to do, Lettice?' I asked.

'When – when it's all over, I am going abroad.' She hesitated and then went on. 'I am going abroad with my mother.'

I looked up, startled.

She nodded.

'Didn't you ever guess? Mrs Lestrange is my mother. She is – is dying, you know. She wanted to see me and so she came down here under an assumed name. Dr Haydock helped her. He's a very old friend of hers – he was keen about her once – you can see that! In a way, he still is. Men always went batty about mother, I believe. She's awfully attractive even now. Any-way, Dr Haydock did everything he could to help her. She didn't come down here under her own name because of the disgusting way people talk and gossip. She went to see father that night and told him she was dying and had a great longing to see some-thing of me. Father was a beast. He said she'd forfeited all claim, and that I thought she was dead – as though I had ever swallowed that story! Men like father never see an inch before their noses!

'But mother is not the sort to give in. She thought it only decent to go to father first, but when he turned her down so brutally she sent a note to me, and I arranged to leave the tennis party early and meet her at the end of the footpath at a quarter past six. We just had a hurried meeting and arranged when to meet again. We left each other before half-past six. Afterwards I was terrified that she would be suspected of having killed father. After all, she *had* got a grudge against him. That's why I got hold of that old picture of her up in the attic and slashed it about. I was afraid the police might go nosing about and get hold of it and recognise it. Dr Haydock was frightened too. Sometimes, I believe, he really thought she had done it! Mother is rather a – desperate kind of person. She doesn't count consequences.'

She paused.

'It's queer. She and I belong to each other. Father and I didn't. But mother – well, anyway, I'm going abroad with her. I shall be with her till – till the end . . .'

She got up and I took her hand.

'God bless you both,' I said. 'Some day, I hope, there is a lot of happiness coming to you, Lettice.'

'There should be,' she said, with an attempt at a laugh. 'There hasn't been much so far – has there? Oh, well, I don't suppose it matters. Goodbye, Mr Clement. You've been frightfully decent to me always – you and Griselda.'

Griselda!

I had to own to her how terribly the anonymous letter had upset me, and first she laughed, and then solemnly read me a lecture.

'However,' she added, 'I'm going to be very sober and god-fearing in future – quite like the Pilgrim Fathers.'

I did not see Griselda in the role of a Pilgrim Father.

She went on:

'You see, Len, I have a steadying influence coming into my life. It's coming into your life, too, but in your case it will be a kind of – of rejuvenating one – at least, I hope so! You can't call me a dear child half so much when we have a real child of our own. And, Len, I've decided that now I'm going to be a real "wife and mother" (as they say in books), I must be a house-keeper too. I've bought two books on Household Management and one on Mother Love, and if that doesn't turn me out a pattern I don't know what will! They are all simply screamingly funny – not intentionally, you know. Especially the one about bringing up children.'

'You haven't bought a book on How to Treat a Husband, have you?' I asked, with sudden apprehension as I drew her to me.

'I don't need to,' said Griselda. 'I'm a very good wife. I love you dearly. What more do you want?'

'Nothing,' I said.

'Could you say, just for once, that you love me madly?'

'Griselda,' I said – 'I adore you! I worship you! I am wildly, hopelessly and quite unclerically crazy about you!'

My wife gave a deep and contented sigh.

Then she drew away suddenly.

'Bother! Here's Miss Marple coming. Don't let her suspect, will you? I don't want everyone offering me cushions and urging me to put my feet up. Tell her I've gone down to the golf links. That will put her off the scent – and it's quite true because I left my yellow pullover there and I want it.'

Miss Marple came to the window, halted apologetically, and asked for Griselda.

'Griselda,' I said, 'has gone to the golf links.'

An expression of concern leaped into Miss Marple's eyes.

'Oh, but surely,' she said, 'that is most unwise – just now.'

And then in a nice, old-fashioned, ladylike, maiden-lady way, she blushed.

And to cover the moment's confusion, we talked hurriedly of the Protheroe case, and of 'Dr Stone', who had turned out to be a well-known cracksman with several different aliases. Miss Cram, by the way, had been cleared of all complicity. She had at last admitted taking the suit-case to the wood, but had done so in all good faith, Dr Stone having told her that he feared the rivalry of other archæologists who would not stick at burglary to gain their object of discrediting his theories. The girl apparently swallowed this not very plausible story. She is now, according to the village, looking out for a more genuine article in the line of an elderly bachelor requiring a secretary.

As we talked, I wondered very much how Miss Marple had discovered our latest secret. But presently, in a discreet fashion, Miss Marple herself supplied me with a clue.

'I hope dear Griselda is not overdoing it,' she murmured, and, after a discreet pause, 'I was in the bookshop in Much Benham yesterday—'

'Poor Griselda – that book on Mother Love has been her undoing!

'I wonder, Miss Marple,' I said suddenly, 'if you were to commit a murder whether you would ever be found out.'

'What a terrible idea,' said Miss Marple, shocked. 'I hope I could never do such a wicked thing.'

'But human nature being what it is,' I murmured.

Miss Marple acknowledged the hit with a pretty old-ladyish laugh.

'How naughty of you, Mr Clement.' She rose. 'But naturally you are in good spirits.'

She paused by the window.

'My love to dear Griselda – and tell her – that any little secret is quite safe with me.'

Really Miss Marple is rather a dear . . .

A MURDER
IS
ANNOUNCED

A MURDER IS ANNOUNCED

I

Between 7.30 and 8.30 every morning except Sundays, Johnnie
Butt made the round of the village of Chipping Cleghorn on his
bicycle, whistling vociferously through his teeth, and alighting
at each house or cottage to shove through the letter-box such
morning papers as had been ordered by the occupants of the
house in question from Mr Totman, stationer, of the High
Street. Thus, at Colonel and Mrs Easterbrook's he delivered *The
Times* and the *Daily Graphic*; at Mrs Swettenham's he left *The
Times* and *The Daily Worker*; at Miss Hinchcliffe and Miss
Murgatroyd's he left the *Daily Telegraph* and the *News Chronicle*; at Miss Blacklock's he left the *Telegraph, The Times* and
The Daily Mail.

At all these houses, and indeed at practically every house in
Chipping Cleghorn, he delivered every Friday a copy of the
North Benham News and Chipping Cleghorn Gazette, known
locally simply as 'the Gazette.'

Thus, on Friday mornings, after a hurried glance at the headlines in the daily paper (*International situation critical! UNO
meets today! Bloodhounds seek blonde typist's killer! Three col-
lieries idle. Twenty-three die of food poisoning in Seaside
Hotel, etc.*) most of the inhabitants of Chipping Cleghorn
eagerly opened the *Gazette* and plunged into the local news.
After a couple of cursory glances at Correspondence (in which
the passionate hates and feuds of rural life found full play) nine
out of ten subscribers then turned to the PERSONAL column.
Here were grouped together higgledy piggledy articles for Sale or
Wanted, frenzied appeals for Domestic Help, innumerable inser-
tions regarding dogs, announcements concerning poultry and
garden equipment; and various other items of an interesting
nature to those living in the small community of Chipping Cleghorn.

This particular Friday, October 29th – was no exception to
the rule—

II

Mrs Swettenham, pushing back the pretty little grey curls from her forehead, opened *The Times*, looked with a lack lustre eye at the left hand centre page, decided that, as usual, if there *was* any exciting news *The Times* had succeeded in camouflaging it in an impeccable manner; took a look at the Births, Marriages and Deaths, particularly the latter; then, her duty done, she put aside *The Times* and eagerly seized the *Chipping Cleghorn Gazette*.

When her son Edmund entered the room a moment later, she was already deep in the Personal Column.

'Good-morning, dear,' said Mrs Swettenham. 'The Smedleys are selling their Daimler. 1935 – that's rather a long time ago, isn't it?'

Her son grunted, poured himself out a cup of coffee, helped himself to a couple of kippers, sat down at the table and opened the *Daily Worker* which he propped up against the toast rack.

'*Bull mastiff puppies*,' read out Mrs Swettenham. 'I really don't know how people manage to feed big dogs nowadays – I really *don't* . . . H'm Selina Lawrence is advertising for a cook again. I could tell her it's just a waste of time advertising in these days. She hasn't put her address, only a box number – that's *quite* fatal – I could have told her so – servants simply insist on knowing where they are going. They like a good address . . . *False teeth* – I can't think why false teeth are so popular. *Best prices paid* . . . *Beautiful bulbs. Our special selection.* They sound rather cheap . . . Here's a girl wants an "*Interesting post – Would travel.*" I dare say! Who wouldn't? . . . *Dachshunds* . . . I've never really cared for dachshunds myself – I don't mean because they're *German*, because we've got over all that – I just don't care for them, that's all. – Yes, Mrs Finch?'

The door had opened to admit the head and torso of a grim-looking female in an aged velvet beret.

'Good-morning, Mum,' said Mrs Finch. 'Can I clear?'

'Not yet. We haven't finished,' said Mrs Swettenham. 'Not quite finished,' she added ingratiatingly.

Casting a look at Edmund and his paper, Mrs Finch sniffed, and withdrew.

'I've only just begun,' said Edmund, just as his mother remarked:

'I do wish you wouldn't read that horrid paper, Edmund. Mrs Finch doesn't like it *at all.*'

'I don't see what my political views have to do with Mrs Finch.'

'And it isn't,' pursued Mrs Swettenham, 'as though you *were* a worker. You don't do any work at all.'

'That's not in the least true,' said Edmund indignantly. 'I'm writing a book.'

'I meant *real* work,' said Mrs Swettenham. 'And Mrs Finch does matter. If she takes a dislike to us and won't come, who else could we get?'

'Advertise in the *Gazette*,' said Edmund, grinning.

'I've just told you that's no use. Oh dear me, nowadays unless one has an old Nannie in the family, who will go into the kitchen and do everything, one is simply *sunk*.'

'Well, why haven't we an old Nannie? How remiss of your not to have provided me with one? What were you thinking about?'

'You had an *ayah*, dear.'

'No foresight,' murmured Edmund.

Mrs Swettenham was once more deep in the Personal Column.

'*Second hand Motor Mower for sale*. Now I wonder.... Goodness, what a *price*! ... More Dachshunds ... '*Do write or communicate desperate Woggles*.' What silly nicknames people have ... *Cocker Spaniels* ... Do you remember darling Susie, Edmund? She really was *human*. Understood every word you said to her ... *Sheraton sideboard for Sale. Genuine family antique. Mrs Lucas, Dayas Hall* ... What a liar that woman is! Sheraton indeed ...!'

Mrs Swettenham sniffed and then continued her reading:

'*All a mistake, darling. Undying love. Friday as usual – J*. ... I suppose they've had a lovers' quarrel – or do you think it's a code for burglars? ... *More dachshunds*! Really, I do think people have gone a little crazy about breeding Dachshunds. I mean, there *are* other dogs. Your Uncle Simon used to breed Manchester Terriers. Such graceful little things. I do like dogs with *legs*... *Lady going abroad will sell her navy two piece suiting* ... no measurements or price given ... *A marriage is announced* – no, a *murder. What? Well*, I never! Edmund, Edmund, listen to this ... *A murder is announced and will take place on Friday, October 29th at Little Paddocks at 6.30 p.m. Friends please accept this, the only intimation*. What an extraordinary thing! *Edmund*!'

'What's that?' Edmund looked up from his newspaper.

'Friday, October 29th ... Why, that's *today*.'

'Let me see.' Her son took the paper from her.

'But what does it mean?' Mrs Swettenham asked with lively curiosity.

Edmund Swettenham rubbed his nose doubtfully.

'Some sort of party, I suppose. The Murder Game – that kind of thing.'

'Oh,' said Mrs Swettenham doubtfully. 'It seems a very odd way of doing it. Just sticking it in the advertisements like that. Not at all like Letitia Blacklock who always seems to me such a sensible woman.'

'Probably got up by the bright young things she has in the house.'

'It's very short notice. Today. Do you think we're just supposed to go?'

'It says "Friends, please accept this, the only intimation?"' her son pointed out.

'Well, I think these new fangled ways of giving invitations are very tiresome,' said Mrs Swettenham decidedly.

'All right, Mother, you needn't go.'

'No,' agreed Mrs Swettenham.

There was a pause.

'Do you really *want* that last piece of toast, Edmund?'

'I should have thought my being properly nourished mattered more than letting that old hag clear the table.'

'Sh, dear, she'll *hear* you . . . Edmund, what happens at a Murder Game?'

'I don't know, exactly . . . They pin pieces of paper upon you, or something . . . No, I think you draw them out of a hat. And somebody's the victim and somebody else is a detective – and then they turn the lights out and somebody taps you on the shoulder and then you scream and lie down and sham dead.'

'It sounds quite exciting.'

'Probably a beastly bore. I'm not going.'

'Nonsense, Edmund,' said Mrs Swettenham resolutely. '*I'm* going and *you're* coming with me. That's *settled!*'

III

'Archie,' said Mrs Easterbrook to her husband, 'listen to *this.*'

Colonel Easterbrook paid no attention, because he was already snorting with impatience over an article in *The Times.*

'Trouble with these fellows is,' he said, 'that none of them knows the first thing about India! Not the first thing!'

'I know, dear, I know.'

'If they did, they wouldn't write such piffle.'

'Yes, I know. Archie, do listen. *A murder is announced and will take place on Friday, October 29th* (that's today), *at Little Paddocks at 6.30 p.m. Friends please accept this, the only intimation.*'

She paused triumphantly. Colonel Easterbrook looked at her indulgently but without much interest.

'Murder Game,' he said.

'Oh.'

'That's all it is. Mind you,' he unbent a little, 'it can be very good fun if it's well done. But it needs good organising by someone who knows the ropes. You draw lots. One person's the murderer, nobody knows who. Lights out. Murderer chooses his victim. The victim has to count twenty before he screams. Then the person who's chosen to be the detective takes charge. Questions everybody. Where they were, what they were doing, tries to trip the real fellow up. Yes, it's a good game – if the detective – er – knows something about police work.'

'Like you, Archie. You had all those interesting cases to try in your district.'

Colonel Easterbrook smiled indulgently and gave his moustache a complacent whirl.

'Yes, Laura,' he said. 'I dare say I could give them a hint or two.'

And he straightened his shoulders.

'Miss Blacklock ought to have asked you to help her in getting the things up.'

The Colonel snorted.

'Oh, well, she's got that young cub staying with her. Expect this is his idea. Nephew or something. Funny idea, though, sticking it in the paper.'

'It was in the Personal Column. We might never have seen it. I suppose it *is* an invitation, Archie?'

'Funny kind of invitation. I can tell you one thing. They can count *me* out.'

'Oh, Archie,' Mrs Easterbrook's voice rose in a shrill wail.

'Short notice. For all they know I might be busy.'

'But you're not, are you, darling?' Mrs Easterbrook lowered her voice persuasively. 'And I do think, Archie, that you really *ought* to go – just to help poor Miss Blacklock out. I'm sure she's counting on you to make the thing a success. I mean, you know so much about police work and procedure. The whole thing will fall flat if you don't go and help to make it a success. After all, one must be *neighbourly.*'

Mrs Easterbrook put her synthetic blonde head on one side and opened her blue eyes very wide.

'Of course, if you put it like that, Laura . . .' Colonel Easterbrook twirled his grey moustache again, importantly, and looked with indulgence on his fluffy little wife. Mrs Easterbrook was at least thirty years younger than her husband.

'If you put it like *that,* Laura,' he said.

'I really do think it's your *duty,* Archie,' said Mrs Easterbrook solemnly.

IV

The *Chipping Cleghorn Gazette* had also been delivered at Boulders, the picturesque three cottages knocked into one inhabited by Miss Hinchcliffe and Miss Murgatroyd.

'Hinch?'

'What is it, Murgatroyd?'

'Where are you?'

'Henhouse.'

'Oh.'

Padding gingerly through the long wet gress, Miss Amy Murgatroyd approached her friend. The latter, attired in corduroy slacks and battledress tunic, was conscientiously stirring in handfuls of balancer meal to a repellently steaming basin full of cooked potato peelings and cabbage stumps.

She turned her head with its short man-like crop and weatherbeaten countenance toward her friend.

Miss Murgatroyd, who was fat and amiable, wore a checked tweed skirt and a shapeless pullover of brilliant royal blue. Her curly bird's nest of grey hair was in a good deal of disorder and she was slightly out of breath.

'In the *Gazette,*' she panted. 'Just listen – what can it *mean? A murder is announced . . . and will take place on Friday, October 29th, at Little Paddocks at 6.30 p.m. Friends please accept this, the only intimation.*'

She paused, breathless, as she finished reading, and awaited some authoritative pronouncement.

'Daft,' said Miss Hinchcliffe.

'Yes, but what do you think it *means*?'

'Means a drink, anyway,' said Miss Hinchcliffe.

'You mean it's a sort of invitation?'

'We'll find out what it means when we get there,' said Miss Hinchcliffe. 'Bad sherry, I expect. You'd better get off the grass, Murgatroyd. You've got your bedroom slippers on still. They're soaked.'

'Oh, dear.' Miss Murgatroyd looked down ruefully at her feet.

'How many eggs today?'

'Seven. That damned hen's still broody. I must get her into the coop.'

'It's a funny way of putting it, don't you think?' Amy Murgatroyd asked, reverting to the notice in the *Gazette*. Her voice was slightly wistful.

But her friend was made of sterner and more single-minded stuff. She was intent on dealing with recalcitrant poultry and no announcement in a paper, however enigmatic, could deflect her.

She squelched heavily through the mud and pounced upon a speckled hen. There was a loud and indignant squawking.

'Give me ducks every time,' said Miss Hinchcliffe. '*Far* less trouble . . .'

V

'Oo, scrumptious!' said Mrs Harmon across the breakfast table to her husband, the Rev. Julian Harmon, 'there's going to be a murder at Miss Blacklock's.'

'A murder?' said her husband, slightly surprised. 'When?'

'This afternoon . . . at least, this evening. 6.30. Oh, bad luck, darling, you've got your preparations for confirmation then. It *is* a shame. And you do so love murders!'

'I don't really know what you're talking about, Bunch.'

Mrs Harmon, the roundness of whose form and face had early led to the soubriquet of 'Bunch' being substituted for her baptismal name of Diana, handed the *Gazette* across the table.

'There. All among the second-hand pianos, and the old teeth.'

'What a very extraordinary announcement.'

'Isn't it?' said Bunch happily. 'You wouldn't think that Miss Blacklock cared about murders and games and things, would you? I suppose it's the young Simmonses put her up to it – though I should have thought Julia Simmons would find murders rather crude. Still, there it is, and I do think, darling, it's a

207

shame you can't be there. Anyway, I'll go and tell you all about
it, though it's rather wasted on me, because I don't really like
games that happen in the dark. They frighten me, and I *do* hope
I shan't have to be the one who's murdered. If someone suddenly
puts a hand on my shoulder and whispers, "You're dead," I know
my heart will give such a big bump that perhaps it really *might*
kill me! Do you think that's likely?'

'No, Bunch. I think you're going to live to be an old, old
woman – with me.'

'And die on the same day and be buried in the same grave.
That would be lovely.'

Bunch beamed from ear to ear at this agreeable prospect.

'You seem very happy, Bunch?' said her husband, smiling.

'Who'd *not* be happy if they were me?' demanded Bunch,
rather confusedly. 'With you and Susan and Edward, and all of
you fond of me and not caring if I'm stupid . . . And the sun
shining! And this lovely big house to live in!'

The Rev. Julian Harmon looked round the big bare dining-
room and assented doubtfully.

'Some people would think it was the last straw to have to live
in this great rambling draughty place.'

'Well, I like big rooms. All the nice smells from outside can
get in and stay there. And you can be untidy and leave things
about and they don't clutter you.'

'No labour saving devices or central heating? It means a lot
of work for you, Bunch.'

'Oh, Julian, it doesn't. I get up at half-past six and light the
boiler and rush around like a steam engine, and by eight it's all
done. And I keep it nice, don't I? With beeswax and polish and
big jars of Autumn leaves. It's not really harder to keep a big
house clean than a small one. You go round with mops and
things much quicker, because your behind isn't always bumping
into things like it is in a small room. And I like sleeping in a big
cold room – it's so cosy to snuggle down with just the tip of your
nose telling you what it's like up above. And whatever size of
house you live in, you peel the same amount of potatoes and
wash up the same amount of plates and all that. Think how nice
it is for Edward and Susan to have a big empty room to play in
where they can have railways and dolls' tea-parties all over the
floor and never have to put them away? And then it's nice to
have extra bits of the house that you can let people have to live
in. Jimmy Symes and Johnnie Finch – they'd have had to live
with their in-laws otherwise. And you know, Julian, it isn't nice

living with your in-laws. You're devoted to Mother, but you wouldn't really have liked to start our married life living with her and Father. And I shouldn't have liked it, either. I'd have gone on feeling like a little girl.'

Julian smiled at her.

'You're rather like a little girl still, Bunch.'

Julian Harmon himself had clearly been a model designed by nature for the age of sixty. He was still about twenty-five years short of achieving Nature's purpose.

'I know I'm stupid—'

'You're not stupid, Bunch. You're very clever.'

'No, I'm not. I'm not a bit intellectual. Though I do try . . . And I really love it when you talk to me about books and history and things. I think perhaps it wasn't an awfully good idea to read aloud Gibbon to me in the evenings, because if it's been a cold wind out, and it's nice and hot by the fire, there's something about Gibbon that does, rather, make you go to sleep.'

Julian laughed.

'But I do love listening to you, Julian. Tell me the story again about the old vicar who preached about Ahasuerus.'

'You know that by heart, Bunch.'

'Just tell it me again. *Please.*'

Her husband complied.

'It was old Scrymgour. Somebody looked into his church one day. He was leaning out of the pulpit and preaching fervently to a couple of old charwomen. He was shaking his finger at them and saying, 'Aha! I know what you are thinking. *You* think that the Great Ahasuerus of the First Lesson was Artaxerxes the Second. But he *wasn't!*' And then with enormous triumph, 'He was Artaxerxes the *Third.*' '

It had never struck Julian Harmon as a particularly funny story himself, but it never failed to amuse Bunch.

Her clear laugh floated out.

'The old pet!' she exclaimed. 'I think you'll be exactly like that some day, Julian.'

Julian looked rather uneasy.

'I know,' he said with humility. 'I do feel very strongly that I can't always get the proper simple approach.'

'I shouldn't worry,' said Bunch, rising and beginning to pile the breakfast plates on a tray. 'Mrs Butt told me yesterday that Butt, who never went to church and used to be practically the local atheist, comes every Sunday now on purpose to hear you preach.

She went on, with a very fair imitation of Mrs Butt's super-refined voice:

'And Butt was saying only the other day, Madam, to Mr Timkins from Little Worsdale, that we'd got real *culture* here in Chipping Cleghorn. *Not* like Mr Goss, at Little Worsdale, who talks to the congregation as though they were children who hadn't had any education. Real culture, Butt said, that's what *we've* got. Our Vicar's a highly educated gentleman – Oxford, not Milchester, and he gives us the full benefit of his education. All about the Romans and the Greeks he knows, and the Babylonians and the Assyrians, too. And even the Vicarage cat, Butt says, is called after an Assyrian king! So there's glory for you,' finished Bunch triumphantly. 'Goodness, I must get on with things or I shall never get done. Come along, Tiglath Pileser, you shall have the herring bones.'

Opening the door and holding it dexterously ajar with her foot, she shot through with the loaded tray, singing in a loud and not particularly tuneful voice, her own version of a sporting song.

> *'It's a fine murdering day,* (sang Bunch)
> *And as balmy as May*
> *And the sleuths from the village are gone.'*

A rattle of crockery being dumped in the sink drowned the next lines, but as the Rev. Julian Harmon left the house, he heard the final triumphant assertion:

> *'And we'll all go a'murdering today!'*

—— 2 ——

BREAKFAST AT LITTLE PADDOCKS

I

At Little Paddocks also, breakfast was in progress.

Miss Blacklock, a woman of sixty odd, the owner of the house, sat at the head of the table. She wore country tweeds – and with them, rather incongruously, a choker necklace of largely false pearls. She was reading Lane Norcott in the *Daily Mail*. Julia

Simmons was languidly glancing through the *Telegraph*. Patrick Simmons was checking up on the crossword in *The Times*. Miss Dora Bunner was giving her attention wholeheartedly to the local weekly paper.

Miss Blacklock gave a subdued chuckle, Patrick muttered: '*Adherent* – not *adhesive* – that's where I went wrong.'

Suddenly a loud cluck, like a started hen, came from Miss Bunner.

'Letty – *Letty* – have you seen this? Whatever *can* it mean?'

'What's the matter, Dora?'

'The most extraordinary advertisement. It says Little Paddocks quite distinctly. But whatever can it *mean*?'

'If you'd let me see, Dora dear—'

Miss Bunner obediently surrendered the paper into Miss Blacklock's outstretched hand, pointing to the item with a tremulous forefinger.

'Just look, Letty.'

Miss Blacklock looked. Her eyebrows went up. She threw a quick scrutinising glance round the table. Then she read the advertisement out loud.

'*A murder is announced and will take place on Friday, October 29th, at Little Paddocks at 6.30 p.m. Friends please accept this, the only intimation.*'

Then she said sharply: 'Patrick, is this your idea?'

Her eyes rested searchingly on the handsome devil-may-care face of the young man at the other end of the table.

Patrick Simmons' disclaimer came quickly.

'No, indeed, Aunt Letty. Whatever put that idea into your head? Why should I know anything about it?'

'I wouldn't put it past you,' said Miss Blacklock grimly. 'I thought it might be your idea of a joke.'

'A joke? Nothing of the kind.'

'And you, Julia?'

Julia, looking bored, said: 'Of course not.'

Miss Bunner murmured: 'Do you think Mrs Haymes—' and looked at an empty place where someone had breakfasted earlier.

'Oh, I don't think our Phillipa would try and be funny,' said Patrick. 'She's a serious girl, she is.'

'But what's the idea, anyway?' said Julia, yawning. 'What does it mean?'

Miss Blacklock said slowly, 'I suppose – it's some silly sort of hoax.'

'But why?' Dora Bunner exclaimed. 'What's the point of it? It seems a very stupid sort of joke. And in very bad taste.'

Her flabby cheeks quivered indignantly, and her short-sighted eyes sparkled with indignation.

Miss Blacklock smiled at her.

'Don't work yourself up over it, Bunny,' she said. 'It's just somebody's idea of humour, but I wish I knew whose.'

'It says today,' pointed out Miss Bunner. 'Today at 6.30 p.m. What do you think is going to happen?'

'*Death!*' said Patrick in sepulchal tones. 'Delicious death.'

'Be quiet, Patrick,' said Miss Blacklock as Miss Bunner gave a little yelp.

'I only meant the special cake that Mitzi makes,' said Patrick apologetically. 'You know we *always* call it delicious death.'

Miss Blacklock smiled a little absentmindedly.

Miss Bunner persisted: 'But Letty, what do you really think—?'

Her friend cut across the words with reassuring cheerfulness.

'I know one thing that will happen at 6.30,' she said dryly. 'We'll have half the village up here, agog with curiosity. I'd better make sure we've got some sherry in the house.'

II

'You *are* worried, aren't you Lotty?'

Miss Blacklock started. She had been sitting at her writing-table, absent-mindedly drawing little fishes on the blotting paper. She looked up into the anxious face of her old friend.

She was not quite sure what to say to Dora Bunner. Bunny, she knew, mustn't be worried or upset. She was silent for a moment or two, thinking.

She and Dora Bunner had been at school together. Dora then had been a pretty, fair-haired, blue-eyed rather stupid girl. Her being stupid hadn't mattered, because her gaiety and high spirits and her prettiness had made her an agreeable companion. She ought, her friend thought, to have married some nice Army officer, or a country solicitor. She had so many good qualities – affection, devotion, loyalty. But life had been unkind to Dora Bunner. She had had to earn her living. She had been painstaking but never competent at anything she undertook.

The two friends had lost sight of each other. But six months ago a letter had come to Miss Blacklock, a rambling, pathetic letter. Dora's health had given way. She was living in one room, trying to subsist on her old age pension. She endeavoured to do needlework, but her fingers were stiff with rheumatism. She mentioned their schooldays – since then life had driven them apart – but could – possibly – her old friend help? Miss Blacklock had responded impulsively. Poor Dora, poor pretty silly fluffy Dora. She had swooped down upon Dora, had carried her off, had installed her at Little Paddocks with the comforting fiction that 'the housework is getting too much for me. I need someone to help me run the house.' It was not for long – the doctor had told her that – but sometimes she found poor old Dora a sad trial. She muddled everything, upset the temperamental foreign 'help,' miscounted the laundry, lost bills and letters – and sometimes reduced the competent Miss Blacklock to an agony of exasperation. Poor old muddle-headed Dora, so loyal, so anxious to help, so pleased and proud to think she was of assistance – and, alas, so completely unreliable.

She said sharply:

'Don't, Dora. You know I asked you—'

'Oh,' Miss Bunner looked guilty. 'I know. I forgot. But – but you *are*, aren't you?'

'Worried? No. At least,' she added truthfully, 'not exactly. You mean about that silly notice in the *Gazette?*'

'Yes – even if it's a joke, it seems to me it's a – a spiteful sort of joke.'

'Spiteful?'

'Yes. It seems to me there's *spite* there somewhere. I mean – it's not a *nice* kind of joke.'

Miss Blacklock looked at her friend. The mild eyes, the long obstinate mouth, the slightly upturned nose. Poor Dora, so maddening, so muddleheaded, so devoted and such a problem. A dear fussy old idiot and yet, in a queer way, with an instinctive sense of value.

'I think you're right, Dora,' said Miss Blacklock. 'It's not a nice joke.'

'I dont like it at all, said Dora Bunner with unsuspected vigour. 'It frightens me. She added, suddenly: 'And it frightens *you*, Letitia.'

'Nonsense,' said Miss Blacklock with spirit.

'It's *dangerous*. I'm sure it is. Like those people who send you bombs done up in parcels.'

'My dear, it's just some silly idiot trying to be funny.'

'But it *isn't* funny.'

It wasn't really very funny . . . Miss Blacklock's face betrayed her thoughts, and Dora cried triumphantly, 'You see. You think so, too!'

'But Dora, my dear—'

She broke off. Through the door there surged a tempestuous young woman with a well-developed bosom heaving under a tight jersey. She had on a dirndl skirt of a bright colour and had greasy plaits wound round and round her head. Her eyes were dark and flashing.

She said gustily:

'I can speak to you, yes, please, no?'

Miss Blacklock sighed.

'Of course, Mitzi, what is it?'

Sometimes she thought it would be preferable to do the entire work of the house as well as the cooking rather than be bothered with the eternal nerve storms of her refugee 'lady help.'

'I tell you at once – it is in order, I hope? I give you my notices and I *go* – I go at *once!*'

'For what reason? Has somebody upset you?'

'Yes, I am upset,' said Mitzi dramatically. 'I do not wish to die! Already in Europe I escape. My family they all die – they are all killed – my mother, my little brother, my so sweet little niece – all, all they are killed. But me I run away – I hide. I get to England. I work. I do work that never – never would I do in my own country – I—'

'I know all that,' said Miss Blacklock crisply. It was, indeed, a constant refrain on Mitzi's lips. 'But why do you want to leave *now?*'

'Because again they come to kill me!'

'Who do?'

'My enemies. The Nazis! Or perhaps this time it is the Bolsheviks. They find out I am here. They come to kill me. I have read it – yes – it is in the newspaper!'

'Oh, you mean in the *Gazette?*'

'*Here*, it is written *here*.' Mitzi produced the *Gazette* from where she had been holding it behind her back. 'See – here it says a *murder*. At Little Paddocks. That is here, is it not? This evening at 6.30. Ah! I do not wait to be murdered – *no.*'

'But why should this apply to *you?* It's – we think it is a joke.'

'A *joke?* It is not a joke to murder someone?'

'No, of course not. But my dear child, if anyone wanted to murder you, they wouldn't advertise the fact in the paper, would they?'

'You do not think they would?' Mitzi seemed a little shaken. 'You think, perhaps, they do not mean to murder anyone at all? Perhaps it is *you* they mean to murder, Miss Blacklock.'

'I certainly can't believe anyone wants to murder me,' said Miss Blacklock lightly. 'And really, Mitzi, I don't see why anyone should want to murder you. After all, why should they?' 'Because they are bad peoples . . . Very bad peoples. I tell you, my mother, my little brother, my so sweet niece . . .' 'Yes, yes.' Miss Blacklock stemmed the flow, adroitly. 'But I cannot really believe *anyone* wants to murder you, Mitzi. Of course, if you want to go off like that at a moment's notice, I can't possibly stop you. But I think you will be very silly if you do.'

She added firmly, as Mitzi looked doubtful: 'We'll have that beef the butcher sent stewed for lunch. It looks very tough.'

'I make you a goulash, a special goulash.'

'If you prefer to call it that, certainly. And perhaps you could use up that rather hard bit of cheese in making some cheese straws. I think some people may come in this evening for drinks.'

'This evening? What do you mean, this evening?'

'At half-past six.'

'But that is the time in the paper? Who should come then? *Why* should they come?'

'They're coming to the funeral,' said Miss Blacklock with a twinkle. 'That'll do now, Mitzi. I'm busy. Shut the door after you, she added firmly.

'And that's settled *her* for the moment,' she said as the door closed behind a puzzled-looking Mitzi.

'You are so efficient, Letty,' said Miss Bunner admiringly.

3

AT 6.30 P.M.

I

'Well, here we are, all set,' said Miss Blacklock. She looked round the double drawing-room with an appraising eye. The rose-patterned chintzes – the two bowls of bronze chrysanthemums, the small vase of violets and the silver cigarette-box on a table by the wall, the tray of drinks on the centre table.

Little Paddocks was a medium-sized house built in the early Victorian style. It had a long shallow veranda and green shuttered windows. The long, narrow drawing-room which lost a good deal of light owing to the veranda roof had originally had double doors at one end leading into a small room with a bay window. A former generation had removed the double doors and replaced them with portières of velvet. Miss Blacklock had dispensed with the portières so that the two rooms had become definitely one. There was a fireplace each end, but neither fire was lit although a gentle warmth pervaded the room.

'You've had the central heating lit,' said Patrick.

Miss Blacklock nodded.

'It's been so misty and damp lately. The whole house felt clammy. I got Evans to light it before he went.'

'The precious precious coke?' said Patrick mockingly.

'As you say, the precious coke. But otherwise there would have been the even more precious coal. You know the Fuel Office won't even let us have the little bit that's due to us each week – not unless we can say definitely that we haven't got any means of cooking.'

'I suppose there was once heaps of coke and coal for everybody?' said Julia with the interest of one hearing about an unknown country.

'Yes, and cheap, too.'

'And anyone could go and buy as much as they wanted, without filling in anything, and there wasn't any shortage? There was lots of it there?'

'All kinds and qualities – and *not* all stones and slates like what we get nowadays.'

'It must have been a wonderful world,' said Julia, with awe in her voice.

Miss Blacklock smiled. 'Looking back on it, *I* certainly think so. But then I'm an old woman. It's natural for me to prefer my own times. But you young things oughtn't to think so.'

'I needn't have had a job then,' said Julia. 'I could just have stayed at home and done the flowers, and written notes . . . Why did one write notes and who were they to?'

'All the people that you now ring up on the telephone,' said Miss Blacklock with a twinkle. 'I don't believe you even know *how* to write, Julia.'

'Not in the style of that delicious "Complete Letter Writer"

216

I found the other day. Heavenly! It told you the correct way of refusing a proposal of marriage from a widower.'

'I doubt if you would have enjoyed staying at home as much as you think,' said Miss Blacklock. 'There were duties, you know.' Her voice was dry. 'However, I don't really know much about it. Bunny and I,' she smiled affectionately at Dora Bunner, 'went into the labour market early.'

'Oh, we did, we did *indeed*,' agreed Miss Bunner. 'Those naughty, naughty children. I'll never forget them. Of course, Letty was clever. She was a business woman, secretary to a big financier.'

The door opened and Phillipa Haymes came in. She was tall and fair and placid looking. She looked round the room in surprise.

'Hallo,' she said. 'Is it a party? Nobody told me.'

'Of course,' cried Patrick. 'Our Phillipa doesn't know. The only woman in Chipping Cleghorn who doesn't, I bet.'

Phillipa looked at him inquiringly.

'Here you behold,' said Patrick dramatically, waving a hand, 'the scene of a murder!'

Phillipa Haymes looked faintly puzzled.

'Here,' Patrick indicated the two big bowls of chrysanthemums, 'are the funeral wreaths and these dishes of cheese straws and olives represent the funeral baked meats.'

Phillipa looked inquiringly at Miss Blacklock.

'Is it a joke?' she asked. 'I'm always terribly stupid at seeing jokes.'

'It's a very nasty joke,' said Dora Bunner with energy. 'I don't like it at all.'

'Show her the advertisement,' said Miss Blacklock. 'I *must* go and shut up the ducks. It's dark. They'll be in by now.'

'Let me do it,' said Phillipa.

'Certainly not, my dear. You've finished your day's work.'

'I'll do it, Aunt Letty,' offered Patrick.

'No, you won't,' said Miss Blacklock with energy. 'Last time you didn't latch the door properly.'

'I'll do it, Letty dear,' cried Miss Bunner. 'Indeed, I should love to. I'll just slip on my goloshes – and now where did I put my cardigan?'

But Miss Blacklock, with a smile, had already left the room.

'It's no good, Bunny,' said Patrick. 'Aunt Letty's so efficient that she can never bear anybody else to do things for her. She really much prefers to do everything herself.'

'She loves it,' said Julia.

'I didn't notice you making any offers of assistance,' said her brother.

Julia smiled lazily.

'You've just said Aunt Letty likes to do things herself,' she pointed out. 'Besides,' she held out a well-shaped leg in a sheer stocking, 'I've got my best stockings on.'

'Death in silk stockings!' declaimed Patrick.

'Not silk – nylons, you idiot.'

'That's not nearly such a good title.'

'Won't somebody please tell me,' cried Phillipa plaintively, 'why there is all this insistence on death?'

Everybody tried to tell her at once – nobody could find the *Gazette* to show her because Mitzi had taken it into the kitchen.

Miss Blacklock returned a few minutes later.

'There,' she said briskly, '*that's* done.' She glanced at the clock. 'Twenty-past six. Somebody ought to be here soon – unless I'm entirely wrong in my estimate of my neighbours.'

'I don't see why anybody should come,' said Phillipa, looking bewildered.

'Don't you, dear? . . . I dare say you wouldn't. But most people are rather more inquisitive than you are.'

'Phillipa's attitude to life is that she just isn't interested,' said Julia, rather nastily.

Phillipa did not reply.

Miss Blacklock was glancing round the room. Mitzi had put the sherry and three dishes containing olives, cheese straws and some little fancy pastries on the table in the middle of the room.

'You might move that tray – or the whole table if you like – round the corner into the bay window in the other room, Patrick, if you don't mind. After all, I am *not* giving a party! I haven't asked anyone. And I don't intend to make it obvious that I expect people to turn up.'

'You wish, Aunt Letty, to disguise your intelligent anticipation?'

'Very nicely put, Patrick. Thank you, my dear boy.'

'Now we can all give a lovely performance of a quiet evening at home,' said Julia, 'and be quite surprised when somebody drops in.'

Miss Blacklock had picked up the sherry bottle. She stood holding it uncertainly in her hand.

Patrick reassured her.

'There's quite half a bottle there. It ought to be enough.'

'Oh, yes – yes . . .' She hesitated. Then, with a slight flush, she said:

'Patrick, would you mind . . . there's a new bottle in the cupboard in the pantry . . . Bring it and a corkscrew. I – we – might as well have a new bottle. This – this has been opened some time.'

Patrick went on his errand without a word. He returned with the new bottle and drew the cork. He looked up curiously at Miss Blacklock as he placed it on the tray.

'Taking things seriously, aren't you, darling?' he asked gently.

'Oh,' cried Dora Bunner, shocked. 'Surely, Letty, you can't imagine—'

'Hush,' said Miss Blacklock quickly. 'That's the bell. You see, my intelligent anticipation is being justified.'

II

Mitzi opened the door of the drawing-room and admitted Colonel and Mrs Easterbrook. She had her own methods of announcing people.

'Here is Colonel and Mrs Easterbrook to see you,' she said conversationally.

Colonel Easterbrook was very bluff and breezy to cover some slight embarrassment.

'Hope you don't mind us dropping in,' he said. (A subdued gurgle came from Julia.) 'Happened to be passing this way – eh what? Quite a mild evening. Notice you've got your central heating on. We haven't started ours yet.'

'Aren't your chrysanthemums *lovely*?' gushed Mrs Easterbrook. '*Such* beauties!'

'They're rather scraggy, really,' said Julia.

Mrs Easterbrook greeted Phillipa Haymes with a little extra cordiality to show that she *quite* understood that Phililipa was not really an agricultural labourer.

'How is Mrs Lucas' garden getting on?' she asked. 'Do you think it will ever be straight again? Completely neglected all through the war – and then only that dreadful old man Ashe who simply did nothing but sweep up a few leaves and put in a few cabbage plants.'

'It's yielding to treatment,' said Phillipa. 'But it will take a little time.'

Mitzi opened the door again and said:
'Here are the ladies from Boulders.'
"Evening,' said Miss Hinchcliffe, striding over and taking
Miss Blacklock's hand in her formidable grip. 'I said to Murga-
troyd: "Let's just drop in at Little Paddocks!" I wanted to ask
you how your ducks are laying.'
'The evenings do draw in so quickly now, don't they?' said
Miss Murgatroyd to Patrick in a rather fluttery way. 'What
lovely chrysanthemums!'
'Scraggy!' said Julia.
'Why can't you be co-operative?' murmured Patrick to her in
a reproachful aside.
'You've got your central heating on,' said Miss Hinchcliffe.
She said it accusingly. 'Very early.'
'The house gets so damp this time of year,' said Miss Blacklock.
Patrick signalled with his eyebrows: 'Sherry yet?' and Miss
Blacklock signalled back: 'Not yet.'
She said to Colonel Easterbrook:
'Are you getting any bulbs from Holland this year?'
The door again opened and Mrs Swettenham came in rather
guiltily, followed by a scowling and uncomfortable Edmund.
'Here we are!' said Mrs Swettenham gaily, gazing round her
with frank curiosity. Then, feeling suddenly uncomfortable, she
went on: 'I just thought I'd pop in and ask you if by any chance
you wanted a kitten, Miss Blacklock? Our cat is just—'
'About to be brought to bed of the progeny of a ginger tom,'
said Edmund. 'The result will, I think, be frightful. Don't say
you haven't been warned!'
'She's a very good mouser,' said Mrs Swettenham hastily. And
added: 'What *lovely* chrysanthemums!'
'You've got your central heating on, haven't you?' asked Edmund, with an air of originality.
'Aren't people just like gramophone records?' murmured
Julia.
'I don't like the news,' said Colonel Easterbrook to Patrick,
buttonholing him fiercely. 'I don't like it at all. If you ask me,
war's inevitable – absolutely inevitable.'
'I never pay any attention to news,' said Patrick.
Once more the door opened and Mrs Harmon came in.
Her battered felt hat was stuck on the back of her head in a
vague attempt to be fashionable and she had put on a rather
limp frilly blouse instead of her usual pullover.
'Hallo, Miss Blacklock,' she exclaimed, beaming all over her

round face. 'I'm not too late, am I? When does the murder begin?'

III

There was an audible series of gasps. Julia gave an approving little giggle, Patrick crinkled up his face and Miss Blacklock smiled at her latest guest.

'Julian is just frantic with rage that he can't be here,' said Mrs Harmon. 'He *adores* murders. That's really why he preached such a good sermon last Sunday – I suppose I oughtn't to say it was a good sermon as he's my husband – but it really was good, didn't you think? – so much better than his usual sermons. But as I was saying it was all because of *Death Does the Hat Trick*. Have you read it? The girl at Boots' kept it for me specially. It's simply *baffling*. You keep thinking you know – and then the whole thing switches round – and there are a lovely lot of murders, four or five of them. Well, I left it in the study when Julian was shutting himself up there to do his sermon, and he just picked it up and simply *could not* put it down! And consequently he had to write his sermon in a frightful hurry and had to just put down what he wanted to say very simply – without any scholarly twists and bits and learned references – and naturally it was heaps better. Oh, dear, I'm talking too much. But do tell me, when is the murder going to begin?'

Miss Blacklock looked at the clock on the mantelpiece.

'If's it going to begin,' she said cheerfully, 'it ought to begin soon. It's just a minute to the half hour. In the meantime, have a glass of sherry.'

Patrick moved with alacrity through the archway. Miss Blacklock went to the table by the Archway where the cigarette-box was.

'I'd love some sherry,' said Mrs Harmon. 'But what do you mean by *if*?'

'Well,' said Miss Blacklock, 'I'm as much in the dark as you are. I don't know what—'

She stopped and turned her head as the little clock on the mantelpiece began to chime. It had a sweet silvery bell-like tone. Everybody was silent and nobody moved. They all stared at the clock.

It chimed a quarter – and then the half. As the last note died away all the lights went out.

IV

Delighted gasps and feminine squeaks of appreciation were heard in the darkness. 'It's beginning,' cried Mrs Harmon in an ecstasy. Dora Bunner's voice cried out plaintively, 'Oh, I don't like it!' Other voices said, 'How terribly terribly frightening!' It gives me the creeps.' 'Archie, where are you?' 'What do I have to *do*?' 'Oh dear – did I step on your foot? I'm so sorry.'

Then, with a crash, the door swung open. A powerful flashlight played rapidly round the room. A man's hoarse nasal voice, reminiscent to all of pleasant afternoons at the cinema directed the company crisply to:

'Stick 'em up!'

'Stick 'em up, I tell you!' the voice barked.

Delightedly, hands were raised willingly above heads.

'Isn't it wonderful?' breathed a female voice. 'I'm *so* thrilled.'

And then, unexpectedly, a revolver spoke. It spoke twice. The ping of two bullets shattered the complacency of the room. Suddenly the game was no longer a game. Somebody screamed . . .

The figure in the doorway whirled suddenly round, it seemed to hesitate, a third shot rang out, it crumpled and then it crashed to the ground. The flashlight dropped and went out.

There was darkness once again. And gently, with a little Victorian protesting moan, the drawing-room door, as was its habit when not propped open, swung gently to and latched with a click.

V

Inside the drawing-room there was pandemonium. Various voices spoke at once. 'Lights.' Can't you find the switch?' 'Who's got a lighter?' 'Oh, I don't like it, I don't *like* it.' 'But those shots were *real*!' 'It was a *real* revolver he had.' 'Was it a burglar?' 'Oh, Archie, I want to get out of here.' 'Please, has somebody got a lighter?'

And then, almost at the same moment, two lighters clicked and burned with small steady flames.

Everybody blinked and peered at each other. Startled face looked into startled face. Against the wall by the archway Miss Blacklock stood with her hand up to her face. The light was too dim to show more than that something dark was trickling over her fingers.

Colonel Easterbrook cleared his throat and rose to the occasion.

'Try the switches, Swettenham,' he ordered.

Edmund, near the door, obediently jerked the switch up and down.

'Off at the main, or a fuse,' said the Colonel. 'Who's making that awful row?'

A female voice had been screaming steadily from somewhere beyond the closed door. It rose now in pitch and with it came the sound of fists hammering on a door.

Dora Bunner, who had been sobbing quietly, called out:

'It's Mitzi. Somebody's murdering Mitzi . . .'

Patrick muttered: 'No such luck.'

Miss Blacklock said: 'We must get candles. Patrick, will you—?'

The Colonel was already opening the door. He and Edmund, their lighters flickering, stepped into the hall. They almost stumbled over a recumbent figure there.

'Seems to have knocked him out,' said the Colonel. 'Where's that woman making that hellish noise?'

'In the dining-room,' said Edmund.

The dining-room was just across the hall. Someone was beating on the panels and howling and screaming.

'She's locked in,' said Edmund, stooping down. He turned the key and Mitzi came out like a bounding tiger.

The dining-room light was still on. Silhouetted against it Mitzi presented a picture of insane terror and continued to scream. A touch of comedy was introduced by the fact that she had been engaged in cleaning silver and was still holding a chamois leather and a large fish slice.

'Be quiet, Mitzi,' said Miss Blacklock.

'Stop it,' said Edmund, and as Mitzi showed no disposition to stop screaming, he leaned forward and gave her a sharp slap on the cheek. Mitzi gasped and hiccupped into silence.

'Get some candles,' said Miss Blacklock. 'In the kitchen cupboard. Patrick, you know where the fusebox is?'

'The passage behind the scullery? Right, I'll see what I can do.'

Miss Blacklock had moved forward into the light thrown from the dining-room and Dora Bunner gave a sobbing gasp. Mitzi let out another full-blooded scream.

'The blood, the *blood*!' she gasped. 'You are shot – Miss Blacklock, you bleed to death.'

'Don't be so stupid,' snapped Miss Blacklock. 'I'm hardly hurt at all. It just grazed my ear.'

'But Aunt Letty,' said Julia, 'the blood.'

And indeed Miss Blacklock's white blouse and pearls and her hands were a horrifyingly gory sight.

'Ears always bleed,' said Miss Blacklock. 'I remember fainting in the hairdresser's when I was a child. The man had only just snipped my ear. There seemed to be a basin of blood at once. But we *must* have some light.'

'I get the candles,' said Mitzi.

Julia went with her and returned with several candles stuck into saucers.

'Now let's have a look at our malefactor,' said the Colonel. 'Hold the candles down low, will you, Swettenham? As many as you can.'

'I'll come the other side,' said Phillipa.

With a steady hand she took a couple of saucers. Colonel Easterbrook knelt down.

The recumbent figure was draped in a roughly-made black cloak with a hood to it. There was a black mask over the face and he wore black cotton gloves. The hood had slipped back disclosing a ruffled fair head.

Colonel Easterbrook turned him over, felt the pulse, the heart . . . then drew away his fingers with an exclamation of distaste, looking down on them. They were sticky and red.

'Shot himself,' he said.

'Is he badly hurt?' asked Miss Blacklock.

'H'm. I'm afraid he's dead . . . May have been suicide – or he may have tripped himself up with that cloak thing and the revolver went off as he fell. If I could see better—'

At that moment, as though by magic, the lights came on again.

With a queer feeling of unreality those inhabitants of Chipping Cleghorn who stood in the hall of Little Paddocks realized that they stood in the presence of violent and sudden death. Colonel Easterbrook's hand was stained red. Blood was still trickling down Miss Blacklock's neck over her blouse and coat and the grotesquely sprawled figure of the intruder lay at their feet. . . .

Patrick, coming from the dining-room, said, 'It seemed to be just one fuse gone . . .' He stopped.

Colonel Easterbrook tugged at the small black mask.

'Better see who the fellow is,' he said. 'Though I don't suppose it's anyone we know . . .'

He detached the mask. Necks were craned forward. Mitzi hiccupped and gasped, but the others were very quiet.

'He's quite young,' said Mrs Harmon with a note of pity in her voice.

And suddenly Dora Bunner cried out excitedly:

'Letty, Letty, it's the young man from the Spa Hotel in Medenham Wells. The one who came out here and wanted you to give him money to get back to Switzerland and you refused. I suppose the whole thing was just a pretext – to spy out the house ... Oh, dear – he might easily have killed you ...'

Miss Blacklock, in command of the situation, said incisively:

'Phillipa, take Bunny into the dining-room and give her a half-glass of brandy. Julia dear, just run up to the bathroom and bring me the sticking plaster out of the bathroom cupboard – it's so messy bleeding like a pig. Patrick, will you ring up the police at once?'

—— 4 ——

THE ROYAL SPA HOTEL

I

George Rydesdale, Chief Constable of Middleshire, was a quiet man. Of medium height, with shrewd eyes under rather bushy brows, he was in the habit of listening rather than talking. Then, in his unemotional voice, he would give a brief order – and the order was obeyed.

He was listening now to Detective-Inspector Dermot Craddock. Craddock was now officially in charge of the case. Rydesdale had recalled him last night from Liverpool where he had been sent to make certain inquiries in connection with another case. Rydesdale had a good opinion of Craddock. He not only had brains and imagination, he had also, which Rydesdale appreciated even more, the self-discipline to go slow, to check and examine each fact, and to keep an open mind until the very end of a case.

'Constable Legg took the call, sir,' Craddock was saying. 'He seems to have acted very well, with promptitude and presence of mind. And it can't have been easy. About a dozen people all trying to talk at once, including one of those Mittel Europas who go off at the deep end at the mere sight of a policeman. Made sure she was going to be locked up, and fairly screamed the place down.

'Deceased has been identified?'

'Yes, sir. Rudi Scherz. Swiss Nationality. Employed at the Royal Spa Hotel, Medenham Wells, as a receptionist. If you agree, sir, I thought I'd take the Royal Spa Hotel first, and go out to Chipping Cleghorn afterwards. Sergeant Fletcher is out there now. He'll see the bus people and then go on to the house.'

Rydesdale nodded approval.

The door opened, and the Chief Constable looked up.

'Come in, Henry,' he said. 'We've got something here that's a little bit out of the ordinary.'

Sir Henry Clithering, ex-Commissioner of Scotland Yard, came in with slightly raised eyebrows. He was a tall, distinguished-looking elderly man.

'It may appeal to even your blasé palate,' went on Rydesdale.

'I was never blasé,' said Sir Henry indignantly.

'The latest idea,' said Rydesdale, 'is to advertise one's murders beforehand. Show Sir Henry that advertisement, Craddock.'

'*The North Benham News and Chipping Cleghorn Gazette,*' said Sir Henry. 'Quite a mouthful.' He read the half inch of print indicated by Craddock's finger. 'H'm, yes, somewhat unusual.'

'Any line on who inserted this advertisement?' asked Rydesdale.

'By the description, sir, it was handed in by Rudi Scherz himself – on Wednesday.'

'Nobody questioned it? The person who accepted it, didn't think it odd?'

'The adenoidal blonde who receives the advertisements is quite incapable of thinking, I should say, sir. She just counted the words and took the money.'

'What was the idea?' asked Sir Henry.

'Get a lot of the locals curious,' suggested Rydesdale. 'Get them all together at a particular place at a particular time, then hold them up and relieve them of their spare cash and valuables. As an idea, it's not without originality.'

'What sort of a place is Chipping Cleghorn?' asked Sir Henry.

'A large sprawling picturesque village. Butcher, baker, grocer, quite a good antique shop – two tea-shops. Self-consciously a beauty spot. Caters for the motoring tourist. Also highly residential. Cottages formerly lived in by agricultural labourers now converted and lived in by elderly spinsters and retired couples.

A certain amount of building done round about in Victorian times.'

'I know,' said Sir Henry. 'Nice old Pussies and retired Colonels. Yes, if they noticed that advertisement they'd all come sniffing round at 6.30 to see what was up. Lord, I wish I had my own particular old Pussy here. Wouldn't she like to get her nice ladylike teeth into this. Right up her street it would be.'

'Who's your own particular Pussy, Henry? An aunt?'

'No, Sir Henry sighed. 'She's no relation.' He said reverently: 'She's just the finest detective God ever made. Natural genius cultivated in a suitable soil.'

He turned upon Craddock.

'Don't you despise the old Pussies in this village of yours, my boy,' he said. 'In case this turns out to be a high-powered mystery, which I don't suppose for a moment it will, remember that an elderly unmarried woman who knits and gardens is streets ahead of any detective sergeant. She can tell you what might have happened and what ought to have happened and even what actually *did* happen! And she can tell you *why* it happened!'

'I'll bear that in mind, sir,' said Detective-Inspector Craddock in his most formal manner, and nobody would have guessed that Dermot Eric Craddock was actually Sir Henry's godson and was on easy and intimate terms with his godfather.

Rydesdale gave a quick outline of the case to his friend.

'They'd all turn up at 6.30, I grant you that,' he said. 'But would that Swiss fellow know they would? And another thing, would they be likely to have much loot on them to be worth the taking?'

'A couple of old-fashioned brooches, a string of seed pearls – a little loose change, perhaps a note or two – not more,' said Sir Henry, thoughtfully. 'Did this Miss Blacklock keep much money in the house?'

'She says not, sir. Five pounds odd, I understand.'

'Mere chicken feed,' said Rydesdale.

'What you're getting at,' said Sir Henry, 'is that this fellow liked to playact – it wasn't the loot, it was the fun of playing and acting the hold-up. Cinema stuff? Eh? It's quite possible. How did he manage to shoot himself?'

Rydesdale drew a paper towards him.

'Preliminary medical report. The revolver was discharged at close range – singeing . . . h'm . . . nothing to show whether accident or suicide. Could have been done deliberately, or he could have tripped and fallen and the revolver which he was holding close to him could have gone off . . . Probably the latter.' He looked at Craddock. 'You'll have to question the witnesses very carefully and make them say exactly what they saw.'

Detective-Inspector Craddock said sadly: 'They'll all have seen something different.'

'It's always interested me,' said Sir Henry, 'what people do see at a moment of intense excitement and nervous strain. What they do see and, even more interesting, what they don't see.'

'Where's the report on the revolver?'

'Foreign make – (fairly common on the Continent) – Scherz did not hold a permit for it – and did not declare it on coming into England.'

'Bad lad,' said Sir Henry.

'Unsatisfactory character all round. Well, Craddock, go and see what you can find out about him at the Royal Spa Hotel.'

II

At the Royal Spa Hotel, Inspector Craddock was taken straight into the Manager's office.

The Manager, Mr Rowlandson, a tall florid man with a hearty manner, greeted Inspector Craddock with expansive geniality.

'Glad to help you in any way we can, Inspector,' he said. 'Really a most surprising business. I'd never have credited it – never. Scherz seemed a very ordinary, pleasant young chap – not at all my idea of a hold-up man.'

'How long has he been with you, Mr Rowlandson?'

'I was looking that up just before you came. A little over three months. Quite good credentials, the usual permits, etc.'

'And you found him satisfactory?'

Without seeming to do so, Craddock marked the infinitesimal pause before Rowlandson replied.

'Quite satisfactory.'

Craddock made use of a technique he had found efficacious before now.

'No, no, Mr Rowlandson,' he said, gently shaking his head. 'That's not really the case, is it?'

'We-ll—' The Manager seemed slightly taken aback.

'Come now, there was something wrong. What was it?'

'That's just it. I don't know.'

'But you *thought* there was something wrong?'

'Well – yes – I did . . . But I've nothing really to go upon. I shouldn't like my conjectures to be written down and quoted against me.'

Craddock smiled pleasantly.

'I know just what you mean. You needn't worry. But I've got to get some idea of what this fellow, Scherz, was like. You suspected him of – what?'

Rowlandson said, rather reluctantly:

'Well, there was trouble, once or twice, about the bills. Items charged that oughtn't to have been there.'

'You mean you suspected that he charged up certain items which didn't appear in the hotel records, and that he pocketed the difference when the bill was paid?'

'Something like that . . . Put it at the best, there was gross carelessness on his part. Once or twice quite a big sum was involved. Frankly, I got our accountant to go over his books suspecting that he was – well, a wrong 'un, but though there were various mistakes and a good deal of slipshod method, the actual cash was quite correct. So I came to the conclusion that I must be mistaken.'

'Supposing you hadn't been wrong? Supposing Scherz had been helping himself to various small sums here and there, he could have covered himself, I suppose, by making good the money?'

'Yes, if he *had* the money. But people who help themselves to "small sums" as you put it – are usually hard up for those sums and spend them offhand.'

'So, if he wanted money to replace missing sums, he would have had to get money – by a hold-up or other means?'

'Yes. I wonder if this is his first attempt . . .'

'Might be. It was certainly a very amateurish one. Is there anyone else he could have got money from? Any women in his life?'

'One of the waitresses in the Grill. Her name's Myrna Harris.'

'I'd better have a talk with her.'

III

Myrna Harris was a pretty girl with a glorious head of red hair and a pert nose.

She was alarmed and wary, and deeply conscious of the indignity of being interviewed by the police.

'I don't know a thing about it, sir. Not a thing,' she protested. 'If I'd known what he was like I'd never have gone out with

Rudi at all. Naturally, seeing as he worked in Reception here, I thought he was all right. Naturally I did. What I say is the hotel ought to be more careful when they employ people – especially foreigners. Because you never know where you are with foreigners. I suppose he might have been in with one of these gangs you read about?'

'We think,' said Craddock, 'that he was working quite on his own.'

'Fancy – and him so quiet and respectable. You'd never think. Though there have been things missed – now I come to think of it. A diamond brooch – and a little gold locket, I believe. But I never dreamed that it could have been Rudi.'

'I'm sure you didn't,' said Craddock. 'Anyone might have been taken in. You knew him fairly well?'

'I don't know that I'd say *well*.'

'But you were friendly?'

'Oh, we were friendly – that's all, just friendly. Nothing serious at all. I'm always on my guard with foreigners, anyway. They've often got a way with them, but you never know, do you? Some of those Poles during the war! And even some of the Americans! Never let on they're married men until it's too late. Rudi talked big and all that – but I always took it with a grain of salt.'

Craddock seized on the phrase.

'Talked big, did he? That's very interesting, Miss Harris. I can see you're going to be a lot of help to us. In what way did he talk big?'

'Well, about how rich his people were in Switzerland – and how important. But that didn't go with his being as short of money as he was. He always said that because of the money regulation he couldn't get money from Switzerland over here. That might be, I suppose, but his things weren't expensive. His clothes, I mean. They weren't really class. I think, too, that a lot of the stories he used to tell me were so much hot air. About climbing in the Alps, and saving people's lives on the edge of a glacier. Why, he turned quite giddy just going along the edge of Boulter's Gorge. Alps, indeed!'

'You went out with him a good deal?'

'Yes – well – yes, I did. He had awfully good manners and he knew how to – to look after a girl. The best seats at the pictures always. And even flowers he'd buy me, sometimes. And he was just a lovely dancer – lovely.'

'Did he mention this Miss Blacklock to you at all?'

'She comes in and lunches here sometimes, doesn't she? And she's stayed here once. No, I don't think Rudi ever mentioned her. I didn't know he knew her.'

'Did he mention Chipping Cleghorn?'

He thought a faintly wary look came into Myrna Harris's eyes but he couldn't be sure.

'I don't think so . . . I think he did once ask about buses – what time they went – but I can't remember if that was Chipping Cleghorn or somewhere else. It wasn't just lately.'

He couldn't get more out of her. Rudi Scherz had seemed just as usual. She hadn't seen him the evening before. She'd no idea – no idea *at all* – she stressed the point, that Rudi Scherz was a crook.

And probably, Craddock thought, that was quite true.

—— 5 ——

MISS BLACKLOCK AND MISS BUNNER

Little Paddocks was very much as Detective-Inspector Craddock had imagined it to be. He noted ducks and chickens and what had been until lately an attractive herbaceous border and in which a few late Michaelmas daisies showed a last dying splash of purple beauty. The lawn and the paths showed signs of neglect.

Summing up, Detective-Inspector Craddock thought: 'Probably not much money to spend on gardeners – fond of flowers and a good eye for planning and massing a border. House needs painting. Most houses do, nowadays. Pleasant little property.'

As Craddock's car stopped before the front door, Sergeant Fletcher came round the side of the house. Sergeant Fletcher looked like a guardsman, with an erect military bearing, and was able to impart several different meanings to the one monosyllable: 'Sir.'

'So there you are, Fletcher.'

'Sir,' said Sergeant Fletcher.

'Anything to report?'

'We've finished going over the house, sir. Scherz doesn't seem to have left any fingerprints anywhere. He wore gloves, of course. No signs of any of the doors or windows being forced to effect an entrance. He seems to have come out from Medenham on the bus, arriving here at six o'clock. Side door of the house was locked at 5.30, I understand. Looks as though he must have walked in through the front door. Miss Blacklock states that that door isn't usually locked until the house is shut up for the night. The maid, on the other hand, states that the front door was locked all the afternoon – but she'd say anything. Very temperamental you'll find her. Mittel Europa refugee of some kind.'

'Difficult, is she?'

'Sir!' said Sergeant Fletcher, with intense feeling.

Craddock smiled.

Fletcher resumed his report.

'Lighting system is quite in order everywhere. We haven't spotted yet how he operated the lights. It was just the one circuit went. Drawing-room and hall. Of course, nowadays the wall brackets and lamps wouldn't all be on one fuse – but this is an old-fashioned installation and wiring. Don't see how he could have tampered with the fuse-box because it's out by the scullery and he'd have had to go through the kitchen, so the maid would have seen him.'

'Unless she was in it with him?'

'That's very possible. Both foreigners – and I wouldn't trust her a yard – not a yard.'

Craddock noticed two enormous frightened black eyes peering out of a window by the front door. The face, flattened against the pane, was hardly visible.

'That her there?'

'That's right, sir.'

The face disappeared.

Craddock rang the front-door bell.

After a long wait the door was opened by a good-looking young woman with chestnut hair and a bored expression.

'Detective-Inspector Craddock,' said Craddock.

The young woman gave him a cool stare out of very attractive hazel eyes and said:

'Come in. Miss Blacklock is expecting you.'

The hall, Craddock noted, was long and narrow and seemed almost incredibly full of doors.

The young woman threw open a door on the left, and said:

'Inspector Craddock, Aunt Letty. Mitzi wouldn't go to the door. She's shut herself up in the kitchen and she's making the most marvellous moaning noises. I shouldn't think we'd get *any* lunch.'

She added in an explanatory manner to Craddock: 'She

doesn't like the police,' and withdrew, shutting the door behind her.

Craddock advanced to meet the owner of Little Paddocks.

He saw a tall active-looking woman of about sixty. Her grey hair had a slight natural wave and made a distinguished setting for an intelligent, resolute face. She had keen grey eyes and a square determined chin. There was a surgical dressing on her left ear. She wore no make-up and was plainly dressed in a well-cut tweed coat and skirt and pullover. Round the neck of the latter she wore, rather unexpectedly, a set of old-fashioned cameos – a Victorian touch which seemed to hint at a sentimental streak not otherwise apparent.

Close behind her, with an eager round face and untidy hair escaping from a hair net, was a woman of about the same age whom Craddock had no difficulty in recognizing as the 'Dora Bunner – companion' of Constable Legg's notes – to which the latter had added an off-the-record commentary of 'Scatty!'

Miss Blacklock spoke in a pleasant well-bred voice.

'Good-morning, Inspector Craddock. This is my friend, Miss Bunner, who helps me run the house. Won't you sit down? You won't smoke, I suppose?'

'Not on duty, I'm afraid, Miss Blacklock.'

'What a shame!'

Craddock's eyes took in the room with a quick, practised glance. Typical Victorian double drawing-room. Two long windows in this room, built out bay window in the other . . . chairs . . . sofa . . . centre table with a big bowl of chrysanthemums – another bowl in window – all fresh and pleasant without much originality. The only incongruous note was a small silver vase with dead violets in it on a table near the archway in the further room. Since he could not imagine Miss Blacklock tolerating dead flowers in a room, he imagined it to be the only indication that something out of the way had occurred to distract the routine of a well-run household.

He said:

'I take it, Miss Blacklock, that this is the room in which the – incident occurred?'

'Yes.'

'And you should have seen it last night,' Miss Bunner exclaimed. 'Such a *mess*. Two little tables knocked over, and the leg off one – people barging about in the dark – and someone put down a lighted cigarette and burnt one of the best bits of furniture. People – young people especially, are so careless about these things . . . Luckily none of the china got broken—'

Miss Blacklock interrupted gently but firmly:

'Dora, all these things, vexatious as they may be, are only trifles. It will be best, I think, if we just answer Inspector Craddock's questions.'

'Thank you, Miss Blacklock. I shall come to what happened last night, presently. First of all I want you to tell me when you first saw the dead man – Rudi Scherz.'

'Rudi Scherz?' Miss Blacklock looked slightly surprised. 'Is that his name? Somehow, I thought . . . Oh, well, it doesn't matter. My first encounter with him was when I was in Medenham Spa for a day's shopping about – let me see, about three weeks ago. We – Miss Bunner and I – were having lunch at the Royal Spa Hotel. As we were just leaving after lunch, I heard my name spoken. It was this young man. He said: "It is Miss Blacklock, is it not?" And went on to say that perhaps I did not remember him, but that he was the son of the proprietor of the Hotel des Alpes at Montreux where my sister and I had stayed for nearly a year during the war.'

'The Hotel des Alpes, Montreux,' noted Craddock. 'And did you remember him, Miss Blacklock?'

'No, I didn't. Actually I had no recollection of ever having seen him before. These boys at hotel reception desks all look exactly alike. We had had a very pleasant time at Montreux and the proprietor there had been extremely obliging, so I tried to be as civil as possible and said I hoped he was enjoying being in England, and he said, yes, that his father had sent him over for six months to learn the hotel business. It all seemed quite natural.'

'And your next encounter?'

'About – yes, it must have been ten days ago, he suddenly turned up here. I was very surprised to see him. He apologised for troubling me, but said I was the only person he knew in England. He told me that he urgently needed money to return to Switzerland as his mother was dangerously ill.'

'But Letty didn't give it to him,' Miss Bunner put in breathlessly.

'It was a thoroughly fishy story,' said Miss Blacklock, with vigour. 'I made up my mind that he was definitely a wrong 'un. That story about wanting the money to return to Switzerland was *nonsense*. His father could easily have wired for arrangements to have been made in this country. These hotel people are

234

all in with each other. I suspected that he'd been embezzling money or something of that kind.' She paused and said dryly: 'In case you think I'm hardhearted, I was secretary for many years to a big financier and one becomes wary about appeals for money. I know simply all the hard luck stories there are.

'The only thing that did surprise me,' she added thoughtfully, 'was that he gave in so easily. He went away at once without any more argument. It's as though he had never expected to get the money.'

'Do you think now, looking back on it, this his coming was really by way of a pretext to spy out the land?'

Miss Blacklock nodded her head vigorously.

'That's exactly what I do think – now. He made certain remarks as I let him out – about the rooms. He said, 'You have a very nice dining-room' (which of course it isn't – it's a horrid dark little room) just as an excuse to look inside. And then he sprang forward and unfastened the front door, said, "Let me." I think now he wanted to have a look at the fastening. Actually, like most people round here, we never lock the front door until it gets dark. *Anyone* could walk in.'

'And the side door? There is a side door to the garden, I understand?'

'Yes. I went out through it to shut up the ducks not long before the people arrived.'

'Was it locked when you went out?'

Miss Blacklock frowned.

'I can't remember . . . I think so. I certainly locked it when I came in.'

'That would be about quarter-past six?'

'Somewhere about then.'

'And the front door?'

'That's not usually locked until later.'

'Then Scherz could have walked in quite easily that way. Or he could have slipped in whilst you were out shutting up the ducks. He'd already spied out the lie of the land and had probably noted various places of concealment – cupboards, etc. Yes, that all seems quite clear.'

'I beg your pardon, it isn't at all clear,' said Miss Blacklock. 'Why on earth should anyone take all that elaborate trouble to come and burgle this house and stage that silly sort of hold-up?'

'Do you keep much money in the house, Miss Blacklock?'

'About five pounds in that desk there, and perhaps a pound or two in my purse.'

'Jewellery?'

'A couple of rings and brooches, and the cameos I'm wearing. You must agree with me, Inspector, that the whole thing's absurd.'

'It wasn't burglary at all,' cried Miss Bunner. 'I've told you so, Letty, all along. It was *revenge*! Because you wouldn't give him that money! He deliberately shot at you – twice.'

'Ah,' said Craddock. 'We'll come now to last night. What happened exactly, Miss Blacklock? Tell me in your own words as nearly as you can remember.'

Miss Blacklock reflected a moment.

'The clock struck,' she said. 'The one on the mantelpiece. I remember saying that if anything were going to happen it would have to happen soon. And then the clock struck. We all listened to it without saying anything. It chimes, you know. It chimed the two quarters and then, quite suddenly, the lights went out.'

'What lights were on?'

'The wall brackets in here and the further room. The standard lamp and the two small reading lamps weren't on.'

'Was there a flash first, or a noise when the lights went out?'

'I don't think so.'

'I'm sure there *was* a flash,' said Dora Bunner. '*And* a crackling noise. Dangerous!'

'And then, Miss Blacklock?'

'The door opened—'

'Which door? There are two in the room.'

'Oh, this door in here. The one in the other room doesn't open. It's a dummy. The door opened and there he was – a masked man with a revolver. It just seemed too fantastic for words, but of course at the time I just thought it was a silly joke. He said something – I forget what—'

'Hands up or I shoot!' supplied Miss Bunner, dramatically.

'Something like that,' said Miss Blacklock, rather doubtfully.

'And you all put your hands up?'

'Oh, yes,' said Miss Bunner. 'We all did. I mean, it was *part* of it.'

'*I* didn't,' said Miss Blacklock crisply. 'It seemed so utterly silly. And I was annoyed by the whole thing.'

'And then?'

'The flashlight was right in my eyes. It dazzled me. And then, quite incredibly, I heard a bullet whizz past me and hit the wall by my head. Somebody shrieked and then I felt a burning pain in my ear and heard the second report.'

'It was *terrifying*,' put in Miss Bunner.

'And what happened next, Miss Blacklock?'

'It's difficult to say – I was so staggered by the pain and the surprise. The – the figure turned away and seemed to stumble and there was another shot and his torch went out and everybody began pushing and calling out. All banging into each other.'

'Where were you standing, Miss Blacklock?'

'She was over by the table. She'd got that vase of violets in her hand,' said Miss Bunner breathlessly.

'I was over here.' Miss Blacklock went over to the small table by the archway. 'Actually it was the cigarette-box I'd got in my hand.'

Inspector Craddock examined the wall behind her. The two bullet holes showed plainly. The bullets themselves had been extracted and had been sent for comparison with the revolver.

He said quietly:

'You had a very near escape, Miss Blacklock.'

'He *did* shoot at her,' said Miss Bunner. 'Deliberately *at* her! I saw him. He turned the flash round on everybody until he found her and then he held it right at her and just fired at *her*. He meant to kill *you*, Letty.'

'Dora dear, you've just got that into your head from mulling the whole thing over and over.'

'He shot at *you*,' repeated Dora stubbornly. 'He meant to shoot you and when he'd missed, he shot himself. I'm *certain* that's the way it was!'

'I don't think he meant to shoot himself for a minute, said Miss Blacklock. 'He wasn't the kind of man who shoots himself.'

'You tell me, Miss Blacklock, that until the revolver was fired you thought the whole business was a joke?'

'Naturally. What else could I think it was?'

'Who do you think was the author of this joke?'

'You thought Patrick had done it at first,' Dora Bunner reminded her.

'Patrick?' asked the Inspector sharply.

'My young cousin, Patrick Simmons,' Miss Blacklock continued sharply, annoyed with her friend. 'It did occur to me when I saw this advertisement that it might be some attempt at humour on his part, but he denied it absolutely.'

'And then you were worried, Letty,' said Miss Bunner. 'You *were* worried, although you pretended not to be. And you were quite right to be worried. It said a murder is announced – and it *was* announced – *your murder*! And if the man hadn't missed, you *would* have been murdered. And then where should we all be?'

Dora Bunner was trembling as she spoke. Her face was puckered up and she looked as though she were going to cry.

Miss Blacklock patted her on the shoulder.

'It's all right, Dora dear – don't get excited. It's so bad for you. Everything's quite all right. We've had a nasty experience, but it's over now.' She added, 'You must pull yourself together for my sake, Dora. I rely on you, you know, to keep the house going. Isn't it the day for the laundry to come?'

'Oh, dear me, Letty, how *fortunate* you reminded me! I wonder if they'll return that missing pillowcase. I must make a note in the book about it. I'll go and see to it at once.'

'And take those violets away,' said Miss Blacklock. 'There's nothing I hate more than dead flowers.'

'What a pity. I picked them fresh yesterday. They haven't lasted at all – oh, dear, I must have forgotten to put any water in the vase. Fancy that! I'm always forgetting things. Now I must go and see about the laundry. They might be here any moment.'

She bustled away, looking quite happy again.

'She's not very strong,' said Miss Blacklock, 'and excitements are bad for her. Is there anything more you want to know, Inspector?'

'I just want to know exactly how many people make up your household here and something about them.'

'Yes, well in addition to myself and Dora Bunner, I have two young cousins living here at present, Patrick and Julia Simmons.'

'Cousins? Not a nephew and niece?'

'No. They call me Aunt Letty, but actually they are distant cousins. Their mother was my second cousin.'

'Have they always made their home with you?'

'Oh, dear no, only for the last two months. They lived in the South of France before the war. Patrick went into the Navy and Julia, I believe, was in one of the Ministries. She was at Llandudno. When the war was over their mother wrote and asked me if they could possible come to me as paying guests – Julia is training as a dispenser in Milchester General Hospital, Patrick is studying for an engineering degree at Milchester University. Milchester, as you know, is only fifty minutes by bus, and I was very glad to have them here. This house is really too large for me. They pay a small sum for board and lodgings and it all works out very well.' She added with a smile, 'I like having somebody young about the place.'

'Then there is a Mrs Haymes, I believe?'

'Yes. She works as an assistant gardener at Dayas Hall, Mrs Lucas's place. The cottage there is occupied by the old gardener and his wife and Mrs Lucas asked if I could billet her here. She's a very nice girl. Her husband was killed in Italy, and she has a boy of eight who is at prep school and whom I have arranged to have here in the holidays.'

'And by way of domestic help?'

'A jobbing gardener comes in on Tuesdays and Fridays. A Mrs Huggins from the village comes up five mornings a week and I have a foreign refugee with a most unpronouncable name as a kind of lady cook help. You will find Mitzi rather difficult, I'm afraid. She has a kind of persecution mania.'

Craddock nodded. He was conscious in his own mind of yet another of Constable Legg's invaluable commentaries. Having appended the word 'Scatty' to Dora Bunner, and 'All right' to Letitia Blacklock, he had embellished Mitzi's record with the one word 'Liar.'

As though she had read his mind Miss Blacklock said:

'Please don't be too prejudiced against the poor thing because she's a liar. I do really believe that, like so many liars, there is a real substratum of truth behind her lies. I mean that though, to take an instance, her atrocity stories have grown and grown until every kind of unpleasant story that has ever appeared in print has happened to her or her relations personally, she did have a bad shock initially and did see one, at least, of her relations killed. I think a lot of these displaced persons feel, perhaps justly, that their claim to our notice and sympathy lies in their atrocity value and so they exaggerate and invent.'

She added: 'Quite frankly, Mitzi is a maddening person. She exasperates and infuriates us all, she is suspicious and sulky, is perpetually having "feelings" and thinking herself insulted. But in spite of it all, I really am sorry for her.' She smiled. 'And also, when she wants to, she can cook very nicely.'

'I'll try not to ruffle her more than I can help,' said Craddock soothingly. 'Was that Miss Julia Simmons who opened the door to me?'

'Yes. Would you like to see her now? Patrick has gone out. Phillipa Haymes you will find working at Dayas Hall.'

'Thank you, Miss Blacklock. I'd like to see Miss Simmons now if I may.'

─── 6 ───

JULIA, MITZI AND PATRICK

I

Julia, when she came into the room, and sat down in the chair vacated by Letitia Blacklock, had an air of composure that Craddock for some reason found annoying. She fixed a limpid gaze on him and waited for his questions.

Miss Blacklock had tactfully left the room.

'Please tell me about last night, Miss Simmons.'

'Last night?' murmured Julia with a blank stare. 'Oh, we all slept like logs. Reaction, I suppose.'

'I mean last night from six o'clock onwards.'

'Oh, I see. Well, a lot of tiresome people came—'

'They were?'

She gave him another limpid stare.

'Don't you know all this already?'

'I'm asking the questions, Miss Simmons,' said Craddock pleasantly.

'My mistake. I always find repetitions so dreary. Apparently you don't . . . Well, there was Colonel and Mrs Easterbrook, Miss Hinchcliffe and Miss Murgatroyd, Mrs Swettenham and Edmund Swettenham, and Mrs Harmon, the Vicar's wife. They arrived in that order. And if you want to know what they said – they all said the same things in turn. "I see you've got your central heating on" and "What *lovely* chrysanthemums!" '

Craddock bit his lip. The mimicry was good.

'The exception was Mrs Harmon. She's rather a pet. She came in with her hat falling off and her shoelaces untied and she asked straight out when the murder was going to happen. It embarrassed everybody because they'd all been pretending they'd dropped in by chance. Aunt Letty said in her dry way that it was due to happen quite soon. And then that clock chimed and just as it finished, the lights went out, the door was flung open and a masked figure said, "Stick 'em up, guys," or something like that. It was exactly like a bad film. Really quite ridiculous. And then he fired two shots at Aunt Letty and suddenly it wasn't ridiculous any more.'

'Where was everybody when this happened?'

'When the lights went out? Well, just standing about, you

know. Mrs Harmon was sitting on the sofa – Hinch (that's Miss Hinchcliffe) had taken up a manly stance in front of the fireplace.'

'You were all in this room, or the far room?'

'Mostly, I think, in this room. Patrick had gone into the other to get the sherry. I think Colonel Easterbrook went after him, but I don't really know. We were – well – as I said, just standing about.'

'Where were you yourself?'

'I think I was over by the window. Aunt Letty went to get the cigarettes.'

'On that table by the archway?'

'Yes – and then the lights went out and the bad film started.'

'The man had a powerful torch. What did he do with it?'

'Well, he shone it on us. Horribly dazzling. It just made you blink.'

'I want you to answer this very carefully, Miss Simmons. Did he hold the torch steady, or did he move it about?'

Julia considered. Her manner was now definitely less weary.

'He moved it,' she said slowly. 'Like a spotlight in a dance hall. It was full in my eyes and then it went on round the room and then the shots came. Two shots.'

'And then?'

'He whirled round – and Mitzi began to scream like a siren from somewhere and his torch went out and there was another shot. And then the door closed (it does, you know, slowly, with a whining noise – quite uncanny) and there we were all in the dark, not knowing what to do, and poor Bunny squealing like a rabbit and Mitzi going all out across the hall.'

'Would it be your opinion that the man shot himself deliberately, or do you think he stumbled and the revolver went off accidentally?'

'I haven't the faintest idea. The whole thing was so stagey. Actually I thought it was still some silly joke – until I saw the blood from Letty's ear. But even if you were actually going to fire a revolver to make the thing more real, you'd be careful to fire it well above someone's head, wouldn't you?'

'You would indeed. Do you think he could see clearly who he was firing at? I mean, was Miss Blacklock clearly outlined in the light of the torch?'

'I've no idea. I wasn't looking at her. I was looking at the man.'

'What I'm getting at is – do you think the man was deliberately aiming at her – at her in particular, I mean?'

Julia seemed a little startled by the idea.

'You mean deliberately picking on Aunt Letty? Oh, I shouldn't think so . . . After all, if he wanted to take a pot shot at Aunt Letty, there would be heaps of more suitable opportunities. There would be no point in collecting all the friends and neighbours just to make it more difficult. He could have shot her from behind a hedge in the good old Irish fashion any day of the week, and probably got away with it.'

And that, thought Craddock, was a very complete reply to Dora Bunner's suggestion of a deliberate attack on Letitia Blacklock.

He said with a sigh, 'Thank you, Miss Simmons. I'd better go and see Mitzi now.'

'Mind her fingernails,' warned Julia. 'She's a tartar!'

II

Craddock, with Fletcher in attendance, found Mitzi in the kitchen. She was rolling pastry and looked up suspiciously as he entered.

Her black hair hung over her eyes; she looked sullen, and the purple jumper and brilliant green skirt she wore were not becoming to her pasty complexion.

'What do you come in my kitchen for, Mr Policeman? You are police, yes? Always, always there is persecution – ah! I should be used to it by now. They say it is different here in England, but no, it is just the same. You come to torture me, yes, to make me say things, but I shall say *nothing*. You will tear off my fingernails, and put lighted matches on my skin – oh, yes, and worse than that. But I will not speak, do you hear? I shall say nothing – nothing at all. And you will send me away to a concentration camp, and I shall not care.'

Craddock looked at her thoughtfully, selecting what was likely to be the best method of attack. Finally he sighed and said:

'O.K., then, get your hat and coat.'

'What is that you say?' Mitzi looked startled.

'Get your hat and coat and come along. I haven't got my nail-pulling apparatus and the rest of the bag of tricks with me. We keep all that down at the station. Got the handcuffs handy, Fletcher?'

'Sir!' said Sergeant Fletcher with appreciation.

'But I do not want to come,' screeched Mitzi, backing away from him.

'Then you'll answer civil questions civilly. If you like, you can have a solicitor present.'

'A lawyer? I do not like a lawyer. I do not want a lawyer.'

She put the rolling pin down, dusted her hands on a cloth and sat down.

'What do you want to know?' she asked sulkily.

'I want your account of what happened here last night.'

'You know very well what happened.'

'I want your account of it.'

'I tried to go away. Did she tell you that? When I saw that in the paper saying about murder. I wanted to go away. She would not let me. She is very hard – not at all sympathetic. She made me stay. But *I* knew – *I* knew what would happen. *I* knew I should be murdered.'

'Well, you weren't murdered, were you?'

'No,' admitted Mitzi grudgingly.

'Come now, tell me what happened.'

'I was nervous. Oh, I was nervous. All that evening. I hear things. People moving about. Once I think someone is in the hall moving stealthily – but it is only that Mrs Haymes coming in through the side door (so as not to dirty the front steps, *she* says. Much *she* cares!). She is a Nazi herself, that one, with her fair hair and her blue eyes, so superior and looking at me and thinking that I – I am only dirt—'

'Never mind Mrs Haymes.'

'Who does she think *she* is? Has she had expensive university education like I have? Has she a degree in Economics? No, she is just a paid labourer. She digs and mows grass and is paid so much every Saturday. Who is she to call herself a lady?'

'Never mind Mrs Haymes, I said. Go on.'

'I take the sherry and the glasses, and the little pastries that I have made so nice into the drawing-room. Then the bell rings and I answer the door. Again and again I answer the door. It is degrading – but I do it. And then I go back into the pantry and I start to polish the silver, and I think it will be very handy, that, because if someone comes to kill me, I have there close at hand the big carving knife, all sharp.'

'Very foresighted of you.'

'And then, suddenly – I hear shots. I think: "It has come – it is happening." I run through the dining-room (the other door – it will not open). I stand a moment to listen and then there comes another shot and a big thud, out there in the hall, and I turn the door handle, but it is locked outside. I am shut in there like a rat in a trap. And I go mad with fear. I scream and I scream and I beat upon the door. And at last – at last they turn the key and let me out. And then I bring candles, many many candles – and the lights go on, and I see blood – blood! Ach, Gott in Himmell, the blood! It is not the first time I have seen blood. My little brother – I see him killed before my eyes – I see blood in the street – people shot, dying – I—'

'Yes,' said Inspector Craddock. 'Thank you very much.'

'And now,' said Mitzi dramatically, 'you can arrest me and take me to prison!'

'Not today,' said Inspector Craddock.

III

As Craddock and Fletcher went through the hall to the front door it was flung open and a tall handsome young man almost collided with them.

'Sleuths as I live,' cried the young man.

'Mr Patrick Simmons?'

'Quite right, Inspector. You're the inspector, aren't you, and the other's the Sergeant?'

'You are quite right, Mr Simmons. Can I have a word with you, please?'

'I am innocent, Inspector. I swear I am innocent.'

'Now then, Mr Simmons, don't play the fool. I've a good many other people to see and I don't want to waste time. What's this room? Can we go in here?'

'It's the so-called study – but nobody studies.'

'I was told that you were studying?' said Craddock.

'I found I couldn't concentrate on mathematics, so I came home.'

In a businesslike manner Inspector Craddock demanded full name, age, details of war service.

'And now, Mr Simmons, will you describe what happened last night?'

'We killed the fatted calf, Inspector. That is, Mitzi set her hand to making savoury pastries, Aunt Letty opened a new bottle of sherry—'

Craddock interrupted.

'A new bottle? Was there an old one?'

'Yes. Half full. But Aunt Letty didn't seem to fancy it.'

'Was she nervous, then?'

'Oh, not really. She's extremely sensible. It was old Bunny, I think, who put the wind up her – prophesying disaster all day.'

'Miss Bunner was definitely apprehensive, then?'

'Oh, yes, she enjoyed herself thoroughly.'

'She took the advertisement seriously?'

'It scared her into fits.'

'Miss Blacklock seems to have thought, when she first read that advertisement, that you had had something to do with it. Why was that?'

'Ah, sure, I get blamed for everything round here!'

'You *didn't* have anything to do with it, did you, Mr Simmons?'

'Me? Never in the world.'

'Had you ever seen or spoken to this Rudi Scherz?'

'Never seen him in my life.'

'It was the kind of joke you might have played, though?'

'Who's been telling you that? Just because I once made Bunny an apple pie bed – and sent Mitzi a postcard saying the Gestapo was on her track—'

'Just give me your account of what happened.'

'I'd just gone into the small drawing-room to fetch the drinks when, Hey Presto, the lights went out. I turned round and there's a fellow standing in the doorway saying, "Stick your hands up," and everybody gasping and squealing, and just when I'm thinking – can I rush him? he starts firing a revolver and then crash down he goes and his torch goes out and we're in the dark again, and Colonel Easterbrook starts shouting orders in his barrack-room voice. "Lights," he says, and will my lighter go on? No, it won't as is the way of those cussed inventions.'

'Did it seem to you that the intruder was definitely aiming at Miss Blacklock?'

'Ah, how could I tell? I should say he just loosed off his revolver for the fun of the thing – and then found, maybe, he'd gone too far.'

'And shot himself?'

'It could be. When I saw the face of him, he looked like the kind of little pasty thief who might easily lose his nerve.'

'And you're sure you had never seen him before?'

'Never.'

'Thank you, Mr Simmons. I shall want to interview the other

people who were here last night. Which would be the best order in which to take them?'

'Well, our Phillipa – Mrs Haymes – works at Dayas Hall. The gates of it are nearly opposite this gate. After that, the Swettenhams are the nearest. Anyone will tell you.'

—— 7 ——

AMONG THOSE PRESENT

I

Dayas Hall had certainly suffered during the war years. Couch grass grew enthusiastically over what had once been an asparagus bed, as evidenced by a few waving tufts of asparagus foliage. Groundsel, bindweed and other garden pests showed every sign of vigorous growth.

A portion of the kitchen garden bore evidence of having been reduced to discipline and here Craddock found a sour-looking old man leaning pensively on a spade.

'It's Mrs 'Aymes you want? I couldn't say where you'd find 'er. 'As 'er own ideas, she 'as, about what she'll do. Not one to take advice. I could show her – show 'er willing – but what's the good, won't listen these young ladies won't! Think they know everything because they've put on breeches and gone for a ride on a tractor. But it's *gardening* that's needed here. And that isn't learned in a day. *Gardening*, that's what's this place needs.'

'It looks as though it does,' said Craddock.

The old man chose to take this remark as an aspersion.

'Now look here, mister, what do you suppose I can do with a place this size? Three men and a boy, that's what it used to 'ave. And that's what it wants. There's not many men could put in the work on it that I do. 'Ere sometimes I am till eight o'clock at night. Eight o'clock.'

'What do you work by? An oil lamp?'

'Naterally I don't mean this time o' year. Naterally. *Summer* evenings I'm talking about.'

'Oh,' said Craddock. 'I'd better go and look for Mrs Haymes.'

The rustic displayed some interest.

'What are you wanting 'er for? Police, aren't you? She been in trouble, or is it the do there was up to Little Paddocks?

Masked men bursting in and holding up a roomful of people with a revolver. An' that sort of thing wouldn't 'ave 'appened afore the war. Deserters, that's what it is. Desperate men roaming the countryside. Why don't the military round 'em up?'

'I've no idea,' said Craddock. 'I suppose this hold-up caused a lot of talk?'

'That it did. What's us coming to? That's what Ned Barker said. Comes of going to the pictures so much, he said. But Tom Riley he says it comes of letting these furriners run about loose. And depend on it, he says, that girl as cooks up there for Miss Blacklock and 'as such a nasty temper – *she's* in it, he said. She's a communist or worse, he says, and we don't like that sort 'ere. And Marlene, who's behind the bar, you understand, she will 'ave it that there must be something very valuable up at Miss Blacklock's. Not that you'd think it, she says, for I'm sure Miss Blacklock goes about as plain as plain, except for them great rows of false pearls she wears. And then she says – Supposin' as them pearls is *real*, and Florrie (what's old Bellamy's daughter) *she* says, "Nonsense," she says – "*noovo ar* – that's what they are – costume jewellery," she says. Costume jewellery – that's a fine way of labelling a string of false pearls. Roman pearls, the gentry used to call 'em once – and Parisian diamonds – my wife was a lady's maid and I know. But what does it all mean – just glass! I suppose it's "costume jewellery" that young Miss Simmons wears – gold ivy leaves and dogs and such like. 'Tisn't often you see a real bit of gold nowadays – even wedding rings they make of this grey plattinghum stuff. Shabby, I call it – for all that it costs the earth.'

Old Ashe paused for breath and then continued:

' "Miss Blacklock don't keep much money in the 'ouse, that I do know," says Jim Huggins, speaking up. He should know, for it's 'is wife as goes up and does for 'em at Little Paddocks, and she's a woman as knows most of what's going on. Nosey, if you take me.'

'Did he say what Mrs Huggins' view was?'

'That awful Mitzi's mixed up in it, that's what she thinks. Awful temper she 'as, and the airs she gives herself! Called Mrs Huggins a working woman to her face the other morning.'

Craddock stood a moment, checking over in his orderly mind the substance of the old gardener's remarks. It gave him a good cross-section of rural opinion in Chipping Cleghorn, but he didn't think there was anything to help him in his task. He turned away and the old man called after him grudgingly:

'Maybe you'd find her in the apple orchard. She's younger than I am for getting the apples down.'

And sure enough in the apple orchard Craddock found Phillipa Haymes. His first view was a pair of nice legs encased in breeches sliding easily down the trunk of a tree. Then Phillipa, her face flushed, her fair hair ruffled by the branches, stood looking at him in a startled fashion.

'Make a good Rosalind,' Craddock thought automatically, for Detective-Inspector Craddock was a Shakespeare enthusiast and had played the part of the melancholy Jaques with great success in a performance of *As You Like It* for the Police Orphanage.

A moment later he amended his views. Phillipa Haymes was too wooden for Rosalind, her fairness and her impassivity were intensely English, but English of the twentieth rather than of the sixteenth century. Well-bred, unemotional English, without a spark of mischief.

'Good-morning, Mrs Haymes. I'm sorry if I startled you. I'm Detective-Inspector Craddock of the Middleshire Police. I wanted to have a word with you.'

'About last night?'

'Yes.'

'Will it take long? Shall we—?'

She looked about her rather doubtfully.

Craddock indicated a fallen tree trunk.

'Rather informal,' he said pleasantly, 'but I don't want to interrupt your work longer than necessary.'

'Thank you.'

'It's just for the record. You came in from work at what time last night?'

'At about half-past five. I'd stayed about twenty minutes later in order to finish some watering in the greenhouse.'

'You came in by which door?'

'The side door. One cuts across by the ducks and the henhouse from the drive. It saves you going round, and besides it avoids dirtying up the front porch. I'm in rather a mucky state sometimes.'

'You always come in that way?'

'Yes.'

'The door was unlocked?'

'Yes. During the summer it's usually wide open. This time of the year it's shut but not locked. We all go out and in a good deal that way. I locked it when I came in.'

'Do you always do that?'

'I've been doing it for the last week. You see, it gets dark at six. Miss Blacklock goes out to shut up the ducks and the hens sometimes in the evening, but she very often goes out through the kitchen door.'

'And you are quite sure that you did lock the side door this time?'

'I really am quite sure about that.'

'Quite so, Mrs Haymes. And what did you do when you came in?'

'Kicked off my muddy footwear and went upstairs and had a bath and changed. Then I came down and found that a kind of party was in progress. I hadn't known anything about this funny advertisement until then.'

'Now please describe just what occurred when the hold-up happened.'

'Well, the lights went out suddenly—'

'Where were you?'

'By the mantelpiece. I was searching for my lighter which I thought I had put down there. The lights went out – and everybody giggled. Then the door was flung open and this man shone a torch on us and flourished a revolver and told us to put our hands up.'

'Which you proceeded to do?'

'Well, I didn't actually. I thought it was just fun, and I was tired and I didn't think I needed really to put them up.'

'In fact, you were bored by the whole thing?'

'I was, rather. And then the revolver went off. The shots sounded deafening and I was really frightened. The torch went whirling round and dropped and went out, and then Mitzi started screaming. It was just like a pig being killed.'

'Did you find the torch very dazzling?'

'No, not particularly. It was quite a strong one, though. It lit up Miss Bunner for a moment and she looked quite like a turnip ghost – you know, all white and staring with her mouth open and her eyes starting out of her head.'

'The man moved the torch?'

'Oh, yes, he played it all round the room.'

'As though he were looking for someone?'

'Not particularly, I should say.'

'And after that, Mrs Haymes?'

Philippa Haymes frowned.

'Oh, it was all a terrible muddle and confusion. Edmund Swettenham and Patrick Simmons switched on their lighters and they went out into the hall and we followed, and someone opened the dining-room door – the lights hadn't fused there – and Edmund Swettenham gave Mitzi a terrific slap on the cheek and brought her out of her screaming fit, and after that it wasn't so bad.'

'You saw the body of the dead man?'

'Yes.'

'Was he known to you? Had you ever seen him before?'

'Never.'

'Have you any opinion as to whether his death was accidental, or do you think he shot himself deliberately?'

'I haven't the faintest idea.'

'You didn't see him when he came to the house previously?'

'No. I believe it was in the middle of the morning and I shouldn't have been there. I'm out all day.'

'Thank you, Mrs Haymes. One thing more. You haven't any valuable jewellery? Rings, bracelets, anything of that kind?'

Phillipa shook her head.

'My engagement ring – a couple of brooches.'

'And as far as you know, there was nothing of particular value in the house?'

'No. I mean there is some quite nice silver – but nothing out of the ordinary.'

'Thank you, Mrs Haymes.'

II

As Craddock retraced his steps through the kitchen garden he came face to face with a large red-faced lady, carefully corseted.

'Good-morning,' she said belligerently. 'What do you want here?'

'Mrs Lucas? I am Detective-Inspector Craddock.'

'Oh, that's who you are? I beg your pardon. I don't like strangers forcing their way into my garden wasting the gardeners' time. But I quite understand you have to do your duty.'

'Quite so.'

'May I ask if we are to expect a repetition of that outrage last night at Miss Blacklock's? Is it a gang?'

'We are satisfied, Mrs Lucas, that it was *not* the work of a gang.'

'There are far too many robberies nowadays. The police are

getting slack.' Craddock did not reply. 'I suppose you've been talking to Phillipa Haymes?'

'I wanted her account as an eye-witness.'

'You couldn't have waited until one o'clock, I suppose? After all, it would be fairer to question her in *her* time, rather than in *mine* . . .'

'I'm anxious to get back to headquarters.'

'Not that one expects consideration nowadays. Or a decent day's work. On duty late, half an hour's pottering. A break for elevenses at ten o'clock. No work done at all the moment the rain starts. When you want the lawn mown there's always something wrong with the mower. And off duty five or ten minutes before the proper time.'

'I understood from Mrs Haymes that she left here at twenty minutes past five yesterday instead of five o'clock.'

'Oh, I dare say she did. Give her her due, Mrs Haymes is quite keen on her work, though there have been days when I have come out here and not been able to find her anywhere. She is a lady by birth, of course, and one feels it's one's duty to do something for these poor young war widows. Not that it isn't very inconvenient. Those long school holidays and the arrangement is that she has extra time off then. I told her that there are really excellent camps nowadays where children can be sent and where they have a delightful time and enjoy it far more than wandering about with their parents. They need practically not come home at all in the summer holidays.'

'But Mrs Haymes didn't take kindly to that idea?'

'She's as obstinate as a mule, that girl. Just the time of year when I want the tennis court mowed and marked nearly every day. Old Ashe gets the lines crooked. But *my* convenience is never considered!'

'I presume Mrs Haymes takes a smaller salary than is usual?'

'Naturally. What else could she expect?'

'Nothing, I'm sure,' said Craddock. 'Good-morning, Mrs Lucas.'

III

'It was dreadful,' said Mrs Swettenham happily. 'Quite – quite – dreadful, and what I say is that they ought to be far more careful what advertisements they accept at the *Gazette* office. At the time, when I read it, I thought it was very odd. I said so, didn't I, Edmund?'

'Do you remember just what you were doing when the lights went out, Mrs Swettenham?' asked the Inspector.

'How that reminds me of my old Nannie! *Where was Moses when the light went out?* The answer, of course, was "In the Dark." Just like us yesterday evening. All standing about and wondering what was going to happen. And then, you know, the *thrill* when it suddenly went pitch black. And the door opening – just a dim figure standing there with a revolver and that blinding light and a menacing voice saying "Your money or your life!" Oh, I've never enjoyed anything so much. And then a minute later, of course, it was all *dreadful*. *Real* bullets, just *whistling* past our ears! It must have been just like the Commandos in the war.'

'Whereabouts were you standing or sitting at the time, Mrs Swettenham?'

'Now let me see, where was I? Who was I talking to, Edmund?'

'I really haven't the least idea, Mother.'

'Was it Miss Hinchcliffe I was asking about giving the hens cod liver oil in the cold weather? Or was it Mrs Harmon – no, she'd only just arrived. I think I was just saying to Colonel Easterbrook that I thought it was really very dangerous to have an atom research station in England. It ought to be on some lonely island in case the radio activity gets loose.'

'You don't remember if you were sitting or standing?'

'Does it really matter, Inspector? I was somewhere over by the window or near the mantelpiece, because I know I was *quite* near the clock when it struck. Such a thrilling moment! Waiting to see if anything might be going to happen.'

'You describe the light from the torch as blinding. Was it turned full on you?'

'It was right in my eyes. I couldn't see a thing.'

'Did the man hold it still, or did he move it about, from person to person?'

'Oh, I don't really know. Which did he do, Edmund?'

'It moved rather slowly over us all, so as to see what we were doing, I suppose, in case we should try and rush him.'

'And where exactly in the room were *you*, Mr Swettenham?'

'I'd been talking to Julia Simmons. We were both standing up in the middle of the room – the long room.'

'Was everyone in that room, or was there anyone in the far room?'

'Phillipa Haymes had moved in there, I think. She was over by that far mantelpiece. I think she was looking for something.'

'Have you any idea as to whether the third shot was suicide or an accident?'

'I've no idea at all. The man seemed to swerve round very suddenly and then crumple up and fall – but it was all very confused. You must realise that you couldn't really see anything. And then that refugee girl started yelling the place down.'

'I understand it was you who unlocked the dining-room door and let her out?'

'Yes.'

'The door was definitely locked on the outside?'

Edmund looked at him curiously.

'Certainly it was. Why, you don't imagine—?'

'I just like to get my facts quite clear. Thank you, Mr Swettenham.'

IV

Inspector Craddock was forced to spend quite a long time with Colonel and Mrs Easterbrook. He had to listen to a long disquisition on the psychological aspect of the case.

'The psychological approach – that's the only thing nowadays,' the Colonel told him. 'You've got to understand your criminal. Now the whole set-up here is quite plain to a man who's had the wide experience that I have. Why does this fellow put that advert in? Psychology. He wants to advertise himself – to focus attention on himself. He's been passed over, perhaps despised as a foreigner by the other employees at the Spa Hotel. A girl has turned him down, perhaps. He wants to rivet her attention on him. Who is the idol of the cinema nowadays – the gangster – the tough guy? Very well, he will be a tough guy. Robbery with violence. A mask? A revolver? But he wants an audience – he must have an audience. So he arranges for an audience. And then, at the supreme moment, his part runs away with him – he's more than a burglar. He's a killer. He shoots – blindly—'

Inspector Craddock caught gladly at a word:

'You say "blindly," Colonel Easterbrook. You didn't think that he was firing deliberately at one particular object – at Miss Blocklock, that is to say?'

'No, no. He just loosed off, as I say, blindly. And that's what actually brought him to himself. The bullet hit someone –

actually it was only a graze, but he didn't know that. He comes
to himself with a bang. All this – this make-believe he's been in-
dulging in – is *real*. He's shot at someone – perhaps killed someone . . . It's all up with him. And so in blind panic he turns the
revolver on himself.'

Colonel Easterbrook paused, cleared his throat appreciatively
and said in a satisfied voice, 'Plain as pikestaff, that's what it is,
plain as a pikestaff.'

'It really is wonderful,' said Mrs Easterbrook, 'the way you
know exactly what happened, Archie.'

Her voice was warm with admiration.

Inspector Craddock thought it was wonderful, too, but he was
not quite so warmly appreciative.

'Exactly where were you in the room, Colonel Easterbrook,
when the actual shooting business took place?'

'I was standing with my wife – near a centre table with some
flowers on it.'

'I caught hold of your arm, didn't I, Archie, when it happened? I was simply scared to death. I just had to hold on to you.'

'Poor little kitten,' said the Colonel playfully.

V

The Inspector ran Miss Hinchcliffe to earth by a pigsty.

'Nice creatures, pigs,' said Miss Hinchcliffe, scratching a
wrinkled pink back. 'Coming on well, isn't he? Good bacon
around about Christmas time. Well, what do you want to see
me about? I told your people last night I hadn't the least idea
who the man was. Never seen him anywhere in the neighbourhood snooping about or anything of that sort. Our Mrs Mopp
says he came from one of the big hotels in Medenham Wells.
Why didn't he hold up someone there if he wanted to? Get a
much better haul.'

That was undeniable – Craddock proceeded with his inquiries.

'Where were you exactly when the incident took place?'

'Incident! Reminds me of my ARP days. Saw some incidents then, I can tell you. Where was I when the shooting
started? That what you want to know?'

'Yes.'

'Leaning up against the mantelpiece hoping to God someone
would offer me a drink soon,' replied Miss Hinchcliffe promptly.

33

'Do you think that the shots were fired blindly, or aimed carefully at one particular person?'

'You mean aimed at Letty Blacklock? How the devil should I know? Damned hard to sort out what your impressions really were or what really happened after it's all over. All I know is the lights went out, and that torch went whirling round dazzling us all, and then the shots were fired and I thought to myself, "If that damned young fool Patrick Simmons is playing his jokes with a loaded revolver somebody will get hurt." '

'You thought it was Patrick Simmons?'

'Well, it seemed likely. Edmund Swettenham is intellectual and writes books and doesn't care for horseplay, and old Colonel Easterbrook wouldn't think that sort of thing funny. But Patrick's a wild boy. However, I apologise to him for the idea.'

'Did your friend think it might be Patrick Simmons?'

'Murgatroyd? You'd better talk to her yourself. Not that you'll get any sense out of her. She's down the orchard. I'll yell for her if you like.'

Miss Hinchcliffe raised her stentorian voice in a powerful bellow:

'Hi-youp, Murgatroyd...'

'Coming...' floated back a thin cry.

'Hurry up – Polieece,' bellowed Miss Hinchcliffe.

Miss Murgatroyd arrived at a brisk trot very much out of breath. Her skirt was down at the hem and her hair was escaping from an inadequate hair net. Her round, good-natured face beamed.

'Is it Scotland Yard?' she asked breathlessly. 'I'd no idea. Or I wouldn't have left the house.'

'We haven't called in Scotland Yard yet, Miss Murgatroyd. I'm Inspector Craddock from Milchester.'

'Well, that's very nice, I'm sure,' said Miss Murgatroyd vaguely. 'Have you found any clues?'

'Where were you at the time of the crime, that's what he wants to know, Murgatroyd?' said Miss Hinchcliffe. She winked at Craddock.

'Oh, dear,' gasped Miss Murgatroyd. 'Of course. I ought to have been prepared. *Alibis*, of course. Now, let me see, I was just with everybody else.'

'You weren't with me,' said Miss Hinchcliffe.

'Oh, dear, Hinch, wasn't I? No, of course, I'd been admiring the chrysanthemums. Very poor specimens, really. And then it all happened – only I didn't really know it had happened – I mean I didn't know that anything like that had happened. I didn't imagine for a moment that it was a real revolver – and all so awkward in the dark, and that dreadful screaming. I got it all wrong, you know. I thought *she* was being murdered – I mean the refugee girl. I thought she was having her throat cut across the hall somewhere. I didn't know it was *him* – I mean, I didn't even know there was a man. It was really just a voice, you know, saying, "Put them up, please." '

' "Stick 'em up!" ' Miss Hinchcliffe corrected. 'And no suggestion of "please" about it.'

'It's so terrible to think that until that girl started screaming I was actually enjoying myself. Only being in the dark was very awkward and I got a knock on my corn. Agony, it was. Is there anything more you want to know, Inspector?'

'No,' said Inspector Craddock, eyeing Miss Murgatroyd speculatively. 'I don't really think there is.'

Her friend gave a short bark of laughter.

'He's got you taped, Murgatroyd.'

'I'm sure, Hinch,' said Miss Murgatroyd, 'that I'm only too willing to say anything I can.'

'He doesn't want that,' said Miss Hinchcliffe.

She looked at the Inspector. 'If you're doing this geographically I suppose you'll go to the Vicarage next. You might get something there. Mrs Harmon looks as vague as they make them – but I sometimes think she's got brains. Anyway, she's got something.'

As they watched the Inspector and Sergeant Fletcher stalk away, Amy Murgatroyd said breathlessly:

'Oh, Hinch, was I very awful? I do get so flustered!'

'Not at all.' Miss Hinchcliffe smiled. 'On the whole, I should say you did very well.'

VI

Inspector Craddock looked round the big shabby room with a sense of pleasure. It reminded him a little of his own Cumberland home. Faded chintz, big shabby chairs, flowers and books strewn about, and a spaniel in a basket. Mrs Harmon, too, with her distraught air, and her general disarray and her eager face he found sympathetic.

But she said at once, frankly, 'I shan't be any help to you. Because I shut my eyes. I hate being dazzled. And then there were shots and I screwed them up tighter than ever. And I did wish, oh, I did wish, that it had been a *quiet* murder. I don't like bangs.'

'So you didn't see anything.' The Inspector smiled at her. 'But you heard—?'

'Oh, my goodness yes, there was plenty to *hear*. Doors opening and shutting, and people saying silly things and gasping and old Mitzi screaming like a steam engine – and poor Bunny squealing like a trapped rabbit. And everyone pushing and falling over everyone else. However, when there really didn't seem to be any more bangs coming, I opened my eyes. Everyone was out in the hall then, with candles. And then the lights came on and suddenly it was all as usual – I don't mean really as usual, but we were ourselves again, not just – people in the dark. People in the dark are quite different, aren't they?'

'I think I know what you mean, Mrs Harmon.'

Mrs Harmon smiled at him.

'And there he was,' she said. 'A rather weaselly-looking foreigner – all pink and surprised looking – lying there dead – with a revolver beside him. It didn't – oh, it didn't seem to make *sense*, somehow.'

It did not make sense to the Inspector, either.

The whole business worried him.

—— 8 ——

ENTER MISS MARPLE

I

Craddock laid the typed transcript of the various interviews before the Chief Constable. The latter had just finished reading the wire received from the Swiss Police.

'So he had a police record all right,' said Rydesdale. 'H'm – very much as one thought.'

'Yes, sir.'

'Jewellery . . . h'm, yes . . . falsified entries . . . yes . . . cheque . . . Definitely a dishonest fellow.'

'Yes, sir – in a small way.'

'Quite so. And small things lead to large things.'

'I wonder, sir.'

The Chief Constable looked up.

'Worried, Craddock?'

'Yes, sir.'

'Why? It's a straightforward story. Or isn't it? Let's see what all these people you've been talking to have to say.

He drew the report towards him and read it through rapidly. 'The usual thing – plenty of inconsistencies and contradictions. Different people's accounts of a few moments of stress never agree. But the main picture seems clear enough.'

'I know, sir – but it's an unsatisfactory picture. If you know what I mean – it's the wrong picture.'

'Well. let's take the facts. Rudi Scherz took the 5.20 bus from Medenham to Chipping Cleghorn arriving there at six o'clock. Evidence of conductor and two passengers. From the bus stop he walked away in the direction of Little Paddocks. He got into the house with no particular difficulty – probably through the front door. He held up the company with a revolver, he fired two shots, one of which slightly wounded Miss Blacklock, then he killed himself with a third shot, whether accidentally or deliberately there is not sufficient evidence to show. The reasons *why* he did all this are profoundly unsatisfactory, I agree. But *why* isn't really a question we are called upon to answer. A Coroner's jury may bring it in suicide – or accidental death. Whichever verdict it is, it's the same as far as we're concerned. We can write finis.'

'You mean we can always fall back upon Colonel Easterbrook's psychology,' said Craddock gloomily.

Rydesdale smiled.

'After all, the Colonel's probably had a good deal of experience,' he said. 'I'm pretty sick of the psychological jargon that's used so glibly about everything nowadays – but we can't really rule it out.'

'I still feel the picture's all wrong, sir.'

'Any reason to believe that somebody in the set-up at Chipping Cleghorn is lying to you?'

Craddock hesitated.

'I think the foreign girl knows more than she lets on. But that may be just prejudice on my part.'

'You think she might possibly have been in it with this fellow? Let him into the house? Put him up to it?'

'Something of the kind. I wouldn't put it past her. But that surely indicates that there really was something valuable, money or jewellery, in the house, and that doesn't seem to have been the case. Miss Blacklock negatived it quite decidedly. So did the others. That leaves us with the proposition that there was something valuable in the house that nobody knew about—'

'Quite a best seller plot.'

'I agree it's ridiculous, sir. The only other point is Miss Bunner's certainty that it was a definite attempt by Scherz to murder Miss Blacklock.'

'Well, from what you say – and from her statement, this Miss Bunner—'

'Oh, I agree, sir,' Craddock put in quickly, 'She's an utterly unreliable witness. Highly suggestible. Anyone could put a thing into her head – but the interesting thing is that this is quite her own theory – no one *has* suggested it to her. Everybody else negatives it. For once she's *not* swimming with the tide. It definitely *is* her own impression.'

'And why should Rudi Scherz want to kill Miss Blacklock?'

'There you are, sir. I don't know. Miss Blacklock doesn't know – unless she's a much better liar than I think she is. Nobody knows. So presumably it isn't true.'

He sighed.

'Cheer up, Craddock,' said the Chief Constable. 'I'm taking you off to lunch with Sir Henry and myself. The best that the Royal Spa Hotel in Medenham Wells can provide.'

'Thank you, sir.' Craddock looked slightly surprised.

'You see, we received a letter—' He broke off as Sir Henry Clithering entered the room. 'Ah, there you are, Henry.'

Sir Henry, informal this time, said, 'Morning, Dermot.'

'I've got something for you, Henry,' said the Chief Constable. 'What's that?'

'Authentic letter from an old Pussy. Staying at the Royal Spa Hotel. Something she thinks we might like to know in connection with this Chipping Cleghorn business.'

'The old Pussies,' said Sir Henry triumphantly. 'What did I tell you? They hear everything. They see everything. And, unlike the famous adage, they speak all evil. What's this particular one got hold of?'

Rydesdale consulted the letter.

'Writes just like my old grandmother,' he complained. 'Spiky. Like a spider in the ink bottle, and all underlined. A good deal about how she hopes it won't be taking up our valuable time, but might possibly be of some slight assistance, etc., etc. What's her name? Jane – something – Murple – no, Marple, Jane Marple.'

'Ye Gods and Little Fishes,' said Sir Henry, 'can it be? George, it's my own particular, one and only, four starred Pussy. The super Pussy of all old Pussies. And she has managed somehow to be at Medenham Wells, instead of peacefully at home in St Mary Mead, just at the right time to be mixed up in a murder. Once more a murder is announced – for the benefit and enjoyment of Miss Marple.'

'Well, Henry,' said Rydesdale sardonically, 'I'll be glad to see your paragon. Come on! We'll lunch at the Royal Spa and we'll interview the lady. Craddock, here, is looking highly sceptical.'

'Not at all, sir,' said Craddock politely.

He thought to himself that sometimes his godfather carried things a bit far.

II

Miss Jane Marple was very nearly, if not quite, as Craddock had pictured her. She was far more benignant that he had imagined and a good deal older. She seemed indeed very old. She had snow-white hair and a pink crinkled face and very soft innocent blue eyes, and she was heavily enmeshed in fleecy wool. Wool round her shoulders in the form of a lacy cape and wool that she was knitting and which turned out to be a baby's shawl.

She was all incoherent delight and pleasure at seeing Sir Henry, and became quite flustered when introduced to the Chief Constable and Detective-Inspector Craddock.

'But really, Sir Henry, how fortunate . . . how very fortunate. So long since I have seen you . . . Yes, my rheumatism. Very bad of late. Of course I couldn't have afforded this hotel (really fantastic what they charge nowadays) but Raymond – my nephew, Raymond West, you may remember him—'

'Everyone knows *his* name.'

'Yes, the dear boy has been so successful with his clever books – he prides himself upon never writing about anything pleasant. The dear boy insisted on paying all my expenses. And his dear wife is making a name for herself, too, as an artist. Mostly jugs of dying flowers and broken combs on windowsills. I never dare tell her, but I still admire Blair Leighton and Alma Tadema. Oh, but I'm chattering. And the Chief Constable himself – indeed I never expected – so afraid I shall be taking up his time—'

'Completely ga-ga,' thought the disgusted Detective-Inspector Craddock.

'Come into the Manager's private room,' said Rydesdale. 'We can talk better there.'

When Miss Marple had been disentangled from her wool, and her spare knitting pins collected, she accompanied them, fluttering and protesting, to Mr Rowlandson's comfortable sitting-room.

'Now, Miss Marple, let's hear what you have to tell us,' said the Chief Constable.

Miss Marple came to the point with unexpected brevity.

'It was a cheque,' she said. 'He altered it.'

'He?'

'The young man at the desk here, the one who is supposed to have staged that hold-up and shot himself.'

'He altered a cheque, you say?'

Miss Marple nodded.

'Yes. I have it here.' She extracted it from her bag and laid it on the table. 'It came this morning with my others from the Bank. You can see, it was for seven pounds, and he altered it to seventeen. A stroke in front of the 7, and *teen* added after the word seven with a nice artistic little blot just blurring the whole word. Really very nicely done. A certain amount of *practice*, I should say. It's the same ink, because I wrote the cheque actually at the desk. I should think he'd done it quite often before, wouldn't you?'

'He picked the wrong person to do it to, this time,' remarked Sir Henry.

Miss Marple nodded agreement.

'Yes. I'm afraid he would never have gone very far in crime. I was quite the wrong person. Some busy young married woman, or some girl having a love affair – that's the kind who write cheques for all sorts of different sums and don't really look through their passbooks carefully. But an old woman who has to be careful of the pennies, and who has formed habits – that's quite the wrong person to choose. Seventeen pounds is a sum I *never* write a cheque for. Twenty pounds, a round sum, for the monthly wages and books. And as for my personal expenditure, I usually cash seven – it used to be five, but everything has gone up so.'

'And perhaps he reminded you of someone?' prompted Sir Henry, mischief in his eye.

Miss Marple smiled and shook her head at him.

'You are very naughty, Sir Henry. As a matter of fact he *did*. Fred Tyler, at the fish shop. Always slipped an extra 1 in the shillings column. Eating so much fish as we do nowadays, it made a long bill, and lots of people never added it up. Just ten shillings in his pocket every time, not much but enough to get himself a few neckties and take Jessie Spragge (the girl in the draper's) to the pictures. Cut a splash, that's what these young fellows want to do. Well, the very first week I was here, there was a mistake in my bill. I pointed it out to the young man and he apologised very nicely and looked very much upset, but I thought to myself then: 'You've got a shifty eye, young man.'"'

'What I mean by a shifty eye,' continued Miss Marple, 'is the kind that looks very straight at you and never looks away or blinks.'

Craddock gave a sudden movement of appreciation. He thought to himself 'Jim Kelly to the life,' remembering a notorious swindler he had helped to put behind bars not long ago.

'Rudi Scherz was a thoroughly unsatisfactory character,' said Rydesdale. 'He's got a police record in Switzerland, we find.'

'Made the place too hot for him, I suppose, and came over here with forged papers?' said Miss Marple.

'Exactly,' said Rydesdale.

'He was going about with the little red-haired waitress from the dining-room,' said Miss Marple. 'Fortunately I don't think her heart's affected at all. She just liked to have someone a bit "different," and he used to give her flowers and chocolates which the English boys don't do much. Has she told you all she knows?' she asked, turning suddenly to Craddock. 'Or not quite all yet?'

'I'm not absolutely sure,' said Craddock cautiously.

'I think there's a little to come,' said Miss Marple. 'She's looking very worried. Brought me kippers instead of herrings this morning, and forgot the milk jug. Usually she's an excellent waitress. Yes, she's worried. Afraid she might have to give evidence or something like that. But I expect' – her candid blue eyes swept over the manly proportions and handsome face of Detective-Inspector Craddock with truly feminine Victorian appreciation – 'that *you* will be able to persuade her to tell you all she knows.'

Detective-Inspector Craddock blushed and Sir Henry chuckled.

'It might be important,' said Miss Marple. 'He may have told her who it was.'

Rydesdale stared at her.

'Who what was?'

'I express myself so badly. Who it was who put him up to it, I mean.'

'So you think someone put him up to it?'

Miss Marple's eyes widened in surprise.

'Oh, but surely – I mean . . . Here's a personable young man – who filches a little bit here and a little bit there – alters a small cheque, perhaps helps himself to a small piece of jewellery if it's left lying around, or takes a little money from the till – all sorts of small petty thefts. Keeps himself going in ready money so that he can dress well, and take a girl about – all that sort of thing. And then suddenly he goes off, with a revolver, and holds up a room full of people, and shoots at someone. He'd *never* have done a thing like that – not for a moment! He wasn't that kind of person. It doesn't make *sense.*'

Craddock drew in his breath sharply. That was what Letitia Blacklock had said. What the Vicar's wife had said. What he himself felt with increasing force. *It didn't make sense.* And now Sir Henry's old Pussy was saying it, too, with complete certainty in her fluting old lady's voice.

'Perhaps you'll tell us, Miss Marple,' he said, and his voice was suddenly aggressive, 'what did happen, then?'

She turned on him in surprise.

'But how should I know what happened? There was an account in the paper – but it says so little. One can make conjectures, of course, but one has no accurate information.'

'George,' said Sir Henry, 'would it be very unorthodox if Miss Marple were allowed to read the notes of the interviews Craddock had with these people at Chipping Cleghorn?'

'It may be unorthodox,' said Rydesdale, 'but I've not got where I am by being orthodox. She can read them. I'd be curious to hear what she has to say.'

Miss Marple was all embarrassment.

'I'm afraid you've been listening to Sir Henry. Sir Henry is always too kind. He thinks too much of any little observations I may have made in the past. Really, I have no gifts – no gifts at all – except perhaps a certain knowledge of human nature. People, I find, are apt to be far too trustful. I'm afraid that I have a tendency always to believe the *worst*. Not a nice trait. But so often justified by subsequent events.'

'Read these,' said Rydesdale, thrusting the typewritten sheets upon her. 'They won't take you long. After all, these people are your kind – you must know a lot of people like them. You may be able to spot something that we haven't. The case is just going to be closed. Let's have an amateur's opinion on it before we shut up the files. I don't mind telling you that Craddock here isn't satisfied. He says, like you, that it doesn't make sense.'

There was silence whilst Miss Marple read. She put the type-written sheets down at last.

'It's very interesting,' she said with a sigh. 'All the different things that people say – and think. The things they see – or think that they see. And all so complex, nearly all so trivial and if one thing isn't trivial, it's so hard to spot which one – like a needle in a haystack.'

Craddock felt a twinge of disappointment. Just for a moment or two, he wondered if Sir Henry might be right about this funny old lady. She might have put her finger on something – old people were often very sharp. He'd never, for instance, been able to conceal anything from his own great aunt Emma. She had finally told him that his nose twitched when he was about to tell a lie.

But just a few fluffy generalities, that was all that Sir Henry's famous Miss Marple could produce. He felt annoyed with her and said rather curtly:

'The truth of the matter is that the facts are indisputable. Whatever conflicting details these people give, they all saw one thing. They saw a masked man with a revolver and a torch open the door and hold them up, and whether they think he said "Stick 'em up" or "Your money or your life," or whatever phrase is associated with a hold-up in their minds, they *saw* him.'

'But surely,' said Miss Marple gently. 'They couldn't – actu-ally – have seen anything at all . . .'

Craddock caught his breath. She'd got it! She was sharp, after all. He was testing her by that speech of his, but she hadn't fallen for it. It didn't actually make any difference to the facts, or to what happened, but she'd realized, as he'd realized, that those people who had seen a masked man holding them up couldn't really have *seen* him at all.

'If I understand rightly,' Miss Marple had a pink flush on her cheeks, her eyes were bright and pleased as a child's, 'there wasn't any light in the hall outside – and not on the landing up-stairs either?'

'That's right,' said Craddock.

'And so, if a man stood in the doorway and flashed a powerful torch into the room, *nobody could see anything but the torch,* could they?

'No, they couldn't. I tried it out.'

'And so when some of them say they saw a masked man, etc., they are really, though they don't realize it, recapitulating from what they saw *afterwards* – when the lights came on. So it really all fits in very well, doesn't it, on the assumption that Rudi Scherz was the – I think, "fall guy" is the expression I mean?'

Rydesdale stared at her in such surprise that she grew pinker still.

'I may have got the term wrong,' she murmured. 'I am not very clever about Americanisms – and I understand they change very quickly. I got it from one of Mr Dashiel Hammett's stories. (I understand from my nephew Raymond that he is considered at the top of the tree in what is called the "tough" style of literature.) A *"fall guy,"* if I understand it rightly, means someone who will be blamed for a crime really committed by someone else. This Rudi Scherz seems to me exactly the right type for that. Rather stupid really, you know, but full of cupidity and probably extremely credulous.'

Rydesdale said, smiling tolerantly:

'Are you suggesting that he was persuaded by someone to go out and take pot shots at a room full of people? Rather a tall order.'

'I think he was told that it was a *joke*,' said Miss Marple. 'He was paid for doing it, of course. Paid, that is, to put an advertisement in the newspaper, to go out and spy out the household premises, and then, on the night in question, he was to go there, assume a mask and a black cloak, and throw open a door, brandishing a torch, and cry "Hands up!" ' '

'And fire off a revolver?'

'No, no,' said Miss Marple. 'He never had a revolver.'

'But everyone says—' began Rydesdale, and stopped.

'Exactly,' said Miss Marple. 'Nobody could possibly have *seen* a revolver even if he had one. And I don't think he had. I think that after he'd called "Hands up" somebody came up quietly behind him in the darkness and fired those two shots over his shoulder. It frightened him to death. He swung round and as he did so, that other person shot him and let the revolver drop beside him . . .'

The three men looked at her. Sir Henry said softly:

'It's a possible theory.'

'But who is Mr X who came up in the darkness?' asked the Chief Constable.

Miss Marple coughed.

'You'll have to find out from Miss Blacklock who wanted to kill her.'

Good for old Dora Bunner, thought Craddock. Instinct against intelligence every time.

'So you think it was a deliberate attempt on Miss Blacklock's life,' asked Rydesdale.

'It certainly has that appearance,' said Miss Marple. 'Though there are one of two difficulties. But what I was really wondering about was whether there mightn't be a short cut. I've no doubt that whoever arranged this with Rudi Scherz took pains to tell him to keep his mouth shut about it, and perhaps he did keep his mouth shut, but if he talked to anybody it would probably be to that girl, Myrna Harris. And he may – he just may – have dropped some hint as to the kind of person who'd suggested the whole thing.'

'I'll see her now,' said Craddock, rising.

Miss Marple nodded.

'Yes, do, Inspector Craddock. I'll feel happier when you have. Because once she's told you anything she knows she'll be much safer.'

'Safer? . . . Yes, I see.'

He left the room. The Chief Constable said doubtfully, but tactfully:

'Well, Miss Marple, you've certainly given us something to think about.'

III

'I'm sorry about it, I am really,' said Myrna Harris. 'It's ever so nice of you not to be ratty about it. But you see Mum's the sort of person who fusses like anything. And it did look as though I'd – what's the phrase? – been an accessory before the fact' (the words ran glibly off her tongue). 'I mean, I was afraid you'd never take my word for it that I only thought it was just a bit of fun.'

Inspector Craddock repeated the reassuring phrase with which he had broken down Myrna's resistance.

'I will. I'll tell you *all* about it. But you will keep me out of it if you can because of Mum? It all started with Rudi breaking a date with me. We were going to the pictures that evening and then he said he wouldn't be able to come and I was a bit stand-offish with him about it – because after all, it had been his idea and I don't fancy being stood up by a foreigner. And he said it wasn't his fault, and I said that was a likely story, and then he said he'd got a bit of a lark on that night – and that he wasn't going to be out of pocket by it and how would I fancy a wrist-watch? So I said, what do you mean by a lark? And he said not to tell anyone, but there was to be a party somewhere and he was to stage a sham hold-up. Then he showed me the advertisement he'd put in and I had to laugh. He was a bit scornful about it all. Said it was kid's stuff, really – but that was just like the English. They never really grew up – and of course, I said what did he mean by talking like that about Us – and we had a bit of an argument, but we made it up. Only you can understand, can't you, sir, that when I read all about it, and it hadn't been a joke at all and Rudi had shot someone and then shot himself – why, I didn't know *what* to do. I thought if I said I knew about it be-forehand, it would look as though I were in on the whole thing. But it really did seem like a joke when he told me about it. I'd have sworn he meant it that way. I didn't even know he'd got a revolver. He never said anything about taking a revolver with him.'

Craddock comforted her and then asked the most important question.

'Who did he say it was who had arranged this party?'

But there he drew a blank.

'He never said who it was that was getting him to do it. I sup-pose nobody was, really. It was all his own doing.'

'He didn't mention a name? Did he say he – or she?'

'He didn't say anything except that it was going to be a scream. "I shall laugh to see all their faces." That's what he said.'

He hadn't had long to laugh, Craddock thought.

IV

'It's only a theory,' said Rydesdale as they drove back to Meden-ham. 'Nothing to support it, nothing at all. Put it down as an old maid's vapourings and let it go, eh?'

'I'd rather not do that, sir.'

'It's all very improbable. A mysterious X appearing suddenly in the darkness behind our Swiss friend, Where did he come from? Who was he? Where had he been?'

'He could have come in through the side door,' said Craddock, 'just as Scherz came. Or,' he added slowly, 'he could have come from the kitchen.'

'*She* could have come from the kitchen, you mean?'

'Yes, sir, it's a possibility. I've not been satisfied about that girl all along. She strikes me as a nasty bit of goods. All that screaming and hysterics – it could have been put on. She could have worked on this young fellow, let him in at the right moment, rigged the whole thing, shot him, bolted back into the dining-room, caught up her bit of silver and her chamois and started her screaming act.'

'Against that we have the fact that – er – what's his name – oh, yes, Edmund Swettenham, definitely says the key was turned on the outside of the door, and that he turned it to release her. Any other door into that part of the house?'

'Yes, there's a door to the back stairs and kitchen just under the stairs, but it seems the handle came off three weeks ago and nobody's come to put it on yet. In the meantime you can't open the door. I'm bound to say that story seems correct. The spindle and the two handles were on a shelf outside the door in the hall and they were thickly coated with dust, but of course a professional would have ways of opening that door all right.'

'Better look up the girl's record. See if her papers are in order. But it seems to me the whole thing is very theoretical.'

Again the Chief Constable looked inquiringly at his subordinate. Craddock replied quietly:

'I know, sir, and of course if you think the case ought to be closed, it must be. But I'd appreciate it if I could work on it for just a little longer.'

Rather to his surprise the Chief Constable said quietly and approvingly:

'Good lad.'

'There's the revolver to work on. If this theory is correct, it wasn't Scherz's revolver and certainly nobody so far has been able to say that Scherz ever had a revolver.'

'It's a German make.'

'I know, sir. But this country's absolutely full of continental makes of guns. All the Americans brought them back and so did our chaps. You can't go by that.'

'True enough. Any other lines of inquiry?'

'There's got to be a motive. If there's anything in this theory at all, it means that last Friday's business wasn't a mere joke, and wasn't an ordinary hold-up, it was a cold blooded attempt at murder. *Somebody tried to murder Miss Blacklock. Now why?*

It seems to me that if anyone knows the answer to that it must be Miss Blacklock herself.'

'I understand she rather poured cold water on that idea?'

'She poured cold water on the idea that *Rudi Scherz* wanted to murder her. And she was quite right. And there's another thing, sir.'

'Yes?'

'Somebody might try again.'

'That would certainly prove the truth of the theory,' said the Chief Constable dryly. 'By the way, look after Miss Marple, won't you?'

'Miss Marple? Why?'

'I gather she is taking up residence at the Vicarage in Chipping Cleghorn and coming into Medenham Wells twice a week for her treatments. It seems that Mrs What'shername is the daughter of an old friend of Miss Marple's. Good sporting instincts, that old bean. Oh, well, I suppose she hasn't much excitement in her life and sniffing round after possible murderers gives her a kick.'

'I wish she wasn't coming,' said Craddock seriously.

'Going to get under your feet?'

'Not that, sir, but she's a nice old thing. I shouldn't like anything to happen to her . . . always supposing, I mean, that there's anything *in* this theory.'

—— 9 ——

CONCERNING A DOOR

I

'I'm sorry to bother you again, Miss Blacklock—'

'Oh, it doesn't matter. I suppose, as the inquest was adjourned for a week, you're hoping to get more evidence?'

Detective-Inspector Craddock nodded.

'To begin with, Miss Blacklock, Rudi Scherz was not the son of the proprietor of the Hotel des Alpes at Montreux. He seems to have started his career as an orderly in a hospital at Berne. A good many of the patients missed small pieces of jewellery. Under another name he was a waiter at one of the small winter sports places. His speciality there was making out duplicate bills in the restaurant with items on one that didn't appear on the other. The difference, of course, went into his pocket. After that he was in a department store in Zürich. There losses from shoplifting were rather above the average whilst he was with them. It seems likely that the shoplifting wasn't entirely due to customers.'

'He was a picker up of unconsidered trifles, in fact?' said Miss Blacklock dryly. 'Then I was right in thinking that I had not seen him before?'

'You were quite right – no doubt you were pointed out to him at the Royal Spa Hotel and he pretended to recognize you. The Swiss police had begun to make his own country rather too hot for him, and he came over here with a very nice set of forged papers and took a job at the Royal Spa.'

'Quite a good hunting ground,' said Miss Blacklock dryly. 'It's extremely expensive and very well-off people stay there. Some of them are careless about their bills, I expect.'

'Yes,' said Craddock. 'There were prospects of a satisfactory harvest.'

Miss Blacklock was frowning.

'I see all that,' she said. 'But why come to Chipping Cleghorn? What does he think we've got here that could probably be better than the rich Royal Spa Hotel?'

'You stick to your statement that there's nothing of especial value in the house?'

'Of course there isn't. *I* should know. I can assure you Inspector, we've not got an unrecognized Rembrandt or anything like that.'

'Then it looks, doesn't it, as though your friend Miss Bunner was right? He came here to attack *you.*'

('There, Letty, what did I tell you!'

'Oh, nonsense, Bunny.')

'But is it nonsense?' said Craddock. 'I think, you know, that it's true.'

Miss Blacklock stared very hard at him.

'New, let's get this straight. You really believe that this young man came out here – having previously arranged by means of an advertisement that half the village would turn up agog at that particular time—'

'But he mayn't have meant *that* to happen,' interrupted Miss Bunner eagerly. 'It may have been just a horrid sort of warning – to *you,* Letty – that's how I read it at the time – '*A murder is announced*' – I felt in my bones that it was sinister – if it had all gone as planned he would have shot you and got away – and how would anyone have ever known who it was?'

'That's true enough,' said Miss Blacklock. 'But—'

'I knew that advertisement wasn't a joke, Letty. I said so. And look at Mitzi – *she* was frightened, too!'

'Ah,' said Craddock, 'Mitzi. I'd like to know rather more about that young woman.'

'Her permit and papers are quite in order.'

'I don't doubt that,' said Craddock dryly. 'Scherz's papers appeared to be quite correct, too.'

'But why should this Rudi Scherz want to murder me? That's what you don't attempt to explain, Inspector Craddock.'

'There may have been someone behind Scherz,' said Craddock slowly. 'Have you thought of that?'

He used the words metaphorically though it flashed across his mind that if Miss Marple's theory was correct, the words would also be true in a literal sense. In any case they made little impression on Miss Blacklock, who still looked sceptical.

'The point remains the same,' she said. 'Why on earth should anyone want to murder *me*?'

'It's the answer to that that I want *you* to give me, Miss Blacklock.'

'Well, I can't! That's flat. I've no enemies. As far as I'm aware I've always lived on perfectly good terms with my neighbours. I don't know any guilty secrets about anyone. The whole idea is ridiculous! And if what you're hinting is that Mitzi has something to do with this, that's absurd, too. As Miss Bunner has just told you she was frightened to death when she saw that advertisement in the *Gazette*. She actually wanted to pack up and leave the house then and there.'

'That may have been a clever move on her part. She may have known you'd press her to stay.'

'Of course, if you've made up your mind about it, you'll find an answer to everything. But I can assure you that if Mitzi had taken an unreasoning dislike to me, she might conceivably poison my food, but I'm sure she wouldn't go in for all this elaborate rigmarole.

'The whole idea's absurd. I believe you police have got an anti-foreigner complex. Mitzi may be a liar but she's *not* a cold-blooded murderer. Go and bully her if you must. But when she's departed in a whirl of indignation, or shut herself up howling in her room, I've a good mind to make *you* cook the dinner. Mrs Harmon is bringing some old lady who is staying with her to tea this afternoon and I wanted Mitzi to make some little cakes – but I suppose you'll upset her completely. Can't you *possibly* go and suspect somebody else?'

II

Craddock went out to the kitchen. He asked Mitzi questions that he had asked her before and received the same answers. Yes, she had locked the front door soon after four o'clock. No, she did not always do so, but that afternoon she had been nervous because of 'that dreadful advertisement.' It was no good locking the side door because Miss Blacklock and Miss Bunner went out that way to shut up the ducks and feed the chickens and Mrs Haymes usually came in that way from work.

'Mrs Haymes says she locked the door when she came in at 5.30.'

'Ah, and you believe her – oh, yes, you believe her . . .'

'Do you think we shouldn't believe her?'

'What does it matter what I think? You will not believe *me*.'

'Supposing you give us a chance. You think Mrs Haymes didn't lock that door?'

'I thinking she was very careful not to lock it.'

'What do you mean by that?' asked Craddock.

'That young man, he does not work alone. No, he knows *where* to come, he knows that *when* he comes a door will be left open for him – oh, very conveniently open!'

'What are you trying to say?'

'What is the use of what I say? You will not listen. You say I am a poor refugee girl who tells lies. You say that a fair-haired English lady, oh, no, *she* does not tell lies – she is so British – so honest. So you believe her and not me. But I could tell you. Oh, yes, I could tell you!'

She banged down a saucepan on the stove.

Craddock was in two minds whether to take notice of what might be only a stream of spite.

'We note everything we are told,' he said.

'I shall not tell you anything at all. Why should I? You are all alike. You persecute and despise poor refugees. If I say to you that when, a week before, that young man comes to ask Miss Blacklock for money and she sends him away, as you say, with a flea in the ear – if I tell you that after I hear him talking with

Mrs Haymes – yes, out there in the summerhouse – all you say is that I make it up!'

And so you probably are making it up, thought Craddock. But he said aloud:

'You couldn't hear what was said out in the summerhouse.'

'There you are wrong,' screamed Mitzi triumphantly. 'I go out to get nettles – it makes very nice vegetables, nettles. They do not think so, but I cook it and not tell them. And I hear them talking in there. He say to her "But where can I hide?" And she say "I will show you" – and then she say, "At a quarter-past six," and I think, "Ach so! That is how you behave, my fine lady! After you come back from work, you go out to meet a man. You bring him into the house." Miss Blacklock, I think, she will not like that. She will turn you out. I will watch, I think, and listen and then I will tell Miss Blacklock. But I understand now I was wrong. It was not love she planned with him, it was to rob and to murder. But you will say I make all this up. Wicked Mitzi, you will say. I will take her to prison.'

Craddock wondered. She might be making it up. But possibly she might not. He asked cautiously:

'You are sure it was this Rudi Scherz she was talking to?'

'Of course I am sure. He just leave and I see him go from the drive across to the summerhouse. And presently,' said Mitzi defiantly, 'I go out to see if there are any nice young green nettles.'

Would there, the Inspector wondered, be any nice young green nettles in October? But he appreciated that Mitzi had had to produce a hurried reason for what had undoubtedly been nothing more than plain snooping.

'You didn't hear any more than what you have told me?'

Mitzi looked aggrieved.

'That Miss Bunner, the one with the long nose, she call and call me. Mitzi! Mitzi! So I have to go. Oh, she is irritating. Always interfering. Says she will teach me to cook. *Her* cooking! It tastes, yes, everything she does, of water, water, *water*!'

'Why didn't you tell me this the other day?' asked Craddock sternly.

'Because I did not remember – I did not think . . . Only afterwards do I say to myself, it was planned then – planned with *her*.

'You are quite sure it was Mrs Haymes?'

'Oh, yes, I am sure. Oh, yes, I am very sure. She is a thief, that Mrs Haymes. A thief and the associate of thieves. What she gets for working in the garden, it is not enough for such a fine lady, no. She has to rob Miss Blacklock who has been kind to her. Oh, she is bad, bad, bad, that one!'

'Supposing,' said the Inspector, watching her closely, 'that someone was to say that *you* had been seen talking to Rudi Scherz?'

The suggestion had less effect than he had hoped for. Mitzi merely snorted and tossed her head.

'If anyone say they see me talking to him, this is lies, lies, lies, lies,' she said contemptuously. 'To tell lies about anyone, that is easy, but in England you have to prove them true. Miss Blacklock tell me that, and it is true, is it not? I do not speak with murderers and thieves. And no English policeman shall say I do. And how can I do cooking for lunch if you are here, talk, talk, talk? Go out of my kitchens, please. I want now to make a very careful sauce.'

Craddock went obediently. He was a little shaken in his suspicions of Mitzi. Her story about Phillipa Haymes had been told with great conviction. Mitzi might be a liar (he thought she was), but he fancied that there might be some substratum of truth in this particular tale. He resolved to speak to Phillipa on the subject. She had seemed to him when he questioned her a quiet, well-bred young woman. He had had no suspicion of her.

Crossing the hall, in his abstraction, he tried to open the wrong door. Miss Bunner, descending the staircase, hastily put him right.

'Not that door,' she said. 'It isn't open. The next one to the left. Very confusing, isn't it? So many doors.'

'There are a good many,' said Craddock, looking up and down the narrow hall.

Miss Bunner amiably enumerated them for him.

'First the door to the cloakroom, and then the cloaks cupboard door and then the dining-room – that's on that side. And on this side, the dummy door that you were trying to get through and then there's the drawing-room door proper, and then the china cupboard and the door of the little flower room, and at the end the side door. Most confusing. Especially these two being so near together. I've often tried the wrong one by mistake. We used to have the hall table against it, as a matter of fact, but then we moved it along against the wall there.'

Craddock had noted, almost mechanically, a thin line horizontally across the panels of the door he had been trying to open. He realized now it was the mark where the table had been. Something stirred vaguely in his mind as he asked, 'Moved? How long ago?'

In questioning Dora Bunner there was fortunately no need to give a reason for any question. Any query on any subject seemed perfectly natural to the garrulous Miss Bunner who delighted in the giving of information, however trivial.

'Now let me see, really quite recently – ten days or a fortnight ago.'

'Why was it moved?'

'I really can't remember. Something to do with the flowers. I think Phillipa did a big vase – she arranges flowers quite beautifully – all autumn colouring and twigs and branches, and it was so big it caught your hair as you went past, and so Phillipa said, "Why not move the table along and anyway the flowers would look much better against the bare wall than against the panels of the door." Only we had to take down Wellington at Waterloo. Not a print I'm really very fond of. We put it under the stairs.'

'It's not really a dummy, then?' Craddock asked looking at the door.'

'Oh, no, it's a *real* door, if that's what you mean. It's the door of the small drawing-room, but when the rooms were thrown into one, one didn't need two doors, so this one was fastened up.'

'Fastened up?' Craddock tried it again, gently. 'You mean it's nailed up? Or just locked?'

'Oh, locked, I think, and bolted too.'

He saw the bolt at the top and tried it. The bolt slid back easily – too easily . . .

'When was it last open?' he asked Miss Bunner.

'Oh, years and years ago, I imagine. It's never been opened since I've been here, I know that.'

'You don't know where the key is?'

'There are a lot of keys in the hall drawer. It's probably among those.'

Craddock followed her and looked at a rusty assortment of old keys pushed far back in the drawer. He scanned them and selected one that looked different from the rest and went back to the door. The key fitted and turned easily. He pushed and the door slid open noiselessly.

'Oh, do be careful,' cried Miss Bunner. 'There may be something resting against it inside. We never open it.'

'Don't you? said the Inspector.'

His face now was grim. He said with emphasis:

'This door's been opened quite recently, Miss Bunner. The lock's been oiled and the hinges.'

She stared at him, her foolish face agape.

'But who could have done that? she asked.

'That's what I mean to find out,' said Craddock grimly. He thought – 'X from outside? No – X was here – in this house – X was in the drawing-room that night....'

—— 10 ——

PIP AND EMMA

I

Miss Blacklock listened to him this time with more attention. She was an intelligent woman, as he had known, and she grasped the implications of what he had to tell her.

'Yes,' she said quietly. 'That does alter things . . . No one had any right to meddle with that door. Nobody *has* meddled with it to my knowledge.'

'You see what it means,' the Inspector urged. 'When the lights went out, *anybody in this room the other night* could have slipped out of that door, come up behind Rudi Scherz and fired at you.'

'Without being seen or heard or noticed?'

'Without being seen or heard or noticed. Remember when the lights went out people moved, exclaimed, bumped into each other. And after that all that could be seen was the blinding light of the electric torch.'

Miss Blacklock said slowly, 'And you believe that one of those people – one of my nice commonplace neighbours – slipped out and tried to murder me? *Me?* But *why?* For goodness' sake, *why?*'

'I've a feeling that you *must* know the answer to that question, Miss Blacklock.'

'But I don't, Inspector. I can assure you, I don't.'

'Well, let's make a start. Who gets your money if you were to die?'

Miss Blacklock said rather reluctantly:

'Patrick and Julia. I've left the furniture in this house and a small annuity to Bunny. Really, I've not much to leave. I had holdings in German and Italian securities which became worthless, and what with taxation, and the lower percentages that are now paid on invested capital, I can assure you I'm not worth murdering – I put most of my money into an annuity about a year ago.'

'Still, you *have* some income, Miss Blacklock, and your nephew and niece would come into it.'

'And so Patrick and Julia would plan to murder me? I simply don't believe it. They're not desperately hard up or anything like that.'

'Do you know that for a fact?'

'No. I suppose I only know it from what they've told me . . . But I really refuse to suspect them. *Some* day I *might* be worth murdering, but not now.'

'What do you mean by someday you might be worth murdering, Miss Blacklock?' Inspector Craddock pounced on the statement.

'Simply that one day – possibly quite soon – I *may* be a very rich woman.'

'That sounds interesting. Will you explain?'

'Certainly. You may not know it, but for more than twenty years I was secretary to and closely associated with Randall Goedler.'

Craddock was interested. Randall Goedler had been a big name in the world of finance. His daring speculations and the rather theatrical publicity with which he surrounded himself had made him a personality not quickly forgotten. He had died, if Craddock remembered rightly, in 1937 or 1938.

'He's rather before your time, I expect,' said Miss Blacklock. 'But you've probably heard of him.'

'Oh, yes. He was a millionaire, wasn't he?'

'Oh, several times over – though his finances fluctuated. He always risked most of what he made on some new *coup*.'

She spoke with a certain animation, her eyes brightened by memory.

'Anyway he died a very rich man. He had no children. He left his fortune in trust for his wife during her lifetime and after death to me absolutely.'

A vague memory stirred in the Inspector's mind.

IMMENSE FORTUNE TO COME TO FAITHFUL SECRETARY – something of that kind.

'For the last twelve years or so,' said Miss Blacklock with a

277

slight twinkle, '*I've* had an excellent motive for murdering Mrs Goedler – but that doesn't help you, does it?'

'Did – excuse me for asking this – did Mrs Goedler resent her husband's disposition of his fortune?'

Miss Blacklock was now looking frankly amused.

'You needn't be so very discreet. What you really mean is, was I Randall Goedler's mistress? No, I wasn't. I don't think Randall ever gave me a sentimental thought, and I certainly didn't give him one. He was in love with Belle (his wife), and remained in love with her until he died. I think in all probability it was gratitude on his part that prompted his making his will. You see, Inspector, in the very early days, when Randall was still on an insecure footing, he came very near to disaster. It was a question of just a few thousands of actual cash. It was a big *coup*, and a very exciting one; daring, as all his schemes were; but he just hadn't got that little bit of cash to tide him over. I came to the rescue. I had a little money of my own. I believed in Randall. I sold every penny I had out and gave it to him. It did the trick. A week later he was an immensely wealthy man.

'After that, he treated me more or less as a junior partner. Oh! they were exciting days.' She sighed. 'I enjoyed it all thoroughly. Then my father died, and my only sister was left a hopeless invalid. I had to give it all up and go and look after her. Randall died a couple of years later. I had made quite a lot of money during our association and I didn't really expect him to leave me anything, but I was very touched, yes, and very proud to find that if Belle predeceased me (and she was one of those delicate creatures whom everyone always says won't live long) I was to inherit his entire fortune. I think really the poor man didn't know who to leave it to. Belle's a dear, and she was delighted about it. She's really a very sweet person. She lives up in Scotland. I haven't seen her for years – we just write at Christmas. You see, I went with my sister to a sanatorium in Switzerland just before the war. She died of consumption out there.'

She was silent for a moment or two, then said:

'I only came back to England just over a year ago.'

'You said you might be a rich woman very soon . . . How soon?'

'I heard from the nurse attendant who looks after Belle Goedler that Belle is sinking rapidly. It may be – only a few weeks.'

She added sadly:

'The money won't mean much to me now. I've got quite

enough for my rather simple needs. Once I should have enjoyed playing the markets again – but now . . . Oh, well, one grows old. Still, you do see, Inspector, don't you, that if Patrick and Julia wanted to kill me for a financial reason they'd be crazy not to wait for another few weeks.'

'Yes, Miss Blacklock, but what happens if you should predecease Mrs Goedler? Who does the money go to then?'

'D'you know, I've never really thought. Pip and Emma, I suppose . . .'

Craddock stared and Miss Blacklock smiled.

'Does that sound rather crazy? I believe, if I predecease Belle, the money would go to the legal offspring – or whatever the term is – of Randall's only sister, Sonia. Randall had quarrelled with his sister. She married a man whom he considered a crook and worse.'

'And was he a crook?'

'Oh, definitely, I should say. But I believe a very attractive pearson to women. He was a Greek or a Roumanian or something – what was his name now – Stamfordis, Dmitri Stamfordis.'

'Randall Goedler cut his sister out of his will when she married this man?'

'Oh, Sonia was a very wealthy woman in her own right. Randall had already settled packets of money on her, as far as possible in a way so that her husband couldn't touch it. But I believe that when the lawyers urged him to put in someone in case I predeceased Belle, he reluctantly put down Sonia's offspring, simply because he couldn't think of anyone else and he wasn't the sort of man to leave money to charities.'

'And there were children of the marriage?'

'Well, there are Pip and Emma.' She laughed. 'I know it sounds ridiculous. All I know is that Sonia wrote once to Belle after her marriage, telling her to tell Randall that she was extremely happy and that she had just had twins and was calling them Pip and Emma. As far as I know she never wrote again. But Belle, of course, may be able to tell you more.'

Miss Blacklock had been amused by her own recital. The Inspector did not look amused.

'It comes to this,' he said. 'If you had been killed the other night, there are presumably at least two people in the world who would have come into a very large fortune. You are wrong, Miss Blacklock, when you say that there is no one who has a motive for desiring your death. There are two people, at least, who are vitally interested. How old would this brother and sister be?'

Miss Blacklock frowned.

'Let me see . . . 1922 . . . no – it's difficult to remember . . I suppose about twenty-five or twenty-six.' Her face had sobered. 'But you surely don't think—?'

'I think somebody shot at you with the intent to kill you. I think it possible that that same person or persons might try again. I would like you, if you will, to be very *very* careful, Miss Blacklock. One murder has been arranged and did not come off. I think it possible that another murder may be arranged very soon.'

II

Phillipa Haymes straightened her back and pushed back a tendril of hair from her damp forehead. She was cleaning a flower border.

'Yes, Inspector?'

She looked at him inquiringly. In return he gave her a rather closer scrunity than he had done before. Yes, a good-looking girl, a very English type with her pale ash-blonde hair and her rather long face. An obstinate chin and mouth. Something of repression – of tautness about her. The eyes were blue, very steady in their glance, and told you nothing at all. The sort of girl, he thought, who would keep a secret well.

'I'm sorry always to bother you when you're at work, Mrs Haymes,' he said, 'but I didn't want to wait until you came back for lunch. Besides, I thought it might be easier to talk to you here, away from Little Paddocks.'

'Yes, Inspector?'

No emotion and little interest in her voice. But there was a note of wariness – or did he imagine it?

'A certain statement has been made to me this morning. This statement concerns you.'

Phillipa raised her eyebrows very slightly.

'You told me, Mrs Haymes, that this man, Rudi Scherz, was quite unknown to you?'

'Yes.'

'That when you saw him there, dead, it was the first time you had set eyes on him. Is that so?'

'Certainly. I had never seen him before.'

'You did not, for instance, have a conversation with him in the summerhouse of Little Paddocks?'

'In the *summer*house?'

He was almost sure he caught a note of fear in her voice.

'Yes, Mrs Haymes.'

'*Who* says so?'

'I am told that you had a conversation with this man, Rudi Scherz, and that he asked you where he could hide and you replied that you would show him, and that a time, a quarter-past six, was definitely mentioned. It would be a quarter-past six, roughly, when Scherz would get here from the bus stop on the evening of the hold-up.'

There was a moment's silence. Then Phillipa gave a short scornful laugh. She looked amused.

'I don't know who told you that,' she said. 'At least I can guess. It's a very silly, clumsy story – spiteful, of course. For some reason Mitzi dislikes me even more than she dislikes the rest of us.'

'You deny it?'

'Of course it's not true . . . I never met or saw Rudi Scherz in my life, and I was working near the house that morning. I was over here, working.'

Inspector Craddock said very gently:

'Which morning?'

There was a momentary pause. Her eyelids flickered.

'Every morning. I'm here every morning. I don't get away until one o'clock.'

She added scornfully:

'It's no good listening to what Mitzi tells you. She tells lies all the time.'

'And that's that,' said Craddock when he was walking away with Sergeant Fletcher. 'Two young women whose stories flatly contradict each other. Which one am I to believe?'

'Everyone seems to agree that this foreign girl tells whoppers,' said Fletcher. 'It's been my experience in dealing with aliens that lying comes more easy than truth telling. Seems to be clear she's got a spite against this Mrs Haymes.'

'So, if you were me, you'd believe Mrs Haymes?'

'Unless you've got reason to think otherwise, sir.'

And Craddock hadn't, not really – only the remembrance of a pair of over-steady blue eyes and the glib enunciation of the words *that morning*. For to the best of his recollection he hadn't said whether the interview in the summerhouse had taken place in the morning or the afternoon.

Still, Miss Blacklock, or if not Miss Blacklock, certainly Miss Bunner, might have mentioned the visit of the young foreigner who had come to cadge his fare back to Switzerland. And Phillipa Haymes might have therefore assumed that the conversation was supposed to have taken place on that particular morning.

But Craddock still thought that there had been a note of fear in her voice as she asked:

'In the *summer*house?'

He decided to keep an open mind on the subject.

III

It was very pleasant in the Vicarage garden. One of those sudden spells of autumn warmth had descended upon England. Inspector Craddock could never remember if it was St Martin's or St Luke's Summer, but he knew that it was very pleasant – and also very enervating. He sat in a deck chair provided for him by an energetic Bunch, just on her way to a Mothers' Meeting, and, well protected with shawls and a large rug round her knees, Miss Marple sat knitting beside him. The sunshine, the peace, the steady click of Miss Marples's knitting needles, all combined to produce a soporific feeling in the Inspector. And yet, at the same time, there was a nightmarish feeling at the back of his mind. It was like a familiar dream where an undertone of menace grows and finally turns Ease into Terror . . .

He said abruptly, 'You oughtn't to be here.'

Miss Marple's needles stopped clicking for a moment. Her placid china blue eyes regarded him thoughtfully.

She said, 'I know what you mean. You're a very conscientious boy. But it's perfectly all right. Bunch's father (he was vicar of our parish, a very fine scholar) and her mother (who is a most remarkable woman – real spiritual power) are very old friends of mine. It's the most natural thing in the world that when I'm at Medenham I should come on here to stay with Bunch for a little.'

'Oh, perhaps,' said Craddock. 'But – but don't snoop around . . . I've a feeling – I have really – that it isn't *safe*.'

Miss Marple smiled a little.

'But I'm afraid,' she said, 'that we old women always do snoop. It would be very odd and much more noticeable if I didn't. Questions about mutual friends in different parts of the world and whether they remember so and so, and do they remember who it was that Lady Somebody's daughter married? All that helps, doesn't it?'

'Helps?' said the Inspector, rather stupidly.

'Helps to find out if people are who they say they are,' said Miss Marple.

She went on:

'Because that's what's worrying you, isn't it? And that's really the particular way the world has changed since the war. Take this place, Chipping Cleghorn, for instance. It's very much like St Mary Mead where I live. Fifteen years ago one *knew* who everybody was. The Bantrys in the big house – and the Hartnells and the Price Ridleys and the Weatherbys . . . They were people whose fathers and mothers and grandfathers and grandmothers, or whose aunts and uncles, had lived there before them. If somebody new came to live there, they brought letters of introduction, or they'd been in the same regiment or served in the same ship as someone there already. If anybody new – really new – really a stranger – came, well, they stuck out – everybody wondered about them and didn't rest till they found out.'

She nodded her head gently.

'But it's not like that any more. Every village and small country place is full of people who've just come and settled there without any ties to bring them. The big houses have been sold, and the cottages have been converted and changed. And people just come – and all you know about them is what they say of themselves. They've come, you see, from all over the world. People from India and Hong Kong and China, and people who used to live in France and Italy in little cheap places and odd islands. And people who've made a little money and can afford to retire. But nobody *knows* any more who anyone is. You can have Benares brassware in your house and talk about *tiffin* and *chota Hazri* – and you can have pictures of Taormina and talk about the English church and the library – like Miss Hinchcliffe and Miss Murgatroyd. You can come from the South of France, or have spent your life in the East. People take you at your own valuation. They don't wait to call until they've had a letter from a friend saying that the So-and-So's are delightful people and she's known them all their lives.'

And that, thought Craddock, was exactly what *was* oppressing him. He didn't *know*. There were just faces and personalities and they were backed up by ration books and identity cards – nice neat identity cards with numbers on them, without photographs or fingerprints. Anybody who took the trouble could have a suitable identity card – and partly because of that, the subtler links that had held together English social rural life had fallen apart. In a town nobody expected to know his neighbour. In the country now nobody knew his neighbour either, though possibly he still thought he did . . .

Because of the oiled door, Craddock knew that there had been somebody in Letitia Blacklock's drawing-room who was not the pleasant friendly country neighbour he or she pretended to be . . .

And because of that he was afraid for Miss Marple who was frail and old and who noticed things . . .

He said: 'We can, to a certain extent, check up on these people . . .' But he knew that that wasn't so easy. India and China and Hong Kong and the South of France . . . It wasn't as easy as it would have been fifteen years ago. There were people, as he knew only too well, who were going about the country with borrowed identities – borrowed from people who had met sudden death by 'incidents' in the cities. There were organisations who bought up identities, who faked identity and ration cards – there were a hundred small rackets springing into being. You *could* check up – but it would take time – and time was what he hadn't got, because Randall Goedler's widow was very near death.

It was then that, worried and tired, lulled by the sunshine, he told Miss Marple about Randall Goedler and about Pip and Emma.

'Just a couple of names,' he said. 'Nicknames at that! They mayn't exist. They may be respectable citizens living in Europe somewhere. On the other hand one, or both, of them may be here in Chipping Cleghorn.'

Twenty-five years old approximately – Who filled that description? He said, thinking aloud:

'That nephew and niece of hers – or cousins or whatever they are . . . I wonder when she saw them last—'

Miss Marple said gently: 'I'll find out for you, shall I?'

'Now, please, Miss Marple, don't—'

'It will be quite simple, Inspector, you really need not worry. And it won't be noticeable if I do it, because, you see, it won't be official. If there is anything wrong you don't want to put them on their guard.'

Pip and Emma, thought Craddock, Pip and Emma? He was getting obsessed by Pip and Emma. That attractive dare-devil young man, the good-looking girl with the cool stare . . .

He said: 'I may find out more about them in the next forty-

eight hours. I'm going up to Scotland. Mrs Goedler, if she's able
to talk, may know a good deal more about them.'
'I think that's a very wise move.' Miss Marple hesitated. 'I
hope,' she murmured, 'that you have warned Miss Blacklock to
be careful?'
'I've warned her, yes. And I shall leave a man here to keep an
unobtrusive eye on things.'
He avoided Miss Marple's eye which said plainly enough that
a policeman keeping an eye on things would be little good if the
danger was in the family circle . . .
'And remember,' said Craddock, looking squarely at her, 'I've
warned *you*.'
'I assure you, Inspector,' said Miss Marple, 'that I can take
care of myself.'

—— I I ——

MISS MARPLE COMES TO TEA

If Letitia Blacklock seemed slightly absentminded when Mrs
Harmon came to tea and brought a guest who was staying with
her, Miss Marple, the guest in question, was hardly likely to
notice the fact since it was the first time she had met her.
The old lady was very charming in her gentle gossipy fashion.
She revealed herself almost at once to be one of those old ladies
who have a constant preoccupation with burglars.
'They can get in anywhere, my dear,' she assured her hostess, 'absolutely *anywhere* nowadays. So many new American
methods. I myself pin my faith to a very old-fashioned device. *A
cabin hook and eye*. They can pick locks and draw back bolts but
a brass hook and eye defeats them. Have you ever tried that?'
'I'm afraid we're not very good at bolts and bars,' said Miss
Blacklock cheerfully. 'There's really nothing much to burgle.'
'A chain on the front door,' Miss Marple advised. 'Then the
maid need only open it a crack and see who is there and they
can't force their way in.'
'I expect Mitzi, our Mittel European, would love that.'
'The hold-up you had must have been very, very frightening,'
said Miss Marple. 'Bunch has been telling me all about it.'
'I was scared stiff,' said Bunch.
'It was an alarming experience,' admitted Miss Blacklock.

'It really seems like Providence that the man tripped himself up and shot himself. These burglars are so *violent* nowadays. How did he get in?'

'Well, I'm afraid we don't lock our doors much.'

'Oh, Letty,' exclaimed Miss Bunner. 'I forgot to tell you the Inspector was most peculiar this morning. He insisted on opening the second door – you know – the one that's never been opened – the one over there. He hunted for the key and everything and said the door had been oiled. But I can't see why because—'

Too late she got Miss Blacklock's signal to be quiet, and paused open-mouthed.

'Oh, Lotty, I'm so – sorry – I mean, oh, I *do* beg your pardon, Letty – oh, how stupid I am.'

'It doesn't matter,' said Miss Blacklock, but she was annoyed. 'Only I don't think Inspector Craddock wants that talked about. I didn't know you had been there when he was experimenting, Dora. You do understand, don't you, Mrs Harmon?'

'Oh, yes,' said Bunch. 'We won't breathe a word, will we, Aunt Jane. But I wonder *why* he—'

She relapsed into thought. Miss Bunner fidgeted and looked miserable, bursting out at last: 'I always say the wrong thing – Oh, dear, I'm nothing but a trial to you, Letty.'

Miss Blacklock said quickly, 'You're my great comfort, Dora. And anyway in a small place like Chipping Cleghorn there aren't really any secrets.'

'Now that is very true,' said Miss Marple. 'I'm afraid, you know, that things do get round in the most extraordinary way. Servants, of course, and yet it can't only be that, because one has so few servants nowadays. Still, there are the daily women and perhaps they are worse, because they go to everybody in turn and pass the news round.'

'Oh!' said Bunch Harmon suddenly. 'I've got it! Of course, if that door could open too, someone might have gone out of here in the dark and done the hold-up – only of course they didn't – because it was the man from the Royal Spa Hotel. Or wasn't it? ... No, I don't see after all ...' She frowned.

'Did it all happen in this room then?' asked Miss Marple, adding apologetically: 'I'm afraid you must think me sadly *curious,* Miss Blacklock – but it really is so very exciting – just like something one reads about in the paper – and actually to have happened to someone one *knows* .. I'm just longing to hear all about it and to picture it all, if you know what I mean—'

4

Immediately Miss Marple received a confused and voluble account from Bunch and Miss Bunner – with occasional emendations and corrections from Miss Blacklock.

In the middle of it Patrick came in and good-naturedly entered into the spirit of the recital – going so far as to enact himself the part of Rudi Scherz.

'And Aunt Letty was there – in the corner by the archway ... Go and stand there, Aunt Letty.'

Miss Blacklock obeyed, and then Miss Marple was shown the actual bullet-holes.

'What a marvellous – what a providential escape,' she gasped.

'I was just going to offer my guests cigarettes—' Miss Blacklock indicated the big silver box on the table.

'People are so careless when they smoke,' said Miss Bunner disapprovingly. 'Nobody really respects good furniture as they used to do. Look at the horrid burn somebody made on this beautiful table by putting a cigarette down on it. *Disgraceful.*'

Miss Blacklock sighed.

'Sometimes, I'm afraid, one thinks too much of one's possessions.'

'But it's such a lovely table, Letty.'

Miss Bunner loved her friend's possessions with as much fervour as though they had been her own. Bunch Harmon had always thought it was a very endearing trait in her. She showed no sign of envy.

'It is a lovely table,' said Miss Marple politely. 'And what a very pretty china lamp on it.'

Again it was Miss Bunner who accepted the compliment as though she and not Miss Blacklock was the owner of the lamp.

'Isn't it delightful? Dresden. There is a pair of them. The other's in the spare room, I think.'

'You know where everything in this house is, Dora – or you think you do,' said Miss Blacklock good-humouredly. 'You care far more about my things than I do.'

Miss Bunner flushed.

'I *do* like nice things,' she said. He voice was half defiant – half wistful.

'I must confess,' said Miss Marple, 'that my own few possessions are very dear to me, too – so many *memories*, you know. It's the same with photographs. People nowadays have so few photographs about. Now I like to keep all the pictures of my nephews and nieces as babies – and then as children – and so on.'

'You've got a horrible one of me, aged three,' said Bunch. 'Holding a fox terrier and squinting.'

'I expect your aunt has many photographs of you,' said Miss Marple, turning to Patrick.

'Oh, we're only distant cousins,' said Patrick.

'I believe Elinor did send me one of you as a baby, Pat,' said Miss Blacklock. 'But I'm afraid I didn't keep it. I'd really forgotten how many children she'd had or what their names were until she wrote me about you two being over here.'

'Another sign of the times,' said Miss Marple. 'Nowadays one so often doesn't know one's younger relations *at all*. In the old days, with all the big family reunions, that would have been impossible.'

'I last saw Pat and Julia's mother at a wedding thirty years ago,' said Miss Blacklock. 'She was a very pretty girl.'

'That's why she has such handsome children,' said Patrick with a grin.

'You've got a marvellous old album,' said Julia. 'Do you remember, Aunt Letty, we looked through it the other day. The hats!'

'And how smart we thought ourselves,' said Miss Blacklock with a sigh.

'Never mind, Aunt Letty,' said Patrick, 'Julia will come across a snapshot of herself in about thirty years' time – and won't she think she looks a guy!'

'Did you do that on purpose?' said Bunch, as she and Miss Marple were walking home. 'Talk about photographs, I mean?'

'Well, my dear, it *is* interesting to know that Miss Blacklock didn't know either of her two young relatives by sight . . . Yes – I think Inspector Craddock will be interested to hear that.'

——— 12 ———

MORNING ACTIVITIES IN CHIPPING CLEGHORN

I

Edmund Swettenham sat down rather precariously on a garden roller.

'Good-morning, Phillipa,' he said.

'Hallo.'

'Are you very busy?'

'Moderately.'

'What are you doing?'

'Can't you see?'

'No. I'm not a gardener. You seem to be playing with earth in some fashion.'

'I'm pricking out winter lettuce.'

'Pricking out? What a curious term! Like pinking. Do you know what pinking is? I only learnt the other day. I always thought it was a term for professional duelling.'

'Do you want anything particular?' asked Phillipa coldly.

'Yes. I want to see you.'

Phillipa gave him a quick glance.

'I wish you wouldn't come here like this. Mrs Lucas won't like it.'

'Doesn't she allow you to have followers?'

'Don't be absurd.'

'Followers. That's another nice word. It describes my attitude perfectly. Respectful – at a distance – but firmly pursuing.'

'Please go away, Edmund. You've no business to come here.'

'You're wrong,' said Edmund triumphantly. 'I *have* business here. Mrs Lucas rang up my mamma this morning and said she had a good many vegetable marrows.'

'Masses of them.'

'And would we like to exchange a pot of honey for a vegetable marrow or so.'

'That's not a fair exchange at all! Vegetable marrows are quite unsaleable at the moment – everybody has such a lot.'

'Naturally. That's why Mrs Lucas rang up. Last time, if I remember rightly, the exchange suggested was some skim milk – *skim* milk, mark you – in exchange for some lettuces. It was then very early in the season for lettuces. They were about a shilling each.'

Phillipa did not speak.

Edmund tugged at his pocket and extracted a pot of honey.

'So here,' he said, 'is my alibi. Used in a loose and quite indefensible meaning of the term. If Mrs Lucas pops her bust round the door of the potting shed, I'm here in quest of vegetable marrows. There is absolutely no question of dalliance.'

'I see.'

'Do you ever read Tennyson?' inquired Edmund conversationally.

'Not very often.'

'You should. Tennyson is shortly going to make a come back in a big way. When you turn on your wireless in the evening it will be the *Idylls of the Kings* you will hear and not interminable Trollope. I always thought the Trollope pose was the most unbearable affectation. Perhaps a little of Trollope, but not to drown in him. But speaking of Tennyson, have you read Maud?'

'Once, long ago.'

'It's got some points about it.' He quoted softly: ' "Faultily faultless, icily regular, splendidly null." That's you, Phillipa.'

'Hardly a compliment!'

'No, it wasn't meant to be. I gather Maud got under the poor fellow's skin just like you've got under mine.'

'Don't be absurd, Edmund.'

'Oh, hell, Phillipa, why are you like you are? What goes on behind your splendidly regular features? What do you think? What do you *feel*? Are you happy, or miserable, or frightened, or what? There must be *something*.'

Phillipa said quietly:

'What I feel is my own business.'

'It's mine, too. I want to make you talk. I want to know what goes on in that quiet head of yours. I've a *right* to know. I have really. I didn't want to fall in love with you. I wanted to sit quietly and write my book. Such a nice book, all about how miserable the world is. It's frightfully easy to be clever about how miserable everybody is. And it's all a habit, really. Yes, I've suddenly become convinced of that. After reading a life of Burne Jones.'

Phillipa had stopped pricking out. She was staring at him with a puzzled frown.

'What has Burne Jones got to do with it?'

'Everything. When you've read all about the pre-Raphaelites you realize just what fashion is. They were all terrifically hearty and slangy and jolly, and laughed and joked, and everything was fine and wonderful. That was fashion, too. They weren't any happier or heartier than we are. And we're not any more miserable than they were. It's all fashion, I tell you. After the last war, we went in for sex. Now it's all frustration. None of it matters. Why are we talking about all this? I started out to talk about *us*. Only I got cold feet and shied off. Because you won't help me.'

'What do you want me to do?'

'*Talk!* Tell me things. Is it your husband? Do you adore him and he's dead and so you've shut up like a clam? Is that it? All right, you adored him, and he's dead. Well, other girls' husbands are dead – lots of them – and some of the girls loved their husbands. They tell you so in bars, and cry a bit when they're drunk enough, and then want to go to bed with you so that they'll feel better. It's one way of getting over it, I suppose. You've got to get over it, Phillipa. You're young – and you're extremely lovely – and I love you like Hell. Talk about your damned husband, tell me about him.'

'There's nothing to tell. We met and got married.'

'You must have been very young.'

'Too young.'

'Then you weren't happy with him? Go *on*, Phillipa.'

'There's nothing to go on about. We were married. We were as happy as most people are, I suppose. Harry was born. Ronald went overseas. He – he was killed in Italy.'

'And now there's Harry?'

'And now there's Harry.'

'I like Harry. He's a really nice kid. He likes me. We get on. What about it, Phillipa? Shall we get married? You can go on gardening and I can go on writing my book and in the holidays we'll leave off working and enjoy ourselves. We can manage, with tact, not to have to live with Mother. She can fork out a bit to support her devoted son. I sponge, I write tripey books, I have defective eyesight and I talk too much. That's the worst. Will you try it?'

Phillipa looked at him. She saw a tall rather solemn young man with an anxious face and large spectacles. His sandy head was rumpled and he was regarding her with a reassuring friendliness.

'No,' said Phillipa.

'Definitely – no?'

'Definitely no.'

'Why?'

'You don't know anything about me.'

'Is that all?'

'No, you don't know anything about anything.'

Edmund considered.

'Perhaps not,' he admitted. 'But who does? Phillipa, my adored one—' He broke off.

A shrill and prolonged yapping was rapidly approaching.

"Pekes in the high hall garden, (said Edmund)
When twilight was falling (only it's eleven a.m.)
Phil, Phil, Phil, Phil,
They were crying and calling

'Your name doesn't lend itself to the rhythm, does it? Sounds like an Ode to a Fountain Pen. Have you got another name?'
'Joan. *Please* go away. That's Mrs Lucas.'
'*Joan, Joan, Joan, Joan.* Better, but still not good. *When greasy Joan the pot doth keel* – that's not a nice picture of married life, either.'
'Mrs Lucas is—'
'Oh, *hell!*' said Edmund. 'Get me a blasted vegetable marrow.'

II

Sergeant Fletcher had the house at Little Paddocks to himself. It was Mitzi's day off. She always went by the eleven o'clock bus into Medenham Wells. By arrangement with Miss Blacklock, Sergeant Fletcher had the run of the house. She and Dora Bunner had gone down to the village.

Fletcher worked fast. Someone in the house had oiled and prepared that door, and whoever had done it, had done it in order to be able to leave the drawing-room unnoticed as soon as the lights went out. That ruled out Mitzi who wouldn't have needed to use the door.

Who was left? The neighbours, Fletcher thought, might also be ruled out. He didn't see how they could have found an opportunity to oil and prepare the door. That left Patrick and Julia Simmons, Phillipa Haymes, and possibly Dora Bunner. The young Simmonses were in Milchester. Phillipa Haymes was at work. Sergeant Fletcher was free to search out any secrets he could. But the house was disappointingly innocent. Fletcher, who was an expert on electricity, could find nothing suggestive in the wiring or appurtenances of the electric fixtures to show how the lights had been fused. Making a rapid survey of the household bedrooms he found an irritating normality. In Phillipa Haymes' room were photographs of a small boy with serious eyes, an earlier photo of the same child, a pile of schoolboy letters, a theatre programme or two. In Julia's room there was a drawer full of snapshots of the south of France. Bathing photos, a villa set amidst mimosa. Patrick's held some souvenirs of Naval days. Dora Bunner's held few personal possessions and they seemed innocent enough.

And yet, thought Fletcher, someone in the house must have oiled that door.

His thoughts broke off at a sound below stairs. He went quickly to the top of the staircase and looked down. Mrs Swettenham was crossing the hall. She had a basket on her arm. She looked into the drawing-room, crossed the hall and went into the dining-room. She came out again without the basket.

Some faint sound that Fletcher made, a board that creaked unexpectedly under his feet, made her turn her head. She called up:

'Is that you, Miss Blacklock?'

'No, Mrs Swettenham, it's me,' said Fletcher.

Mrs Swettenham gave a faint scream.

'Oh! how you startled me. I thought it might be another burglar.'

Fletcher came down the stairs.

'This house doesn't seem very well protected against burglars,' he said. 'Can anybody always walk in and out just as they like?'

'I just brought up some of my quinces,' explained Mrs Swettenham. 'Miss Blacklock wants to make quince jelly and she hasn't got a quince tree here. I left them in the dining-room.'

Then she smiled.

'Oh, I see, you mean how did I get in? Well, I just came in through the side door. We all walk in and out of each other's houses, Sergeant. Nobody dreams of locking a door until it's dark. I mean it would be so awkward, wouldn't it, if you brought things and couldn't get in to leave them? It's not like the old days when you rang a bell and a servant always came to answer it.' Mrs Swettenham sighed. 'In India, I remember,' she said mournfully, 'we had eighteen servants – eighteen. Not counting the ayah. Just as a matter of course. And at home, when I was a girl, we always had three – though Mother always felt it was terribly poverty stricken not to be able to afford a kitchen-maid. I must say that I find life very odd nowadays, Sergeant, though I know one mustn't complain. So much worse for the miners always getting psittiscosis (or is that parrot disease?) and having to come out of the mines and try to be gardeners though they don't know weeds from spinach.'

She added, as she tripped towards the door, 'I mustn't keep

you. I expect you're very busy. Nothing else is going to happen, is it?'

'Why should it, Mrs Swettenham?'

'I just wondered, seeing you here. I thought it might be a *gang*. You'll tell Miss Blacklock about the quinces, won't you?'

Mrs Swettenham departed. Fletcher felt like a man who has received an unexpected jolt. He had been assuming – erroneously, he now perceived – that it must have been someone in the house who had done the oiling of the door. He saw now that he was wrong. An outsider had only to wait until Mitzi had departed by bus and Letitia Blacklock and Dora Bunner were both out of the house. Such an opportunity must have been simplicity itself. That meant that he couldn't rule out anybody who had been in the drawing-room that night.

III

'Murgatroyd!'

'Yes, Hinch?'

'I've been doing a bit of thinking.'

'Have you, Hinch?'

'Yes, the great brain has been working. You know, Murgatroyd, the whole set-up the other evening was decidedly fishy.'

'Fishy?'

'Yes. Tuck your hair up, Murgatroyd, and take this trowel. Pretend it's a revolver.'

'Oh,' said Miss Murgatroyd, nervously.

'All right. It won't bite you. Now come along to the kitchen door. You're going to be the burglar. You stand *here*. Now you're going into the kitchen to hold up a lot of nit-wits. Take the torch. Switch it on.'

'But it's broad daylight!'

'Use your imagination, Murgatroyd. Switch it on.'

Miss Murgatroyd did so, rather clumsily, shifting the trowel under one arm while she did so.

'Now then,' said Miss Hinchcliffe, 'off you go. Remember the time you played Hermia in *A Midsummer Night's Dream* at the Woman's Institute? Act. Give it all you've got. "Stick 'em up!" Those are your lines – and don't ruin them by saying "Please." '

Obediently Miss Murgatroyd raised her torch, flourished the trowel and advanced on the kitchen door.

Transferring the torch to her right hand she swiftly turned the handle and stepped forward, resuming the torch in her left hand.

'Stick 'em up!' she fluted, adding vexedly: 'Dear me, this is very difficult, Hinch.'

'Why?'

'The door. It's a swing door, it keeps coming back and I've got both hands full.'

'Exactly,' boomed Miss Hinchcliffe. 'And the drawing-room door at Little Paddocks always swings to. It isn't a swing door like this, but it won't stay open. That's why Letty Blacklock bought that absolutely delectable heavy glass door-stop from Elliot's in the High Street. I don't mind saying I've never forgiven her for getting in ahead of me there. I was beating the old brute down most successfully. He'd come down from eight guineas to six pound ten, and then Blacklock comes along and buys the damned thing. I'd never seen as attractive a doorstop, you don't often get those glass bubbles in that big size.'

'Perhaps the burglar put the doorstop against the door to keep it open,' suggested Miss Murgatroyd.

'Use your common sense, Murgatroyd. What does he do? Throw the door open, say "Excuse me a moment," stoop and put the stop into position and then resume business by saying "Hands up"? Try holding the door with your shoulder.'

'It's still very awkward,' complained Miss Murgatroyd.

'Exactly,' said Miss Hinchcliffe. 'A revolver, a torch and a door to hold open – a bit too much, isn't it? So what's the answer?'

Miss Murgatroyd did not attempt to supply an answer. She looked inquiringly and admiringly at her masterful friend and waited to be enlightened.

'We know he'd got a revolver, because he fired it,' said Miss Hinchcliffe. 'And we know he had a torch because we all saw it – that is unless we're all the victims of mass hypnotism like explanations of the Indian Rope Trick (what a bore that old Easterbrook is with his Indian stories) so the question is, did someone hold the door open for him?'

'But who could have done that?'

'Well, *you* could have for one, Murgatroyd. As far as I remember, you were standing directly behind it when the lights went out.' Miss Hinchcliffe laughed heartily. 'Highly suspicious character, aren't you, Murgatroyd? But who'd think it to look at you. Here, give me that trowel – thank heavens it isn't really a revolver. You'd have shot yourself by now!'

IV

'It's a most extraordinary thing,' muttered Colonel Easterbrook. 'Most extraordinary. Laura.'

'Yes, darling?'

'Come into my dressing-room a moment.'

'What is it, darling?'

Mrs Easterbrook appeared through the open door.

'Remember my showing you that revolver of mine?'

'Oh, yes, Archie, a nasty horrid black thing.'

'Yes. Hun souvenir. Was in this drawer, wasn't it?'

'Yes, it was.'

'Well, it's not there now.'

'Archie, how *extraordinary*!'

'You haven't moved it or anything?'

'Oh, no, I'd never dare to touch the horrid thing.'

'Think old mother whatsername did?'

'Oh, I shouldn't think so for a minute. Mrs Butt would never do a thing like that. Shall I ask her?'

'No – no, better not. Don't want to start a lot of talk. Tell me, do you remember when it was I showed it to you?'

'Oh, about a week ago. You were grumbling about your collars and the laundry and you opened this drawer wide and there it was at the back and I asked you what it was.'

'Yes, that's right. About a week ago. You don't remember the date?'

Mrs Easterbrook considered, eyelids down over her eyes, a shrewd brain working.

'Of course,' she said. 'It was Saturday. The day we were to have gone in to the pictures, but we didn't.'

'H'm – sure it wasn't before that? Wednesday? Thursday or even the week before that again?'

'No, dear,' said Mrs Easterbrook. 'I remember *quite* distinctly. It was Saturday the 30th. It just seems a long time because of all the trouble there's been. And I can tell you *how* I remember. It's because it was the day after the hold-up at Miss Blacklock's. Because when I saw your revolver it reminded me of the shooting the night before.'

'Ah,' said Colonel Easterbrook, 'then that's a great load off my mind.'

'Oh, Archie, why?'

'Just because if that revolver had disappeared before the shooting – well, it might possibly have been my revolver that was pinched by that Swiss fellow.'

'But how would he have known you had one?'

'These gangs have a most extraordinary communication service. They get to know everything about a place and who lives there.'

'What a lot you do know, Archie.'

'Ha. Yes. Seen a thing or two in my time. Still as you definitely remember seeing my revolver *after* the hold-up – well, that settles it. The revolver that Swiss fellow used can't have been mine, can it?'

'Of course it can't.'

'A great relief. I should have had to go to the police about it. And they ask a lot of awkward questions. Bound to. As a matter of fact I never took out a licence for it. Somehow, after a war, one forgets these peacetime regulations. I looked on it as a war souvenir, not as a firearm.'

'Yes, I see. Of course.'

'But all the same – where on earth can the damned thing be?'

'Perhaps Mrs Butt took it. She's always seemed quite honest, but perhaps she felt nervous after the hold-up and thought she'd like to – to have a revolver in the house. Of course, she'll never admit doing that. I shan't even ask her. She might get offended. And what should we do then? This is such a big house – I simply couldn't—'

'Quite so,' said Colonel Easterbrook. 'Better not say anything.'

—— 13 ——

MORNING ACTIVITIES IN CHIPPING CLEGHORN (CONTINUED)

Miss Marple came out of the Vicarage gate and walked down the little lane that led into the main street.

She walked fairly briskly with the aid of the Rev. Julian Harmon's stout ashplant stick.

She passed the Red Cow and the butcher's and stopped for a brief moment to look into the window of Mr Elliot's antique shop. This was cunningly situated next door to the Bluebird Tearooms and Café so that rich motorists, after stopping for a nice cup of tea and somewhat euphemistically named 'Home Made Cakes' of a bright saffron colour, could be tempted by Mr Elliot's judiciously planned shop window.

In this antique bow frame, Mr Elliot catered for all tastes. Two pieces of Waterford glass reposed on an impeccable wine cooler. A walnut bureau, made up of various bits and pieces proclaimed itself a Genuine Bargain and on a table, in the window itself, were a nice assortment of cheap doorknockers and quaint pixies, a few chipped bits of Dresden, a couple of sad-looking bead necklaces, a mug with 'A Present from Tunbridge Wells' on it, and some tit-bits of Victorian silver.

Miss Marple gave the window her rapt attention, and Mr Elliot, an elderly obese spider, peeped out of his web to appraise the possibilities of this new fly.

But just as he decided that the charms of the Present from Tunbridge Wells were about to be too much for the lady who was staying at the Vicarage (for of course Mr Elliot, like everybody else, knew exactly who she was), Miss Marple saw out of the corner of her eye Miss Dora Bunner entering the Bluebird Café, and immediately decided that what she needed to counteract the cold wind was a nice cup of morning coffee.

Four or five ladies were already engaged in sweetening their morning shopping by a pause for refreshment. Miss Marple, blinking a little in the gloom of the interior of the Bluebird, and hovering artistically, was greeted by the voice of Dora Bunner at her elbow.

'Oh, good-morning, Miss Marple. Do sit down here. I'm all alone.'

'Thank you.'

Miss Marple subsided gratefully on to the rather angular little blue-painted arm-chair which the Bluebird affected.

'Such a sharp wind,' she complained. 'And I can't walk very fast because of my rheumatic leg.'

Oh, I know. I had sciatica one year – and really most of the time I was in *agony*.'

The two ladies talked rheumatism, sciatica and neuritis for some moments with avidity. A sulky looking girl in a pink overall with a flight of bluebirds down the front of it took their order for coffee and cakes with a yawn and an air of weary patience.

'The cakes,' Miss Bunner said in a conspiratorial whisper, 'are really *quite* good here.'

'I was so interested in that very pretty girl I met as we were coming away from Miss Blacklock's the other day,' said Miss

Marple. 'I think she said she does gardening. Or is she on the land? Hynes – was that her name?'

'Oh, yes, Phillipa Haymes. Our "Lodger," as we call her.' Miss Bunner laughed at her own humour. 'Such a nice quiet girl. A *lady*, if you know what I mean.'

'I wonder now. I knew a Colonel Haymes – in the Indian cavalry. Her father perhaps?'

'She's *Mrs* Haymes. A widow. Her husband was killed in Sicily or Italy. Of course, it might be *his* father.'

'I wondered, perhaps, if there might be a little romance on the way?' Miss Marple suggested roguishly. 'With that tall young man?'

'With Patrick, do you mean? Oh, I don't—'

'No, I meant a young man with spectacles. I've seen him about.'

'Oh, of course, Edmund Swettenham. Sh! That's his mother, Mrs Swettenham, over in the corner. I don't know, I'm sure. You think he admires her? He's such an odd young man – says the most disturbing things sometimes. He's supposed to be *clever*, you know,' said Miss Bunner with frank disapproval.

'Cleverness isn't everything,' said Miss Marples, shaking her head. 'Ah, here is our coffee.'

The sulky girl deposited it with a clatter. Miss Marple and Miss Bunner pressed cakes on each other.

'I was so interested to hear you were at school with Miss Blacklock. Yours is indeed an old friendship.'

'Yes, indeed.' Miss Bunner sighed. 'Very few people would be as loyal to their old friends as dear Miss Blacklock is. Oh, dear, those days seem a long time ago. Such a pretty girl and enjoyed life so much. It all seemed so *sad*.'

Miss Marple, though with no idea of what had seemed so sad, sighed and shook her head.

'Life is indeed hard,' she murmured.

'*And sad affliction bravely borne*,' murmured Miss Bunner, her eyes suffusing with tears. 'I always think of that verse. True patience; true resignation. Such courage and patience *ought* to be rewarded, that is what I say. What I feel is that *nothing* is too good for dear Miss Blacklock, and whatever good comes to her, she truly *deserves* them.'

'Money,' said Miss Marple, 'can do a lot to ease one's path in life.'

She felt herself safe in this observation since she judged that it must be Miss Blacklock's prospects of future affluence to which her friend referred.

The remark, however, started Miss Bunner on another train of thought.

'Money!' she exclaimed with bitterness. 'I don't believe, you know, that until one has really experienced it, one can know what money, or rather the lack of it, *means.*'

Miss Marple nodded her white head sympathetically.

Miss Bunner went on rapidly, working herself up, and speaking with a flushed face:

'I've heard people say so often "I'd rather have flowers on the table than a meal without them." But how many meals have those people ever missed? They don't know what it is – nobody knows who hasn't been through it – to be really *hungry.* Bread, you know, and a jar of meat paste, and a scrape of margarine. Day after day, and how one longs for a good plate of meat and two vegetables. And the *shabbiness.* Darning one's clothes and hoping it won't show. And applying for jobs and always being told you're too old. And then perhaps getting a job and after all one isn't strong enough. One faints. And you're back again. It's the *rent* – always the *rent* – that's *got* to be paid – otherwise you're out in the street. And in these days it leaves so little over. One's old age pension doesn't go far – indeed it doesn't.'

'I know,' said Miss Marple gently. She looked with compassion at Miss Bunner's twitching face.

'I wrote to Letty. I just happened to see her name in the paper. It was a luncheon in aid of Milchester Hospital. There it was in black and white, Miss Letitia Blacklock. It brought the past back to me. I hadn't heard of her for years and years. She'd been secretary, you know, to that very rich man, Goedler. She was always a clever girl – the kind that gets on in the world. Not so much looks – as *character.* I thought – well, I thought – perhaps she'll remember me – and she's one of the people I *could* ask for a little help. I mean someone you've known as a girl – been at school with – well, they do *know* about you – they know you're not just a – begging letter-writer—'

Tears came into Dora Bunner's eyes.

'And then Lotty came and took me away – said she needed someone to help her. Of course, I was very surprised – *very* surprised – but then newspapers do get things wrong. How kind she was – and how *sympathetic.* And remembering all the old days so well . . . I'd do anything for her – I really would. And I try *very* hard, but I'm afraid sometimes I muddle things – my head's not what it was. I make mistakes. And I forget and say foolish things. She's very patient. What's so nice about her is that she always pretends that I *am* useful to her. That's real kindness, isn't it?'

Miss Marple said gently: 'Yes, that's real kindness.'

'I used to worry, you know, even after I came to Little Paddocks – about what would become of me if – if anything were to happen to Miss Blacklock. After all, there are so many accidents – these motors dashing about – one never knows, does one? But naturally I never *said* anything – but she must have guessed. Suddenly, one day she told me that she'd left me a small annuity in her will – and – what I value far more – all her beautiful furniture. I was quite *overcome* . . . But she said nobody else would value it as I should – and that is quite true – I can't bear to see some lovely piece of china smashed – or wet glasses put down on a table and leaving a mark. I do really look after her things. Some people – some people especially, are so terribly careless – and sometimes worse than careless!'

'I'm not really as stupid as I look,' Miss Bunned continued with simplicity. 'I can see, you know, when Letty's being imposed upon. Some people – I won't name names – but they take *advantage*. Dear Miss Blacklock is, perhaps, just a shade too *trusting*.'

Miss Marple shook her head.

'*That's* a mistake.'

'Yes, it is. You and I, Miss Marple, know the world. Dear Miss Blacklock—' She shook her head.

Miss Marple thought that as the secretary of a big financier Miss Blacklock might be presumed to know the world too. But probably what Dora Bunner meant was that Letty Blacklock had always been comfortably off, and that the comfortably off do not know the deeper abysses of human nature.

'That Patrick!' said Miss Bunner with a suddenness and an asperity that made Miss Marple jump. 'Twice, at least, to my knowledge, he's got money out of her. Pretending he's hard up. Run into debt. All that sort of thing. She's far too generous. All she said to me when I remonstrated with her was: "The boy's young, Dora. Youth is the time to have your fling." '

'Well, that's true enough,' said Miss Marple. 'Such a handsome young man, too.'

'Handsome is as handsome does,' said Dora Bunner. 'Much too fond of poking fun at people. And a lot of going on with girls, I expect. I'm just a figure of fun to him – that's all. He doesn't seem to realize that people have their feelings.'

'Young people *are* rather careless that way,' said Miss Marple.

Miss Bunner leaned forward suddenly with a mysterious air.

'You won't breathe a word, will you, my dear?' she demanded. 'But I can't help feeling that he *was* mixed up in this dreadful business. I think he knew that young man – or else Julia did. I daren't hint at such a thing to dear Miss Blacklock – at least I did, and she just snapped my head off. And, of course, it's *awkward* – because he's her nephew – or at any rate her *cousin* – and if the Swiss young man shot himself Patrick might be held morally responsible, mightn't he? If he'd put him up to it, I mean. I'm really terribly confused about the whole thing. Everyone making such a fuss about that other door into the drawing-room. That's another thing that worries me – the detective saying it had been oiled. Because you see, I saw—'

She came to an abrupt stop.

Miss Marple paused to select a phrase.

'Most difficult for you,' she said sympathetically. 'Naturally you wouldn't want anything to get round to the police.'

'That's just it,' Dora Bunner cried. 'I lie awake at nights and worry . . . because, you see, I came upon Patrick in the shubbery the other day. I was looking for eggs – one hen lays out – and there he was holding a feather and a cup – an oily cup. And he jumped most guiltily when he saw me and he said: "I was just wondering what this was doing here." Well, of course, he's a quick thinker. I should say he thought that up quickly when I startled him. And how did he come to find a thing like that in the shrubbery unless he was looking for it, knowing perfectly well it was there. Of course, I didn't *say* anything.'

'No, no, of course not.'

'But I gave him a *look*, if you know what I mean.'

Dora Bunner stretched out her hand and bit abstractedly into a lurid salmon-coloured cake.

'And then another day I happened to overhear him having a very curious conversation with Julia. They seemed to be having a kind of quarrel. He was saying: "If I thought you had anything to do with a thing like that!" and Julia (she's always so calm, you know) said: "Well, little brother, what would you do about it?" And then, *most* unfortunately, I trod on that board that always squeaks, and they saw me. So I said, quite gaily: "You two having a quarrel?" and Patrick said, "I'm warning Julia not to go in for these black market deals." Oh, it was all very slick, but I don't believe they were talking about anything of the sort! And if you ask me, I believe Patrick had tampered with that lamp in the drawing-room – to make the lights go out, because I remember distinctly that it was the shepherdess – *not* the shepherd. And the next day—'

She stopped and her face grew pink. Miss Marple turned her head to see Miss Blacklock standing behind them – she must just have come in.

'Coffee and gossip, Bunny?' said Miss Blacklock, with quite a shade of reproach in her voice. 'Good-morning, Miss Marple. Cold isn't it?'

'We were just talking,' said Miss Bunner, hurriedly. 'So many rules and regulations nowadays. One really doesn't know where one is.'

The doors flew open with a clang and Bunch Harmon came into the Bluebird with a rush.

'Hallo,' she said, 'am I too late for coffee?'

'No, dear,' said Miss Marple. 'Sit down and have a cup.'

'We must get home,' said Miss Blacklock. 'Done your shopping, Bunny?'

Her tone was indulgent once more, but her eyes still held a slight reproach.

'Yes – yes, thank you, Letty. I must just pop into the chemists in passing and get some aspirin and some cornplasters.'

As the doors of the Bluebird swung to behind them, Bunch asked:

'What were you talking about?'

Miss Marple did not reply at once. She waited whilst Bunch gave the order, then she said:

'Family solidarity is a very strong thing. Very strong. Do you remember some famous case – I really can't remember what it was. They said the husband poisoned his wife. In a glass of wine. Then, at the trial, the daughter said she'd drunk half her mother's glass – so that knocked the case against her father to pieces. They do say – but that may be just rumour – that she never spoke to her father or lived with him again. Of course, a father is one thing – and a nephew or a distant cousin is another. But still there it is – no one wants a member of their own family hanged, do they?'

'No,' said Bunch, considering. 'I shouldn't think they would.'

Miss Marple leaned back in her chair. She murmured under her breath, 'People are really very alike, everywhere.'

'Who am I like?'

'Well, really, dear, you are very much like yourself. I don't know that you remind me of anyone in particular. Except perhaps—'

'Here it comes,' said Bunch.

'I was just thinking of a parlourmaid of mine, dear.'

'A parlourmaid? I should make a terrible parlourmaid.'

'Yes, dear, so did she. She was no good at all at waiting at table. Put everything on the table crooked, mixed up the kitchen knives with the dining-room ones, and her cap (this was a long time ago, dear) her cap was *never* straight.'

Bunch adjusted her hat automatically.

'Anything else?' she demanded anxiously.

'I kept her because she was so pleasant to have about the house – and because she used to make me laugh. I liked the way she said things straight out. Came to me one day, "Of course, I don't know, ma'am," she says, "but Florrie, they way she sits down, it's just like a married woman." And sure enough poor Florrie was in trouble – the gentlemanly assistant at the hairdresser's. Fortunately it was in good time, and I was able to have a little talk with him, and they had a very nice wedding and settled down quite happily. She was a good girl, Florrie, but inclined to be taken in by a gentlemanly appearance.'

'She didn't do a murder, did she?' asked Bunch. 'The parlourmaid, I mean.'

'No, indeed,' said Miss Marple. 'She married a Baptist Minister and they had a family of five.'

'Just like me,' said Bunch. 'Though I've only got as far as Edward and Susan up to date.'

She added, after a minute or two:

'Who are you thinking about now, Aunt Jane?'

'Quite a lot of people, dear, quite a lot of people,' said Miss Marple, vaguely.

'In St Mary Mead?'

'Mostly . . . I was really thinking about Nurse Ellerton – really an excellent kindly woman. Took care of an old lady, seemed really fond of her. Then the old lady died. And another came and *she* died. Morphia. It all came out. Done in the kindest way, and the shocking thing was that the woman herself really couldn't see that she'd done anything wrong. They hadn't long to live in any case, she said, and one of them had cancer and quite a lot of pain.'

'You mean – it was a mercy killing?'

'No, *no*. They signed their money away to her. She liked money, you know . . .'

'And then there was that young man in the liner – Mrs Pusey at the paper shop, *her* nephew. Brought home stuff he'd stolen and got her to dispose of it. Said it was things that he'd bought abroad. She was quit taken in. And then when the police came round and started asking questions, he tried to bash her on the head, so that she shouldn't be able to give him away. . . . Not a nice young man – but very good looking. Had two girls in love with him. He spent a lot of money on one of them.'

'The nastiest one, I suppose,' said Bunch.

'Yes, dear. And there was Mrs Cray at the wool shop. Devoted to her son, spoilt him, of course. He got in with a very queer lot. Do you remember, Joan Croft, Bunch?'

'N-no, I don't think so.'

'I thought you might have seen her when you were with me on a visit. Used to stalk about smoking a cigar or a pipe. We had a Bank hold-up once, and Joan Croft was in the Bank at the time. She knocked the man down and took his revolver away from him. She was congratulated on her courage by the Bench.'

Bunch listened attentively. She seemed to be learning by heart.

'And—?' she prompted.

'That girl at St Jean des Collines that summer. Such a quiet girl – not so much quiet as silent. Everybody liked her, but they never got to know her much better . . . We heard afterwards that her husband was a *forger*. It made her feel cut off from people. It made her, in the end, a little queer. Brooding does, you know.'

'Any Anglo-Indian Colonels in your reminiscences, darling?'

'Naturally, dear. There was Major Vaughan at The Larches and Colonel Wright at Simla Lodge. Nothing wrong with either of them. But I do remember Mr Hodgson, the Bank Manager, went on a cruise and married a woman young enough to be his daughter. No idea of where she came from – except what she told him of course.'

'And that wasn't true?'

'No, dear, it definitely wasn't.'

'Not bad,' said Bunch, nodding, and ticking off on her fingers. 'We've had devoted Dora, and handsome Patrick, and Mrs Swettenham and Edmund, and Phillipa Haymes, and Colonel Easterbrook and Mrs Easterbrook – and if you ask me, I should say you're absolutely right about *her*. But there wouldn't be any reason for her murdering Letty Blacklock.'

'Miss Blacklock, of course, might know something about her that she didn't want known.'

'Oh, darling, that old Tanqueray stuff? Surely that's dead as the hills.'

'It might not be. You see, Bunch, you are not the kind that minds much about what people think of you.'

'I see what you mean,' said Bunch suddenly. 'If you'd been up against it, and then, rather like a shivering stray cat, you'd found a home and cream and a warm stroking hand and you were called Pretty Pussy and somebody thought the world of you . . . You'd do a lot to keep that . . . Well, I must say, you've presented with a very complete gallery of people.'

'You didn't get them all right, you know,' said Miss Marple, mildly.

'Didn't I? Where did I slip up? Julia? *Julia, pretty Julia is peculiar.*'

'Three and sixpence,' said the sulky waitress, materialising out of the gloom.

'And,' she added, her bosom heaving beneath the bluebirds, 'I'd like to know, Mrs Harmon, why you call me peculiar. I had an Aunt who joined the Peculiar People, but I've always been good Church of England myself, as the late Rev. Hopkinson can tell you.'

'I'm terribly sorry,' said Bunch. 'I was just quoting a song. I didn't mean you at all. I didn't know your name was Julia.'

'Quite a coincidence,' said the sulky waitress, cheering up. 'No offence, I'm sure, but hearing my name, as I thought – well, naturally if you think someone's talking about you, it's only human to listen. Thank you.'

She departed with her tip.

'Aunt Jane,' said Bunch, 'don't look so upset. What is it?'

'But surely,' murmured Miss Marple. 'That couldn't be so. There's no *reason*—'

'Aunt Jane!'

Miss Marple sighed and then smiled brightly.

'It's nothing, dear,' she said.

'Did you think you knew who did the murder?' asked Bunch. 'Who was it?'

'I don't know at all,' said Miss Marple. 'I got an idea for a moment – but it's gone. I wish I did know. Time's so short. So terribly short.'

'What do you mean short?'

'That old lady up in Scotland may die any moment.'

Bunch said, staring:
'Then you really do believe in Pip and Emma. You think it was them – and that they'll try again?'
'Of course they'll try again,' said Miss Marple, almost absent-mindedly. 'If they tried once, they'll try again. If you've made up your mind to murder someone, you don't stop because the first time it didn't come off. Especially if you're fairly sure you're not suspected.'
'But if it's Pip and Emma,' said Bunch, 'there are only two people it *could* be. It *must* be Patrick and Julia. They're brother and sister and they're the only ones who are the right age.'
'My dear, it isn't nearly as simple as that. There are all sorts of ramifications and combinations. There's Pip's wife if he's married, or Emma's husband. There's their mother – she's an interested party even if she doesn't inherit direct. If Letty Blacklock hasn't seen her for thirty years, she'd probably not recognize her now. One elderly woman is very like another. You remember Mrs Wotherspoon drew her own and Mrs Bartlett's Old Age Pension although Mrs Bartlett had been dead for years. Anyway, Miss Blacklock's short-sighted. Haven't you noticed how she peers at people? And then there's the father. Apparently he was a real bad lot.'
'Yes, but he's a foreigner.'
'By birth. But there's no reason to believe he speaks broken English and gesticulates with his hands. I dare say he could play the part of – of an Anglo-Indian Colonel as well as anybody else.'
'Is *that* what you think?'
'No, I don't. I don't indeed, dear. I just think that there's a great deal of money at stake, a great deal of money. And I'm afraid I know only too well the really terrible things that people will do to lay their hands on a lot of money.'
'I suppose they will,' said Bunch. 'It doesn't really do them any good, does it? Not in the end?'
'No – but they don't usually know that.'
'I can understand it.' Bunch smiled suddenly, her sweet rather crooked smile. 'One feels it would be different for oneself . . . Even I feel that.' She considered: 'You pretend to yourself that you'd do a lot of good with all that money. Schemes . . . Homes for Unwanted Children . . . Tired Mothers . . . A lovely rest abroad somewhere for elderly women who have worked too hard . . .'
Her face grew sombre. Her eyes were suddenly dark and tragic.

'I know what you're thinking,' she said to Miss Marple. 'You're thinking that I'd be the worst kind. Because I'd kid myself. If you just wanted the money for selfish reasons you'd at any rate *see* what you were like. But once you began to pretend about doing good with it, you'd be able to persuade yourself, perhaps, that it wouldn't very much matter killing someone . . .'
Then her eyes cleared.
'But I shouldn't,' she said. 'I shouldn't really kill anyone. Not even if they were old, or ill, or doing a lot of harm in the world. Not even if they were blackmailers or – or absolute *beasts*.' She fished a fly carefully out of the dregs of the coffee and arranged it on the table to dry. 'Because people like living, don't they? So do flies. Even if you'd old and in pain and can just crawl out in the sun. Julian says those people like living even more than young strong people do. It's harder, he says, for them to die, the struggle's greater. I like living myself – not just being happy and enjoying myself and having a good time. I mean *living* – waking up and feeling, all over me, that I'm *there* – ticking over.'
She blew on the fly gently; it waved its legs, and flew rather drunkenly away.
'Cheer up, darling Aunt Jane,' said Bunch. '*I*'d never kill anybody.'

—— 14 ——

EXCURSION INTO THE PAST

After a night in the train, Inspector Craddock alighted at a small station in the Highlands.
It struck him for a moment as strange that the wealthy Mrs Goedler – an invalid – with a choice of a London house in a fashionable square, an estate in Hampshire, and a villa in the South of France, should have selected this remote Scottish home as her residence. Surely she was cut off here from many friends and distractions. It must be a lonely life – or was she too ill to notice or care about her surroundings?
A car was waiting to meet him. A big old-fashioned Daimler with an elderly chauffeur driving it. It was a sunny morning and the Inspector enjoyed the twenty-mile drive, though he marvelled anew at this preference for isolation. A tentative remark to the chauffeur brought partial enlightenment.

'It's her own home as a girl. Ay, she's the last of the family. And she and Mr Goedler were always happier here than anywhere, though it wasn't often he could get away from London. But when he did they enjoyed themselves like a couple of bairns.'

When the grey walls of the old keep came in sight, Craddock felt that time was slipping backwards. An elderly butler received him, and after a wash and a shave he was shown into a room with a huge fire burning in the grate, and breakfast was served to him.

After breakfast, a tall, middle-aged woman in nurse's dress, with a pleasant and competent manner, came in and introduced herself as Sister McClelland.

'I have my patient all ready for you, Mr Craddock. She is, indeed, looking forward to seeing you.'

'I'll do my best not to excite her,' Craddock promised.

'I had better warn you of what will happen. You will find Mrs Goedler apparently quite normal. She will talk and enjoy talking and then – quite suddenly – her powers will fail. Come away at once, then, and send for me. She is, you see, kept almost entirely under the influence of morphia. She drowses most of the time. In preparation for your visit, I have given her a strong stimulant. As soon as the effect of the stimulant wears off, she will relapse into semi-consciousness.'

'I quite understand, Miss McClelland. Would it be in order for you to tell me exactly what the state of Mrs Goedler's health is?'

'Well, Mr Craddock, she is a dying woman. Her life cannot be prolonged for more than a few weeks. To say that she should have been dead years ago would strike you as odd, yet it is the truth. What has kept Mrs Goedler alive is her intense enjoyment and love of being alive. That sounds, perhaps, an odd thing to say of someone who has lived the life of an invalid for many years and has not left her home here for fifteen years, but it is true. Mrs Goedler has never been a strong woman – but she has retained to an astonishing degree the will to live.' She added with a smile, 'She is a very charming woman, too, as you will find.'

Craddock was shown into a large bedroom where a fire was burning and where an old lady lay in a large canopied bed. Though she was only about seven or eight years older than Letitia Blacklock, her fragility made her seem older than her years.

Her white hair was carefully arranged, a froth of pale blue

wool enveloped her neck and shoulders. There were lines of pain on the face, but lines of sweetness, too. And there was strangely enough, what Craddock could only describe as a roguish twinkle in her faded blue eyes.

'Well, this is interesting,' she said. 'It's not often I receive a visit from the police. I hear Letitia Blacklock wasn't much hurt by this attempt on her? How is my dear Blackie?'

'She's very well, Mrs Goedler. She sent you her love.'

'It's a long time since I've seen her . . . For many years now, it's been just a card at Christmas. I asked her to come up here when she came back to England after Charlotte's death, but she said it would be painful after so long and perhaps she was right . . . Blackie always had a lot of sense. I had an old school friend to see me about a year ago, and, lor!' – she smiled – 'we bored each other to death. After we'd finished all the "Do you remembers?" there wasn't anything to say. *Most* embarrassing.'

Craddock was content to let her talk before pressing his questions. He wanted, as it were, to get back into the past, to get the feel of the Goedler-Blacklock ménage.

'I suppose,' said Belle shrewdly, 'that you want to ask about the money? Randall left it all to go to Blackie after my death. Really, of course, Randall never dreamed that I'd outlive him. He was a big strong man, never a day's illness, and I was always a mass of aches and pains and complaints and doctors coming and pulling long faces over me.'

'I don't think complaints would be the right word, Mrs Goedler.'

The old lady chuckled.

'I didn't mean it in the complaining sense. I've never been *too* sorry for myself. But it was always taken for granted that I, being the weakly one, would go first. It didn't work out that way. No – it didn't work out that way . . .'

'Why, exactly, did your husband leave his money the way he did?'

'You mean, why did he leave it to Blackie? Not for the reason you've probably been thinking.' The roguish twinkle was very apparent. 'What minds you policemen have! Randall was never in the least in love with her and she wasn't with him. Letitia, you know, has really got a man's mind. She hasn't any feminine feelings or weaknesses. I don't believe she was ever in love with any man. She was never particularly pretty and she didn't care for clothes. She used a little make-up in deference to prevailing custom, but not to make herself look prettier.' There was pity in the old voice as she went on: 'She never knew any of the fun of being a woman.'

Craddock looked at the frail little figure in the big bed with interest. Belle Goedler, he realised, *had* enjoyed – still enjoyed – being a woman. She twinkled at him.

'I've always thought,' she said, 'it must be terribly dull to be a man.'

Then she said thoughtfully:

'I think Randall looked on Blackie very much as a kind of younger brother. He relied on her judgment which was always excellent. She kept him out of trouble more than once, you know.'

'She told me that she came to his rescue once with money?'

'That, yes, but I meant more than that. One can speak the truth after all these years. Randall couldn't really distinguish between what was crooked and what wasn't. His conscience wasn't sensitive. The poor dear really didn't know what was just smart – and what was dishonest. Blackie kept him straight. That's one thing about Letitia Blacklock, she's absolutely dead straight. She would never do anything that was dishonest. She's a very fine character, you know. I've always admired her. They had a terrible girlhood, those girls. The father was an old country doctor – terrifically pig-headed and narrow-minded – the complete family tyrant. Letitia broke away, came to London, and trained herself as a chartered accountant. The other sister was an invalid, there was a deformity of kinds and she never saw people or went out. That's why when the old man died, Letitia gave up everything to go home and look after her sister. Randall was wild with her – but it made no difference. If Letitia thought a thing was her duty she'd do it. And you couldn't move her.'

'How long was that before your husband died?'

'A couple of years, I think. Randall made his will before she left the firm, and he didn't alter it. He said to me: "We've no one of our own." (Our little boy died, you know, when he was two years old.) "After you and I are gone, Blackie had better have the money. She'll play the markets and make 'em sit up.'

'You see,' Belle went on,' 'Randall enjoyed the whole money making game so much – it wasn't just the money – it was the adventure, the risks, the excitement of it all. And Blackie liked it too. She had the same adventurous spirit and the same judgment. Poor darling, she'd never had any of the usual fun – being in love, and leading men on and teasing them – and having a home and children and all the real fun of life.'

Craddock thought it was odd, the real pity and indulgent contempt felt by this woman, a woman whose life had been hampered by illness, whose only child had died, whose husband had
died, leaving her to a lonely widowhood, and who had been a
hopeless invalid for years.

She nodded her head at him.

'I know what you're thinking. But I've *had* all the things that
make life worth while – they may have been taken from me – but
I have had them. I was pretty and gay as a girl, I married the
man I loved, and he never stopped loving me . . . My child died,
but I had him for two precious years . . . I've had a lot of physical
pain – but if you have pain, you know how to enjoy the exquisite
pleasure of the times when pain stops. And everyone's been kind
to me, always . . . I'm a lucky woman, really.'

Craddock seized upon an opening in her former remarks.

'You said just now, Mrs Goedler, that your husband left his
fortune to Miss Blacklock because he had no one else to leave it
to. But that's not strictly true, is it? He had a sister.'

'Oh, Sonia. But they quarrelled years ago and made a clean
break of it.'

'He disapproved of her marriage?'

'Yes, she married a man called – now what was his name—?'

'Stamfordis.'

'That's it. Dmitri Stamfordis. Randall always said he was a
crook. The two men didn't like each other from the first. But
Sonia was wildly in love with him and quite determined to
marry him. And I really never saw why she couldn't. Men have
such odd ideas about these things. Sonia wasn't a mere girl – she
was twenty-five, and she knew exactly what she was doing. He
was a crook, I dare say – I mean really a crook. I believe he had
a criminal record – and Randall always suspected the name he
was passing under wasn't his own. Sonia knew all that. The point
was, which of course Randall couldn't appreciate, that Dmitri
was really a wildly attractive person to women. And he was just
as much in love with Sonia as she was with him. Randall insisted
that he was just marrying her for her money – but that wasn't
true. Sonia was very handsome, you know. And she had plenty of
spirit. If the marriage had turned out badly, if Dmitri had been
unkind to her or unfaithful to her, she would just have cut her
losses and walked out on him. She was a rich woman and could
do as she chose with her life.'

'The quarrel was never made up?'

'No. Randall and Sonia never had got on very well. She resented his trying to prevent the marriage. She said, "Very well. You're quite impossible! This is the last you hear of me!"'

'But it was not the last you heard of her?'

Belle smiled.

'No, I got a letter from her about eighteen months afterwards. She wrote from Budapest, I remember, but she didn't give an address. She told me to tell Randall that she was extremely happy and that she'd just had twins.'

'And she told you their names?'

Again Belle smiled. 'She said they were born just after mid-day – and she intended to call them Pip and Emma. That may have been just a joke, of course.'

'Didn't you hear from her again?'

'No. She said she and her husband and the babies were going to America on a short stay. I never heard any more . . .'

'You don't happen, I suppose, to have kept that letter?'

'No, I'm afraid not . . . I read it to Randall and he just grunted: 'She'll regret marrying that fellow one of these days.' That's all he ever said about it. We really forgot about her. She went right out of our lives . . .'

'Nevertheless Mr Goedler left his estate to her children in the event of Miss Blacklock predeceasing you?'

'Oh, that was my doing. I said to him, when he told me about the will: "And suppose Blackie dies before I do?" He was quite surprised. I said, "Oh, I know Blackie is as strong as a horse and I'm a delicate creature – but there's such a thing as accidents, you know, and there's such a thing as creaking gates . . ." And he said, "There's no one – absolutely no one." I said, "There's Sonia." And he said at once, "And let that fellow get hold of my money? No – indeed!" I said, "Well, her children then. Pip and Emma, and there may be lots more by now" – and so he grumbled, but he did put it in.'

'And from that day to this,' Craddock said slowly, 'you've heard nothing of your sister-in-law or her children?'

'Nothing – they may be dead – they may be – anywhere.'

They may be in Chipping Cleghorn, thought Craddock.

As though she read his thoughts, a look of alarm came into Belle Goedler's eyes. She said, 'Don't let them hurt Blackie. Blackie's *good* –really good – you mustn't let harm come to—'

Her voice trailed off suddenly. Craddock saw the sudden grey shadows round her mouth and eyes.

'You're tired,' he said. 'I'll go.'

She nodded.

'Send Mac to me,' she whispered. 'Yes, tired . . .' She made a feeble motion of her hand. 'Look after Blackie . . . Nothing must happen to Blackie . . . look after her . . .'

'I'll do my very best, Mrs Goedler.' He rose and went to the door.

Her voice, a thin thread of sound, followed him . . .

'Not long now – until I'm dead – dangerous for her— Take care . . .'

Sister McClelland passed him as he went out. He said, uneasily:

'I hope I haven't done her harm.'

'Oh, I don't think so, Mr Craddock. I told you she would tire quite suddenly.'

Later, he asked the nurse:

'The only thing I hadn't time to ask Mrs Goedler was whether she had any old photographs? If so, I wonder—'

She interrupted him.

'I'm afraid there's nothing of that kind. All her personal papers and things were stored with their furniture from the London house at the beginning of the war. Mrs Goedler was desperately ill at the time. Then the storage depository was blitzed. Mrs Goedler was very upset at losing so many personal souvenirs and family papers. I'm afraid there's nothing of that kind.'

So that was that, Craddock thought.

Yet he felt his journey had not been in vain. Pip and Emma, those twin wraiths, were not quite wraiths.

Craddock thought, 'Here's a brother and sister brought up somewhere in Europe. Sonia Goedler was a rich woman at the time of her marriage, but money in Europe hasn't remained money. Queer things have happened to money during these war years. And so there are two young people, the son and daughter of a man who had a criminal record. Suppose they came to England, more or less penniless. What would they do? Find out about any rich relatives. Their uncle, a man of vast fortune, is dead. Possibly the first thing they'd do would be to look up their uncle's will. See if by any chance money had been left to them or to their mother. So they go to Somerset House and learn the contents of his will, and then, perhaps, they learn of the existence of Miss Letitia Blacklock. Then they make inquiries about Randall Goedler's widow. She's an invalid, living up in Scotland, and they find out she hasn't long to live. *If this Letitia Blacklock dies before her,* they will come into a vast fortune. What then?'

Craddock thought, 'They wouldn't go to Scotland. They'd find out where Letitia Blacklock is living now. And they'd go there – but not as themselves . . . They'd go together – or separately? Emma . . . I wonder? . . . Pip and Emma . . , I'll eat my hat if Pip, or Emma, or both of them, aren't in Chipping Cleghorn now . . .'

—— 15 ——

DELICIOUS DEATH

I

In the kitchen at Little Paddocks, Miss Blacklock was giving instructions to Mitzi.

'Sardine sandwiches as well as the tomato ones. And some of those little scones you make so nicely. And I'd like you to make that special cake of yours.'

'Is it a party then, that you want all these things?'

'It's Miss Bunner's birthday, and some people will be coming to tea.'

'At her age one does not have birthdays. It is better to forget.'

'Well, she doesn't want to forget. Several people are bringing her presents – and it will be nice to make a little party of it.'

'That is what you say last time – and see what happened!'

Miss Blacklock controlled her temper.

'Well, it won't happen this time.'

'How do you know what may happen in this house? All day long I shiver and at night I lock my door and I look in the wardrobe to see no one is hidden there.'

'That ought to keep you nice and safe,' said Miss Blacklock, coldly.

'The cake that you want me to make, it is the—?' Mitzi uttered a sound that to Miss Blacklock's English ear sounded like Schwitzebzr or alternatively like cats spitting at each other.

'That's the one. The rich one.'

'Yes. It is rich. For it I have *nothing*! Impossible to make such a cake. I need for it chocolate and much butter, and sugar and raisins.'

'You can use this tin of butter that was sent us from America. And some of the raisins we were keeping for Christmas, and here is a slab of chocolate and a pound of sugar.'

Mitzi's face suddenly burst into radiant smiles.

'So, I make him for you good – good,' she cried, in an ecstasy. 'It will be rich, rich, of a melting richness! And on top I will put the icing – chocolate icing – I make him so nice – and write on it *Good Wishes*. These English people with their cakes that tastes of sand, never *never*, will they have tasted such a cake. Delicious, they will say – delicious—'

Her face clouded again.

'Mr Patrick. He called it Delicious Death. My cake! I will not have my cake called that!'

'It was a compliment really,' said Miss Blacklock. 'He meant it was worth dying to eat such a cake.'

Mitzi looked at her doubtfully.

'Well, I do not like that word – *death*. They are not dying because they eat my cake, no, they feel much, much better . . .'

'I'm sure we all shall.'

Miss Blacklock turned away and left the kitchen with a sigh of relief at the successful ending of the interview. With Mitzi one never knew.

She ran into Dora Bunner outside.

'Oh, Letty, shall I run in and tell Mitzi just how to cut the sandwiches?'

'No,' said Miss Blacklock, steering her friend firmly into the hall. 'She's in a good mood now and I don't want her disturbed.'

'But I could just show her—'

'Please don't show her *anything*, Dora. These Central Europeans don't *like* being shown. They hate it.'

Dora looked at her doubtfully. Then she suddenly broke into smiles.

'Edmund Swettenham just rang up. He wished me many happy returns of the day and said he was bringing me a pot of honey as a present this afternoon. Isn't it kind? I can't imagine how he knew it was my birthday.'

'Everybody seems to know. You must have been talking about it, Dora.'

'Well, I did just happen to mention that today I should be fifty-nine.'

'You're sixty-four,' said Miss Blacklock with a twinkle.

'And Miss Hinchcliffe said, 'You don't look it. What age do you think *I* am?'' Which was rather awkward because Miss Hinchcliffe always looks so peculiar that she might be any age. She said she was bringing me some eggs, by the way. I said our hens hadn't been laying very well, lately.'

'We're not doing so badly out of your birthday,' said Miss Blacklock. 'Honey, eggs – a magnificent box of chocolates from Julia—'

'I don't know where she gets such things.'

'Better not ask. Her methods are probably strictly illegal.'

'And your lovely brooch.' Miss Bunner looked down proudly at her bosom on which was pinned a small diamond leaf.

'Do you like it? I'm glad. I never cared for jewellery.'

'I love it.'

'Good. Let's go and feed the ducks.'

II

'Ha,' cried Patrick dramatically, as the party took their places round the dining-room table. 'What do I see before me? *Delicious Death.*'

'Hush,' said Miss Blacklock. 'Don't let Mitzi hear you. She objects to your name for her cake very much.'

'Nevertheless, Delicious Death it is! Is it Bunny's birthday cake?'

'Yes, it is,' said Miss Bunner. 'I really am having the most wonderful birthday.'

Her cheeks were flushed with excitement and had been ever since Colonel Easterbrook had handed her a small box of sweets and declaimed with a bow, 'Sweets to the Sweet!'

Julia had turned her head away hurriedly, and had been frowned at by Miss Blacklock.

Full justice was done to the good things on the tea table and they rose from their seats after a round of crackers.

'I feel slightly sick,' said Julia. 'It's that cake. I remember I felt just the same last time.'

'It's worth it,' said Patrick.

'These foreigners certainly understand confectionery,' said Miss Hinchcliffe. 'What they can't make is a plain boiled pudding.'

Everybody was respectfully silent, though it seemed to be hovering on Patrick's lips to ask if anyone really *wanted* a plain boiled pudding.

317

'Got a new gardener?' asked Miss Hinchcliffe of Miss Black-lock as they returned to the drawing-room.

'No, why?'

'Saw a man snooping round the henhouse. Quite a decent-looking Army type.'

'Oh, *that*,' said Julia. 'That's our detective.'

Mrs Easterbrook dropped her handbag.

'Detective?' she exclaimed. 'But – but – why?'

'I don't know,' said Julia. 'He prowls about and keeps an eye on the house. He's protecting Aunt Letty, I suppose.'

'Absolute nonsense,' said Miss Blacklock. 'I can protect my-self, thank you.'

'But surely it's all over now,' cried Mrs Easterbrook. 'Though I meant to ask you, why did they adjourn the inquest?'

'Police aren't satisfied,' said her husband. 'That's what that means.'

'But aren't satisfied of what?'

Colonel Easterbrook shook his head with the air of a man who could say a good deal more if he chose. Edmund Swetten-ham, who disliked the Colonel said, 'The truth of it is, we're all under suspicion.'

'But suspicion of *what*?' repeated Mrs Easterbrook.

'Never mind kitten,' said her husband.

'Loitering with intent,' said Edmund. 'The intent being to commit murder upon the first opportunity.'

'Oh, don't, please, don't, Mr Swettenham.' Dora Bunner be-gan to cry. 'I'm sure nobody here could possibly want to kill dear, dear Letty.'

There was a moment of horrible embarrassment, Edmund turned scarlet, murmured, 'Just a joke.' Phillipa suggested in a high clear voice that they might listen to the six o'clock news and the suggestion was received with enthusiastic assent.

'Patrick murmured to Julia: 'We need Mrs Harmon here. She'd be sure to say in that high clear voice of hers, "But I sup-pose somebody *is* still waiting for a good chance to murder you, Miss Blacklock?"'

'I'm glad she and that old Miss Marple couldn't come,' said Julia. 'That old woman is the prying kind. And a mind like a sink, I should think. Real Victorian type.'

Listening to the news led easily into a pleasant discussion on the horrors of atomic warfare. Colonel Easterbrook said that the real menace to civilisation was undoubtedly Russia, and Edmund said that he had several charming Russian friends – which announcement was coldly received.

The party broke up with renewed thanks to the hostess.

'Enjoy yourself, Bunny?' asked Miss Blacklock, as the last guest was sped.

'Oh, I did. But I've got a terrible headache. It's the excitement, I think.'

'It's the cake,' said Patrick. 'I feel a bit liverish myself. And you've been nibbling chocolates all the morning.'

'I'll go and lie down, I think,' said Miss Bunner. 'I'll take a couple of aspirins and try and have a nice sleep.'

'That would be a very good plan,' said Miss Blacklock.

Miss Bunner departed upstairs.

'Shall I shut up the ducks for you, Aunt Letty?'

Miss Blacklock looked at Patrick severely.

'If you'll be sure to latch that door properly.'

'I will. I swear I will.'

'Have a glass of sherry, Aunt Letty,' said Julia. 'As my old nurse used to say, "It will settle your stomach." A revolting phrase, but curiously apposite at this moment.'

'Well, I dare say it might be a good thing. The truth is one isn't used to rich things. Oh, Bunny, how you made me jump. What is it?'

'I can't find my aspirin,' said Miss Bunner disconsolately.

'Well, take some of mine, dear, they're by my bed.'

'There's a bottle on my dressing-table,' said Phillipa.

'Thank you – thank you very much. If I can't find mine – but I know I've got it *somewhere*. A new bottle. Now where could I have put it?'

'There's heaps in the bathroom,' said Julia impatiently. 'This house is chock full of aspirin.'

'It vexes me to be so careless and mislay things,' replied Miss Bunner, retreating up the stairs again.

'Poor old Bunny,' said Julia, holding up her glass. 'Do you think we ought to have given her some sherry?'

'Better not, I think,' said Miss Blacklock. 'She's had a lot of excitement today, and it isn't really good for her. I'm afraid she'll be the worse for it tomorrow. Still, I really do think she has enjoyed herself!'

'She's loved it,' said Phillipa.

'Let's give Mitzi a glass of sherry,' suggested Julia. 'Hi, Pat,' she called as she heard him entering the side door. 'Fetch Mitzi.'

So Mitzi was brought in and Julia poured her out a glass of sherry.

'Here's to the best cook in the world,' said Patrick.

Mitzi was gratified – but felt nevertheless that a protest was due.

'That is not so. I am not really a cook. In my country I do intellectual work.'

'Then you're wasted,' said Patrick. 'What's intellectual work compared to a *chef d'œuvre* like Delicious Death?'

'Oo – I say to you I do not like—'

'Never mind what you like, my girl,' said Patrick. 'That's my name for it and here's to it. Let's all drink to Delicious Death and to hell with the after effects.'

III

'Phillipa, my dear, I want to talk to you.'

'Yes, Miss Blacklock?'

Phillipa Haymes looked up in slight surprise.

'You're not worrying about anything, are you?'

'Worrying?'

'I've noticed that you've looked worried lately. There isn't anything wrong, is there?'

'Oh no, Miss Blacklock. Why should there be?'

'Well – I wondered. I thought, perhaps that you and Patrick—?'

'Patrick?' Phillipa looked really surprised.

'It's not so, then. Please forgive me if I've been impertinent. But you've been thrown together a lot – and although Patrick is my cousin, I don't think he's the type to make a satisfactory husband. Not for some time to come, at all events.'

Phillipa's face had frozen into a hard immobility.

'I shan't marry again,' she said.

'Oh, yes, you will someday, my child. You're wrong. But we needn't discuss that. There's no other trouble. You're not worried about – money, for instance?'

'No, I'm quite all right.'

'I know you get anxious sometimes about your boy's education. That's why I want to tell you something. I drove into Milchester this afternoon to see Mr Beddingfeld, my lawyer. Things haven't been very settled lately and I thought I would like to

make a new will – in view of certain eventalities. Apart from
Bunny's legacy, everything goes to you, Phillipa.'
'What?' Phillipa spun round. Her eyes stared. She looked dis-
mayed, almost frightened.
'But I don't want it – really I don't . . . Oh, I'd rather not . . .
And anyhow, why? Why to *me*?'
'Perhaps,' said Miss Blacklock in a peculiar voice, 'because
there's no one else.'
'But there's Patrick and Julia.'
'Yes, there's Patrick and Julia.' The odd note in Miss Black-
lock's voice was still there.
'They are your relations.'
'Very distant ones. They have no claim on me.'
'But I – I haven't either – I don't know what you think . . .
Oh, I don't want it.'
Her gaze held more hostility than gratitude. There was some-
thing almost like fear in her manner.
'I know what I'm doing, Phillipa. I've become fond of you –
and there's the boy . . . You won't get very much if I should die
now – but in a few weeks' time it might be different.'
Her eyes met Phillipa's steadily.
'But you're not going to die!' Phillipa protested.
'Not if I can avoid it by taking due precautions.'
'Precautions?'
'Yes. Think it over . . . And don't worry any more.'
She left the room abruptly. Phillipa heard her speaking to
Julia in the hall.
Julia entered the drawing-room a few moments later.
There was a slightly steely glitter in her eyes.
'Played your cards rather well, haven't you, Phillipa? I see
you're one of those quiet ones . . . a dark horse.'
'So you heard—?'
'Yes, I heard. I rather think I was meant to hear.'
'What do you mean?'
'Our Letty's no fool . . . Well, anyway, you're all right, Phil-
lipa. Sitting pretty, aren't you?'
'Oh, Julia – I didn't mean – I never meant—'
'Didn't you? Of course you did. You're fairly up against
things, aren't you? Hard up for money. But just remember this
– if anyone bumps off Aunt Letty now, *you'll* be suspect No. 1.'
'But I shan't be. It would be idiotic if I killed her now when
– if I waited—'
'So you *do* know about old Mrs Whatsername dying up in

Scotland? I wondered . . . Phillipa, I'm beginning to believe you're a very dark horse indeed.'

'I don't want to do you and Patrick out of anything.'

'Don't you, my dear? I'm sorry – but I don't believe you.'

—— 16 ——

INSPECTOR CRADDOCK RETURNS

Inspector Craddock had had a bad night on his night journey home. His dreams had been less dreams than nightmares. Again and again he was racing through the grey corridors of an old-world castle in a desperate attempt to get somewhere, or to prevent something, in time. Finally he dreamt that he awoke. An enormous relief surged over him. Then the door of his compartment slid slowly open, and Letitia Blacklock looked in at him with blood running down her face, and said reproachfully: 'Why didn't you save me? You could have if you'd tried.'

This time he really awoke.

Altogether, the Inspector was thankful finally to reach Milchester. He went straight away to make his report to Rydesdale who listened carefully.

'It doesn't take us much further,' he said. 'But it confirms what Miss Blacklock told you. Pip and Emma – h'm, I wonder.'

'Patrick and Julia Simmons are the right age, sir. If we could establish that Miss Blacklock hadn't seen them since they were children—'

With a very faint chuckle, Rydesdale said: 'Our ally, Miss Marple, has established that for us. Actually Miss Blacklock had never seen either of them at all until two months ago.'

'Then, surely, sir—'

'It's not so easy as all that, Craddock. We've been checking up. On what we've got, Patrick and Julia seem definitely to be out of it. His Naval record is genuine – quite a good record bar a tendency to "insubordination." We've checked with Cannes, and an indignant Mrs Simmons says of course her son and daughter are at Chipping Cleghorn with her cousin Letitia Blacklock. So that's that!'

'And Mrs Simmons *is* Mrs Simmons?'

'She's been Mrs Simmons for a very long time, that's all I can say,' said Rydesdale dryly.

'That seems clear enough. Only – those two fitted. Right age. Not known to Miss Blacklock, personally. If we wanted Pip and Emma – well, there they were.'

The Chief Constable nooded thoughtfully, then he pushed across a paper to Craddock.

'Here's a little something we've dug up on Mrs Easterbrook.'

The Inspector read with lifted eyebrows.

'Very interesting,' he remarked. 'Hoodwinked that old ass pretty well, hasn't she? It doesn't tie in with this business though, as far as I can see.'

'Apparently not.'

'And here's an item that concerns Mrs Haymes.'

Again Craddock's eyebrows rose.

'I think I'll have another talk with the lady,' he said.

'You think this information might be relevant?'

'I think it might be. It would be a long shot, of course . . .'

The two men were silent for a moment or two.

'How has Fletcher got on, sir?'

'Fletcher has been exceedingly active. He's made a routine search of the house by agreement with Miss Blacklock – but he didn't find anything significant. Then he's been checking up on who could have had the opportunity of oiling that door. Checking who was up at the house on the days that that foreign girl was out. A little more complicated than we thought, because it appears she goes for a walk most afternoons. Usually down to the village where she has a cup of coffee at the Bluebird. So that when Miss Blacklock and Miss Bunner are out – which is most afternoons – they go blackberrying – the coast is clear.'

'And the doors are always left unlocked?'

'They used to be. I don't suppose they are now.'

'What are Fletcher's results? Who's known to have been in the house when it was left empty?'

'Practically the whole lot of them.'

Rydesdale consulted a page in front of him.

'Miss Murgatroyd was there with a hen to sit on some eggs. (Sounds complicated but that's what she says.) Very flustered about it all and contradicts herself, but Fletcher thinks that's temperamental and not a sign of guilt.'

'Might be,' Craddock admitted. 'She flaps.'

'Then Mrs Swettenham came up to fetch some horse meat that Miss Blacklock had left for her on the kitchen table because Miss Blacklock had been in to Milchester in the car that day and always gets Mrs Swettenham's horse meat for her. That make sense to you?'

Craddock considered.

'Why didn't Miss Blacklock leave the horse meat when she passed Mrs Swettenham's house on her way back from Milchester?'

'I don't know, but she didn't. Mrs Swettenham says she (Miss B.) always leaves it on the kitchen table, and she (Mrs S.) likes to fetch it when Mitzi isn't there because Mitzi is sometimes so rude.'

'Hangs together quite well. And the next?'

'Miss Hinchcliffe. Says she wasn't there at all lately. But she was. Because Mitzi saw her coming out of the side door one day and so did a Mrs Butt (she's one of the locals). Miss H. then admitted she might have been there but had forgotten. Can't remember what she went for. Says she probably just dropped in.'

'That's rather odd.'

'So was her manner, apparently. Then there's Mrs Easterbrook. She was exercising the dear dogs out that way and she just popped in to see if Miss Blacklock would lend her a knitting pattern but Miss Blacklock wasn't in. She says she waited a little.'

'Just so. Might be snooping round. Or might be oiling a door. And the Colonel?'

'Went there one day with a book on India that Miss Blacklock had expressed a desire to read.'

'Had she?'

'Her account is that she tried to get out of having to read it, but it was no use.'

'And that's fair enough,' sighed Craddock. 'If anyone is really determined to lend you a book, you never can get out of it!'

'We don't know if Edmund Swettenham was up there. He's extremely vague. Said he did drop in occasionally on errands for his mother, but thinks not lately.

'In fact, it's all inconclusive.'

'Yes.'

Rydesdale said, with a slight grin:

'Miss Marple has also been active. Fletcher reports that she had morning coffee at the Bluebird. She's been to sherry at Boulders, and to tea at Little Paddocks. She's admired Mrs Swettenham's garden – and dropped in to see Colonel Easterbrook's Indian curios.'

'She may be able to tell us if Colonel Easterbrook's a pukka Colonel or not.'

'She'd know, I agree – he seems all right. We'd have to check with the Far Eastern Authorities to get certain identification.'

'And in the meantime' – Craddock broke off – 'do you think Miss Blacklock would consent to go away?'

'Go away from Chipping Cleghorn?'

'Yes. Take the faithful Bunner with her, perhaps, and leave for an unknown destination. Why shouldn't she go up to Scotland and stay with Belle Goedler. It's a pretty unget-at-able place.'

'Stop there and wait for her to die? I don't think she'd do that. I don't think any nice-natured woman would like that suggestion.'

'If it's a matter of saving her life—'

'Come now, Craddock, it isn't quite so easy to bump someone off as you seem to think.'

'Isn't it, sir?'

'Well – in one way – it's easy enough I agree. Plenty of methods. Weed-killer. A bash on the head when she's out shutting up the poultry, a pot shot from behind a hedge. All quite simple. But to bump someone off and not be suspected of bumping them off – that's not quite so easy. And they must realize by now that they're all under observation. The original carefully planned scheme failed. Our unknown murdered has got to think up something else.'

'I know that, sir. But there's the time element to consider. Mrs Goedler's a dying woman – she might pop off any minute. That means that our murderer can't afford to wait.'

'True.'

'And another thing, sir. He – or she – must know that we're checking up on everybody.'

'And that takes time,' said Rydesdale with a sigh. 'It means checking with the East, with India. Yes, it's a long tedious business.'

'So that's another reason for – hurry. I'm sure, sir, that the danger is very real. It's a very large sum that's at stake. If Belle Goedler dies—'

He broke off as a constable entered.

'Constable Legg on the line from Chipping Cleghorn, sir.'

'Put him through here.'

Inspector Craddock, watching the Chief Constable, saw his features harden and stiffen.

'Very good,' barked Rydesdale. 'Detective-Inspector Craddock will be coming out immediately.'

He put the receiver down.

'Is it—? Craddock broke off.

Rydesdale shook his head.

'No,' he said. 'It's Dora Bunner. She wanted some aspirin. Apparently she took some from a bottle beside Letitia Blacklock's bed. There were only a few tablets left in the bottle. She took two and left one. The doctor's got that one and is sending it to be analysed. He says it's definitely *not* aspirin,'

'She's dead?'

'Yes, found dead in her bed this morning. Died in her sleep, doctor says. He doesn't think it was natural though her health was in a bad state. Narcotic poisoning, that's his guess. Autopsy's fixed for tonight.'

'Aspirin tablets by Letitia Blacklock's bed. The clever clever devil. Patrick told me Miss Blacklock threw away a half bottle of sherry – opened a new one. I don't suppose she'd have thought of doing that with an open bottle of aspirin. Who had been in the house this time – within the last day or two? The tablets can't have been there long.'

Rydesdale looked at him.

'All our lot were there yesterday,' he said. 'Birthday party for Miss Bunner. Any of them could have nipped upstairs and done a neat little substitution. Or of course anyone living in the house could have done it any time.'

17

THE ALBUM

Standing by the Vicarage Gate, well wrapped up, Miss Marple took the note from Bunch's hand.

'Tell Miss Blacklock,' said Bunch, 'that Julian is terribly sorry he can't come up himself. He's got a parishioner dying out at Locke Hamlet. He'll come up after lunch if Miss Blacklock would like to see him. The note's about the arrangements for the funeral. He suggests Wednesday if the inquest's on Tuesday. Poor old Bunny. It's so typical of her, somehow, to get hold of poisoned aspirin meant for someone else. Goodbye, darling. I hope the walk won't be too much for you. But I've simply got to get that child to hospital at once.'

Miss Marple said the walk wouldn't be too much for her, and Bunch rushed off.

Whilst waiting for Miss Blacklock, Miss Marple looked round the drawing-room, and wondered just exactly what Dora Bunner had meant that morning in the Bluebird by saying that she believed Patrick had 'tampered with the lamp' to 'make the lights go out.' What lamp? And how had he 'tampered' with it?'

She must, Miss Marple decided, have meant the small lamp that stood on the table by the archway. She had said something about a shepherdess or a shepherd – and this was actually a delicate piece of Dresden china, a shepherd in a blue coat and pink breeches holding what had originally been a candlestick and had now been adapted to electricity. The shade was of plain vellum and a little too big so that it almost masked the figure. What else was it that Dora Bunner had said? 'I remember distinctly that it was the shepherdess. And the next day—' Certainly it was a shepherd now.

Miss Marple remembered that when she and Bunch had come to tea, Dora Bunner had said something about the lamp being one of a *pair*. Of course – a shepherd and a shepherdess. And it had been the shepherdess on the day of the hold-up – and the next morning it had been the *other* lamp – the lamp that was here now, the shepherd. The lamps had been changed over during the night. And Dora Bunner had had reason to believe (or had believed without reason) that it was Patrick who had changed them.

Why? Because, if the original lamp were examined, it would show just how Patrick had managed to 'make the lights go out.' How had he managed? Miss Marple looked earnestly at the lamp in front of her. The flex ran along the table over the edge and was plugged into the wall. There was a small pear-shaped switch half-way along the flex. None of it suggested anything to Miss Marples because she knew very little about electricity.

Where was the shepherdess lamp? she wondered. In the 'spare room' or thrown away, or – where was it Dora Bunner had come upon Patrick Simmons with a feather and an oily cup? In the shrubbery? Miss Marple made up her mind to put all these points to Inspector Craddock.

At the very beginning Miss Blacklock had leaped to the conclusion that her nephew Patrick had been behind the insertion of that advertisement. That kind of instinctive belief was often justified, or so Miss Marple believed. Because, if you knew people fairly well, you knew the kind of things they thought of . . .

Patrick Simmons . . .

A handsome young man. An engaging young man. A young man whom women liked, both young women and old women. The kind of man, perhaps, that Randall Goedler's sister had married. Could Patrick Simmons be 'Pip'? But he'd been in the Navy during the war. The police could soon check up on that.

Only – sometimes – the most amazing impersonations *did* happen.

You could get away with a great deal if you had enough audacity . . .

The door opened and Miss Blacklock came in. She looked, Miss Marple thought, many years older. All the life and energy had gone out of her.

'I'm very sorry, disturbing you like this,' said Miss Marple. 'But the Vicar had a dying parishioner and Bunch had to rush a sick child to hospital. The Vicar wrote you a note.'

She held it out and Miss Blacklock took it and opened it.

'Do sit down, Miss Marple,' she said. 'It's very kind of you to have brought this.'

She read the note through.

'The Vicar's a very understanding man,' she said quietly. 'He doesn't offer one fatuous consolation . . . Tell him that these arrangements will do very well. Her – her favourite hymn was *Lead Kindly Light.*'

Her voice broke suddenly.

Miss Marple said gently:

'I am only a stranger, but I am so very very sorry.'

And suddenly, uncontrollably, Letitia Blacklock wept. It was a piteous overmastering grief, with a kind of hopelessness about it. Miss Marple sat quite still.

Miss Blacklock sat up at last. Her face was swollen and blotched with tears.

'I'm sorry,' she said. 'It – it just came over me. What I've lost. She – she was the only link with the past, you see. The only one who – who *remembered*. Now that she's gone I'm quite alone.'

'I know what you mean,' said Miss Marple. 'One *is* alone when the last one who *remembers* is gone. I have nephews and nieces and kind friends – but there's no one who knew me as a young girl – no one who belongs to the old days. I've been alone for quite a long time now.'

Both women sat silent for some moments.

'You understand very well,' said Letitia Blacklock. She rose and went over to her desk. 'I must write a few words to the Vicar.' She held the pen rather awkwardly and wrote slowly.

'Arthritic,' she explained. 'Sometimes I can hardly write at all.'

She sealed up the envelope and addressed it.

'If you wouldn't mind taking it, it would be very kind.'

Hearing a man's voice in the hall she said quickly:

'That's Inspector Craddock.'

She went to the mirror over the fireplace and applied a small powder puff to her face.

Craddock came in with a grim, angry face.

He looked at Miss Marple with disapprobation.

'Oh,' he said. 'So *you're* here.'

Miss Blacklock turned from the mantelpiece.

'Miss Marple kindly came up with a note from the Vicar.'

Miss Marple said in a flurried manner:

'I am going at once – at once. Please don't let me hamper you in *any* way.'

'Were you at the tea party here yesterday afternoon?'

Miss Marple said nervously:

'No – no, I wasn't. Bunch drove me over to call on some friends.'

'Then there's nothing you can tell me.' Craddock held the door open in a pointed manner, and Miss Marples scuttled out in a somewhat abashed fashion.

'Nosey Parkers, these old women,' said Craddock.

'I think you're being unfair to her,' said Miss Blacklock. 'She really did come with a note from the Vicar.'

'I bet she did.'

'I don't think it was idle curiosity.'

'Well, perhaps you're right, Miss Blacklock, but my own diagnosis would be a severe attack of Nosey Parkeritis . . .'

'She's a very harmless old creature,' said Miss Blacklock.

'Dangerous as a rattlesnake if you only knew,' the Inspector thought grimly. But he had no intention of taking anyone into his confidence unnecessarily. Now that he knew definitely there was a killer at large, he felt that the less said the better. He didn't want the next person bumped off to be Jane Marple.

Somewhere – a killer . . . Where?

'I won't waste time offering sympathy, Miss Blacklock,' he said. 'As a matter of fact I feel pretty bad about Miss Bunner's death. We ought to have been able to prevent it.'

I don't see what you could have done.'

'No – well, it wouldn't have been easy. But now we've got to work fast. Who's doing this, Miss Blacklock? Who's had two shots at killing you, and will probably, if we don't work fast enough, soon have another?'

Letitia Blacklock shivered. 'I don't know, Inspector – I don't know *at all*!'

'I've checked up with Mrs Goedler. She's given me all the help she can. It wasn't very much. There are just a few people who would definitely profit by your death. First Pip and Emma. Patrick and Julia Simmons are the right age, but their background seems clear enough. Anyway, we can't concentrate on these two alone. Tell me, Miss Blacklock, would you recognize Sonia Goedler if you saw her?'

'Recognize Sonia? Why, of course—' She stopped suddenly. 'No,' she said slowly, 'I don't know that I would. It's a long time. Thirty years . . . She'd be an elderly woman now.'

'What was she like when you remember her?'

'Sonia?' Miss Blacklock considered for some moments. 'She was rather small, dark . . .'

'Any special peculiarities? Mannerisms?'

'No – no, I don't think so. She was gay – very gay.'

'She mayn't be so gay now,' said the Inspector. 'Have you got a photograph of her?'

'Of Sonia? Let me see – not a proper photograph. I've got some old snapshots – in an album somewhere – at least I think there's one of her.'

'Ah. Can I have a look at it?'

'Yes, of course. Now where did I put that album?'

'Tell me, Miss Blacklock, do you consider it remotely possible that Mrs Swettenham might be Sonia Goedler?'

'*Mrs Swettenham?*' Miss Blacklock looked at him in lively astonishment. 'But her husband was in the Government Service – in India first, I think, and then in Hong Kong.'

'What you mean is, that that's the story she's told you. You don't, as we say in the Courts, know it of your own knowledge, do you?'

'No,' said Miss Blacklock slowly. 'When you put it like that, I don't . . . But Mrs Swettenham? Oh, it's absurd!'

'Did Sonia Goedler ever do any acting? Amateur theatricals?'

'Oh, yes. She was good.'

'There you are! Another thing, Mrs Swettenham wears a wig. At least,' the Inspector corrected himself, 'Mrs Harmon says she does.'

'Yes – yes, I suppose it might be a wig. All those little grey curls. But I still think it's absurd. She's really very nice and exceedingly funny sometimes.'

'Then there's Miss Hinchcliffe and Miss Murgatroyd. Could either of them be Sonia Goedler?'

Miss Hinchcliffe is too tall. She's as tall as a man.'

'Miss Murgatroyd then?'

'Oh, but – oh no, I'm sure Miss Murgatroyd couldn't be Sonia.'

'You don't see very well, do you, Miss Blacklock?'

'I'm short-sighted; is that what you mean?'

'Yes. What I'd like to see is a snapshot of this Sonia Goedler, even if it's a long time ago and not a good likeness. We're trained, you know, to pick our resemblances, in a way no amateur can ever do.'

'I'll try and find it for you.'

'Now?'

'What, at once?'

'I'd prefer it.'

'Very well. Now let me see. I saw that album when we were tidying a lot of books out of the cupboard. Julia was helping me. She laughed, I remember, at the clothes we used to wear in those days . . . The books we put in the shelf in the drawing-room. Where did we put the albums and the big bound volumes of the Art Journal? What a wretched memory I have! Perhaps Julia will remember. She's at home today.'

'I'll find her.'

The Inspector departed on his quest. He did not find Julia in any of the downstairs rooms. Mitzi, asked where Miss Simmons was, said crossly that it was not her affair.

'Me! I stay in my kitchen and concern myself with the lunch. And nothing do I eat that I have not cooked myself. Nothing, do you hear?'

The Inspector called up the stairs 'Miss Simmons,' and getting no response, went up.

He met Julia fact to face just as he turned the corner of the landing. She had just emerged from a door that showed behind it a small twisty staircase.

'I was up in the attic,' she explained. 'What is it?'

Inspector Craddock explained.

'Those old photograph albums? Yes, I remember them quite well. We put them in the big cupboard in the study, I think. I'll find them for you.'

She led the way downstairs and pushed open the study door. Near the window there was a large cupboard. Julia pulled it open and disclosed a heterogenous mass of objects.

'Junk,' said Julia. 'All junk. But elderly people simply will *not* throw things away.'

The Inspector knelt down and took a couple of old-fashioned albums from the bottom shelf.

'Are these they?'

'Yes.'

Miss Blacklock came in and joined them.

'Oh, so *that's* where we put them. I couldn't remember.'

Craddock had the books on the table and was turning the pages.

Women in large cartwheel hats, women with dresses tapering down to their feet so that they could hardly walk. The photos had captions neatly printed underneath them, but the ink was old and faded.

'It would be in this one,' said Miss Blacklock. 'On about the second or third page. The other book is after Sonia had married and gone away.' She turned a page. 'It ought to be here.' She stopped.

There were several empty spaces on the page. Craddock bent down and deciphered the faded writing. 'Sonia . . . Self . . . R.G.' A little further along, 'Sonia and Belle on beach.' And again on the opposite page, 'Picnic at Skeyne.' He turned over another page, 'Charlotte, Self, Sonia, R.G.'

Craddock stood up. His lips were grim.

'*Somebody has removed these photographs* – not long ago, I should say.'

'There weren't any blank spaces when we looked at them the other day. Were there, Julia?'

'I didn't look very closely – only at some of the dresses. But no . . . you're right, Aunt Letty, there *weren't* any blank spaces.'

Craddock looked grimmer still.

'Somebody,' he said, 'has removed every photo of Sonia Goedler from this album.'

—— 18 ——

THE LETTERS

I

'Sorry to worry you again, Mrs Haymes.'

'It doesn't matter,' said Phillipa coldly.

'Shall we go into this room here?'

'The study? Yes, if you like, Inspector. It's very cold. There's no fire.'

'It doesn't matter. It's not for long. And we're not so likely to be overheard here.'

'Does that matter?'

'Not to me, Mrs Haymes. It might to you.'

'What do you mean?'

'I think you told me, Mrs Haymes, that your husband was killed fighting in Italy?'

'Well?'

'Wouldn't it have been simpler to have told me the truth – that he was a deserter from his regiment.'

He saw her face grow white, and her hands close and unclose themselves.

She said bitterly:

'Do you have to rake up *everything*?'

Craddock said dryly:

'We expect people to tell us the truth about themselves.'

She was silent. Then she said:

'Well?'

'What do you mean by "Well?", Mrs Haymes?'

'I mean, what are you going to do about it? Tell everybody? Is that necessary – or fair – or kind?'

'Does nobody know?'

'Nobody here. Harry' – her voice changed – 'my son, he doesn't know. I don't want him to know. I don't want him to know – ever.'

'Then let me tell you that you're taking a very big risk, Mrs Haymes. When the boy is old enough to understand, tell him the truth. If he finds out by himself some day – it won't be good for him. If you go on stuffing him up with tales of his father dying like a hero—'

'I don't do that. I'm not completely dishonest. I just don't talk about it. His father was – killed in the war. After all, that's what it amounts to – for us.'

'But your husband is still alive?'

'Perhaps. How should I know?'

'When did you see him last, Mrs Haymes?'

Phillipa said quickly:

'I haven't seen him for years.'

'Are you quite sure that's true? You didn't, for instance, see him about a fortnight ago?'

'What are you suggesting?'

'It never seemed to me very likely that you met Rudi Scherz in the summerhouse here. But Mitzi's story was very emphatic. I suggest, Mrs Haymes, that the man you came back from work to meet that morning was your husband.'

'I didn't meet anybody in the summerhouse.'

'He was hard up for money, perhaps, and you supplied him with some?'

'I've not seen him, I tell you. I didn't meet anybody in the summerhouse.'

'Deserters are often rather desperate men. They often take part in robberies, you know. Hold-ups. Things of that kind. *And they have foreign revolvers very often that they've brought back from abroad.*'

'I don't know where my husband is. I haven't seen him for years.'

'Is that your last word, Mrs Haymes?'

'I've nothing else to say.'

II

Craddock came away from his interview with Phillipa Haymes feeling angry and baffled.

'Obstinate as a mule,' he said to himself angrily.

He was fairly sure that Phillipa was lying, but he hadn't succeeded in breaking down her obstinate denials.

He wished he knew a little more about ex-Captain Haymes. His information was meagre. An unsatisfactory Army record, but nothing to suggest that Haymes was likely to turn criminal.

And anyway Haymes didn't fit in with the oiled door.

Someone in the house had done that, or someone with easy access to it.

He stood looking up the staircase, and suddenly he wondered

what Julia had been doing up in the attic. An attic, he thought, was an unlikely place for the fastidious Julia to visit.

What had she been doing up there?

He ran lightly up to the first floor There was no one about. He opened the door out of which Julia had come and went up the narrow stairs to the attic.

There were trunks there, old suitcases, various broken articles of furniture, a chair with a leg off, a broken china lamp, part of an old dinner service.

He turned to the trunks and opened the lid of one.

Clothes. Old fashioned, quite good quality women's clothes. Clothes belonging, he supposed, to Miss Blacklock, or to her sister who had died.

He opened another trunk.

Curtains.

He passed to a small attaché-case. It had papers in it and letters. Very old letters, yellowed with time.

He looked at the outside of the case which had the initials C.L.B. on it. He deduced correctly that it had belonged to Letitia's sister Charlotte. He unfolded one of the letters. It began *Dearest Charlotte. Yesterday Belle felt well enough to go for a picnic. R.G. also took a day off. The Asvogel flotation has gone splendidly, R.G. is terribly pleased about it. The Preference shares are at a premium.*

He skipped the rest and looked at the signature:

Your loving sister, Letitia.

He picked up another.

Darling Charlotte. I wish you would sometimes make up your mind to see people. You do exaggerate, you know. It isn't nearly as bad as you think. And people really don't mind things like that. It's not the disfigurement you think it is.

He nodded his head. He remembered Belle Goedler saying that Charlotte Blacklock had a disfigurement or deformity of some kind. Letitia had, in the end, resigned her job, to go and look after her sister. These letters all breathed the anxious spirit of her affection and love for an invalid. She had written her sister, apparently, long accounts of everyday happenings, of any little detail that she thought might interest the sick girl. And Charlotte had kept these letters. Occasionally odd snapshots had been enclosed.

Excitement suddenly flooded Craddock's mind. Here, it might be, he would find a clue. In these letters there would be written down things that Letitia herself had long forgotten.

Here was a faithful picture of the past and somewhere amongst it, there might be a clue that would help him to identify the unknown. Photographs, too. There might, just possibly, be a photograph of Sonia Goedler here that the person who had taken the other photos out of the album did not know about.

Inspector Craddock packed the letters up again, carefully, closed the case, and started down the stairs.

Letitia Blacklock, standing on the landing below, looked at him in amazement.

'Was that you up in the attic? I heard footsteps. I couldn't imagine who—'

'Miss Blacklock, I have found some letters here, written by you to your sister Charlotte many years ago. Will you allow me to take them away and read them?'

She flushed angrily.

'Must you do a thing like that? Why? What good can they be to you?'

'They might give me a picture of Sonia Goedler, of her character – there may be some allusion – some incident – that will help.'

'They are private letters, Inspector.'

'I know.'

'I suppose you will take them anyway . . . You have the power to do so, I suppose, or you can easily get it. Take them – take them! But you'll find very little about Sonia. She married and went away only a year or two after I began to work for Randall Goedler.'

Craddock said obstinately:

'There may be *something*.' He added, 'We've got to try everything. I assure you the danger is very real.'

She said, biting her lips:

'I know. Bunny is dead – from taking an aspirin tablet that was meant for me. It may be Patrick, or Julia, or Phillipa, or Mitzi next – somebody young with their life in front of them. Somebody who drinks a glass of wine that is poured out for me, or eats a chocolate that is sent to me. Oh! take the letters – take them away. And afterwards burn them. They don't mean anything to anyone but me and Charlotte. It's all over – gone – past. Nobody remembers now . . .'

Her hand went to the choker of false pearls she was wearing. Craddock thought how incongruous it looked with her tweed coat and skirt.

She said again:
'Take the letters.'

III

It was the following afternoon that the Inspector called at the Vicarage.

It was a dark gusty day.

Miss Marple had her chair pulled close to the fire and was knitting. Bunch was on hands and knees, crawling about the floor, cutting out material to a pattern.

She sat back and pushed a mop of hair out of her eyes, looking up expectantly at Craddock.

'I don't know if it's a breach of confidence,' said the Inspector, addressing himself to Miss Marple, 'but I'd like you to look at this letter.'

He explained the circumstances of his discovery in the attic.

'It's rather a touching collection of letters,' he said. 'Miss Blacklock poured out everything in the hopes of sustaining her sister's interest in life and keeping her health good. There's a very clear picture of an old father in the background – old Dr Blacklock. A real old pig-headed bully, absolutely set in his ways, and convinced that everything he thought and said was right. Probably killed thousands of patients through obstinacy. He wouldn't stand for any new ideas or methods.'

'I don't really know that I blame him there,' said Miss Marple. 'I always feel that the young doctors are only too anxious to experiment. After they've whipped out all our teeth, and administered quantities of very peculiar glands, and removed bits of our insides, they then confess that nothing can be done for us. I really prefer the old-fashioned remedy of big black bottles of medicine. After all, one can always pour those down the sink.'

She took the letter that Craddock handed her.

He said: 'I want you to read it because I think that that generation is more easily understood by you than by me. I don't know really quite how these people's minds worked.'

Miss Marple unfolded the fragile paper.

Dearest Charlotte,
I've not written for two days because we've been having the most terrible domestic complications. Randall's sister Sonia (you

remember her? She came to take you out in the car that day? How I wish you would go out more). Sonia has declared her intention of marrying one, Dmitri Stamfordis. I have only seen him once. Very attractive – not to be trusted I should say. R.G. raves against him and says he is a crook and a swindler. Belle, bless her, just smiles and lies on her sofa. Sonia, who though she looks so impassive has really a terrific temper, is simply wild with R.G. I really thought yesterday she was going to murder him!

I've done my best. I've talked to Sonia and I've talked to R.G. and I've got them both into a more reasonable frame of mind and then they come together and it all starts over again! You've no idea how tiring *it is. R.G. has been making enquiries – and it does really seem as though this Stamfordis man was thoroughly undesirable.*

In the meantime business is being neglected. I carry on at the office and in a way it's rather fun because R.G. gives me a free hand. He said to me yesterday: 'Thank Heaven, there's one sane person in the world. You're never likely to fall in love with a crook, Blackie, are *you?' I said I didn't think I was likely to fall in love with anybody. R.G. said: 'Let's start a few new hares in the City.' He's really rather a mischievous devil sometimes and he sails terribly near the wind. 'You're quite determined to keep me on the straight and narrow path aren't you, Blackie?' he said the other day. And I shall too! I can't understand how people can't* see *when a thing's dishonest – but R.G. really and truly* doesn't. *He only knows what is actually against the law.'*

Belle only laughs at all this. She thinks the fuss about Sonia is all nonsense. 'Sonia has her own money,' she said. 'Why shouldn't she marry this man if she wants to?' I said it might turn out to be a terrible mistake and Belle said, 'It's never a mistake to marry a man you want to marry – even if you regret it.' And then she said, 'I suppose Sonia doesn't want to break with Randall because of money. Sonia's very fond of money.'

No more now. How is father? I won't say Give him my love. But you can if you think it's better to do so. Have you seen more people? You really must not be morbid, *darling.*

Sonia asks to be remembered to you. She has just come in and is closing and unclosing her hands like an angry cat sharpening its claws. I think she and R.G. have had another row. Of course Sonia can be very irritating. She stares you down with that cool stare of hers.

Lots of love, darling, and buck up. This iodine treatment may

make a lot of difference. I've been enquiring about it and it
really does seem to have good results.
Your loving sister,
Letitia.

Miss Marple folded the letter and handed it back. She looked abstracted.

'Well, what do you think about her?' Craddock urged. 'What picture do you get of her?'

'Of Sonia? It's difficult, you know, to see anyone through another person's mind . . . Determined to get her own way – that, definitely, I think. And wanting the best of two worlds . . .'

'*Closing and unclosing her hands like an angry cat,*' murmured Craddock. 'You know, that reminds me of someone . . .'
He frowned.

'Making enquiries . . .' murmured Miss Marple.

'If we could get hold of the result of those inquiries,' said Craddock.

'Does that letter remind you of anything in St Mary Mead?' asked Bunch, rather indistinctly since her mouth was full of pins.

'I really can't say it does, dear . . . Dr Blacklock is, perhaps, a little like Mr Curtiss the Wesleyan Minister. He wouldn't let his child wear a plate on her teeth. Said it was the Lord's Will if her teeth stuck out. "After all," I said to him, "you do trim your beard and cut your hair. It might be the Lord's Will that your hair should grow out." He said that was quite different. So like a man. But that doesn't help us with our present problem.'

'We've never traced that revolver, you know. It wasn't Rudi Scherz. If I knew who had had a revolver in Chipping Cleghorn—'

'Colonel Easterbrook has one,' said Bunch. 'He keeps it in his collar drawer.'

'How do you know, Mrs Harmon?'

'Mrs Butt told me. She's my daily. Or rather, my twice weekly. Being a military gentleman, she said, he'd naturally have a revolver and very handy it would be if burglars were to come along.'

'When did she tell you this?'

'Ages ago. About six months ago, I should think.'

'Colonel Easterbrook?' murmured Craddock.

'It's like those pointer things at fairs, isn't it?' said Bunch,

339

still speaking through a mouthful of pins. 'Go round and round and stop at something different every time.'

'You're telling me?' said Craddock and groaned.

'Colonel Easterbrook was up at Little Paddocks to leave a book there one day. He could have oiled that door then. He was quite straightforward about being there though. Not like Miss Hinchcliffe.

Miss Marple coughed gently. 'You must make allowances for the times we live in, Inspector,' she said.

Craddock looked at her, uncomprehendingly.

'After all,' said Miss Marple, 'you *are* the Police, aren't you? People can't say everything they'd like to say to the Police, can they?'

'I don't see why not,' said Craddock. 'Unless they've got some criminal matter to conceal.'

'She means butter,' said Bunch, crawling actively round a table leg to anchor a floating bit of paper. 'Butter and corn for hens, and sometimes cream – and sometimes, even, a side of bacon.

'Show him that note from Miss Blacklock,' said Miss Marple. 'It's some time ago now, but it reads like a first-class mystery story.'

'What have I done with it? Is this the one you mean, Aunt Jane?'

Miss Marple took it and looked at it.

'Yes,' she said with satisfaction. 'That's the one.'

She handed it to the Inspector.

'*I have made enquiries – Thursday is the day,*' Miss Blacklock had written. '*Any time after three. If there is any for me leave it in the usual place.*'

Bunch spat out her pins and laughed. Miss Marple was watching the Inspector's face.

The Vicar's wife took upon herself to explain.

'Thursday is the day one of the farms round here makes butter. They let anybody they like have a bit. It's usually Miss Hinchcliffe who collects it. She's very much in with all the farmers – because of her pigs, I think. But it's all a bit hush hush, you know, a kind of local scheme of barter. One person gets butter, and sends along cucumbers, or something like that – and a little something when a pig's killed. And now and then an animal has an accident and has to be destroyed. Oh, you know the sort of thing. Only one can't, very well, say it right out to the Police. Because I suppose quite a lot of this barter is illegal –

only nobody really knows because it's all so complicated. But I expect Hinch had slipped into Little Paddocks with a pound of butter or something and had put it in the *usual place*. That's a flour bin under the dresser, by the way. It doesn't have flour in it.'

Craddock sighed.

'I'm glad I came here to you ladies,' he said.

'There used to be clothing coupons, too,' said Bunch. 'Not usually bought – that wasn't considered honest. No money passes. But people like Mrs Butt or Mrs Finch or Mrs Huggins like a nice woollen dress or a winter coat that hasn't seen too much wear and they pay for it with coupons instead of money.'

'You'd better not tell me any more,' said Craddock. 'It's all against the law.'

'Then there oughtn't to be such silly laws,' said Bunch, filling her mouth with pins again. '*I* don't do it, of course, because Julian doesn't like me to, so I don't. But I know what's going on, of course.'

A kind of despair was coming over the Inspector.

'It all sounds so pleasant and ordinary,' he said. 'Funny and petty and simple. And yet one woman and a man have been killed, and another woman may be killed before I can get anything definite to go on. I've left off worrying about Pip and Emma for the moment. I'm concentrating on Sonia. I wish I knew what she looked like. There was a snapshot or two in with these letters, but none of the snaps could have been of her.'

'How do you know it couldn't have been her? Do you know what she looked like?'

'She was small and dark, Miss Blacklock said.'

'Really,' said Miss Marple, 'that's *very* interesting.'

'There was one snap that reminded me vaguely of someone. A tall fair girl with her hair all done up on top of her head. I don't know who she could have been. Anyway, it can't have been Sonia. Do you think Mrs Swettenham could have been dark when she was a girl?'

'Not very dark,' said Bunch. 'She's got blue eyes.'

'I hoped there might be a photo of Dmitri Stamfordis – but I suppose that was too much to hope for . . . Well' – he took up the letter – 'I'm sorry this doesn't suggest anything to you, Miss Marple.'

'Oh! but it does,' said Miss Marple. 'It suggests a good deal. Just read it through again, Inspector – especially where it says that Randall Goedler was making inquiries about Dmitri Stamfordis.'

Craddock stared at her.

The telephone rang.

Bunch got up from the floor and went out into the hall where, in accordance with the best Victorian traditions, the telephone had originally been placed and where it still was.

She re-entered the room to say to Craddock:

'It's for you.'

Slightly surprised, the Inspector went out to the instrument – carefully shutting the door of the living-room behind him.

'Craddock? Rydesdale here.'

'Yes, sir.'

'I've been looking through your report. In the interview you had with Phillipa Haymes I see she states positively that she hasn't seen her husband since his desertion from the Army?'

'That's right, sir – she was most emphatic. But in my opinion she wasn't speaking the truth.'

'I agree with you. Do you remember a case about ten days ago – man run over by a lorry – taken to Milchester General with concussion and a fractured pelvis?'

'The fellow who snatched a child practically from under the wheels of a lorry, and got run down himself?'

'That's the one. No papers of any kind on him and nobody came forward to identify him. Looked as though he might be on the run. He died last night without regaining consciousness. But he's been identified – deserted from the Army – Ronald Haymes, ex-Captain in the South Loamshires.'

'Phillipa Haymes' husband?'

'Yes. He'd got an old Chipping Cleghorn bus ticket on him, by the way – and quite a reasonable amount of money.'

'So he did get money from his wife? I always thought he was the man Mitzi overheard talking to her in the summerhouse. She denied it flatly, of course. But surely, sir, that lorry accident was before—'

Rydesdale took the words out of his mouth.

'Yes, he was taken to Milchester General on the 28th. The hold-up at Little Paddocks was on the 29th. That lets him out of any possible connection with it. But his wife, of course, knew nothing about the accident. She may have been thinking all along that he *was* concerned in it. She'd hold her tongue – naturally – after all he *was* her husband.'

'It was a fairly gallant bit of work, wasn't it, sir?' said Craddock slowly.

'Rescuing that child from the lorry? Yes. Plucky. Don't suppose it was cowardice that made Haymes desert. Well, all that's past history. For a man who'd blotted his copybook, it was a good death.'

'I'm glad for her sake,' said the Inspector. 'And for that boy of theirs.'

'Yes, he needn't be too ashamed of his father. And the young woman will be able to marry again now.'

Craddock said slowly:

'I was thinking of that, sir . . . It opens up – possibilities.'

'You'd better break the news to her as you're on the spot.'

'I will, sir. I'll push along there now. Or perhaps I'd better wait until she's back at Little Paddocks. It may be rather a shock – and there's someone else I rather want to have a word with first.'

—— 19 ——

RECONSTRUCTION OF THE CRIME

I

'I'll put a lamp by you before I go' said Bunch. 'It's so dark in here. There's going to be a storm, I think.'

She lifted the small reading lamp to the other side of the table where it would throw light on Miss Marple's knitting as she sat in a wide highbacked chair.

As the flex pulled across the table, Tiglath Pileser the cat leapt upon it and bit and clawed it violently.

'No, Tiglath Pileser, you mustn't . . . He really is awful. Look, he's nearly bitten it through – it's all frayed. Don't you understand, you idiotic puss, that you may get a nasty electric shock if you do that?'

'Thank you, dear,' said Miss Marple, and put out a hand to turn on the lamp.

'It doesn't turn on there. You have to press that silly little switch half-way along the flex. Wait a minute. I'll take these flowers out of the way.'

She lifted a bowl of Christmas roses across the table. Tiglath

Pileser, his tail switching, put out a mischievous paw and clawed Bunch's arm. She spilled some of the water out of the vase. It fell on the frayed area of flex and on Tiglath Pileser himself, who leapt to the floor with an indignant hiss.

Miss Marple pressed the small pear-shaped switch. Where the water had soaked the frayed flex there was a flash and a crackle.

'Oh, dear,' said Bunch. 'It's fused. Now I suppose all the lights in here are off.' She tried them. 'Yes, they are. So stupid being all on the same thingummibob. And it's made a burn on the table, too. Naughty Tiglath Pileser – it's all his fault. Aunt Jane – what's the matter? Did it startle you?'

'It's nothing, dear. Just something I saw quite suddenly which I ought to have seen before . . .'

'I'll go and fix the fuse and get the lamp from Julian's study.'

'No, dear, don't bother. You'll miss your bus. I don't want any more light. I just want to sit quietly and – think about something. Hurry dear, or you won't catch your bus.'

When Bunch had gone, Miss Marple sat quite still for about two minutes. The air of the room was heavy and menacing with the gathering storm outside.

Miss Marple drew a sheet of paper towards her.

She wrote first: '*Lamp?* and underlined it heavily.

After a moment or two, she wrote another word.

Her pencil travelled down the paper, making brief cryptic notes. . . .

II

In the rather dark living-room of Boulders with its low ceiling and latticed window panes, Miss Hinchcliffe and Miss Murgatroyd were having an argument.

'The trouble with you, Murgatroyd,' said Miss Hinchcliffe, 'is that you won't *try*.'

'But I tell you, Hinch, I can't remember a thing.'

'Now look here, Amy Murtatroyd, we're going to do some constructive thinking. So far we haven't shone on the detective angle. I was quite wrong over that door business. You didn't hold the door open for the murderer after all. You're cleared, Murgatroyd!'

Miss Murgatroyd gave a rather watery smile.

'It's just our luck to have the only silent cleaning woman in Chipping Cleghorn,' continued Miss Hinchcliffe. 'Usually I'm thankful for it, but this time it means we've got off to a bad start. Everybody else in the place knows about that second door in the drawing-room being used – and we only heard about it yester-day—'

'I still don't quite understand how—'

'It's perfectly simple. Our original premises were quite right. You can't hold open a door, wave a torch and shoot with a re-volver all at the same time. We kept in the revolver and the torch and cut out the door. Well, we were wrong. It was the revolver we ought to have cut out.'

'But he *did* have a revolver,' said Miss Murgatroyd. 'I saw it. It was there on the floor beside him.'

'When he was dead, yes. It's all quite clear. *He* didn't fire that revolver—'

'Then who did?'

'That's what we're going to find out. But whoever did it, the same person put a couple of poisoned aspirin tablets by Letty Blacklock's bed – and thereby bumped off poor Dora Bunner. And that couldn't have been Rudi Scherz, because he's as dead as a doornail. It was someone who was in the room that night of the hold-up and probably someone who was at the birthday party, too. And the only person *that* lets out is Mrs Harmon.'

'You think someone put those aspirins there the day of the birthday party?'

'Why not?'

'But how could they?'

'Well, we all went to the loo, didn't we?' said Miss Hinchcliffe coarsely. 'And I washed my hands in the bathroom because of that sticky cake. And little Sweetie Easterbrook powdered her grubby little face in Blacklock's bedroom, didn't she?'

'Hinch! Do you think *she*—?'

'I don't know yet. Rather obvious, if she did. I don't think if you were going to plant some tablets, that you'd want to be seen in the bedroom at all. Oh, yes, there were plenty of opportuni-ties.'

'The men didn't go upstairs.'

'There are back stairs. After all, if a man leaves the room, you don't follow him to see if he really is going where you think he is going. It wouldn't be delicate! Anyway, don't *argue*, Murga-troyd. I want to get back to the original attempt on Letty Black-lock. Now, to begin with, get the facts firmly into your head, because it's all going to depend upon you.'

Miss Murgatroyd looked alarmed.

'Oh, dear, Hinch, you know what a muddle I get into!'

'It's not a question of your brains, or the grey fluff that passes for brains with you. It's a question of *eyes.* It's a question of what you *saw.*'

'But I didn't see *anything.*'

'The trouble with you is, Murgatroyd, as I said just now, that you won't *try.* Now pay attention. This is what happened. Whoever it is that's got it in for Letty Blacklock was there in the room that evening. He (I say *he* because it's easier, but there's no reason why it should be a man more than a woman except, of course, that men are dirty dogs), well, he has previously oiled that second door that leads out of the drawing-room and which is supposed to be nailed up or something. Don't ask me *when* he did it, because that confuses things. Actually, by choosing my time, I could walk into any house in Chipping Cleghorn and do anything I liked there for half an hour or so with no one being the wiser. It's just a question of working out where the daily woman are and when the occupiers are out and exactly where they've gone and how long they'll be. Just good staff work. Now, to continue. He's oiled that second door. It will open without a sound. Here's the set-up: Lights go out, door A (the regular door) opens with a flourish. Business with torch and hold-up lines. In the meantime, while we're all goggling, X (that's the best term to use) slips quietly out by door B into the dark hall, comes up behind that Swiss idiot, takes a couple of shots at Letty Blacklock and then shoots the Swiss. Drops the revolver, where lazy thinkers like you will assume its evidence that the Swiss did the shooting, and nips back into the room again by the time that someone gets a lighter going. Got it?'

'Yes – ye-es, but who was it?'

'Well, if *you* don't know, Murgatroyd, nobody does!'

'*Me?*' Miss Murgatroyd fairly twittered in alarm. 'But I don't know anything *at all.* I don't *really,* Hinch!'

'Use that fluff of yours you call a brain. To begin with, where was everybody when the lights went out?'

'I don't know.'

'Yes, you do. You're maddening, Murgatroyd. You know where *you* were, don't you? You were behind the door.'

'Yes – yes, I was. It knocked against my corn when it flew open.'

'Why don't you go to a proper chiropodist instead of messing about yourself with your feet. You'll give yourself blood poisoning one of these days. Come on, now – *you're* behind the door.

I'm standing against the mantelpiece with my tongue hanging out for a drink. Letty Blacklock is by the table near the archway, getting the cigarettes. Patrick Simmons has gone through the archway into the small room where Letty Blacklock has had the drinks put. Agreed?'

'Yes, yes, I remember all that.'

'Good, now somebody else followed Patrick into that room or was just starting to follow him. One of the men. The annoying thing is that I can't remember whether it was Easterbrook or Edmund Swettenham. Do you remember?'

'No, I don't.'

'You wouldn't! And there was someone else who went through to the small room; Phillipa Haymes. I remember that distinctly because I remember noticing what a nice flat back she has, and I thought to myself "that girl would look well on a horse.' I was watching her and thinking just that. She went over to the mantelpiece in the other room. I don't know what it was she wanted there, because at that moment the lights went out.

'So that's the position. In the far drawing-room are Patrick Simmons, Phillipa Haymes, and *either* Colonel Easterbrook or Edmund Swettenham – we don't know which. Now, Murgatroyd, pay attention. The most probable thing is that it was *one of those three* who did it. If anyone wanted to get out of that far door, they'd naturally take care to put themselves in a convenient place when the lights went out. So, as I say, in all probability, it's one of those three. And in that case, Murgatroyd, there's not a thing you can do about it!'

Miss Murgatroyd brightened perceptibly.

'On the other hand,' continued Miss Hinchcliffe, 'there's the possibility that it *wasn't* one of those three. And that's where you come in, Murgatroyd.'

'But how should *I* know anything about it?'

'As I said before if you don't nobody does.'

'But I don't! I really *don't*! I couldn't see anything *at all*!'

'Oh, yes, you could. You're the only person who *could* see. You were standing behind the door. You couldn't look *at* the torch – because the door was between you and it. You were facing the other way, the same way as the torch was pointing. The rest of us were dazzled. But *you* weren't dazzled.'

'No – no, perhaps not, but I didn't *see* anything, the torch went round and round—'

'Showing you *what*? It rested on *faces*, didn't it? And on tables? And on chairs?'

'Yes – yes, it did . . . Miss Bunner, her mouth wide open and her eyes popping out of her head, staring and blinking.'

'That's the stuff!' Miss Hinchcliffe gave a sigh of relief. 'The difficulty there is in making you use that grey fluff of yours! Now then, keep it up.'

'But I didn't see any more, I didn't, really.'

'You mean you saw an empty room? Nobody standing about? Nobody sitting down?'

'No, of course not *that*. Miss Bunner with her mouth open and Mrs Harmon was sitting on the arm of a chair. She had her eyes tight shut and her knuckles all doubled up to her face – like a child.'

'Good, that's Mrs Harmon and Miss Bunner. Don't you see yet what I'm getting at? The difficulty is that I don't want to put ideas into your head. But when we've eliminated who you *did* see – we can get on to the important point which is, was there anyone you *didn't* see. Got it? Besides the tables and the chairs and the chrysanthemums and the rest of it, there were certain people: Julia Simmons, Mrs Swettenham, Mrs Easterbrook, – *either* Colonel Easterbrook or Edmund Swettenham – Dora Bunner and Bunch Harmon. All right, you saw Bunch Harmon and Dora Bunner. Cross them off. Now *think*, Murgatroyd, *think*, was there one of those people who definitely *wasn't* there?'

Miss Murgatroyd jumped slightly as a branch knocked against the open window. She shut her eyes. She murmured to herself . . .

'The flowers . . . on the table . . . the big arm-chair . . . the torch didn't come round as far as you, Hinch – Mrs Harmon, yes . . .'

The telephone rang sharply. Miss Hinchcliffe went to it.

'Hallo, yes? The station?'

The obedient Miss Murgatroyd, her eyes closed, was reliving the night of the 29th. The torch, sweeping slowly round . . . a group of people . . . the windows . . . the sofa . . . Dora Bunner . . . the wall . . . the table with lamp . . . the archway . . . the sudden spat of the revolver . . .

'. . . but that's *extraordinary*!' said Miss Murgatroyd.

'What?' Miss Hinchcliffe was barking angrily into the telephone. 'Been there since this morning? What time? Damn and blast you, and you only ring me up *now*? I'll set the S.P.C.A. after you. An oversight? It *that* all you've got to say?'

She banged down the receiver. 'It's that dog,' she said. 'The red setter. Been at the station since this morning – since this morning at eight o'clock. Without a drop of water! And the idiots only ring me up now. I'm going to get her right away.'

She plunged out of the room, Miss Murgatroyd squeaking shrilly in her wake.

'But listen, Hinch, a most extraordinary thing . . . I don't understand it . . .'

Miss Hinchcliffe had dashed out of the door and across to the shed which served as a garage.

'We'll go on with it when I come back,' she called. 'I can't wait for you to come with me. You've got your bedroom slippers on as usual.'

She pressed the starter of the car and backed out of the garage with a jerk. Miss Murgatroyd skipped nimbly sideways.

'But listen, Hinch, I *must* tell you—'

'When I come back . . .'

The car jerked and shot forwards. Miss Murgatroyd's voice came faintly after it on a high excited note.

'But Hinch, *she wasn't there* . . .'

III

Overhead, the clouds had been gathering thick and blue. As Miss Murgatroyd stood looking after the retreating car, the first big drops began to fall.

In an agitated fashion, Miss Murgatroyd plunged across to a line of string on which she had, some hours previously, hung out a couple of jumpers and a pair of woollen combinations to dry.

She was murmuring under her breath:

'Really *most* extraordinary . . . Oh, dear, I shall never get these down in time . . . And they were nearly dry . . .'

She struggled with a recalcitrant clothes peg, then turned her head as she heard someone approaching.

Then she smiled a pleased welcome.

'Hallo – do go inside, you'll get wet.'

'Let me help you.'

'Oh, if you don't mind . . . so annoying if they all get soaked again. I really ought to let down the line, but I think I can just reach.'

'Here's your scarf. Shall I put it round your neck?'

'Oh, thank you . . . Yes, perhaps . . . If I could just reach this peg . . .'

The woollen scarf was slipped round her neck and then, suddenly, pulled tight . . .

Miss Murgatroyd's mouth opened, but no sound came except a small choking gurgle.

And the scarf was pulled tighter still . . .

IV

On her way back from the station, Miss Hinchcliffe stopped the car to pick up Miss Marple who was hurrying along the street.

'Hallo,' she shouted. 'You'll get very wet. Come and have tea with us. I saw Bunch waiting for the bus. You'll be all alone at the Vicarage. Come and join us. Murgatroyd and I are doing a bit of reconstruction of the crime. I rather think we're just getting somewhere. Mind the dog. She's rather nervous.'

'What a beauty!'

'Yes, lovely bitch, isn't she? Those fools kept her at the station since this morning without letting me know. I told them off, the lazy b——s. Oh, excuse my language. I was brought up by grooms at home in Ireland.'

The little car turned with a jerk into the small backyard of Boulders.

A crowd of eager ducks and fowls encircled the two ladies as they descended.

'Curse Murgatroyd,' said Miss Hinchcliffe, 'she hasn't given 'em their corn.'

'Is it difficult to get corn?' Miss Marple inquired.

Miss Hinchcliffe winked.

'I'm in with most of the farmers,' she said.

Shooing away the hens, she escorted Miss Marple towards the cottage.

'Hope you're not too wet?'

'No, this is a very good mackintosh.'

'I'll light the fire if Murgatroyd hasn't lit it. Hiyah, Murgatroyd? Where is the woman? Murgatroyd! Where's that dog? *She's* disappeared now.'

A slow dismal howl came from outside.

'Curse the silly bitch.' Miss Hinchcliffe tramped to the door and called:

'Hyoup, Cutie – Cutie. Damn' silly name but that's what they called her apparently. We must find her another name. Hiyah, Cutie.'

The red setter was sniffing at something lying below the taut string where a row of garments swirled in the wind.

'Murgatroyd's not even had the sense to bring the washing in. Where *is* she?'

Again the red setter nosed at what seemed to be a pile of clothes, and raised her nose high in the air and howled again.

'What's the *matter* with the dog?'

Miss Hinchcliffe strode across the grass.

And quickly, apprehensively, Miss Marple ran after her. They stood there, side by side, the rain beating down on them and the older woman's arm went round the younger one's shoulders.

She felt the muscles go stiff and taut as Miss Hinchcliffe stood looking down on the thing lying there, with the blue congested face and the protruding tongue.

'I'll kill whoever did this,' said Miss Hinchcliffe in a low quiet voice, 'if I once get my hands on her . . .'

Miss Marple said questioningly:

'*Her?*'

Miss Hinchcliffe turned a ravaged face towards her.

'Yes. I know who it is – near enough . . . That is, it's one of three possibles.'

She stood for another moment, looking down at her dead friend, and then turned towards the house. Her voice was dry and hard.

'We must ring up the police,' she said. 'And while we're waiting for them, I'll tell you. My fault, in a way, that Murgatroyd's lying out there. I made a game of it . . . Murder isn't a game . . .'

'No,' said Miss Marple. 'Murder isn't a game.'

'You know something about it, don't you?' said Miss Hinchcliffe as she lifted the receiver and dialled.

She made a brief report and hung up.

'They'll be here in a few minutes . . . Yes, I heard that you'd been mixed up in this sort of business before . . . I think it was Edmund Swettenham told me so . . . Do you want to hear what we were doing, Murgatroyd and I?'

Succinctly she described the conversation held before her departure for the station.

'She called after me, you know, just as I was leaving . . . That's how I know it's a woman and not a man . . . If I'd waited – if only I'd *listened*! God dammit, the dog could have stopped where she was for another quarter of an hour.'

'Don't blame yourself, my dear. That does no good. One can't foresee.'

'No, one can't . . . Something tapped against the window, I remember. Perhaps *she* was outside there, then – yes, of course, she must have been . . . coming to the house . . . and there were Murgatroyd and I shouting at each other. Top of our voices . . . She heard . . . She heard it all . . .'

'You haven't told me yet what your friend said.'

'Just one sentence! *"She wasn't there."* '

She paused. 'You see? There were three women we hadn't eliminated. Mrs Swettenham, Mrs Easterbrook, Julia Simmons. And one of those three – *wasn't there* . . . She wasn't there in the drawing-room because she had slipped out through the other door and was out in the hall.'

'Yes,' said Miss Marple, 'I see.'

'It's *one* of those three women. I don't know which. But I'll find out!'

'Excuse me,' said Miss Marple. 'But did she – did Miss Murgatroyd, I mean, say it exactly as you said it?'

'How d'you mean – as I said it?'

'Oh, dear, how can I explain? You said it like this. She-wasn't-there. An equal emphasis on every word. You see, there are three ways you could say it. You could say, "*She* wasn't there." Very personal. Or again, "She *wasn't* there." Confirming some suspicion already held. Or else you could say (and this is nearer to the way you said it just now), "She wasn't *there* . . ." quite blankly – with the emphasis, if there was emphasis – on the "*there*." '

'I don't know,' Miss Hinchcliffe shook her head. 'I can't remember . . . How the hell can I remember? I think, yes, surely she'd say "*She* wasn't there." That would be the natural way, I should think. But I simply don't know. Does it make any difference?'

'Yes,' said Miss Marple, thoughtfully. 'I think so. It's a very *slight* indication, of course, but I think it *is* an indication. Yes, I should think it makes a lot of difference . . .'

——— 20 ———

MISS MARPLE IS MISSING

I

The postman, rather to his disgust, had lately been given orders to make an afternoon delivery of letters in Chipping Cleghorn as well as a morning one.

On this particular afternoon he left three letters at Little Paddocks at exactly ten minutes to five.

One was addressed to Phillipa Haymes in a schoolboy's hand; the other two were for Miss Blacklock. She opened them as she and Phillipa sat down at the tea table. The torrential rain had enabled Phillipa to leave Dayas Hall early today, since once she had shut up the greenhouses there was nothing more to do.

Miss Blacklock tore open her first letter which was a bill for repairing a kitchen boiler. She snorted angrily.

'Dymond's prices are *preposterous* – quite preposterous. Still, I suppose all the other people are just as bad.'

She opened the second letter which was in a handwriting quite unknown to her.

Dear Cousin Letty (it said),

I hope it will be all right for me to come to you on Tuesday? I wrote to Patrick two days ago but he hasn't answered. So I presume it's all right. Mother is coming to England next month and hopes to see you then.

My train arrives at Chipping Cleghorn at 6.15 if that's convenient?

Yours affectionately,
Julia Simmons.

Miss Blacklock read the letter once with astonishment pure and simple, and then again with a certain grimness. She looked up at Phillipa who was smiling over her son's letter.

'Are Julia and Patrick back, do you know?'

Phillipa looked up.

'Yes, they came in just after I did. They went upstairs to change. They were wet.'

'Perhaps you'd not mind going and calling them.'

'Of course I will.'

'Wait a moment – I'd like you to read this.'

She handed Phillipa the letter she had received.

Phillipa read it and frowned. 'I don't understand . . .'

'Nor do I, quite . . . I think it's about time I did. Call Patrick and Julia, Phillipa.'

Phillipa called from the bottom of the stairs:

'Patrick! Julia! Miss Blacklock wants you.'

Patrick came running down the stairs and entered the room.

'Don't go, Phillipa,' said Miss Blacklock.

'Hallo, Aunt Letty,' said Patrick cheerfully. 'Want me?'

'Yes, I do. Perhaps you'll give me an explanation of *this*?'

Patrick's face showed in almost comical dismay as he read.

'I meant to telegraph her! What an ass I am!'

'This letter, I presume, is from your sister Julia?'

'Yes – yes, it is.'

Miss Blacklock said grimly:

'*Then who, may I ask, is the young woman whom you brought here as Julia Simmons,* and whom I was given to understand was your sister and my cousin?'

'Well – you see – Aunt Letty – the fact of the matter is – I can explain it all – I know I oughtn't to have done it – but it really seemed more of a lark than anything else. If you'll just let me explain—'

'I am waiting for you to explain. *Who is this young woman?*'

'Well, I met her at a cocktail party soon after I got demobbed. We got talking and I said I was coming here and then – well, we thought it might be rather a good wheeze if I brought her along . . . You see, Julia, the real Julia, was mad to go on the stage and Mother had seven fits at the idea – however, Julia got a chance to join a jolly good repertory company up in Perth or somewhere and she thought she'd give it a try – but she thought she'd keep Mum calm by letting Mum think that she was here with me studying to be a dispenser like a good little girl.'

'I still want to know who this other young woman *is*.'

Patrick turned with relief as Julia, cool and aloof, came into the room.

'The balloon's gone up,' he said.

Julia raised her eyebrows. Then, still cool, she came forward and sat down.

'O.K.,' she said. 'That's that. I suppose you're very angry? She studied Miss Blacklock's face with almost dispassionate interest. 'I should be if I were you.'

'*Who are you?*'

354

Julia sighed.

'I think the moment's come when I make a clean breast of things. Here we go. I'm one half of the Pip and Emma combination. To be exact, my christened name is Emma Jocelyn Stamfordis – only father soon dropped the Stamfordis. I think he called himself De Courcy next.'

'My father and mother, let me tell you, split up about three years after Pip and I were born. Each of them went their own way. And they split us up. I was Father's part of the loot. He was a bad parent on the whole, though quite a charming one. I had various desert spells of being educated in convents – when Father hadn't any money, or was preparing to engage in some particularly nefarious deal. He used to pay the first term with every sign of affluence and then depart and leave me on the nuns' hands for a year or two. In the intervals, he and I had some very good times together, moving in cosmopolitan society. However, the war separated us completely. I've no idea of what's happened to him. I had a few adventures myself. I was with the French Resistance for a time. Quite exciting. To cut a long story short, I landed up in London and began to think about my future. I knew that Mother's brother with whom she'd had a frightful row, had died a very rich man. I looked up his will to see if there was anything for me. There wasn't – not directly, that is to say. I made a few inquiries about his widow – it seemed she was quite gaga and kept under drugs and was dying by inches. Frankly, it looked as though *you* were my best bet. You were going to come into a hell of a lot of money and from all I could find out, you didn't seem to have anyone much to spend it on. I'll be quite frank. It occurred to me that if I could get to know you in a friendly kind of way, and if you took a fancy to me – well, after all, conditions have changed a bit, haven't they, since Uncle Randall died? I mean any money we ever had has been swept away in the cataclysm of Europe. I thought you might pity a poor orphan girl, all alone in the world, and make her, perhaps, a small allowance.'

'Oh, you did, did you?' said Miss Blacklock grimly.

'Yes. Of course, I hadn't seen you then . . . I visualised a kind of sob stuff approach . . . Then, by a marvellous stroke of luck, I met Patrick here – and he turned out to be your nephew or your cousin, or something. Well, that struck me as a marvellous chance. I went bull-headed for Patrick and he fell for me in a most gratifying way. The real Julia was all wet about this acting stuff and I soon persuaded her it was her duty to Art to go and fix herself up in some uncomfortable lodgings in Perth and train to be the new Sarah Bernhardt.

'You mustn't blame Patrick too much. He felt awfully sorry for me, all alone in the world – and he soon thought it would be a really marvellous idea for me to come here as his sister and do my stuff.'

'And he also approved of your continuing to tell a tissue of lies to the police?'

'Have a heart, Letty. Don't you see that when that ridiculous hold-up business happened – or rather after it happened – I began to feel I was in a bit of a spot. Let's face it, I've got a perfectly good motive for putting you out of the way. You've only got my word for it now that I wasn't the one who tried to do it. You can't expect me deliberately to go and incriminate myself. Even Patrick got nasty ideas about me from time to time, and if even *he* could think things like that, what on earth would the police think? That Detective-Inspector struck me as a man of singularly sceptical mind. No, I figured out the only thing for me to do was to sit tight as Julia and just fade away when term came to an end.

'How was I to know that fool Julia, the real Julia, would go and have a row with the producer, and fling the whole thing up in a fit of temperament? She writes to Patrick and asks if she can come here, and instead of wiring her "Keep away" he goes and forgets to do anything at all!' She cast an angry glance at Patrick. 'Of all the utter *idiots*!'

She sighed.

'You don't know the straits I've been put to in Milchester! Of course, I haven't been to the hospital at all. But I had to go *somewhere*. Hours and hours I've spent in the pictures seeing the most frightful films over and over again.'

'*Pip and Emma*,' murmured Miss Blacklock. 'I never believed, somehow, in spite of what the Inspector said, that they were *real*—'

She looked searchingly at Julia.

'You're Emma,' she said. 'Where's Pip?'

Julia's eyes, limpid and innocent, met hers.

'I don't know,' she said. 'I haven't the faintest idea.'

'I think you're lying, Julia. When did you see him last?'

Was there a momentary hesitation before Julia spoke?

She said clearly and deliberately:

'I haven't seen him since we were both three years old –

when my mother took him away. I haven't seen either him or my mother. I don't know where they are.'

'And that's all you have to say?'

Julia sighed.

'I could say I was sorry. But it wouldn't really be true; because actually I'd do the same thing again – though not if I'd known about this murder business, of course.'

'Julia,' said Miss Blacklock, 'I call you that because I'm used to it. You were with the French Resistance, you say?'

'Yes. For eighteen months.'

'Then I suppose you learned to shoot?'

Again those cool blue eyes met hers.

'I can shoot all right. I'm a first-class shot. I didn't shoot at you, Letitia Blacklock, though you've only got my word for that. But I can tell you this, that if *I* had shot at you, I wouldn't have been likely to miss.'

II

The sound of a car driving up to the door broke through the tenseness of the moment.

'Who can that be?' asked Miss Blacklock.

Mitzi put a tousled head in. She was showing the whites of her eyes.

'It is the police come again,' she said. 'This, it is persecution! Why will they not leave us alone? I will not bear it. I will write to the Prime Minister. I will write to your King.'

Craddock's hand put her firmly and not too kindly aside. He came in with such a grim set to his lips that they all looked at him apprehensively. This was a new Inspector Craddock.

He said sternly:

'Miss Murgatroyd has been murdered. She was strangled – not more than an hour ago.' His eye singled out Julia. 'You – Miss Simmons – where have you been all day?'

Julia said warily:

'In Milchester. I've just got in.'

'And you?' The eye went on to Patrick.

'Yes.'

'Did you both come back here together?'

'Yes – yes, we did,' said Patrick.

'No,' said Julia. 'It's no good, Patrick. That's the kind of lie that will be found out at once. The bus people know us well. I

357

came back on the earlier bus, Inspector – the one that gets here at four o'clock.'

'And what did you do then?'

'I went for a walk.'

'In the direction of Boulders?'

'No. I went across the fields.'

He stared at her. Julia, her face pale, her lips tense, stared back.

Before anyone could speak, the telephone rang.

Miss Blacklock, with an inquiring glance at Craddock, picked up the receiver.

'Yes. Who? Oh, Bunch. What? No. No, she hasn't. I've no idea . . . Yes, he's here now.'

She lowered the instrument and said:

'Mrs Harmon would like to speak to you, Inspector. Miss Marple has not come back to the Vicarage and Mrs Harmon is worried about her.'

Craddock took two strides forward and gripped the telephone.

'Craddock speaking.'

'I'm worried, Inspector.' Bunch's voice came through with a childish tremor in it. 'Aunt Jane's out somewhere – and I don't know where. And they say that Miss Murgatroyd's been killed. Is it true?'

'Yes, it's true, Mrs Harmon. Miss Marple was there with Miss Hinchcliffe when they found the body.'

'Oh, so *that's* where she is.' Bunch sounded relieved.

'No – no, I'm afraid she isn't. Not now. She left there about – let me see – half an hour ago. She hasn't got home?'

'No – she hasn't. It's only ten minutes' walk. Where can she be?'

'Perhaps she's called in on one of your neighbours?'

'I've rung them up – *all of them*. She's not there. I'm frightened, Inspector.'

'So am I,' thought Craddock.

He said quickly:

'I'll come round to you – at once.'

'Oh, *do* – there's a piece of paper. She was writing on it before she went out. I don't know if it means anything . . . It just seems gibberish to me.'

Craddock replaced the receiver.

Miss Blacklock said anxiously:

'Has something happened to Miss Marple? Oh, I hope not.'

'I hope not, too.' His mouth was grim.

'She's so old – and frail.'

'I know.'

Miss Blacklock, standing with her hand pulling at the choker of pearls round her neck, said in a hoarse voice:

'It's getting worse and worse. Whoever's doing these things must be mad, Inspector – quite mad . . .'

'I wonder.'

The choker of pearls round Miss Blacklock's neck broke under the clutch of her nervous fingers. The smooth white globules rolled all over the room.

Letitia cried out in an anguished tone.

'My pearls – my *pearls*—' The agony in her voice was so acute that they all looked at her in astonishment. She turned, her hand to her throat, and rushed sobbing out of the room.

Phillipa began picking up the pearls.

'I've never seen her so upset over anything,' she said. 'Of course – she always wears them. Do you think, perhaps, that someone special gave them to her? Randall Goedler, perhaps?'

'It's possible,' said the Inspector slowly.

'They're not – they couldn't be – *real* by any chance?' Phillipa asked from where, on her knees, she was still collecting the white shining globules.

Taking one in his hand, Craddock was just about to reply contemptuously, 'Real? Of course not!' when he suddenly stifled the words.

After all, *could* the pearls be real?

They were so large, so even, so white that their falseness seemed palpable, but Craddock remembered suddenly a police case where a string of real pearls had been bought for a few shillings in a pawnbroker's shop.

Letitia Blacklock had assured him that there was no jewellery of any value in the house. If these pearls were, by any chance, genuine, they must be worth a fabulous sum. And if Randall Goedler had given them to her then they might be worth any sum you cared to name.

They looked false – they *must* be false, but – if they were real?'

Why not? She might herself be unaware of their value. Or she might choose to protect her treasure by treating it as though it were a cheap ornament worth a couple of guines at most. What would they be worth if real? A fabulous sum . . . Worth doing murder for – *if anybody knew about them.*

With a start, the Inspector wrenched himself away from his

359

speculations. Miss Marple was missing. He must go to the Vicarage.

III

He found Bunch and her husband waiting for him, their faces anxious and drawn.

'She hasn't come back,' said Bunch.

'Did she say she was coming back here when she left Boulders?' asked Julian.

'She didn't actually say so,' said Craddock slowly, throwing his mind back to the last time he had seen Jane Marple.

He remembered the grimness of her lips and the severe frosty light in those usually gentle blue eyes.

Grimness, an inexorable determination . . . to do what? To go where?

'She was talking to Sergeant Fletcher when I last saw her,' he said. 'Just by the gate. And then she went through it and out. I took it she was going straight home to the Vicarage. I would have sent her in the car – but there was so much to attend to, and she slipped away very quietly. Fletcher may know something! Where's Fletcher?'

But Sergeant Fletcher, it seemed, as Craddock learned when he rang up Boulders, was neither to be found there nor had he left any message where he had gone. There was some idea that he had returned to Milchester for some reason.

The Inspector rang up headquarters in Milchester, but no news of Fletcher was to be found there.

Then Craddock turned to Bunch as he remembered what she had told him over the telephone.

'Where's that paper? You said she'd been writing something on a bit of paper.'

Bunch brought it to him. He spread it out on the table and looked down on it. Bunch leant over his shoulder and spelled it it out as he read. The writing was shaky and not easy to read:

Lamp.

Then came the word '*Violets.*'

Then came a space:

Where is bottle of aspirin?

The next item in this curious list was more difficult to make out. '*Delicious Death,*' Bunch read. 'That's Mitzi's cake.'

'*Making enquiries,*' read Craddock.

'Inquiries? What about, I wonder? What's this? *Severe afflic-tion bravely borne* . . . What on earth—!'

'*Iodine,*' read the Inspector. '*Pearls.* Ah, pearls.'

'And then *Lotty* – no, Letty. Her *e*'s look like *o*'s. And then *Berne.* And what's this? *Old Age Pension* . . .'

They looked at each other in bewilderment.

Craddock recapitulated swiftly:

'Lamp. Violets. Where is bottle of aspirin? Delicious Death. Making enquiries. Severe affliction bravely borne. Iodine. Pearls. Letty. Berne. Old Age Pension.'

Bunch asked: 'Does it mean anything? Anything at all? I can't see any connection.'

Craddock said slowly: 'I've just a glimmer – but I don't see. It's odd that she should have put that down about pearls.'

'What about pearls? What does it mean?'

'Does Miss Blacklock always wear that three-tiered choker of pearls?'

'Yes, she does. We laugh about it sometimes. They're so dread-fully false looking, aren't they? But I suppose she thinks it's fashionable.'

'There might be another reason,' said Craddock slowly.

'You don't mean that they're *real*. Oh! they *couldn't be!*'

'How often have you had an opportunity of seeing real pearls of that size, Mrs Harmon?'

'But they're so glassy.'

Craddock shrugged his shoulders.

'Anyway, they don't matter now. It's Miss Marple that matters. We've got to find her.'

They'd got to find her before it was too late – but perhaps it was already too late? Those pencilled words showed that she was on the track . . . But that was dangerous – horribly dangerous. And where the hell was Fletcher?

Craddock strode out of the Vicarage to where he'd left his car. Search – that was all he could do – search.

A voice spoke to him out of the dripping laurels.

Sir!' said Sergeant Fletcher urgently. '*Sir* . . .'

21

THREE WOMEN

Dinner was over at Little Paddocks. It had been a silent and uncomfortable meal.

Patrick, uneasily aware of having fallen from grace, only made spasmodic attempts at conversation – and such as he did make were not well received. Phillipa Haymes was sunk in abstraction. Miss Blacklock herself had abandoned the effort to behave with her normal cheerfulness. She had changed for dinner and had come down wearing her necklace of camoes but for the first time fear showed from her darkly-circled eyes, and betrayed itself by her twitching hands.

Julia, alone, had maintained her air of cynical detachment throughout the evening.

'I'm sorry, Letty,' she said, 'that I can't pack my bag and go. But I presume the police wouldn't allow it. I don't suppose I'll darken your roof – or whatever the expression is – for long. I should imagine that Inspector Craddock will be round with a warrant and the handcuffs any moment. In fact I can't imagine why something of the kind hasn't happened already.'

'He's looking for the old lady – for Miss Marple,' said Miss Blacklock.

'Do you think she's been murdered, too?' Patrick asked with scientific curiosity. 'But why? What could she know?'

'I don't know,' said Miss Blacklock dully. 'Perhaps Miss Murgatroyd told her something.'

'If she's been murdered too,' said Patrick, 'there seems to be logically only one person who could have done it.'

'Who?'

'Hinchcliffe, of course,' said Patrick triumphantly. 'That's where she was last seen alive – at Boulders. My solution would be that she never left Boulders.'

'My head aches,' said Miss Blacklock in a dull voice. She pressed her fingers to her forehead. 'Why should Hinch murder Miss Marple? It doesn't make sense.'

'It would if Hinch had really murdered Murgatroyd,' said Patrick triumphantly.

Phillipa came out of her apathy to say:

'Hinch wouldn't murder Murgatroyd.'

Patrick was in an argumentative mood.

'She might have if Murgatroyd had blundered on something to show that she – Hinch – was the criminal.'

'Anyway, Hinch was at the station when Murgatroyd was killed.'

'She could have murdered Murgatroyd before she left.'

Startling them all, Letitia Blacklock suddenly screamed out:

'Murder, murder, *murder*—! Can't you talk of *anything* else? I'm frightened, don't you understand? I'm frightened. I wasn't before. I thought I could take care of myself . . . But what can you do against a murderer who's waiting – and watching – and biding his time! Oh, God!'

She dropped her head forward on her hands. A moment later she looked up and apologised stiffly.

'I'm sorry. I – I lost control.'

'That's all right, Aunt Letty,' said Patrick affectionately. 'I'll look after you.'

'You?' was all Letitia Blacklock said, but the disillusionment behind the word was almost an accusation.

That had been shortly before dinner, and Mitzi had then created a diversion by coming and declaring that she was not going to cook the dinner.

'I do not do anything more in this house. I go to my room. I lock myself in. I stay there until it is daylight. I am afraid – people are being killed – that Miss Murgatroyd with her stupid English face – who would want to kill *her*? Only a maniac! Then it is a maniac that is about! And a maniac does not care *who* he kills. But me, I do not want to be killed. There are shadows in that kitchen – and I hear noises – I think there is someone out in the yard and then I think I see a shadow by the larder door and then it is footsteps I hear. So I go now to my room and I lock the door and perhaps even I put the chest of drawers against it. And in the morning I tell that cruel hard policeman that I go away from here. And if he will not let me I say: "I scream and I scream and I scream until you have to let me go!"'

Everybody, with a vivid recollection of what Mitzi could do in the screaming line, shuddered at the threat.

'So I go to my room,' said Mitzi, repeating the statement once more to make her intentions quite clear. With a symbolic action she cast off the cretonne apron she had been wearing. 'Goodnight Miss Blacklock. Perhaps in the morning, you may not be alive. So in case that is so, I say goodbye.'

She departed abruptly and the door, with its usual gentle little whine, closed softly after her.

Julia got up.

'I'll see to dinner,' she said in a matter of fact way. 'Rather a good arrangement – less embarrassing for you all than having me sit down at table with you. Patrick (since he's constituted himself your protector, Aunt Letty) has better taste every dish first. I don't want to be accused of poisoning you on top of everything else.'

So Julia had cooked and served a really excellent meal.

Phillipa had come out to the kitchen with an offer of assistance but Julia had said firmly that she didn't want any help.

'Julia, there's something I want to say—'

'This is no time for girlish confidences,' said Julia firmly. 'Go on back in the dining-room, Phillipa.'

Now dinner was over and they were in the drawing-room with coffee on the small table by the fire – and nobody seemed to have anything to say. They were waiting – that was all.

At 8.30 Inspector Craddock rang up.

'I shall be with you in about a quarter of an hour's time,' he announced. 'I'm bringing Colonel and Mrs Easterbrook and Mrs Swettenham and her son with me.'

'But really, Inspector . . . I can't cope with people tonight—'

Miss Blacklock's voice sounded as though she were at the end of her tether.

'I know how you feel, Miss Blacklock. I'm sorry. But this is urgent.'

'Have you – found Miss Marple?'

'No,' said the Inspector, and rang off.

Julia took the coffee tray out to the kitchen where, to her surprise, she found Mitzi contemplating the piled-up dishes and plates by the sink.

Mitzi burst into a torrent of words.

'See what you do in my so nice kitchen! That frying pan – only, *only* for omelettes do I use it! And you, what have you used it for?'

'Frying onions.'

'Ruined – *ruined*. It will have now to be *washed* and never – never – do I wash my omelette pan. I rub it carefully over with a greasy newspaper, that is all. And this saucepan here that you have used – that one, I use him only for milk—'

'Well, I don't know what pans you use for what,' said Julia crossly. 'You chose to go to bed and why on earth you've chosen to get up again, I can't imagine. Go away again and leave me to wash up in peace.'

'No, I will not let you use my kitchen.'

'Oh, Mitzi, you *are* impossible!'

Julia stalked angrily out of the kitchen and at that moment the door-bell rang.

'I do not go to the door,' Mitzi called from the kitchen. Julia muttered an impolite Continental expression under her breath and stalked to the front door.

It was Miss Hinchcliffe.

'Evening,' she said in her gruff voice. 'Sorry to barge in. Inspector's rung up, I expect?'

'He didn't tell us you were coming,' said Julia, leading the way to the drawing-room.

'He said I needn't come unless I liked,' said Miss Hinchcliffe. 'But I do like.'

Nobody offered Miss Hinchcliffe sympathy or mentioned Miss Murgatroyd's death. The ravaged face of the tall vigorous woman told its own tale, and would have made any expression of sympathy an impertinence.

'Turn all the lights on,' said Miss Blacklock. 'And put more coal on the fire. I'm cold – horribly cold. Come and sit here by the fire, Miss Hinchcliffe. The Inspector said he would be here in a quarter of an hour. It must be nearly that now.'

'Mitzi's come down again,' said Julia.

'Has she? Sometimes I think that girl's mad – quite mad. But then perhaps we're all mad.'

'I've no patience with this saying that all people who commit crimes are mad,' barked Miss Hinchcliffe. 'Horribly and intelligently sane – that's what I think a criminal is!'

The sound of a car was heard outside and presently Craddock came in with Colonel and Mrs Easterbrook and Edmund and Mrs Swettenham.

They were all curiously subdued.

Colonel Easterbrook said in a voice that was like an echo of his usual tones:

'Ha! A good fire.'

Mrs Easterbrook wouldn't take off her fur coat and sat down close to her husband. Her face, usually pretty and rather vapid, was like a little pinched weasel face. Edmund was in one of his furious moods and scowled at everybody. Mrs Swettenham made what was evidently a great effort. and which resulted in a kind of parody of herself.

'It's awful – isn't it?' she said conversationally. 'Everything, I mean. And really the less one says, the better. Because one doesn't know *who next* – like the Plague. Dear Miss Blacklock, don't you think you ought to have a little brandy? Just half a wineglass even? I always think there's nothing like brandy – such a wonderful stimulant. I – it seems so terrible of us – forcing our way in here like this, but Inspector Craddock *made* us come. And it seems so terrible – she hasn't been found, you know. That poor old thing from the Vicarage, I mean. Bunch Harmon is nearly frantic. Nobody knows *where* she went instead of going home. She didn't come to us. I've not even seen her today. And I should know if she *had* come to the house because I was in the drawing-room – at the back, you know, and Edmund was in his study writing – and that's at the front – so if she'd come either way we *should* have seen. And oh, I do hope and pray that nothing has happened to that dear sweet old thing – all her faculties still and *everything*.'

'Mother,' said Edmund in a voice of acute suffering, 'can't you shut up?'

'I'm sure, dear, I don't want to say a *word*,' said Mrs Swettenham, and sat down on the sofa by Julia.

Inspector Craddock stood near the door. Facing him, almost in a row, were the three women. Julia and Mrs Swettenham on the sofa. Mrs Easterbrook on the arm of her husband's chair. He had not brought about this arrangement, but it suited him very well.

Miss Blacklock and Miss Hinchcliffe were crouching over the fire. Edmund stood near them. Phillipa was far back in the shadows.

Craddock began without preamble.

'You all know that Miss Murgatroyd's been killed,' he began. 'We've reason to believe that the person who killed her was a woman. And for certain other reasons we can narrow it down still more. I'm about to ask certain ladies here to account for what they were doing between the hours of four and four-twenty this afternoon. I have already had an account of her movements from – from the young lady who has been calling herself Miss Simmons. I will ask her to repeat that statement. At the same time, Miss Simmons, I must caution you that you need not answer if you think your answers may incriminate you, and anything you say will be taken down by Constable Edwards and may be used as evidence in court.'

'You have to say that, don't you?' said Julia. She was rather pale, but composed. 'I repeat that between four and four-thirty I was walking along the field leading down to the brook by Compton Farm. I came back to the road by that field with three poplars in it. I didn't meet anyone as far as I can remember. I did not go near Boulders.'

'Mrs Swettenham?'

Edmund said, 'Are you cautioning all of us?'

The Inspector turned to him.

'No. At the moment only Miss Simmons. I have no reason to believe that any other statement will be incriminating, but anyone, of course, is entitled to have a solicitor present and to refuse to answer questions unless he *is* present.'

'Oh, but that would be very silly and a complete waste of time,' cried Mrs Swettenham. 'I'm sure I can tell you at once exactly what I was doing. That's what you want, isn't it? Shall I begin now?'

'Yes, please, Mrs Swettenham.'

'Now, let me see.' Mrs Swettenham closed her eyes, opened them again. 'Of course I had nothing *at all* to do with killing Miss Murgatroyd. I'm sure *everybody* here knows *that*. But I'm a woman of the world, I know quite well that the police have to ask all the most unnecessary questions and write the answers down very carefully, because it's all for what they call "the record." That's it, isn't it?' Mrs Swettenham flashed the question at the diligent Constable Edwards, and added graciously, 'I'm not going too fast for you, I hope?'

Constable Edwards, a good shorthand writer, but with little social *savoir faire*, turned red to the ears and replied:

'It's quite all right, madam. Well, perhaps a *little* slower would be better.'

Mrs Swettenham resumed her discourse with emphatic pauses where she considered a comma or a full stop might be appropriate.

'Well, of course it's difficult to say – exactly – because I've not got, really, a very good sense of time. And ever since the war quite half our clocks haven't gone at all, and the ones that do go are often fast or slow or stop because we haven't wound them up.' Mrs Swettenham paused to let this picture of confused time sink in and then went on earnestly, 'What I *think* I was doing at four o'clock was turning the heel of my sock (and for some extraordinary reason I was going round the wrong way – in purl, you know, not plain) but if I *wasn't* doing that, I must have been outside snipping off the dead chrysanthemums – no, that was earlier – before the rain.'

'The rain,' said the Inspector, 'started at 4.10 exactly.'

'Did it now? That helps a lot. Of course, I was upstairs putting a wash basin in the passage where the rain always comes through. And it was coming through so fast that I guessed at once that the gutter was stopped up again. So I came down and got my mackintosh and rubber boots. I called Edmund, but he didn't answer, so I thought perhaps he'd got to a very important place in his novel and I wouldn't disturb him, and I've done it quite often myself before. With the broom handle, you know, tied in to that long thing you push up windows with.'

'You mean,' said Craddock, noting bewilderment on his subordinate's face, 'that you were cleaning out the gutter?'

'Yes, it was all choked up with leaves. It took a long time and I got rather wet, but I got it clear at last. And then I went in and got changed and washed – so *smelly*, dead leaves – and then I went into the kitchen and put the kettle on. It was 6.15 by the kitchen clock.'

Constable Edwards blinked.

'Which means,' finished Mrs Swettenham triumphantly, 'that it was exactly twenty minutes to five.'

'Or near enough,' she added.

'Did anybody see what you were doing whilst you were out cleaning the gutter?'

'No, indeed,' said Mrs Swettenham. 'I'd soon have roped them in to help if they had! It's a most difficult thing to do single-handed.'

'So, by your own statement, you were outside, in a mackintosh and boots, at the time when the rain was coming down, and according to you, you were employed during that time in cleaning out a gutter but you have no one who can substantiate that statement?'

'You can look at the gutter,' said Mrs Swettenham. 'It's beautifully clear.'

'Did you hear your mother call to you, Mr Swettenham?'

'No,' said Edmund. 'I was fast asleep.'

'Edmund,' said his mother reproachfully, 'I thought you were *writing*.'

Inspector Craddock turned to Mrs Easterbrook.

'Now, Mrs Easterbrook?'

'I was sitting with Archie in his study,' said Mrs Easterbrook, fixing wide innocent eyes on him. 'We were listening to the wireless together, weren't we, Archie?'

There was a pause. Colonel Easterbrook was very red in the face. He took his wife's hand in his.

'You don't understand these things, kitten,' he said. 'I – well, I must say, Inspector, you've rather sprung this business on us. My wife, you know, has been terribly upset by all this. She's nervous and highly strung and doesn't appreciate the importance of – of taking due consideration before she makes a statement.'

'Archie,' cried Mrs Easterbrook reproachfully, 'are you going to say you weren't with me?'

'Well, I wasn't, was I, my dear? I mean one's got to stick to the facts. Very important in this sort of inquiry. I was talking to Lampson, the farmer at Croft End, about some chicken netting. That was about a quarter to four. I didn't get home until after the rain had stopped. Just before tea. A quarter to five. Laura was toasting the scones.'

'And had *you* been out also, Mrs Easterbrook?'

The pretty face looked more like a weasel's than ever. Her eyes had a trapped look.

'No – no, I just sat listening to the wireless. I didn't go out. Not then. I'd been out earlier. About – about half-past three. Just for a little walk. Not far.'

She looked as though she expected more questions, but Craddock said quietly:

'That's all, Mrs Easterbrook.'

He went on: 'These statements will be typed out. You can read them and sign them if they are substantially correct.'

Mrs Easterbrook looked at him with sudden venom.

'Why don't you ask the others where they were? That Haymes woman? And Edmund Swettenham? How do you know he *was* asleep indoors? Nobody saw him.'

Inspector Craddock said quietly:

'Miss Murgatroyd, before she died, made a certain statement. On the night of the hold-up here, *someone* was absent from this room. Someone who was supposed to have been in the room all the time. Miss Murgatroyd told her friend the names of all the people she *did* see. By a process of elimination, she made the discovery that there was someone she did *not* see.'

'Nobody could see anything,' said Julia.

'Murgatroyd could,' said Miss Hinchcliffe, speaking suddenly in her deep voice. 'She was over there behind the door, where Inspector Craddock is now. She was the only person who could see anything of what was happening.'

'*Aha! That is what you think is it!*' demanded Mitzi.

She made one of her dramatic entrances, flinging open the door and almost knocking Craddock sideways. She was in a frenzy of excitement.

'Ah, you do not ask Mitzi to come in here with the others, do you, you stiff policemen? I am only Mitzi! Mitzi in the kitchen! Let her stay in the kitchen where she belongs! But I tell you that Mitzi, as well as anyone else, and perhaps better, yes, better, can see things. Yes, I see things. I see something the night of the burglary. I see something and I do not quite believe it, and I hold my tongue till now. I think to myself I will not tell what it is I have seen, not yet. I will wait.'

'And when everything has calmed down, you meant to ask for a little money from a certain person, eh?' said Craddock.

Mitzi turned on him like an angry cat.

'And why not? Why look down your nose? Why should I not be paid for it if I have been so generous as to keep silence? Especially if some day there will be money – much *much* money. Oh! I have heard things – I know what goes on. I know this Pippemmer – this secret society of which *she*' – she flung a dramatic finger towards Julia – 'is an agent. Yes, I would have waited and asked for money – but now I am afraid I would rather be *safe*. For soon, perhaps, someone will kill *me*. So I will tell what I know.'

'All right then,' said the Inspector sceptically. 'What *do* you know?'

'I tell you.' Mitzi spoke solemnly. 'On that night I am *not* in the pantry cleaning silver as I say – I am already in the dining-room when I hear the gun go off. I look through the keyhole. The hall it is black, but the gun go off again and the torch it falls – and it swings round as it falls – and I see *her*. I see *her* there close to him with the gun in her hand. I see Miss Black-lock.'

'Me?' Miss Blacklock sat up in astonishment. 'You must be mad!'

'But that's impossible,' cried Edmund. 'Mitzi couldn't have seen Miss Blacklock.'

Craddock cut in and his voice had the corrosive quality of a deadly acid.

'*Couldn't she, Mr Swettenham? And why not?* Because it

wasn't Miss Blacklock who was standing there with the gun? It was *you*, wasn't it?'

'I – of course not – what the *hell*!'

'*You* took Colonel Easterbrook's revolver. *You* fixed up the business with Rudi Scherz – as a good joke. You had followed Patrick Simmons into the far room and when the lights went out you slipped out through the carefully oiled door. You shot at Miss Blacklock and then you killed Rudi Scherz. A few seconds later you were back in the drawing-room clicking your lighter.'

For a moment Edmund seemed at a loss for words, then he spluttered out:

'The whole idea is *monstrous*. Why *me*? What earthly motive had *I* got?'

'If Miss Blacklock dies before Mrs Goedler, two people inherit, remember. The two we know of as Pip and Emma. Julia Simmons has turned out to be Emma—'

'And you think I'm Pip?' Edmund laughed. 'Fantastic – absolutely *fantastic*! I'm about the right age – nothing else. And I can prove to you, you damned fool, that I *am* Edmund Swettenham. Birth certificate, schools, university – everything.'

'He isn't Pip.' The voice came from the shadows in the corner. Phillipa Haymes came forward, her face pale. '*I'm Pip*, Inspector.'

'*You*, Mrs Haymes?'

'Yes. Everybody seems to have assumed that Pip was a boy – Julia knew, of course, that her twin was another girl – I don't know why she didn't say so this afternoon—'

'Family solidarity,' said Julia. 'I suddenly realized who you were. I'd had no idea till that moment.'

'I'd had the same idea as Julia did,' said Phillipa, her voice trembling a little. 'After I – lost my husband and the war was over, I wondered what I was going to do. My mother died many years ago. I found out about my Goedler relations. Mrs Goedler was dying and at her death the money would go to a Miss Blacklock. I found out where Miss Blacklock lived and I – I came here. I took a job with Mrs Lucas. I hoped that, since this Miss Blacklock was an elderly woman without relatives, she might, perhaps, be willing to help. Not me, because I could work, but help with Harry's education. After all, it *was* Goedler money and she'd no one particular of her own to spend it on.

'And then,' Phillipa spoke faster, it was as though, now her long reserve had broken down, she couldn't get the words out fast enough, 'that hold-up happened and I began to be frightened. Because it seemed to me that the only possible person with a motive for killing Miss Blacklock was *me*. I hadn't the least idea who Julia was – we aren't identical twins and we're not much alike to look at. No, it seemed as though I was the only one bound to be suspected.'

She stopped and pushed her fair hair back from her face, and Craddock suddenly realized that the faded snapshot in the box of letters must have been a photograph of Phillipa's mother. The likeness was undeniable. He knew too why that mention of closing and unclosing hands had seemed familiar – Phillipa was doing it now.

'Miss Blacklock has been good to me. Very *very* good to me – I didn't try to kill her. I never thought of killing her. But all the same, I'm Pip.' She added, 'you see, you needn't suspect Edmund any more.'

'Needn't I?' said Craddock. Again there was that acid biting tone in his voice. 'Edmund Swettenham's a young man who's fond of money. A young man, perhaps, who would like to marry a rich wife. But she wouldn't be a rich wife *unless Miss Blacklock died before Mrs Goedler.* And since it seemed almost certain that Mrs Goedler would die before Miss Blacklock, well – he had to do something about it – *didn't you, Mr Swettenham?*'

'It's a damned lie!' Edmund shouted.

And then, suddenly, a sound rose on the air. It came from the kitchen – a long unearthly shriek of terror.

'That isn't Mitzi!' cried Julia.

'No,' said Inspector Craddock, 'it's someone who's murdered three people . . .'

22

THE TRUTH

When the Inspector turned on Edmund Swettenham, Mitzi had crept quietly out of the room and back to the kitchen. She was running water into the sink when Miss Blacklock entered.

Mitzi gave her a shamefaced sideways look.

'What a liar you are, Mitzi,' said Miss Blacklock pleasantly. 'Here – that isn't the way to wash up. The silver first, and fill the sink right up. You can't wash up in about two inches of water.'

Mitzi turned the taps on obediently.

'You are not angry at what I say, Miss Blacklock?' she asked.

'If I were to be angry at all the lies you tell, I should never be out of a temper,' said Miss Blacklock.

'I will go and say to the Inspector that I make it all up, shall I?' asked Mitzi.

'He knows that already,' said Miss Blacklock, pleasantly.

Mitzi turned off the taps and as she did so two hands came up behind her head and with one swift movement forced it down into the water-filled sink.

'Only *I* know that you're telling the truth for once,' said Miss Blacklock viciously.

Mitzi thrashed and struggled but Miss Blacklock was strong and her hands held the girl's head firmly under water.

Then, from somewhere quite close behind her, Dora Bunner's voice rose piteously on the air:

'*Oh Lotty – Lotty – don't do it . . . Lotty.*'

Miss Blacklock screamed. Her hands flew up in the air, and Mitzi, released, came up choking and spluttering.

Miss Blacklock screamed again and again. For there was no one there in the kitchen with her . . .

'*Dora, Dora, forgive me. I had to . . . I had to—*'

She rushed distractedly towards the scullery door – and the bulk of Sergeant Fletcher barred her way, just as Miss Marple stepped, flushed and triumphant, out of the broom cupboard.

'I could always mimic people's voices,' said Miss Marple.

'You'll have to come with me, Madam,' said Sergeant Fletcher. 'I was a witness of your attempt to drown this girl. And there will be other charges. I must warn you, Letitia Blacklock—'

'Charlotte Blacklock,' corrected Miss Marple. 'That's who she is, you know. Under that choker of pearls she always wears you'll find the scar of the operation.'

'Operation?'

'Operation for goitre.'

Miss Blacklock, quite calm now, looked at Miss Marple.

'So you know all about it?' she said.

'Yes, I've known for some time.'

Charlotte Blacklock sat down by the table and began to cry.

'You shouldn't have done that,' she said. 'Not made Dora's voice come. I loved Dora. I really loved Dora.'

Inspector Craddock and the others had crowded in the doorway.

Constable Edwards, who added a knowledge of first aid and artificial respiration to his other accomplishments, was busy with

Mitzi. As soon as Mitzi could speak she was lyrical with self praise.

'I do that good, do I not? I am clever! And I am brave! Oh, I am brave! Very nearly was *I* murdered, too. But I was so brave I risk *everything*.'

With a rush Miss Hinchcliffe thrust aside the others and leapt upon the weeping figure of Charlotte Blacklock by the table.

It took all Sergeant Fletcher's strength to hold her off.

'Now then—' he said. 'Now then – no, no, Miss Hinchcliffe—'

Between clenched teeth Miss Hinchcliffe was muttering:

'Let me get at her. Just let me get at her. It was she who killed Amy Murgatroyd.'

Charlotte Blacklock looked up and sniffed.

' I didn't want to kill her. I didn't want to kill anybody – I had to – but it's Dora I mind about – after Dora was dead, I was all alone – ever since she died – I've been alone – oh, Dora – Dora—'

And once again she dropped her head on her hands and wept.

—— 23 ——

EVENING AT THE VICARAGE

Miss Marple sat in the tall arm-chair. Bunch was on the floor in front of the fire with her arms round her knees.

The Reverend Julian Harmon was leaning forward and was for once looking more like a schoolboy than a man foreshadowing his own maturity. And Inspector Craddock was smoking his pipe and drinking a whisky and soda and was clearly very much off duty. An outer circle was composed of Julia, Patrick, Edmund and Phillipa.

'I think it's your story, Miss Marple,' said Craddock.

'Oh no, my dear boy. I only just helped a little, here and there. *You* were in charge of the whole thing, and conducted it all, and you know so much that I don't.'

'Well, tell it together,' said Bunch impatiently. 'Bit each. Only let Aunt Jane start because I like the muddly way her mind works. When did you first think that the whole thing was a put-up job by Blacklock?'

'Well, my dear Bunch, it's hard to say. Of course, right at the very beginning, it did seem as though the ideal person – or rather the *obvious* person, I should say – to have arranged the hold-up *was* Miss Blacklock herself. She was the only person who was known to have been in contact with Rudi Scherz, and how much easier to arrange something like that when it's your own house. The central heating, for instance. No fires – because that would have meant light in the room. But the only person who could have arranged *not* to have a fire was the mistress of the house herself.

'Not that I thought of all that at the time – it just seemed to me that it was a pity it *couldn't* be as simple as that! Oh, no, I was taken in like everyone else, I thought that someone really did want to kill Letitia Blacklock.'

'I think I'd like to get clear first on what really happened,' said Bunch. 'Did this Swiss boy recognize her?'

'Yes. He'd worked in—'

She hesitated and looked at Craddock.

In Dr Adolf Koch's clinic in Berne,' said Craddock. 'Koch was a world famous specialist on operations for goitre. Charlotte Blacklock went there to have her goitre removed and Rudi Scherz was one of the orderlies. When he came to England he recognized in the hotel a lady who had been a patient and on the spur of the moment he spoke to her. I dare say he mightn't have done that if he'd paused to think, because he left the place under a cloud, but that was some time after Charlotte had been there, so she wouldn't know anything about it.'

'So he never said anything to her about Montreux and his father being a hotel proprietor?'

'Oh, no, she made that up to account for his having spoken to her.'

'It must have been a great shock to her,' said Miss Marple, thoughtfully. 'She felt reasonably safe – and then – the almost impossible mischance of somebody turning up who had known her – not as one of the two Miss Blacklocks – she was prepared for *that* – but definitely as *Charlotte* Blacklock, a patient who'd been operated on for goitre.

'But you wanted to go through it all from the beginning. Well, the beginning, I think – if Inspector Craddock agrees with me – was when Charlotte Blacklock, a pretty, light-hearted affectionate girl, developed that enlargement of the thyriod gland that's called a goitre. It ruined her life, because she was a very sensitive girl. A girl, too, who had always set a lot of stress on her personal appearance. And girls just at that age in their teens are particularly sensitive about themselves. If she'd had a mother, or a reaesonable father, I don't think she would have got into the morbid state she undoubtedly did get into. She had no one, you see, to take her out of herself, and force her to see people and lead a normal life and not think too much about her infirmity. And, of course, in a different household, she might have been sent for an operation many years earlier.

But Dr Blacklock, I think, was an old-fashioned, narrow-minded tyrannical and obstinate man. He didn't believe in these operations. Charlotte must take it from him that nothing could be done – apart from dosage with iodine and other drugs. Charlotte *did* take it from him, and I think her sister also placed more faith in Dr Blacklock's powers as a physician than he deserved.

'Charlotte was devoted to her father in a rather weak and soppy way. She thought, definitely, that her father knew best. But she shut herself up more and more as the goitre became larger and more unsightly, and refused to see people. She was actually a kindly affectionate creature.'

'That's an odd description of a murderess,' said Edmund.

'I don't know that it is,' said Miss Marple. 'Weak and kindly people are often very treacherous. And if they've got a grudge against life it saps the little moral strength that they may possess.

Letitia Blacklock, of course, had quite a different personality. Inspector Craddock told me that Belle Goedler described her as really *good* – and I think Letitia *was* good. She was a woman of great integrity who found – as she put it herself – a great difficulty in understanding how people couldn't see what was dishonest. Letitia Blacklock, however tempted, would never have contemplated any kind of fraud for a moment.

'Letitia was devoted to her sister. She wrote her long accounts of everything that happened in an effort to keep her sister in touch with life. She was worried by the morbid state Charlotte was getting into.

'Finally Dr Blacklock died. Letitia, without hesitation, threw up her position with Randall Goedler and devoted herself to Charlotte. She took her to Switzerland, to consult authorities there on the possibility of operating. It had been left very late – but as we know the operation was successful. The deformity was gone – and the scar this operation had left was easily hidden by a choker of pearls or beads.

'The war had broken out. A return to England was difficult and the two sisters stayed in Switzerland doing various Red Cross and other work. That's right, isn't it, Inspector?'

'Yes, Miss Marple.'

'They got occasional news from England – amongst other things, I expect, they heard that Belle Goedler could not live long. I'm sure it would be only human nature for them both to have planned and talked together of the days ahead when a big fortune would be theirs to spend. One has got to realize, I think, that this prospect meant much more to *Charlotte* than it did to Letitia. For the first time in her life, Charlotte could go about feeling herself a normal woman, a woman at whom no one looked with either repulsion or pity. She was free at last to enjoy life – and she had a whole lifetime, as it were, to crowd into her remaining years. To travel, to have a house and beautiful grounds – to have clothes and jewels, and go to plays and concerts, to gratify every whim – it was all a kind of fairy tale come true to Charlotte.

'And then Letitia, the strong healthy Letitia, got flu which turned to pneumonia and died within the space of a week! Not only had Charlotte lost her sister, but the whole dream existence she had planned for herself was cancelled. I think, you know, that she may have felt almost resentful towards Letitia. Why need Letitia have died, just then, when they had just had a letter saying Belle Goedler could not last long? Just one more month, perhaps, and the money would have been Letitia's – and hers when Letitia died . . .

'Now this is where I think the difference between the two came in. Charlotte didn't really feel that what she suddenly thought of doing was wrong – not really wrong. The money was meant to come to Letitia – it *would* have come to Letitia in the course of a few months – and she regarded herself and Letitia as one.

'Perhaps the idea didn't occur to her until the doctor or someone asked her her sister's Christian name – and then she realized how to nearly everyone they had appeared as the two Miss Blacklocks – elderly, well-bred Englishwomen, dressed much the same, with a strong family resemblance – (and, as I pointed out to Bunch, one elderly woman is *so* like another). Why shouldn't it be Charlotte who had died and *Letitia* who was alive?

It was an impulse, perhaps, more than a plan. Letitia was buried under Charlotte's name. "Charlotte" was dead, "Letitia" came to England. All the natural initiative and energy, dormant for so many years, were now in the ascendant. As Charlotte she had played second fiddle. She now assumed the airs of command, the feeling of command that had been Letitia's. They were not really so unlike in mentality – though there was, I think, a big difference *morally*.

'Charlotte had, of course, to take one or two obvious precautions. She bought a house in a part of England quite unknown to her. The only people she had to avoid were a few people in her own native town in Cumberland (where in any case she'd lived as a recluse) and, of couse, Belle Goedler who had known Letitia so well that any impersonation would have been out of the question. Handwriting difficulties were got over by the arthritic condition of her hands. It was really very easy because so few people had ever really known Charlotte.'

'But supposing she'd met people who'd known Letitia?' asked Bunch. 'There must have been plenty of those.'

'They wouldn't matter in the same way. Someone might say: "I came across Letitia Blacklock the other day. She's changed so much I really wouldn't have known her.' But there still wouldn't be any suspicion in their minds that she wasn't Letitia. People *do* change in the course of ten years. *Her* failure to recognize *them* could always be put down to her short-sightedness; and you must remember that she knew every detail of Letitia's life in London – the people she met – the places she went. She'd got Letitia's letters to refer to, and she could quickly have disarmed any suspicion by mention of some incident, or an inquiry after a mutual friend. No, it was recognition as *Charlotte* that was the only thing she had to fear.

'She settled down at Little Paddocks, got to know her neighbours and, when she got a letter asking dear Letitia to be kind, she accepted with pleasure the visit of two young cousins she had never seen. Their acceptance of her as Aunt Letty increased her security.

'The whole thing was going splendidly. And then – she made her big mistake. It was a mistake that arose solely from her kindness of heart and her naturally affectionate nature. She got a letter from an old friend who had fallen on evil days, and she hurried to the rescue. Perhaps it may have been partly because she was, in spite of everything, lonely. Her secret kept her in a way apart from people. And she had been genuinely fond of Dora Bunner and remembered her as a symbol of her own gay carefree days at school. Anyway, on an impulse, she answered Dora's letter in person. And very surprised Dora must have been! She'd written to *Letitia* and the sister who turned up in answer to her letter was *Charlotte*. There was never any question of pretending to be Letitia to Dora. Dora was one of the few friends who had been admitted to see Charlotte in her lonely and unhappy days.

'And because she knew that Dora would look at the matter in exactly the same way as she did herself, she told Dora what she had done. Dora approved wholeheartedly. In her confused muddle-headed mind it seemed only right that dear Lotty should not be done out of her inheritance by Letty's untimely death. Lotty *deserved* a reward for all the patient suffering she had borne so bravely. It would have been most unfair if all that money should have gone to somebody nobody had ever heard of.

'She quite understood that nothing must be allowed to get out. It was like an extra pound of butter. You couldn't talk about it but there was nothing wrong about having it. So Dora came to Little Paddocks – and very soon Charlotte began to understand that she had made a terrible mistake. It was not merely the fact that Dora Bunner, with her muddles and her mistakes and her bungling, was quite maddening to live with. Charlotte could have put up with that – because she really cared for Dora, and anyway knew from the doctor that Dora hadn't got a very long time to live. But Dora very soon became a real danger. Though Charlotte and Letitia had called each other by their full names, Dora was the kind of person who always uses abbreviations. To her the sisters had always been Letty and Lotty. And though she schooled her tongue resolutely to call her friend Letty – the old name often slipped out. Memories of the past, too, were rather apt to come to her tongue – and Charlotte had constantly to be on the watch to check these forgetful allusions. It began to get on her nerves.

'Still, nobody was likely to pay much attention to Dora's inconsistencies. The real blow to Charlotte's security came, as I say, when she was recognized and spoken to by Rudi Scherz at the Royal Spa Hotel.

'I think that the money Rudi Scherz used to replace his earlier defalcations at the hotel may have come from Charlotte Blacklock. Inspector Craddock doesn't believe – and I don't either – that Rudi Scherz applied to her for money with any idea of blackmail in his head.'

'He hadn't the faintest idea he knew anything to blackmail her about,' said Inspector Craddock. 'He knew that he was quite a personable young man – and he was aware by experience that personable young men sometimes can get money out of elderly ladies if the tell a hard luck story convincingly enough.

'But she may have seen it differently. She may have thought

that it was a form of insidious blackmail, that perhaps he suspected something – and that later, if there was publicity in the
papers as there might be after Belle Goedler's death, he would
realize that in her he had found a gold mine.

'And she was committed to the fraud now. She'd established
herself as Letitia Blacklock. With the Bank. With Mrs Goedler.
The only snag was this rather dubious Swiss hotel clerk, an unreliable character, and possibly a blackmailer. If only he were
out of the way – she'd be safe.

'Perhaps she made it all up as a kind of fantasy first. She'd
been starved of emotion and drama in her life. She pleased herself by working out the details. How would she go about getting
rid of him?

'She made her plan. And at last she decided to act on it. She
told her story of a sham hold-up at a party to Rudi Scherz, explained that she wanted a stranger to act the part of the
"gangster," and offered him a generous sum for his co-operation.

'And the fact that he agreed without any suspicion is what
makes me quite certain that Scherz had no idea that he had any
kind of hold over her. To him she was just a rather foolish old
woman, very ready to part with money.

'She gave him the advertisement to insert, arranged for him
to pay a visit to Little Paddocks to study the geography of the
house, and showed him the spot where she would meet him and
let him into the house on the night in question. Dora Bunner,
of course, knew nothing about all this.

'The day came—' He paused.

Miss Marple took up the tale in her gentle voice.

'She must have spent a very miserable day. You see, it still
wasn't too late to draw back . . . Dora Bunner told us that Letty
was frightened that day and she must have been frightened.
Frightened of what she was going to do, frightened of the plan
going wrong – but not frightened enough to draw back.

'It had been fun, perhaps, getting the revolver out of Colonel
Easterbrook's collar drawer. Taking along eggs, or jam – slipping upstairs in the empty house. It had been fun getting the
second door in the drawing-room oiled, so that it would open
and shut noiselessly. Fun suggesting the moving of the table outside the door so that Phillipa's flower arrangements would show
to better advantage. It may have all seemed like a game. But
what was going to happen next definitely wasn't a game any
longer. Oh, yes, she was frightened . . . Dora Bunner was right
about that.'

'All the same, she went through with it,' said Craddock. 'And it all went according to plan. She went out just after six to "shut up the ducks," and she let Scherz in then and gave him the mask and cloak and gloves and the torch. Then, at 6.30, when the clock begins to chime, she's ready by that table near the archway with her hand on the cigarette-box. It's all so natural. Patrick, acting as host, has gone for the drinks. She, the hostess, is fetching cigarettes. She'd judged, quite correctly, that when the clock begins to chime, everyone will look at the clock. They did. Only one person, the devoted Dora, kept her eyes fixed on her friend. And she told us, in her very first statement, exactly what Miss Blacklock did. She said that Miss Blacklock had picked up the vase of violets.

'She'd previously frayed the cord of the lamp so that the wires were nearly bare. The whole thing only took a second. The cigarette-box, the vase and the little switch were all close together. She picked up the violets, spilt the water on the frayed place and switched on the lamp. Water's a good conductor of electricity. The wires fused.'

'Just like the other afternoon at the Vicarage,' said Bunch. 'That's what startled you so, wasn't it, Aunt Jane?'

'Yes, my dear. I've been puzzling about those lights. I'd realized that there were two lamps, a pair, and that one had been changed for the other – probably during the night.'

'That's right,' said Craddock. 'When Fletcher examined that lamp the next morning it was, like all the others, perfectly in order, no frayed flex or fused wires.'

'I'd understood what Dora Bunner meant by saying it had been the *shepherdess* the night before,' said Miss Marple, 'but I fell into the error of thinking, as she thought, that *Patrick* had been responsible. The interesting thing about Dora Bunner was that she was quite unreliable in repeating things she had heard – she always used her imagination to exaggerate or distort them, and she was usually wrong in what she *thought* – but she was quite accurate about the things she *saw*. She saw Letitia pick up the violets—'

'And she saw what she described as a flash and a crackle,' put in Craddock.

'And, of course, when dear Bunch spilt the water from the Christmas roses on to the lamp wire – I realized at once that only Miss Blacklock herself could have fused the lights because only she was near the table.'

'I could kick myself,' said Craddock. 'Dora Bunner even prattled about a burn on the table where someone had "put their cigarette down" – but nobody had even lit a cigarette . . . And the violets were dead because there was no water in the vase – a slip on Letitia's part – she ought to have filled it up again. But I suppose she thought nobody would notice and as a matter of fact Miss Bunner was quite ready to believe that she herself had put no water in the vase to begin with.'

He went on:

'She was highly suggestible, of course. And Miss Blacklock took advantage of that more than once. Bunny's suspicions of Patrick were, I think, induced by her.'

'Why pick on me?' demanded Patrick in an aggrieved tone.

'It was not, I think, a serious suggestion – but it would keep Bunny distracted from any suspicion that Miss Blacklock might be stage managing the business. Well, we know what happened next. As soon as the lights went and everybody was exclaiming, she slipped out through the previously oiled door and up behind Rudi Scherz who was flashing his torch round the room and playing his part with gusto. I don't suppose he realized for a moment she was there behind him with her gardening gloves pulled on and the revolver in her hand. She waits till the torch reaches the spot she must aim for – the wall near which she is supposed to be standing. Then she fires rapidly twice and as he swings round startled, she holds the revolver close to his body and fires again. She lets the revolver fall by his body, throws her gloves carelessly on the hall table, then back through the other door and across to where she had been standing when the lights went out. She nicked her ear – I don't quite know how—'

'Nail scissors, I expect,' said Miss Marple. 'Just a snip on the lobe of the ear lets out a lot of blood. That was very good psychology, of course. The actual blood running down over her white blouse made it seem certain that she *had* been shot at, and that it had been a near miss.'

'It ought to have gone off quite all right,' said Craddock. 'Dora Bunner's insistence that Scherz had definitely aimed at Miss Blacklock had its uses. Without meaning it, Dora Bunner conveyed the impression that she'd actually seen her friend wounded. It might have been brought in Suicide or Accidental Death. And the case would have been closed. That it was kept open is due to Miss Marple here.'

'Oh, no, no.' Miss Marple shook her head energetically. 'Any little efforts on my part were quite incidental. It was you who weren't satisfied, Mr Craddock. It was *you* who wouldn't let the case be closed.'

'I wasn't happy about it,' said Craddock. 'I knew it was all wrong somewhere. But I didn't see *where* it was wrong, till you showed me. And after that Miss Blacklock had a real piece of bad luck. I discovered that that second door had been tampered with. Until that moment, whatever we agreed *might* have happened – we'd nothing to go on but a pretty theory. But that oiled door was *evidence*. And I hit upon it by pure chance – by catching hold of a handle by mistake.'

'I think you were *led* to it, Inspector,' said Miss Marple. 'But then I'm old-fashioned.'

'So the hunt was up again,' said Craddock. 'But this time with a difference. We were looking now for someone with a motive to kill Letitia Blacklock.'

'And there *was* someone with a motive, and Miss Blacklock knew it,' said Miss Marple. 'I think she recognised Phillipa almost at once. Because Sonia Goedler seems to have been one of the very few people who had been admitted to Charlotte's privacy. And when one is old (you wouldn't know this yet, Mr Craddock) one has a much better memory for a face you've seen when you were young than you have for anyone you've only met a year or two ago. Phillipa must have been just about the same age as her mother was when Charlotte remembered her, and she was very like her mother. The odd thing is that I think Charlotte was very pleased to recognise Phillipa. She became very fond of Phillipa and I think, unconsciously, it helped to stifle any qualms of conscience she may have had. She told herself that when she inherited the money, she was going to look after Phillipa. She would treat her as a daughter. Phillipa and Harry should live with her. She felt quite happy and beneficent about it. But once the Inspector began asking questions and finding out about "Pip and Emma" Charlotte became very uneasy. She didn't want to make a scapegoat of Phillipa. Her whole idea had been to make the business look like a hold-up by a young criminal and his accidental death. But now, with the discovery of the oiled door, the whole viewpoint was changed. And, except for Phillipa, there wasn't (as far as *she* knew, for she had absolutely no idea of Julia's identity) anyone with the least possible motive for wishing to kill her. She did her best to shield Phillipa's identity. She was quick witted enough to tell you when you asked her, that Sonia was small and dark and she took the old snapshots out of the album so that you shouldn't notice any resemblance at the same time as she removed snapshots of Letitia herself.'

'And to think I suspected Mrs Swettenham of being Sonia Goedler,' said Craddock disgustedly.

'My poor Mamma,' murmured Edmund. 'A woman of blameless life – or so I have always believed.'

'But of course,' Miss Marple went on, 'it was Dora Bunner who was the real danger. Every day Dora got more forgetful and more talkative. I remember the way Miss Blacklock looked at her the day we went to tea there. Do you know why? Dora had just called her Lotty again. It seemed to us a mere harmless slip of the tongue. But it frightened Charlotte. And so it went on. Poor Dora could not stop herself talking. That day we had coffee together in the Bluebird, I had the oddest impression that Dora was talking about *two* people, not one – and so, of course, she was. At one moment she spoke of her friend as not pretty but having so much character – but almost at the same moment she described her as a pretty light-hearted girl. She'd talk of Letty as so clever and so successful – and then say what a sad life she'd had, and then there was that quotation about stern affliction bravely borne – which really didn't seem to fit Letitia's life at all. Charlotte must, I think, have overheard a good deal that morning she came into the café. She certainly must have heard Dora mention about the lamp having been changed – about its being the shepherd and not the shepherdess. And she realized then what a very real danger to her security poor devoted Dora Bunner was.

'I'm afraid that that conversation with me in the café really sealed Dora's fate – if you'll excuse such a melodramatic expression. But I think it would have come to the same in the end . . . Because life couldn't be safe for Charlotte while Dora Bunner was alive. She loved Dora – she didn't want to kill Dora – but she couldn't see any other way. And, I expect (like Nurse Ellerton that I was telling you about, Bunch) she persuaded herself that it was really almost a *kindness*. Poor Bunny – not long to live anyway and perhaps a painful end. The queer thing is that she did her best to make Bunny's last day a happy day. The birthday party – and the special cake . . .'

'Delicious Death,' said Phillipa with a shudder.

'Yes – yes, it was rather like that . . . she tried to give her friend a delicious death . . . The party, and all the things she liked to eat, and trying to stop people saying things to upset her. And then the tablets, whatever they were, in the aspirin bottle by her bed so that Bunny, when she couldn't find the new bottle of aspirin she'd just bought, would go there to get some. And it would look, as it did look, that the tablets had been meant for *Letitia* . . .

'And so Bunny died in her sleep, quite happily, and Charlotte felt safe again. But she missed Dora Bunner – she missed her affection and her loyalty, she missed being able to talk to her about the old days . . . She cried bitterly the day I came up with that note from Julian – and her grief was quite genuine. She'd killed her own dear friend . . .'

'That's horrible,' said Bunch. 'Horrible.'

'But it's very human,' said Julian Harmon. 'One forgets how human murderers are.'

'I know,' said Miss Marple. 'Human. And often very much to be pitied. But very dangerous, too. Especially a weak kindly murderer like Charlotte Blacklock. Because, once a weak person gets *really* frightened, they get quite savage with terror and they've no self control at all.'

'Murgatroyd?' said Julian.

'Yes, poor Miss Murgatroyd. Charlotte must have come up to the cottage and heard them rehearsing the murder. The window was open and she listened. It had never occurred to her until that moment that there was anyone else who could be a danger to her. Miss Hinchcliffe was urging her friend to remember what she'd seen and until that moment Charlotte hadn't realized that anyone could have seen anything at all. She'd assumed that everybody would automatically be looking at Rudi Scherz. She must have held her breath outside the window and listened. Was it going to be all right? And then, just as Miss Hinchcliffe rushed off to the station Miss Murgatroyd got to a point which showed that she had stumbled on the truth. She called after Miss Hinchcliffe: "She wasn't *there* . . ."

'I asked Miss Hinchcliffe, you know, if that was the way she said it . . . Because if she'd said "*She* wasn't there" it wouldn't have meant the same thing.'

'Now that's too subtle a point for me,' said Craddock.

Miss Marple turned her eager pink and white face to him.

'Just think what's going on in Miss Murgatroyd's mind . . . One does see things, you know, and not know one sees them. In a railway accident once, I remember noticing a large blister of paint at the side of the carriage. I could have *drawn* it for you afterwards. And once, when there was a fly bomb in London – splinters of glass everywhere – and the shock – but what I remember best is a woman standing in front of me who had a big hole half-way up the leg of her stockings and the stockings didn't match. So when Miss Murgatroyd stopped thinking and just tried to remember what she *saw*, she remembered a good deal.

'She started, I think, near the mantelpiece, where the torch must have hit first – then it went along the two windows and there were people in between the windows and her. Mrs Harmon with her knuckles screwed into her eyes for instance. She went on in her mind following the torch past Miss Bunner with her mouth open and her eyes staring – past a blank wall and a table lamp and a cigarette-box. And then came the shots – and quite suddenly she remembered a most incredible thing. She'd seen the wall where, later, there were the two bullet holes, the wall where Letitia Blacklock had been standing when she was shot, and at the moment when the revolver went off and Letty was shot, *Letty hadn't been there* ...

'You see what I mean now? She'd been thinking of the three women Miss Hinchcliffe had told her to think about. If one of them hadn't been there, it would have been the *personality* she'd have fastened upon. She'd have said – in effect – *"That's the one!"* *She* wasn't there;" But it was a *place* that was in her mind – a place where someone should have been – but the place wasn't filled – there was nobody there. The place was there – but the person wasn't. And she couldn't take it in all at once. "How extraordinary, Hinch," she said. "She wasn't *there*." ... So that could only mean Letitia Blacklock ...'

'But you knew before that, didn't you?' said Bunch. 'When the lamp fused. When you wrote down those things on the paper.'

'Yes, my dear. It all came together then, you see – all the various isolated bits – and made a coherent pattern.'

Bunch quoted softly:

'*Lamp?* Yes. *Violets?* Yes. *Bottle of Aspirin*. You meant that Bunny had been going to buy a new bottle that day, and so she ought not to have needed to take Letitia's?'

'Not unless her own bottle had been taken or hidden. It had to appear as though Letitia Blacklock was the one meant to be killed.'

'Yes, I see. And then "Delicious Death." The cake – but more than the cake. The whole party set-up A happy day for Bunny before she died. Treating her rather like a dog you were going to destroy. That's what I find the most horrible thing of all – the sort of – of spurious kindness.'

'She *was* quite a kindly woman. What she said at the last in the kitchen was quite true. "I didn't want to kill anybody." What she wanted was a great deal of money that didn't belong to her! And before that desire – (and it had become a kind of obsession – the money was to pay her back for all the suffering life had inflicted on her) – everything else went to the wall. People with a grudge against the world are always dangerous. They seem to think life owes them something. I've known many an invalid who has suffered far worse and been cut off from life much more than Charlotte Blacklock – and they've managed to lead happy contented lives. It's what's in *yourself* that makes you happy or unhappy. But, oh dear, I'm afraid I'm straying away from what we were talking about. Where were we?'

'Going over your list,' said Bunch. 'What did you mean by "Making enquiries?" Inquiries about what?'

Miss Marple shook her head playfully at Inspector Craddock.

'You ought to have seen that, Inspector Craddock. You showed me that letter from Letitia Blacklock to her sister. It had the word "enquiries" in it twice – each time spelt with an *e*. But in the note I asked Bunch to show you, Miss Blacklock had written "inquiries" with an *i*. People don't often alter their spelling as they get older. It seemed to me very significant.'

'Yes,' Craddock agreed. 'I ought to have spotted that.'

Bunch was continuing. '*Severe afflictions bravely borne.* That's what Bunny said to you in the café and of course Letitia hadn't had any affliction. *Iodine.* That put you on the track of goitre?'

'Yes, dear. Switzerland, you know, and Miss Blacklock giving the impression that her sister had died of consumption. But I remember then that the greatest authorities on goitre and the most skilful surgeons operating on it are Swiss. And it linked up with those really preposterous pearls that Letitia Blacklock always wore. Not really her *style* – but just right for concealing the scar.'

'I understand now her agitation the night the string broke,' said Craddock. 'It seemed at the time quite disproportionate.'

'And after that, it *was* Lotty you wrote not Letty as we thought,' said Bunch.

'Yes, I remembered that the sister's name was Charlotte, and that Dora Bunner had called Miss Blacklock Lotty once or twice – and that each time she did so, she had been very upset afterwards.'

'And what about Berne and Old Age Pensions?'

'Rudi Scherz had been an orderly in a hospital in Berne.'

'And Old Age Pension?'

'Oh, my dear Bunch, I mentioned that to you in the Bluebird though I didn't really see the application then. How Mrs Wotherspoon drew Mrs Bartlett's Old Age Pension as well as her own – though Mrs Bartlett had been dead for years – simply because one old woman is so unlike another old woman – yes, it all made a pattern and I felt so worked up I went out to cool my head a little and think what could be done about proving all this. Then Miss Hinchcliffe picked me up and we found Miss Murgatroyd . . .'

Miss Marple's voice dropped. It was no longer excited and pleased. It was quiet and remorseless.

'I knew then something had *got* to be done. Quickly! But there still wasn't any *proof*. I thought out a possible plan and I talked to Sergeant Fletcher.'

'And I have had Fletcher on the carpet for it!' said Craddock. 'He'd no business to go agreeing to your plans without reporting first to me.'

'He didn't like it, but I talked him into it,' said Miss Marple. 'We went up to Little Paddocks and I got hold of Mitzi.'

Julia drew a deep breath and said, 'I can't imagine how you ever got her to do it.'

'I worked on her, my dear,' said Miss Marple. 'She thinks far too much about herself anyway, and it will be good for her to have done something for others. I flattered her up, of course, and said I was sure if she'd been in her own country she'd have been in the Resistance movement, and she said, "Yes, indeed." And I said I could see she had got just the temperament for that sort of work. She was brave, didn't mind taking risks, and could act a part. I told her stories of deeds done by girls in the Resistance movements, some of them true, and some of them, I'm afraid, invented. She got tremendously worked up!'

'Marvellous,' said Patrick.

'And then I got her to agree to do her part. I rehearsed her till she was word perfect. Then I told her to go upstairs to her room and not come down until Inspector Craddock came. The worst of these excitable people is that they're apt to go off half-cocked and start the whole thing before the time.'

'She did it very well,' said Julia.

'I don't quite see the point,' said Bunch. 'Of course, I wasn't there—' she added apologetically.

'The point was a little complicated – and rather touch and go.

388

The idea was that Mitzi whilst admitting, as though casually, that blackmail *had* been in her mind, was now so worked up and terrified that she was willing to come out with the truth. She'd seen, through the keyhole of the dining-room, Miss Blacklock in the hall with a revolver behind Rudi Scherz. She'd seen, that is, *what had actually taken place*. Now the only danger was that Charlotte Blacklock might have reaized that, as the key was in the keyhole, Mitzi couldn't possibly have seen anything at all. But I banked on the fact that you don't think of things like that when you've just had a bad shock. All she could take in was that Mitzi had seen her.'

Craddock took over the story.

'But – and this was essential – I pretended to receive this with scepticism, and I made an immediate attack as though unmasking my batteries at last, upon someone who had not been previously suspected. I accused Edmund—'

'And very nicely *I* played *my* part,' said Edmund. 'Hot denial. All according to plan. What wasn't according to plan, Phillipa, my love, was you throwing in your little chirp and coming out into the open as "Pip." Neither the Inspector nor I had any idea you were Pip. *I* was going to be Pip! It threw us off our stride for the moment, but the Inspector made a masterly comeback and made some perfectly filthy insinuations about my wanting a rich wife which will probably stick in your subconscious and make irreparable trouble between us one day.'

'I don't see why that was necessary?'

'Don't you? It meant that, *from Charlotte Blacklock's point of view*, the only person who suspected or knew the truth, was *Mitzi*. The suspicions of the police were elsewhere. They had treated Mitzi for the moment as a liar. But if Mitzi were to persist, they might listen to her and take her seriously. So Mitzi had got to be silenced.'

'Mitzi went straight out of the room and back to the kitchen – just like I had told her,' said Miss Marple. 'Miss Blacklock came out after her almost immediately. Mitzi was apparently alone in the kitchen. Sergeant Fletcher was behind the scullery door. And I was in the broom cupboard in the kitchen. Luckily I'm very thin.'

Bunch looked at Miss Marple.

'What did you expect to happen, Aunt Jane?'

'One of two things. Either Charlotte would offer Mitzi money to hold her tongue – and Sergeant Fletcher would be a witness to that offer, or else – or else I thought she'd try to kill Mitzi.'

'But she couldn't hope to get away with *that*? She'd have been suspected at once.'

'Oh, my dear, she was past reasoning. She was just a snapping terrified cornered rat. Think what had happened that day. The scene between Miss Hinchcliffe and Miss Murgatroyd. Miss Hinchcliffe driving off to the station. As soon as she comes back Miss Murgatroyd will explain that Letitia Blacklock wasn't in the room that night. There's just a few minutes in which to make sure Miss Murgatroyd can't tell anything. No time to make a plan or set a stage. Just crude murder. She greets the poor woman and strangles her. Then a quick rush home to change, to be sitting by the fire when the others come in, as though she'd never been out.

'And then came the revelation of Julia's identity. She breaks her pearls and is terrified they may notice her scar. Later, the Inspector telephones that he's bringing everyone there. No time to think, to rest. Up to her neck in murder now, no mercy killing – or undesirable young man to be put out of the way. Crude plain murder. Is she safe? Yes, so far. And then comes Mitzi – yet *another* danger. Kill Mitzi, stop her tongue! She's beside herself with fear. Not human any longer. Just a dangerous animal.'

'But why were you in the broom cupboard, Aunt Jane?' asked Bunch. 'Couldn't you have left it to Sergeant Fletcher?'

'It was safer with two of us, my dear. And besides, I knew I could mimic Dora Bunner's voice. If anything could break Charlotte Blacklock down – that would.'

'And it did ...!'

'Yes ... she went to pieces.'

There was a long silence as memory laid hold of them and then, speaking with determined lightness, to ease the strain, Julia said:

'It's made a wonderful difference to Mitzi. She told me yesterday that she was taking a post near Southampton. And she said (Julia produced a very good imitation of Mitzi's accent):

'"I go there and if they say to me you have to register with the police – you are an alien, I say to them, 'Yes, I will register! The police, they know me very well. I assist the police! Without me the police never would they have made the arrest of a very dangerous criminal. I risked my life because I am brave – brave like a lion – I do not care about risks.' 'Mitzi,' they say to me, 'you are a *heroine*, you are superb.' 'Ach, it is nothing, I say.'"'

Julia stopped.

'And a great deal more,' she added.

'I think,' said Edmund thoughtfully, 'that soon Mitzi will have assisted the police in not one but hundreds of cases!'

'She's softened towards me,' said Phillipa. 'She actually presented me with the recipe for Delicious Death as a kind of wedding present. She added that I was on no account to divulge the secret to Julia, because Julia had ruined her omelette pan.'

'Mrs Lucas,' said Edmund, 'is all over Phillipa now that since Belle Goedler's death Phillipa and Julia have inherited the Goedler millions. She sent us some silver asparagus tongs as a wedding present. I shall have enormous pleasure in *not* asking her to the wedding!'

'And so they lived happily ever after,' said Patrick. 'Edmund and Phillipa – and Julia and Patrick?' he added tentatively.

'Not with me, you won't live happily ever after,' said Julia. 'The remarks that Inspector Craddock improvised to address to Edmund apply far more aptly to you. You *are* the sort of soft young man who would like a rich wife. Nothing doing!'

'There's gratitude for you,' said Patrick. 'After all I did for that girl.'

'Nearly landed me in prison on a murder charge – that's what your forgetfulness nearly did for me,' said Julia. 'I shall never forget that evening when your sister's letter came. I really thought I was for it. I couldn't see any way out.'

'As it is,' she added musingly, 'I think I shall go on the stage.'

'What? You, too?' groaned Patrick.

'Yes. I might go to Perth. See if I can get your Julia's place in the Rep there. Then, when I've learnt my job, I shall go into theatre management –and put on Edmund's plays, perhaps.'

'I thought you wrote novels,' said Julian Harmon.

'Well, so did I,' said Edmund. 'I began writing a novel. Rather good it was. Pages about an unshaven man getting out of bed and what he smelt like, and the grey streets, and a horrible old woman with dropsy and a vicious young tart who dribbled down her chin – and they all talked interminably about the state of the world and wondered what they were alive for. And suddenly I began to wonder too . . . And then a rather comic idea occurred to me . . . and I jotted it down – and then I worked up rather a good little scene . . . All very obvious stuff. But somehow, I got interested . . . And before I knew what I was doing I'd finished a roaring farce in three acts.'

'What's it called?' asked Patrick. ' "*What the butler saw*'?"

'Well, it easily might be . . . As a matter of fact I've called it

Elephants Do Forget. What's more, it's been accepted and it's going to be produced!'

'Elephants Do Forget,' murmured Bunch. 'I thought they didn't?'

The Rev. Julian Harmon gave a guilty start.

'My goodness. I've been so interested. My *sermon*!'

'Detective stories again,' said Bunch. 'Real life ones this time.'

'You might preach on Thou Shall Do No Murder,' suggested Patrick.

'No,' said Julian Harmon quietly. 'I shan't take that as my text.'

'No,' said Bunch. 'You're quite right, Julian. I know a much nicer text, a happy text.' She quoted in a fresh voice, 'For lo the Spring is here and the Voice of the Turtle is heard in the Land – I haven't got it quite right – but you know the one I mean. Though why a *turtle* I can't think. I shouldn't think turtles have got nice voices at all.'

'The word turtle,' explained the Rev. Julian Harmon, 'is not very happily translated. It doesn't mean a reptile but the turtle dove. The Hebrew word in the original is—'

Bunch interrupted him by giving him a hug and saying:

'I know one thing – *You* think that the Ahasuerus of the Bible is Artaxerxes the Second, but between you and me it was Artaxerxes the Third.'

As always, Julian Harmon wondered why his wife should think that story so particularly funny.

'Tiglath Pileser wants to go and help you,' said Bunch. 'He ought to be a very proud cat. *He* showed us how the lights fused.'

EPILOGUE

'We ought to order some papers,' said Edmund to Phillipa upon the day of their return to Chipping Cleghorn after the honeymoon. 'Let's go along to Totman's.'

Mr Totman, a heavy-breathing, slow-moving man, received them with affability.

'Glad to see you back, sir. *And* madam.'

'We want to order some papers.'

'Certainly sir. And your mother is keeping well, I hope? Quite settled down at Bournemouth?'

'She loves it,' said Edmund, who had not the faintest idea whether this was so or not, but like most sons, preferred to believe that all was well with those loved, but frequently irritating beings, parents.

'Yes, sir. Very agreeable place. Went there for my holiday last year. Mrs Totman enjoyed it very much.'

'I'm glad. About papers, we'd like—'

'And I hear you have a play on in London, sir. Very amusing, so they tell me.'

'Yes, it's doing very well.'

'Called *Elephants Do Forget*, so I hear. You'll excuse me, sir, asking you, but I always thought that they *didn't* – forget, I mean.'

'Yes – yes, exactly – I've begun to think it was a mistake calling it that. So many people have said just what you say.'

'A kind of natural history fact, I've always understood.'

'Yes – yes. Like earwigs making good mothers.'

'Do they indeed, sir? Now, that a fact I *didn't* know.'

'About the papers—'

'*The Times*, sir, I think it was?' Mr Totman paused with pencil uplifted.

'*The Daily Worker*,' said Edmund firmly. 'And the *Daily Telegraph*,' said Phillipa. 'And the *New Statesman*,' said Edmund. '*The Radio Times*,' said Phillipa. '*The Spectator*,' said Edmund. '*The Gardener's Chronicle*,' said Phillipa.

They both paused to take breath.

'Thank you, sir,' said Mr Totman. '*And* the *Gazette*, I suppose?'

'No,' said Edmund.

'No,' said Phillipa.

'Excuse me, you *do* want the *Gazette*?'

'No.'

'No.'

'You mean' – Mr Totman liked to get things perfectly clear – 'You *don't* want the *Gazette*!'

'No, we don't.'

'Certainly not.'

'You don't want the *North Benham News and the Chipping Cleghorn Gazette*?'

'No.'

'You don't want me to send it along to you every week?'

'*No*.' Edmund added: 'Is that quite clear now?'

'Oh, yes, sir – yes.'

Edmund and Phillipa went out, and Mr Totman padded into his back parlour.

'Got a pencil, Mother?' he said. 'My pen's run out.'

'Here you are,' said Mrs Totman, seizing the order book. 'I'll do it. What do they want?'

'*Daily Worker, Daily Telegraph, Radio Times, New Statesman, Spectator* – let me see – *Gardener's Chronicle.*'

'*Gardener's Chronicle,*' repeated Mrs Totman, writing busily. 'And the *Gazette.*'

'They don't want the *Gazette.*'

'What?'

'They don't want the *Gazette.* They said so.'

'Nonsense,' said Mrs Totman. 'You don't hear properly. Of course they want the *Gazette*! Everybody has the *Gazette.* How else would they know what's going on round here?'

A
POCKET FULL
OF RYE

It was Miss Somers's turn to make the tea. Miss Somers was the newest and the most inefficient of the typists. She was no longer young and had a mild worried face like a sheep. The kettle was not quite boiling when Miss Somers poured the water on to the tea, but poor Miss Somers was never quite sure when a kettle *was* boiling. It was one of the many worries that afflicted her in life.

She poured out the tea and took the cups round with a couple of limp, sweet biscuits in each saucer.

Miss Griffith, the efficient head typist, a grey-haired martinet who had been with Consolidated Investments Trust for sixteen years, said sharply: 'Water not boiling *again*, Somers!' and Miss Somers's worried meek face went pink and she said, 'Oh dear, I *did* think it was boiling *this* time.'

Miss Griffith thought to herself: 'She'll last for another month, perhaps, just while we're so busy . . . But really! The mess the silly idiot made of that letter to Eastern Developments – a perfectly straightforward job, and always so stupid over the tea. If it weren't so difficult to get hold of any intelligent typists – and the biscuit tin lid wasn't shut tightly last time, either. *Really*—'

Like so many of Miss Griffith's indignant inner communings the sentence went unfinished.

At that moment Miss Grosvenor sailed in to make Mr Fortescue's sacred tea. Mr Fortescue had different tea, and different china and special biscuits. Only the kettle and the water from the cloakroom tap were the same. But on this occasion, being Mr Fortescue's tea, the water boiled. Miss Grosvenor saw to that.

Miss Grosvenor was an incredibly glamorous blonde. She wore an expensively cut little black suit and her shapely legs were encased in the very best and most expensive black-market nylons.

She sailed back through the typists' room without deigning to give anyone a word or a glance. The typists might have been so many blackbeetles. Miss Grosvenor was Mr Fortescue's own special personal secretary; unkind rumour always hinted that she was something more, but actually this was not true. Mr Fortescue had recently married a second wife, both glamorous and expensive, and fully capable of absorbing all his attention. Miss Grosvenor was to Mr Fortescue just a necessary part of the office décor – which was all very luxurious and very expensive.

Miss Grosvenor sailed back with the tray held out in front of her like a ritual offering. Through the inner office and through the waiting-room, where the more important clients were allowed to sit, and through her own ante-room, and finally with a light tap on the door she entered the holy of holies, Mr Fortescue's office.

It was a large room with a gleaming expanse of parquet floor on which were dotted expensive oriental rugs. It was delicately panelled in pale wood and there were some enormous stuffed chairs upholstered in pale buff leather. Behind a colossal sycamore desk, the centre and focus of the room, sat Mr Fortescue himself.

Mr Forestcue was less impressive than he should have been to match the room, but he did his best. He was a large flabby man with a gleaming bald head. It was his affection to wear loosely cut country tweeds in his city office. He was frowning down at some papers on his desk when Miss Grosvenor glided up to him in her swanlike manner. Placing the tray on the desk at his elbow, she murmured in a low impersonal voice, 'Your tea, Mr Fortescue,' and withdrew.

Mr Fortescue's contribution to the ritual was a grunt.

Seated at her own desk again Miss Grosvenor proceeded with the business in hand. She made two telephone calls, corrected some letters that were lying there typed ready for Mr Fortescue to sign and took one incoming call.

'Ay'm afraid it's impossible just now,' she said in haughty accents. 'Mr Fortescue is in conference.'

As she laid down the receiver she glanced at the clock. It was ten minutes past eleven.

It was just then that an unusual sound penetrated through the almost sound-proof door of Mr Fortescue's office. Muffled, it was yet fully recognisable, a strangled agonised cry. At the same moment the buzzer on Miss Grosvenor's desk sounded in a long-drawn frenzied summons. Miss Grosvenor, startled for a moment into complete immobility, rose uncertainly to her feet. Confronted by the unexpected, her poise was shaken. However, she moved towards Mr Fortescue's door in her usual statuesque fashion, tapped and entered.

398

What she saw upset her poise still further. Her employer behind his desk seemed contorted with agony. His convulsive
movements were alarming to watch.

Miss Grosvenor said, 'Oh dear, Mr Fortescue, are you ill?'
and was immediately conscious of the idiocy of the question.
There was no doubt but that Mr Fortescue was very seriously
ill. Even as she came up to him, his body was convulsed in a
painful spasmodic movement.

Words came out in jerky gasps.

'Tea – what the hell – you put in the tea – get help – quick
get a doctor—'

Miss Grosvenor fled from the room. She was no longer the
supercilious blonde secretary – she was a thoroughly frightened
woman who had lost her head.

She came running into the typists' office crying out:

'Mr Fortescue's having a fit – he's dying – we must get a
doctor – he looks awful – I'm sure he's dying.'

Reactions were immediate and varied a good deal.

Miss Bell, the youngest typist said, 'If it's epilepsy we ought
to put a cork in his mouth. Who's got a cork?'

Nobody has a cork.

Miss Somers said, 'At his age it's probably apoplexy.'

Miss Griffith said, 'We must get a doctor – *at once.*'

But she was hampered in her usual efficiency because in all
her sixteen years of service it had never been necessary to call
a doctor to the city office. There was her own doctor but that
was at Streatham Hill. Where was there a doctor near here?

Nobody knew. Miss Bell seized a telephone directory and
began looking up Doctors under D. But it was not a classified
directory and doctors were not automatically listed like taxi
ranks. Someone suggested a hospital – but which hospital? 'It
has to be the right hospital,' Miss Somers insisted, 'or else they
won't come. Because of the National Health, I mean. It's got
to be in the area.'

Someone suggested 999 but Miss Griffith was shocked at that
and said it would mean the police and that would never do.
For citizens of a country which enjoyed the benefits of Medical
Service for all, a group of quite reasonably intelligent women
showed incredible ignorance of correct procedure. Miss Bell
started looking up Ambulances under A. Miss Griffith said,
'There's his own doctor – he must *have* a doctor.' Someone
rushed for the private address book. Miss Griffith instructed the
office boy to go out and find a doctor – somehow, *anywhere.* In

the private address book, Miss Griffith found Sir Edwin Sandeman with an address in Harley Street. Miss Grosvenor, collapsed in a chair, wailed in a voice whose accent was noticeably less Mayfair than usual, 'I made the tea just as usual – really I did there couldn't have been anything wrong in it.'

'*Wrong* in it?' Miss Griffith paused, her hand on the dial of the telephone. 'Why do you say that?'

'*He* said it – Mr Fortescue – he said it was the tea—'

Miss Griffith's hand hovered irresolutely between Welbeck and 999. Miss Bell, young and hopeful, said: 'We ought to give him some mustard and water – *now*. Isn't there any mustard in the office?'

There was no mustard in the office.

Some short while later Dr Isaacs of Bethnal Green, and Sir Edwin Sandeman met in the elevator just as two different ambulances drew up in front of the building. The telephone and the office boy had done their work.

2

Inspector Neele sat in Mr Fortescue's sanctum behind Mr Fortescue's vast sycamore desk. One of his underlings with a notebook sat unobtrusively against the wall near the door.

Inspector Neele had a smart soldierly appearance with crisp brown hair growing back from the rather low forehead. When he uttered the phrase 'just a matter of routine' those addressed were wont to think spitefully: 'And routine is about all *you*'re capable of!' They would have been quite wrong. Behind his unimaginative appearance, Inspector Neele was a highly imaginative thinker, and one of his methods of investigation was to propound to himself fantastic theories of guilt which he applied to such persons as he was interrogating at the time.

Miss Griffith, whom he had at once picked out with an unerring eye as being the most suitable person to give him a succint account of the events which had led to his being seated where he was, had just left the room having given him an admirable résumé of the morning's happenings. Inspector Neele propounded to himself three separate highly coloured reasons why the faithful doyenne of the typists' room should have poisoned her employer's mid-morning cup of tea, and rejected them as unlikely.

He classified Miss Griffith as (a) Not the type of a poisoner, (b) Not in love with her employer, (c) No pronounced mental instability, (d) Not a woman who cherished grudges. That really seemed to dispose of Miss Griffith except as a source of accurate information.

Inspector Neele glanced at the telephone. He was expecting a call from St Jude's Hospital at any moment now.

It was possible, of course, that Mr Fortescue's sudden illness was due to natural causes, but Dr Isaacs of Bethnal Green had not thought so and Sir Edwin Sandeman of Harley Street had not thought so.

Inspector Neele pressed a buzzer conveniently situated at his left hand and demanded that Mr Fortescue's personal secretary should be sent in to him.

Miss Grosvenor had recovered a little of her poise, but not much. She came in apprehensively, with nothing of the swan-like glide about her motions, and said at once defensively:

'I didn't do it!'

Inspector Neele murmured conversationally: 'No?'

He indicated the chair where Miss Grosvenor was wont to place herself, pad in hand, when summoned to take down Mr Fortescue's letters. She sat down now with reluctance and eyed Inspector Neele in alarm. Inspector Neele, his mind playing imaginatively on the themes Seduction? Blackmail? Platinum Blonde in Court? etc., looked reassuring and just a little stupid.

'There wasn't anything wrong with the tea,' said Miss Grosvenor. 'There couldn't have been.'

'*I* see,' said Inspector Neele. 'Your name and address, please?'

'Grosvenor. Irene Grosvenor.'

'How do you spell it?'

'Oh. Like the Square.'

'And your address?'

'14 Rushmoor Road, Muswell Hill.'

Inspector Neele nodded in a satisfied fashion.

'No seduction,' he said to himself. 'No Love Nest. Respectable home with parents. No blackmail.'

Another good set of speculative theories washed out.

'And so it was you who made the tea?' he said pleasantly.

'Well, I had to. I always do, I mean.'

Unhurried, Inspector Neele took her closely through the morning ritual of Mr Fortescue's tea. The cup and saucer and teapot had already been packed up and dispatched to the appropriate quarter for analysis. Now Inspector Neele learned that Irene Grosvenor and only Irene Grosvenor had handled that cup and saucer and teapot. The kettle had been used for making the office tea and had been refilled from the cloakroom tap by Miss Grosvenor.

'And the tea itself?'

'It was Mr Fortescue's own tea, special China tea. It's kept on the shelf in my room next door.'

Inspector Neele nodded. He inquired about sugar and heard that Mr Fortescue didn't take sugar.

The telephone rang. Inspector Neele picked up the receiver. His face changed a little.

'St Jude's?'

He nodded to Miss Grosvenor in dismissal.

'That's all for now, thank you, Miss Grosvenor.'

Miss Grosvenor sped out of the room hurriedly.

Inspector Neele listened carefully to the thin unemotional tones speaking from St Jude's Hospital. As the voice spoke he made a few cryptic signs with a pencil on the corner of the blotter in front of him.

'Died five minutes ago, you say?' he asked. His eye went to the watch on his wrist. *Twelve forty-three,* he wrote on the blotter.

The unemotional voice said that Doctor Bernsdorff himself would like to speak to Inspector Neele.

Inspector Neele said, 'Right. Put him through,' which rather scandalised the owner of the voice who had allowed a certain amount of reverence to seep into the official accents.

There were then various clicks, buzzes, and far-off ghostly murmurs. Inspector Neele sat patiently waiting.

Then without warning a deep bass roar caused him to shift the receiver an inch or two away from his ear.

'Hallo, Neele, you old vulture. At it again with your corpses?'

Inspector Neele and Professor Bernsdorff of St Jude's had been brought together over a case of poisoning just over a year ago and had remained on friendly terms.

'Our man's dead, I hear, doc.'

'Yes. We couldn't do anything by the time he got here.'

'And the cause of death?'

'There will have to be an autopsy, naturally. Very interesting case. Very interesting indeed. Glad I was able to be in on it.'

The professional gusto in Bernsdorff's rich tones told Inspector Neele one thing at least.

'I gather you don't think it was natural death,' he said dryly.

'Not a dog's chance of it,' said Dr Bernsdorff robustly. 'I'm speaking unofficially, of course,' he added with belated caution.

'Of course. Of course. That's understood. He was poisoned?'

'Definitely. And what's more – this is quite unofficial, you understand – just between you and me – I'd be prepared to make a bet on what the poison was.'

'In-deed?'

'Taxine, my boy. Taxine.'

'Taxine? Never heard of it.'

'I know. *Most* unusual. Really delightfully unusual! I don't say I'd have spotted it myself if I hadn't had a case only three or four weeks ago. Couple of kids playing dolls' tea-parties – pulled berries off a yew tree and used them for tea.'

'Is that what it is? Yew berries?'

'Berries or leaves. Highly poisonous. Taxine, of course, is the alkaloid. Don't think I've heard of a case where it was used deliberately. Really *most* interesting and unusual . . . You've no idea, Neele, how tired one gets of the inevitable weed-killer. Taxine is a real treat. Of course, I *may* be wrong – don't quote me, for Heaven's sake – but I don't think so. Interesting for you, too, I should think. Varies the routine!'

'A good time is to be had by all, is that the idea? With the exception of the victim.'

'Yes, yes, poor fellow.' Dr Bernsdorff's tone was perfunctory. 'Very bad luck on him.'

'Did he say anything before he died?'

'Well, one of your fellows was sitting by him with a notebook. He'll have the exact details. He muttered something once about tea – that he'd been given somthing in his tea at the office – but that's nonsense, of course.'

'Why is it nonsense?' Inspector Neele, who had been reviewing speculatively the picture of the glamorous Miss Grosvenor adding yew berries to a brew of tea, and finding it incongruous, spoke sharply.

'Because the stuff couldn't possibly have worked so soon. I understand the symptoms came on immediately he had drunk the tea?'

'That's what they say.'

'Well, there are very few poisons that act as quickly as that apart from the cyanides, of course – and possibly pure nicotine—'

'And it definitely wasn't cyanide or nicotine?'

'My dear fellow. He'd have been dead before the ambulance arrived. Oh no, there's no question of anything of that kind. I *did* suspect strychnine, but the convulsions were not at all typical. Still unofficial, of course, but I'll stake my reputation it's taxine.'

'How long would that take to work?'

'Depends. An hour. Two hours, three hours. Deceased looked like a hearty eater. If he had had a big breakfast, that would slow things up.'

'Breakfast,' said Inspector Neele thoughtfully. 'Yes, it looks like breakfast.'

'Breakfast with the Borgias.' Dr Bernsdorff laughed cheerfully. 'Well, good hunting, my lad.'

'Thanks, doctor. I'd like to speak to my sergeant before you ring off.'

Again there were clicks and buzzes and far-off ghostly voices. And then the sound of heavy breathing came through, an inevitable prelude to Sergeant Hay's conversation.

'Sir,' he said urgently. '*Sir.*'

'Neele here. Did the deceased say anything I ought to know?'

'Said it was the tea. The tea he had at the office. But the MO says not ...'

'Yes, I know about that. Nothing else?'

'No, sir. But there's one thing that's odd. The suit he was wearing – I checked the contents of the pockets. The usual stuff – handkerchief, keys, change, wallet – but there was one thing that's downright peculiar. The right-hand pocket of his jacket. It had *cereal* in it.'

'Cereal?'

'Yes, sir.'

'What do you mean by cereal? Do you mean a breakfast food? Farmer's Glory or Wheatifax? Or do you mean corn or barley—'

'That's right, sir. Grain it was. Looked like rye to me. Quite a lot of it.'

'I see ... Odd ... But it might have been a sample – something to do with a business deal.'

'Quite so, sir – but I thought I'd better mention it.'

'Quite right, Hay.'

Inspector Neele sat staring ahead of him for a few moments after he had replaced the telephone receiver. His orderly mind was moving from Phase I to Phase II of the inquiry – from suspicion of poisoning to certainty of poisoning. Professor Bernsdorff's words may have been unofficial, but Professor Bernsdorff was not a man to be mistaken in his beliefs. Rex Fortescue had been poisoned and the poison had probably been administered one to three hours before the onset of the first symptoms. It seemed probable, therefore, that the office staff could be given a clean bill of health.

Neele got up and went into the outer office. A little desultory work was being done but the typewriters were not going at full speed.

'Miss Griffith? Can I have another word with you?'

'Certainly, Mr Neele. Could some of the girls go out to lunch? It's long past their regular time. Or would you prefer that we get something sent in?'

'No. They can go to lunch. But they must return afterwards.'

'Of course.'

Miss Griffith followed Neele back into the private office. She sat down in her composed efficient way.

Without preamble, Inspector Neele said:

'I have heard from St Jude's Hospital. Mr Fortescue died at 12.43.'

Miss Griffith received the news without surprise, merely shook her head.

'I was afraid he was very ill,' she said.

She was not, Neele noted, at all distressed.

'Will you please give me particulars of his home and family?'

'Certainly. I have already tried to get into communication with Mrs Fortescue, but it seems she is out playing golf. She was not expected home to lunch. There is some uncertainty as to which course she is playing on.' She added in an explanatory manner, 'They live at Baydon Heath, you know, which is a centre for three well-known golf courses.'

Inspector Neele nodded. Baydon Heath was almost entirely inhabited by rich city men. It had an excellent train service, was only twenty miles from London and was comparatively easy to reach by car even in the rush of morning and evening traffic.

'The exact address, please, and the telephone number?'

'Baydon Heath 3400. The name of the house is Yewtree Lodge.'

'*What?*' The sharp query slipped out before Inspector Neele could control it. 'Did you say *Yewtree* Lodge?'

'Yes.'

Miss Griffith looked faintly curious, but Inspector Neele had himself in hand again.

'Can you give me particulars of his family?'

'Mrs Fortescue is his second wife. She is much younger than he is. They were married about two years ago. The first Mrs Fortescue has been dead a long time. There are two sons and a daughter of the first marriage. The daughter lives at home and so does the elder son who is a partner in the firm. Unfortunately he is away in the North of England today on business. He is expected to return tomorrow.'

'When did he go away?'

'The day before yesterday.'

'Have you tried to get in touch with him?'

'Yes. After Mr Fortescue was removed to hospital I rang up the Midland Hotel in Manchester where I thought he might be staying, but he had left early this morning. I believe he was also going to Sheffield and Leicester, but I am not sure about that. I can give you the names of certain firms in those cities whom he might be visiting.'

Certainly an efficient woman, thought the Inspector, and if she murdered a man she would probably murder him very efficiently, too. But he forced himself to abandon these speculations and concentrate once more on Mr Fortescue's home front.

'There is a second son you said?'

'Yes. But owing to a disagreement with his father he lives abroad.'

'Are both sons married?'

'Yes. Mr Percival has been married for three years. He and his wife occupy a self-contained flat in Yewtree Lodge, though they are moving into their own house at Baydon Heath very shortly.'

'You were not able to get in touch with Mrs Percival Fortescue when you rang up this morning?'

'She had gone to London for the day.' Miss Griffith went on, 'Mr Lancelot got married less than a year ago. To the widow of Lord Frederick Anstice. I expect you've seen pictures of her. In the *Tatler* – with horses, you know. And at point-to-points.'

Miss Griffith sounded a little breathless and her cheeks were faintly flushed. Neele, who was quick to catch the moods of human beings, realized that this marriage had thrilled the snob and the romantic in Miss Griffith. The aristocracy was the aristocracy to Miss Griffith and the fact that the late Lord Frederick Anstice had had a somewhat unsavoury reputation in sporting circles was almost certainly not known to her. Freddie Anstice had blown his brains out just before an inquiry by the Stewards into the running of one of his horses. Neele remembered something vaguely about his wife. She had been the daughter of an Irish Peer and had been married before to an airman who had been killed in the Battle of Britain.

And now, it seemed, she was married to the black sheep of the Fortescue family, for Neele assumed that the disagreement with his father referred to primly by Miss Griffith, stood for some disgraceful incident in young Lancelot Fortescue's career.

Lancelot Fortescue! What a name! And what was the other son – Percival? He wondered what the first Mrs Fortescue had been like? She'd had a curious taste in Christian names. . . .

He drew the phone towards him and dialled TOL. He asked for Baydon Heath 3400.

Presently a man's voice said:

'Baydon Heath 3400.'

'I want to speak to Mrs Fortescue or Miss Fortescue.'

'Sorry. They aren't in, either of 'em.'

The voice struck Inspector Neele as slightly alcoholic.

'Are you the butler?'

'That's right.'

'Mr Fortescue has been taken seriously ill.'

'I know. They rung up and said so. But there's nothing I can do about it. Mr Val's away up North and Mrs Fortescue's out playing golf. Mrs Val's gone up to London but she'll be back for dinner and Miss Elaine's out with her Brownies.'

'Is there no one in the house I can speak to about Mr Fortescue's illness? It's important.'

'Well – I don't know.' The man sounded doubtful. 'There's Miss Ramsbottom – but she don't ever speak over the phone. Or there's Miss Dove – she's what you might call the 'ousekeeper.'

'I'll speak to Miss Dove, please.'

'I'll try and get hold of her.'

His retreating footsteps were audible through the phone. Inspector Neele heard no approaching footsteps but a minute or two later a woman's voice spoke.

'This is Miss Dove speaking.'

The voice was low and well poised, with clear-cut enunciation. Inspector Neele formed a favourable picture of Miss Dove.

'I am sorry to have to tell you, Miss Dove, that Mr Fortescue died in St Jude's Hospital a short time ago. He was taken suddenly ill in his office. I am anxious to get in touch with his relatives—'

'Of course. I had no idea—' She broke off. Her voice held no agitation, but it was shocked. She went on: 'It is all most unfortunate. The person you really want to get in touch with is Mr Percival Fortescue. He would be the one to see to all the necessary arrangements. You might be able to get in touch with him at the Midland in Manchester or possibly at the Grand in Leicester. Or you might try Shearer and Bonds of Leicester. I don't know their telephone number, I'm afraid, but I know they are a firm on whom he was going to call and they might be able to inform you where he would be likely to be today. Mrs Fortescue will certainly be in to dinner and she may be in to tea. It will be a great shock to her. It must have been very sudden? Mr Fortescue was quite well when he left here this morning.'

'You saw him before he left?'

'Oh yes. What was it? Heart?'

'Did he suffer from heart trouble?'

'No – no – I don't think so— But I thought as it was so sudden—' She broke off. 'Are you speaking from St Jude's Hospital? Are you a doctor?'

'No, Miss Dove, I'm not a doctor. I'm speaking from Mr Fortescue's office in the city. I am Detective-Inspector Neele of the CID and I shall be coming down to see you as soon as I can get there.'

'Detective Inspector? Do you mean – what *do* you mean?'

It was a case of sudden death, Miss Dove; and when there is a sudden death we get called to the scene, especially when the deceased man hasn't seen a doctor lately – which I gather was the case?'

It was only the faintest suspicion of a question mark but the young woman responded.

'I know. Percival made an appointment twice for him, but he wouldn't keep it. He was quite unreasonable – they've all been worried—'

She broke off and then resumed in her former assured manner:

'If Mrs Fortescue returns to the house before you arrive, what do you want me to tell her?'

Practical as they make 'em, thought Inspector Neele.

Aloud he said:

'Just tell her that in a case of sudden death we have to make a few inquiries. Routine inquiries.'

He hung up.

3

Neele pushed the telephone away and looked sharply at Miss Griffith.

'So they've been worried about him lately,' he said. 'Wanted him to see a doctor. You didn't tell me that.'

'I didn't think of it,' said Miss Griffith, and added: 'He never seemed to me really *ill*—'

'Not ill – but what?'

'Well, just odd. Unlike himself. Peculiar in his manner.'

'Worried about something?'

'Oh no, not *worried*. It's *we* who were worried—'

Inspector Neele waited patiently.

'It's difficult to say, really,' said Miss Griffith. 'He had moods, you know. Sometimes he was quite boisterous. Once or twice, frankly, I thought he had been drinking. . . . He boasted and told the most extraordinary stories which I'm sure couldn't possibly have been true. For most of the time I've been here he was always very close about his affairs – not giving anything away, you know. But lately he's been quite different, expansive, and positively – well – flinging money about. Most unlike his usual manner. Why, when the office boy had to go to his grand-mother's funeral, Mr Fortescue called him in and gave him a five pound note and told him to put it on the second favourite and then roared with laughter. He wasn't – well, he just wasn't like himself. That's all I can say.'

'As though, perhaps, he had something on his mind?'

'Not in the usual meaning of the term. It was as though he were looking forward to something pleasurable – exciting—'

'Possibly a big deal that he was going to pull off?'

Miss Griffith agreed with more conviction.

'Yes – yes, that's much more what I mean. As though every-day things didn't matter any more. He was excited. And some very odd-looking people came to see him on business. People who'd never been here before. It worried Mr Percival dread-fully.'

'Oh it worried him, did it?'

'Yes. Mr Percival's always been very much in his father's confidence, you see. His father relied on him. But lately—'

'Lately they weren't getting along so well.'

'Well, Mr Fortescue was doing a lot of things that Mr Percival thought unwise. Mr Percival is always very careful and prudent. But suddenly his father didn't listen to him any more and Mr Percival was very upset.'

'And they had a real row about it all?'

Inspector Neele was still probing.

'I don't know about a *row*. . . . Of course, I realize now Mr Fortescue can't have been himself – shouting like that.'

'Shouted, did he? What did he say?'

'He came right out in the typists' room—'

'So that you all heard?'

'Well – yes.'

'And he called Percival names – abused him – swore at him . . .? What did he say Percival had done?'

'It was more that he hadn't done anything . . . he called him a miserable pettifogging little clerk. He said he had no large outlook, no conception of doing business in a big way. He said "I shall get Lance home again. He's worth ten of you – *and* he's married well. Lance has got guts even if he did risk a criminal prosecution once—" Oh dear, I oughtn't to have said that!' Miss Griffith, carried away as others before her had been under Inspector Neele's expert handling, was suddenly overcome with confusion.

'Don't worry,' said Inspector Neele comfortingly. 'What's past is past.'

'Oh yes, it was a long time ago. Mr Lance was just young and high spirited and didn't really realize what he was doing.'

Inspector Neele had heard that view before and didn't agree with it. But he passed on to fresh questions.

'Tell me a little more about the staff here.'

Miss Griffith, hurrying to get away from her indiscretion, poured out information about the various personalities in the firm. Inspector Neele thanked her and then said he would like to see Miss Grosvenor again.

Detective-Constable Waite sharpened his pencil. He remarked wistfully that this was a Ritzy joint. His glance wandered appreciatively over the huge chairs, the big desk and the indirect lighting.

'All these people have got Ritzy names, too,' he said. 'Grosvenor – that's something to do with a Duke. And Fortescue – that's a classy name, too.'

Inspector Neele smiled.

'His father's name wasn't Fortescue. Fontescu – and he came

from somewhere in Central Europe. I suppose this man thought
Fortescue sounded better.'

Detective-Constable Waite looked at his superior officer with
awe.

'So you know all about him?'

'I just looked up a few things before coming along on the
call.'

'Not got a record, had he?'

'Oh no. Mr Fortescue was much too clever for that. He's
had certain connections with the Black Market and put through
one or two deals that are questionable to say the least of it, but
they've always been just within the law.'

'I see,' said Waite. 'Not a nice man,'

'A twister,' said Neele. 'But we've got nothing on him. The
Inland Revenue have been after him for a long time but he's
been too clever for them. Quite a financial genius, the late Mr
Fortescue.'

'The sort of man,' said Constable Waite, 'who might have
enemies?'

He spoke hopefully.

'Oh yes – certainly enemies. But he was poisoned at home
remember. Or so it would seem. You know, Waite, I see a kind
of pattern emerging. An old-fashioned familiar kind of pattern.
The good boy, Percival. The bad boy, Lance – attractive to
women. The wife who's younger than her husband and who's
vague about which course she's going to play golf on. It's all
very very familiar. But there's one thing that sticks out in a most
incongruous way.'

Constable Waite asked 'What's that?' just as the door opened
and Miss Grosvenor, her poise restored, and once more her
glamorous self, inquired haughtily:

'You wished to see me?'

'I wanted to ask you a few questions about your employer
– your late employer perhaps I should say.'

'Poor soul,' said Miss Grosvenor unconvincingly.

'I want to know if you have noticed any difference in him
lately.'

'Well, yes. I did, as a matter of fact.'

'In what way?'

'I couldn't really say. . . . He seemed to talk a lot of nonsense.
I couldn't really believe half of what he said. And then he lost
his temper very easily – especially with Mr Percival. Not with

me, because of course I *never* argue. I just say, "Yes, Mr Fortescue," whatever peculiar thing he says – said, I mean.'

'Did he – ever – well – make any passes at you?'

Miss Grosvenor replied rather regretfully:

'Well, no, I couldn't exactly say *that*.'

'There's just one other thing, Miss Grosvenor. Was Mr Fortescue in the habit of carrying grain about in his pocket?'

Miss Grosvenor displayed a lively surprise.

'Grain? In his pocket? Do you mean to feed pigeons or something?'

'It could have been for that purpose.'

'Oh I'm sure he didn't. Mr Fortescue? Feed pigeons? Oh no.'

'Could he have had barley – or rye – in his pocket today for any special reason? A sample, perhaps? Some deal in grain?'

'Oh no. He was expecting the Asiatic Oil people this afternoon. And the President of the Atticus Building Society. . . . No one else.'

'Oh well—' Neele dismissed the subject and Miss Grosvenor with a wave of the hand.

'Lovely legs she's got,' said Constable Waite with a sigh. 'And super nylons—'

'Legs are no help to me,' said Inspector Neele. 'I'm left with what I had before. A pocketful of rye – and no explanation of it.'

4

Mary Dove paused on her way downstairs and looked out through the big window on the stairs. A car had just driven up from which two men were alighting. The taller of the two stood for a moment with his back to the house surveying his surroundings. Mary Dove appraised the two men thoughtfully. Inspector Neele and presumably a subordinate.

She turned from the window and looked at herself in the full length mirror that hung on the wall where the staircase turned. . . . She saw a small demure figure with immaculate white collar and cuffs on a beige grey dress. Her dark hair was parted in the middle and drawn back in two shining waves to a knot in the back of the neck. . . . The lipstick she used was a pale rose colour.

On the whole Mary Dove was satisfied with her appearance. A very faint smile on her lips, she went on down the stairs.

Inspector Neele, surveying the house, was saying to himself:

Call it a lodge, indeed! Yewtree Lodge! The affectation of these rich people! The house was what he, Inspector Neele, would call a mansion. He knew what a lodge was. He'd been brought up in one! The lodge at the gates of Hartington Park, that vast unwieldy Palladian house with its twenty-nine bedrooms which had now been taken over by the National Trust. The lodge had been small and attractive from the outside, and had been damp, uncomfortable and devoid of anything but the most primitive form of sanitation within. Fortunately these facts had been accepted as quite proper and fitting by Inspector Neele's parents. They had no rent to pay and nothing whatever to do except open and shut the gates when required, and there were always plenty of rabbits and an occasional pheasant or so for the pot. Mrs Neele had never discovered the pleasure of elctric irons, slow combustion stoves, airing cupboards, hot and cold water from taps, and the switching on of light by a mere flick of a finger. In winter the Neeles had an oil lamp and in summer they went to bed when it got dark. They were a healthy family and a happy one, all thoroughly behind the times.

So when Inspector Neele heard the word Lodge, it was his childhood memories that stirred. But this place, this pretentiously named Yewtree Lodge was just the kind of mansion that rich people built themselves and then called it 'their little place in the country.' It wasn't in the country either, according to Inspector Neele's idea of the country. The house was a large solid red brick structure, sprawling lengthwise rather than upward, with too many gables, and a vast number of leaded paned windows. The gardens were highly artificial – all laid out in rose beds and pergolas and pools, and living up to the name of the house with large numbers of clipped yew hedges.

Plenty of yew here for anybody with a desire to obtain the raw material of taxine. Over on the right, behind the rose pergola, there was a bit of actual nature left – a vast yew tree of the kind one associates with churchyards, its branches held up by stakes – like a kind of Moses of the forest world. That tree, the Inspector thought, had been there long before the rash of newly built red brick houses had begun to spread over the countryside. It had been there before the golf courses had been laid out and the fashionable architects had walked round with their rich clients, pointing out the advantages of the various sites. And since it was a valuable antique, the tree had been kept and incorporated in the new set-up and had, perhaps, given its name to the new desirable residence. Yewtree Lodge. And possibly the berries from that very tree—

Inspector Neele cut off these unprofitable speculations. Must get on with the job. He rang the bell.

It was opened promptly by a middle-aged man who fitted in quite accurately with the mental image Inspector Neele had formed of him over the phone. A man with a rather spurious air of smartness, a shifty eye and a rather unsteady hand.

Inspector Neele announced himself and his subordinate and had the pleasure of seeing an instant look of alarm come into the butler's eye. . . . Neele did not attach too much importance to that. It might easily have nothing to do with the death of Rex Fortescue. It was quite possibly a purely automatic reaction.

'Has Mrs Fortescue returned yet?'

'No, sir.'

'Nor Mr Percival Fortescue? Nor Miss Fortescue?'

'No, sir.'

'Then I would like to see Miss Dove, please.'

The man turned his head slightly.

'Here's Miss Dove now – coming downstairs.'

Inspector Neele took in Miss Dove as she came composedly down the wide staircase. This time the mental picture did not correspond with the reality. Unconsciously the word housekeeper had conjured up a vague impression of someone large and authoritative dressed in black with somewhere concealed about her a jingle of keys.

The Inspector was quite unprepared for the small trim figure descending towards him. The soft dove-coloured tones of her dress, the white collar and cuffs, the neat waves of hair, the faint Mona Lisa smile. It all seemed, somehow, just a little unreal, as though this young woman of under thirty was playing a part: not, he thought, the part of a housekeeper, but the part of Mary Dove. Her appearance was directed towards living up to her name.

She greeted him composedly.

'Inspector Neele?'

'Yes. This is Sergeant Hay. Mr Fortescue, as I told you through the phone, died in St Jude's Hospital at 12.43. It seems likely that his death was the result of something he ate at breakfast this morning. I should be glad therefore if Sergeant Hay

414

could be taken to the kitchen where he can make inquiries as to the food served.'

Her eyes met his for a moment, thoughtfully, then she nodded.

'Of course,' she said. She turned to the uneasily hovering butler. 'Crump, will you take Sergeant Hay and show him whatever he wants to see.'

The two men departed together. Mary Dove said to Neele: 'Will you come in here?'

She opened the door of a room and preceded him into it. It was a characterless apartment, clearly labelled 'Smoking Room,' with panelling, rich upholstery, large stuffed chairs, and a suitable set of sporting prints on the walls.

'Please sit down.'

He sat and Mary Dove sat opposite him. She chose, he noticed, to face the light. An unusual preference for a woman. Still more unusual if a woman had anything to hide. But perhaps Mary Dove had nothing to hide.

'It is very unfortunate,' she said, 'that none of the family is available. Mrs Fortescue may return at any minute. And so may Mrs Val. I have sent wires to Mr Percival Fortescue at various places.'

'Thank you, Miss Dove.'

'You say that Mr Fortescue's death was caused by something he may have eaten for breakfast? Food poisoning, you mean?'

'Possibly.' He watched her.

She said composedly, 'It seems unlikely. For breakfast this morning there were bacon and scrambled eggs, coffee, toast and marmalade. There was also a cold ham on the sideboard, but that had been cut yesterday, and no one felt any ill effects. No fish of any kind was served, no sausages – nothing like that.'

'I see you know exactly what was served.'

'Naturally. I order the meals. For dinner last night—'

'No.' Inspector Neele interrupted her. 'It would not be a question of dinner last night.'

'I thought the onset of food poisoning could sometimes be delayed as much as twenty-four hours.'

'Not in this case. . . . Will you tell me exactly what Mr Fortescue ate and drank before leaving the house this morning?'

'He had early tea brought to his room at eight o'clock. Breakfast was at a quarter past nine. Mr Fortescue, as I have told you, had scrambled eggs, bacon, coffee, toast and marmalade.'

'Any cereal?'

'No, he didn't like cereals.'

'The sugar for the coffee – is it lump sugar or granulated?'

'Lump. But Mr Fortescue did not take sugar in his coffee.'

'Was he in the habit of taking any medicines in the morning? Salts? A tonic? Some digestive remedy?'

'No, nothing of that kind.'

'Did you have breakfast with him also?'

'No. I do not take meals with the family.'

'Who was at breakfast?'

'Mrs Fortescue. Miss Fortescue. Mrs Val Fortescue. Mr Percival Fortescue, of course, was away.'

'And Mrs and Miss Fortescue ate the same things for breakfast?'

'Mrs Fortescue has only coffee, orange juice and toast, Mrs Val and Miss Fortescue always ate a hearty breakfast. Besides eating scrambled eggs and cold ham, they would probably have a cereal as well. Mrs Val drinks tea, not coffee.'

Inspector Neele reflected for a moment. The opportunities seemed at least to be narrowing down. Three people and three people only had had breakfast with the deceased, his wife, his daughter and his daughter-in-law. Either of them might have seized an opportunity to add taxine to his cup of coffee. The bitterness of the coffee would have masked the bitter taste of the taxine. There was the early morning tea, of course, but Bernsdorff had intimated that the taste would be noticeable in tea. But perhaps, first thing in the morning, before the senses were alert . . . He looked up to find Mary Dove watching him.

'Your questions about tonic and medicines seem to me rather odd, Inspector,' she said. 'It seems to imply that either there was something wrong with a medicine, or that something had been added to it. Surely neither of those processes could be described as food poisoning.'

Neele eyed her steadily.

'I did not say – definitely – that Mr Fortescue died of food poisoning.'

'But some kind of poisoning. In fact – just poisoning.'

She repeated softly 'Poisoning. . . .'

She appeared neither startled nor dismayed, merely interested. Her attitude was of one sampling a new experience.

In fact she said as much, remarking after a moment's reflection: 'I have never had anything to do with a poisoning case before.'

'It's not very pleasant,' Neele informed her dryly.

'No – I suppose not. . . .'

She thought about it for a moment and then looked up at him with a sudden smile.

'I didn't do it,' she said. 'But I suppose everybody will tell you that!'

'Have you any idea who did do it, Miss Dove?'

She shrugged her shoulders.

'Frankly, he was an odious man. Anybody might have done it.'

'But people aren't poisoned just for being "odious," Miss Dove. There usually has to be a pretty solid motive.'

'Yes, of course.'

She was thoughtful.

'Do you care to tell me something about the household here?'

She looked up at him. He was a little startled to find her eyes cool and amused.

'This isn't exactly a statement you're asking me to make, is it? No, it couldn't be, because your Sergeant is busy upsetting the domestic staff. I shouldn't like to have what I say read out in court – but all the same I should rather like to say it – unofficially. Off the record, so to speak?'

'Go ahead then, Miss Dove. I've no witness, as you've already observed.'

She leaned back, swinging one slim foot and narrowing her eyes.

'Let me start by saying that I've no feeling of loyalty to my employers. I work for them because it's a job that pays well and I insist that it should pay well.'

'I was a little surprised to find you doing this type of job. It struck me that with your brains and education—'

'I ought to be confined in an office? Or compiling files in a Ministry? My dear Inspector Neele, this is the perfect racket. People will pay anything – *anything* – to be spared domestic worries. To find and engage a staff is a thoroughly tedious job. Writing to agencies, putting in advertisements, interviewng people, making arrangements for interviews, and finally keeping the whole thing running smoothly – it takes a certain capacity which most of these people haven't got.'

'And suppose your staff when you've assembled it, runs out on you? I've heard of such things.'

Mary smiled.

'If necessary, I can make the beds, dust the rooms, cook a meal *and* serve it without anyone noticing the difference. Of course I don't advertise that fact. It might give rise to ideas. But

I can always be sure of tiding over any little gap. But there aren't often gaps. I work only for the extremely rich who will pay anything to be comfortable. I pay top prices and so I get the best of what's going.'

'Such as the butler?'

She threw him an amused, appreciative glance.

'There's always that trouble with a couple. Crump stays because of Mrs Crump, who is one of the best cooks I've ever come across. She's a jewel and one would put up with a good deal to keep her. Our Mr Fortescue likes his food – liked, I should say, In this household nobody has any scruples and they have plenty of money. Butter, eggs, cream, Mrs Crump can command what she likes. As for Crump, he just makes the grade. His silver's all right, and his waiting at table is not too bad. I keep the key of the wine cellar and a sharp eye on the whisky, and gin, and supervise his valeting.'

Inspector Neele raised his eyebrows.

'The admirable Miss Crichton.'

'I find one must *know* how to do everything oneself. Then – one need never do it. But you wanted to know my impressions of the family.'

'If you don't mind.'

'They are really all quite odious. The late Mr Fortescue was the kind of crook who is always careful to play safe. He boasted a great deal of his various smart dealings. He was rude and overbearing in manner and was a definite bully. Mrs Fortescue, Adele – was his second wife and about thirty years younger than he was. He came across her at Brighton. She was a manicurist on the look-out for big money. She is very good looking – a real sexy piece, if you know what I mean.'

Inspector Neele was shocked but managed not to show it. A girl like Mary Dove ought not to say such things, he felt.

The young lady was continuing composedly:

'Adele married him for his money, of course, and his son, Percival, and his daughter, Elaine, were simply livid about it. They're as nasty as they can be to her, but very wisely she doesn't care or even notice. She knows she's got the old man where she wants him. Oh dear, the wrong tense again. I haven't really grasped yet that he's dead. . . .'

'Let's hear about the son.'

'Dear Percival? Val as his wife calls him. Percival is a mealy-mouthed hypocrite. He's prim and sly and cunning. He's terrified of his father and has always let himself be bullied, but he's quite clever at getting his own way. Unlike his father he's mean about money. Economy is one of his passions. That's why he's been so long about finding a house of his own. Having a suite of rooms here saved his pocket.'

'And his wife?'

'Jennifer's meek and seems very stupid. But I'm not so sure. She was a hospital nurse before her marriage – nursed Percival through pneumonia to a romantic conclusion. The old man was disappointed by the marriage. He was a snob and wanted Percival to make what he called a "good marriage." He despised poor Mrs Val and snubbed her. She dislikes – disliked him a good deal, I think. Her principal interests are shopping and the cinema; her principal grievance is that her husband keeps her short of money.'

'What about the daughter?'

'Elaine? I'm rather sorry for Elaine. She's not a bad sort. One of those great schoolgirls who never grow up. She plays games quite well, and runs Guides and Brownies and all that sort of thing. There was some sort of affair not long ago with a disgruntled young schoolmaster, but Father discovered the young man had communistic ideas and came down on the romance like a ton of bricks.'

'She hadn't got the spirit to stand up to him?'

'*She* had. It was the young man who ratted. A question of money yet again, I fancy. Elaine is not particularly attractive, poor dear.'

'And the other son?'

'I've never seen him. He's attractive, by all accounts, and a thoroughly bad lot. Some little matter of a forged cheque in the past. He lives in East Africa.'

'And was estranged from his father.'

'Yes, Mr Fortescue couldn't cut him off with a shilling because he'd already made him a junior partner in the firm, but he held no communication with him for years, and in fact if Lance was ever mentioned, he used to say "Don't talk to me of that rascal. He's no son of mine." All the same—'

'Yes, Miss Dove?'

Mary said slowly: 'All the same, I shouldn't be surprised if old Fortescue hadn't been planning to get him back here.'

'What makes you think that?'

'Because, about a month ago, old Fortescue had a terrific row with Percival – he found out something that Percival had been doing behind his back – I don't know what it was – and he was absolutely furious. Percival suddenly stopped being the white-headed boy. He's been quite different lately, too.'

'Mr Fortescue was quite different?'

'No. I mean Percival. He's gone about looking worried to death.'

'Now what about servants? You've alyready described the Crumps. Who else is there?'

'Gladys Martin is the parlourmaid or waitress, as they like to call themselves nowadays. She does the downstairs rooms, lays the table, clears away and helps Crump wait at table. Quite a decent sort of girl but very nearly half-witted. The adenoidal type.'

Neele nodded.

'The housemaid is Ellen Curtis. Elderly, very crabbed, and very cross, but has been in good service and is a first-class house-maid. The rest is outside help – odd women who come in.'

'And those are the only people living here?'

'There's old Miss Ramsbottom.'

'Who is she?'

'Mr Fortescue's sister-in-law – his first wife's sister. His wife was a good deal older than he was and her sister again was a good deal older than her – which makes her well over seventy. She has a room of her own on the second floor – does her own cooking and all that, with just a woman coming in to clean. She's rather eccentric and she never liked her brother-in-law, but she came here while her sister was alive and stayed on when she died. Mr Fortescue never bothered about her much. She's quite a character, though, is Aunt Effie.'

'And that is all.'

'That's all.'

'So we come to you, Miss Dove.'

'You want particulars? I'm an orphan. I took a secretarial course at the St Alfred's Secretarial College. I took a job as short-hand typist, left it and took another, decided I was in the wrong racket, and started on my present career. I have been with three different employers. After about a year or eighteen months I get tired of a particular place and move on. I have been at Yewtree Lodge just over a year. I will type out the names and addresses of my various employers and give them, with a copy of my refer-ences to Sergeant – Hay, is it? Will that be satisfactory?'

'Perfectly, Miss Dove.' Neele was silent for a moment, enjoy-ing a mental image of Miss Dove tampering with Mr Fortescue's breakfast. His mind went back farther, and he saw her methodically gathering yew berries in a little basket. With a sigh he returned to the present and reality. 'Now, I would like to see the girl – er Gladys – and then the housemaid, Ellen.' He added as he rose, 'By the way, Miss Dove, can you give me any idea why Mr Fortescue would be carrying loose grain in his pocket?'

'Grain?' She stared at him with what appeared to be genuine surprise.

'Yes – grain. Does that suggest something to you, Miss Dove?'

'Nothing at all.'

'Who looked after his clothes?'

'Crump.'

'I see. Did Mr Fortescue and Mrs Fortescue occupy the same bedroom?'

'Yes. He had a dressing-room and bath, of course, and so did she. . . .' Mary glanced down at her wrist-watch. 'I really think that she ought to be back very soon now.'

The Inspector had risen. He said in a pleasant voice:

'Do you know one thing, Miss Dove? It strikes me as very odd that even though there are three golf courses in the immediate neighbourhood, it has yet not been possible to find Mrs Fortescue on one of them before now?'

'It would not be so odd, Inspector, if she did not actually happen to be playing golf at all.'

Mary's voice was dry. The Inspector said sharply:

'I was distinctly informed that she was playing golf.'

'She took her golf clubs and announced her intention of doing so. She was driving her own car, of course.'

He looked at her steadily, perceiving the inference.

'Who was she playing with? Do you know?'

'I think it possible that it might be Mr Vivian Dubois.'

Neele contented himself by saying: 'I see.'

'I'll send Gladys in to you. She'll probably be scared to death.'

Mary paused for a moment by the door, then she said:

'I should hardly advise you to go too much by all I've told you. I'm a malicious creature.'

She went out. Inspector Neele looked at the closed door and wondered. Whether actuated by malice or not, what she had told him could not fail to be suggestive. If Rex Fortescue had been deliberately poisoned, and it seemed almost certain that that was the case, then the set-up at Yewtree Lodge seemed highly promising. Motives appeard to be lying thick on the ground.

5

The girl who entered the room with obvious unwillingness was an unattractive, frightened looking girl, who managed to look faintly sluttish in spite of being tall and smartly dressed in a claret-coloured uniform.

She said at once, fixing imploring eyes upon him.

'I didn't do anything. I didn't really. I don't know anything about it.'

'That's all right,' said Neele heartily. His voice had changed slightly. It sounded more cheerful and a good deal commoner in intonation. He wanted to put the frightened rabbit Gladys at her ease.

'Sit down here,' he went on. 'I just want to know about breakfast this morning.'

'I didn't do anything at all.'

'Well, you laid the breakfast, didnt you?'

'Yes, I did that.' Even that admission came unwillingly. She looked both guilty and terrified, but Inspector Neele was used to witnesses who looked like that. He went on cheerfully, trying to put her at her ease, asking questions: who had come down first? And who next?

Elaine Fortescue had been the first down to breakfast. She'd come in just as Crump was bringing in the coffee pot. Mrs Fortescue was down next, and then Mrs Val, and the master last. They waited on themselves. The tea and coffee and the hot dishes were all on hot plates on the sideboard.

He learnt little of importance from her that he did not know already. The food and drink was as Mary Dove had described it. The master and Mrs Fortescue and Miss Elaine took coffee and Mrs Val took tea. Everything had been quite as usual.

Neele questioned her about herself and here she answered more readily. She'd been in private service first and after that in various cafés. Then she thought she'd like to go back to private service and had come to Yewtree Lodge last September. She'd been there two months.

'And you like it?'

'Well, it's all right, I suppose.' She added: 'It's not so hard on your feet – but you don't get so much freedom. . . .'

'Tell me about Mr Fortescue's clothes – his suits. Who looked after them? Brushed them and all that?'

Gladys looked faintly resentful.

'Mr Crump's supposed to. But half the time he makes me do it.'

'Who brushed and pressed the suit Mr Fortescue had on today?'

'I don't remember which one he wore. He's got ever so many.'

'Have you ever found grain in the pocket of one of his suits?'

'Grain?' She looked puzzled.

'Rye, to be exact.'

'Rye? That's bread, isn't it? A sort of black bread – got a nasty taste, I always think.'

'That's bread made from rye. Rye is the grain itself. There was some found in the pocket of your master's coat.'

'In his coat pocket?'

'Yes. Do you know how it got there?'

'I couldn't say I'm sure. I never saw any.'

He could get no more from her. For a moment or two he wondered if she knew more about the matter than she was willing to admit. She certainly seemed embarrassed and on the defensive – but on the whole he put it down to a natural fear of the police.

When he finally dismissed her, she asked:

'It's really true, is it. He's dead?'

'Yes, he's dead.'

'Very sudden, wasn't it? They said when they rang up from the office that he'd had a kind of fit.'

'Yes – it was a kind of fit.'

Gladys said: 'A girl I used to know had fits. Come on any time, they did. Used to scare me.'

For the moment this reminiscence seemed to overcome her suspicions.

Inspector Neele made his way to the kitchen.

His reception was immediate and alarming. A woman of vast proportions, with a red face and armed with a rolling-pin stepped towards him in a menacing fashion.

'Police, indeed,' she said. 'Coming here and saying things like that! Nothing of the kind, I'd have you know. Anything I've sent in to the dining-room has been just what it should be. Coming here and saying I poisoned the master. I'll have the law on you, police or no police. No bad food's ever been served in this house.'

It was some time before Inspector Neele could appease the irate artist. Sergeant Hay looked in grinning from the pantry and Inspector Neele gathered that he had already run the gauntlet of Mrs Crump's wrath.

The scene was terminated by the ringing of the telephone.

Neele went out into the hall to find Mary Dove taking the call. She was writing down a message on a pad. Turning her head over her shoulder she said: 'It's a telegram.'

The call concluded, she replaced the receiver and handed the pad on which she had been writing to the Inspector. The place or origin was Paris and the message ran as follows:

'FORTESCUE YEWTREE LODGE BAYDON HEATH SURREY. SORRY YOUR LETTER DELAYED. WILL BE WITH YOU TOMORROW ABOUT TEATIME. SHALL EXPECT ROAST VEAL FOR DINNER. LANCE.

Inspector Neele raised his eyebrows.

'So the Prodigal Son had been summoned home,' he said.

—— 6 ——

At the moment when Rex Fortescue had been drinking his last cup of tea, Lance Fortescue and his wife had been sitting under the trees on the Champs Elysées watching the people walking past.

'It's all very well to say "describe him," Pat. I'm a rotten hand at descriptions. What do you want to know? The Guvnor's a bit of an old crook, you know. But you won't mind that? You must be used to that more or less.'

'Oh yes,' said Pat. 'Yes – as you say – I'm acclimatised.'

She tried to keep a certain forlornness out of her voice. Perhaps, she reflected, the whole world was really crooked – or was it just that she herself had been unfortunate?

She was a tall, long-legged girl, not beautiful but with a charm that was made up of vitality and a warm-hearted personality. She moved well, and had lovely gleaming chestnut brown hair. Perhaps from a long association with horses, she had acquired the look of a thoroughbred filly.

Crookedness in the racing world she knew about – now, it seemed, she was to encounter crookedness in the financial world. Though for all that, it seemed that her father-in-law whom she had not yet met, was, as far as the law was concerned, a pillar

424

of rectitude. All these people who went about boasting of 'smart work' were the same – technically they always managed to be within the law. Yet it seemed to her that her Lance, whom she loved, and who had admittedly strayed outside the ringed fence in earlier days, had an honesty that these successful practitioners of the crooked lacked.

'I don't mean,' said Lance, 'that he's a swindler – not anything like that. But he knows how to put over a fast one.'

'Sometimes,' said Pat, 'I feel I hate people who put over fast ones.' She added: 'You're fond of him.' It was a statement, not a question.

Lance considered it for a moment, and then said in a surprised kind of voice:

'Do you know darling, I believe I am.'

Pat laughed. He turned his head to look at her. His eyes narrowed. What a darling she was! He loved her. The whole thing was worth it for her sake.

'In a way, you know,' he said, 'it's hell going back. City life. Home on the 5.18. It's not my kind of life. I'm far more at home among the down and outs. But one's got to settle down sometime, I suppose. And with you to hold my hand the process may even be quite a pleasant one. And since the old boy has come round, one ought to take advantage of it. I must say I was surprised when I got his letter. . . . Percival, of all people, blotting his copybook. Percival, the good little boy. Mind you, Percy was always sly. Yes, he was always sly.'

'I don't think,' said Patricia Fortescue, 'that I'm going to like your brother Percival.'

'Don't let me put you against him. Percy and I never got on – that's all there is to it. I blued my pocket money, he saved his. I had disreputable but entertaining friends. Percy made what's called "worth while contacts." Poles apart we were, he and I. I always thought him a poor fish, and he – sometimes, you know, I think he almost hated me, I don't know why exactly. . . .'

'I think I can see why.'

'Can you, darling? You're so brainy. You know I've always wondered – it's a fantastic thing to say – but—'

'Well? Say it.'

'I've wondered if it wasn't Percival who was behind that cheque business – you know, when the old man kicked me out – and was he mad that he'd given me a share in the firm and so he couldn't disinherit me! Because the queer thing was that I never forged that cheque – though of course nobody would believe that after that time I swiped funds out of the till and put it on a horse. I was dead sure I could put it back, and anyway it was my own cash in a manner of speaking. But that cheque business – no. I don't know why I've got the ridiculous idea that Percival did that – but I have, somehow.'

'But it wouldn't have done *him* any good? It was paid into your account.'

'I know. So it doesn't make sense, does it?'

Pat turned sharply towards him.

'You mean – he did it to get you chucked out of the firm?'

'I wondered. Oh well – it's a rotten thing to say. Forget it. I wonder what old Percy will say when he sees the Prodigal returned. Those pale, boiled, gooseberry eyes of his will pop right out of his head!'

'Does he know you are coming?'

'I shouldn't be surprised if he didn't know a damned thing!' The old man's got rather a funny sense of humour, you know.'

'But what has your brother *done* to upset your father so much?'

'That's what *I'd* like to know. Something must have made the old man livid. Writing off to me the way he did.'

'When was it you got his first letter?'

'Must be four – no five months ago. A cagey letter, but a distinct holding out of the olive branch. "Your elder brother has proved himself unsatisfactory in many ways." "You seem to have sown your wild oats and settled down." "I can promise you that it will be well worth your while financially." "Shall welcome you and your wife." You know, darling, I think my marrying you had a lot to do with it. The old boy was impressed that I'd married into a class above me.'

Pat laughed.

'What? Into the aristocratic riff-raff?'

He grinned. 'That's right. But riff-raff didn't register and aristocracy did. You should see Percival's wife. She's the kind who says "Pass the preserves, please" and talks about a postage stamp.'

Pat did not laugh. She was considering the women of the family into which she had married. It was a point of view which Lance had not taken into account.

'And your sister?' she asked.

'Elaine—? Oh she's all right. She was pretty young when I left home. Sort of an earnest girl – but probably she's grown out of that. Very intense over things.'

It did not sound very reassuring. Pat said:

'She never wrote to you – after you went away?'

'I didn't leave an address. But she wouldn't have, anyway. We're not a devoted family.'

'No.'

He shot a quick look at her.

'Got the wind up? About my family? You needn't. We're not going to live with them, or anything like that. We'll have our own little place somewhere. Horses, dogs, anything you like.'

'But there will still be the 5.18.'

'For me, yes. To and fro to the city, all togged up. But don't worry, sweet – there are rural pockets, even round London. And lately I've felt the sap of financial affairs rising in me. After all, it's in my blood – from both sides of the family.'

'You hardly remember your mother, do you?'

'She always seemed to me incredibly old. She was old, of course. Nearly fifty when Elaine was born. She wore lots of clinking things and lay on a sofa and used to read me stories about knights and ladies which bored me stiff. Tennyson's "Idylls of the King." I suppose I was fond of her. . . . She was very – colourless, you know. I realize that, looking back.'

'You don't seem to have been particularly fond of anybody,' said Pat disapprovingly.

Lance grasped and squeezed her arm.

'I'm fond of you,' he said.

— 7 —

Inspector Neele was still holding the telegraph message in his hand when he heard a car drive up to the front door and stop with a careless scrunching of brakes.

Mary Dove said, 'That will be Mrs Fortescue now.'

Inspector Neele moved forwards to the front door. Out of the tail of his eye, he saw Mary Dove melt unobtrusively into the background and disappear. Clearly she intended to take no part in the forthcoming scene. A remarkable display of tact and discretion – and also a rather remarkable lack of curiosity. Most women, Inspector Neele decided, would have remained. . . .

As he reached the front door he was aware of the butler, Crump, coming forward from the back of the hall. So he had heard the car.

The car was a Rolls Bentley sports model coupé. Two people got out of it and came towards the house. As they reached the door, it opened. Surprised, Adele Fortescue stared at Inspector Neele.

He realized at once that she was a very beautiful woman, and he realized too, the force of Mary Dove's comment which had so shocked him at the time. Adele Fortescue *was* a sexy piece. In figure and type she resembled the blonde Miss Grosvenor, but whereas Miss Grosvenor was all glamour without and all respectability within, Adele Fortescue was glamour all through. Her appeal was obvious, not subtle. It said simply to every man 'Here am I. I'm a woman.' She spoke and moved and breathed sex – and yet, within it all, her eyes had a shrewd appraising quality. Adele Fortescue, he thought, liked men – but she would always like money even better.

His eyes went on to the figure behind her who carried her golf clubs. He knew the type very well. It was the type that specialised in the young wives of rich and elderly men. Mr Vivian Dubois, if this was he, had that rather forced masculinity which is, in reality, nothing of the kind. He was the type of man who 'understands' women.

'Mrs Fortescue?'

'Yes.' It was a wide blue-eyed gaze. 'But I don't know—'

'I am Inspector Neele. I'm afraid I have bad news for you.'

'Do you mean – a burglary – something of that kind?'

'No, nothing of that kind. It is about your husband. He was taken seriously ill this morning.'

'Rex? Ill?'

'We have been trying to get in touch with you since half-past eleven this morning.'

'Where is he? Here? Or in hospital?'

'He was taken to St Jude's Hospital. I'm afraid you must prepare yourself for a shock.

'You don't mean – he isn't – *dead.*'

She lurched forward a little and clutched his arm. Gravely feeling like someone playing a part in a stage performance, the Inspector supported her into the hall. Crump was hovering eagerly.

'Brandy she'll be needing,' he said.

The deep voice of Mr Dubois said:

'That's right, Crump. Get the brandy.' To the Inspector he said: 'In here.'

He opened a door on the left. The procession filed in. The Inspector and Adele Fortescue, Vivian Dubois, and Crump with a decanter and two glasses.

Adele Fortescue sank on to an easy chair, her eyes covered with her hand. She accepted the glass that the Inspector offered and took a tiny sip, then pushed it away.

'I don't want it,' she said. 'I'm all right. But tell me, what was it? A stroke, I suppose? Poor Rex.'

'It wasn't a stroke, Mrs Fortescue.'

'Did you say you were an Inspector?' It was Mr Dubois who made the inquiry.

Neele turned to him. 'That's right,' he said pleasantly. 'Inspector Neele of the CID.'

He saw the alarm grow in the dark eyes. Mr Dubois did not like the appearance of an Inspector of the CID. He didn't like it at all.

'What's up?' he said. 'Something wrong – eh?'

Quite unconsciously he backed away a little towards the door. Inspector Neele noted the movement.

'I'm afraid,' he said to Mrs Fortescue, 'that there will have to be an inquest.'

'An inquest? Do you mean – what *do* you mean?'

'I'm afraid this is all very distressing for you, Mrs Fortescue.' The words came smoothly. 'It seemed advisable to find out as soon as possible exactly what Mr Fortescue had to eat or drink before leaving for the office this morning.'

'Do you mean he might have been *poisoned*?'

'Well, yes, it would seem so.'

'I can't believe it. Oh – you mean *food* poisoning.'

Her voice dropped half an octave on the last words. His face wooden, his voice still smooth, Inspector Neele said:

'Madam? What did you think I meant?'

She ignored that question, hurrying on.

'But we've been all right – all of us.'

'You can speak for all the members of the family?'

'Well – no – of course – I can't really.'

Dubois said with a great show of consulting his watch:

'I'll have to push off, Adele. Dreadfully sorry. You'll be all right, won't you? I mean, there are the maids, and the little Dove and all that—'

'Oh Vivian, don't. Don't go.'

It was quite a wail, and it affected Mr Dubois adversely. His retreat quickened.

'Awfully sorry, old girl. Important engagement. I'm putting up at the Dormy House, by the way, Inspector. If you – er want me for anything.'

Inspector Neele nodded. He had no wish to detain Mr Dubois. But he recognised Mr Dubois's departure for what it was. Mr Dubois was running away from trouble.

Adele Fortescue said, in an attempt to carry off the situation:

'It's such a shock, to come back and find the *police* in the house.'

'I'm sure it must be. But you see, it was necessary to act promptly in order to obtain the necessary specimens of foodstuffs, coffee, tea, etc.'

'Tea and coffee? But they're not poisonous? I expect it's the awful bacon we sometimes get. It's quite uneatable sometimes.'

'We shall find out, Mrs Fortescue. Don't worry. You'd be surprised at some of the things that can happen. We once had a case of digitalis poisoning. It turned out that foxglove leaves had been picked in mistake for horseradish.'

'You think something like that could happen here?'

'We shall know better after the autopsy, Mrs Fortescue.'

'The autop – oh I see.' She shivered.

The Inspector went on: 'You've got a lot of yew round the house, haven't you, madam. There's no possibility, I suppose, of the berries or leaves having got – mixed up in anything?'

He was watching her closely. She stared at him.

'Yew berries? Are they poisonous?'

The wonder seemed a little too wide-eyed and innocent.

'Children have been known to eat them with unfortunate results.'

Adele clasped her hands to her head.

'I can't bear to talk about it any more. Must I? I want to go and lie down. I can't stand any more. Mr Percival Fortescue will arrange everything – I can't – I can't – it isn't fair to ask me.'

'We are getting in touch with Mr Percival Fortescue as soon as possible. Unfortunately he is away in the North of England.'

'Oh yes, I forgot.'

'There's just one thing, Mrs Fortescue. There was a small quantity of grain in your husband's pocket. Could you give me some explanation of that?'

She shook her head. She appeared quite bewildered.

'Would anyone have slipped it in there as a joke?'

'I don't see why it would be a joke?'

Inspector Neele did not see either. He said:

'I won't trouble you any further at present, Mrs Fortescue. Shall I send one of the maids to you? Or Miss Dove?'

'What?' The word came abstractedly. He wondered what she had been thinking about.

She fumbled with her bag and pulled out a handkerchief. Her voice trembled.

'It's so awful,' she said unsteadily. 'I'm only just beginning to take it in. I've really been *numbed* up to now. Poor Rex. Poor dear Rex.'

She sobbed in a manner that was almost convincing.

Inspector Neele watched her respectfully for a moment or two.

'It's been very sudden, I know,' he said. 'I'll send someone to you.'

He went towards the door, opened it and passed through. He paused for a moment before looking back into the room.

Adele Fortescue still held the handkerchief to her eyes. The ends of it hung down but did not quite obscure her mouth. On her lips was a very faint smile.

8

'I've got what I could, sir.' So Sergeant Hay reporting. 'The marmalade, bit of the ham. Samples of tea, coffee and sugar, for what they're worth. Actual brews have been thrown out by now, of course, but there's one point. There was a good lot of coffee left over and they had it in the servants' hall at elevenses – that's important, I should say.'

'Yes, that's important. Shows that if he took it in his coffee, it must have been slipped into the actual cup.'

'By one of those present. Exactly. I've inquired, cautious like, about this yew stuff – berries or leaves – there's been none of it seen about the house. Nobody seems to know anything about the cereal in his pocket, either. . . . It just seems daft to them. Seems daft to me, too. He doesn't seem to have been one of those food faddists who'll eat any mortal thing so long as it isn't cooked. My sister's husband's like that. Raw carrots, raw peas, raw turnips. But even he doesn't eat raw grain. Why, I should say it would swell up in your inside something awful.'

The telephone rang and on a nod from the Inspector, Sergeant Hay sprinted off to answer it. Following him, Neele found that it was headquarters on the line. Contact had been made with Mr Percival Fortescue, who was returning to London immediately.

As the Inspector replaced the telephone, a car drew up at the front door. Crump went to the door and opened it. The woman who stood there had her arms full of parcels. Crump took them from her.

'Thanks, Crump. Pay the taxi, will you? I'll have tea now. Is Mrs Fortescue or Miss Elaine in?'

The butler hesitated, looking back over his shoulder.

'We've had bad news, ma'am,' he said. 'About the master.'

'About Mr Fortescue?'

Neele came forward. Crump said: 'This is Mrs Percival, sir.'

'What is it? What's happened? An accident?'

The Inspector looked her over as he replied. Mrs Percival Fortescue was a plump woman with a discontented mouth. Her age he judged to be about thirty. Her questions came with a kind of eagerness. The thought flashed across his mind that she must be very bored.

'I'm sorry to have to tell you that Mr Fortescue was taken to St Jude's Hospital this morning seriously ill and has since died.'

'Died? You mean he's dead?' The news was clearly even more sensational than she had hoped for. 'Dear me – this is a surprise. My husband's away. You'll have to get in touch with him. He's in the North somewhere. I dare say they'll know at the office. He'll have to see to everything. Things always happen at the most awkward moment, don't they.'

She paused for a moment, turning things over in her mind.

'It all depends, I suppose,' she said, 'where they'll have the funeral. Down here, I suppose. Or will it be in London?'

'That will be for the family to say.'

'Of course. I only just wondered.' For the first time she took direct cognisance of the man who was speaking to her.

'Are you from the office?' she asked. 'You're not a doctor, are you?'

'I'm a police officer. Mr Fortescue's death was very sudden and—'

She interrupted him.

'Do you mean he was *murdered*?'

It was the first time that word had been spoken. Neele surveyed her eager questioning face carefully.

'Now why should you think that, madam?'

'Well, people are sometimes. You said sudden. And you're police. Have you seen her about it? What did she say?'

'I don't quite understand to whom you are referring?'

'Adele, of course. I always told Val his father was crazy to go marrying a woman years younger than himself. There's no fool like an old fool. Besotted about that awful creature, he was. And now look what comes of it. . . . A nice mess we're all in. Pictures in the paper and reporters coming round.'

She paused, obviously visualising the future in a series of crude highly-coloured pictures. He thought that the prospect was still not wholly unpleasing. She turned back to him.

'What was it? Arsenic?'

In a repressive voice Inspector Neele said:

'The cause of death has yet to be ascertained. There will be an autopsy and an inquest.'

'But you know already, don't you? Or you wouldn't come down here.'

There was a sudden shrewdness in her plump rather foolish face.

'You've been asking about what he ate and drank, I suppose? Dinner last night. Breakfast this morning. And all the drinks, of course.'

He could see her mind ranging vividly over all the possibilities. He said, with caution:

'It seems possible that Mr Fortescue's illness resulted from something he ate at breakfast.'

'Breakfast?' She seemed surprised. 'That's difficult. I don't see how . . .'

She paused and shook her head.

'I don't see how she could have done it, then . . . unless she slipped something into the coffee – when Elaine and I weren't looking. . . .'

A quiet voice spoke softly beside them:

'Your tea is all ready in the library, Mrs Val.'

Mrs Val jumped.

'Oh thank you, Miss Dove. Yes, I could do with a cup of tea. Really, I feel quite bowled over. What about you, Mr – Inspector—'

'Thank you, not just now.'

433

The plump figure hesitated and then went slowly away.

As she disappeared through a doorway, Mary Dove murmured softly:

'I don't think she's ever heard of the term slander.'

Inspector Neele did not reply.

Mary Dove went on:

'Is there anything I can do for you?'

'Where can I find the housemaid, Ellen?'

'I will take you to her. She's just gone upstairs.'

II

Ellen proved to be grim but unafraid. Her sour old face looked triumphantly at the Inspector.

'It's a shocking business, sir. And I never thought I'd live to find myself in a house where that sort of thing has been going on. But in a way I can't say that it surprises me. I ought to have given my notice in long ago and that's a fact. I don't like the language that's used in this house, and I don't like the amount of drink that's taken, and I don't approve of the goings on there've been. I've nothing against Mrs Crump, but Crump and that girl Gladys just don't know what proper service is. But it's the goings on that I mind about most.'

'What goings on do you mean exactly?'

'You'll soon hear about them if you don't know already. It's common talk all over the place. They've been seen here there and everywhere. All this pretending to play golf – or tennis— And I've seen things – with my own eyes – in this house. The library door was open and there they were, kissing and canoodling.'

The venom of the spinster was deadly. Neele really felt it unnecessary to say 'Whom do you mean?' but he said it nevertheless.

'Who should I mean? The mistress – and that man. No shame about it, they hadn't. But if you ask me, the master had got wise to it. Put someone on to watch them, he had. Divorce, that's what it would have come to. Instead, it's come to *this*.'

'When you say this, you mean—'

'You've been asking questions, sir, about what the master ate and drank and who gave it to him. They're in it together, sir, that's what I'd say. He got the stuff from somewhere and she gave it to the master, that was the way of it, I've no doubt.'

'Have you ever seen any yew berries in the house – or thrown away anywhere.'

The small eyes glinted curiously.

'Yew? Nasty poisonous stuff. Never you touch those berries, my mother said to me when I was a child. Was *that* what was used, sir?'

'We don't know yet what was used.'

'I've never seen her fiddling about with yew.' Ellen sounded disappointed. 'No, I can't say I've seen anything of that kind.'

Neele questioned her about the grain found in Fortescue's pocket but here again he drew a blank.

'No, sir. I know nothing about that.'

He went on to further questions, but with no gainful result. Finally he asked if he could see Miss Ramsbottom.

Ellen looked doubtful.

'I could ask her, but it's not everyone she'll see. She's a very old lady, you know, and she's a bit odd.'

The Inspector pressed his demand, and rather unwillingly Ellen led him along a passage and up a short flight of stairs to what he thought had probably been designed as a nursery suite.

He glanced out of a passage window as he followed her and saw Sergeant Hay standing by the yew tree talking to a man who was evidently a gardener.

Ellen tapped on a door, and when she received an answer, opened it and said:

'There's a police gentleman here who would like to speak to you, miss.'

The answer was apparently in the affirmative for she drew back and motioned Neele to go in.

The room he entered was almost fantastically over-furnished. The Inspector felt rather as though he had taken a step back-ward into not merely Edwardian but Victorian times. At a table drawn up to a gas fire an old lady was sitting laying out a patience. She wore a maroon-coloured dress and her sparse grey hair was slicked down each side of her face.

Without looking up or discontinuing her game she said impatiently:

'Well, come in, come in. Sit down if you like.'

The invitation was not easy to accept as every chair appeared to be covered with tracts or publications of a religious nature.

As he moved them slightly aside on the sofa Miss Rams-bottom asked sharply:

'Interested in mission work?'

'Well, I'm afraid I'm not very, ma'am.'

'Wrong. You should be. That's where the Christian spirit is nowadays. Darkest Africa. Had a young clergyman here last week. Black as your hat. But a true Christian.'

Inspector Neele found it a little difficult to know what to say.

The old lady further disconcerted him by snapping:

'I haven't got a wireless.'

'I beg your pardon?'

'Oh I thought perhaps you came about a wireless licence. Or one of these silly forms. Well, man, what is it?'

'I'm sorry to have to tell you, Miss Ramsbottom, that your brother-in-law, Mr Fortescue, was taken suddenly ill and died this morning.'

Miss Ramsbottom continued with her patience without any sign of perturbation, merely remarking in a conversational way:

'Struck down at last in his arrogance and sinful pride. Well, it had to come.'

'I hope it's not a shock to you?'

It obviously wasn't but the Inspector wanted to hear what she would say.

Miss Ramsbottom gave him a sharp glance over the top of her spectacles and said:

'If you mean I am not distressed, that is quite right. Rex Fortescue was always a sinful man and I never liked him.'

'His death was very sudden—'

'As befits the ungodly,' said the old lady with satisfaction.

'It seems possible that he may have been poisoned—'

The Inspector paused to observe the effect he had made.

He did not seem to have made any. Miss Ramsbottom merely murmured 'Red seven on black eight. Now I can move up the King.'

Struck apparently by the Inspector's silence, she stopped with a card poised in her hand and said sharply:

'Well, what did you expect me to say? I didn't poison him if that's what you want to know.'

'Have you any idea who might have done so?'

'That's a very improper question,' said the old lady sharply. 'Living in this house are two of my dead sister's children. I decline to believe that anybody with Ramsbottom blood in them could be guilty of murder. Because it's murder you're meaning, isn't it?'

'I didn't say so, madam.'

'Of course it's murder. Plenty of people have wanted to murder Rex in their time. A very unscrupulous man. And old sins have long shadows, as the saying goes.'

'Have you anyone in particular in mind?'

Miss Ramsbottom swept up the cards and rose to her feet. She was a tall woman.

'I think you'd better go now,' she said.

She spoke without anger but with a kind of cold finality.

'If you want my opinion,' she went on, 'it was probably one of the servants. The butler looks to me a bit of a rascal, and that parlourmaid is definitely subnormal. Good evening.'

Inspector Neele found himself meekly walking out. Certainly a remarkable old lady. Nothing to be got out of her.

He came down the stairs into the square hall to find himself suddenly face to face with a tall dark girl. She was wearing a damp mackintosh and she stared into his face with a curious blankness.

'I've just come back,' she said. 'And they told me – about Father – that he's dead.'

'I'm afraid that's true.'

She pushed out a hand behind her as though blindly seeking for support. She touched an oak chest and slowly, stiffly, she sat down on it.

'Oh no,' she said. 'No . . .'

Slowly two tears ran down her cheeks.

'It's awful,' she said. 'I didn't think that I even liked him. . . . I thought I hated him. . . . But that can't be so, or I wouldn't mind. I do mind.'

She sat there, staring in front of her and again tears forced themselves from her eyes and down her cheeks.

Presently she spoke again, rather breathlessly.

'The awful thing is that it makes everything come right. I mean, Gerald and I can get married now. I can do everything that I want to do. But I hate it happening this way. I don't want Father to be dead. . . . Oh, I don't. Oh Daddy – Daddy. . . .'

For the first time since he had come to Yewtree Lodge, Inspector Neele was startled by what seemed to be genuine grief for the dead man.

9

'Sounds like the wife to me,' said the Assistant Commissioner. He had been listening attentively to Inspector Neele's report.

It had been an admirable précis of the case. Short, but with no relevant detail left out.

'Yes,' said the AC. 'It looks like the wife. What do you think yourself, Neele, eh?'

Inspector Neele said that it looked life the wife to him too. He reflected cynically that it usually was the wife – or the husband as the case might be.

'She had the opportunity all right. And motive?' The AC paused. 'There *is* motive?'

'Oh, I think so, sir. This Mr Dubois, you know.'

'Think he was in it, too?'

'No, I shouldn't say that, sir.' Inspector Neele weighed the idea. 'A bit too fond of his own skin for that. He may have guessed what was in her mind, but I shouldn't imagine that he instigated it.'

'No, too careful.'

'Much too careful.'

'Well, we mustn't jump to conclusions, but it seems a good working hypothesis. What about the other two who had opportunity?'

'That's the daughter and the daughter-in-law. The daughter was mixed up with a young man whom her father didn't want her to marry. And he definitely wasn't marrying her unless she had the money. That gives *her* a motive. As to the daughter-in-law, I wouldn't like to say. Don't know enough about her yet. But any of the three of them *could* have poisoned him, and I don't see how anyone else could have done so. The parlourmaid, the butler, the cook, they all handled the breakfast or brought it in, but I don't see how any of them could have been sure of Fortescue himself getting the taxine and nobody else. That is, if it *was* taxine.'

The AC said, 'It was taxine all right. I've just got the preliminary report.'

'That settles that, then,' said Inspector Neele. 'We can go ahead.'

'Servants seem all right?'

'The butler and the parlourmaid both seem nervous. There's

438

nothing uncommon about that. Often happens. The cook's fighting mad and the housemaid was grimly pleased. In fact all quite natural and normal.'

'There's nobody else whom you consider suspicious in any way?'

'No, I don't think so, sir.' Involuntarily, Inspector Neele's mind went back to Mary Dove and her enigmatic smile. There had surely been a faint yet definite look of antagonism. Aloud he said, 'Now that we know it's taxine, there ought to be some evidence to be got as to how it was obtained or prepared.'

'Just so. Well, go ahead, Neele. By the way, Mr Percival Fortescue is here now. I've had a word or two with him and he's waiting to see you. We've located the other son, too. He's in Paris at the Bristol, leaving today. You'll have him met at the airport, I suppose?'

'Yes, sir. That was my idea. . . .'

'Well, you'd better see Percival Fortescue now.' The AC chuckled. 'Percy Prim, that's what he is.'

Mr Percival Fortescue was a neat fair man of thirty odd, with pale hair and eyelashes and a slightly pendantic way of speech.

'This has been a terrible shock to me, Inspector Neele, as you can well imagine.'

'It must have been, Mr Fortescue,' said Inspector Neele.

'I can only say that my father was perfectly well when I left home the day before yesterday. This food poisoning, or whatever it was, must have been very sudden?'

'It was very sudden, yes. But it wasn't food poisoning, Mr Fortescue.'

Percival stared and frowned.

'No? So that's why—' he broke off.

'Your father,' said Inspector Neele, 'was poisoned by the administration of taxine.'

'Taxine? I never heard of it.'

'Very few people have, I should imagine. It is a poison that takes effect very suddenly and drastically.'

The frown deepened.

'Are you telling me, Inspector, that my father was deliberately poisoned by someone?'

'It would seem so, yes, sir.'

'That's terrible!'

'Yes indeed, Mr Fortescue.'

Percival murmured: 'I understand now their attitude in the

439

hospital – their referring me here.' He broke off. After a pause he went on, 'The funeral?' He spoke interrogatively.

'The inquest is fixed for tomorrow after the post-mortem. The proceedings at the inquest will be purely formal and the inquest will be adjourned.'

'I understand. That is usually the case?'

'Yes, sir. Nowadays.'

'May I ask have you formed any ideas, any suspicions of who could— Really, I—' again he broke off.

'It's rather early days for that, Mr Fortescue,' murmured Neele.

'Yes, I suppose so.'

'All the same it would be helpful to us, Mr Fortescue, if you could give us some idea of your father's testamentary dispositions. Or perhaps you could put me in touch with his solicitor.'

'His solicitors are Billingsby, Horsethorpe & Walters of Bedford Square. As far as his Will goes I think I can more or less tell you its main dispositions.'

'If you will be kind enough to do so, Mr Fortescue. It's a routine that has to be gone through, I'm afraid.'

'My father made a new Will on the occasion of his marriage two years ago,' said Percival precisely. 'My father left the sum of £100,000 to his wife absolutely and £50,000 to my sister, Elaine. I am his residuary legatee. I am already, of course, a partner in the firm.'

'There was no bequest to your brother, Lancelot Fortescue?'

'No, there is an estrangement of long standing between my father and my brother.'

Neele threw a sharp glance at him – but Percival seemed quite sure of his statement.

'So as the Will stands,' said Inspector Neele, 'the three people who stand to gain are Mrs Fortescue, Miss Elaine Fortescue and yourself?'

'I don't think I shall be much of a gainer.' Percival sighed. 'There are death duties, you know, Inspector. And of late my father has been – well, all I can say is, highly injudicious in some of his financial dealings.'

'You and your father have not seen eye to eye lately about the conduct of the business?' Inspector Neele threw out the question in a genial manner.

'I put my point of view to him, but alas—' Percival shrugged his shoulders.

'Put it rather forcibly, didn't you?' Neele inquired. 'In fact, not to put too fine a point on it there was quite a row about it, wasn't there?'

'I should hardly say that, Inspector.' A red flush of annoyance mounted to Percival's forehead.

'Perhaps the dispute you had was about some other matter then, Mr Fortescue.'

'There was no dispute, Inspector.'

'Quite sure of that, Mr Fortescue? Well, no matter. Did I understand that your father and brother are still estranged?'

'That is so.'

'Then perhaps you can tell me what this means?'

Neele handed him hte telephone message Mary Dove had jotted down.

Percival read it and uttered an exclamation of surprise and annoyance. He seemed both incredulous and angry.

'I can't understand it, I really can't. I can hardly believe it.'

'It seems to be true, though, Mr Fortescue. Your brother is arriving from Paris today.'

'But it's extraordinary, quite extraordinary. No, I really *can't* understand it.'

'Your father said nothing to you about it?'

'He certainly did *not*. How outrageous of him. To go behind my back and send for Lance.'

'You've no idea, I suppose, *why* he did such a thing?'

'Of course I haven't. 'It's all on a par with his behaviour lately – Crazy! Unaccountable. It's got to be stopped – I—'

Percival came to an abrup stop. The colour ebbed away again from his pale face.

'I'd forgotten—' he said. 'For the moment I'd forgotten that my father was dead—'

Inspector Neele shook his head sympathetically.

Percival Fortescue prepared to take his departure – as he picked up his hat he said:

'Call upon me if there is anything I can do. But I suppose—' he paused – 'you will be coming down to Yewtree Lodge?'

'Yes, Mr Fortescue – I've got a man in charge there now.'

Percival shuddered in a fastidious way.

'It will all be most unpleasant. To think such a thing should happen to us—'

He sighed and moved towards the door.

'I shall be at the office most of the day. There is a lot to be seen to here. But I shall get down to Yewtree Lodge this evening.'

'Quite so, sir.'

Percival Fortescue went out.

'Percy Prim,' murmured Neele.

Sergeant Hay who was sitting unobtrusively by the wall looked up and said 'Sir?' interrogatively.

Then as Neele did not reply, he asked, 'What do you make of it all, sir?'

'I don't know,' said Neele. He quoted softly, "They're all very unpleasant people." '

Sergeant Hay looked somewhat puzzled.

'Alice in Wonderland,' said Neele. 'Don't you know your Alice, Hay?'

'It's a classic, isn't it, sir?' said Hay. 'Third Programme stuff. I don't listen to the Third Programme.'

—— 10 ——

It was about five minutes after leaving Le Bourget that Lance Fortescue opened his copy of the continental *Daily Mail*. A minute or two later he uttered a startled exclamation. Pat, in the seat beside him, turned her head inquiringly.

'It's the old man,' said Lance. 'He's dead.'

'Dead! Your father?'

'Yes, he seems to have been taken suddenly ill at the office, was taken to St Jude's Hospital and died there soon after arrival.'

'Darling, I'm so sorry. What was it, a stroke?'

'I suppose so. Sounds like it.'

'Did he ever have a stroke before?'

'No. Not that I know of.'

'I thought people never died from a first one.'

'Poor old boy,' said Lance. 'I never thought I was particularly fond of him, but somehow, now that he's dead . . .'

'Of course you were fond of him.'

'We haven't all got your nice nature, Pat. Oh well, it looks as though my luck's out again, doesn't it.'

'Yes. It's odd that it should happen now. Just when you were on the point of coming home.'

He turned his head sharply towards her.

'Odd? What do you mean by odd, Pat?'

She looked at him with slight surprise.

'Well, a sort of coincidence.'

'You mean that whatever I set out to do goes wrong?'

'No, darling, I didn't mean that. But there is such a thing as a run of bad luck.'

'Yes, I suppose there is.'

Pat said again: 'I'm so sorry.'

When they arrived at Heath Row and were waiting to disembark from the plane, an official of the air company called out in a clear voice:

'Is Mr Lancelot Fortescue aboard?'

'Here,' said Lance.

'Would you just step this way, Mr Fortescue.'

Lance and Pat followed him out of the plane, preceding the other passengers. As they passed a couple in the last seat, they heard the man whisper to his wife:

'Well-known smugglers, I expect. Caught in the act.'

II

'It's fantastic,' said Lance. 'Quite fantastic.' He stared across the table at Detective-Inspector Neele.

Inspector Neele nodded his head sympathetically.

'Taxine – yewberries – the whole thing seems like some kind of melodrama. I dare say this sort of thing seems ordinary enough to you, Inspector. All in the day's work. But poisoning, in our family, seems wildly far-fetched.'

'You've no idea then at all,' asked Inspector Neele, 'who might have poisoned your father?'

'Good lord, no. I expect the old man's made a lot of enemies in business, lots of people who'd like to skin him alive, do him down financially – all that sort of thing. But poisoning? Anyway I wouldn't be in the know. I've been abroad for a good many years and have known very little of what's going on at home.'

'That's really what I wanted to ask you about, Mr Fortescue. I understand from your brother that there was an estrangement between you and your father which had lasted for many years. Would you like to tell me the circumstances that led to your coming home at this time?'

'Certainly, Inspector. I heard from my father, let me see it must be about – yes, six months ago now. It was soon after my marriage. My father wrote and hinted that he would like to let bygones be bygones. He suggested that I should come home and enter the firm. He was rather vague in his terms and I wasn't really sure that I wanted to do what he asked. Anyway, the upshot was that I came over to England last – yes, last August, just about three months ago. I went down to see him at Yewtree Lodge and he made me, I must say, a very advantageous offer. I told him that I'd have to think about it and I'd have to consult my wife. He quite understood that. I flew back to East Africa, talked it over with Pat. The upshot was that I decided to accept the old boy's offer. I had to wind up my affairs there, but I agreed to do so before the end of last month. I told him I would wire to him the date of my actual arrival in England.'

Inspector Neele coughed.

'Your arrival back seems to have caused your brother some surprise.'

Lance gave a sudden grin. His rather attractive face lit up with the spirit of pure mischief.

'Don't believe old Percy knew a thing about it,' he said. 'He was away on his holiday in Norway at the time. If you ask me, the old man picked that particular time on purpose. He was going behind Percy's back. In fact I've a very shrewd suspicion that my father's offer to me was actuated by the fact that he had a blazing row with poor old Percy – or Val as he prefers to be called. Val, I think, had been more or less trying to run the old man. Well, the old man would never stand for anything of that kind. What the exact row was about I don't know, but he was furious. And I think he thought it a jolly good idea to get me there and thereby spike poor old Val's guns. For one thing he never liked Percy's wife much and he was rather pleased, in a snobbish kind of way, with my marriage. It would be just his idea of a good joke to get me home and suddenly confront Percy with the accomplished fact.'

'How long were you at Yewtree Lodge on this occasion?'

'Oh, not more than an hour or two. He didn't ask me to stay the night. The whole idea, I'm sure, was a kind of secret offensive behind Percy's back. I don't thing he even wanted the servants to report upon it. As I say, things were left that I'd think it over, talk about it to Pat and then write him my decision, which I did. I wrote giving him the approximate date of my arrival, and I finally sent him a telegram yesterday from Paris.'

Inspector Neele nodded.

33

'A telegram which surprised your brother very much.'

'I bet it did. However, as usual, Percy wins. I've arrived too late.'

'Yes,' said Inspector Neele thoughtfully, 'You've arrived too late.' He went on briskly, 'On the occasion of your visit last August, did you meet any other members of the family?'

'My stepmother was there at tea.'

'You had not met her previously?'

'No.' He grinned suddenly. 'The old boy certainly knew how to pick them. She must be thirty years younger than him at least.'

'You will excuse my asking, but did you resent your father's remarriage, or did your brother do so?'

Lance looked surprised.

'I certainly didn't, and I shouldn't think Percy did either. After all, our own mother died when we were about – oh, ten, twelve years old. What I'm really surprised at is that the old man didn't marry again before.'

Inspector Neele murmured:

'It may be considered taking rather a risk to marry a woman very much younger than yourself.'

'Did my dear brother say that to you? It sounds rather like him. Percy is a great master of the art of insinuation. Is that the set up, Inspector? Is my stepmother suspected of poisoning my father?'

Inspector Neele's face became blank.

'It's early days to have any definite ideas about anything, Mr Fortescue,' he said pleasantly. 'Now, may I ask you what your plans are?'

'Plans?' Lance considered. 'I shall have to make new plans, I suppose. Where is the family? All down at Yewtree Lodge?'

'Yes.'

'I'd better go down there straight away.' He turned to his wife. 'You'd better go to an hotel, Pat.'

She protested quickly. 'No, no, Lance, I'll come with you.'

'No, darling.'

'But I want to.'

'Really, I'd rather you didn't. Go and stay at the – oh it's so long since I stayed in London – Barnes's. Barnes's Hotel used to be a nice, quiet sort of place. That's still going, I suppose?'

'Oh, yes, Mr Fortescue.'

'Right, Pat, I'll settle you in there if they've got a room, then I'll go on down to Yewtree Lodge.'

'But why can't I come with you, Lance?'

Lance's face took suddenly a rather grim line.

'Frankly, Pat, I'm not sure of my welcome. It was Father who invited me there, but Father's dead. I don't know who the place belongs to now. Percy, I suppose, or perhaps Adele. Anyway, I'd like to see what reception I get before I bring you there. Besides—'

'Besides what?'

'I don't want to take you to a house where there's a poisoner at large.'

'Oh, what nonsense.'

Lance said firmly:

'Where you're concerned, Pat, I'm taking no risks.'

—— I I ——

Mr Dubois was annoyed. He tore Adele Fortescue's letter angrily across and threw it into the waste-paper basket. Then, with a sudden caution, he fished out the various pieces, struck a match and watched them burn to ashes. He muttered under his breath:

'Why have women got to be such damned fools? Surely common prudence . . .' But then, Mr Dubois reflected gloomily, women never had any prudence. Though he had profited by this lack many a time, it annoyed him now. He himself had taken every precaution. If Mrs Fortescue rang up they had instructions to say that he was out. Already Adele Fortescue had rung him up three times, and now she had written. On the whole, writing was far worse. He reflected for a moment or two, then he went to the telephone.

'Can I speak to Mrs Fortescue, please? Yes, Mr Dubois.' A minute or two later he heard her voice.

'Vivian, at last!'

'Yes, yes, Adele, but be careful. Where are you speaking from?'

'From the library.'

'Sure nobody's listening in, in the hall?'

'Why should they?'

'Well, you never know. Are the police still about the house?'

'No, they've gone for the moment, anyhow. Oh, Vivian dear, it's been *awful*.'

'Yes, yes, it must have I'm sure. But look here, Adele, we've got to be careful.'

'Oh, of course, darling.'

'Don't call me darling through the phone. It isn't safe.'

'Aren't you being a little bit panicky, Vivian? After all, everybody says darling nowadays.'

'Yes, yes, that's true enough. But listen. *Don't telephone to me and don't write.*'

'But Vivian—'

'It's just for the present, you understand. *We must be careful.*'

'Oh. All right.' Her voice sounded offended.

'Adele, listen. My letters to you. You did burn them, didn't you?'

There was a momentary hesitation before Adele Fortescue said:

'Of course. I told you I was going to do so.'

'That's all right, then. Well I'll ring off now. Don't phone and don't write. You'll hear from me in good time.'

He put the receiver back in its hook. He stroked his cheek thoughtfully. He didn't like that moment's hesitation. Had Adele burnt his letters? Women were all the same. They promised to burn things and then didn't.

Letters, Mr Dubois thought to himself. Women always wanted you to write them letters. He himself tried to be careful but sometimes one could not get out of it. What had he said exactly in the few letters he had written to Adele Fortescue? 'It was the usual sort of gup,' he thought, gloomily. But were there any special words – special phrases that the police could twist to make them say what they wanted them to say. He remembered the Edith Thompson case. His letters were innocent enough, he thought, but he could not be sure. His uneasiness grew. Even if Adele had not already burnt his letters, would she have the sense to burn them now? Or had the police already got hold of them? Where did she keep them, he wondered. Probably in that sitting-room of hers upstairs. That gimcrack little desk, probably. Sham antique Louis XIV. She had said something to him once about there being a secret drawer in it. Secret drawer! That would not fool the police long. But there were no police about the house now. She had said so. They had been there that morning, and now they had all gone away.

Up to now they had probably been busy looking for possible

sources of poison in the food. They would not, he hoped, have got round to a room by room search of the house. Perhaps they would have to ask permission or get a search warrant to do that. It was possible that if he acted now, at once—

He visualised the house clearly in his mind's eye. It would be getting towards dusk. Tea would be brought in, either into the library or into the drawing-room. Everyone would be assembled downstairs and the servants would be having tea in the servants' hall. There would be no one upstairs on the first floor. Easy to walk up through the garden, skirting the yew hedges that provided such admirable cover. Then there was the little door at the side on to the terrace. That was never locked until just before bedtime. One could slip through there and, choosing one's moment, slip upstairs.

Vincent Dubois considered very carefully what it behove him to do next. If Fortescue's death had been put down to a seizure or to a stroke as surely it ought to have been, the position would be very different. As it was – Dubois murmured under his breath, 'Better be safe than sorry.'

II

Mary Dove came slowly down the big staircase. She paused a moment at the window on the half landing, from which she had seen Inspector Neele arrive on the preceding day. Now, as she looked out in the fading light, she noticed a man's figure just disappearing round the yew hedge. She wondered if it was Lancelot Fortescue, the prodigal son. He had, perhaps, dismissed his car at the gate and was wandering round the garden recollecting old times there before tackling a possibly hostile family. Mary Dove felt rather sympathetic towards Lance. A faint smile on her lips, she went on downstairs. In the hall she encountered Gladys, who jumped nervously at the sight of her.

'Was that the telephone I heard just now?' Mary asked. 'Who was it?'

'Oh, that was a wrong number. Thought we were the laundry.' Gladys sounded breathless and rather hurried. 'And before that, it was Mr Dubois. He wanted to speak to the mistress.'

'I see.'

Mary went on across the hall. Turning her head, she said:] 'It's tea-time, I think. Haven't you brought it in yet?'

Gladys said: 'I don't think its half-past four yet, is it, miss?'

'It's twenty minutes to five. Bring it in now, will you?'

Mary Dove went on into the library where Adele Fortescue, sitting on the sofa, was staring at the fire, picking with her fingers at a small lace handkerchief. Adele said fretfully:

'Where's tea?'

Mary Dove said: 'It's just coming in.'

A log had fallen out of the fireplace and Mary Dove knelt down at the grate and replaced it with the tongs, adding another piece of wood and a little coal.

Gladys went out into the kitchen where Mrs Crump raised a red and wrathful face from the kitchen table where she was mixing pastry in a large bowl.

'The library bell's been ringing and ringing. Time you took in the tea, my girl.'

'All right, all right, Mrs Crump.'

'What I'll say to Crump tonight,' muttered Mrs Crump. 'I'll tell him off.'

Gladys went on into the pantry. She had not cut any sandwiches. Well, she jolly well wasn't going to cut sandwiches. They'd got plenty to eat without that, hadn't they? Two cakes, biscuits and scones and honey. Fresh black market farm butter. Plenty without her bothering to cut tomato or fois gras sandwiches. She'd got other things to think about. Fair temper Mrs Crump was in, all because Mr Crump had gone out this afternoon. Well, it was his day out, wasn't it? Quite right of him, Gladys thought. Mrs Crump called out from the kitchen:

'The kettle's boiling its head off. Aren't you ever going to make that tea?'

'Coming.'

She jerked some tea without measuring it into the big silver pot, carried it into the kitchen and poured the boiling water on it. She added the teapot and the kettle to the big silver tray and carried the whole thing through to the library where she set it on the small table near the sofa. She went back hurriedly for the other tray with the eatables on it. She carried the latter as far as the hall when the sudden jarring noise of the grandfather clock preparing itself to strike made her jump.

In the library, Adele Fortescue said querulously, to Mary Dove.

'Where *is* everybody this afternoon?'

'I really don't know, Mrs Fortescue. Miss Fortescue came in

some time ago. I think Mrs Percival's writing letters in her room.'

Adele said pettishly, 'Writing letters, writing letters. That woman never stops writing letters. She's like all people of her class. She takes an absolute delight in death and misfortune. Ghoulish, that's what I call it. Absolutely ghoulish.'

Mary murmured tactfully, 'I'll tell her that tea is ready.'

Going towards the door she drew back a little in the doorway as Elaine Fortescue came into the room. Elaine said:

'It's cold,' and dropped down by the fireplace, rubbing her hands before the blaze.

Mary stood for a moment in the hall. A large tray with cakes on it was standing on one of the hall chests. Since it was getting dark in the hall, Mary switched on the light. As she did so she thought she heard Jennifer Fortescue walking along the passage upstairs. Nobody, however, came down the stairs and Mary went up the staircase and along the corridor.

Percival Fortescue and his wife occupied a self-contained suite in one wing of the house. Mary tapped on the sitting-room door. Mrs Percival liked you to tap on doors, a fact which always roused Crump's scorn of her. Her voice said briskly:

'Come in.'

Mary opened the door and murmured:

'Tea is just coming in, Mrs Percival.'

She was rather surprised to see Jennifer Fortescue with her outdoor clothes on. She was just divesting herself of a long camel-hair coat.

'I didn't know you'd been out,' said Mary.

Mrs Percival sounded slightly out of breath.

'Oh, I was just in the garden, that's all. Just getting a little air. Really, though, it was too cold. I shall be glad to get down to the fire. The central heating here isn't as good as it might be. Somebody must speak to the gardeners about it, Miss Dove.'

'I'll do so,' Mary promised.

Jennifer Fortescue dropped her coat on a chair and followed Mary out of the room. She went down the stairs ahead of Mary, who drew back a little to give her precedence. In the hall, rather to Mary's surprise, she noticed the tray of eatables was still there. She was about to go out to the pantry and call to Gladys when Adele Fortescue appeared in the door of the library, saying in an irritable voice:

'Aren't we ever going to have anything to eat for tea?'

Quickly Mary picked up the tray and took it into the library, disposing the various things on low tables near the fireplace. She was carrying the empty tray out to the hall again when the front-door bell rang. Setting down the tray, Mary went to the door herself. If this was the prodigal son at last she was rather curious to see him. 'How unlike the rest of the Fortescues,' Mary thought, as she opened the door and looked up into the dark lean face and the faint quizzical twist of the mouth. She said quietly:

'Mr Lancelot Fortescue?'

'Himself.'

Mary peered beyond him.

'Your luggage?'

'I've paid off the taxi. This is all I've got.'

He picked up a medium-sized zip bag. Some faint feeling of surprise in her mind, Mary said:

'Oh, you did come in a taxi. I thought perhaps you'd walked up. And your wife?'

His face set in a rather grim line, Lance said:

'My wife won't be coming. At least, not just yet.'

'I see. Come this way, will you, Mr Fortescue. Everyone is in the library, having tea.'

She took him to the library door and left him there. She thought to herself that Lancelot Fortescue was a very attractive person. A second thought followed the first. Probably a great many other women thought so, too.

III

'Lance!'

Elaine came hurrying forward towards him. She flung her arms round his neck and hugged him with a schoolgirl abandon that Lance found quite surprising.

'Hallo. Here I am.'

He disengaged himself gently.

'This is Jennifer?'

Jennifer Fortescue looked at him with eager curiosity.

'I'm afraid Val's been detained in town,' she said. 'There's so much to see to, you know. All the arrangements to make and everything. Of course it all comes on Val. He has to see to *everything*. You can really have no idea what we're all going through.'

'It must be terrible for you,' said Lance gravely.

He turned to the woman on the sofa, who was sitting with a

piece of scone and honey in her hand, quietly appraising him.

'Of course,' cried Jennifer, 'you don't know Adele, do you?'

Lance murmured, 'Oh yes, I do,' as he took Adele Fortescue's hand in his. As he looked down at her, her eyelids fluttered. She set down the scone she was eating with her left hand and just touched the arrangement of her hair. It was a feminine gesture. It marked her recognition of the entry to the room of a personable man. She said in her thick, soft voice:

'Sit down here on the sofa beside me, Lance.' She poured out a cup of tea for him. 'I'm so glad you've come,' she went on. 'We badly need another man in the house.'

Lance said:

'You must let me do everything I can to help.'

'You know – but perhaps you don't know – we've had the police here. They think – they think—' she broke off and cried out passionately: 'Oh, it's awful! Awful!'

'I know.' Lance was grave and sympathetic. 'As a matter of fact they met me at London Airport.'

'The police met you?'

'Yes.'

'What did they say?'

'Well,' Lance was deprecating. 'They told me what had happened.'

'He was poisoned,' said Adele, 'that's what they think, what they say. Not food poisoning. Real poisoning, by someone. I believe, I really do believe they think it's one of *us*.'

Lance gave her a sudden quick smile.

'That's their pigeon,' he said consolingly. 'It's no good our worrying. What a scrumptious tea! It's a long time since I've seen a good English tea.'

The others fell in with his mood soon enough. Adele said suddenly:

'But your wife – haven't you got a wife, Lance?'

'I've got a wife, yes. She's in London.'

'But aren't you – hadn't you better bring her down here?'

'Plenty of time to make plans,' said Lance. 'Pat – oh, Pat's quite all right where she is.'

Elaine said sharply:

'You don't mean – you don't think—'

Lance said quickly:

'What a wonderful-looking chocolate cake. I must have some.'

Cutting himself a slice, he asked:

'Is Aunt Effie alive still?'

'Oh, yes, Lance. She won't come down and have meals with us or anything, but she's quite well. Only she's getting very peculiar.'

'She always was peculiar,' said Lance. 'I must go up and see her after tea.'

Jennifer Fortescue murmured:

'At her age one does really feel that she ought to be in some kind of a home. I mean somewhere where she will be properly looked after.'

'Heaven help any old ladies' home that got Aunt Effie in their midst,' said Lance. He added, 'Who's the demure piece of goods who let me in?'

Adele looked surprised.

'Didn't Crump let you in? The butler? Oh no, I forgot. It's his day out today. But surely Gladys—'

Lance gave a description. 'Blue eyes, hair parted in the middle, soft voice, butter wouldn't melt in the mouth. What goes on behind it all, I wouldn't like to say.'

'That,' said Jennifer, 'would be Mary Dove.'

Elaine said:

'She sort of runs things for us.'

'Does she, now?'

Adele said:

'She's really very useful.'

'Yes,' said Lance thoughtfully, 'I should think she might be.'

'But what is so nice is,' said Jennifer, 'that she knows her place. She never presumes, if you know what I mean.'

'Clever Mary Dove,' said Lance, and helped himself to another piece of chocolate cake.

—— 12 ——

'So you've turned up again like a bad penny,' said Miss Ramsbottom.

Lance grinned at her. 'Just as you say, Aunt Effie.'

'Humph!' Miss Ramsbottom sniffed disapprovingly. 'You've chosen a nice time to do it. Your father got himself murdered yesterday, the house is full of police poking about everywhere, grubbing in the dustbins, even. I've seen them out of the window.' She paused, sniffed again, and asked, 'Got your wife with you?'

'No. I left Pat in London.'

'That shows some sense. I shouldn't bring her *here* if I were you. You never know what might happen.'

'To her? To Pat?'

'To anybody,' said Miss Ramsbottom.

Lance Fortescue looked at her thoughtfully.

'Got any ideas about it all, Aunt Effie?' he asked.

Miss Ramsbottom did not reply directly. 'I had an Inspector here yesterday asking me questions. He didn't get much change out of me. But he wasn't such a fool as he looked, not by a long way.' She added with some indignation, 'What your grandfather would feel if he knew we had the police in the house – it's enough to make him turn in his grave. A strict Plymouth Brother he was all his life. The fuss there was when he found out I'd been attending Church of England services in the evening! And I'm sure *that* was harmless enough compared to murder.'

Normally Lance would have smiled at this, but his long, dark face remained serious. He said:

'D'you know, I'm quite in the dark after having been away so long. What's been going on here of late?'

Miss Ramsbottom raised her eyes to heaven.

'Godless doings,' she said firmly.

'Yes, yes, Aunt Effie, you would say that anyway. But what gives the police the idea that Dad was killed here, in this house?'

'Adultery is one thing and murder is another,' said Miss Ramsbottom. 'I shouldn't like to think it of her, I shouldn't indeed.'

Lance looked alert. 'Adele?' he asked.

'My lips are sealed,' said Miss Ramsbottom.

'Come on, old dear,' said Lance. 'It's a lovely phrase, but it doesn't mean a thing. Adele had a boy friend? Adele and the boy friend fed him henbane in the morning tea. Is that the set up?'

'I'll trouble you not to joke about it.'

'I wasn't really joking, you know.'

'I'll tell you one thing,' said Miss Ramsbottom suddenly. 'I believe that girl knows something about it.'

'Which girl?' Lance looked surprised.

'The one that sniffs,' said Miss Ramsbottom. 'The one that

ought to have brought me up my tea this afternoon, but didn't. Gone out without leave, so they say. I shouldn't wonder if she had gone to the police. Who let you in?'

'Someone called Mary Dove, I understand. Very meek and mild – but not really. Is she the one who's gone to the police?'

'*She* wouldn't go to the police,' said Miss Ramsbottom. 'No – I mean that silly little parlourmaid. She's been twitching and jumping like a rabbit all day. "What's the matter with you?" I said. "Have you got a guilty conscience?" She said "*I* never did anything – I wouldn't do a thing like that." "I hope you wouldn't," I said to her, "but there's something worrying you now, isn't there?" Then she began to sniff and said she didn't want to get anybody into trouble, she was sure it must be all a mistake. I said to her, I said, "Now, my girl, you speak the truth and shame the devil." That's what I said. "You go to the police," I said, "and tell them anything you know, because no good ever came," I said, "of hushing up the truth, however unpleasant it is." Then she talked a lot of nonsense about she couldn't go to the police, they'd never believe her and what on earth should she say? She ended up by saying anyway she didn't know anything at all.'

'You don't think,' Lance hesitated, 'that she was just making herself important?'

'No, I don't. I think she was scared. I think she saw something or heard something that's given her some idea about the whole thing. It may be important, or it mayn't be of the least consequence.'

'You don't think she herself could've had a grudge against Father and—' Lance hesitated.

Miss Ramsbottom was shaking her head decidedly.

'She's not the kind of girl your father would have taken the least notice of. No man ever will take much notice of her, poor girl. Ah, well, it's all the better for her soul, that, I dare say.'

Lance took no interest in Gladys's soul. He asked:

'You think she may have run along to the police station?'

Aunt Effie nodded vigorously.

'Yes. I think she mayn't like to've said anything to them in this house in case somebody overheard her.'

Lance asked. 'Do you think she may have seen someone tampering with the food?'

Aunt Effie threw him a sharp glance.

'It's possible, isn't it?' she said.

'Yes, I suppose so.' Then he added apologetically. 'The whole thing still seems so wildly improbable. Like a detective story.'

'Percival's wife is a hospital nurse,' said Miss Ramsbottom.

The remark seemed so unconnected with what had gone before that Lance looked at her in a puzzled fashion.

'Hospital nurses are used to handling drugs,' said Miss Ramsbottom.

Lance looked doubtful.

'This stuff – taxine – is it ever used in medicine?'

'They get it from yewberries, I gather. Children eat yewberries sometimes,' said Miss Ramsbottom. 'Makes them very ill, too. I remember a case when I was a child. It made a great impression on me. I never forgot it. Things you remember come in useful sometimes.'

Lance raised his head sharply and stared at her.

'Natural affection is one thing,' said Miss Ramsbottom, 'and I hope I've got as much of it as anyone. But I won't stand for wickedness. Wickedness has to be destroyed.'

II

'Went off without a word to me,' said Mrs Crump, raising her red, wrathful face from the pastry she was now rolling out on the board. 'Slipped out without a word to anybody. Sly, that's what it is. Sly! Afraid she'd be stopped, and I *would* have stopped her if I'd caught her! The idea! There's the master dead, Mr Lance coming home that hasn't been home for years and I said to Crump, I said, "Day out or no day out, I know my duty. There's not going to be cold supper tonight as is usual on a Thursday, but a proper dinner. A gentleman coming home from abroad with his wife, what was formerly married in the aristocracy, things must be properly done." You know me, miss, you know I take a pride in my work.'

Mary Dove, the recipient of these confidences, nodded her head gently.

'And what does Crump say?' Mrs Crump's voice rose angrily. ' "It's my day off and I'm goin' of," that's what he says. "And a fig for the aristocracy," he says. No pride in his work, Crump hasn't. So off he goes and I tell Gladys she'll have to manage alone tonight. She just says, "Alright, Mrs Crump," then, when my back's turned out *she* sneaks. It wasn't *her* day out, anyway. Friday's *her* day. How we're going to manage now, I don't know! Thank goodness Mr Lance hasn't brought his wife here with him today.'

'We shall manage, Mrs Crump,' Mary's voice was both soothing and authoritative, 'if we just simplify the menu a little.' She outlined a few suggestions. Mrs Crump nodded unwilling acquiescence. 'I shall be able to serve that quite easily,' Mary concluded.

'You mean you'll wait at table yourself, Miss?' Mrs Crump sounded doubtful.

'If Gladys doesn't come back in time.'

'*She* won't come back,' said Mrs Crump. 'Gallivanting off, wasting her money somewhere in the shops. She's got a young man, you know, miss, though you wouldn't think it to look at her. Albert his name is. Going to get married next spring, so she tells me. Don't know what the married state's like, these girls don't. What I've been through with Crump.' She sighed, then said in an ordinary voice. 'What about tea, miss. Who's going to clear it away and wash it up?'

'I'll do that,' said Mary. 'I'll go and do it now.'

The lights had not been turned on in the drawing-room though Adele Fortescue was still sitting on the sofa behind the tea tray.

'Shall I switch the lights on, Mrs Fortescue?' Mary asked. Adele did not answer.

Mary switched on the lights and went across to the window where she pulled the curtains across. It was only then that she turned her head and saw the face of the woman who had sagged back against the cushions. A half-eaten scone spread with honey was beside her and her tea cup was still half full. Death had come to Adele Fortescue suddenly and swiftly.

III

'Well?' demanded Inspector Neele impatiently.

The doctor said promptly:

'Cyanide – potassium cyanide probably – in the tea.'

'Cyanide,' muttered Neele.

The doctor looked at him with slight curiosity.

'You're taking this hard – any special reason—'

'She was cast as a murderess,' said Neele.

'And she turns out to be a victim. H'm. You'll have to think again, won't you?'

Neele nodded. His face was bitter and his jaw was grimly set.

Poisoned! Right under his nose. Taxine in Rex Fortescue's breakfast coffee, cyanide in Adele Fortescue's tea. Still an intimate family affair. Or so it seemed.

Adele Fortescue, Jennifer Fortescue, Elaine Fortescue and the newly arrived Lance Fortescue had had tea together in the library. Lance had gone up to see Miss Ramsbottom, Jennifer had gone to her own sitting-room to write letters, Elaine had been the last to leave the library. According to her Adele had then been in perfect health and had just been pouring herself out a last cup of tea.

A last cup of tea! Yes, it *had* indeed been her last cup of tea.

And after that a blank twenty minutes, perhaps, until Mary Dove had come into the room and discovered the body.

And during that twenty minutes—

Inspector Neele swore to himself and went out into the kitchen.

Sitting in a chair by the kitchen table, the vast figure of Mrs Crump, her belligerence pricked like a balloon, hardly stirred as he came in.

'Where's that girl? Has she come back yet?'

'Gladys? No – she's not back— Won't be, I suspect, until eleven o'clock.'

'She made the tea, you say, and took it in.'

'I didn't touch it, sir, as God's my witness. And what's more I don't believe Gladys did anything she shouldn't. She wouldn't do a thing like that – not Gladys. She's a good enough girl, sir – a bit foolish like, that's all – not wicked.'

No, Neele did not think that Gladys was wicked. He did not think that Gladys was a poisoner. And in any case the cyanide had not been in the teapot.

'But what made her go off suddenly – like this? It wasn't her day out, you say.'

'No, sir, tomorrow's her day out.'

'Does Crump—'

Mrs Crump's belligerence suddenly revived. Her voice rose wrathfully.

'Don't you go fastening anything on Crump. Crump's out of it. He went off at three o'clock – and thankful I am now that he did. He's as much out of it as Mr Percival himself.'

Percival Fortescue had only just returned from London – to be greeted by the astounding news of this second tragedy.

'I wasn't accusing Crump,' said Neele mildly. 'I just wondered if he knew anything about Gladys's plans.'

'She had her best nylons on,' said Mrs Crump. 'She was up to something. Don't tell me! Didn't cut any sandwiches for tea, either. Oh yes, she was up to something. *I'*ll give her a piece of my mind when she comes back.'

When she comes back—

A faint uneasiness possessed Neele. To shake it off he went upstairs to Adele Fortescue's bedroom. A lavish apartment – all rose brocade hanging and a vast gilt bed. On one side of the room was a door into a mirror-lined bathroom with a sunk orchid-pink porcelain bath. Beyond the bathroom, reached by a communicating door, was Rex Fortescue's dressing room. Neele went back into Adele's bedroom, and through the door on the farther side of the room into her sitting-room.

The room was furnished in Empire style with a rose pile carpet. Neele only gave it a cursory glance for that particular room had had his close attention on the preceding day – with special attention paid to the small elegant desk.

Now, however, he stiffened to sudden attention. On the centre of the rose pile carpet was a small piece of caked mud.

Neele went over to it and picked it up. The mud was still damp.

He looked round – there were no footprints visible – only this one isolated fragment of wet earth.

IV

Inspector Neele looked round the bedroom that belonged to Gladys Martin. It was past eleven o'clock – Crump had come in half an hour ago – but there was still no sign of Gladys. Inspector Neele looked round him. Whatever Gladys's training had been, her own natural instincts were slovenly. The bed, Inspector Neele judged, was seldom made, the windows seldom opened. Gladys's personal habits, however, were not his immediate concern. Instead, he went carefully through her possessions.

They consisted for the most part of cheap and rather pathetic finery. There was little that was durable or of good quality. The elderly Ellen, whom he had called upon to assist him, had not been helpful. She didn't know what clothes Gladys had or hadn't. She couldn't say what, if anything, was missing. He turned from the clothes and the underclothes to the contents of the chest of drawers. There Gladys kept her treasures. There were picture postcards and newspaper cuttings, knitting patterns, hints on beauty culture, dressmaking and fashion advice.

Inspector Neele sorted them neatly into various categories. The picture postcards consisted mainly of views of various places where he presumed Gladys had spent her holidays. Amongst them were three picture postcards signed 'Bert.' Bert, he took to be the 'young man' referred to by Mrs Crump. The first postcard said – in an illiterate hand 'All the best. Missing you a lot. Yours ever, Bert.' The second said, 'Lots of nice looking girls here but not one that's a patch on you. Be seeing you soon. Don't forget our date. And remember after that – it's thumbs up and living happy ever after.' The third said merely, 'Don't forget. I'm trusting you. Love B.'

Next, Neele looked through the newspaper cuttings and sorted them into three piles. There were the dressmaking and beauty hints, there were items about cinema stars to which Gladys had appeared greatly addicted and she had also, it appeared, been attracted by the latest marvels of science. There were cuttings about flying saucers, about secret weapons, about truth drugs used by Russians, and claims for fantastic drugs discovered by American doctors. All the witchcraft, so Neele thought, of our twentieth century. But in all the contents of the room there was nothing to give him a clue to her disappearance. She had kept no diary, not that he had expected that. It was a remote possibility. There was no unfinished letter, no record at all of anything she might have seen in the house which could have had a bearing on Rex Fortescue's death. Whatever Gladys had seen, whatever Gladys had known, there was no record of it. It would still have to be guesswork why the second tea tray had been left in the hall, and Gladys herself had so suddenly vanished.

Sighing, Neele left the room, shutting the door behind him.

As he prepared to descend the small winding stairs he heard a noise of running feet coming along the landing below.

The agitated face of Sergeant Hay looked up at him from the bottom of the stairs. Sergeant Hay was panting a little.

'Sir,' he said urgently. 'Sir! We've found her—'

'Found her?'

'It was the housemaid, sir – Ellen – remembered as she hadn't brought the clothes in from where they were hanging on the line – just round the corner from the back door. So she went out with a torch to take them in and she almost fell over the body

– the girl's body – strangled, she was, with a stocking round her throat – been dead for hours, I'd say. And, sir, it's a wicked kind of joke – there was a *clothes peg clipped to her nose—*'

——— 13 ———

An elderly lady travelling by train had bought three morning papers, and each of them as she finished it, folded it and laid it aside, showed the same headline. It was no longer a question now of a small paragraph hidden away in the corner of the papers. There were headlines with flaring announcements of Triple Tragedy at Yewtree Lodge.

The old lady sat very upright, looking out of the window of the train, her lips pursed together, an expression of distress and disapproval on her pink and white wrinkled face. Miss Marple had left St Mary Mead by the early train, changing at the junction and going on to London where she took a Circle train to another London terminus and thence on to Baydon Heath.

At the station she signalled a taxi and asked to be taken to Yewtree Lodge. So charming, so innocent, such a fluffy and pink and white old lady was Miss Marple that she gained admittance to what was now practically a fortress in a state of siege far more easily than could have been believed possible. Though an army of reporters and photographers were being kept at bay by the police, Miss Marple was allowed to drive in without question, so impossible would it have been to believe that she was anyone but an elderly relative of the family.

Miss Marple paid off the taxi in a careful assortment of small change, and rang the front-door bell. Crump opened it and Miss Marple summed him up with an experienced glance. 'A shifty eye,' she said to herself. 'Scared to death, too.'

Crump saw a tall, elderly lady wearing an old-fashioned tweed coat and skirt, a couple of scarves and a small felt hat with a bird's wing. The old lady carried a capacious handbag and an aged but good quality suitcase reposed by her feet. Crump recognised a lady when he saw one and said:

'Yes, madam?' in his best and most respectful voice.

'Could I see the mistress of the house, please?' said Miss Marple.

Crump drew back to let her in. He picked up the suitcase and put it carefully down in the hall.

'Well, madam,' he said rather dubiously, 'I don't know who exactly—'

Miss Marple helped him out.

'I have come,' she said, 'to speak about the poor girl who was killed. Gladys Martin.'

'Oh, I see, madam. Well in that case—' he broke off, and looked towards the library door from which a tall young woman had just emerged. 'This is Mrs Lance Fortescue, madam,' he said.

Pat came forward and she and Miss Marple looked at each other. Miss Marple was aware of a faint feeling of surprise. She had not expected to see someone like Patricia Fortescue in this particular house. Its interior was much as she had pictured it, but Pat did not somehow match with that interior.

'It's about Gladys, madam,' said Crump helpfully.

Pat said rather hesitatingly:

'Will you come in here? We shall be quite alone.'

She led the way into the library and Miss Marple followed her.

'There wasn't anyone specially you wanted to see, was there?' said Pat, 'because perhaps I shan't be much good. You see my husband and I only came back from Africa a few days ago. We don't really know anything much about the household. But I can fetch my sister-in-law or my brother-in-law's wife.'

Miss Marple looked at the girl and liked her. She liked her gravity and her simplicity. For some strange reason she felt sorry for her. A background of shabby chintz and horses and dogs, Miss Marple felt vaguely, would have been much more suitable than this richly furnished interior décor. At the pony show and gymkhanas held locally round St Mary Mead, Miss Marple had met many Pats and knew them well. She felt at home with this rather unhappy looking girl.

'It's very simple, really,' said Miss Marple, taking off her gloves carefully and smoothing out the fingers of them. 'I read in the paper, you see, about Gladys Martin having been killed. And of course I know all about her. She comes from my part of the country. I trained her, in fact, for domestic service. And since this terrible thing has happened to her, I felt – well, I felt that I ought to come and see if there was anything I could do about it.'

'Yes,' said Pat. 'Of course. I see.'

462

And she did see. Miss Marple's action appeared to her natural and inevitable.

'I think it's a very good thing you have come,' said Pat. 'Nobody seems to know very much about her. I mean relations and all that.'

'No,' said Miss Marple, 'of course not. She hadn't got any relations. She came to me from the orphanage. St Faith's. A very well run place though sadly short of funds. We do our best for the girls there, try to give them a good training and all that. Gladys came to me when she was seventeen and I taught her how to wait at table and keep the silver and everything like that. Of course she didn't stay long. They never do. As soon as she got a little experience, she went and took a job in a café. The girls nearly always want to do that. They think it's freer, you know, and a gayer life. Perhaps it may be. I really don't know.'

'I never even saw her,' said Pat. 'Was she a pretty girl?'

'Oh, no,' said Miss Marple, 'not at all. Adenoids, and a good many spots. She was rather pathetically stupid, too. I don't suppose,' went on Miss Marple thoughtfully, 'that she ever made many friends anywhere. She was very keen on men, poor girl. But men didn't take much notice of her and other girls rather made use of her.'

'It sounds rather cruel,' said Pat.

'Yes, my dear,' said Miss Marple, 'life is cruel, I'm afraid. One doesn't really know what to do with the Gladyses. They enjoy going to the pictures and all that, but they're always thinking of impossible things that can't possibly happen to them. Perhaps that's happiness of a kind. But they get disappointed. I think Gladys was disappointed in café and restaurant life. Nothing very glamorous or interesting happened to her and it was just hard on the feet. Probably that's why she came back into private service. Do you know how long she'd been here?'

Pat shook her head.

'Not very long, I should think. Only a month or two.' Pat paused and then went on, 'It seems so horrible and futile that she should have been caught up in this thing. I suppose she'd seen something or noticed something.'

'It was the clothes peg that really worried me,' said Miss Marple in her gentle voice.

'The clothes peg?'

'Yes. I read about it in the paper. I suppose it is true? That when she was found there was a clothes peg clipped on to her nose.'

Pat nodded. The colour rose to Miss Marple's pink cheeks.

'That's what made me so very angry, if you can understand, my dear. It was such a cruel, contemptuous gesture. It gave me a kind of picture of the murderer. To do a thing like that! It's very wicked, you know, to affront human dignity. Particularly if you've already killed.'

Pat said slowly:

'I think I see what you mean.' She got up. 'I think you'd better come and see Inspector Neele. He's in charge of the case and he's here now. You'll like him, I think. He's a very human person.' She gave a sudden, quick shiver. 'The whole thing is such a horrible nightmare. Pointless. Mad. Without rhyme or reason in it.'

'I wouldn't say that, you know,' said Miss Marple. 'No, I wouldn't say that.'

Inspector Neele was looking tired and haggard. Three deaths and the press of the whole country whooping down the trail. A case that seemed to be shaping in well-known fashion had gone suddenly haywire. Adele Fortescue, that appropriate suspect, was now the second victim of an incomprehensible murder case. At the close of that fatal day the Assistant Commissioner had sent for Neele and the two men had talked far into the night.

In spite of his dismay, or rather behind it, Inspector Neele had felt a faint inward satisfaction. That pattern of the wife and the lover. It had been too slick, too easy. He had always mistrusted it. And now that mistrust of his was justified.

'The whole thing takes on an entirely different aspect,' the AC had said, striding up and down his room and frowning 'It looks to me, Neele, as though we'd got someone mentally unhinged to deal with. First the husband, then the wife. But the very circumstances of the case seem to show that it's an inside job. It's all there, in the family. Someone who sat down to break-fast with Fortescue put taxine in his coffee or on his food, some-one who had tea with the family that day put potassium cyanide in Adele Fortescue's cup of tea. Someone trusted, unnoticed, one of the family. Which of 'em, Neele?'

Neele said dryly:

'Percival wasn't there, so that lets him out again. That lets him out again,' Inspector Neele repeated.

The AC looked at him sharply. Something in the repetition had attracted his attention.

'What's the idea, Neele? Out with it, man.'

Inspector Neele looked stolid.

'Nothing, sir. Not so much as an idea. All I say is it was very convenient for him.

'A bit too convenient, eh?' the AC reflected and shook his head. 'You think he might have managed it somehow? Can't see how, Neele. No, I can't see how.'

He added, 'And he's a cautious type, too.'

'But quite intelligent, sir.'

'You don't fancy the women. Is that it? Yet the women are indicated. Elaine Fortescue and Percival's wife. They were at breakfast and they were at tea that day. Either of them could have done it. No signs of anything abnormal about them? Well, it doesn't always show. There might be something in their past medical record.'

Inspector Neele did not answer. He was thinking of Mary Dove. He had no definite reason for suspecting her, but that was the way his thoughts lay. There was something unexplained about her, unsatisfactory. A faint, amused antagonism. That had been her attitude after the death of Rex Fortescue. What was her attitude now? Her behaviour and manner were, as always, exemplary. There was no longer, he thought, amusement. Perhaps not even antagonism, but he wondered whether, once or twice, he had not seen a trace of fear. He had been to blame, culpably to blame, in the matter of Gladys Martin. That guilty confusion of hers he had put down to no more than a natural nervousness of the police. He had come across that guilty ner-vousness so often. In this case it had been something more. Gladys had seen or heard something which had aroused her sus-picions. It was probably, he thought, some quite small thing, something so vague and indefinite that she had hardly liked to speak about it. And now, poor little rabbit, she would never speak.

Inspector Neele looked with some interest at the mild, earnest face of the old lady who confronted him now at Yewtree Lodge. He had been in two minds at first how to treat her, but he quickly made up his mind. Miss Marple would be useful to him. She was upright, of unimpeachable rectitude and she had, like most old ladies, time on her hands and an old maid's nose for scenting bits of gossip. She'd get things out of servants and out of the women of the Fortescue family perhaps, that he and his policemen would never get. Talk, conjecture, reminiscences, repetitions of things said and done, out of it all she would pick the salient facts. So Inspector Neele was gracious.

'It's uncommonly good of you to have come here, Miss Marple,' he said.

'It was my duty, Inspector Neele. The girl had lived in my house. I feel, in a sense, responsible for her. She was a very silly girl, you know.'

Inspector Neele looked at her appreciatively.

'Yes,' he said, 'just so.'

She had gone, he felt, to the heart of the matter.

'She wouldn't know,' said Miss Marple, 'what she ought to do. If, I mean, something came up. Oh, dear, I'm expressing myself very badly.'

Inspector Neele said that he understood.

'She hadn't got good judgment as to what was important or not, that's what you mean, isn't it?'

'Oh yes, exactly, Inspector.'

'When you say that she was silly—' Inspector Neele broke off.

Miss Marple took up the theme.

'She was the credulous type. She was the sort of girl who would have given her savings to a swindler, if she'd had any savings. Of course, she never did have any savings because she always spent her money on most unsuitable clothes.'

'What about men?' asked the Inspector.

'She wanted a young man badly,' said Miss Marple. 'In fact that's really, I think, why she left St Mary Mead. The competition there is very keen. So few men. She did have hopes of the young man who delivered the fish. Young Fred had a pleasant word for all the girls, but of course he didn't mean anything by it. That upset poor Gladys quite a lot. Still, I gather she did get herself a young man in the end?'

Inspector Neele nodded.

'It seems so. Albert Evans, I gather, his name was. She seems to have met him at some holiday camp. He didn't give her a ring or anything so maybe she made it all up. He was a mining engineer, so she told the cook.'

'That seems *most* unlikely,' said Miss Marple, 'but I dare say it's what he *told* her. As I say, she'd believe anything. You don't connect *him* with this business at all?'

Inspector Neele shook his head.

'No. I don't think there are any complications of that kind. He never seems to have visited her. He sent her a postcard from time to time, usually from a seaport – probably 4th Engineer on a boat on the Baltic run.'

'Well,' said Miss Marple, 'I'm glad she had her little romance. Since her life has been cut short in this way—' She tightened her lips. 'You know, Inspector, it makes me very, very angry.' And she added, as she had said to Pat Fortescue, 'Especially the clothes peg. That, Inspector, was really wicked.'

Inspector Neele looked at her with interest.

'I know just what you mean, Miss Marple,' he said.

Miss Marple coughed apologetically.

'I wonder – I suppose it would be great presumtion on my part – if only I could assist you in my very humble and, I'm afraid, very *feminine* way. This is a wicked murderer, Inspector Neele, and the wicked should not go unpunished.'

'That's an unfashionable belief nowadays, Miss Marple,' Inspector Neele said rather grimly. 'Not that I don't agree with you.'

'There is an hotel near the station, or there's the Golf Hotel,' said Miss Marple tentatively, 'and I believe there's a Miss Ramsbottom in this house who is interested in foreign missions.'

Inspector Neele looked at Miss Marple appraisingly.

'Yes,' he said. 'You've got something there, maybe. I can't say that I've had great success with the lady.'

'It's really very kind of you, Inspector Neele,' said Miss Marple. 'I'm so glad you don't think I'm just a sensation hunter.'

Inspector Neele gave a sudden, rather unexpected smile. He was thinking to himself that Miss Marple was very unlike the popular idea of an avenging fury. And yet, he thought that was perhaps exactly what she was.

'Newspapers, said Miss Marple, 'are often so sensational in their accounts. But hardly, I fear, as accurate as one might wish.' She looked inquiringly at Inspector Neele. 'If one could be sure of having just the sober facts.'

'They're not particularly sober,' said Neele. 'Shorn of undue sensation, they're as follows. Mr Fortescue died in his office as a result of taxine poisoning. Taxine is obtained from the berries and leaves of yew trees.'

'Very convenient,' Miss Marple said.

'Possibly,' said Inspector Neele, 'but we've no evidence as to that. As yet, that is.' He stressed the point because it was here that he thought Miss Marple might be useful. If any brew or concoction of yewberries had been made in the house, Miss Marple was quite likely to come upon traces of it. She was the sort of old pussy who would make homemade liqueurs, cordials and herb teas herself. She would know methods of making and methods of disposal.

'And Mrs Fortescue?'

'Mrs Fortescue had tea with the family in the library. The last person to leave the room and the tea table was Miss Elaine Fortescue, her step-daughter. She states that as she left the room Mrs Fortescue was pouring herself out another cup of tea. Some twenty minutes or half-hour later Miss Dove, who acts as housekeeper, went in to remove the tea-tray. Mrs Fortescue was still sitting on the sofa, dead. Beside her was a tea cup a quarter full and in the dregs of it was potassium cyanide.'

'Which is almost immediate in its action, I believe,' said Miss Marple.

'Exactly.'

'Such dangerous stuff,' murmured Miss Marple. 'One has it to take wasps' nests but I'm always very, very careful.'

'You're quite right,' said Inspector Neele. 'There was a packet of it in the gardener's shed here.'

'Again very convenient,' said Miss Marple. She added, 'Was Mrs Fortescue eating anything?'

'Oh, yes. They'd had quite a sumptuous tea.'

'Cake, I suppose? Bread and butter? Scones, perhaps? Jam? Honey?'

'Yes, there was honey and scones, chocolate cake and swiss roll and various other plates of things.' He looked at her curiously. 'The potassium cyanide was in the tea, Miss Marple.'

'Oh, yes, yes. I quite understand that. I was just getting the whole picture, so to speak. Rather significant, don't you think?'

He looked at her in a slightly puzzled fashion. Her cheeks were pink, her eyes were bright.

'And the third death, Inspector Neele?'

'Well, the facts there seem clear enough, too. The girl, Gladys, took in the tea-tray, then she brought the next tray into the hall, but left it there. She'd been rather absent-minded all the day, apparently. After that no one saw her. The cook, Mrs Crump, jumped to the conclusion that the girl had gone out for the evening without telling anybody. She based her belief, I think, on the fact that the girl was wearing a good pair of nylon stockings and her best shoes. There, however, she was proved quite wrong. The girl had obviously remembered suddenly that she had not taken in some clothes that were drying outside on the clothes line. She ran out to fetch them in, had taken down half

of them apparently, when somebody took her unawares by slipping a stocking round her neck and – well, that was that.'

'Someone from outside?' said Miss Marple.

'Perhaps,' said Inspector Neele. 'But perhaps someone from
inside. Someone who'd been waiting his or her opportunity to
get the girl alone. The girl was upset, nervous, when we first
questioned her, but I'm afraid we didn't quite appreciate the
importance of that.'

'Oh, but how could you,' cried Miss Marple, 'because people
so often do look guilty and embarrassed when they are questioned by the police.'

'That's just it. But this time, Miss Marple it was rather more
than that. I think the girl Gladys had seen someone performing
some action that seemed to her needed explanation. It can't, I
think, have been anything very definite. Otherwise she *would*
have spoken out. But I think she did betray the fact to the person in question. That person realized that Gladys was a danger.'

'And so Gladys was strangled and a clothes peg clipped on her
nose,' murmured Miss Marple to herself.

'Yes, that's a nasty touch. A nasty, sneering sort of touch. Just
a nasty bit of unnecessary bravado.'

Miss Marple shook her head.

'Hardly *unnecessary*. It does all make a pattern, doesn't it?'

Inspector Neele looked at her curiously.

'I don't quite follow you, Miss Marple. What do you mean
by a pattern?'

Miss Marple immediately became flustered.

'Well, I mean it does seem – I mean, regarded as a sequence,
if you understand – well, one can't get away from facts, can
one?'

'I don't think I quite understand.'

'Well, I mean – first we have Mr Fortescue. *Rex* Fortescue.
Killed in his office in the city. And then we have Mrs Fortescue,
sitting here in the library and having tea. There were scones
and *honey*. And then poor Gladys with the clothes peg on her
nose. Just to *point* the whole thing. That very charming Mrs
Lance Fortescue said to me that there didn't seem to be any
rhyme or reason in it, but I couldn't agree with her, because it's
the rhyme that strikes one, isn't it?'

Inspector Neele said slowly: 'I don't think—'

Miss Marple went on quickly.

'I expect you're about thirty-five or thirty-six, aren't you,
Inspector Neele? I think there was rather a reaction just then,

469

when you were a little boy, I mean, against nursery rhymes. But if one has been brought up on Mother Goose – I mean it is really highly significant, isn't it? What I wondered was,' Miss Marple paused, then appearing to take her courage in her hands went on bravely: 'Of course it is great impertinence I know, on my part, saying this sort of thing to you.'

'Please say anything you like, Miss Marple.'

'Well, that's very kind of you. I shall. Though, as I say, I do it with the utmost diffidence because I know I am very old and rather muddle headed, and I dare say my idea is of no value at all. But what I mean to say is have you gone into the question of blackbirds?'

—— 14 ——

For about ten seconds Inspector Neele stared at Miss Marple with the utmost bewilderment. His first idea was that the old lady had gone off her head.

'Blackbirds?' he repeated.

Miss Marple nodded her head vigorously.

'Yes,' she said, and forthwith recited:

" '*Sing a song of sixpence, a pocketful of rye,*
Four and twenty blackbirds baked in a pie.
When the pie was opened the birds began to sing.
Wasn't that a dainty dish to set before the king?

The king was in his counting house, counting out his money,
The queen was in the parlour eating bread and honey,
The maid was in the garden hanging out the clothes,
When there came a little dickey bird and nipped off her nose." '

'Good Lord,' Inspector Neele said.

'I mean, it does fit,' said Miss Marple. 'It *was* rye in his pocket, wasn't it? One newspaper said so. The others just said cereal which might mean anything. Farmer's Glory or Corn-flakes – or even maize – but it *was* rye?'

Inspector Neele nodded.

'There you are,' said Miss Marple, triumphantly. '*Rex*

Fortescue. Rex means *King.* In his *Counting House.* And Mrs Fortescue the Queen in the parlour, eating bread and honey. And so, of course, the murderer had to put that clothes peg on poor Gladys's nose.'

Inspector Neele said:

'You mean the whole set up is crazy?'

'Well, one mustn't jump to conclusions – but it is certainly very *odd.* But you really must make inquiries about blackbirds. Because there must *be* blackbirds!'

It was at this point that Sergeant Hay came into the room saying urgently, 'Sir.'

He broke off at sight of Miss Marple. Inspector Neele, recovering himself said:

'Thank you, Miss Marple. I'll look into the matter. Since you are interested in the girl, perhaps you would care to look over the things from her room. Sergeant Hay will show you them presently.'

Miss Marple, accepting her dismissal, twittered her way out.

'Blackbirds!' murmured Inspector Neele to himself.

Sergeant Hay stared.

'Yes, Hay, what is it?'

'Sir,' said Sergeant Hay, urgently, again. 'Look at this.'

He produced an article wrapped in a somewhat grubby handkerchief.

'Found it in the shrubbery,' said Sergeant Hay. 'Could have been chucked there from one of the back windows.'

He tipped the object down on the desk in front of the Inspector who leaned forward and inspected it with rising excitement. The exhibit was a nearly full pot of marmalade.

The Inspector stared at it without speech. His face assumed a peculiarly wooden and stupid appearance. In actual fact this meant that Inspector Neele's mind was racing once more round an imaginary track. A moving picture was enacting itself before the eyes of his mind. He saw a new pot of marmalade, he saw hands carefully removing its cover, he saw a small quantity of marmalade removed, mixed with a preparation of taxine and replaced in the pot, the top smoothed over and the lid carefully replaced. He broke off at this point to ask Sergeant Hay:

'They don't take marmalade out of the pot and put it into fancy pots?'

'No, sir. Got into the way of serving it in its own pot during the war when things were scarce, and it's gone on like that ever since.'

Neele murmured:

'That made it easier, of course.'

'What's more,' said Sergeant Hay, 'Mr Fortescue was the only one that took marmalade for breakfast (and Mr Percival when he was at home). The others had jam or honey.'

Neele nodded.

'Yes,' he said. 'That made it very simple, didn't it?'

After a slight gap the moving picture went on in his mind. It was the breakfast table now. Rex Fortescue stretching out his hand for the marmalade pot, taking out a spoonful of marmalade and spreading it on his toast and butter. Easier, far easier that way than the risk and difficulty of insinuating it into his coffee cup. A foolproof method of administering the poison! And afterwards? Another gap and a picture that was not quite so clear. The replacing of that pot of marmalade by another with exactly the same amount taken from it. And then an open window. A hand and an arm flinging out that pot into the shrubbery. Whose hand and arm?

Inspector Neele said in a businesslike voice:

'Well, we'll have of course to get this analysed. See if there are any traces of taxine. We can't jump to conclusions.'

'No, sir. There may be fingerprints too.'

'Probably not the ones we want,' said Inspector Neele gloomily. 'There'll be Gladys's, of course, and Crump's and Fortescue's own. Then probably Mrs Crump's, the grocer's assistant and a few others! If anyone put taxine in here they'd take care not to go playing about with their own fingers all over the pot. Anyway, as I say, we mustn't jump to conclusions. How do they order marmalade and where is it kept?'

The industrious Sergeant Hay had his answer pat for all these questions.

'Marmalade and jams comes in in batches of six at a time. A new pot would be taken into the pantry when the old one was getting low.'

'That means,' said Neele, 'that it could have been tampered with several days before it was actually brought on to the breakfast table. And anyone who was in the house or had access to the house could have tampered with it.'

The term 'access to the house' puzzled Sergeant Hay slightly. He did not see in what way his superior's mind was working.

But Neele was postulating what seemed to him a logical assumption.

If the marmalade had been tampered with *beforehand* – then

surely that ruled out *those persons who were actually at the breakfast table on the fatal morning.*

Which opened up some interesting new possibilities.

He planned in his mind interviews with various people – this time with rather a different angle of approach.

He'd keep an open mind. . . .

He'd even consider seriously that old Miss Whatshername's suggestions about the nursery rhyme. Because there was no doubt that that nursery rhyme fitted in a rather startling way. It fitted with a point that had worried him from the beginning. The pocketful of rye.

'Blackbirds?' murmured Inspector Neele to himself.

Sergeant Hay stared.

'It's not blackberry jelly, sir,' he said. 'It's *marmalade.*'

II

Inspector Neele went in search of Mary Dove.

He found her in one of the bedrooms on the first floor super-intending Ellen, who was denuding the bed of what seemed to be clean sheets. A little pile of clean towels lay on a chair.

Inspector Neele looked puzzled.

'Somebody coming to stay?' he asked.

Mary Dove smiled at him. In contrast to Ellen, who looked grim and truculent, Mary was her usual imperturbable self.

'Actually,' she said, 'the opposite is the case.'

Neele looked inquiringly at her.

'This is the guest room we had prepared for Mr Gerald Wright.'

'Gerald Wright? Who is he?'

'He's a friend of Miss Elaine Fortescue's.' Mary's voice was carefully devoid of inflection.

'He was coming here – when?'

'I believe he arrived at the Golf Hotel the day after Mr Fortescue's death.'

'The day *after.*'

'So Miss Fortescue said.' Mary's voice was still impersonal. 'She told me she wanted him to come and stay in the house – so I had a room prepared. Now – after these other two – tragedies – it seems more suitable that he should remain at the hotel.'

'The Golf Hotel?'

'Yes.'

'Quite,' said Inspector Neele.

Ellen gathered up the sheets and towels and went out of the room.

Mary Dove looked inquiringly at Neele.

'You wanted to see me about something?'

Neele said pleasantly:

'It's becoming important to get exact times very clearly stated. Members of the family all seem a little vague about time – perhaps understandably. You, on the other hand, Miss Dove, I have found extremely accurate in your statements as to times.'

'Again understandably!'

'Yes – perhaps – I must certainly congratulate you on the way you kept this house going in spite of the – well panic – these last deaths must have caused.' He paused and then asked curiously: 'How did you do it?'

He had realized, astutely, that the one chink in the armour of Mary Dove's inscrutability was her pleasure in her own efficiency. She unbent slightly now as she answered.

'The Crumps wanted to leave at once, of course.'

'We couldn't have allowed that.'

'I know. But I also told them that Mr Percival Fortescue would be more likely to be – well – generous – to those who had spared him inconvenience.'

'And Ellen?'

'Ellen does not wish to leave.'

'Ellen does not wish to leave,' Neele repeated. 'She has good nerves.'

'She enjoys disasters,' said Mary Dove. 'Like Mrs Percival, she finds in disaster a kind of pleasurable drama.'

'Interesting. Do you think Mrs Percival has – enjoyed the tragedies?'

'No – of course not. That is going too far. I would merely say that it has enabled her to – well – stand up to them—'

'And how have you yourself been affected, Miss Dove?'

Mary Dove shrugged her shoulders.

'It has not been a pleasant experience,' she said dryly.

Inspector Neele felt again a longing to break down this cool young woman's defences – to find out what was really going on behind the careful and efficient understatement of her whole attitude.

He merely said brusquely:

'Now – to recapitulate times and places: the last time you

474

saw Gladys Martin was in the hall before tea, and that was at twenty minutes to five?'

'Yes – I told her to bring in tea.'

'You yourself were coming from where?'

'From upstairs – I thought I had heard the telephone a few minutes before.'

'Gladys, presumably, had answered the telephone?'

'Yes. It was a wrong number. Someone who wanted the Baydon Heath Laundry.'

'And that was the last time you saw her?'

'She brought the tea-tray into the library about ten minutes or so later.'

'After that Miss Elaine Fortescue came in?'

'Yes, about three or four minutes later. Then I went up to tell Mrs Percival tea was ready.'

'Did you usually do that?'

'Oh no – people came in to tea when they pleased – but Mrs Fortescue asked where everybody was. I thought I heard Mrs Percival coming – but that was a mistake—'

Neele interrupted. Here was something new.

'You mean you heard someone upstairs moving about?'

'Yes – at the head of the stairs, I thought. But no one came down so I went up. Mrs Percival was in her bedroom. She had just come in. She had been out for a walk—'

'Out for a walk – I see. The time being then—'

'Oh – nearly five o'clock, I think—'

'And Mr Lancelot Fortescue arrived – when?'

'A few minutes after I came downstairs again – I thought he had arrived earlier – but—'

Inspector Neele interrupted:

'Why did you think he had arrived earlier?'

'Because I thought I had caught sight of him through the landing window.'

'In the garden, you mean?'

'Yes – I caught a glimpse of someone through the yew hedge – and I thought it would probably be him.'

'This was when you were coming down after telling Mrs Percival Fortescue tea was ready?'

Mary corrected him.

'No – not then – it was earlier – when I came down the first time.'

Inspector Neele stared.

'Are you sure about that, Miss Dove?'

'Yes, I'm perfectly sure. That's why I was surprised to see him – when he actually did ring the bell.'

Inspector Neele shook his head. He kept his inner excitement out of his voice as he said:

'It couldn't have been Lancelot Fortescue you saw in the garden. His train – which was due at 4.28, was nine minutes late. He arrived at Baydon Heath Station at 4.37. He had to wait a few minutes for a taxi – that train is always very full. It was actually nearly a quarter to five (five minutes *after* you had seen the man in the garden) when he left the station and it is a ten-minute drive. He paid off the taxi at the gate here at about five minutes to five at the earliest. No – it wasn't Lancelot Fortescue you saw.'

'I'm sure I did see someone.'

'Yes, you saw someone. It was getting dark. You couldn't have seen the man clearly?'

'Oh no – I couldn't see his face or anything like that – just his build – tall and slender. We were expecting Lancelot Fortescue – so I jumped to the conclusion that that's who it was.'

'He was going – which way?'

'Along behind the yew hedge towards the east side of the house.'

'There is a side door there. Is it kept locked?'

'Not until the house is locked up for the night.'

'Anyone could have come in by that side door without being observed by any of the household.'

Mary Dove considered.

'I think so. Yes.' She added quickly: 'You mean – the person I heard later upstairs could have come in that way? Could have been hiding – upstairs?'

'Something of the kind.'

'But who—?'

'That remains to be seen. Thank you, Miss Dove.'

As she turned to go away Inspector Neele said in a casual voice: 'By the way, you can't tell me anything about *blackbirds*, I suppose?'

For the first time, so it seemed, Mary Dove was taken aback. She turned back sharply.

'I – what did you say?'

'I was just asking you about blackbirds.'

'Do you mean—'

'Blackbirds,' said Inspector Neele.

He had on his most stupid expression.

'You mean that silly business last summer? But surely that can't . . .' She broke off.

Inspector Neele said pleasantly:

'There's been a bit of talk about it, but I was sure I'd get a clear account from you.'

Mary Dove was her calm, practical self again.

'It must, I think, have been some silly, spiteful joke,' she said. 'Four dead blackbirds were on Mr Fortescue's desk in his study here. It was summer and the windows were open, and we rather thought it must have been the gardener's boy, though he insisted he'd never done anything of the kind. But they were actually blackbirds the gardener had shot which had been hanging up by the fruit bushes.'

'And somebody had cut them down and put them on Mr Fortescue's desk?'

'Yes.'

'Any sort of reason behind it – any association with blackbirds?'

Mary shook her head.

'I don't think so.'

'How did Mr Fortescue take it? Was he annoyed?'

'Naturally he was annoyed.'

'But not upset in any way?'

'I really can't remember.'

'I see,' said Inspector Neele.

He said no more. Mary Dove once more turned away, but this time, he thought, she went rather unwillingly as though she would have liked to know more of what was in his mind. Ungratefully, all that Inspector Neele felt was annoyance with Miss Marple. She had suggested to him that there would be blackbirds and sure enough, there the blackbirds were! Not four and twenty of them, that was true. What might be called a token consignment.

That had been as long ago as last summer and where it fitted in, Inspector Neele could not imagine. He was not going to let this blackbird bogey divert him from the logical and sober investigation of murder by a sane murderer for a sane reason, but he would be forced from now on to keep the crazier possibilities of the case in mind.

15

'I'm sorry, Miss Fortescue, to bother you again, but I want to be quite, quite clear about this. As far as we know you were the last person – or rather the last person but one – to see Mrs Fortescue alive. It was about twenty-past five when you left the drawing-room?'

'About then,' said Elaine, 'I can't say exactly.' She added defensively. 'One doesn't look at clocks the whole time.'

'No, of course not. During the time that you were alone with Mrs Fortescue after the others had left, what did you talk about?'

'Does it matter what we talked about?'

'Probably not,' said Inspector Neele, 'but it might give me some clue as to what was in Mrs Fortescue's mind.'

'You mean – you think she might have done it herself?'

Inspector Neele noticed the brightening on her face. It would certainly be a very convenient solution as far as the family was concerned. Inspector Neele did not think it was true for a moment. Adele Fortescue was not to his mind a suicidal type. Even if she had poisoned her husband and was convinced the crime was about to be brought home to her, she would not, he thought, have ever thought of killing herself. She would have been sure optimistically that even if she were tried for murder she would be sure to be acquitted. He was not, however, averse to Elaine Fortescue's entertaining the hypothesis. He said, therefore, quite truthfully:

'There's a possibility of it at least, Miss Fortescue. Now perhaps you'll tell me just what your conversation was about?'

'Well, it was really about my affairs.' Elaine hesitated.

'Your affairs being . . .?' he paused questioningly with a genial expression.

'I – a friend of mine had just arrived in the neighbourhood, and I was asking Adele if she would have any objection to – to my asking him to stay here at the house.'

'Ah. And who is this friend?'

'It's a Mr Gerald Wright. He's a schoolmaster. He – he's staying at the Golf Hotel.'

'A very close friend, perhaps?'

Inspector Neele gave an avuncular beam which added at least fifteen years to his age.

'We may expect an interesting announcement shortly, perhaps?'

He felt almost compunction as he saw the awkward gesture of the girl's hand and the flush on her face. She was in love with the fellow all right.

'We – we're not actually engaged and of course we couldn't have it announced just now, but – well, yes I think we do— I mean we are going to get married.'

'Congratulations,' said Inspector Neele pleasantly. 'Mr Wright is staying at the Golf Hotel, you say? How long has he been there?'

'I wired him when Father died.'

'And he came at once. *I* see,' said Inspector Neele.

He used this favourite phrase of his in a friendly and reassuring way.

'What did Mrs Fortescue say when you asked her about his coming here?'

'Oh, she said, all right, I could have anybody I pleased.'

'She was nice about it then?'

'Not exactly nice. I mean, she said—'

'Yes, what else did she say?'

Again Elaine flushed.

'Oh, something stupid about my being able to do a lot better for myself now. It was the sort of thing Adele would say.'

'Ah, well,' said Inspector Neele soothingly, 'relations say these sort of things.'

'Yes, yes, they do. But people often find it difficult to – to appreciate Gerald properly. He's an intellectual you see, and he's got a lot of unconventional and progressive ideas that people don't like.'

'That's why he didn't get on with your father?'

Elaine flushed hotly.

'Father was very prejudiced and unjust. He hurt Gerald's feelings. In fact, Gerald was so upset by my father's attitude that he went off and I didn't hear from him for weeks.'

And probably wouldn't have heard from him now if your father hadn't died and left you a packet of money, Inspector Neele thought. Aloud he said:

'Was there any more conversation between you and Mrs Fortescue?'

'No. No, I don't think so.'

'And that was about twenty-five-past five and Mrs Fortescue

479

was found dead at five minutes to six. You didn't return to the room during that half-hour?'

'No.'

'What were you doing?'

'I – I went out for a short walk.'

'To the Golf Hotel?'

'I – well, yes, but Gerald wasn't in.'

Inspector Neele said, 'I see' again, but this time with a rather dismissive effect. Elaine Fortescue got up and said:

'Is that all?'

'That's all, thank you, Miss Fortescue.'

As she got up to go, Neele said casually:

'You can't tell me anything about blackbirds, can you?'

She stared at him.

'Blackbirds? You mean the ones in the pie?'

They *would* be in the pie, the Inspector thought to himself. He merely said, 'When was this?'

'Oh! Three or four months ago – and there were some on Father's desk, too. He was furious—'

'Furious, was he? Did he ask a lot of questions?'

'Yes – of course – but we couldn't find out who put them there.'

'Have you any idea why he was so angry?'

'Well – it was rather a horrid thing to do, wasn't it?'

Neele looked thoughtfully at her – but he did not see any signs of evasion in her face. He said:

'Oh, just one more thing, Miss Fortescue. Do you know if your stepmother made a will at any time?'

Elaine shook her head.

'I've no idea – I – suppose so. People usually do, don't they?'

'They should do – but it doesn't always follow. Have you made a will yourself, Miss Fortescue?'

'No – no – I haven't – up to now I haven't had anything to leave – now, of course—'

He saw the realization of the changed position come into the eyes.

'Yes,' he said. 'Fifty thousand pounds is quite a responsibility – it changes a lot of things, Miss Fortescue.'

II

For some minutes after Elaine Fortescue left the room, Inspector Neele sat staring in front of him thoughtfully. He had, indeed, new food for thought. Mary Dove's statement that she had seen a man in the garden at approximately 4.35 opened up certain new possibilities. That is, of course, if Mary Dove was speaking the truth. It was never Inspector Neele's habit to assume that *anyone* was speaking the truth. But, examine her statement as he might, he could see no real reason why she should have lied. He was inclined to think that Mary Dove was speaking the truth when she spoke of having seen a man in the garden. It was quite clear that that man could not have been Lancelot Fortescue, although her reason for assuming that it was he was quite natural under the circumstances. It had not been Lancelot Fortescue, but it had been a man about the height and build of Lancelot Fortescue, and if there had been a man in the garden at that particular time, moreover a man moving furtively, as it seemed, to judge from the way he had crept behind the yew hedges, then that certainly opened up a line of thought.

Added to this statement of hers, there had been the further statement that she had heard someone moving about upstairs. That, in its turn, tied up with something else. The small piece of mud he had found on the floor of Adele Fortescue's boudoir. Inspector Neele's mind dwelt on the small dainty desk in that room. Pretty little sham antique with a rather obvious secret drawer in it. There had been three letters in that drawer, letters written by Vivian Dubois to Adele Fortescue. A great many love letters of one kind or another had passed through Inspector Neele's hands in the course of his career. He was acquainted with passionate letters, foolish letters, sentimental letters and nagging letters. There had also been cautious letters. Inspector Neele was inclined to classify these three as of the latter kind. Even if read in the divorce court, they could pass as inspired by a merely platonic friendship. Though in this case: 'Platonic friendship my foot!' thought the Inspector inelegantly. Neele, when he had found the letters, had sent them up at once to the Yard since at that time the main question was whether the Public Prosecutor's office thought that there was sufficient evidence to proceed with the case against Adele Fortescue or Adele Fortescue and Vivian Dubois together. Everything had pointed towards Rex Fortescue having been poisoned by his wife with or without her lover's connivance. These letters, though cautious, made it fairly clear that Vivian Dubois was her lover, but there had not been in the wording, so far as Inspector Neele could see, any signs of incitement to crime. There might have been incitement of a spoken kind, but Vivian Dubois would be far too cautious to put anything of that kind down on paper.

Inspector Neele surmised accurately that Vivian Dubois had asked Adele Fortescue to destroy his letters and that Adele Fortescue had told him she had done so.

Well, now they had two more deaths on their hands. And that meant, or should mean, that Adele Fortescue had not killed her husband.

Unless, that is – Inspector Neele considered a new hypothesis – Adele Fortescue had wanted to marry Vivian Dubois and Vivian Dubois had wanted, not Adele Fortescue, but Adele Fortescue's hundred thousand pounds which would come to her on the death of her husband. He had assumed, perhaps, that Rex Fortescue's death would be put down to natural causes. Some kind of seizure or stroke. After all, everybody seemed to be worried over Rex Fortescue's health during the last year. (Parenthetically, Inspector Neele said to himself that he must look into that question. He had a subconscious feeling that it might be important in some way.) To continue, Rex Fortescue's death had not gone according to plan. It had been diagnosed without loss of time as poisoning, and the correct poison named.

Supposing that Adele Fortescue and Vivian Dubois had been guilty, what state would they be in then? Vivian Dubois would have been scared and Adele Fortescue would have lost her head. She might have done or said foolish things. She might have rung up Dubois on the telephone, talking indiscreetly in a way that he would have realized might have been overheard in Yewtree Lodge. What would Vivian Dubois have done next?

It was early as yet to try and answer that question, but Inspector Neele proposed very shortly to make inquiries at the Golf Hotel as to whether Dubois had been in or out of the hotel between the hours of 4.15 and 6 o'clock. Vivian Dubois was tall and dark like Lance Fortescue. He might have slipped through the garden to the side door, made his way upstairs and then what? Looked for the letters and found them gone? Waited there, perhaps, till the coast was clear, then come down into the library when tea was over and Adele Fortescue was alone?

But all this was going too fast—

Neele had questioned Mary Dove and Elaine Fortescue; he must see now what Percival Fortescue's wife had to say.

16

Inspector Neele found Mrs Percival in her own sitting-room upstairs, writing letters. She got up rather nervously when he came in.

'Is there anything – what – are there—'

'Please sit down, Mrs Fortescue. There are only just a few more questions I would like to ask you.'

'Oh, yes. Yes, of course, Inspector. It's all so dreadful, isn't it? So very dreadful.'

She sat down rather nervously in an armchair. Inspector Neele sat down in the small, straight chair near her. He studied her rather more carefully than he had done heretofore. In some ways a mediocre type of woman, he thought – and thought also that she was not very happy. Restless, unsatisfied, limited in mental outlook, yet he thought she might have been efficient and skilled in her own profession of hospital nurse. Though she had achieved leisure by her marriage with a well-to-do man, leisure had not satisfied her. She bought clothes, read novels and ate sweets, but he remembered her avid excitement on the night of Rex Fortescue's death, and he saw in it not so much a ghoulish satisfaction but rather a revelation of the arid deserts of boredom which encompassed her life. Her eyelids fluttered and fell before his searching glance. They gave her the appearance of being both nervous and guilty, but he could not be sure that that was really the case.

'I'm afraid,' he said soothingly, 'we have to ask people questions again and again. It must be very tiresome for you all. I do appreciate that, but so much hangs, you understand, on the exact *timing* of events. You came down to tea rather late, I understand? In fact, Miss Dove came up and fetched you.'

'Yes. Yes, she did. She came and said tea was in. I had no idea it was so late. I'd been writing letters.'

Inspector Neele just glanced over at the writing-desk.

'I see,' he said. 'Somehow, or other, I thought you'd been out for a walk.'

'Did she say so? Yes – now I believe you're right. I had been writing letters; then it was so stuffy and my head ached so I went out and – er – went for a walk. Only round the garden.'

'I see. You didn't meet anyone?'

'Meet anyone?' She stared at him. 'What do you mean?'

'I just wondered if you'd seen anybody or anybody had seen you during this walk of yours.'

'I saw the gardener in the distance, that's all.' She was looking at him suspiciously.

'Then you came in, came up here to your room and you were just taking your things off when Miss Dove came to tell you that tea was ready?'

'Yes. Yes, and so I came down.'

'And who was there?'

'Adele and Elaine, and a minute or two later Lance arrived. My brother-in-law, you know. The one who's come back from Kenya.'

'And then you all had tea?'

'Yes, we had tea. Then Lance went up to see Aunt Effie and I came up here to finish my letters. I left Elaine there with Adele.'

He nodded reassuringly.

'Yes. Miss Fortescue seems to have been with Mrs Fortescue for quite five or ten minutes after you left. Your husband hadn't come home yet?'

'Oh no. Percy – Val – didn't get home until about half-past six or seven. He'd been kept up in town.'

'He came back by train?'

'Yes. He took a taxi from the station.'

'Was it unusual for him to come back by train?'

'He does sometimes. Not very often. I think he'd been to places in the city where it's rather difficult to park the car. It was easier for him to take a train home from Cannon Street.'

'I see,' said Inspector Neele. He went on, 'I asked your husband if Mrs Fortescue had made a will before she died. He said he thought not. I suppose you don't happen to have any idea?'

To his surprise Jennifer Fortescue nodded vigorously.

'Oh, yes,' she said. 'Adele made a will. She told me so.'

'Indeed! When was this?'

'Oh, it wasn't very long ago. About a month ago, I think.'

'That's very interesting,' said Inspector Neele.

Mrs Percival leant forward eagerly. Her face now was all animation. She clearly enjoyed exhibiting her superior knowledge.

'Val didn't know about it,' she said. 'Nobody knew. It just happened that I found out about it. I was in the street. I had just come out of the stationer's, then I saw Adele coming out of the solicitor's office. Ansell and Worrall's you know. In the High Street.'

'Ah,' said Neele, 'the local solicitors?'

'Yes. And I said to Adele "Whatever have you been doing there?" I said. And she laughed and said "Wouldn't you like to know?" And then as we walked along together she said "I'll tell you, Jennifer. I've been making my will." "Well," I said, "why are you doing that, Adele, you're not ill or anything, are you?" And she said no, of course she wasn't ill. She'd never felt better. But everyone ought to make a will. She said she wasn't going to those stuck up family solicitors in London, Mr Billingsley. She said the old sneak would go round and tell the family. "No," she said, "My will's my own business, Jennifer, and I'll make it my own way and nobody's going to know about it." "Well, Adele," I said, "*I* shan't tell anybody." She said "It doesn't matter if you do. You won't know what's in it." But I didn't tell anyone. No, not even Percy. I do think women ought to stick together, don't you, Inspector Neele?'

'I'm sure that's a very nice feeling on your part, Mrs Fortescue,' said Inspector Neele, diplomatically.

'I'm sure I'm never ill-natured,' said Jennifer. 'I didn't particularly care for Adele, if you know what I mean. I always thought she was the kind of woman who would stick at nothing in order to get what she wanted. Now she's dead, perhaps I misjudged her, poor soul.'

'Well, thank you very much, Mrs Fortescue, for being so helpful to me.'

'You're welcome, I'm sure. I'm only too glad to do anything I can. It's all so very terrible, isn't it? Who is the old lady who's arrived this morning?'

'She's a Miss Marple. She very kindly came here to give us what information she could about the girl Gladys. It seems Gladys Martin was once in service with her.'

'Really? How interesting.'

'There's one other thing, Mrs Percival. Do you know anything about blackbirds?'

Jennifer Fortescue started violently. She dropped her handbag on the floor and bent to pick it up.

'Blackbirds, Inspector? Blackbirds? What kind of blackbirds?'

Her voice was rather breathless. Smiling a little, Inspector Neele said:

'Just blackbirds. Alive or dead or even, shall we say, symbolical?'

Jennifer Fortescue said sharply:

'I don't know what you mean. I don't know what you're talking about.'

'You don't know anything about blackbirds, then, Mrs Fortescue?'

She said slowly:

'I suppose you mean the ones last summer in the pie. All very silly.'

'There were some left on the library table, too, weren't there?'

'It was all a very silly practical joke. I don't know who's been talking to you about it. Mr Fortescue, my father-in-law, was very much annoyed by it.'

'Just annoyed? Nothing more?'

'Oh. I see what you mean. Yes, I suppose – yes, it's true. He asked us if there were any strangers about the place.'

'Strangers!' Inspector Neele raised his eyebrows.

'Well, that's what he said,' said Mrs Percival defensively.

'Strangers,' repeated Inspector Neele thoughtfully. Then he asked, 'Did he seem afraid in any way?'

'Afraid? I don't know what you mean.'

'Nervous. About strangers, I mean.'

'Yes. Yes, he did, rather. Of course I don't remember very well. It was several months ago, you know. I don't think it was anything except a silly practical joke. Crump perhaps. I really do think that Crump is a very unbalanced man, and I'm perfectly certain that he drinks. He's really very insolent in his manner sometimes. I've sometimes wondered if he could have had a grudge against Mr Fortescue. Do you think that's possible, Inspector?'

'Anything's possible,' said Inspector Neele and went away.

II

Percival Fortescue was in London, but Inspector Neele found Lancelot sitting with his wife in the library. They were playing chess together.

'I don't want to interrupt you,' said Neele, apologetically.

'We're only killing time, Inspector, aren't we, Pat?'

Pat nodded.

'I expect you'll think it's rather a foolish question I'm asking you,' said Neele. 'Do you know anything about blackbirds, Mr Fortescue?'

'Blackbirds?' Lance looked amused. 'What kind of blackbirds? Do you mean genuine birds, or the slave trade?'

Inspector Neele said with a sudden, disarming smile:

'I'm not sure what I mean, Mr Fortescue: It's just that a mention of blackbirds has turned up.'

'Good Lord.' Lancelot looked suddenly alert, 'Not the old Blackbird Mine, I suppose?'

Inspector Neele said sharply:

'The Blackbird Mine? What was that?'

Lance frowned in a puzzled fashion.

'The trouble is, Inspector, that I can't really remember much myself. I just have a vague idea about some shady transaction in my papa's past. Something on the West Coast of Africa. Aunt Effie I believe, once threw it in his teeth, but I can't remember anything definite about it.'

'Aunt Effie? That will be Miss Ramsbottom, won't it?'

'Yes.'

'I'll go and ask her about it,' said Inspector Neele. He added ruefully, 'She's rather a formidable old lady, Mr Fortescue. Always makes me feel quite nervous.'

Lance laughed.

'Yes. Aunt Effie is certainly a character, but she may be helpful to you, Inspector, if you get on the right side of her. Especially if you're delving into the past. She's got an excellent memory, she takes a positive pleasure in remembering anything that's detrimental in any way.' He added thoughtfully, 'There's something else. I went up to see her, you know, soon after I got back home. Immediately after tea that day, as a matter of fact. And she was talking about Gladys. The maid who got killed. Not that we knew she was dead then, of course. But Aunt Effie was saying she was quite convinced that Gladys knew something that she hadn't told the police.'

'That seems fairly certain,' said Inspector Neele. 'She'll never tell it now, poor girl.'

'No. It seems Aunt Effie had given her good advice as to spilling anything she knew. Pity the girl didn't take it.'

Inspector Neele nodded. Bracing himself for the encounter he penetrated to Miss Ramsbottom's fortress. Rather to his surprise, he found Miss Marple there. The two ladies appeared to be discussing foreign missions.

'I'll go away, Inspector.' Miss Marple rose hurriedly to her feet.

'No need, madam,' said Inspector Neele.

'I've asked Miss Marple to come and stay in the house,' said Miss Ramsbottom. 'No sense in spending money in that ridiculous Golf Hotel. A wicked nest of profiteers, that is. Drinking and card playing all the evening. She'd better come and stay in a decent Christian household. There's a room next door to mine. Dr Mary Peters, the missionary, had it last.'

'It's very, very kind of you,' said Miss Marple, 'but I really think I mustn't intrude in a house of mourning.'

'Mourning? Fiddlesticks,' said Miss Ramsbottom. 'Who'll weep for Rex in this house? Or Adele either? Or is it the police you're worried about? Any objections, Inspector?'

'None from me, madam.'

'There you are,' said Miss Ramsbottom.

'It's very kind of you,' said Miss Marple gratefully. 'I'll go and telephone to the hotel to cancel my booking.' She left the room and Miss Ramsbottom said sharply to the Inspector:

'Well, and what do *you* want?'

'I wondered if you could tell me anything about the Blackbird Mine, ma'am.'

Miss Ramsbottom uttered a sudden, shrill cackle of laughter.

'Ha. You've got on to *that*, have you! Took the hint I gave you the other day. Well, what do you want to know about it?'

'Anything you can tell me, madam.'

'I can't tell you much. It's a long time ago now – oh, twenty to twenty-five years maybe. Some concession or other in East Africa. My brother-in-law went into it with a man called MacKenzie. They went out there to investigate the mine together and MacKenzie died out there of fever. Rex came home and said the claim or the concession or whatever you call it was worthless. That's all *I* know.'

'I think you know a little more than that, ma'am,' said Neele persuasively.

'Anything else is hearsay. You don't like hearsay in the law, so I've been told.'

'We're not in court yet, ma'am.'

'Well, *I* can't tell you anything. The MacKenzies kicked up a fuss. That's all I know. They insisted that Rex had swindled MacKenzie. I daresay he did. He was a clever, unscrupulous fellow, but I've no doubt whatever he did it was all legal. They couldn't prove anything. Mrs MacKenzie was an unbalanced sort of woman. She came here and made a lot of threats of revenge. Said Rex had murdered her husband. Silly, melo-dramatic fuss! I think she was a bit off her head – in fact, I believe she went into an asylum not long after. Came here dragging along a couple of young children who looked scared to death. Said she'd bring up her children to have revenge. Something like that. Tomfoolery, all of it. Well, that's all I can tell you. And mind you, the Blackbird Mine wasn't the only swindle that Rex put over in his lifetime. You'll find a good many more if you look for them. What put you on to the Black-bird? Did you come across some trail leading to the MacKenzies?'

'You don't know what became of the family, ma'am?'

'No idea,' said Miss Ramsbottom. 'Mind you, I don't think Rex would have actually murdered MacKenzie, but he might have left him to die. The same thing before the Lord, but not the same thing before the law. If he did, retribution's caught up with him. The mills of God grind slowly, but they grind exceeding small – you'd better go away now, I can't tell you any more and it's no good your asking.'

'Thank you very much for what you have told me,' said Inspector Neele.

'Send that Marple woman back,' Miss Ramsbottom called after him. 'She's frivolous, like all Church of England people, but she knows how to run a charity in a sensible way.'

Inspector Neele made a couple of telephone calls, the first to Ansell and Worrall and the second to the Golf Hotel, then he summoned Sergeant Hay and told him that he was leaving the house for a short period.

'I've a call to pay at a solicitor's office – after that, you can get me at the Golf Hotel if anything urgent turns up.'

'Yes, sir.'

'And find out anything you can about blackbirds,' added Neele over his shoulder.

'Blackbirds, sir?' Sergeant Hay repeated, thoroughly mystified.

'That's what I said – not blackberry jelly – blackbirds.'

'Very good, sir,' said Sergeant Hay bewilderedly.

17

Inspector Neele found Mr Ansel the type of solicitor who was more easily intimidated than intimidating. A member of a small and not very prosperous firm, he was anxious not to stand upon his rights but instead to assist the police in every way possible.

Yes, he said, he had made a will for the late Mrs Adele Fortescue. She had called at his office about five weeks previously. It had seemed to him rather a peculiar business but naturally he had not said anything. Peculiar things did happen in a solicitor's business, and of course the Inspector would understand that discretion, etc., etc. The Inspector nodded to show he understood. He had already discovered Mr Ansel had not transacted any legal business previously for Mrs Fortescue or for any of the Fortescue family.

'Naturally,' said Mr Ansell, 'she didn't want to go to her husband's firm of lawyers about this.'

Shorn of verbiage, the facts were simple. Adele Fortescue had made a will leaving everything of which she died possessed to Vivian Dubois.

'But I gathered,' said Mr Ansell, looking at Neele in an interrogating manner, 'that she hadn't actually much to leave.'

Inspector Neele nodded. At the time Adele Fortescue made her will that was true enough. But since then Rex Fortescue had died, and Adele Fortescue had inherited £100,000 and presumably that £100,000 (less death duties) now belonged to Vivian Edward Dubois.

II

At the Golf Hotel, Inspector Neele found Vivian Dubois nervously awaiting his arrival. Dubois had been on the point of leaving, indeed his bags were packed, when he had received over the telephone a civil request from Inspector Neele to remain. Inspector Neele had been very pleasant about it, quite apologetic. But behind the conventional words the request had been an order. Vivian Dubois had demurred, but not too much.

He said now:

'I do hope you realize, Inspector Neele, that it is very incon-

venient for me to have to stay on. I really have urgent business
that needs attending to.'

'I didn't know you were in business, Mr Dubois,' said Inspector Neele, genially.

'I'm afraid none of us can be as leisured as we would like to
appear to be nowadays.'

'Mrs Fortescue's death must have been a great shock to you,
Mr Dubois. You were great friends, were you not?'

'Yes,' said Dubois, 'she was a charming woman. We played
golf quite often together.'

'I expect you'll miss her very much.'

'Yes, indeed.' Dubois sighed. 'The whole thing is really quite,
quite terrible.'

'You actually telephoned her, I believe, on the afternoon of
her death?'

'Did I? I really cannot remember now.'

'About four o'clock, I understand.'

'Yes, I believe I did.'

'Don't you remember what your conversation was about, Mr
Dubois?'

'It wasn't of any significance. I think I asked her how she was
feeling and if there was any further news about her husband's
death – a more or less conventional inquiry.'

'*I* see,' said Inspector Neele. He added, 'And then you went
out for a walk?'

'Er – yes – yes, I – I did, I think. At least, not a walk, I played
a few holes of golf.'

Inspector Neele said gently:

'I think not, Mr Dubois. . . . Not that particular day. . . . The
porter here noticed you walking down the road towards Yewtree
Lodge.'

Dubois's eyes met his, then shied away again nervously.

'I'm afraid I can't remember, Inspector.'

'Perhaps you actually went to call upon Mrs Fortescue?'

Dubois said sharply:

'No. No, I didn't do that. I never went near the house.'

'Where did you go, then?'

'Oh, I – went on down the road, down as far as the Three
Pigeons and then I turned around and came back by the links.'

'You're quite sure you didn't go to Yewtree Lodge?'

'Quite sure, Inspector.'

The Inspector shook his head.

'Come, now, Mr Dubois,' he said, 'it's much better to be frank with us, you know. You may have had some quite innocent reason for going there.'

'I tell you I never went to see Mrs Fortescue that day.'

The Inspector stood up.

'You know, Mr Dubois,' he said pleasantly, 'I think we'll have to ask you for a statement and you'll be well advised and quite within your rights in having a solicitor present when you are making that statement.'

The colour fled from Mr. Dubois's face, leaving it a sickly greenish colour.

'You're threatening me,' he said. 'You're threatening me.'

'No, no, nothing of the kind.' Inspector Neele spoke in a shocked voice. 'We're not allowed to do anything of that sort. Quite the contrary. I'm actually pointing out to you that you have certain rights.'

'I had nothing to do with it at all, I tell you! Nothing to do with it.'

'Come now, Mr Dubois, you were at Yewtree Lodge round about half-past four on that day. Somebody looked out of the window, you know, and saw you.'

'I was only in the garden. I didn't go into the house.'

'Didn't you?' said Inspector Neele. 'Are you sure? Didn't you go in by the side door and up the stairs to Mrs Fortescue's sitting-room on the first floor? You were looking for something weren't you, in the desk there?'

'*You've* got them, I suppose,' said Dubois sullenly. 'That fool Adele kept them, then – she swore she burnt them – But they don't mean what you think they mean.'

'You're not denying, are you, Mr Dubois, that you were a very *close* friend of Mrs Fortescue's?'

'No, of course I'm not. How can I when you've got the letters. All I say is, there's no need to go reading any sinister meaning into them. Don't think for a moment that we – that she – ever thought of getting rid of Rex Fortescue. Good God, I'm not *that* kind of man!'

'But perhaps she was that kind of woman?'

'Nonsense,' cried Vivian Dubois, 'wasn't she killed too?'

'Oh yes, yes.'

'Well, isn't it natural to believe that the same person who killed her husband killed her?'

'It might be. It certainly might be. But there are other solutions. For instance – (this is quite a hypothetical case, Mr Dubois) it's possible that Mrs Fortescue got rid of her husband

and that after his death she became somewhat of a danger to someone else. Someone who had, perhaps, not helped her in what she had done but who had at least encouraged her and provided, shall we say, the *motive* for the deed. She might be, you know, a danger to that particular person.'

Dubois stammered:

'You c-c-can't build up a case against me. You can't.'

'She made a will, you know,' said Inspector Neele. 'She left all her money to you. Everything she possessed.'

'I don't want the money. I don't want a penny of it.'

'Of course, it isn't very much really,' said Inspector Neele. 'There's jewellery and some furs, but I imagine very little actual cash.'

Dubois stared at him, his jaw dropping.

'But I thought her husband—'

He stopped dead.

'Did you, Mr Dubois?' said Inspector Neele, and there was steel now in his voice. 'That's very interesting. I wondered if you knew the terms of Rex Fortescue's will—'

III

Inspector Neele's second interview at the Golf Hotel was with Mr Gerald Wright. Mr Gerald Wright was a thin, intellectual and very superior young man. He was, Inspector Neele noted, not unlike Vivian Dubois in build.

'What can I do for you, Inspector Neele?' he asked.

'I thought you might be able to help us with a little information, Mr Wright.'

'Information? Really? It seems very unlikely.'

'It's in connection with the recent events at Yewtree Lodge. You've heard of them, of course?'

Inspector Neele put a little irony into the question. Mr Wright smiled patronisingly.

'Heard of them,' he said, 'is hardly the right word. The newspapers appear to be full of nothing else. How incredibly bloodthirsty our public press is! What an age we live in! On one side the manufacture of atom bombs, on the other our newspapers delight in reporting brutal murders! But you said you had some questions to ask. Really, I cannot see what they can be. I know nothing about this Yewtree Lodge affair. I was actually in the Isle of Man when Mr Rex Fortescue was killed.'

493

'You arrived here very shortly afterwards, didn't you, Mr Wright? You had a telegram, I believe, from Miss Elaine Fortescue.'

'Our police know everything, do they not? Yes, Elaine sent for me. I came, of course, at once.'

'And you are, I understand, shortly to be married?'

'Quite right, Inspector Neele. You have no objections, I hope.'

'It is entirely Miss Fortescue's business. I understand the attachment between you dates from some time back? Six or seven months ago, in fact?'

'Quite correct.'

'You and Miss Fortescue became engaged to be married. Mr Fortescue refused to give his consent, informed you that if his daughter married against his wishes he did not propose to give her an income of any kind. Whereupon, I understand, you broke off the engagement and departed.'

Gerald Wright smiled rather pityingly.

'A very crude way of putting things, Inspector Neele. Actually, I was victimised for my political opinions. Rex Fortescue was the worst type of capitalist. Naturally I could not sacrifice my political beliefs and convictions for money.'

'But you have no objections to marrying a wife who has just inherited £50,000?'

Gerald Wright gave a thin satisfied smile.

'Not at all, Inspector Neele. The money will be used for the benefit of the community. But surely you did not come here to discuss with me either my financial circumstances – or my political convictions?'

'No, Mr Wright. I wanted to talk to you about a simple question of fact. As you are aware, Mrs Adele Fortescue died as a result of cyanide poisoning on the afternoon of November the 5th.

'Since you were in the neighbourhood of Yewtree Lodge on that afternoon I thought it possible that you might have seen or heard something that had a bearing on the case.'

'And what leads you to believe that I was, as you call it, in the neighbourhood of Yewtree Lodge at the time?'

'You left this hotel at a quarter past four on that particular afternoon, Mr Wright. On leaving the hotel you walked down the road in the direction of Yewtree Lodge. It seems natural to suppose that you were going there.'

'I thought of it,' said Gerald Wright, 'but I considered that

494

it would be a rather pointless thing to do. I already had an arrangement to meet Miss Fortescue – Elaine – at the hotel at six o'clock. I went for a walk along a lane that branches off from the main road and returned to the Golf Hotel just before six o'clock. Elaine did not keep her appointment. Quite naturally, under the circumstances.'

'Anybody see you on this walk of yours, Mr Wright?'

'A few cars passed me, I think, on the road. I did not see anyone I knew, if that's what you mean. The lane was little more than a cart-track and too muddy for cars.'

'So between the time you left the hotel at a quarter past four until six o'clock when you arrived back again, I've only your word for it as to where you were?'

Gerald Wright continued to smile in a superior fashion.

'Very distressing for us both, Inspector, but there it is.'

Inspector Neele said softly:

'Then if someone said they looked out of a landing window and saw you in the garden of Yewtree Lodge at about 4.35—' he paused and left the sentence unfinished.

Gerald Wright raised his eyebrows and shook his head.

'Visibility must have been very bad by then,' he said. 'I think it would be difficult for anyone to be sure.'

'Are you acquainted with Mr Vivian Dubois, who is also staying here?'

'Dubois. Dubois? No, I don't think so. Is that the tall dark man with a pretty taste in suede shoes?'

'Yes. He also was out for a walk that afternoon, and he also left the hotel and walked past Yewtree Lodge. You did not notice him in the road by any chance?'

'No. No. I can't say I did.'

Gerald Wright looked for the first time faintly worried. Inspector Neele said thoughtfully:

'It wasn't really a very nice afternoon for walking, especially after dark in a muddy lane. Curious how energetic everyone seems to have felt.'

IV

On Inspector Neele's return to the house he was greeted by Sergeant Hay with an air of satisfaction.

'I've found out about the blackbirds for you, sir,' he said.

'You have, have you?'

495

'Yes, sir, in a pie they were. Cold pie was left out for Sunday night's supper. Somebody got at that pie in the larder or somewhere. They'd taken off the crust and they'd taken out the veal and 'am what was inside it, and what d'you think they put in instead? Some stinkin' blackbirds they got out of the gardener's shed. Nasty sort of trick to play, wasn't it?'

' "*Wasn't that a dainty dish to set before the king*"?' said Inspector Neele.

He left Sergeant Hay staring after him.

—— 18 ——

'Just wait a minute,' said Miss Ramsbottom. 'This Patience is going to come out.'

She transferred a king and his various impedimenta into an empty space, put a red seven on a black eight, built up the four, five and six of spades on her foundation heap, made a few more rapid transfers of cards and then leaned back with a sigh of satisfaction.

'That's the Double Jester,' she said. 'It doesn't often come out.'

She leaned back in a satisfied fashion, then raised her eyes at the girl standing by the fireplace.

'So you're Lance's wife,' she said.

Pat, who had been summoned upstairs to Miss Ramsbottom's presence, nodded her head.

'Yes,' she said.

'You're a tall girl,' said Miss Ramsbottom, 'and you look healthy.'

'I'm very healthy.'

Miss Ramsbottom nodded in a satisfied manner.

'Percival's wife is pasty,' she said. 'Eats too many sweets and doesn't take enough exercise. Well, sit down, child, sit down. Where did you meet my nephew?'

'I met him out in Kenya when I was staying there with some friends.'

'You've been married before, I understand.'

'Yes. Twice.'

Miss Ramsbottom gave a profound sniff.

'Divorce, I suppose.'

496

'No,' said Pat. Her voice trembled a little. 'They both – died. My first husband was a fighter pilot. He was killed in the war.'

'And your second husband? Let me see – somebody told me. Shot himself, didn't he?'

Pat nodded.

'Your fault?'

'No,' said Pat. 'It wasn't my fault.'

'Racing man, wasn't he?'

'Yes.'

'I've never been on a race-course in my life,' said Miss Ramsbottom. 'Betting and card playing – all devices of the devil!'

Pat did not reply.

'I wouldn't go inside a theatre or a cinema,' said Miss Ramsbottom. 'Ah, well, it's a wicked world nowadays. A lot of wickedness was going on in this house, but the Lord struck them down.'

Pat still found it difficult to say anything. She wondered if Lance's Aunt Effie was really quite all there. She was, however, a trifle disconcerted by the old lady's shrewd glance at her.

'How much,' demanded Aunt Effie, 'do you know about the family you've married into?'

'I suppose,' said Pat, 'as much as one ever knows of the family one marries into.'

'H'm, something in that, something in that. Well, I'll tell you this. My sister was a fool, my brother-in-law was a rogue, Percival is a sneak, and your Lance was always the bad boy of the family.'

'I think that's all nonsense,' said Pat robustly.

'Maybe you're right,' said Miss Ramsbottom, unexpectedly. 'You can't just stick labels on people. But don't underestimate Percival. There's a tendency to believe that those who are labelled good are also stupid. Percival isn't the least bit stupid. He's quite clever in a sanctimonious kind of way. I've never cared for him. Mind you, I don't *trust* Lance and I don't *approve* of him, but I can't help being fond of him. . . . He's a reckless sort of fellow – always has been. You've got to look after him and see he doesn't go too far. Tell him not to under-estimate Percival, my dear. Tell him not to believe everything that Percival says. They're all liars in this house.' The old lady added with satisfaction, 'Fire and brimstone shall be their portion.'

II

Inspector Neele was finishing a telephone conversation with Scotland Yard.

The Assistant Commissioner at the other end said:

'We ought to be able to get that information for you – by circularising the various private sanatoriums. Of course she *may* be dead.'

'Probably is. It's a long time ago.'

Old sins cast long shadows. Miss Ramsbottom had said that – said it with a significance, too – as though she was giving him a hint.

'It's a fantastic theory,' said the AC.

'Don't I know it, sir. But I don't feel we can ignore it altogether. Too much fits in—'

'Yes – yes – rye – blackbirds – the man's Christian name—'

Neele said:

'I'm concentrating on the other lines too – Dubois is a possibility – so is Wright – the girl Gladys could have caught sight of either of them outside the side door – she could have left the tea-tray in the hall and gone out to see who it was and what they were doing – whoever it was could have strangled her then and there and then carried her body round to the clothes line and put the peg on her nose—'

'A crazy thing to do in all conscience! A nasty one too.'

'Yes, sir. That's what upset the old lady – Miss Marple. I mean. Nice old lady – and very shrewd. She's moved into the house – to be near old Miss Ramsbottom – and I've no doubt she'll get to hear anything that's going.'

'What's your next move, Neele?'

'I've an appointment with the London solicitors. I want to find out a little more about Rex Fortescue's affairs. And though it's old history, I want to hear a little more about the Blackbird Mine.'

III

Mr Billingsley, of Billingsley, Horsethorpe & Walters, was an urban man whose discretion was concealed habitually by a misleadingly forthcoming manner. It was the second interview that Inspector Neele had had with him, and on this occasion Mr Billingsley's discretion was less noticeable than it had been on the former one. The triple tragedy at Yewtree Lodge had shaken Mr Billingsley out of his professional reserve. He was now only too anxious to put all the facts he could before the police.

'Most extraordinary business, this whole thing,' he said. 'A most extraordinary business. I don't remember anything like it in all my professional career.'

'Frankly, Mr Billingsley,' said Inspector Neele, 'we need all the help we can get.'

'You can count on me, my dear sir. I shall be only too happy to assist you in every way I can.'

'First let me ask you how well you knew the late Mr Fortescue, and how well do you know the affairs of his firm?'

'I knew Rex Fortescue fairly well. That is to say I've known him for a period of, well, sixteen years I should say. Mind you, we are not the only firm of solicitors he employed, not by a long way.'

Inspector Neele nodded. He knew that. Billingsley, Horsethorpe & Walters were what one might describe as Rex Fortescue's reputable solicitors. For his less reputable dealings he had employed several different and slightly less scrupulous firms.

'Now what do you want to know?' continued Mr Billingsley. 'I've told you about his will. Percival Fortescue is the residuary legatee.'

'I'm interested now,' said Inspector Neele, 'in the will of his widow. On Mr Fortescue's death she came into the sum of one hundred thousand pounds, I understand?'

Billingsley nodded his head.

'A considerable sum of money,' he said, 'and I may tell you in confidence, Inspector, that it is one the firm could ill have afforded to pay out.'

'The firm, then, is not prosperous?'

'Frankly,' said Mr Billingsley, 'and strictly between ourselves, it's drifting on to the rocks and has been for the last year and a half.'

'For any particular reason?'

'Why yes. I should say the reason was Rex Fortescue himself. For the last year Rex Fortescue's been acting like a madman. Selling good stock here, buying speculative stuff there, talking big about it all the time in the most extraordinary way. Wouldn't listen to advice. Percival – the son, you know – he came here urging me to use my influence with his father. *He'd* tried, apparently and been swept aside. Well, I did what I could, but

Fortescue wouldn't listen to reason. Really, he seems to have been a changed man.'

'But not, I gather, a depressed man,' said Inspector Neele.

'No, no. Quite the contrary. Flamboyant, bombastic.'

Inspector Neele nodded. An idea which had already taken form in his mind was strengthened. He thought he was beginning to understand some of the causes of friction between Percival and his father. Mr Billingsley was continuing.

'But it's no good asking me about the wife's will. *I* didn't make any will for her.'

'No. I know that,' said Neele. 'I'm merely verifying that she had something to leave. In short, a hundred thousand pounds.'

Mr Billingsley was shaking his head violently.

'No, no, my dear sir. You're wrong there.'

'Do you mean the hundred thousand pounds was only left to her for her lifetime?'

'No – no – it was left to her outright. But there was a clause in the will governing that bequest. That is to say, Fortescue's wife did not inherit the sum unless she survived him for one month. That, I may say, is a clause fairly common nowadays. It has come into operation owing to the uncertainties of air travel. If two people are killed in an air accident, it becomes exceedingly difficult to say who was the survivor and a lot of very curious problems arise.'

Inspector Neele was staring at him.

'Then Adele Fortescue had not got a hundred thousand pounds to leave. What happens to that money?'

'It goes back into the firm. Or rather, I should say, it goes to the residuary legatee.'

'And the residuary legatee is Mr Percival Fortescue.'

'That's right,' said Billingsley, 'it goes to Percival Fortescue. And with the state the firm's affairs are in,' he added unguardedly, 'I should say that he'll need it!'

IV

'The things you policemen want to know,' said Inspector Neele's doctor friend.

'Come on, Bob, spill it.'

'Well, as we're alone together you can't quote me, fortunately! But I should say, you know, that your idea's dead right. GPI by the sound of it all. The family suspected it and wanted to get him to see a doctor. He wouldn't. It acts just in the way you describe. Loss of judgment, megalomania, violent fits of irritation and anger – boastfulness – delusions of grandeur – of being a great financial genius. Anyone suffering from that would soon put a solvent firm on the rocks – unless he could be restrained – and that's not so easy to do – especially if the man himself has an idea of what you're after. Yes – I should say it was a bit of luck for your friends that he died.'

'They're no friends of mine,' said Neele. He repeated what he had once said before:

'*They're all very unpleasant people. . . .*'

—— 19 ——

In the drawing-room at Yewtree Lodge, the whole Fortescue family was assembled. Percival Fortescue, leaning against the mantelpiece was addressing the meeting.

'It's all very well,' said Percival. 'But the whole position is most unsatisfactory. The police come and go and don't tell us anything. One supposes they're pursuing some line of research. In the meantime everything's at a standstill. One can't make plans, one can't arrange things for the future.'

'It's all so inconsiderate,' said Jennifer. 'And so stupid.'

'There still seems to be this ban against anyone leaving the house,' went on Percival. 'Still, I think among ourselves we might discuss future plans. What about you, Elaine? I gather you're going to marry – what's-his-name – Gerald Wright? Have you any idea when?'

'As soon as possible,' said Elaine.

Percival frowned.

'You mean, in about six months' time?'

'No, I don't. Why should we wait six months?'

'I think it would be more decent,' said Percival.

'Rubbish,' said Elaine. 'A month. That's the longest we'll wait.'

'Well, it's for you to say,' said Percival. 'And what are your plans when you are married, if you have any?'

'We're thinking of starting a school.'

Percival shook his head.

'That's a very risky speculation in these times. What with the shortage of domestic labour, the difficulty of getting an adequate teaching staff – really, Elaine, it sounds all right. But I should think twice about it if I were you.'

'We have thought. Gerald feels that the whole future of this country lies in right education.'

'I am seeing Mr Billingsley the day after tomorrow,' said Percival. 'We've got to go into various questions of finance. He was suggesting that you might like to make this money that's been left to you by father into a trust for yourself and your children. It's a very sound thing to do nowadays.'

'I don't want to do that,' said Elaine. 'We shall need the money to start up our school. There's a very suitable house we've heard of for sale. It's in Cornwall. Beautiful grounds and quite a good house. It would have to be built on to a good deal – several wings added.'

'You mean – you mean you're going to take all your money out of the business? Really, Elaine, I *don't* think you're wise.'

'Much wiser to take it out than leave it in, I should say,' said Elaine. 'Businesses are going phut all over the place. You said yourself, Val, before father died, that things were getting into a pretty bad state.'

'One says that sort of thing,' said Percival vaguely, 'but I must say, Elaine, to take out all your capital and sink it in the buying, equipping and running of a school is crazy. If it's not a success look what happens? You're left without a penny.'

'It *will* be a success,' said Elaine, doggedly.

'I'm with you.' Lance, lying sprawled out in a chair, spoke up encouragingly. 'Have a crack at it, Elaine. In my opinion it'll be a damned odd sort of school, but it's what you want to do – you and Gerald. If you do lose your money you'll at any rate have had the satisfaction of doing what you wanted to do.'

'Just what one might have expected you to say, Lance,' said Percival, acidly.

'I know, I know,' said Lance. 'I'm the spendthrift prodigal son. But I still think I've had more fun out of life than you have, Percy, old boy.'

'It depends on what you call fun,' said Percival coldly. 'Which brings us to your own plans, Lance. I suppose you'll be off again back to Kenya – or Canada – or climbing Mount Everest or something fairly fantastic?'

'Now what makes you think that?' said Lance.

'Well, you've never had much use for a stay-at-home life in England, have you?'

'One changes as one gets older,' said Lance. 'One settles down. D'you know, Percy my boy, I'm quite looking forward to having a crack at being a sober business man.'

'Do you mean . . .'

'I mean I'm coming into the firm with you, old boy.' Lance grinned. 'Oh, you're the senior partner, of course. You've got the lion's share. I'm only a very junior partner. But I *have* got a holding in it that gives me the right to be in on things, doesn't it?'

'Well – yes – of course, if you put it that way. But I can assure you, my dear boy, you'll be very, very bored.'

'I wonder now. I don't believe I shall be bored.'

Percival frowned.

'You don't seriously mean, Lance, that you're coming into the business?'

'Having a finger in the pie? Yes, that's exactly what I am doing.'

Percival shook his head.

'Things are in a very bad way, you know. You'll find that out. It's going to be about all we can do to pay out Elaine her share, if she insists on having it paid out.'

'There you are, Elaine,' said Lance. 'You see how wise you were to insist on grabbing your money while it's still there to grab.'

'Really, Lance,' Percival spoke angrily, 'these jokes of yours are in very bad taste.'

'I do think, Lance, you might be more careful what you say,' said Jennifer.

Sitting a little way away near the window, Pat studied them one by one. If this was what Lance had meant by twisting Percival's tail, she could see that he was achieving his object. Percival's neat impassivity was quite ruffled. He snapped again, angrily:

'Are you serious, Lance?'

'Dead serious.'

'It won't work, you know. You'll soon get fed up.'

'Not me. Think what a lovely change it'll be for me. A city office, typists coming and going. I shall have a blonde secretary like Miss Grosvenor – is it Grosvenor? I suppose you've snaffled her. But I shall get one just like her. "Yes, Mr Lancelot; no, Mr Lancelot. Your tea, Mr Lancelot." '

'Oh, don't play the fool,' snapped Percival.

'Why are you so angry, my dear brother? Don't you look forward to having me sharing your city cares?'

'You haven't the least conception of the mess everything's in.'

'No. You'll have to put me wise to all that.'

'First you've got to understand that for the last six months – no, more, a year, father's not been himself. He's done the most incredibly foolish things, financially. Sold out good stock, acquired various wild-cat holdings. Sometimes he's really thrown away money hand over fist. Just, one might say, for the fun of spending it.'

'In fact,' said Lance, 'it's just as well for the family that he had taxine in his tea.'

'That's a very ugly way of putting it, but in essence you're quite right. It's about the only thing that saved us from bankruptcy. But we shall have to be extremely conservative and go very cautiously for a bit.'

Lance shook his head.

'I don't agree with you. Caution never does anyone any good. You must take a few risks, strike out. You must go for something big.'

'I don't agree,' said Percy. 'Caution and economy. Those are our watchwords.'

'Not mine,' said Lance.

'You're only the junior partner, remember,' said Percival.

'All right, all right. But I've got a little say-so all the same.'

Percival walked up and down the room agitatedly.

'It's no good, Lance. I'm fond of you and all that—'

'Are you?' Lance interpolated. Percival did not appear to hear him.

'. . . but I really don't think we're going to pull together at all. Our outlooks are totally different.'

'That may be an advantage,' said Lance.

'The only sensible thing,' said Percival, 'is to dissolve the partnership.'

'You're going to buy me out – is that the idea?'

'My dear boy, it's the only sensible thing to do, with our ideas so different.'

'If you find it hard to pay Elaine out her legacy, how are you going to manage to pay me my share?'

'Well, I didn't mean in cash,' said Percival. 'We could – er – divide up the holdings.'

'With you keeping the gilt-edged and me taking the worst of the speculative off you, I suppose?'

'They seem to be what you prefer,' said Percival.

Lance grinned suddenly.

'You're right in a way, Percy, old boy. But I can't indulge my own taste entirely. I've got Pat here to think of.'

Both men looked towards her. Pat opened her mouth, then shut it again. Whatever game Lance was playing, it was best that she should not interfere. That Lance was driving at something special, she was quite sure, but she was still a little uncertain as to what his actual object was.

'Line 'em up, Percy,' said Lance, laughing. 'Bogus Diamond Mines, Inaccessible Rubies, the Oil Concessions where no oil is. Do you think I'm quite as big a fool as I look?'

Percival said:

'Of course, some of these holdings are highly speculative, but remember, they *may* turn out immensely valuable.'

'Changed your tune, haven't you?' said Lance, grinning. 'Going to offer me father's latest wildcat acquisition as well as the old Blackbird Mine and things of that kind. By the way, has the Inspector been asking you about this Blackbird Mine?'

Percival frowned.

'Yes, he did. I can't imagine what he wanted to know about it. I couldn't tell him much. You and I were children at the time. I just remember vaguely that father went out there and came back saying the whole thing was no good.'

'What was it – a gold mine?'

'I believe so. Father came back pretty certain that there was no gold there. And, mind you, he wasn't the sort of man to be mistaken.'

'Who got him into it? A man called MacKenzie, wasn't it?'

'Yes. MacKenzie died out there.'

'MacKenzie died out there,' said Lance thoughtfully. 'Wasn't there a terrific scene? I seem to remember . . . Mrs MacKenzie, wasn't it? Came here. Ranted and stormed at father. Hurled down curses on his head. She accused him, if I remember rightly, of murdering her husband.'

'Really,' said Percival repressively. 'I can't recollect anything of the kind.'

'I remember it, though,' said Lance. 'I was a good bit younger than you, of course. Perhaps that's why it appealed to me. As a child it struck me as full of drama. Where was Blackbird? West Africa wasn't it?'

'Yes, I think so.'

'I must look up the concession sometime,' said Lance, 'when I'm at the office.'

'You can be quite sure,' said Percival, 'that father made no mistake. If he came back saying there was no gold, there was no gold.'

'You're probably right there,' said Lance. 'Poor Mrs MacKenzie. I wonder what happened to her and to those two kids she brought along. Funny – they must be grown up by now.'

—— 20 ——

At the Pinewood Private Sanatorium, Inspector Neele, sitting in the visitors' parlour, was facing a grey-haired, elderly lady. Helen MacKenzie was sixty-three, though she looked younger. She had pale blue, rather vacant-looking eyes, and a weak, indeterminate chin. She had a long upper lip which occasionally twitched. She held a large book in her lap and was looking down at it as Inspector Neele talked to her. In Inspector Neele's mind was the conversation he had just had with Doctor Crosbie, the head of the establishment.

'She's a voluntary patient, of course,' said Doctor Crosbie, 'not certified.'

'She's not dangerous, then?'

'Oh, no. Most of the time she's as sane to talk to as you or me. It's one of her good periods now so that you'll be able to have a perfectly normal conversation with her.'

Bearing this in mind, Inspector Neele started his first conversational essay.

'It's very kind of you to see me, madam,' he said. 'My name is Neele. I've come to see you about a Mr Fortescue who has recently died. A Mr Rex Fortescue. I expect you know the name.'

Mrs MacKenzie's eyes were fixed on her book. She said:

'I don't know what you're talking about.'

'Mr Fortescue, madam. Mr Rex Fortescue.'

'No,' said Mrs MacKenzie. 'No. Certainly not.'

Inspector Neele was slightly taken aback. He wondered whether this was what Doctor Crosbie called being completely normal.

'I think, Mrs MacKenzie, you knew him a good many years ago.'

'Not really,' said Mrs MacKenzie. 'It was yesterday.'

'I see,' said Inspector Neele, falling back upon his formula rather uncertainly. 'I believe,' he went on, 'that you paid him a visit many years ago at his residence, Yewtree Lodge.'

'A very ostentatious house,' said Mrs MacKenzie.

'Yes. Yes, you might call it that. He had been connected with your husband, I believe, over a certain mine in Africa. The Blackbird Mine, I believe it was called.'

'I have to read my book,' said Mrs MacKenzie. 'There's not much time and I have to read my book.'

'Yes, madam. Yes, I quite see that.' There was a pause, then Inspector Neele went on, 'Mr MacKenzie and Mr Fortescue went out together to Africa to survey the mine.'

'It was my husband's mine,' said Mrs MacKenzie. 'He found it and staked a claim to it. He wanted money to capitalise it. He went to Rex Fortescue. If I'd been wiser, if I'd known more, I wouldn't have let him do it.'

'No, I see that. As it was, they went out together to Africa, and there your husband died of fever.'

'I must read my book,' said Mrs MacKenzie.

'Do you think Mr Fortescue swindled your husband over the Blackbird Mine, Mrs MacKenzie?'

Without raising her eyes from the book, Mrs MacKenzie said:

'How stupid you are.'

'Yes, yes, I dare say. . . . But you see it's all a long time ago and making inquiries about a thing that is over a long time ago is rather difficult.'

'Who said it was over?'

'I see. You don't think it is over?'

'*No question is ever settled until it is settled right.* Kipling said that. Nobody reads Kipling nowadays, but he was a great man.'

'Do you think the question will be settled right one of these days?'

'Rex Fortescue is dead, isn't he? You said so.'

'He was poisoned,' said Inspector Neele.

Rather disconcertingly, Mrs MacKenzie laughed.

'What nonsense,' she said, 'he died of fever.'

'I'm talking about Mr Rex Fortescue.'

'So am I.' She looked up suddenly and her pale blue eyes

fixed his. 'Come now,' she said, 'he died in his bed, didn't he? He died in his bed?'

'He died in St Jude's Hospital,' said Inspector Neele.

'Nobody knows where my husband died,' said Mrs MacKenzie. 'Nobody knows how he died or where he was buried. . . . All anyone knows is what Rex Fortescue *said*. And Rex Fortescue was a liar!'

'Do you think there may have been foul play?'

'Foul play, foul play, fowls lay eggs, don't they?'

'You think that Rex Fortescue was responsible for your husband's death?'

'I had an egg for breakfast this morning,' said Mrs MacKenzie. 'Quite fresh, too. Surprising, isn't it, when one thinks that it was thirty years ago?'

Neele drew a deep breath. It seemed unlikely that he was ever going to get anywhere at this rate, but he persevered.

'Somebody put dead blackbirds on Rex Fortescue's desk about a month or two before he died.'

'That's interesting. That's very, very interesting.'

'Have you any idea, madam, who might have done that?'

'Ideas aren't any help to one. One has to have action. I brought them up for that, you know, to take action.'

'You're talking about your children?'

She nodded her head rapidly.

'Yes. Donald and Ruby. They were nine and seven and left without a father. I told them. I told them every day. I made them swear it every night.'

Inspector Neele leant forward.

'What did you make them swear?'

'That't they'd kill him, of course.'

'I see.'

Inspector Neele spoke as though it was the most reasonable remark in the world.

'Did they?'

'Donald went to Dunkirk. He never came back. They sent me a wire saying he was dead, "Deeply regret killed in action." Action, you see, the wrong kind of action.'

'I'm sorry to hear that, madam. What about your daughter?'

'I haven't got a daughter,' said Mrs MacKenzie.

'You spoke of her just now,' said Neele. 'Your daughter, Ruby.'

'Ruby. Yes, Ruby.' She leaned forward. 'Do you know what I've done to Ruby?'

4

'No, madam. What have you done to her?'

She whispered suddenly:

'Look here at the Book.'

He saw then that what she was holding in her lap was a Bible. It was a very old Bible and as she opened it, on the front page, Inspector Neele saw that various names had been written. It was obviously a family Bible in which the old-fashioned custom had been continued of entering each new birth. Mrs MacKenzie's thin forefinger pointed to the two last names. 'Donald MacKenzie' with the date of his birth, and 'Ruby MacKenzie' with the date of hers. But a thick line was drawn through Ruby MacKenzie's name.

'You see?' said Mrs MacKenzie. 'I struck her out of the Book. I cut her off for ever! The Recording Angel won't find her name there.'

'You cut her name out of the book? Now, why, madam?'

Mrs MacKenzie looked at him cunningly.

'You know why,' she said.

'But I don't. Really, madam, I don't.'

'She didn't keep faith. You know she didn't keep faith.'

'Where is your daughter now, madam?'

'I've told you. I have no daughter. There isn't such a person as Ruby MacKenzie any longer.'

'You mean she's dead?'

'Dead?' The woman laughed suddenly. 'It would be better for her if she were dead. Much better. Much, much better.' She sighed and turned restlessly in her seat. Then her manner reverted to a kind of formal courtesy, she said, 'I'm so sorry, but really I'm afraid I can't talk to you any longer. You see, the time is getting very short, and I *must* read my book.'

To Inspector Neele's further remarks Mrs MacKenzie returned no reply. She merely made a faint gesture of annoyance and continued to read her Bible with her finger following the line of the verse she was reading.

Neele got up and left. He had another brief interview with the Superintendent.

'Do any of her relations come to see her?' he asked. 'A daughter, for instance?'

'I believe a daughter did come to see her in my predecessor's time, but her visit agitated the patient so much that he advised her not to come again. Since then everything is arranged through solicitors.'

'And you've no idea where this Ruby MacKenzie is now?'

The Superintendent shook his head.

'No idea whatsoever.'

'You've no idea whether she's married, for instance?'

'I don't know, all I can do is to give you the address of the solicitors who deal with us.'

Inspector Neele had already tracked down those solicitors. They were unable, or said they were unable, to tell him anything. A trust fund had been established for Mrs MacKenzie which they managed. These arrangements had been made some years previously and they had not seen Miss MacKenzie since.

Inspector Neele tried to get a description of Ruby MacKenzie but the results were not encouraging. So many relations came to visit patients that after a lapse of years they were bound to be remembered dimly, with the appearance of one mixed up with the appearance of another. The Matron who had been there for many years, seemed to remember that Miss MacKenzie was small and dark. The only other nurse who had been there for any length of time recalled that she was heavily built and fair.

'So there we are, sir,' said Inspector Neele as he reported to the Assistant Commissioner. 'There's a whole crazy set-up and it fits together. It *must* mean something.'

The AC nodded thoughtfully.

'The blackbirds in the pie tying up with the Blackbird Mine, rye in the dead man's pocket, bread and honey with Adele Fortescue's tea – (not that that is conclusive. After all, anyone might have had bread and honey for tea!) The third murder, that girl strangled with a stocking and a clothes peg nipped on to her nose. Yes, crazy as the set-up is, it certainly can't be ignored.'

'Half a minute, sir,' said Inspector Neele.

'What is it?'

Neele was frowning.

'You know, what you've just said. It didn't ring true. It was wrong somewhere.' He shook his head and sighed. 'No. I can't place it.'

—— 21 ——

Lance and Pat wandered round the well kept grounds surrounding Yewtree Lodge.

'I hope I'm not hurting your feelings, Lance,' Pat murmured, 'if I say this is quite the nastiest garden I've ever been in.'

'It won't hurt my feelings,' said Lance. 'Is it? Really I don't know. It seems to have three gardeners working on it very industriously.'

Pat said:

'Probably that's what's wrong with it. No expense spared, no signs of any individual taste. All the right rhododendrons and all the right bedding out done in the proper season, I expect.'

'Well, what would *you* put in an English garden, Pat, if you had one?'

'My garden,' said Pat, 'would have hollyhocks, lark-spurs and Canterbury bells, no bedding out and none of these horrible yews.'

She glanced up at the dark yew hedges, disparagingly.

'Association of ideas,' said Lance easily.

'There's something awfully frightening about a poisoner,' said Pat. 'I mean it must be a horrid, brooding, revengeful mind.'

'So that's how you see it? Funny! I just think of it as business-like and cold-blooded.'

'I suppose one could look at it that way.' She resumed, with a slight shiver, 'All the same to do *three* murders . . . Whoever did it *must* be mad.'

'Yes,' said Lance, in a low voice. 'I'm afraid so.' Then breaking out sharply, he said, 'For God's sake, Pat, do go away from here. Go back to London. Go down to Devonshire or up to the Lakes. Go to Stratford-on-Avon or go and look at the Norfolk Broads. The police wouldn't mind your going – you had nothing to do with all this. You were in Paris when the old man was killed and in London when the other two died. I tell you it worries me to death to have you here.'

Pat paused a moment before saying quietly:

'You know who it is, don't you?'

'No, I don't.'

'But you *think* you know. . . . That's why you're frightened for me . . . I wish you'd tell me.'

'I can't tell you. I don't know anything. But I wish to God you'd go away from here.'

'Darling,' said Pat. 'I'm not going. I'm staying here. For better, for worse. That's how I feel about it.' She added, with a sudden catch in her voice, 'Only with me its always for worse.'

'What on earth do you mean, Pat?'

'I bring bad luck. That's what I mean. I bring bad luck to anybody I come in contact with.'

'My dear adorable nitwit, you haven't brought bad luck to me. Look how after I married you the old man sent for me to come home and make friends with him.'

'Yes, and what happened when you did come home? I tell you, I'm unlucky to people.'

'Look here, my sweet, you've got a thing about all this. It's superstition, pure and simple.'

'I can't help it. Some people do bring bad luck. I'm one of them.'

Lance took her by the shoulders and shook her violently. 'You're my Pat and to be married to you is the greatest luck in the world. So get that into your silly head.' Then, calming down, he said in a more sober voice, 'But, seriously, Pat, do be very careful. If there *is* someone unhinged round here, I don't want you to be the one who stops the bullet or drinks the henbane.'

'Or drinks the henbane as you say.'

'When I'm not around, stick to that old lady. What's-her-name Marple. Why do you think Aunt Effie asked her to stay here?'

'Goodness knows why Aunt Effie does anything. Lance, how long are *we* going to stay here?'

Lance shrugged his shoulders.

'Difficult to say.'

'I don't think,' said Pat, 'that we're really awfully welcome.' She hesitated as she spoke the words. 'The house belongs to your brother now, I suppose? He doesn't really want us here, does he?'

Lance chuckled suddenly.

'Not he, but he's got to stick us for the present at any rate.'

'And afterwards? What are we going to do, Lance? Are we going back to East Africa or what?'

'Is that what you'd like to do, Pat?'

She nodded vigorously.

'That's lucky,' said Lance, 'because it's what I'd like to do, too. I don't take much to this country nowadays.'

Pat's face brightened.

'How lovely. From what you said the other day, I was afraid you might want to stop here.'

A devilish glint appeared in Lance's eyes.

'You're to hold your tongue about our plans, Pat,' he said. 'I have it in my mind to twist dear brother Percival's tail a bit.'

'Oh, Lance, do be careful.'

'I'll be careful, my sweet, but I don't see why old Percy should get away with everything.'

II

With her head a little on one side looking like an amiable cockatoo, Miss Marple sat in the large drawing-room listening to Mrs Percival Fortescue. Miss Marple looked particularly incongruous in the drawing-room. Her light spare figure was alien to the vast brocaded sofa in which she sat with its many-hued cushions strewn round her. Miss Marple sat very upright because she had been taught to use a back-board as a girl, and not to loll. In a large armchair beside her, dressed in elaborate black, was Mrs Percival, talking away volubly at nineteen to the dozen. 'Exactly,' thought Miss Marple, 'like poor Mrs Emmett, the bank manager's wife.' She remembered how one day Mrs Emmett had come to call and talk about the selling arrangements for Poppy Day, and how after the preliminary business had been settled, Mrs Emmett had suddenly begun to talk and talk and talk. Mrs Emmett occupied rather a difficult position in St Mary Mead. She did not belong to the old guard of ladies in reduced circumstances who lived in neat houses round the church, and who knew intimately all the ramifications of the county families even though they might not be strictly county themselves. Mr Emmett, the bank manager, had undeniably married beneath him and the result was that his wife was in a position of great loneliness since she could not, of course, associate with the wives of the trades people. Snobbery here raised its hideous head and marooned Mrs Emmett on a permanent island of loneliness.

The necessity to talk grew upon Mrs Emmett, and on that particular day it had burst its bounds, and Miss Marple had received the full flood of the torrent. She had been sorry for Mrs Emmett then, and today she was rather sorry for Mrs Percival Fortescue.

Mrs Percival had had a lot of grievances to bear and the relief of airing them to a more or less total stranger was enormous.

'Of course I never want to complain,' said Mrs Percival. 'I've never been of the complaining kind. What I always say is that one must put up with things. What can't be cured must be endured and I'm sure I've never said a word to *anyone*. It's really difficult to know who I *could* have spoken to. In some ways one is very isolated here – very isolated. It's very convenient, of course, and a great saving of expense to have our own set of rooms in this house. But of course it's not at all like having a place of your own. I'm sure you agree.'

Miss Marple said she agreed.

'Fortunately our new house is almost ready to move into. It is a question really of getting the painters and decorators out. These men are so slow. My husband, of course, has been quite satisfied living here. But then it's different for a man. That's what I always say – it's so different for a man. Don't you agree?'

Miss Marple agreed that it was very different for a man. She could say this without a qualm as it was what she really believed. 'The gentlemen' were, in Miss Marple's mind, in a totally different category to her own sex. They required two eggs plus bacon for breakfast, three good nuorishing meals a day and were never to be contradicted or argued with before dinner. Mrs Percival went on:

'My husband, you see, is away all day in the city. When he comes home he's just tired and wants to sit down and read. But I, on the contrary, am alone here all day with no congenial company *at all*. I've been perfectly comfortable and all that. Excellent food. But what I do feel one needs is a really pleasant social circle. The people round here are really not my kind. Part of them are what I call a flashy, bridge-playing lot. Not *nice* bridge. I like a hand at bridge myself as well as anyone, but of course, they're all very rich down here. They play for enormously high stakes, and there's a great deal of drinking. In fact, the sort of life that I call really fast society. Then, of course, there's a sprinkling of – well, you can only call them *old pussies* who love to potter round with a trowel and do gardening.'

Miss Marple looked slightly guilty since she was herself an inveterate gardener.

'I don't want to say anything against the dead,' resumed Mrs Percy rapidly, 'but there's no doubt about it, Mr Fortescue, my father-in-law, I mean, made a very foolish second marriage. My – well I can't call her my mother-in-law, she was the same age as I am. The real truth of it is she was man-mad. Absolutely man-mad. And the way she spent money! My father-in-law

was an absolute fool about her. Didn't care what bills she ran
up. It vexed Percy very much, very much indeed. Percy is
always so careful about money matters. He hates waste. And
then what with Mr Fortescue being so peculiar and so bad
tempered, flashing out in these terrible rages, spending money
like water backing wildcat schemes. Well – it wasn't at all nice.'

Miss Marple ventured upon making a remark.

'That must have worried your husband, too?'

'Oh, yes, it did. For the last year Percy's been very worried
indeed. It's really made him quite different. His manner, you
know, changed even towards me. Sometimes when I talked to
him he used not to answer.' Mrs Percy sighed, then went on,
'Then Elaine, my sister-in-law, you know, she's a *very* odd sort
of girl. Very out of doors and all that. Not exactly unfriendly,
but not sympathetic, you know. She never wanted to go to London and shop, or go to a matinée or anything of that kind. She
wasn't even interested in clothes.' Mrs Percival sighed again
and murmured, 'But of course I don't want to complain in any
way.' A qualm of compunction came over her. She said, hurriedly: 'You must think it most odd, talking to you like this
when you are a comparative stranger. But really, what with all
the strain and shock – I think really it's the shock that matters
most. Delayed shock. I feel so nervous, you know, that I really –
well, I really must speak to *someone*. You remind me so much of
a dear old lady, Miss Trefusis James. She fractured her femur
when she was seventy-five. It was a very long business nursing
her and we became great friends. She gave me a fox fur cape
when I left and I did think it was kind of her.'

'I know just how you feel,' said Miss Marple.

And this again was true. Mrs Percival's husband was obviously
bored by her and paid very little attention to her, and the poor
woman had managed to make no local friends. Running up to
London and shopping, matinées and a luxurious house to live
in did not make up for the lack of humanity in her relations
with her husband's family.

'I hope it's not rude of me to say so,' said Miss Marple in a
gentle old lady's voice, 'but I really feel that the late Mr Fortescue cannot have been a very nice man.'

'He wasn't,' said his daughter-in-law. 'Quite frankly my dear,
between you and me, he was a detestable old man. I don't
wonder – I really don't that someone put him out of the way.'

'You've no idea at all who—' began Miss Marple and broke

515

off. 'Oh dear, perhaps this is a question I should not ask – **not** even an idea who – who – well, who it might have been?'

'Oh, I think it was that horrible man, Crump,' said Mrs Percival. 'I've always disliked him very much. He's got a manner, not really rude, you know, but yet it *is* rude. Impertinent, that's more it.'

'Still, there would have to be a motive, I suppose.'

'I really don't know that that sort of person requires much motive. I dare say Mr Fortescue ticked him off about something, and I rather suspect that sometimes he drinks too much. But what I really think is that he's a bit unbalanced, you know. Like that footman, or butler, whoever it was, who went round the house shooting everybody. Of course, to be quite honest with you, I *did* suspect that it was *Adele* who poisoned Mr Fortescue. But now, of course, one can't suspect that since she's been poisoned herself. She may have accused Crump, you know. And then he lost his head and perhaps managed to put something in the sandwiches and Gladys saw him do it and so he killed her too – I think it's really dangerous having him in the house at all. Oh dear, I wish I could get away, but I suppose those horrible policemen won't let one do anything of the kind.' She leant forward impulsively and put a plump hand on Miss Marple's arm. 'Sometimes I feel I must get away – that if it doesn't all stop soon I shall – I shall actually *run away*.'

She leant back studying Miss Marple's face.

'But perhaps – that wouldn't be wise?'

'No – I don't think it would be very wise – the police could soon find you, you know.'

'Could they? Could they really? You think they're clever enough for that?'

'It is very foolish to under-estimate the police. Inspector Neele strikes me as a particularly intelligent man.'

'Oh! I thought he was rather stupid.'

Miss Marple shook her head.

'I can't help feeling' – Jennifer Fortescue hesitated – 'that it's dangerous to stay here.'

'Dangerous for you, you mean?'

'Ye-es – well, yes—'

'Because of something you – know?'

Mrs Percival seemed to take breath.

'Oh no – of course I don't know anything. What should I know? It's just – just that I'm nervous. That man Crump—'

But it was not, Miss Marple thought, of Crump that Mrs

Percival Fortescue was thinking – watching the clenching and unclenching of Jennifer's hands. Miss Marple thought that for some reason Jennifer Fortescue was very badly frightened indeed.

—— 22 ——

It was growing dark. Miss Marple had taken her knitting over to the window in the library. Looking out of the glass pane she saw Pat Fortescue walking up and down the terrace outside. Miss Marple unlatched the window and called through it.

'Come in, my dear. Do come in. I'm sure it's much too cold and damp for you to be out there without a coat on.'

Pat obeyed the summons. She came in and shut the window and turned on two of the lamps.

'Yes,' she said, 'it's not a very nice afternoon.' She sat down on the sofa by Miss Marple. 'What are you knitting?'

'Oh, just a little matinée coat, dear. For a baby, you know. I always say young mothers can't have too many matinée coats for their babies. It's the second size. I always knit the second size. Babies so soon grow out of the first size.'

Pat stretched out long legs towards the fire.

'It's nice in here today,' she said. 'With the fire and the lamps and you knitting things for babies. It all seems cosy and homely and like England ought to be.'

'It's like England is,' said Miss Marple. 'There are not so many Yewtree Lodges, my dear.'

'I think that's a good thing,' said Pat. 'I don't believe this was ever a happy house. I don't believe anybody was ever happy in it, in spite of all the money they spent and the things they had.'

'No,' Miss Marple agreed. 'I shouldn't say it had been a happy house.'

'I suppose Adele may have been happy,' said Pat. 'I never met her, of course, so I don't know, but Jennifer is pretty miserable and Elaine's been eating her heart out over a young man whom she probably knows in her heart of hearts doesn't care for her. Oh, *how* I want to get away from here!' She looked at Miss Marple and smiled suddenly. 'D'you know,' she said, 'that Lance told me to stick as close to you as I could. He seemed to think I should be safe that way.'

'Your husband's no fool,' said Miss Marple.

'No. Lance isn't a fool. At least, he is in some ways. But I wish he'd tell me exactly what he's afraid of. One thing seems clear enough. Somebody in this house is mad, and madness is always frightening because you don't know how mad people's minds will work. You don't know what they'll do next.'

'My poor child,' said Miss Marple.

'Oh, I'm all right, really. I ought to be tough enough by now.'

Miss Marple said gently:

'You've had a good deal of unhappiness, haven't you, my dear?'

'Oh, I've had some very good times, too. I had a lovely childhood in Ireland, riding, hunting, and a great big, bare, draughty house with lots and lots of sun in it. If you've had a happy childhood, nobody can take that away from you, can they? It was afterwards – when I grew up – that things seemed always to go wrong. To begin with, I suppose, it was the war.'

'Your husband was a fighter pilot, wasn't he?'

'Yes. We'd only been married about a month when Don was shot down.' She stared ahead of her into the fire. 'I thought at first I wanted to die too. It seemed so unfair, so cruel. And yet – in the end – I almost began to see that it had been the best thing. Don was wonderful in the war. Brave and reckless and gay. He had all the qualities that are needed, wanted in a war. But I don't believe, somehow, peace would have suited him. He had a kind of – oh, how shall I put it? – arrogant insubordination. He wouldn't have fitted in or settled down. He'd have fought against things. He was – well, anti-social in a way. No, he wouldn't have fitted in.'

'It's wise of you to see that, my dear.' Miss Marple bent over her knitting, picked up a stitch, counted under her breath, 'Three plain, two purl, slip one, knit two together,' and then said aloud: 'And your second husband, my dear?'

'Freddy? Freddy shot himself.'

'Oh ear. How very sad. What a tragedy.'

'We were very happy together,' said Pat. 'I began to realize, about two years after we were married, that Freddy wasn't – well, wasn't always straight. I began to find out the sort of things that were going on. But it didn't seem to matter, between us two, that is. Because, you see, Freddy loved me and I loved

him. I tried not to know what was going on. That was cowardly
of me, I suppose, but I couldn't have changed him you know.
You can't change people.'

'No,' said Miss Marple, 'you can't change people.'

'I'd taken him and loved him and married him for what he
was, and I sort of felt that I just had to – put up with it. Then
things went wrong and he couldn't face it, and he shot himself.
After he died I went out to Kenya to stay with some friends
there. I couldn't stop on in England and go on meeting all –
all the old crowd that knew about it all. And out in Kenya I
met Lance.' Her face changed and softened. She went on looking into the fire, and Miss Marple looked at her. Presently
Pat turned her head and said, 'Tell me, Miss Marple, what do
you really think of Percival?'

'Well, I've not seen very much of him. Just at breakfast
usually. That's all. I don't think he very much likes my being
here.'

Pat laughed suddenly.

'He's mean, you know. Terribly mean about money. Lance
says he always was. Jennifer complains of it, too. Goes over the
housekeeping accounts with Miss Dove. Complaining of every
item. But Miss Dove manages to hold her own. She's really
rather a wonderful person. Don't you think so?'

'Yes, indeed. She reminds me of Mrs Latimer in my own
village, St Mary Mead. She ran the WVS, you know, and the
Girl Guides, and indeed, she ran practically everything there.
It wasn't for quite five years that we discovered that – oh, but
I mustn't gossip. Nothing is more boring than people talking
to you about places and people whom you've never seen and
know nothing about. You must forgive me, my dear.'

'Is St Mary Mead a very nice village?'

'Well, I don't know what you would call a nice village, my
dear. It's quite a *pretty* village. There are some nice people living in it and some extremely unpleasant people as well. Very
curious things go on there just as in any other village. Human
nature is much the same everywhere, is it not?'

'You go up and see Miss Ramsbottom a good deal, don't you?'
said Pat. 'Now she *really* frightens me.'

'Frightens you? Why?'

'Because I think she's crazy. I think she's got religious mania.
You don't think she could be – really – *mad*, do you?'

'In what way, mad?'

'Oh, you know what I mean, Miss Marple, well enough. She

sits up there and never goes out, and broods about sin. Well, she might have felt in the end that it was her mission in life to execute judgment.'

'Is that what your husband thinks?'

'I don't know what Lance thinks. He won't tell me. But I'm quite sure of one thing – that he believes that it's someone who's mad, and it's someone in the family. Well, Percival's sane enough, I should say. Jennifer's just stupid and rather pathetic. She's a bit nervy but that's all, and Elaine is one of those queer, tempestuous, tense girls. She's desperately in love with this young man of hers and she'll never admit to herself for a moment that he's marrying her for her money.'

'You think he is marrying her for money?'

'Yes, I do. Don't you think so?'

'I should say quite certainly,' said Miss Marple. 'Like young Ellis who married Marion Bates, the rich ironmonger's daughter. She was a very plain girl and absolutely besotted about him. However, it turned out quite well. People like young Ellis and this Gerald Wright are only really disagreeable when they've married a poor girl for love. They are so annoyed with themselves for doing it that they take it out of the girl. But if they marry a rich girl they continue to respect her.'

'I don't see,' went on Pat, frowning, 'how it can be anybody from outside. And so – and so that accounts for the atmosphere that is here. Everyone watching everybody else. Only something's got to happen soon—'

'There won't be any more deaths,' said Miss Marple. 'At least, I shouldn't think so.'

'You can't be sure of that.'

'Well, as a matter of fact, I am fairly sure. The murderer's accomplished his purpose, you see.'

'His?'

'Well, his or her. One says his for convenience.'

'You say his or her purpose. What sort of purpose?'

Miss Marple shook her head – she was not yet quite sure herself.

—— 23 ——

Once again Miss Somers had just made tea in the typists' room, and once again the kettle had not been boiling when Miss Somers poured the water on to the tea. History repeats itself. Miss Griffith, accepting her cup, thought to herself, 'I really *must* speak to Mr Percival about Somers. I'm sure we can do better. But with all this terrible business going on, one doesn't like to bother him over office details.'

As so often before Miss Griffith said sharply:

'Water not boiling *again*, Somers,' and Miss Somers, going pink, replied in her usual formula:

'Oh, dear, I was sure it was boiling *this* time.'

Further developments on the same line were interrupted by the entrance of Lance Fortescue. He looked round him somewhat vaguely, and Miss Griffith, jumped up, came forward to meet him.

'Mr Lance,' she exclaimed.

He swung round towards her and his face lit up in a smile.

'Hallo. Why, it's Miss Griffith.'

Miss Griffith was delighted. Eleven years since he had seen her and he knew her name. She said in a confused voice:

'Fancy you remembering.'

And Lance said easily, with all his charm to the fore:

'Of course I remember.'

A flicker of excitement was running round the typists' room. Miss Somers's troubles over the tea were forgotten. She was gaping at Lance with her mouth slightly open. Miss Bell gazed eagerly over the top of her typewriter and Miss Chase unobtrusively drew out her compact and powdered her nose. Lance Fortescue looked round him.

'So everything's still going on just the same here,' he said.

'Not many changes, Mr Lance. How brown you look and how well! I suppose you must have had a very interesting life abroad.'

'You could call it that,' said Lance, 'but perhaps I am now going to try and have an interesting life in London.'

'You're coming back here to the office?'

'Maybe.'

'Oh, but how delightful.'

'You'll find me very rusty,' said Lance. 'You'll have to show me all the ropes, Miss Griffith.'

Miss Griffith laughed delightedly.

'It will be very nice to have you back, Mr Lance. Very nice indeed.'

Lance threw her an appreciative glance.

'That's sweet of you,' he said, 'that's very sweet of you.'

'We never believed – none of us thought . . .' Miss Griffith broke off and flushed.

Lance patted her on the arm.

'You didn't believe the devil was as black as he was painted? Well, perhaps he wasn't. But that's all old history now. There's no good going back over it. The future's the thing.' He added, 'Is my brother here?'

'He's in the inner office, I think.'

Lance nodded easily and passed on. In the ante-room to the inner sanctum a hard-faced woman of middle age rose behind a desk and said forbiddingly:

'Your name and business, please?'

Lance looked at her doubtfully.

'Are you – Miss Grosvenor?' he asked.

Miss Grosvenor had been described to him as a glamorous blonde. She had indeed appeared so in the pictures that had appeared in the newspapers reporting the inquest on Rex Fortescue. This, surely, could not be Miss Grosvenor.

'Miss Grosvenor left last week. I am Mrs Hardcastle, Mr Percival Fortescue's personal secretary.'

'How like old Percy,' thought Lance. 'To get rid of a glamorous blonde and take on a Gorgon instead. I wonder why? Was it safety or was it because this one comes cheaper?' Aloud he said easily:

'I'm Lancelot Fortescue. You haven't met me yet.'

'Oh, I'm so sorry, Mr Lancelot,' Mrs Hardcastle apologised, 'this is the first time, I think, you've been to the office?'

'The first time but not the last,' said Lance, smiling.

He crossed the room and opened the door of what had been his father's private office. Somewhat to his surprise it was not Percival who was sitting behind the desk there, but Inspector Neele. Inspector Neele looked up from a large wad of papers which he was sorting, and nodded his head.

'Good morning, Mr Fortescue, you've come to take up your duties, I suppose.'

'So you've heard I decided to come into the firm?'

'Your brother told me so.'

'He did, did he? With enthusiasm?'

Inspector Neele endeavoured to conceal a smile.

'The enthusiasm was not marked,' he said gravely.

'Poor Percy,' commented Lance.

Inspector Neele looked at him curiously.

'Are you really going to become a City man?'

'You don't think it's likely, Inspector Neele?'

'It doesn't seem quite in character, Mr Fortescue.'

'Why not? I'm my father's son.'

'And your mother's.'

Lance shook his head.

'You haven't got anything there, Inspector. My mother was a Victorian romantic. Her favourite reading was the *Idylls of the King*, as indeed you may have deduced from our curious Christian names. She was an invalid and always, I should imagine, out of touch with reality. I'm not like that at all. I have no sentiment, very little sense of romance and I'm a realist first and last.'

'People aren't always what they think themselves to be,' Inspector Neele pointed out.

'No, I suppose that's true,' said Lance.

He sat down in a chair and stretched his long legs out in his own characteristic fashion. He was smiling to himself. Then he said unexpectedly:

'You're shrewder than my brother, Inspector.'

'In what way, Mr Fortescue?'

'I've put the wind up Percy all right. He thinks I'm all set for the City life. He thinks he's going to have my fingers fiddling about in his pie. He thinks I'll launch out and spend the firm's money and try and embroil him in wildcat schemes. It would be almost worth doing just for the fun of it! Almost, but not quite. I couldn't really stand an office life, Inspector. I like the open air and some possibilities of adventure. I'd stifle in a place like this.' He added quickly, 'This is off the record, mind. Don't give me away to Percy, will you?'

'I don't suppose the subject will arise, Mr Fortescue.'

'I must have my bit of fun with Percy,' said Lance. 'I want to make him sweat a bit. I've got to get a bit of my own back.'

'That's rather a curious phrase, Mr Fortescue,' said Neele. 'Your own back – for what?'

Lance shrugged his shoulders.

'Oh, it's old history now. Not worth going back over.'

'There was a little matter of a cheque, I understand, in the past. Would that be what you're referring to?'

'How much you know, Inspector!'

'There was no question of prosecution, I understand,' said Neele. 'Your father wouldn't have done that.'

'No. He just kicked me out, that's all.'

Inspector Neele eyed him speculatively, but it was not Lance Fortescue of whom he was thinking, but of Percival. The honest, industrious, parsimonious Percival. It seemed to him that whenever he got in the case he was always coming up against the enigma of Percival Fortescue, a man of whom everybody knew the outer aspects, but whose inner personality was much harder to gauge. One would have said from observing him, a somewhat colourless and insignificant character, a man who had been very much under his father's thumb. Percy Prim in fact, as the AC had once said. Neele was trying now, through Lance, to get at a closer appreciation of Percival's personality. He murmured in a tentative manner:

'Your brother seems always to have been very much – well, how shall I put it – under your father's thumb.'

'I wonder.' Lance seemed definitely to be considering the point. 'I wonder. Yes, that would be the effect, I think, given. But I'm not sure that it was really the truth. It's astonishing, you know, when I look back through life, to see how Percy always got his own way without seeming to do so, if you know what I mean.'

Yes, Inspector Neele thought, it was indeed astonishing. He sorted through the papers in front of him, fished out a letter and shoved it across the desk towards Lance.

'This is a letter you wrote last August, isn't it, Mr Fortescue?'

Lance took it, glanced at it and returned it.

'Yes,' he said, 'I wrote it after I got back to Kenya last summer. Dad kept it, did he? Where was it – here in the office?'

'No, Mr Fortescue, it was among your father's papers in Yewtree Lodge.'

The Inspector considered it speculatively as it lay on the desk in front of him. It was not a long letter.

'*Dear Dad,*
I've talked things over with Pat and I agree to your prop-osition. It will take me a little time to get things fixed up here, say about the end of October or beginning of November.

I'll let you know nearer the time. I hope we'll pull together better than we used to. Anyway, I'll do my best. I can't say more. Look after yourself.

Yours, Lance.'

'Where did you address this letter, Mr Fortescue. To the office or Yewtree Lodge?'

Lance frowned in an effort of recollection.

'It's difficult. I can't remember. You see it's almost three months now. The office, I think. Yes, I'm almost sure. Here to the office.' He paused a moment before asking with frank curiosity, 'Why?'

'I wondered,' said Inspector Neele. 'Your father did not put it on the file here among his private papers. He took it back with him to Yewtree Lodge, and I found it in his desk there. I wondered why he should have done that.'

Lance laughed.

'To keep it out of Percy's way, I suppose.'

'Yes,' said Inspector Neele, 'it would seem so. Your brother, then, had access to your father's private papers here?'

'Well,' Lance hesitated and frowned, 'not exactly. I mean, I suppose he could have looked through them at any time if he liked, but he wouldn't be . . .'

Inspector Neele finished the sentence for him.

'Wouldn't be supposed to do so?'

Lance grinned broadly. 'That's right. Frankly, it would have been snooping. But Percy, I should imagine, always did snoop.'

Inspector Neele nodded. He also thought it probable that Percival Fortescue snooped. It would be in keeping with what the Inspector was beginning to learn of his character.

'And talk of the devil,' murmured Lance, as at that moment the door opened and Percival Fortescue came in. About to speak to the Inspector he stopped, frowning, as he saw Lance.

'Hallo,' he said. 'You here? You didn't tell me you were coming here today.'

'I felt a kind of zeal for work coming over me,' said Lance, 'so here I am ready to make myself useful. What do you want me to do?'

Percival said testily:

'Nothing at present. Nothing at all. We shall have to come to some kind of arrangement as to what side of the business you're going to look after. We shall have to arrange for an office for you.'

Lance inquired with a grin:

'By the way, why did you get rid of glamorous Grosvenor, old boy, and replace her by Horsefaced Hetty out there?'

'Really, Lance,' Percival protested sharply.

'Definitely a change for the worse,' said Lance. 'I've been looking forward to the glamorous Grosvenor. Why did you sack her? Thought she knew a bit too much?'

'Of course not. What an idea!' Percy spoke angrily, a flush mounting his pale face. He turned to the Inspector. 'You mustn't pay any attention to my brother,' he said coldly. 'He has a rather peculiar sense of humour.' He added, 'I never had a very high opinion of Miss Grosvenor's intelligence. Mrs Hardcastle has excellent references and is most capable besides being very moderate in her terms.'

'Very moderate in her terms,' murmured Lance, casting his eyes towards the ceiling. 'You know, Percy, I don't really approve of skimping over the office personnel. By the way, considering how loyally the staff has stood by us during these last tragic weeks, don't you think we ought to raise their salaries all round?'

'Certainly not,' snapped Percival Fortescue. 'Quite uncalled for and unnecessary.'

Inspector Neele noticed the gleam of devilry in Lance's eyes. Percival, however, was far too much upset to notice it.

'You always had the most extraordinary extravagant ideas,' he stuttered. 'In the state in which this firm has been left, economy is our only hope.'

Inspector Neele coughed apologetically.

'That's one of the things I wanted to talk to you about, Mr Fortescue,' he said to Percival.

'Yes, Inspector?' Percival switched his attention to Neele.

'I want to put certain suggestions before you, Mr Fortescue. I understand that for the past six months or longer, possibly a year, your father's general behaviour and conduct has been a source of increasing anxiety to you.'

'He wasn't well,' said Percival, with finality. 'He certainly wasn't at all well.'

'You tried to induce him to see a doctor but you failed. He refused categorically?'

'That is so.'

'May I ask you if you suspected that your father was suffering from what is familiarly referred to as GPI. General Paralysis of the Insane, a condition with signs of megalomania and irritability which terminates sooner or later in hopeless insanity?'

Percival looked surprised. 'It is remarkably astute of you, Inspector. That is exactly what I did fear. That is why I was so anxious for my father to submit to medical treatment.'

Neele went on:

'In the meantime, until you could persuade your father to do that, he was capable of causing a great deal of havoc to the business?'

'He certainly was,' Percival agreed.

'A very unfortunate state of affairs,' said the Inspector.

'Quite terrible. No one knows the anxiety I have been through.'

Neel said gently:

'From the business point of view, your father's death was an extremely fortunate circumstance.'

Percival said sharply:

'You can hardly think I would regard my father's death in that light.'

'It is not a question of how you regard it, Mr Fortescue. I'm speaking merely of a question of fact. Your father died before his finances were completely on the rocks.'

Percival said impatiently:

'Yes, yes. As a matter of actual fact, you are right.'

'It was a fortunate occurrence for your whole family, since they are dependent on this business.'

'Yes. But really, Inspector, I don't see what you're driving at . . .' Percival broke off.

'Oh, I'm not driving at anything, Mr Fortescue,' said Neele. 'I just like getting my facts straight. Now there's another thing. I understood you to say that you'd had no communication of any kind with your brother here since he left England many years ago.'

'Quite so,' said Percival.

'Yes, but it isn't quite so, is it, Mr Fortescue? I mean that last spring when you were so worried about your father's health, you actually wrote to your brother in Africa, told him of your anxiety about your father's behaviour. You wanted, I think, your brother to combine with you in getting your father medically examined and put under restraint, if necessary.'

'I – I – really, I don't see . . .' Percival was badly shaken.

'That is so, isn't it, Mr Fortescue?'

'Well, actually, I thought it only right. After all, Lancelot *was* a junior partner.'

Inspector Neele transferred his gaze to Lance. Lance was grinning.

'You received that letter?' Inspector Neele asked.

Lance Fortescue nodded.

'What did you reply to it?'

Lance's grin widened.

'I told Percy to go and boil his head and to let the old man alone. I said the old man probably knew what he was doing quite well.'

Inspector Neele's gaze went back again to Percival.

'Were those the terms of your brother's answer?'

'I – I – well, I suppose roughly, yes. Far more offensively couched, however.'

'I thought the Inspector had better have a bowdlerised version,' said Lance. He went on, 'Frankly, Inspector Neele, that is one of the reasons why, when I got a letter from my father, I came home to see for myself what I thought. In the short interview I had with my father, frankly I couldn't see anything much wrong with him. He was slightly excitable, that was all. He appeared to me perfectly capable of managing his own affairs. Anyway, after I got back to Africa and had talked things over with Pat, I decided that I'd come home and – what shall we say – see fair play.'

He shot a glance at Percival as he spoke.

'I object,' said Percival Fortescue. 'I object strongly to what you are suggesting. I was not intending to victimise my father, I was concerned for his health. I admit that I was also concerned . . .' he paused.

Lance filled the pause quickly.

'You were also concerned for your pocket, eh? For Percy's little pocket.' He got up and all of a sudden his manner changed. 'All right, Percy, I'm through. I was going to string you along a bit by pretending to work here. I wasn't going to let you have things all your own sweet way, but I'm damned if I'm going on with it. Frankly, it makes me sick to be in the same room with you. You've always been a dirty, mean little skunk all your life. Prying and snooping and lying and making trouble. I'll tell you another thing. I can't prove it, but I've always believed it was you who forged that cheque there was all the row about, that got me shot out of here. For one thing it was a damn bad forgery, a forgery that drew attention to itself in letters a foot high. My record was too bad for me to be able to protest effectively, but I often wondered that the old boy didn't realize that if I *had* forged his name I could have made a much better job of it than that.'

Lance swept on, his voice rising. 'Well, Percy, I'm not going on with this silly game. I'm sick of this country, and of the City. I'm sick of little men like you with their pin-stripe trousers and their black coats and their mincing voices and their mean, shoddy financial deals. We'll share out as you suggested, and I'll get back with Pat to a different country – a country where there's room to breathe and move about. You can make your own division of securities. Keep the gilt-edged and the conservative ones, keep the safe 2 per cent and 3 per cent and $3\frac{1}{2}$ per cent. Give me father's latest wildcat speculations as you call them. Most of them are probably duds. But I'll bet that one or two of them will pay better in the end than all your playing safe with three per cent Trustee Stocks will do. Father was a shrewd old devil. He took chances, plenty of them. Some of those chances paid five and six and seven hundred per cent. I'll back his judgment and his luck. As for you, you little worm . . .' Lance advanced towards his brother, who retreated rapidly, round the end of the desk towards Inspector Neele. 'All right,' said Lance, 'I'm not going to touch you. You wanted me out of here, you're getting me out of here. You ought to be satisfied.' He added as he strode towards the door, 'You can throw in the old Blackbird Mine concession too, if you like. If we've got the murdering MacKenzies on our trail, I'll draw them off to Africa.' He added as he swung through the doorway. 'Revenge – after all these years – scarcely seems credible. But Inspector Neele seems to take it seriously, don't you, Inspector?'

'Nonsense,' said Percival. 'Such a thing is impossible!'

'Ask him,' said Lance. 'Ask him why he's making all these inquiries into blackbirds and rye in father's pocket.'

Gently stroking his upper lip, Inspector Neele said:

'You remember the blackbirds last summer, Mr Fortescue. There *are* certain grounds for inquiry.'

'Nonsense,' said Percival again. 'Nobody's heard of the MacKenzies for years.'

'And yet,' said Lance, 'I'd almost dare to swear that there's a MacKenzie in our midst. I rather imagine the Inspector thinks so, too.'

II

Inspector Neele caught up Lancelot Fortescue as the latter emerged into the street below.

Lance grinned at him rather sheepishly.

'I didn't mean to do that,' he said. 'But I suddenly lost my temper. Oh! well – it would have come to the same before long. I'm meeting Pat at the Savoy – are you coming my way, Inspector?'

'No, I'm returning to Baydon Heath. But there's just something I'd like to ask you, Mr Fortescue.'

'Yes!'

'When you came into the inner office and saw me there – you were surprised. Why?'

'Because I didn't expect to see you, I suppose. I thought I'd find Percy there.'

'You weren't told that he'd gone out?'

Lance looked at him curiously.

'No. They said he was in his office.'

'I see – nobody knew he'd gone out. There's no second door out of the inner office – but there is a door leading straight into the corridor from the little ante-chamber – I suppose your brother went out that way – but I'm surprised Mrs Hardcastle didn't tell you so.'

Lance laughed.

'She'd probably been to collect her cup of tea.'

'Yes – yes – quite so.'

Lance looked at him.

'What's the idea, Inspector?'

'Just puzzling over a few little things, that's all, Mr Fortescue—'

—— 24 ——

In the train on the way down to Baydon Heath, Inspector Neele had singularly little success doing *The Times* crossword. His mind was distracted by various possibilities. In the same way he read the news with only half his brain taking it in. He read of an earthquake in Japan, of the discovery of uranium deposits in Tanganyika, of the body of a merchant seaman washed up near Southampton, and of the imminent strike among the dockers. He read of the latest victims of the cosh and of a new drug that had achieved wonders in advanced cases of tuberculosis.

All these items made a queer kind of pattern in the back of his mind. Presently he returned to the crossword puzzle and was able to put down three clues in rapid succession.

When he reached Yewtree Lodge he had come to a certain decision. He said to Sergeant Hay:

'Where's that old lady? Is she still here?'

'Miss Marple? Oh, yes, she's here still. Great buddies with the old lady upstairs.'

'I see.' Neele paused for a moment and then said: 'Where is she now? I'd like to see her.'

Miss Marple arrived in a few minutes' time, looking rather flushed and breathing fast.

'You want to see me, Inspector Neele? I do hope I haven't kept you waiting. Sergeant Hay couldn't find me at first. I was in the kitchen, talking to Mrs Crump. I was congratulating her on her pastry and how light her hand is, and telling her how delicious the soufflé was last night. I always think, you know, it's better to approach a subject gradually, don't you? At least, I suppose it isn't so easy for you. You more or less have to come almost straight away to the questions you want to ask. But of course for an old lady like me who has all the time in the world, as you might say, it's really *expected* of her that there should be a great deal of unnecessary talk. And the way to a cook's heart, as they say, is through her pastry.'

'What you really wanted to talk to her about,' said Inspector Neele, 'was Gladys Martin?'

Miss Marple nodded.

'Yes. Gladys. You see, Mrs Crump could really tell me a lot about the girl. Not in connection with the murder. I don't mean that. But about her spirits lately and the odd things she said. I don't mean odd in the sense of peculiar. I mean just the odds and ends of conversation.'

'Did you find it helpful?' asked Inspector Neele.

'Yes,' said Miss Marple. 'I found it very helpful indeed. I really think, you know, that things are becoming very much clearer, don't you?'

'I do and I don't,' said Inspector Neele.

Sergeant Hay, he noticed, had left the room. He was glad

of it because what he was about to do now was, to say the least of it, slightly unorthodox.

'Look here, Miss Marple,' he said, 'I want to talk to you seriously.'

'Yes, Inspector Neele?'

'In a way,' said Inspector Neele, 'you and I represent different points of view. I admit, Miss Marple, that I've heard something about you at the Yard.' He smiled, 'It seems you're fairly well known there.'

'I don't know how it is,' fluttered Miss Marple, 'but I so often seem to get mixed up in the things that are really *no* concern of mine. Crimes I mean, and peculiar happenings.'

'You've got a reputation,' said Inspector Neele.

'Sir Henry Clithering, of course,' said Miss Marple, 'is a *very* old friend of mine.'

'As I said before,' Neele went on, 'you and I represent opposite points of view. One might almost call them sanity and insanity.'

Miss Marple put her head a little on one side.

'Now what exactly do you mean by that, I wonder, Inspector?'

'Well, Miss Marple, there's a sane way of looking at things. This murder benefits certain people. One person, I may say, in particular. The second murder benefits the same person. The third murder one might call a murder for safety.'

'But which do you call the third murder?' Miss Marple asked.

Her eyes, a very bright china blue, looked shrewdly at the Inspector. He nodded.

'Yes. You've got something there perhaps. You know, the other day when the AC was speaking to me of these murders, something that he said seemed to me to be wrong. That was it. I was thinking, of course, of the nursery rhyme. The king in his counting-house, the queen in the parlour and the maid hanging out the clothes.'

'Exactly,' said Miss Marple. 'A sequence in that order, but actually Gladys must have been murdered *before* Mrs Fortescue, mustn't she?'

'I think so,' said Neele. 'I take it it's quite certainly so. Her body wasn't discovered till late that night, and of course it was difficult then to say exactly how long she'd been dead. But I think myself that she must almost certainly have been murdered round about five o'clock, because otherwise . . .'

Miss Marple cut in. 'Because otherwise she would certainly have taken the second tray into the drawing-room?'

'Quite so. She took one tray in with the tea on it, she brought the second tray into the hall, and then *something happened*. She saw something or heard something. The question is what that something was. It *might* have been Dubois coming down the stairs from Mrs Fortescue's room. It *might* have been Elaine Fortescue's young man, Gerald Wright, coming in at the side door. Whoever it was, lured her away from the tea-tray and out into the garden. And once that had happened I don't see any possibility of her death being long delayed. It was cold out and she was only wearing her thin uniform.'

'Of course you're quite right,' said Miss Marple. 'I mean it was never a case of "the maid was in the garden hanging up the clothes." She wouldn't be hanging up clothes at that time of the evening and she wouldn't go out to the clothes line without putting a coat on. That was all camouflage, like the clothes peg, to make the thing fit in with the rhyme.'

'Exactly,' said Inspector Neele, 'crazy. That's where I can't yet see eye to eye with you. I can't – I simply can't swallow this nursery rhyme business.'

'But it *fits*, Inspector. You must agree it fits.'

'It fits,' said Neele heavily, 'but all the same the sequence is wrong. I mean the rhyme definitely suggests that the maid was the third murder. But we know that the Queen was the third murder. Adele Fortescue was not killed until between twenty-five-past five and five minutes to six. By then Gladys must already have been dead.'

'And that's all wrong, isn't it?' said Miss Marple. 'All wrong for the nursery rhyme – that's very significant, isn't it?'

Inspector Neele shrugged his shoulders.

'It's probably splitting hairs. The deaths fulfil the conditions of the rhyme, and I suppose that's all that was needed. But I'm talking now as though I were on your side. I'm going to outline *my* side of the case now, Miss Marple. I'm washing out the blackbirds and the rye and all the rest of it. I'm going by sober facts and common sense and the reasons for which sane people do murders. First, the death of Rex Fortescue, and *who benefits by his death*. Well, it benefits quite a lot of people, but most of all it benefits his son, Percival. His son Percival wasn't at Yewtree Lodge that morning. He couldn't have put poison in his father's coffee or in anything that he ate for breakfast. Or that's what we thought at first.'

'Ah,' Miss Marple's eyes brightened. 'So there *was* a method, was there? I've been thinking about it, you know, a good deal, and I've had several ideas. But of course no evidence or proof.'

'There's no harm in my letting you know,' said Inspector Neele. 'Taxine was added to a new jar of marmalade. That jar of marmalade was placed on the breakfast table and the top layer of it was eaten by Mr Fortescue at breakfast. Later that jar of marmalade was thrown out into the bushes and a similar jar with a similar amount taken out of it was placed in the pantry. The jar in the bushes was found and I've just had the result of the analysis. It shows definite evidence of taxine.'

'So that was it,' murmured Miss Marple. 'So simple and easy to do.'

'Consolidated Investments,' Neele went on, 'was in a bad way. If the firm had had to pay out a hundred thousand pounds to Adele Fortescue under her husband's will, it would, I think, have crashed. If Mrs Fortescue had survived her husband for a month that money would have *had* to be paid out to her. *She* would have had no feeling for the firm or its difficulties. But she didn't survive her husband for a month. She died, and as a result of her death the gainer was the residuary legatee of Rex Fortescue's will. In other words, Percival Fortescue again.'

'Always Percival Fortescue,' the Inspector continued bitterly. 'And though he *could* have tampered with the marmalade, he couldn't have poisoned his stepmother or strangled Gladys. According to his secretary he was in his city office at five o'clock that afternoon, and he didn't arrive back here until nearly seven.'

'That makes it *very* difficult, doesn't it?' said Miss Marple.

'It makes it impossible,' said Inspector Neele gloomily. 'In other words, Percival is *out*.' Abandoning restraint and prudence, he spoke with some bitterness, almost unaware of his listener. 'Wherever I go, wherever I turn, I always come up against the same person. Percival Fortescue! Yet it *can't* be Percival Fortescue.' Calming himself a little he said, 'Oh, there are other possibilities, other people who had a perfectly good motive.'

'Mr Dubois, of course,' said Miss Marple sharply. 'And that young Mr Wright. I do so agree with you, Inspector. Wherever there is a question of *gain*, one has to be *very suspicious*. The great thing to avoid is having in any way a trustful mind.'

In spite of himself, Neele smiled.

'Always think the worst, eh?' he asked.

It seemed a curious doctrine to be proceeding from this charming and fragile looking old lady.

'Oh yes,' said Miss Marple fervently. 'I always believe the worst. What is so sad is that one is usually justified in doing so.'

'All right,' said Neele, 'let's think the worst. Dubois could have done it, Gerald Wright could have done it, (that is to say if he'd been acting in collusion with Elaine Fortescue and she tampered with the marmalade), Mrs Percival could have done it, I suppose. She was on the spot. But none of the people I have mentioned tie up with the crazy angle. They don't tie up with blackbirds and pockets full of rye. That's *your* theory and it may be that you're right. If so, it boils down to one person, doesn't it? Mrs MacKenzie's in a mental home and has been for a good number of years. She hasn't been messing about with marmalade pots or putting cyanide in the drawing-room afternoon tea. Her son Donald was killed at Dunkirk. That leaves the daughter, Ruby MacKenzie. And if your theory is correct, if this whole series of murders arises out of the old Blackbird Mine business, then Ruby MacKenzie must be here in this house, and there's only one person that Ruby MacKenzie could be.'

'I think, you know,' said Miss Marple, 'that you're being a little too dogmatic.'

Inspector Neele paid no attention.

'Just one person,' he said grimly.

He got up and went out of the room.

II

Mary Dove was in her own sitting-room. It was a small, rather austerely furnished room, but comfortable. That is to say Miss Dove herself had made it comfortable. When Inspector Neele tapped at the door Mary Dove raised her head, which had been bent over a pile of tradesmen's books, and said in her clear voice:

'Come in.'

The Inspector entered.

'Do sit down, Inspector.' Miss Dove indicated a chair. 'Could you wait just one moment? The total of the fishmonger's account does not seem to be correct and I must check it.'

Inspector Neele sat in silence watching her as she totted up the column. How wonderfully calm and self-possessed the girl

535

was, he thought. He was intrigued, as so often before, by the personality that underlay that self-assured manner. He tried to trace in her features any resemblance to those of the woman he had talked to at the Pinewood Sanatorium. The colouring was not unlike, but he could detect no real facial resemblance. Presently Mary Dove raised her head from her accounts and said:

'Yes, Inspector? What can I do for you?'

Inspector Neele said quietly:

'You know, Miss Dove, there are certain very peculiar features about this case.'

'Yes?'

'To begin with there is the odd circumstance of the rye found in Mr Fortescue's pocket.'

'That was very extraordinary,' Mary Dove agreed. 'You know I really cannot think of any explanation for that.'

'Then there is the curious circumstance of the blackbirds. Those four blackbirds on Mr Fortescue's desk last summer, and also the incident of the blackbirds being substituted for the veal and ham in the pie. You were here, I think, Miss Dove, at the time of both those occurrences?'

'Yes, I was. I remember now. It was most upsetting. It seemed such a very purposeless, spiteful thing to do, especially at the time.'

'Perhaps not entirely purposeless. What do you know, Miss Dove, about the Blackbird Mine?'

'I don't think I've ever heard of the Blackbird Mine?'

'Your name, you told me, is Mary Dove. Is that your real name, Miss Dove?'

Mary Dove raised her eyebrows. Inspector Neele was almost sure that a wary expression had come into her blue eyes.

'What an extraordinary question, Inspector. Are you suggesting that my name is *not* Mary Dove?'

'That is exactly what I am suggesting. I'm suggesting,' said Neele pleasantly, 'that your name is Ruby MacKenzie.'

She stared at him. For a moment her face was entirely blank with neither protest on it nor surprise. There was, Inspector Neele thought, a very definite effect of calculation. After a minute or two she said in a quiet, colourless voice:

'What do you expect me to say?'

'Please answer me. Is your name Ruby MacKenzie?'

'I have told you my name is Mary Dove.'

'Yes, but have you proof of that, Miss Dove?'

'What do you want to see? My birth certificate?'

'That might be helpful or it might not. You might, I mean, be in possession of the birth certificate of *a* Mary Dove. That Mary Dove might be a friend of yours or might be someone who had died.'

'Yes, there are a lot of possibilities, aren't there?' Amusement had crept back into Mary Dove's voice. 'It's really quite a dilemma for you, isn't it, Inspector?'

'They might possibly be able to recognise you at Pinewood Sanatorium,' said Neele.

'Pinewood Sanatorium!' Mary raised her eyebrows. 'What or where is Pinewood Sanatorium?'

'I think you know very well, Miss Dove.'

'I assure you I am quite in the dark.'

'And you deny categorically that you are Ruby MacKenzie?'

'I shouldn't really like to deny *anything*. I think, you know, Inspector, that it's up to you to prove I *am* this Ruby MacKenzie, whoever she is.' There was definite amusement now in her blue eyes, amusement and challenge. Looking him straight in the eyes, Mary Dove said, 'Yes, it's up to you, Inspector. Prove that I'm Ruby MacKenzie if you can.'

—— 25 ——

'The old tabby's looking for you, sir,' said Sergeant Hay in a conspiratorial whisper, as Inspector Neele descended the stairs. 'It appears as how she's got a lot more to say to you.'

'Hell and damnation,' said Inspector Neele.

'Yes, sir,' said Sergeant Hay, not a muscle of his face moving.

He was about to move away when Neele called him back.

'Go over those notes given us by Miss Dove, Hay, notes as to her former employment and situations. Check up on them – and, yes, there are just one or two other things that I would like to know. Put these inquiries in hand, will you?'

He jotted down a few lines on a sheet of paper and gave them to Sergeant Hay who said:

'I'll get on to it at once, sir.'

Hearing a murmur of voices in the library as he passed, Inspector Neele looked in. Whether Miss Marple had been looking for him or not, she was now fully engaged talking to

Mrs Percival Fortescue while her knitting needles clicked busily. The middle of the sentence which Inspector Neele caught was:

'. . . I have really always thought it was a vocation you needed for nursing. It certainly is very noble work.'

Inspector Neele withdrew quietly. Miss Marple had noticed him, he thought, but she had taken no notice of his presence.

She went on in her gentle, soft voice:

'I had such a charming nurse looking after me when I once broke my wrist. She went on from me to nurse Mrs Sparrow's son, a very nice young naval officer. Quite a romance, really, because they became engaged. So romantic I thought it. They were married and were very happy and had two dear little children.' Miss Marple sighed sentimentally. 'It was pneumonia, you know. So much depends on nursing in pneumonia, does it not.'

'Oh, yes,' said Jennifer Fortescue, 'nursing is nearly everything in pneumonia, though of course nowadays M and B works wonders, and it's not the long, protracted battle it used to be.'

'I'm sure you must have been an excellent nurse, my dear,' said Miss Marple. 'That was the beginning of *your* romance, was it not? I mean you came here to nurse Mr Percival Fortescue, did you not?'

'Yes,' said Jennifer. 'Yes, yes – that's how it did happen.'

Her voice was not encouraging, but Miss Marple seemed to take no notice.

'I understand. One should not listen to servants' gossip, of course, but I'm afraid an old lady like myself is always interested to hear about the people in the house. Now what was I saying? Oh, yes. There was another nurse at first, was there not, and she got sent away – something like that. Carelessness, I believe.'

'I don't think it was carelessness,' said Jennifer. 'I believe her father or something was desperately ill, and so I came to replace her.'

'I see,' said Miss Marple. 'And you fell in love and that was that. Yes, very nice indeed, very nice.'

'I'm not so sure about that,' said Jennifer Fortescue. 'I often wish' – her voice trembled – 'I often wish I was back in the wards again.'

'Yes, yes, I understand. You were keen on your profession.'

'I wasn't so much at the time, but now when I think of it –

life's so monotonous, you know. Day after day with nothing to do, and Val so absorbed in business.'

Miss Marple shook her head.

'Gentlemen have to work so hard nowadays,' she said. 'There really doesn't seem any leisure, no matter how much money there is.'

'Yes, it makes it very lonely and dull for a wife sometimes. I often wish I'd never come here,' said Jennifer. 'Oh, well, I dare say it serves me right. I ought never to have done it.'

'Ought never to have done what, my dear?'

'I ought never to have married Val. Oh, well—' she sighed abruptly. 'Don't let's talk of it any more.'

Obligingly Miss Marple began to talk about the new skirts that were being worn in Paris.

II

'So kind of you not to interrupt just now,' said Miss Marple when, having tapped at the door of the study, Inspector Neele had told her to come in. 'There were just one or two little points, you know, that I wanted to verify.' She added reproachfully, 'We didn't really finish our talk just now.'

'I'm so sorry, Miss Marple,' Inspector Neele summoned up a charming smile. 'I'm afraid I was rather rude. I summoned you to a consultation and did all the talking myself.'

'Oh, that's quite all right,' said Miss Marple immediately, 'because, you see, I wasn't really quite ready then to put all *my* cards on the table. I mean I wouldn't like to make any accusation unless I was absolutely sure about it. Sure, that is, in *my own mind*. And I *am* sure, now.'

'You're sure about what, Miss Marple?'

'Well, certainly about who killed Mr Fortescue. What you told me about the marmalade, I mean, just clinches the matter. Showing *how*, I mean, as well as *who,* and well within the mental capacity.'

Inspector Neele blinked a little.

'I'm so sorry,' said Miss Marple, perceiving this reaction on his part, 'I'm afraid I find it difficult sometimes to make myself perfectly clear.'

'I'm not quite sure yet, Miss Marple, what we're talking about.'

'Well, perhaps,' said Miss Marple, 'we'd better begin all over again. I mean if you could spare the time. I would rather like to put my own point of view before you. You see, I've talked a good deal to people, to old Miss Ramsbottom and to Mrs Crump and to her husband. He, of course, is a liar, but that doesn't really matter because if you know liars are liars, it comes to the same thing. But I did want to get the telephone calls clear and the nylon stockings and all that.'

Inspector Neele blinked again and wondered what he had let himself in for and why he had ever thought that Miss Marple might be a desirable and clear-headed colleague. Still, he thought to himself, however muddle-headed she was, she might have picked up some useful bits of information. All Inspector Neele's success in his profession had come from listening well. He was prepared to listen now.

'Please tell me all about it, Miss Marple,' he said, 'but start at the beginning, won't you.'

'Yes, of course,' said Miss Marple, 'and the beginning is Gladys. I mean I came here because of Gladys. And you very kindly let me look through all her things. And what with that and the nylon stockings and the telephone calls and one thing and another, it did come out perfectly clear. I mean about Mr Fortescue and the taxine.'

'You have a theory?' asked Inspector Neele, 'as to who put the taxine into Mr Fortescue's marmalade.'

'It isn't a theory,' said Miss Marple. 'I know.'

For the third time Inspector Neele blinked.

'It was Gladys, of course,' said Miss Marple.

—— 26 ——

Inspector Neele stared at Miss Marple and slowly shook his head.

'Are you saying,' he said incredulously, 'that Gladys Martin deliberately murdered Rex Fortescue? I'm sorry, Miss Marple, but I simply don't believe it.'

'No, of course she didn't *mean* to murder him,' said Miss Marple, 'but she did it all the same! You said yourself that she was nervous and upset when you questioned her. And that she looked guilty.'

'Yes, but not guilty of *murder*.'

'Oh, no, I agree. As I say, she didn't *mean* to murder anybody, but she put the taxine in the marmalade. She didn't think it was poison, of course.'

'What *did* she think it was?' Inspector Neele's voice still sounded incredulous.

'I rather imagine she thought it was a truth drug,' said Miss Marple. 'It's very interesting, you know, and very instructive – the things these girls cut out of papers and keep. It's always been the same, you know, all through the ages. Recipes for beauty, for attracting the man you love. And witchcraft and charms and marvellous happenings. Nowadays they're mostly lumped together under the heading of Science. Nobody believes in magicians any more, nobody believes that anyone can come along and wave a wand and turn you into a frog. But if you read in the paper that by injecting certain glands scientists can alter your vital tissues and you'll develop froglike characteristics, well, everybody would believe that. And having read in the papers about truth drugs, of course Gladys would believe it absolutely when he told her that that's what it was.'

'When who told her?' asked Inspector Neele.

'Albert Evans,' said Miss Marple. 'Not of course that that is *really* his name. But anyway he met her last summer at a holiday camp, and he flattered her up and made love to her, and I should imagine told her some story of injustice or persecution, or something like that. Anyway, the point was that Rex Fortescue had to be made to confess what he had done and make restitution. I don't *know* this, of course, Inspector Neele, but I'm pretty sure about it. He got her to take a post here, and it's really very easy nowadays with the shortage of domestic staff, to obtain a post where you want one. Staffs are changing the whole time. They then arranged a date together. You remember on that last postcard he said, "Remember our date." That was to be the great day they were working for. Gladys would put the drug that he gave her into the top of the marmalade, so that Mr Fortescue would eat it at breakfast and she would also put the rye in his pocket. I don't know what story he told her to account for the rye, but as I told you from the beginning, Inspector Neele, Gladys Martin was a *very* credulous girl. In fact, there's hardly anything she wouldn't believe if a personable young man put it to her the right way.'

'Go on,' said Inspector Neele in a dazed voice.

'The idea probably was,' continued Miss Marple, 'that Albert was going to call upon him at the office that day, and that by that time the truth drug would have worked, and that Mr Fortescue would have confessed everything and so on and so on. You can imagine the poor girl's feelings when she heard that Mr Fortescue is dead.'

'But, surely,' Inspector Neele objected, 'she would have told?'

Miss Marple asked sharply:

'What was the first thing she said to you when you questioned her?'

'She said "I didn't do it," ' Inspector Neele said.

'Exactly,' said Miss Marple, triumphantly. 'Don't you see that's exactly what she *would* say? If she broke an ornament, you know, Gladys would always say, "I didn't do it, Miss Marple. I can't think *how* it happened." They can't help it, poor dears. They're very upset at what they've done and their great idea is to avoid blame. You don't think that a nervous young woman who had murdered someone when she didn't mean to murder him, is going to admit it, do you? That would have been *quite* out of character.'

'Yes,' Neele said, 'I suppose it would.'

He ran his mind back over his interview with Gladys. Nervous, upset, guilty, shifty-eyed, all those things. They might have had small significance, or a big one. He could not really blame himself for having failed to come to the right conclusion.

'Her first idea, as I say,' went on Miss Marple, 'would be to deny it all. Then in a confused way she would try to sort it all out in her mind. Perhaps Albert hadn't known how strong the stuff was, or he'd made a mistake and given her too much of it. She'd think of excuses for him and explanations. She'd hope he'd get in touch with her, which, of course, he did. By telephone.'

'Do you know that?' asked Neele sharply.

Miss Marple shook her head.

'No. I admit I'm assuming it. But there were unexplained calls that day. That is to say, people rang up and when Crump, or Mrs Crump answered, the phone was hung up. That's what he'd do, you know. Ring up and wait until Gladys answered the phone, and then he'd make an appointment with her to meet him.'

'I see,' said Neele. 'You mean she had an appointment to meet him on the day she died.'

Miss Marple nodded vigorously.

'Yes, that was indicated. Mrs Crump was right about one thing. The girl had on her best nylon stockings and her good shoes. She was going to meet someone. Only she wasn't going *out* to meet him. He was coming to Yewtree Lodge. That's why she was on the look-out that day and flustered and late with tea. Then, as she brought the second tray into the hall, I think she looked along the passage to the side door, and saw him there, beckoning to her. She put the tray down and went out to meet him.'

'And then he strangled her,' said Neele.

Miss Marple pursed her lips together. 'It would only take a minute,' she said, 'but he couldn't risk her talking. She had to die, poor, silly, credulous girl. And then – he put a clothes peg on her nose!' Stern anger vibrated the old lady's voice. 'To make it fit in with the rhyme. The rye, the blackbirds, the counting-house, the bread and honey, and the clothes peg – the nearest he could get to a little dicky bird that nipped off her nose—'

'And I suppose at the end of it all he'll go to Broadmoor and we shan't be able to hang him because he's crazy!' said Neele slowly.

'I think you'll hang him all right,' said Miss Marple. 'And he's not crazy, Inspector, not for a moment!'

Inspector Neele looked hard at her.

'Now see here, Miss Marple, you've outlined a theory to me. Yes – yes – although you say you *know*, it's only a *theory*. You're saying that a man is responsible for these crimes, who called himself Albert Evans, who picked up the girl Gladys at a holiday camp and used her for his own purposes. This Albert Evans was someone who wanted revenge for the old Blackbird Mine business. You're suggesting, aren't you, that Mrs MacKenzie's son, Don MacKenzie, didn't die at Dunkirk. That he's still alive, that he's behind all this?'

But to Inspector Neele's surprise, Miss Marple was shaking her head violently.

'Oh no!' she said, 'oh *no*! I'm not suggesting that *at all*. Don't you see, Inspector Neele, all this blackbird business is really a complete *fake*. It was *used*, that was all, used by somebody who heard about the blackbirds – the ones in the library and in the pie. The blackbirds were genuine enough. They were put there by someone who knew about the old business, who wanted revenge for it. But only the revenge of trying to frighten Mr Fortescue or to make him uncomfortable. I don't believe, you know, Inspector Neele, that children can really be brought up and taught to wait and brood and carry out revenge. Children, after all, have got a lot of *sense*. But anyone whose father had been swindled and perhaps left to die, might be willing to play a malicious trick on the person who was supposed to have done it. That's what happened, I think. And the killer used it.'

'The killer,' said Inspector Neele. 'Come now, Miss Marple, let's have your ideas about the killer. Who was he?'

'You won't be surprised,' said Miss Marple. 'Not really. Because you'll see, as soon as I tell you who he is, or rather who I think he is, for one must be accurate must one not? – you'll see that he's just the type of person who *would* commit these murders. He's sane, brilliant and quite unscrupulous. And he did it, of course, for money, probably for a good deal of money.'

'Percival Fortescue?' Inspector Neele spoke almost imploringly, but he knew as he spoke that he was wrong. The picture of the man that Miss Marple had built up for him had no resemblance to Percival Fortescue.

'Oh, no,' said Miss Marple. 'Not Percival. Lance.'

—— 27 ——

'It's impossible,' said Inspector Neele.

He leaned back in his chair and watched Miss Marple with fascinated eyes. As Miss Marple had said, he was not surprised. His words were a denial, not of probability, but of possibility. Lance Fortescue fitted the description: Miss Marple had outlined it well enough. But Inspector Neele simply could not see how Lance could be the answer.

Miss Marple leaned forward in her chair and gently, persuasively, and rather in the manner of someone explaining the simple facts of arithmetic to a small child, outlined her theory.

'He's always been like that, you see. I mean, he's always been *bad*. Bad all through, although with it he's always been *attractive*. Especially attractive to *women*. He's got a brilliant mind and he'll take risks. He's always taken risks and because of his charm people have always believed the best and not the worst about him. He came home in the summer to see his father. I don't believe for a moment that his father wrote to him or sent for him – unless, of course, you've got actual evidence to that effect.' She paused inquiringly.

Neele shook his head. 'No,' he said, 'I've no evidence of his father sending for him. I've got a letter that Lance is supposed to have written to him after being here. But Lance could quite easily have slipped that among his father's papers in the study here the day he arrived.'

'Sharp of him,' said Miss Marple, nodding her head. 'Well, as I say, he probably flew over here and attempted a reconciliation with his father, but Mr Fortescue wouldn't have it. You see, Lance had recently got married and the small pittance he was living on and which he had doubtless been supplementing in various dishonest ways, was not enough for him any more. He was very much in love with Pat (who is a dear, sweet girl) and he wanted a respectable, settled life with her – nothing shifty. And that, from his point of view, meant having a lot of money. When he was at Yewtree Lodge he must have heard about these blackbirds. Perhaps his father mentioned them. Perhaps Adele did. He jumped to the conclusion that MacKenzie's daughter was established in the house and it occurred to him that she would make a very good scapegoat for murder. Because, you see, when he realized that he couldn't get his father to do what he wanted, he must have cold-bloodedly decided that murder it would have to be. He may have realized that his father wasn't – er, very well – and have feared that by the time his father died there would have been a complete crash.'

'He knew about his father's health all right,' said the Inspector.

'Ah – that explains a good deal. Perhaps the coincidence of his father's Christian name being *Rex* together with the blackbird incident suggested the idea of the nursery rhyme. Make a crazy business of the whole thing – and tie it up with that old revenge threat of the MacKenzies. Then, you see, he could dispose of Adele, too, and that hundred thousand pounds going out of the firm. But there would have to be a third character, the "maid in the garden hanging up the clothes" – and I suppose that suggested the whole wicked plan to him. An innocent accomplice whom he could silence before she could talk. And that would give him what he wanted – a genuine alibi for the first murder. The rest was easy. He arrived here from the station just before five o'clock, which was the time when Gladys brought the second tray into the hall. He came to the side door, saw her and beckoned to her. Strangling her and carrying her body round the house to where the clothes lines were would only have taken three or four minutes. Then he rang the front-door bell, was admitted to the house, and joined the family for tea. After tea he went up to see Miss Ramsbottom. When he came

down, he slipped into the drawing-room, found Adele alone
there drinking a last cup of tea and sat down by her on the sofa,
and while he was talking to her, he managed to slip the cyanide
into her tea. It wouldn't be difficult, you know. A little piece of
white stuff, like sugar. He might have stretched out his hand to
the sugar basin and taken a lump and apparently dropped it
into her cup. He'd laugh and say "Look, I've dropped more
sugar into your tea." She'd say she didn't mind, stir and drink
it. It would be as easy and audacious as that. Yes, he's an
audacious fellow.'

Inspector Neele said slowly:

'It's actually possible – yes. But I cannot see – really, Miss
Marple, I cannot see – what he stood to gain by it. Granted that
unless old Fortescue died the business would soon be on the
rocks, is Lance's share big enough to cause him to plan three
murders? I don't think so. I really don't think so.'

'That *is* a little difficult,' admitted Miss Marple. 'Yes, I agree
with you. That does present difficulties. I suppose . . .' She
hesitated, looking at the Inspector. 'I suppose – I am so very
ignorant in financial matters – but I suppose it is really true
that the Blackbird Mine *is* worthless?'

Neele reflected. Various scraps fitted together in his mind.
Lance's willingness to take the various speculative or worthless
shares off Percival's hands. His parting words today in London
that Percival had better get rid of the Blackbird and its hoodoo.
A gold mine. A worthless gold mine. But perhaps the mine had
not been worthless. And yet, somehow, that seemed unlikely.
Old Rex Fortescue was hardly likely to have made a mistake
on that point, although of course there might have been sound-
ings recently. Where *was* the mine? West Africa, Lance had
said. Yes but somebody else – was it Miss Ramsbottom – had
said it was in *East* Africa. Had Lance been deliberately misleading when he said West instead of East? Miss Ramsbottom
was old and forgetful, and yet *she* might have been right and
not Lance. East Africa. Lance had just come from East Africa.
Had he perhaps some recent knowledge?

Suddenly with a click another piece fitted into the Inspector's
puzzle. Sitting in the train, reading *The Times. Uranium deposits found in Tanganyika.* Supposing that the uranium deposits were on the site of the old Blackbird? That would explain
everything. Lance had come to have knowledge of that, being
on the spot, and with uranium deposits there, there was a for-

tune to be grasped. An enormous fortune! He sighed. He looked
at Miss Marple.

'How do you think?' he asked reproachfully, 'that I'm ever
going to be able to prove all this?'

Miss Marple nodded at him encouragingly, as an aunt might
have encouraged a bright nephew who was going in for a
scholarship exam.

'You'll prove it,' she said. 'You're a very, *very* clever man,
Inspector Neele. I've seen that from the first. Now you know
who it is you ought to be able to get the evidence. At that
holiday camp, for instance, they'll recognise his photograph.
He'll find it hard to explain why he stayed there for a week
calling himself Albert Evans.'

Yes, Inspector Neele thought, Lance Fortescue was brilliant
and unscrupulous – but he was foolhardy, too. The risks he
took were just a little too great.

Neele thought to himself, 'I'll get him!' Then, doubt sweeping over him, he looked at Miss Marple.

'It's all pure assumption, you know,' he said.

'Yes – but you are sure, aren't you?'

'I suppose so. After all, I've known his kind before.'

The old lady nodded.

'Yes – that matters so much – that's really why *I*'m sure.'

Neele looked at her playfully.

'Because of your knowledge of criminals.'

'Oh no – of course not. Because of Pat – a dear girl – and
the kind that always marries a bad lot – that's really what drew
my attention to him at the start—'

'I may be sure – in my own mind,' said the Inspector – 'but
there's a lot that needs explaining – the Ruby MacKenzie
business for instance. I could swear that—'

Miss Marple interrupted:

'And you're quite right. But you've been thinking of the
wrong person. Go and talk to Mrs Percy.'

II

'Mrs Fortescue,' said Inspector Neele, 'do you mind telling me
your name before you were married.'

'Oh!' Jennifer gasped. She looked frightened.

'You needn't be nervous madam,' said Inspector Neele, 'but
it's much better to come out with the truth. I'm right, I think,

in saying that your name before you were married was Ruby
MacKenzie?'

'My – well, oh well – oh dear – well, why shouldn't it be?'
said Mrs Percival Fortescue.

'No reason at all,' said Inspector Neele gently, and added,
'I was talking to your mother a few days ago at Pinewood
Sanatorium.'

'She's very angry with me,' said Jennifer. 'I never go and see
her now because it only upsets her. Poor Mumsy, she was so
devoted to Dad, you know.'

'And she brought you up to have very melodramatic ideas of
revenge?'

'Yes,' said Jennifer. 'She kept making us swear on the Bible
that we'd never forget and that we'd kill him one day. Of
course, once I'd gone into hospital and started my training, I
began to realize that her mental balance wasn't what it should
be.'

'You yourself must have felt revengeful though, Mrs Fortescue?'

'Well, of course I did. Rex Fortescue practically murdered
my father! I don't mean he actually shot him, or knifed him
or anything like that. But I'm quite certain that he *did* leave
Father to die. That's the same thing, isn't it?'

'It's the same thing morally – yes.'

'So I did want to pay him back,' said Jennifer. 'When a friend
of mine came to nurse his son I got her to leave and to propose
my replacing her. I don't know exactly what I meant to do . . .
I didn't, really I didn't, Inspector, I never meant to *kill* Mr
Fortescue. I had some idea, I think, of nursing his son so badly
that the son would die. But of course, if you *are* a nurse by profession you can't do that sort of thing. Actually I had quite
a job pulling Val through. And then he got fond of me and
asked me to marry him and I thought, 'Well, really that's a far
more sensible revenge than anything else.' I mean, to marry
Mr Fortescue's eldest son and get the money he swindled Father
out of back that way. I think it was a far more sensible way.'

'Yes, indeed,' said Inspector Neele, 'far more sensible.' He
added, 'It was you, I suppose, who put the blackbirds on the
desk and in the pie?'

Mrs Percival flushed.

'Yes. I suppose it was silly of me really. . . . But Mr Fortescue
had been talking about suckers one day and boasting of how
he'd swindled people – got the best of them. Oh, in quite a

legal way. And I thought I'd just like to give him – well, a kind of fright. And it *did* give him a fright! He was awfully upset.' She added anxiously, 'But I didn't do anything *else*! I didn't really, Inspector. You don't – you don't honestly think I would *murder* anyone, do you?'

Inspector Neele smiled.

'No,' he said, 'I don't.' He added, 'By the way, have you given Miss Dove any money lately?'

Jennifer's jaw dropped.

'How did you know?'

'We know a lot of things,' said Inspector Neele and added to himself: 'And guess a good many, too.'

Jennifer continued, speaking rapidly.

'She came to me and said that you'd accused her of being Ruby MacKenzie. She said if I'd get hold of five hundred pounds she'd let you go on thinking so. She said if you knew that I was Ruby MacKenzie, I'd be suspected of murdering Mr Fortescue and my stepmother. I had an awful job getting the money, because of course I couldn't tell Percival. He doesn't know about me. I had to sell my diamond engagement ring and a very beautiful necklace Mr Fortescue gave me.'

'Don't worry, Mrs Percival,' said Inspector Neele, 'I think we can get your money back for you.'

III

It was on the following day that Inspector Neele had another interview with Miss Mary Dove.

'I wonder, Miss Dove,' he said, 'if you'd give me a cheque for five hundred pounds payable to Mrs Percival Fortescue.'

He had the pleasure of seeing Mary Doyle lose countenance for once.

'The silly fool told you, I suppose,' she said.

'Yes Blackmail, Miss Dove is rather a serious charge.'

'It wasn't exactly blackmail, Inspector. I think you'd find it hard to make out a case of blackmail against me. I was just doing Mrs Percival a special service to oblige her.'

'Well, if you'll give me that cheque, Miss Dove, we'll leave it like that.'

Mary Dove got her cheque book and took out her fountain pen.

'It's very annoying,' she said with a sigh. 'I'm particularly hard up at the moment.'

'You'll be looking for another job soon, I suppose?'

'Yes. This one hasn't turned out quite according to plan. It's all been very unfortunate from my point of view.'

Inspector Neele agreed.

'Yes, it put you in rather a difficult position, didn't it? I mean, it was quite likely that at any moment we might have to look into your antecedents.'

Mary Dove, cool once more, allowed her eyebrows to rise.

'Really, Inspector, my past is quite blameless, I assure you.'

'Yes, it is,' Inspector Neele agreed, cheerfully. 'We've nothing against you at all, Miss Dove. It's a curious coincidence, though, that in the last three places which you have filled so admirably, there have happened to be robberies about three months after you left. The thieves have seemed remarkably well informed as to where mink coats, jewels, etc., were kept. Curious coincidence, isn't it?'

'Coincidences do happen, Inspector.'

'Oh, yes,' said Neele. 'They happen. But they mustn't happen too often, Miss Dove. I dare say,' he added, 'that we may meet in the future.'

'I hope' – said Mary Dove – 'I don't mean to be rude, Inspector Neele – but I hope we don't.'

28

Miss Marple smoothed over the top of her suitcase, tucked in an end of woolly shawl and shut the lid down. She looked round her bedroom. No, she had left nothing behind. Crump came in to fetch down her luggage. Miss Marple went into the next room to say goodbye to Miss Ramsbottom.

'I'm afraid,' said Miss Marple, 'that I've made a very poor return for your hospitality. I hope you will be able to forgive me some day.'

'Hah,' said Miss Ramsbottom.

She was as usual playing patience.

'Black knave, red queen,' she observed, then she darted a shrewd, sideways glance at Miss Marple. 'You found out what you wanted to, I suppose,' she said.

'Yes.'

'And I suppose you've told that police inspector all about it? Will he be able to prove a case?'

'I'm almost sure he will,' said Miss Marple. 'It may take a little time.'

'I'm not asking you any questions,' said Miss Ramsbottom. 'You're a shrewd woman. I knew that as soon as I saw you. I don't blame you for what you've done. Wickedness is wickedness and has got to be punished. There's a bad streak in this family. It didn't come from our side, I'm thankful to say. Elvira, my sister, was a fool. Nothing worse.

'Black knave,' repeated Miss Ramsbottom, fingering the card. 'Handsome, but a black heart. Yes, I was afraid of it. Ah, well, you can't always help loving a sinner. The boy always had a way with him. Even got round me. . . . Told a lie about the time he left me that day. I didn't contradict him, but I wondered. . . . I've wondered ever since. But he was Elvira's boy – I couldn't bring myself to say anything. Ah well, you're a righteous woman, Jane Marple, and right must prevail. I'm sorry for his wife, though.'

'So am I,' said Miss Marple.

In the hall Pat Fortescue was waiting to say goodbye.

'I wish you weren't going,' she said. 'I shall miss you.'

'It's time for me to go,' said Miss Marple. 'I've finished what I came here to do. It hasn't been – altogether pleasant. But it's important, you know, that wickedness shouldn't triumph.'

Pat looked puzzled.

'I don't understand.'

'No, my dear. But perhaps you will, some day. If I might venture to advise, if anything ever – goes wrong in your life – I think the happiest thing for you would be to go back to where you were happy as a child. Go back to Ireland, my dear. Horses and dogs. All that.'

Pat nodded.

'Sometimes I wish I'd done just that when Freddy died. But if I had' – her voice changed and softened – 'I'd never have met Lance.'

Miss Marpe sighed.

'We're not staying here, you know,' said Pat. 'We're going back to East Africa as soon as everything's cleared up. I'm so glad.'

'God bless you, dear child,' said Miss Marple. 'One needs a great deal of courage to get through life. I think you have it.'

She patted the girl's hand and, releasing it, went through the front door to the waiting taxi.

II

Miss Marple reached home late that evening.

Kitty – the latest graduate from St Faith's Home – let her in and greeted her with a beaming face.

'I've got a herring for your supper, miss. I'm so glad to see you home – you'll find everything very nice in the house. Regular spring cleaning I've had.'

'That's very nice, Kitty – I'm glad to be home.'

Six spiders webs on the cornice, Miss Marple noted. These girls never raised their heads! She was none the less too kind to say so.

'Your letters is on the hall table, miss. And there's one as went to Daisymead by mistake. Always doing that, aren't they? Does look a bit alike, Dane and Daisy, and the writing's so bad I don't wonder this time. They've been away there and the house shut up, they only got back and sent it round today. Said as how they hoped it wasn't important.'

Miss Marple picked up her correspondence. The letter to which Kitty had referred was on top of the others. A faint chord of remembrance stirred in Miss Marple's mind at the sight of the blotted scrawled handwriting. She tore it open.

DEAR MADAM,

I hope as you'll forgive me writing this but I really don't know what to do indeed I don't and I never meant no harm. Dear madam, you'll have seen the newspapers it was murder they say but it wasn't me that did it, not really, because I would never do anything wicked like that and I know as how he wouldn't either. Albert, I mean. I'm telling this badly, but you see we met last summer and was going to be married only Bert hadn't got his rights, he'd been done out of them, swindled by this Mr Fortescue who's dead. And Mr Fortescue he just denied everything and of course everybody believed him and not Bert because he was rich and Bert was poor. But Bert had a friend who works in a place where they make these new drugs and there's what they call a truth drug you've read about it perhaps in the paper and it makes people speak the truth whether they want to or not. Bert was going to see Mr Fortescue in his office on Nov. 5th and taking a lawyer with him and I was to be sure to give him the drug at breakfast that morning and then it would work just right for when they came and he'd admit as all what Bert said was quite true. Well, madam, I put it in the marmalade but now he's dead and I think as how it must have been too strong but it wasn't Bert's fault because Bert would never do a thing like that but I can't tell the police because maybe they'd think Bert did it on purpose which I know he didn't Oh, madam, I don't know what to do or what to say and the police are here in the house and it's awful and they ask you questions and look at you so stern and I don't know what to do and I haven't heard from Bert. Oh, madam, I don't like to ask it of you but if you could only come here and help me they'd listen to you and you were always so kind to me, and I didn't mean anything wrong and Bert didn't either. If you could only help us. Yours respectfully,

GLADYS MARTIN.

P.S. – I'm enclosing a snap of Bert and me. One of the boys took it at the camp and give it me. Bert doesn't know I've got it – he hates being snapped. But you can see, madam, what a nice boy he is.

Miss Marple, her lips pursed together, stared down at the photograph. The pair pictured there were looking at each other. Miss Marple's eyes went from Gladys's pathetic adoring face, the mouth slightly open, to the other face – the dark handsome smiling face of Lance Fortescue.

The last words of the pathetic letter echoed in her mind:
You can see what a nice boy he is.

The tears rose in Miss Marple's eyes. Succeeding pity, there came anger – anger against a heartless killer.

And then, displacing both these emotions, there came a surge of triumph – the triumph some specialist might feel who has successfully reconstructed an extinct animal from a fragment of jawbone and a couple of teeth.

THE MIRROR CRACK'D FROM SIDE TO SIDE

Out flew the web and floated wide;
*   The mirror crack'd from side to side:*
'The curse is come upon me,' cried
*   The Lady of Shalott.*

ALFRED TENNYSON

Miss Jane Marple was sitting by her window. The window looked over her garden, once a source of pride to her. That was no longer so. Nowadays she looked out of the window and winced. Active gardening had been forbidden her for some time now. No stooping, no digging, no planting – at most a little light pruning. Old Ladycock who came three times a week, did his best, no doubt. But his best, such as it was (which was not much) was only the best according to *his* lights, and not according to those of his employer. Miss Marple knew exactly what she wanted done, and when she wanted it done, and instructed him duly. Old Laycock then displayed his particular genius which was that of enthusiastic agreement and subsequent lack of performance.

'That's right, missus. We'll have them mecosoapies there and the Canterburys along the wall and as you say it ought to be got on with first thing next week.'

Laycock's excuses were always reasonable, and strongly resembled those of Captain George's in *Three Men in a Boat* for avoiding going to sea. In the captain's case the wind was always wrong, either blowing off shore or in shore, or coming from the unreliable west, or the even more treacherous east. Laycock's was the weather. Too dry – too wet – waterlogged – a nip of frost in the air. Or else something of great importance had to come first (usually to do with cabbages or brussels sprouts of which he liked to grow inordinate quantities). Laycock's own principles of gardening were simple, and no employer, however knowledgeable, could wean him from them.

They consisted of a great many cups of tea, sweet and strong, as an encouragement to effort, a good deal of sweeping up of leaves in the autumn, and a certain amount of bedding out of his own favourite plants, mainly asters and salvias – to 'make a nice show,' as he put it, in summer. He was all in favour of syringeing roses for green-fly, but was slow to get around to it, and a demand for deep trenching for sweet peas was usually countered by the remark that you ought to see his own sweet peas! A proper treat last year, and no fancy stuff done beforehand.

To be fair, he was attached to his employers, humoured their fancies in horticulture (so far as no actual hard work was involved) but vegetables he knew to be the real stuff of life; a nice Savoy, or a bit of curly kale; flowers were fancy stuff such as ladies liked to go in for, having nothing better to do with their time. He showed his affection by producing presents of the aforementioned asters, salvias, lobelia edging, and summer chrysanthemums.

'Been doing some work at them new houses over at the Development. Want their gardens laid out nice, they do. More plants than they needed so I brought along a few, and I've put 'em in where them old-fashioned roses ain't looking so well.'

Thinking of these things, Miss Marple averted her eyes from the garden, and picked up her knitting.

One had to face the fact: St Mary Mead was *not* the place it had been. In a sense, of course, nothing was what it had been. You could blame the war (both the wars) or the younger generation, or women going out to work, or the atom bomb, or just the Government – but what one really meant was the simple fact that one was growing old. Miss Marple who was a very sensible old lady, knew that quite well. It was just that, in a queer way, she felt it more in St Mary Mead, because it had been her home for so long.

St Mary Mead, the old world core of it, was still there. The Blue Boar was there, and the church and the vicarage and the little nest of Queen Anne and Georgian houses, of which hers was one. Miss Hartnell's house was still there, and also Miss Hartnell, fighting progress to the last gasp. Miss Wetherby had passed on and her house was now inhabited by the bank manager and his family, having been given a face-lift by the painting of doors and windows a bright royal blue. There were new people in most of the other old houses, but the houses themselves were little changed in appearance since the people who had bought them had done so because they liked what the house agent called 'old world charm.' They just added another bathroom, and spent a good deal of money on plumbing, electric cookers, and dishwashers.

But though the houses looked much as before, the same could hardly be said of the village street. When shops changed hands there, it was with a view to immediate and intemperate modernisation. The fishmonger was unrecognisable with new super windows behind which the refrigerated fish gleamed. The butcher had remained conservative – good meat is good meat, if you have the money to pay for it. If not, you take the cheaper cuts and the tough joints and like it! Barnes, the grocer, was still there, unchanged, for which Miss Hartnell and Miss Marple and others daily thanked Heaven. So *obliging*, comfortable chairs to sit in by the counter, and cosy discussions as to cuts of bacon, and varieties of cheese. At the end of the street, however, where Mr Toms had once had his basket shop stood a glittering new supermarket – anathema to the elderly ladies of St Mary Mead.

'Packets of things one's never even *heard* of,' exclaimed Miss Hartnell. 'All these great packets of breakfast cereal instead of cooking a child a proper breakfast of bacon and eggs. *And* you're expected to take a basket *yourself* and go round looking for things – it takes a quarter of an hour sometimes to find all one wants – and usually made up in inconvenient sizes, too much or too little. And then a long queue waiting to pay as you go out. Most tiring. Of course it's all very well for the people from the Development—'

At this point she stopped.

Because, as was now usual, the sentence came to an end there. The Development, Period, as they would say in modern terms. It had an entity of its own, and a capital letter.

II

Miss Marple uttered a sharp exclamation of annoyance. She'd dropped a stitch again. Not only that, she must have dropped it some time ago. Not until now, when she had to decrease for the neck and count the stitches, had she realized the fact. She took up a spare pin, held the knitting sideways to the light and peered anxiously. Even her new spectacles didn't seem to do any good. And that, she reflected, was because obviously there came a time when oculists, in spite of their luxurious waiting-rooms, their up-to-date instruments, the bright lights they flashed into your eyes, and the very high fees they charged, couldn't do anything much more for you. Miss Marple reflected with some nostalgia on how good her eyesight had been a few (well, not perhaps a *few*) years ago. From the vantage point of her garden, so admirably placed to see all that was going on in St Mary Mead, how little had escaped her noticing eye! And with the help of her bird glasses – (an interest in birds was *so* useful!) – she had been able to see— She broke off there and let her thoughts run back over the past. Ann Protheroe in her summer frock going along to the Vicarage garden. And Colonel Protheroe – poor man – a very tiresome and unpleasant man, to be sure – but to be murdered like that— She shook her head and went on to thoughts of Griselda, the vicar's pretty young wife. Dear Griselda – such a faithful friend – a Christmas card every year. That attractive baby of hers was a strapping young man now, and with a very good job. Engineering, was it? He always *had* enjoyed taking his mechanical trains to pieces. Beyond the Vicarage, there had been the stile and the field path with Farmer Giles's cattle beyond in the meadows where now – now . . .

The Development.

And why not? Miss Marple asked herself sternly. These things had to be. The houses were necessary, and they were very well built, or so she had been told. 'Planning,' or whatever they called it. Though why everything had to be called a Close she couldn't imagine. Aubrey Close and Longwood Close, and Grandison Close and all the rest of them. Not really Closes at all. Miss Marple knew what a Close was perfectly. Her uncle had been a Canon of Chichester Cathedral. As a child she had gone to stay with him in the Close.

It was like Cherry Baker who always called Miss Marple's old-world overcrowded drawing-room the 'lounge.' Miss Marple corrected her gently, 'It's the drawing-room, Cherry.' And Cherry, because she was young and kind, endeavoured to remember, though it was obvious that to her 'drawing-room' was a very funny word to use – and 'lounge' came slipping out. She had of late, however, compromised on 'living-room.' Miss Marple liked Cherry very much. Her name was Mrs Baker and she came from the Development. She was one of the detatchment of young wives who shopped at the supermarket and wheeled prams about the quiet streets of St Mary Mead. They were all smart and well turned out. Their hair was crisp and curled. They laughed and talked and called to one another. They were like a happy flock of birds. Owing to the insidious snares of Hire Purchase, they were always in need of ready money, though their husbands all earned good wages; and so they came and did housework or cooking. Cherry was a quick and efficient cook, she was an intelligent girl, took telephone calls correctly and was quick to spot inaccuracies in the tradesmen's books. She was not much given to turning mattresses, and as far as washing up went Miss Marple always now passed the pantry door with her head turned away so as not to observe Cherry's method which was that of thrusting everything into the sink together and letting loose a snowstorm of detergent on it. Miss Marple had quietly removed her old Worcester teaset from daily circulation and put it in the corner cabinet whence it only emerged on special occasions. Instead she had purchased a modern service with a pattern of pale grey on white and no gilt on it whatsoever to be washed away in the sink.

How different it had been in the past. . . . Faithful Florence, for instance, that grenadier of a parlourmaid – and there had been Amy and Clara and Alice, those 'nice little maids' – arriving from St Faith's Orphanage, to be 'trained,' and then going on to better paid jobs elsewhere. Rather simple, some of them had been, and frequently adenoidal, and Amy distinctly moronic. They had gossiped and chattered with the other maids in the village and walked out with the fishmonger's assistant, or the under-gardener at the Hall, or one of Mr Barnes the grocer's numerous assistants. Miss Marple's mind went back over them affectionately thinking of all the little woolly coats she had knitted for their subsequent offspring. They had not been very good with the telephone, and no good at all at arithmetic. On the other hand, they knew how to wash up, and how to make a bed. They had had skills, rather than education. It was odd that nowadays it should be the educated girls who went in for all the domestic chores. Students from abroad, girls *au pair*, university students in the vacation, young married women like Cherry Baker, who lived in spurious Closes on new building developments.

There were still, of course, people like Miss Knight. This last thought came suddenly as Miss Knight's tread overhead made the lustres on the mantelpiece tinkle warningly. Miss Knight had obviously had her afternoon rest and would now go out for her afternoon walk. In a moment she would come to ask Miss Marple if she could get her anything in the town. The thought of Miss Knight brought the usual reaction to Miss Marple's mind. Of course, it was very generous of dear Raymond (her nephew) and nobody could be kinder than Miss Knight, and of course that attack of bronchitis *had* left her very weak, and Dr Haydock had said very firmly that she must not go on sleeping alone in the house with only someone coming in daily, but— She stopped there. Because it was no use going on with the thought which was 'If only it could have been someone other than Miss Knight.' But there wasn't much choice for elderly ladies nowadays. Devoted maidservants had gone out of fashion. In real illness you could have a proper hospital nurse, at vast expense and procured with difficulty, or you could go to hospital. But after that critical phase of illness had passed, you were down to the Miss Knights.

There wasn't, Miss Marple reflected, anything wrong about the Miss Knights other than the fact that they were madly irritating. They were full of kindness, ready to feel affection towards their charges, to humour them, to be bright and cheerful with them and in general to treat them as slightly mentally afflicted children.

'But I,' said Miss Marple to herself, 'although I may be old, am *not* a mentally afflicted child.'

At this moment, breathing rather heavily, as was her custom, Miss Knight bounced brightly into the room. She was a big, rather flabby woman of fifty-six with yellowing grey hair very elaborately arranged, glasses, a long thin nose, and below it a good-natured mouth and a weak chin.

'Here we are!' she exclaimed with a kind of beaming boisterousness, meant to cheer and enliven the sad twilight of the aged. 'I hope *we*'ve had out little snooze?'

'*I* have been knitting,' Miss Marple replied, putting some emphasis on the pronoun, 'and,' she went on, confessing her weakness with distaste and shame, 'I've dropped a stitch.'

'Oh dear, dear,' said Miss Knight. 'Well, we'll soon put that right, won't we?'

'*You* will,' said Miss Marple. '*I*, alas, am unable to do so.'

The slight acerbity of her tone passed quite unnoticed. Miss Knight, as always, was eager to help.

'There,' she said after a few moments. 'There you are, dear. Quite all right now.'

Though Miss Marple was perfectly agreeable to be called 'dear' (and even 'ducks') by the woman at the greengrocer or the girl at the paper shop, it annoyed her intensely to be called 'dear' by Miss Knight. Another of those things that elderly ladies have to bear. She thanked Miss Knight politely.

'And now I'm just going out for my wee toddle,' said Miss Knight humorously. 'Shan't be long.'

'Please don't dream of hurrying back,' said Miss Marple politely and sincerely.

'Well, I don't like to leave you too long on your own, dear, in case you get moped.'

'I assure you I am quite happy,' said Miss Marple. 'I probably shall have' (she closed her eyes) 'a little nap.'

'That's right, dear. Anything I can get you?'

Miss Marple opened her eyes and considered.

'You might go into Longdon's and see if the curtains are ready. And perhaps another skein of the blue wool from Mrs Wisley. And a box of blackcurrant lozenges at the chemist's. And change my book at the library – but don't let them give you anything that isn't on my list. This last one was too terrible. I couldn't read it.' She held out *The Spring Awakens*.

'Oh dear dear! Didn't you like it? I thought you'd love it. Such a pretty story.'

'And if it isn't too far for you, perhaps you wouldn't mind going as far as Halletts and see if they have one of those up-and-down egg whisks – *not* the turn-the-handle kind.'

(She knew very well they had nothing of the kind, but Halletts was the farthest shop possible.)

'If all this isn't too much—' she murmured.

But Miss Knight replied with obvious sincerity.

'Not at all. I shall be delighted.'

Miss Knight loved shopping. It was the breath of life to her. One met acquaintances, and had the chance of a chat, one gossiped with the assistants, and had the opportunity of examining various articles in the various shops. And one could spend quite a long time engaged in these pleasant occupations without any guilty feeling that it was one's duty to hurry back.

So Miss Knight started off happily, after a last glance at the frail old lady resting so peacefully by the window.

After waiting a few minutes in case Miss Knight should return for a shopping bag, or her purse, or a handkerchief (she was a great forgetter and returner), and also to recover from the slight mental fatigue induced by thinking of so many unwanted things to ask Miss Knight to get, Miss Marple rose briskly to her feet, cast aside her knitting and strode purposefully across the room and into the hall. She took down her summer coat from its peg, a stick from the hall stand and exchanged her bedroom slippers for a pair of stout walking shoes. Then she left the house by the side door.

'It will take her at least an hour and a half,' Miss Marple estimated to herself. 'Quite that – with all the people from the Development doing their shopping.'

Miss Marple visualised Miss Knight at Longdon's making abortive inquiries re curtains. Her surmises were remarkably accurate. At this moment Miss Knight was exclaiming, 'Of course, I felt quite sure in my own mind they wouldn't be ready yet. But of course I said I'd come along and see when the old lady spoke about it. Poor old dears, they've got so little to look forward to. One must humour them. And she's a sweet old lady. Failing a little now, it's only to be expected – their faculties get dimmed. Now that's a pretty material you've got there. Do you have it in any other colours?'

A pleasant twenty minutes passed. When Miss Knight had finally departed, the senior assistant remarked with a sniff, 'Failing, is she? I'll believe that when I see it for myself. Old Miss Marple has always been as sharp as a needle, and I'd say she still is.' She then gave her attention to a young woman in tight trousers and a sail-cloth jersey who wanted plastic material with crabs on it for bathroom curtains.

'Emily Waters, that's who she reminds me of,' Miss Marple was saying to herself, with the satisfaction it always gave her to match up a human personality with one known in the past. 'Just the same bird brain. Let me see, what happened to Emily?'

Nothing much, was her conclusion. She had once nearly got engaged to a curate, but after an understanding of several years the affair had fizzled out. Miss Marple dismissed her nurse attendant from her mind and gave her attention to her surroundings. She had traversed the garden rapidly only observing as it were from the corner of her eye that Laycock had cut down the old-fashioned roses in a way more suitable to hybrid teas, but she did not allow this to distress her, or distract her from the delicious pleasure of having escaped for an outing entirely on her own. She had a happy feeling of adventure. She turned to the right, entered the Vicarage gate, took the path through the Vicarage garden and came out on the right of way. Where the stile had been there was now an iron swing gate giving on to a tarred asphalt path. This led to a neat little bridge over the stream and on the other side of the stream where once there had been meadows with cows, there was the Development.

With the feeling of Columbus setting out to discover a new world, Miss Marple passed over the bridge, continued on to the path and within four minutes was actually in Aubrey Close.

Of course Miss Marple had seen the Development from the Market Basing Road, that is, had seen from afar its Closes and rows of neat well-built houses, with their television masts and their blue and pink and yellow and green painted doors and windows. But until now it had only had the reality of a map, as it were. She had not been in it and of it. But now she was here, observing the brave new world that was springing up, the world that by all accounts was foreign to all she had known. It was like a neat model built with child's bricks. It hardly seemed real to Miss Marple.

The people, too, looked unreal. The trousered young women, the rather sinister-looking young men and boys, the exuberant bosoms of the fifteen year old girls. Miss Marple couldn't help thinking that it all looked terribly depraved. Nobody noticed her much as she trudged along. She turned out of Aubrey Close and was presently in Darlington Close. She went slowly and as she went she listened avidly to the snippits of conversation between mothers wheeling prams, to the girls addressing young men, to the sinister-looking Teds (she supposed they were Teds) exchanging dark remarks with each other. Mothers came out on doorsteps calling to their children who, as usual, were busy doing all the things they had been told not to do. Children, Miss Marple reflected gratefully, never changed. And presently she began to smile, and noted down in her mind her usual series of recognitions.

That woman is just like Carry Edwards – and the dark one is just like that Hooper girl – she'll make a mess of her marriage just like Mary Hooper did. Those boys – the dark one is just like Edward Leeke, a lot of wild talk but no harm in him – a nice boy really – the fair one is Mrs Bedwell's Josh all over again. Nice boys, both of them. The one like Gregory Binns won't do very well, I'm afraid. I expect he's got the same sort of mother. . . .

She turned a corner into Walsingham Close and her spirits rose every moment.

The new world was the same as the old. The houses were different, the streets were called Closes, the clothes were different, the voices were different, but the human beings were the same as they always had been. And though using slightly different phraseology, the subjects of conversation were the same.

By dint of turning corners in her exploration, Miss Marple had rather lost her sense of direction and had arrived at the edge of the housing estate again. She was now in Carrisbrook Close, half of which was still 'under construction.' At the first-floor window of a nearly finished house a young couple were standing. Their voices floated down as they discussed the amenities.

'You must admit it's a nice position, Harry.'

'Other one was just as good.'

'This one's got two more rooms.'

'And you've got to pay for 'em.'

'Well, I *like* this one.'

'You would!'

'Ow, don't be such a spoil-sport. You know what Mum said.

'Your Mum never stops saying.'

'Don't you say nothing against Mum. Where'd I have been without her? And she might have cut up nastier than she did, I can tell you that. She could have taken you to court.'

'Oh, come off it, Lily.'

'It's a good view of the hills. You can almost see—' She leaned far out, twisting her body to the left. 'You can almost see the reservoir—'

She leant farther still, not realizing that she was resting her weight on loose boards that had been laid across the sill. They slipped under the pressure of her body, sliding outwards, carrying her with them. She screamed, trying to regain her balance.

'Harry—!'

The young man stood motionless – a foot or two behind her. He took one step backwards—

Desperately, clawing at the wall, the girl righted herself.

'Oo!' She let out a frightened breath. 'I near as nothing fell out. Why didn't you get hold of me?'

'It was all so quick. Anyway you're all right.'

'That's all you know about it. I nearly went, I tell you. And look at the front of my jumper, it's all mussed.'

Miss Marple went on a little way, then on impulse, she turned back.

Lily was outside in the road waiting for the young man to lock up the house.

Miss Marple went up to her and spoke rapidly in a low voice.

'If I were you, my dear, I shouldn't marry that young man. You want someone whom you can rely upon if you're in danger. You must excuse me for saying this to you – but I feel you ought to be warned.'

She turned away and Lily stared after her.

'Well, of all the—'

Her young man approached.

'What was she saying to you, Lil?'

Lily opened her mouth – then shut it again.

'Giving me the gipsy's warning, if you want to know.'

She eyed him in a thoughtful manner.

Miss Marple in her anxiety to get away quickly, turned a corner, stumbled over some loose stones and fell.

A woman came running out of one of the houses.

'Oh dear, what a nasty spill! I hope you haven't hurt yourself?'

With almost excessive goodwill she put her arms round Miss Marple and tugged her to her feet.

'No bones broken, I hope? There we are. I expect you feel rather shaken.'

Her voice was loud and friendly. She was a plump squarely built woman of about forty, brown hair just turning grey, blue eyes, and a big generous mouth that seemed to Miss Marple's rather shaken gaze to be far too full of white shining teeth.

'You'd better come inside and sit down and rest a bit. I'll make you a cup of tea.'

Miss Marple thanked her. She allowed herself to be led through the blue-painted door and into a small room full of bright cretonne-covered chairs and sofas.

'There you are,' said her rescuer, establishing her on a cushioned arm-chair. 'You sit quiet and I'll put the kettle on.'

She hurried out of the room which seemed rather restfully quiet after her departure. Miss Marple took a deep breath. She was not really hurt, but the fall had shaken her. Falls at her age were not to be encouraged. With luck, however, she thought guiltily, Miss Knight need never know. She moved her arms and legs gingerly. Nothing broken. If she could only get home all right. Perhaps, after a cup of tea—

The cup of tea arrived almost as the thought came to her. Brought on a tray with four sweet biscuits on a little plate.

'There you are.' It was placed on a small table in front of her. 'Shall I pour it out for you? Better have plenty of sugar.'

'No sugar, thank you.'

'You must have sugar. Shock, you know. I was abroad with ambulances during the war. Sugar's wonderful for shock.' She put four lumps in the cup and stirred vigorously. 'Now you get that down, and you'll feel as right as rain.'

Miss Marple accepted the dictum.

'A kind woman,' she thought. 'She reminds me of someone – now who is it?'

'You've been very kind to me,' she said, smiling.

'Oh, that's nothing. The little ministering angel, that's me. I love helping people.' She looked out of the window as the latch of the outer gate clicked. 'Here's my husband home. Arthur – we've got a visitor.'

She went out into the hall and returned with Arthur who looked rather bewildered. He was a thin pale man, rather slow in speech.

'This lady fell down – right outside out gate, so of course I brought her in.'

'Your wife is very kind, Mr—? '

'Badcock's the name.'

'Mr Badcock. I'm afraid I've given her a lot of trouble.'

'Oh, no trouble to Heather. Heather enjoys doing things for people.' He looked at her curiously. 'Were you on your way anywhere in particular?'

'No, I was just taking a walk. I live in St Mary Mead, the house beyond the Vicarage. My name is Marple.'

'Well, I never!' exclaimed Heather. 'So *you*'re Miss Marple. I've heard about you. You're the one who does all the murders.'

'Heather! What *do* you—'

'Oh, you know what I mean. Not actually *do* murders – find out about them. That's right, isn't it?'

Miss Marple murmured modestly that she *had* been mixed up in murders once or twice.

'I heard there have been murders here, in this village. They were talking about it the other night at the Bingo Club. There was one at Gossington Hall. I wouldn't buy a place where there'd been a murder. I'd be sure it was haunted.'

'The murder wasn't committed in Gossington Hall. A dead body was brought there.'

'Found in the library on the hearthrug, that's what they said?'

Miss Marples nodded.

'Did you ever? Perhaps they're going to make a film of it. Perhaps that's why Marina Gregg has bought Gossington Hall.'

'Marina Gregg?'

'Yes. She and her husband. I forget his name – he's a producer, I think, or a director – Jason something. But Marina Gregg, she's lovely, isn't she? Of course she hasn't been in so many pictures of late years – she was ill for a long time. But I still think there's never anybody like her. Did you see her in *Carmanella*? And *The Price of Love,* and *Mary of Scotland*? She's not so young any more, but she'll always be a wonderful actress. I've always been a terrific fan of hers. When I was a teenager I used to dream about her. The big thrill of my life was when there was a big show in aid of the St John's Ambulance in Bermuda, and Marina Gregg came to open it. I was mad with excitement, and then on the very day I went down with a temperature and the doctor said I couldn't go. But I wasn't going to be beaten. I didn't actually feel too bad. So I got up and put a lot of make-up on my face and went along. I was introduced to her and she talked to me for quite three minutes and gave me her autograph. It was wonderful. I've never forgotten that day.'

Miss Marple stared at her.

'I hope there were no – unfortunate after-effects?' she said anxiously.

Heather Badcock laughed.

'None at all. Never felt better. What I say is, if you want a thing you've got to take risks. I always do.'

She laughed again, a happy strident laugh.

Arthur Badcock said admiringly, 'There's never any holding Heather. She always gets away with things.'

'Alison Wilde,' murmured Miss Marple, with a nod of satisfaction.

'Pardon?' said Mr Badcock.

'Nothing. Just someone I used to know.'

Heather looked at her inquiringly.

'You reminded me of her, that is all.'

'Did I? I hope she was nice.'

'She was very nice indeed,' said Miss Marple slowly. 'Kind, healthy, full of life.'

'But she had her faults, I suppose?' laughed Heather. 'I have.'

'Well, Alison always saw her own point of view so clearly that she didn't always see how things might appear to, or affect, other people.'

'Like the time you took in that evacuated family from a condemned cottage and they went off with all our teaspoons,' Arthur said.

'But Arthur! – I couldn't have turned them away. It wouldn't have been kind.'

'They were family spoons,' said Mr Babcock sadly. 'Georgian. Belonged to my mother's grandmother.'

'Oh, do forget those old spoons, Arthur. You do harp so.'

'I'm not very good at forgetting, I'm afraid.'

Miss Marple looked at him thoughtfully.

'What's your friend doing now?' asked Heather of Miss Marple with kindly interest.

Miss Marple paused a moment before answering.

'Alison Wilde? Oh – she died.'

—— 3 ——

'I'm glad to be back,' said Mrs Bantry. 'Although, of course, I've had a wonderful time.'

Miss Marple nodded appreciatively, and accepted a cup of tea from her friend's hand.

When her husband, Colonel Bantry, had died some years ago, Mrs Bantry had sold Gossington Hall and the considerable amount of land attached to it, retaining for herself what had been the East Lodge, a charming porticoed little building replete with inconvenience, where even a gardener had refused to live. Mrs Bantry had added to it the essentials of modern life, a built-on kitchen of the latest type, a new water supply from the main, electricity, and a bathroom. This had all cost her a great deal, but not nearly so much as an attempt to live at Gossington Hall would have done. She had also retained the essentials of privacy, about three quarters of an acre of garden nicely ringed with trees, so that, as she explained, 'Whatever they do with Gossington I shan't really see it or worry.'

For the last few years she had spent a good deal of the year travelling about, visiting children and grandchildren in various parts of the globe, and coming back from time to time to enjoy the privacies of her own home. Gossington Hall itself had changed hands once or twice. It had been run as a guest house, failed, and been bought by four people who had shared it as four roughtly divided flats and subsequently quarrelled. Finally the Ministry of Health had bought it for some obscure purpose for which they eventually did not want it. The Ministry had now resold it – and it was this sale which the two friends were discussing.

'I have heard rumours, of course,' said Miss Marple.

'Naturally,' said Mrs Bantry. 'It was even said that Charlie Chaplin and all his children were coming to live here. That would have been wonderful fun; unfortunately there isn't a word of truth in it. No, it's definitely Marina Gregg.'

'How very lovely she was,' said Miss Marple with a sigh. 'I always remember those early films of hers. *Bird of Passage* with that handsome Joel Roberts. And the Mary, Queen of Scots film. And of course it was very sentimental, but I *did* enjoy *Comin' Thru the Rye*. Oh dear, that was a long time ago.'

'Yes,' said Mrs Bantry. 'She must be – what do you think? Forty-five? Fifty?'

Miss Marple thought nearer fifty.

'Has she been in anything lately? Of course I don't go very often to the cinema nowadays.'

'Only small parts, I think,' said Mrs Bantry. 'She hasn't been a star for quite a long time. She had that bad nervous breakdown. After one of her divorces.'

'Such a lot of husbands they all have,' said Miss Marple. 'It must be very tiring.'

'It wouldn't suit *me*,' said Mrs Bantry. 'After you've fallen in love with a man and married him and got used to his ways and settled down comfortably – to go and throw it all up and start again! It seems to me madness.'

'I can't presume to speak,' said Miss Marple with a little spinsterish cough, 'never having married. But it seems, you know, a *pity*.'

'I suppose they can't help it really,' said Mrs Bantry vaguely. 'With the kind of lives they have to live. So public, you know. I met her,' she added. 'Marina Gregg, I mean, when I was in California.'

'What was she like?' Miss Marple asked with interest.

'Charming,' said Mrs Bantry. 'So natural and unspoiled.' She added thoughtfully, 'it's like a kind of livery really.'

'What is?'

'Being unspoiled and natural. You learn how to do it, and then you have to go on being it all the time. Just think of the hell of it – never to be able to chuck something, and say, "Oh, for the Lord's sake stop bothering me." I dare say that in sheer self-defence you have to have drunken parties, or orgies.'

'She's had five husbands, hasn't she?' Miss Marple asked.

'At least. An early one that didn't count, and then a foreign Prince or Count, and then another film star, Robert Truscott, wasn't it? That was built up as a great romance. But it only lasted four years. And then Isidore Wright, the playwright. That was rather serious and quiet, and she had a baby – apparently she'd always longed to have a child – she's even half-adopted a few strays – anyway this was the real thing. Very much built up. Motherhood with a capital M. And then, I believe, it was an imbecile, or queer or something – and it was after that, that she had this breakdown and started to take drugs and all that, and threw up her parts.'

'You seem to know a lot about her,' said Miss Marple.

'Well, naturally,' said Mrs Bantry. 'When she bought Gossington I was interested. She married the present man about two years ago, and they say she's quite all right again now. He's a producer – or do I mean a director? I always get mixed. He was in love with her when they were quite young, but he didn't amount to very much in those days. But now, I believe, he's got quite famous. What's his name now? Jason – Jason something – Jason Hudd, no, Rudd, that's it. They've bought Gossington because it's handy for' – she hesitated – 'Elstree?' she hazarded.

Miss Marple shook her head.

'I don't think so,' she said. 'Elstree's in North London.'

'It's the fairly new studios. Hellingforth – that's it. Sounds so Finnish, I always think. About six miles from Market Basing. She's going to do a film on Elizabeth of Austria, I believe.'

'What a lot you know,' said Miss Marple. 'About the private lives of film stars. Did you learn it all in California?'

'Not really,' said Mrs Bantry. 'Actually I get it from the extraordinary magazines I read at my hairdresser's. Most of the stars I don't even know by name, but as I said because Marina Gregg and her husband have bought Gossington, I was interested. Really the things those magazines say! I don't suppose half of it is true – probably not a quarter. I *don't* believe Marina Gregg is a nymphomaniac, I *don't* think she drinks, probably she doesn't even take drugs, and quite likely she just went away to have a nice rest and didn't have a nervous breakdown at all! – but it's true that she is coming here to live.'

'Next week, I heard,' said Miss Marple.

As soon as that? I know she's lending Gossington for a big fête on the twenty-third in aid of St John's Ambulance Corps. I suppose they've done a lot to the house?'

'Practically everything,' said Miss Marple. 'Really, it would have been much simpler, and probably cheaper, to have pulled it down and built a new house.'

'Bathrooms, I suppose?'

'Six new ones, I hear. And a palm court. And a pool. And what I believe they call picture windows, and they've knocked your husband's study and library into one to make a music room.'

'Arthur will turn in his grave. You know how he hated music. Tone deaf, poor dear. His face, when some kind friend took us to the opera! He'll probably come back and haunt them.' She stopped and then said abruptly, 'Does anyone ever hint that Gossington might be haunted?'

Miss Marple shook her head.

'It isn't,' she said with certainty.

'That wouldn't prevent people saying it was,' Mrs Bantry pointed out.

'Nobody ever has said so.' Miss Marple paused and then said, 'People aren't really foolish, you know. Not in villages.'

Mrs Bantry shot her a quick look. 'You've always stuck to that, Jane. And I won't say that you're not right.'

She suddenly smiled.

'Marina Gregg asked me, very sweetly and delicately, if I wouldn't find it very painful to see my old home occupied by strangers? I assured her that it wouldn't hurt me at all. I don't think she quite believed me. But after all, as you know, Jane, Gossington wasn't our home. We weren't brought up there as children – that's what really counts. It was just a house with a nice bit of shooting and fishing attached, that we bought when Arthur retired. We thought of it, I remember, as a house that would be nice and easy to run! How we can ever have thought that, I can't imagine! All those staircases and passages. Only four servants! *Only!* Those were the days, ha ha!' She added suddenly: 'What's all this about your falling down? That Knight woman ought not to let you go out by yourself.'

'It wasn't poor Miss Knight's fault. I gave her a lot of shopping to do and then I—'

'Deliberately gave her the slip? I see. Well, you shouldn't do it, Jane. Not at your age.'

'How did you hear about it?'

Mrs Bantry grinned.

'You can't keep any secrets in St Mary Mead. You've often told me so. Mrs Meavy told me.'

'Mrs Meavy?' Miss Marple looked at sea.

'She comes in daily. She's from the Development.'

'Oh, the Development.' The usual pause happened.

'What were you doing in the Development?' asked Mrs Bantry, curiously.

'I just wanted to see it. To see what the people were like.'

'And what did you think they were like?'

'Just the same as everyone else. I don't quite know if that was disappointing or reassuring.'

'Disappointing, I should think.'

'No. I think it's reassuring. It makes you – well – recognise certain types – so that when anything occurs – one will understand quite well why and for what reason.'

'Murder, do you mean?'

Miss Marple looked shocked.

'I don't know why you should assume that I think of murder *all* the time.'

'Nonsense, Jane. Why don't you come out boldly, and call yourself a criminologist and have done with it?'

'Because I am nothing of the sort,' said Miss Marple with spirit. 'It is simply that I have a certain knowledge of human nature – that is only natural after having lived in a small village all my life.'

'You probably have something there,' said Mrs Bantry thoughtfully, 'though most people wouldn't agree, of course. Your nephew Raymond always used to say this place was a complete backwater.'

'Dear Raymond,' said Miss Marple indulgently. She added: 'He's always been so kind. He's paying for Miss Knight, you know.'

The thought of Miss Knight induced a new train of thought and she rose and said: 'I'd better be going back now, I suppose.'

'You didn't walk all the way here, did you?'

'Of course not. I came in Inch.'

This somewhat enigmatic pronouncement was received with complete understanding. In days very long past, Mr Inch had been the proprietor of two cabs which met trains at the local station and which were also hired by the local ladies to take them 'calling,' out to tea parties, and occasionally, with their daughters, to such frivolous entertainments as dances. In the fullness of time Inch, a cheery red-faced man of seventy odd gave place to his son – known as 'young Inch' (he was then aged forty-five) though old Inch still continued to drive such elderly ladies as considered his son to young and irresponsible. To keep up with the times, young Inch abandoned horse vehicles for motor cars. He was not very good with machinery and in due course a certain Mr Bardwell took over from him. The name Inch persisted. Mr Bardwell in due course sold out to Mr Roberts, but in the telephone book *Inch's Taxi Service* was still the official name, and the older ladies of the community continued to refer to their journeys as going somewhere 'in Inch,' as though they were Jonah and Inch was a whale.

II

'Dr Haydock called,' said Miss Knight reproachfully. 'I told him you'd gone to tea with Mrs Bantry. He said he'd call in again to-morrow.'

She helped Miss Marple off with her wraps.

'And now, I expect, we're tired out,' she said accusingly.

'*You* may be,' said Miss Marple. '*I* am not.'

'You come and sit cosy by the fire,' said Miss Knight, as usual paying no attention. ('You don't need to take much notice of what the old dears say. I just humour them.') 'And how would we fancy a nice cup of Ovaltine? Or Horlicks for a change?'

Miss Marple thanked her and said she would like a small glass of dry sherry. Miss Knight looked disapproving.

'I don't know what the doctor would say to that, I'm sure,' she said, when she returned with the glass.

'We will make a point of asking him tomorrow morning,' said Miss Marple.

On the following morning Miss Knight met Dr Haydock in the hall, and did some agitated whispering.

The elderly doctor came into the room rubbing his hands, for it was a chilly morning.

'Here's our doctor to see us,' said Miss Knight gaily. 'Can I take your gloves, Doctor?'

'They'll be all right here,' said Haydock, casting them carelessly on a table. 'Quite a nippy morning.'

'A little glass of sherry perhaps?' suggested Miss Marple.

'I heard you were taking to drink. Well, you should never drink alone.'

The decanter and glasses were already on a small table by Miss Marple. Miss Knight left the room.

Dr Haydock was a very old friend. He had semi-retired, but came to attend certain of his old patients.

'I hear you've been falling about,' he said as he finished his glass. 'It won't do, you know, not at your age. I'm warning you. And I hear you didn't want to send for Sandford.'

Sandford was Haydock's partner.

'That Miss Knight of yours sent for him anyway – and she was quite right.'

'I was only bruised and shaken a little. Dr Sandford said so. I could have waited quite well until you were back.'

'Now look here, my dear. I can't go on for ever. And Sandford, let me tell you, has better qualifications than I have. He's a first class man.'

'The younger doctors are all the same,' said Miss Marple. 'They take your blood pressure, and whatever's the matter with you, you get some kind of mass produced variety of new pills. Pink ones, yellow ones, brown ones. Medicine nowadays is just like a supermarket – all packaged up.'

'Serve you right if I prescribed leeches, and black draught, and rubbed your chest with camphorated oil.'

'I do that myself when I've got a cough,' said Miss Marple with spirit, 'and very comforting it is.'

'We don't like getting old, that's what it is,' said Haydock gently. 'I hate it.'

'You're quite a young man compared to me,' said Miss Marple. 'And I don't really mind getting old – not that in itself. It's the lesser indignities.'

'I think I know what you mean.'

'Never being alone! The difficulty of getting out for a few minutes by oneself. And even my knitting – such a comfort that has always been, and I really am a good knitter. Now I drop stitches all the time – and quite often I don't even know I've dropped them.'

Haydock looked at her thoughtfully.

Then his eyes twinkled.

'There's always the opposite.'

'Now what do you mean by that?'

'If you can't knit, what about unravelling for a change? Penelope did.'

'I'm hardly in her position.'

'But unravelling's rather in your line, isn't it?'

He rose to his feet.

'I must be getting along. What I'd prescribe for you is a nice juicy murder.'

'That's an outrageous thing to say!'

576

'Isn't it? However, you can always make do with the depth the parsley sank into the butter on a summer's day. I always wondered about that. Good old Holmes. A period piece, nowadays, I suppose. But he'll never be forgotten.'

Miss Knight bustled in after the doctor had gone.

'There,' she said, 'we look *much* more cheerful. Did the doctor recommend a tonic?'

'He recommended me to take an interest in murder.'

'A nice detective story?'

'No,' said Miss Marple. 'Real life.'

'Goodness,' exclaimed Miss Knight. 'But there's not likely to be a murder in this quiet spot.'

'Murders,' said Miss Marple, 'can happen anywhere. And do.'

'At the Development, perhaps?' mused Miss Knight. 'A lot of those Teddy-looking boys carry knives.'

But the murder, when it came, was not at the Development.

—— 4 ——

Mrs Bantry stepped back a foot or two, surveyed herself in the glass, made a slight adjustment to her hat (she was not used to wearing hats), drew on a pair of good quality leather gloves and left the lodge, closing the door carefully behind her. She had the most pleasurable anticipations of what lay in front of her. Some three weeks had passed since her talk with Miss Marple. Marina Gregg and her husband had arrived at Gossington Hall and were now more or less installed there.

There was to be a meeting there this afternoon of the main persons involved in the arrangements for the fête in aid of the St John's Ambulance. Mrs Bantry was not among those on the committee, but she had received a note from Marina Gregg asking her to come and have tea beforehand. It had recalled their meeting in California and had been signed, 'Cordially, Marina Gregg.' It had been handwritten, not typewritten. There is no denying that Mrs Bantry was both pleased and flattered. After all, a celebrated film star is a celebrated film star and elderly ladies, though they may be of local importance, are aware of their complete unimportance in the world of celebrities. So Mrs Bantry had the pleased feeling of a child for whom a special treat had been arranged.

As she walked up the drive Mrs Bantry's keen eyes went from side to side registering her impressions. The place had been smartened up since the days when it had passed from hand to hand. 'No expense spared,' said Mrs Bantry to herself, nodding in satisfaction. The drive afforded no view of the flower garden and for that Mrs Bantry was just as pleased. The flower garden and its special herbaceous border had been her own particular delight in the far-off days when she had lived at Gossington Hall. She permitted regretful and nostalgic memories of her irises. The best iris garden of any in the country, she told herself with a fierce pride.

Faced by a new front door in a blaze of new paint she pressed the bell. The door was opened with gratifying promptness by what was undeniably an Italian butler. She was ushered by him straight to the room which had been Colonel Bantry's library. This, as she had already heard, had been thrown into one with the study. The result was impressive. The walls were panelled, the floor was parquet. At one end was a grand piano and half-way along the wall was a superb record player. At the other end of the room was a small island, as it were, which comprised Persian rugs, a tea-table and some chairs. By the tea-table sat Marina Gregg, and leaning against the mantelpiece was what Mrs Bantry at first thought to be the ugliest man she had ever seen.

Just a few moments previously when Mrs Bantry's hand had been advanced to press the bell, Marina Gregg had been saying in a soft, enthusiastic voice, to her husband:

'This place is right for me, Jinks, just right. It's what I've always wanted. *Quiet.* English quiet and the English countryside. I can see myself living here, living here all my life if need be. And we'll adopt the English way of life. We'll have afternoon tea every afternoon with China tea and my lovely Georgian tea service. And we'll look out of the window on those lawns and that English herbaceous border. I've come *home* at last, that's what I feel. I feel that I can settle down here, that I can be quiet and happy. It's going to be home, this place. That's what I feel. *Home.*'

And Jason Rudd (known to his wife as Jinks) had smiled at her. It was an acquiescent smile, indulgent, but it held its reserve because, after all, he had heard it very often before. Perhaps this time it would be true. Perhaps this *was* the place that Marina Gregg might feel at home. But he knew her early enthusiasms so well. She was always so sure that at last she had found exactly what she wanted. He said in his deep voice:

'That's grand, honey. That's just grand. I'm glad you like it.'

'Like it? I adore it. Don't you adore it too?'

'Sure,' said Jason Rudd. 'Sure.'

It wasn't too bad, he reflected to himself. Good, solidly built, rather ugly Victorian. It had, he admitted, a feeling of solidity and security. Now that the worst of its fantastic inconveniences had been ironed out, it would be quite reasonably comfortable to live in. Not a bad place to come back to from time to time. With luck, he thought, Marina wouldn't start taking a dislike to it for perhaps two years to two year and a half. It all depended.

Marina said, sighing softly:

'It's so wonderful to feel well again. Well and strong. Able to cope with things.'

And he said again: 'Sure, honey, sure.'

And it was at that moment that the door opened and the Italian butler had ushered in Mrs Bantry.

Marina Gregg's welcome was all that was charming. She came forward, hands outstretched, saying how delightful it was to meet Mrs Bantry again. And what a coincidence that they should have met that time in San Francisco and that two years later she and Jinks should actually buy the house that had once belonged to Mrs Bantry. And she did hope, she really did hope that Mrs Bantry wouldn't mind terribly the way they'd pulled the house about and done things to it and she hoped she wouldn't feel that they were terrible intruders living here.

'Your coming to live here is one of the most exciting things that has ever happened in this place,' said Mrs Bantry cheerfully and she looked towards the mantelpiece. Whereupon, almost as an after-thought, Marina Gregg said:

'You don't know my husband, do you? Jason, this is Mrs Bantry.'

Mrs Bantry looked at Jason Rudd with some interest. Her first impression was that this was one of the ugliest men she had ever seen became qualified. He had interesting eyes. They were, she thought, more deeply sunk in his head than any eyes she had seen. Deep quiet pools, said Mrs Bantry to herself, and felt like a romantic lady novelist. The rest of his face was distinctly craggy, almost ludicrously out of proportion. His nose jutted upwards and a little red paint would have transformed it into the nose of a clown very easily. He had, too, a clown's big sad mouth. Whether he was at this moment in a furious temper or whether he always looked as though he were in a furious temper she did not quite know. His voice when he spoke was unexpectedly pleasant. Deep and slow.

'A husband,' he said, 'is always an afterthought. But let me say with my wife that we're very glad to welcome you here. I hope you don't feel that it ought to be the other way about.'

'You must get it out of your head,' said Mrs Bantry, 'that I've been driven forth from my old home. It never *was* my old home. I've been congratulating myself ever since I sold it. It was a most inconvenient house to run. I liked the garden but the house became more and more of a worry. I've had a perfectly splendid time ever since, travelling abroad and going and seeing my married daughters and my grandchildren and my friends in all the different parts of the world.'

'Daughters,' said Marina Gregg, 'you have daughters and sons?'

'Two sons and two daughters,' said Mrs Bantry, 'and pretty widely spaced. One in Kenya, one in South Africa. One near Texas and the other, thank goodness, in London.'

'Four,' said Marina Gregg. 'Four – and grandchildren?'

'Nine up to date,' said Mrs Bantry. 'It's great fun being a grandmother. You don't have any of the worry of parental responsibility. You can spoil them in the most unbridled way—'

Jason Rudd interrupted her. 'I'm afraid the sun catches your eyes,' he said, and went to a window to adjust the blind. 'You must tell us all about this delightful village,' he said as he came back.

He handed her a cup of tea.

'Will you have a hot scone or a sandwich, or this cake? We have an Italian cook and she makes quite good pastry and cakes. You see we have quite taken to your English afternoon tea.'

'Delicious tea too,' said Mrs Bantry, sipping the fragrant beverage.

Marina Gregg smiled and looked pleased. The sudden nervous movement of her fingers which Jason Rudd's eye had noticed a minute or two previously, was stilled again. Mrs Bantry looked at her hostess with great admiration. Marina Gregg's heyday had been before the rise to supreme importance of vital statistics. She could not have been described as Sex Incarnate, or 'The Bust' or 'The Torso.' She had been long and slim and willowy. The bones of her face and head had had some of the beauty associated with those of Garbo. She had brought personality to her pictures rather than mere sex. The sudden turn of her head, the opening of the deep lovely eyes, the faint quiver of her mouth, all these were what brought to one suddenly that feeling of breath-taking loveliness that comes not from regularity of feature but from some sudden magic of the flesh that catches the onlooker unawares. She still had this quality though it was not now so easily apparent. Like many film and stage actresses she had what seemed to be a habit of turning off personality at will. She could retire into herself, be quiet, gentle, aloof, disappointing to an eager fan. And then suddenly the turn of the head, the movement of the hands, the sudden smile and the magic was there.

One of her greatest pictures had been *Mary, Queen of Scots,* and it was of her performance in that picture that Mrs Bantry was reminded now as she watched her. Mrs Bantry's eye switched to the husband. He too was watching Marina. Off guard for a moment, his face expressed clearly his feelings. 'Good Lord,' said Mrs Bantry to herself. 'the man adores her.'

She didn't know why she should feel so surprised. Perhaps because film stars and their love affairs and their devotion were so written up in the Press, that one never expected to see the real thing with one's own eyes. On an impulse she said:

'I do hope you'll enjoy it here and that you'll be able to stay here some time. Do you expect to have the house for long?'

Marina opened wide surprised eyes as she turned her head. 'I want to stay here always,' she said. 'Oh, I don't mean that I shan't have to go away a lot. I shall, of course. There's a possibility of my making a film in North Africa next year although nothing's settled yet. No, but this will be my home. I shall come back here. I shall always be able to come back here.' She sighed. 'That's what's so wonderful. That's what's so very wonderful. To have found a *home* at last.'

'I see,' said Mrs Bantry, but at the same time she thought to herself, 'All the same I don't believe for a moment that it *will* be like that. I don't believe you're the kind that can ever settle down.'

Again she shot a quick surreptitious glance at Jason Rudd. He was not scowling now. Instead he was smiling, a sudden very sweet and unexpected smile, but it was a sad smile. 'He knows it too,' thought Mrs Bantry.

The door opened and a woman came in. 'Bartletts want you on the telephone, Jason,' she said.

'Tell them to call back.'

'They said it was urgent.'

He sighed and rose. 'Let me introduce you to Mrs Bantry,' he said. Ella Zielinsky, my secretary.'

'Have a cup of tea, Ella,' said Marina as Ella Zielinsky acknowledged the introduction with a smiling 'pleased to meet you.'

'I'll have a sandwich,' said Ella. 'I don't go for China tea.'

Ella Zielinsky was at a guess thirty-five. She wore a well cut suit, a ruffled blouse and appeared to breathe self-confidence. She had short-cut black hair and a wide forehead.

'You used to live here, so they tell me,' she said to Mrs Bantry.

'It's a good many years ago now,' said Mrs Bantry. 'After my husband's death I sold it and it's passed through several hands since then.'

'Mrs Bantry really says she doesn't hate the things we've done to it,' said Marina.

'I should be frightfully disappointed if you hadn't,' said Mrs Bantry. 'I came up here all agog. I can tell you the most splendid rumours have been going around the village.'

'Never knew how difficult it was to get hold of plumbers in this country,' said Miss Zielinsky, champing a sandwich in a businesslike way. 'Not that that's been really my job,' she went on.

'Everything is your job,' said Marina, 'and you know it is, Ella. The domestic staff and the plumbing and arguing with the builders.'

'They don't seem ever to have heard of a picture window in this country.'

Ella looked towards the window. 'It's a nice view, I must admit.'

'A lovely old-fashioned rural English scene,' said Marina. 'This house has got *atmosphere*.'

'It wouldn't look so rural if it wasn't for the trees,' said Ella Zielinsky. 'That housing estate down there grows while you look at it.'

'That's new since my time,' said Mrs Bantry.

'You mean there was nothing but the village when you lived here?'

Mrs Bantry nodded.

'It must have been hard to do your shopping.'

'I don't think so,' said Mrs Bantry. 'I think it was frightfully easy.'

'I understand having a flower garden,' said Ella Zielinsky, 'but you folk over here seem to grow all your vegetables as well.

Wouldn't it be much easier to buy them – there's a super-market?'

'It's probably coming to that,' said Mrs Bantry, with a sigh. 'They don't taste the same, though.'

'Don't spoil the atmosphere, Ella,' said Marina.

The door opened and Jason looked in. 'Darling,' he said to Marina, 'I hate to bother you but would you mind? They just want your private view about this.'

Marina sighed and rose. She trailed languidly towards the door. 'Always something,' she murmured. 'I'm so sorry, Mrs Bantry. I don't really think that this will take longer than a minute or two.'

'Atmosphere,' said Ella Zielinsky, as Marina went out and closed the door. 'Do you think the house has got atmosphere?'

'I can't say I ever thought of it that way,' said Mrs Bantry. 'It was just a house. Rather inconvenient in some ways and very nice and cosy in other ways.'

'That's what I should have thought,' said Ella Zielinsky. She cast a quick direct look at Mrs Bantry. 'Talking of atmosphere, when did the murder take place here?'

'No murder ever took place here,' said Mrs Bantry.

'Oh come now. The stories I've heard. There are always stories, Mrs Bantry. On the hearthrug, right there, wasn't it?' said Miss Zielinsky nodding towards the fireplace.

'Yes,' said Mrs Bantry. 'That was the place.'

'So there *was* a murder?'

Mrs Bantry shook her head. 'The murder didn't take place here. The girl who had been killed was brought here and planted in this room. She'd nothing to do with us.'

Miss Zielinsky looked interested.

'Possibly you had a bit of difficulty making people believe that?' she remarked.

'You're quite right there,' said Mrs Bantry.

'When did you find it?'

'The housemaid came in in the morning,' said Mrs Bantry, 'with early morning tea. We had housemaids then, you know.'

'I know,' said Miss Zielinsky, 'wearing print dresses that rustled.'

'I'm not sure about the print dress,' said Mrs Bantry, 'it may have been overalls by then. At any rate, she burst in and said there was a body in the library. I said "nonsense," then I woke up my husband and we came down to see.'

'And there it was,' said Miss Zielinsky. 'My, the way things happen.' She turned her head sharply towards the door and then back again. 'Don't talk about it to Miss Gregg, if you don't mind,' she said. 'It's not good for her, that sort of thing.'

'Of course. I won't say a word,' said Mrs Bantry. 'I never do talk about it, as a matter of fact. It all happened so long ago. But won't she – Miss Gregg I mean – won't she hear it anyway?'

'She doesn't come very much in contact with reality,' said Ella Zielinsky. 'Film stars can lead a fairly insulated life, you know. In fact very often one has to take care that they do. Things upset them. Things upset *her*. She's been seriously ill the last year or two, you know. She only started making a come-back a year ago.'

'She seems to like the house,' said Mrs Bantry, 'and to feel she will be happy here.'

'I expect it'll last a year or two,' said Ella Zielinsky.

'Not longer than that?'

'Well, I rather doubt it. Marina is one of those people, you know, who are always thinking they've found their heart's desire. But life isn't as easy as that, is it?'

'No,' said Mrs Bantry forcefully, 'it isn't.'

'It'll mean a lot to him if she's happy here,' said Miss Zielinsky. She ate two more sandwiches in an absorbed, rather gobbling fashion in the manner of one who crams food into themselves as though they have an important train to catch. 'He's a genius, you know,' she went on. 'Have you seen any of the pictures he's directed?'

Mrs Bantry felt slightly embarrassed. She was of the type of woman who when she went to the cinema went entirely for the picture. The long lists of casts, directors, producers, photography and the rest of it passed her by. Very frequently, indeed, she did not even notice the names of the stars. She was not, however, anxious to call attention to this failing on her part.

'I get so mixed up,' she said.

'Of course he's got a lot to contend with,' said Ella Zielinsky. 'He's got her as well as everything else and she's not easy. You've got to keep her happy, you see; and it's not really easy, I suppose, to keep people happy. Unless – that is – they – they are—' she hesitated.

'Unless they're the happy kind,' suggested Mrs Bantry. 'Some people,' she added thoughtfully, 'enjoy being miserable.'

'Oh, Marina isn't like that,' said Ella Zielinsky, shaking her head. 'It's more that her ups and downs are so violent. You know – far too happy one moment, far too pleased with everything and delighted with everything and how wonderful she feels. Then of course some little thing happens and down she goes to the opposite extreme.'

'I suppose that's temperament,' said Mrs Bantry vaguely.

'That's right,' said Ella Zielinsky. 'Temperament. They've all got it, more or less, but Marina Gregg has got it more than most people. Don't we know it! The stories I could tell you!' She ate the last sandwich. 'Thank God I'm only the social secretary.'

5

The throwing open of the grounds of Gossington Hall for the benefit of the St John's Ambulance Association was attended by a quite unprecedented number of people. Shilling admission fees mounted up in a highly satisfactory fashion. For one thing, the weather was good, a clear sunny day. But the preponderant attraction was undoubtedly the enormous local curiosity to know exactly what these 'film people' had done to Gossington Hall. The most extravangant assumptions were entertained. The swimming pool in particular caused immense satisfaction. Most people's ideas of Hollywood stars were of sun-bathing by a pool in exotic surroundings and in exotic company. That the climate of Hollywood might be more suited to swimming pools, than that of St Mary Mead failed to be considered. After all, England always has one fine hot week in the summer and there is always one day that the Sunday papers publish articles on How to Keep Cool, How to Have Cool Suppers and How to Make Cool Drinks. The pool was almost exactly what everyone had imagined it might be. It was large, its waters were blue, it had a kind of exotic pavilion for changing and was surrounded with a highly artificial plantation of hedges and shrubs. The reactions of the multitude were exactly as might have been expected and hovered over a wide range of remarks.

'O-oh, isn't it lovely!'

'Two penn'orth of splash here, all right!'

'Reminds me of that holiday camp I went to.'

'Wicked luxury I call it. It oughtn't to be allowed.'

'Look at all that fancy marble. It must have cost the earth!'

'Don't see why these people think they can come over here and spend all the money they like.'

'Perhaps this'll be on the telly sometime. That'll be fun.'

Even Mr Sampson, the oldest man in St Mary Mead, boasting proudly of being ninety-six though his relations insisted that he was only eighty-eight, had staggered along supporting his rheumatic legs with a stick, to see the excitement. He gave it his highest praise: 'Wicked, this!' He smacked his lips doubtfully. 'Ah, there'll be a lot of wickedness here, I don't doubt. Naked men and women drinking and smoking what they call in the papers them reefers. There'll be all that, I expect. Ah yes,' said Mr Sampson with enormous pleasure, 'there'll be a lot of wickedness.'

It was felt that the final seal of approval had been set on the afternoon's entertainment. For an extra shilling people were allowed to go into the house, and study the new music room, the drawing-room, the completely unrecognisable dining-room, now done in dark oak and Spanish leather, and a few other joys.

'Never think this was Gossington Hall, would you, now?' said Mr Sampson's daughter-in-law.

Mrs Bantry strolled up fairly late and observed with pleasure that the money was coming in well and that the attendance was phenomenal.

The large marquee in which tea was being served was jammed with people. Mrs Bantry hoped the buns were going to go round. There seemed some very competent women, however, in charge. She herself made a bee-line for the herbaceous border and regarded it with a jealous eye. No expense had been spared on the herbaceous border, she was glad to note, and it was a proper herbaceous border, well planned and arranged and expensively stocked. No personal labours had gone into it, she was sure of that. Some good gardening firm had been given the contract, no doubt. But aided by *carte blanche* and the weather, they had turned out a very good job.

Looking round her, she felt there was a faint flavour of a Buckingham Palace garden party about the scene. Everybody was craning to see all they could see, and from time to time a chosen few were led into one of the more secret recesses of the house. She herself was presently approached by a willowy young man with long wavy hair.

'Mrs Bantry? You *are* Mrs Bantry?'

'I'm Mrs Bantry, yes.'

'Hailey Preston.' He shook hands with her. 'I work for Mr Rudd. Will you come up to the second floor? Mr and Mrs Rudd are asking a few special friends up there.'

Duly honoured Mrs Bantry followed him. They went in through what had been called in her time the garden door. A red cord cordoned off the bottom of the main stairs. Hailey Preston unhooked it and she passed through. Just in front of her Mrs Bantry observed Councillor and Mrs Allcock. The latter who was stout was breathing heavily.

'Wonderful what they've done, isn't it, Mrs Bantry?' panted Mrs Allcock. 'I'd like to have a look at the bathrooms, I must say, but I suppose I shan't get the chance.' Her voice was wistful.

At the top of the stairs Marina Gregg and Jason Rudd were receiving this specially chosen elite. What had once been a spare bedroom had been thrown into the landing so as to make a wide lounge-like effect. Guiseppe the butler was officiating with drinks.

A stout man in livery was announcing guests.

'Councillor and Mrs Allcock,' he boomed.

Marina Gregg was being, as Mrs Bantry had described her to Miss Marple, completely natural and charming. She could already hear Mrs Allcock saying later: '—and so *unspoiled*, you know, in spite of being so famous.'

How very nice of Mrs Allcock to come, *and* the Councillor, and she did hope that they'd enjoy their afternoon. 'Jason, please look after Mrs Allcock.'

Councillor and Mrs Allcock were passed on to Jason and drinks.

'Oh, Mrs Bantry, it *is* nice of you to come.'

'I wouldn't have missed it for the world,' said Mrs Bantry and moved on purposefully towards the Martinis.

The young man called Hailey Preston ministered to her in a tender manner and then made off, consulting a little list in his hand, to fetch, no doubt, more of the Chosen to the Presence. It was all being managed very well, Mrs Bantry thought, turning, Martini in hand, to watch the next arrivals. The vicar, a lean, ascetic man, was looking vague and slightly bewildered. He said earnestly to Marina Gregg:

'Very nice of you to ask me. I'm afraid, you know, I haven't got a television set myself, but of course I – er – I – well, of course my young people keep me up to the mark.'

Nobody knew what he meant. Miss Zielinsky, who was also on duty, administered a lemonade to him with a kindly smile. Mr and Mrs Badcock were next up the stairs. Heather Badcock, flushed and triumphant, came a little ahead of her husband.

'Mr and Mrs Badcock,' boomed the man in livery.

'Mrs Badcock,' said the vicar, turning back, lemonade in hand, 'the indefatigable secretary of the association. She's one of our hardest workers. In fact I don't know what St John's would do without her.'

'I'm sure you've been wonderful,' said Marina.

'You don't remember me?' said Heather, in an arch manner. 'How should you, with all the hundreds of people you meet. And anyway, it was years ago. In Bermuda of all places in the world. I was there with one of our ambulance units. Oh, it's a long time ago now.'

'Of course,' said Marina Gregg, once more all charm and smiles.

'I remember it all so well,' said Mrs Badcock. 'I was thrilled, you know, absolutely thrilled. I was only a girl at the time. To think there was a chance of seeing Marina Gregg in the flesh – Oh! I was a mad fan of yours always.'

'It's too kind of you, really too kind of you,' said Marina sweetly, her eyes beginning to hover faintly over Heather's shoulder towards the next arrivals.

'I'm not going to detain you,' said Heather – 'but I must—'

'Poor Marina Gregg,' said Mrs Bantry to herself. 'I suppose this kind of thing is always happening to her! The patience they need!'

Heather was continuing in a determined manner with her story.

Mrs Allcock breathed heavily at Mrs Bantry's shoulder.

'The changes they've made here! You wouldn't believe till you saw for yourself. What it must have *cost* . . .'

'—I didn't feel really ill – and I thought I just must—'

'This is vodka,' Mrs Allcock regarded her glass suspiciously, 'Mr Rudd asked if I'd like to try it. Sounds very Russian. I don't think I like it very much . . .'

'—I said to myself: I won't be beaten! I put a lot of make-up on my face—'

'I suppose it would be rude if I just put it down somewhere.' Mrs Allcock sounded desperate.

Mrs Bantry reassured her kindly.

'Not at all. Vodka ought really to be thrown straight down the throat' – Mrs Allcock looked startled – 'but that needs practice. Put it down on the table and get yourself a Martini from that tray the butler's carrying.'

She turned back to hear Heather Badcock's triumphant peroration.

'I've never forgotten how wonderful you were that day. It was a hundred times worth it.'

Marina's response was this time not so automatic. Her eyes which had wavered over Heather Badcock's shoulder, now seemed to be fixed on the wall midway up the stairs. She was staring and there was something so ghastly in her expression that Mrs Bantry half took a step forward. Was the woman going to faint? What on earth could she be seeing that gave her that basilisk look? But before she could reach Marina's side the latter had recovered herself. Her eyes, vague and unfocused, returned to Heather and the charm of manner was turned on once more, albeit a shade mechanically.

'What a nice little story. Now, what will you have to drink? Jason! A cocktail?'

'Well, really I usually have lemonade or orange juice.'

'You must have something better than that,' said Marina. 'This is a feast day, remember.'

'Let me persuade you to an American daiquiri,' said Jason, appearing with a couple in his hand. 'They're Marina's favourites, too.'

He handed one to his wife.

'I shouldn't drink any more,' said Marina, 'I've had three already.' But she accepted the glass.

Heather took her drink from Jason. Marina turned away to meet the next person who was arriving.

Mrs Bantry said to Mrs Allcock, 'Let's go and see the bathrooms.'

'Oh, do you think we can? Wouldn't it look rather rude?'

'I'm sure it wouldn't,' said Mrs Bantry. She spoke to Jason Rudd. 'We want to explore your wonderful new bathrooms, Mr Rudd. May we satisfy this purely domestic curiosity?'

'Sure,' said Jason, grinning. 'Go and enjoy yourselves, girls. Draw yourselves baths if you like.'

Mrs Allcock followed Mrs Bantry along the passage.

'That was ever so kind of you, Mrs Bantry. I must say I wouldn't have dared myself.'

'One has to dare if one wants to get anywhere,' said Mrs Bantry.

They went along the passage, opening various doors. Presently 'Ahs' and 'Ohs' began to escape Mrs Allcock and two other women who had joined the party.

'I do like the pink one,' said Mrs Allcock. 'Oh, I like the pink one a lot.'

'I like the one with the dolphin tiles,' said one of the other women.

Mrs Bantry acted the part of hostess with complete enjoyment. For a moment she had really forgotten that the house no longer belonged to her.

'All those showers!' said Mrs Allcock with awe. 'Not that I really *like* showers. I never know how you keep your head dry.'

'It'd be nice to have a peep into the bedrooms,' said one of the other women, wistfully, 'but I suppose it'd be a bit *too* nosy. What do *you* think?'

'Oh, I don't think we could do *that*,' said Mrs Allcock. They both looked hopefully at Mrs Bantry.

'Well,' said Mrs Bantry, 'no, I suppose we oughtn't to—' then she took pity on them, 'But – I don't think anyone would know if we have one peep.' She put her hand on a door-handle.

But that had been attended to. The bedrooms were locked. Everyone was very disappointed.

'I suppose they've got to have some privacy,' said Mrs Bantry kindly.

They retraced their steps along the corridor. Mrs Bantry looked out of one of the landing windows. She noted below her Mrs Meavy (from the Development) looking incredibly smart in a ruffled organdie dress. With Mrs Meavy, she noticed, was Miss Marple's Cherry, whose last name for the moment Mrs Bantry could not remember. They seemed to be enjoying themselves and were laughing and talking.

Suddenly the house felt to Mrs Bantry old, worn-out and highly artificial. In spite of its new gleaming paint, its altera- tions, it was in essence a tired old Victorian Mansion. 'I was wise to go,' thought Mrs Bantry. 'Houses are like everything else. There comes a time when they've just had their day. This has had its day. It's been given a face lift, but I don't really think it's done it any good.'

Suddenly a slight rise in the hum of voices reached her. The two women with her started forward.

'What's happening?' said one. 'It sounds as though some- thing's happening.'

They stepped back along the corridor towards the stairs. Ella Zielinsky came rapidly along and passed them. She tried a bed- room door and said quickly, 'Oh, damn. Of course they've locked them all.'

'Is anything the matter?' asked Mrs Bantry.

'Someone's taken ill,' said Miss Zielinsky shortly.

'Oh dear, I'm sorry. Can I do anything?'

'I suppose there's a doctor here somewhere?'

'I haven't seen any of our local doctors,' said Mrs Bantry, 'but there's almost sure to be one here.'

'Jason's telephoning,' said Ella Zielinsky, 'but she seems pretty bad.'

'Who is it?' asked Mrs Bantry.

'A Mrs Badcock, I think.'

'Heather Badcock? But she looked so well just now.'

Ella Zielinsky said impatiently, 'She's had a seizure, or a fit, or something. Do you know if there's anything wrong with her heart or anything like that?'

'I don't really know anything about her,' said Mrs Bantry. 'She's new since my day. She comes from the Development.'

'The Development? Oh, you mean that housing estate. I don't even know where her husband is or what he looks like.'

'Middle-aged, fair, unobtrusive,' said Mrs Bantry. 'He came in with her so he must be about somewhere.'

Ella Zielinsky went into a bathroom. 'I don't know really what to give her,' she said. 'Sal volatile, do you think, something like that?'

'Is she faint?' said Mrs Bantry.

'It's more than that,' said Ella Zielinsky.

'I'll see if there's anything I can do,' said Mrs Bantry. She turned away and walked rapidly back towards the head of the stairs. Turning a corner she cannoned into Jason Rudd.

'Have you seen Ella?' he said, 'Ella Zielinsky?'

'She went along there into one of the bathrooms. She was looking for something. Sal volatile – something like that.'

'She needn't bother,' said Jason Rudd.

Something in his tone struck Mrs Bantry. She looked up sharply. 'Is it bad?' she said, 'really bad?'

'You could call it that,' said Jason Rudd. 'The poor woman's dead.'

'Dead!' Mrs Bantry was really shocked. She said, as she had said before, 'But she looked so well just now.'

'I know. I know.' said Jason. He stood there, scowling. 'What a thing to happen!'

6

'Here we are,' said Miss Knight, settling a breakfast tray on the bed-table beside Miss Marple. 'And how are we this morning? I see we've got out curtains pulled back,' she added with a slight note of disapproval in her voice.'

'I wake early,' said Miss Marple. 'You probably will, when you're my age,' she added.

'Mrs Bantry rang up,' said Miss Knight, 'about half an hour ago. She wanted to talk to you but I said she'd better ring up again after you'd had your breakfast. I wasn't going to disturb you at that hour, before you'd even had a cup of tea or anything to eat.'

'When my friends ring up,' said Miss Marple, 'I prefer to be told.'

'I'm sorry, I'm sure,' said Miss Knight, 'but it seemed to me very inconsiderate. When you've had your nice tea and your boiled egg and your toast and butter, we'll see.'

'Half an hour ago,' said Miss Marple, thoughtfully, 'that would have been – let me see – eight o'clock.'

'Much too early,' reiterated Miss Knight.

'I don't believe Mrs Bantry would have rung me up then unless it was for some particular reason,' said Miss Marple thoughtfully. 'She doesn't usually ring up in the early morning.'

'Oh well, dear, don't fuss your head about it,' said Miss Knight, soothingly. 'I expect she'll be ringing up again very shortly. Or would you like me to get her for you?'

'No thank you,' said Miss Marple. 'I prefer to eat my breakfast while it's hot.'

'Hope I haven't forgotten anything,' said Miss Knight, cheerfully.

But nothing had been forgotten. The tea had been properly made with boiling water, the egg had been boiled exactly three and three-quarter minutes, the toast was evenly browned, the butter was arranged in a nice little pat and the small jar of honey stood beside it. In many ways undeniably Miss Knight was a treasure. Miss Marple ate her breakfast and enjoyed it. Presently the whirr of a vacuum cleaner began below. Cherry had arrived.

Competing with the whirr of the vacuum cleaner was a fresh tuneful voice singing one of the latest popular tunes of the day. Miss Knight, coming in for the breakfast tray, shook her head.

'I really wish that young woman wouldn't go singing all over the house,' she said. 'It's not what I call respectful.'

Miss Marple smiled a little. 'It would never enter Cherry's head that she would have to be respectful,' she remarked. 'Why should she?'

Miss Knight sniffed and said, 'Very different to what things used to be.'

'Naturally,' said Miss Marple. 'Times change. That is a thing which has to be accepted.' She added, 'Perhaps you'll ring up Mrs Bantry now and find out what it was she wanted.'

Miss Knight bustled away. A minute or two later there was a rap on the door and Cherry entered. She was looking bright and excited and extremely pretty. A plastic overall rakishly patterned with sailors and naval emblems was tied round her dark blue dress.

'Your hair looks nice,' said Miss Marple.

'Went for a perm yesterday,' said Cherry. 'A bit stiff still, but it's going to be all right. I came up to see if you'd heard the news.'

'What news?' said Miss Marple.

'About what happened at Gossington Hall yesterday. You know there was a big do there for the St John's Ambulance?'

Miss Marple nodded. 'What happened?' she asked.

'Somebody died in the middle of it. A Mrs Badcock. Lives round the corner from us. I don't suppose you'd know her.'

'Mrs Badcock?' Miss Marple sounded alert. 'But I do know her. I think – yes, that was the name – she came out and picked me up when I fell down the other day. She was very kind.'

'Oh, Heather Badcock's kind all right,' said Cherry. 'Over-kind, some people say. They call it interfering. Well, anyway, she up and died. Just like that.'

'Died! But what of?'

'Search me,' said Cherry. 'She'd been taken into the house because of her being the secretary of the St John's Ambulance, I suppose. She and the mayor and a lot of others. As far as I heard, she had a glass of something and about five minutes later she was took bad and died before you could snap your fingers.'

'What a shocking occurrence,' said Miss Marple. 'Did she suffer from heart trouble?'

'Sound as a bell, so they say,' Cherry said. 'Of course, you never know, do you? I suppose you can have something wrong with your heart and nobody knowing about it. Anyway, I can tell you this. They've not sent her home.'

Miss Marple looked puzzled. 'What do you mean, not sent her home?'

'The body,' said Cherry, her cheerfulness unimpaired. 'The doctor said there'd have to be an autopsy. Post-mortem – whatever you call it. He said he hadn't attended her for anything and there was nothing to show the cause of death. Looks funny to me,' she added.

'Now what do you mean by funny?' said Miss Marple.

'Well.' Cherry considered. 'Funny. As though there was something behind it.'

'Is her husband terribly upset?'

'Looks as white as a sheet. Never saw a man as badly hit, to look at – that is to say.'

Miss Marple's ears, long attuned to delicate nuances, led her to cock her head slightly on one side like an inquisitive bird.

'Was he so very devoted to her?'

'He did what she told him and gave her her own way,' said Cherry, 'but that doesn't always mean you're devoted, does it? It may mean you haven't got the courage to stick up for yourself.'

'You didn't like her?' asked Miss Marple.

'I hardly know her really,' said Cherry. 'Knew her, I mean. I don't – didn't – dislike her. But she's just not my type. Too interfering.'

'You mean inquisitive, nosy?'

'No, I don't,' said Cherry. 'I don't mean that at all. She was a very kind woman and she was always doing things for people. And she was always quite sure she knew the best thing to do. What they thought about it wouldn't have mattered. I had an aunt like that. Very fond of seed cake herself and she used to bake seed cakes for people and take them to them, and she never troubled to find out whether they liked seed cake or not. There are people can't bear it, just can't stand the flavour of caraway. Well, Heather Badcock was a bit like that.'

'Yes,' said Miss Marple thoughtfully, 'yes, she would have been. I knew someone a little like that. Such people,' she added, 'live dangerously – though they don't know it themselves.'

Cherry stared at her. 'That's a funny thing to say. I don't quite get what you mean.'

Miss Knight bustled in. 'Mrs Bantry seems to have gone out,' she said. 'She didn't say where she was going.'

'I can guess where she's going,' said Miss Marple. 'She's coming here. I shall get up now,' she added.

594

II

Miss Marple had just ensconced herself in her favourite chair by the window when Mrs Bantry arrived. She was slightly out of breath.

'I've got plenty to tell you, Jane,' she said.

'About the fête?' asked Miss Knight, 'you went to the fête yesterday, didn't you? I was there myself for a short time early in the afternoon. The tea tent was very crowded. An astonishing lot of people seemed to be there. I didn't catch a glimpse of Marina Gregg, though, which was rather disappointing.'

She flicked a little dust off a table and said brightly, 'Now I'm sure you two want to have a nice little chat together,' and went out of the room.

'She doesn't seem to know anything about it,' said Mrs Bantry. She fixed her friend with a keen glance. 'Jane, I believe you *do* know.'

'You mean about the death yesterday?'

'You always know everything,' said Mrs Bantry. 'I cannot think how.'

'Well, really dear,' said Miss Marple, 'in the same way one always has known everything. My daily helper, Cherry Baker, brought the news. I expect the butcher will be telling Miss Knight presently.'

'And what do you think of it?' said Mrs Bantry.

'What do I think of what?' said Miss Marple.

'Now don't be aggravating, Jane, you know perfectly what I mean. There's this woman – whatever her name is—'

'Heather Badcock,' said Miss Marple.

'She arrives full of life and spirit. I was there when she came. And about a quarter of an hour later she sits down in a chair, says she doesn't feel well, gasps a bit and dies. What do you think of *that*?'

'One mustn't jump to conclusions,' said Miss Marple. 'The point is, of course, what did a medical man think of it?'

Mrs Bantry nodded. 'There's to be an inquest and a post-mortem,' she said. 'That shows what they think of it, doesn't it?'

'Not necessarily,' said Miss Marple. 'Anyone may be taken ill and die suddenly and they have to have a post-mortem to find out the cause.'

'It's more than that,' said Mrs Bantry.

'How do you know?' said Miss Marple.

'Dr Sandford went home and rang up the police.'

'Who told you that?' said Miss Marple, with great interest.

'Old Briggs,' said Mrs Bantry. 'At least, he didn't tell me. You know he goes down after hours in the evening to see to Dr Sandford's garden, and he was clipping something quite close to the study and he heard the doctor ringing up the police station in Much Benham. Briggs told his daughter and his daughter mentioned it to the post-woman and she told me,' said Mrs Bantry.

Miss Marple smiled. 'I see,' she said, 'that St Mary Mead has not changed very much from what it used to be.'

'The grape-vine is much the same,' agreed Mrs Bantry. 'Well, now, Jane, tell me what you think?'

'One thinks, of course, of the husband,' said Miss Marple reflectively. 'Was he there?'

'Yes, he was there. You don't think it would be suicide,' said Mrs Bantry.

'Certainly not suicide,' said Miss Marple decisively. 'She wasn't the type.'

'How did you come across her, Jane?'

'It was the day I went for a walk to the Development, and fell down near her house. She was kindness itself. She was a very kind woman.'

'Did you see the husband? Did he look as though he'd like to poison her?

'You know what I mean,' Mrs Bantry went on as Miss Marple showed some slight signs of protesting. 'Did he remind you of Major Smith or Bertie Jones or someone you've known years ago who did poison a wife, or tried to?'

'No,' said Miss Marple, 'he didn't remind me of anyone I know.' She added, 'But she did.'

'Who – Mrs Badcock?'

'Yes,' said Miss Marple, 'she reminded me of someone called Alison Wilde.'

'And what was Alison Wilde like?'

'She didn't know at all,' said Miss Marple slowly, 'what the world was like. She didn't know what people were like. She'd never thought about them. And so, you see, she couldn't guard against things happening to her.'

'I don't really think I understand a word of what you're saying,' said Mrs Bantry.

'It's very difficult to explain exactly,' said Miss Marple, apologetically. 'It comes really from being self-centred and I don't mean selfish by that,' she added. 'You can be kind and unselfish and even thoughtful. But if you're like Alison Wilde, you never really know what you may be doing. And so you never know what may happen to you.'

'Can't you make that a little clearer?' said Mrs Bantry.

'Well, I suppose I could give you a sort of figurative example. This isn't anything that actually happened, it's just something I'm inventing.'

'Go on,' said Mrs Bantry.

'Well, supposing you went into a shop, say, and you knew the proprietress had a son who was the spivvy young juvenile delinquent type. He was there listening while you told his mother about some money you had in the house, or some silver or a piece of jewellery. It was something you were excited and pleased about and you wanted to talk about it. And you also perhaps mention an evening that you were going out. You even say that you never lock the house. You're interested in what you're saying, what you're telling her, because it's so very much in your mind. And then, say, on that particular evening you come home because you've forgotten something and there's this bad lot of a boy in the house, caught in the act, and he turned round and coshes you.'

'That might happen to almost anybody nowadays,' said Mrs Bantry.

'Not quite,' said Miss Marple, 'most people have a sense of protection. They realize when it's unwise to say or do something because of the person or persons who are taking in what you say, and because of the kind of character that those people have. But as I say, Alison Wilde never thought of anybody else but herself— She was the sort of person who tells you what they've done and what they've seen and what they've felt and what they've heard. They never mention what any other people said or did. Life is a kind of one-way track – just their own progress through it. Other people seem to them just like – like wallpaper in a room.' She paused and then said, 'I think Heather Badcock was that kind of person.'

Mrs Bantry said, 'You think she was the sort of person who might have butted into something without knowing what she was doing?'

'And without realizing that it was a dangerous thing to do,' said Miss Marple. She added, 'It's the only reason I can possibly think of why she should have been killed. If, of course,' added Miss Marple, 'we are right in assuming that murder *has* been committed.'

'You don't think she was blackmailing someone?' Mrs Bantry suggested.

'Oh, no,' Miss Marple assured her. 'She was a kind, good woman. She'd never have done anything of *that* kind.' She added vexedly, 'The whole thing seems to me very unlikely. I suppose it can't have been—'

'Well?' Mrs Bantry urged her.

'I just wondered if it might have been the wrong murder,' said Miss Marple thoughtfully.

The door opened and Dr Haydock breezed in, Miss Knight twittering behind him.

'Ah, at it already, I see,' said Dr Haydock, looking at the two ladies. 'I came in to see how your health was,' he said to Miss Marple, 'but I needn't ask. I see you've begun to adopt the treatment that I suggested.'

'Treatment, Doctor?'

Dr Haydock pointed a finger at the knitting that lay on the table beside her. 'Unravelling,' he said. 'I'm right, aren't I?'

Miss Marple twinkled very slightly in a discreet, old-ladyish kind of way.

'You will have your joke, Doctor Haydock,' she said.

'You can't pull the wool over my eyes, my dear lady. I've known you too many years. Sudden death at Gossington Hall and all the tongues of St Mary Mead are wagging. Isn't that so? Murder suggested long before anybody even knows the result of the inquest.'

'When is the inquest to be held?' asked Miss Marple.

'The day after tomorrow,' said Dr Haydock, 'and by that time,' he said, 'you ladies will have reviewed the whole story, decided on the verdict and decided on a good many other points too, I expect. Well,' he added, 'I shan't waste my time here. It's no good wasting time on a patient that doesn't need my ministrations. Your cheeks are pink, your eyes are bright, you've begun to enjoy yourself. Nothing like having an interest in life. I'll be on my way.' He stomped out again.

'I'd rather have him than Sandford any day,' said Mrs Bantry.

'So would I,' said Miss Marple. 'He's a good friend, too,' she added thoughtfully. 'He came, I think, to give me the go-ahead sign.'

'Then it *was* murder,' said Mrs Bantry. They looked at each other. 'At any rate, the doctors think so.'

Miss Knight brought in cups of coffee. For once in their lives, both ladies were too impatient to welcome this interruption. When Miss Knight had gone Miss Marple started immediately.

'Now then, Dolly, you were there—'

'I practically saw it happen,' said Mrs Bantry, with modest pride.

'Splendid,' said Miss Marple. 'I mean – well, you know what I mean. So you can tell me just exactly what happened from the moment she arrived.'

'I'd been taken into the house,' said Mrs Bantry. 'Snob status.'

'Who took you in?'

'Oh, a willowy-looking young man. I think he's Marina Gregg's secretary or something like that. He took me in, up the staircase. They were having a kind of reunion reception committee at the top of the stairs.'

'On the landing?' said Miss Marple, surprised.

'Oh, they've altered all that. They've knocked the dressing-room and bedroom down so that you've got a big sort of alcove, practically a room. It's very attractive looking.'

'I see. And who was there?'

'Marina Gregg, being natural and charming, looking lovely in a sort of willowy grey-green dress. And the husband, of course, and that woman, Ella Zielinsky I told you about. She's their social secretary. And there were about – oh, eight or ten people I should think. Some of them I knew, some of them I didn't. Some I think were from the studios – the ones I didn't know. There was the vicar and Doctor Sandford's wife. He wasn't there himself until later, and Colonel and Mrs Clittering and the High Sheriff. And I think there was someone from the Press there. And a young woman with a big camera taking photographs.'

Miss Marple nodded.

'Go on.'

'Heather Badcock and her husband arrived just after me. Marina Gregg said nice things to me, then to somebody else, oh yes, – the vicar – and then Heather Badcock and her husband came. She's the secretary, you know, of the St John's Ambulance. Somebody said something about that and how hard she worked and how valuable she was. And Marina Gregg said some pretty things. Then Mrs Badcock, who struck me, I must say, Jane, as rather a tiresome sort of woman, began some long rigmarole of how years before she'd met Marina Gregg somewhere. She wasn't awfully tactful about it since she urged exactly how long ago and the year it was and everything like that. I'm sure that actresses and film stars and people don't really like being reminded of the exact age they are. Still, she wouldn't think of that, I suppose.'

'No,' said Miss Marple, 'she wasn't the kind of woman who would have thought of that. Well?'

'Well, there was nothing particular in that except for the fact that Marina Gregg didn't do her usual stuff.'

'You mean she was annoyed?'

'No, no, I don't mean that. As a matter of fact I'm not at all sure that she heard a word of it. She was staring, you know, over Mrs Badcock's shoulder and when Mrs Badcock had finished her rather silly story of how she got out of a bed of sickness and sneaked out of the house to go and meet Marina and get her autograph, there was a sort of odd silence. Then I saw her face.'

'Whose face? Mrs Badcock's?'

'No. Marina Gregg's. It was as though she hadn't heard a word the Badcock woman was saying. She was staring over her shoulder right at the wall opposite. Staring with – I can't explain it to you—'

'But do try, Dolly,' said Miss Marple, 'because I think perhaps that this might be important.'

'She had a kind of frozen look,' said Mrs Bantry, struggling with words, 'as though she'd seen something that – oh dear me, how hard it is to describe things. Do you remember the Lady of Shalott? *The mirror crack'd from side to side: "The doom has come upon me," cried the Lady of Shalott.* Well, that's what she looked like. People laugh at Tennyson nowadays, but the Lady of Shalott always thrilled me when I was young and it still does.'

'She had a frozen look,' repeated Miss Marple thoughtfully. 'And she was looking *over* Mrs Badcock's shoulder at the wall. What was on that wall?'

'Oh! A picture of some kind, I think,' said Mrs Bantry. 'You know, Italian. I think it was a copy of a Bellini Madonna, but I'm not sure. A picture where the Virgin is holding up a laughing child.'

Miss Marple frowned. 'I can't see that a *picture* could give her that expression.'

'Especially as she must see it every day,' agreed Mrs Bantry.

'There were people coming up the stairs still, I suppose?'

'Oh yes, there were.'

'Who were they, do you remember?'

'You mean she might have been looking at one of the people coming up the stairs?'

'Well, it's possible, isn't it?' said Miss Marple.

'Yes – of course— Now let me see. There was the mayor, all dressed up too with his chains and all, and his wife, and there was a man with long hair and one of those funny beards they wear nowadays. Quite a young man. And there was the girl with the camera. She'd taken her position on the stairs so as to get photos of people coming up and having their hands shaken by Marina, and – let me see, two people I didn't know. Studio people, I think, and the Grices from Lower Farm. There may have been others, but that's all I can remember now.'

'Doesn't sound very promising,' said Miss Marple. 'What happened next?'

'I think Jason Rudd nudged her or something because all of a sudden she seemed to pull herself together and she smiled at Mrs Badcock, and she began to say all the usual things. You know, sweet, unspoilt, natural, charming, the usual bag of tricks.'

'And then?'

'And then Jason Rudd gave them drinks.'

'What kind of drinks?'

'Daiquiris, I think. He said they were his wife's favourites. He gave one to her and one to the Badcock woman.'

'That's very interesting,' said Miss Marple. 'Very interesting indeed. And what happened after that?'

'I don't know, because I took a gaggle of women to look at the bathrooms. The next thing I knew was when the secretary woman came rushing along and said someone had been taken ill.'

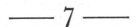

7

The inquest, when it was held, was short and disappointing. Evidence of identification was given by the husband, and the only other evidence was medical. Heather Badcock had died as a result of four grains of hy-ethyl-dexyl-barboquindelorytate, or, let us be frank, some such name! There was no evidence to show how the drug was administered.

The inquest was adjourned for a fortnight.

After it was concluded, Detective-Inspector Frank Cornish joined Arthur Badcock.

'Could I have a word with you, Mr Badcock?'

'Of course, of course.'

Arthur Badcock looked more like a chewed-out bit of string than ever. 'I can't understand it,' he muttered. 'I simply can't understand it.'

'I've got a car here,' said Cornish. 'We'll drive back to your house, shall we? Nicer and more private there.'

'Thank you, sir. Yes, yes, I'm sure that would be much better.'

They drew up at the neat little blue-painted gate of No. 3 Arlington Close. Arthur Badcock led the way and the inspector followed him. He drew out his latch-key but before he had inserted it into the door, it was opened from inside. The woman who opened it stood back looking slightly embarrassed. Arthur Badcock looked startled.

'Mary,' he said.

'I was just getting you ready some tea, Arthur. I thought you'd need it when you came back from the inquest.'

'That's very kind of you, I'm sure,' said Arthur Badcock gratefully. 'Er—' he hesitated. 'This is Inspector Cornish, Mrs Bain. She's a neighbour of mine.'

'I see,' said Inspector Cornish.

'I'll get another cup,' said Mrs Bain.

She disappeared and rather doubtfully Arthur Badcock showed the inspector into the bright cretonne-covered sitting-room to the right of the hall.

'She's very kind,' said Arthur Badcock. 'Very kind always.'

'You've known her a long time?'

'Oh no. Only since we came here.'

'You've been here two years, I believe, or is it three?'

'Just about three now,' said Arthur. 'Mrs Bain only got here about six months ago,' he explained. 'Her son works near here and so, after her husband's death, she came down to live here and he boards with her.'

Mrs Bain appeared at this point bringing the tray from the kitchen. She was a dark, rather intense-looking woman of about forty years of age. She had gipsy colouring that went with her dark hair and eyes. There was something a little odd about her eyes. They had a watchful look. She put down the tray on the table and Inspector Cornish said something pleasant and non-committal. Something in him, some professional instinct, was on the alert. The watchful look in the woman's eyes, the slight start she had given when Arthur introduced him had not passed unnoticed. He was familiar with that slight uneasiness in the presence of the police. There were two kinds of uneasiness. One was the kind of natural alarm and distrust as of those who might have offended unwittingly against the majesty of the law, but there was a second kind. And it was the second kind that he felt sure was present here. Mrs Bain, he thought, had had at some time some connexion with the police, something that had left her wary and ill at ease. He made a mental note to find out a little more about Mary Bain. Having set down the tea tray, and refused to partake herself saying she had to get home, she departed.

'Seems a nice woman,' said Inspector Cornish.

'Yes, indeed. She's very kind, a very good neighbour, a very sympathetic woman,' said Arthur Badcock.

'Was she a great friend of your wife?'

'No. No, I wouldn't say that. They were neighbourly and on pleasant terms. Nothing special about it though.'

'I see. Now, Mr Badcock, we want as much information as we can from you. The finishings of the inquest have been a shock to you, I expect?'

'Oh, they have, Inspector. Of course I realized that you must think something was wrong and I almost thought so myself because Heather has always been such a healthy woman. Practically never a day's illness. I said to myself, "There *must* be something wrong." But it seems so incredible, if you understand what I mean, Inspector. Really quite incredible. What is this stuff – this Bi-ethyl-hex—' he came to a stop.

'There is an easier name for it,' said the inspector. 'It's sold under a trade name, the trade name of Calmo. Ever come across it?'

Arthur Badcock shook his head, perplexed.

'It's more used in America than here,' said the inspector. 'They prescribe it very freely over there, I understand.'

'What's it for?'

'It induces, or so I understand, a happy and tranquil state of mind,' said Cornish. 'It's prescribed for those under strain; suffering anxiety, depression, melancholy, sleeplessness and a good many other things. The properly prescribed dose is not dangerous, but overdoses are not to be advised. It would seem that your wife took something like six times the ordinary dose.'

Badcock stared. 'Heather never took anything like that in her life,' he said. 'I'm sure of it. She wasn't one for taking medicines anyway. She was never depressed or worried. She was one of the most cheerful women you could possibly imagine.'

The inspector nodded. 'I see. And no doctor had prescribed anything of this kind for her?'

'No. Certainly not. I'm sure of that.'

'Who was her doctor?'

'She's on Dr Sims's panel, but I don't think she's been to him once since we've been here.'

Inspector Cornish said thoughtfully, 'So she doesn't seem the kind of woman to have been likely to need such a thing, or to have taken it?'

'She didn't, Inspector, I'm sure she didn't. She must have taken it by a mistake of some kind.'

'It's a very difficult mistake to imagine,' said Inspector Cornish. 'What did she have to eat and drink that afternoon?'

'Well, let me see. For lunch—'

'You needn't go back as far as lunch,' said Cornish. Given in such quantity the drug would act quickly and suddenly. Tea. Go back to tea.'

'Well, we went into the marquee in the grounds. It was a terrible scrum in there, but we managed in the end to get a bun each and a cup of tea. We finished it as quickly as possible because it was very hot in the marquee and we came out again.'

'And that's all she had, a bun and a cup of tea there?'

'That's right, sir.'

'And after that you went into the house. Is that right?'

'Yes. The young lady came and said that Miss Marina Gregg would be very pleased to see my wife if she would like to come into the house. Of course my wife was delighted. She had been talking about Marina Gregg for days. Everybody was excited. Oh well, you know that, Inspector, as well as anyone does.'

'Yes, indeed,' said Cornish. 'My wife was excited, too. Why, from all around people were paying their shilling to go in and see Gossington Hall and what had been done there, and hoped to catch a glimpse of Marina Gregg herself.'

'The young lady took us into the house,' said Arthur Badcock, 'and up the stairs. That's where the party was. On the landing up there. But it looked quite different from what it used to look like, so I understand. It was more like a room, a sort of big hollowed out place with chairs and tables with drinks on them. There were about ten or twelve people there, I suppose.'

Inspector Cornish nodded. 'And you were received there – by whom?'

'By Miss Marina Gregg herself. Her husband was with her. I've forgotten his name now.'

33

'Jason Rudd,' said Inspector Cornish.

'Oh, yes, not that I noticed him at first. Well, anyway, Miss Gregg greeted Heather very nicely and seemed very pleased to see her, and Heather was talking and telling a story of how she'd once met Miss Gregg years ago in the West Indies and everything seemed as right as rain.'

'Everything seemed as right as rain,' echoed the inspector. 'And then?'

'And then Miss Gregg said what would we have? And Miss Gregg's husband, Mr Rudd, got Heather a kind of cocktail. A dickery or something like that.'

'A daiquiri.'

'That's right, sir. He brought two. One for her and one for Miss Gregg.'

'And you, what did you have?'

'I had a sherry.'

'I see. And you three stood there drinking your drinks together?'

'Well, not quite like that. You see there were more people coming up the stairs. There was the mayor, for one, and some other people – an American gentleman and lady, I think – so we moved off a bit.'

'And your wife drank her daiquiri then?'

'Well, no, not then, she didn't.'

'Well, if she didn't drink it then, when did she drink it?'

Arthur Badcock stood frowning in remembrance. 'I think – she sat it down on one of the tables. She saw some friends there. I think it was someone to do with St John's Ambulance who'd driven over from Much Benham or somewhere like that. Anyway they got to talking together.'

'And when did she drink her drink?'

Arthur Badcock again frowned. 'It was a little after that,' he said. 'It was getting rather more crowded by then. Somebody jogged Heather's elbow and her glass got spilt.'

'What's that?' Inspector Cornish looked up sharply. 'Her drink was spilt?'

'Yes, that's how I remember it . . . She'd picked it up and I think she took a little sip and made rather a face. She didn't really like cocktails, you know, but all the same she wasn't going to be downed by that. Anyway, as she stood there, somebody jogged her elbow and the glass spilled over. It went down her dress and I think it went on Miss Gregg's dress too. Miss Gregg couldn't have been nicer. She said it didn't matter at all and it would make no stain and she gave Heather her handkerchief to wipe up Heather's dress, and then she passed over the drink she was holding and said, "Have this, I haven't touched it yet." '

'She handed over her own drink, did she?' said the inspector. 'You're sure of that?'

Arthur Badcock paused a moment while he thought. 'Yes, I'm quite sure of that,' he said.

'And your wife took the drink?'

'Well, she didn't want to at first, sir. She said "Oh no, I couldn't do that" and Miss Gregg laughed and said, "I've had far too much to drink already." '

'And so your wife took that glass and did what with it?'

'She turned away a little and drank it, rather quick, I think. And then we walked a little way along the corridor looking at some of the pictures and the curtains. Lovely curtain stuff it was, like nothing we'd seen before. Then I met a pal of mine, Councillor Allcock, and I was just passing the time of day with him when I looked round and saw Heather was sitting on a chair looking rather odd, so I came to her and said, "What's the matter?" She said she felt a little queer.'

'What kind of queerness?'

'I don't know, sir. I didn't have time. Her voice sounded very queer and thick and her head was rolling a little. All of a sudden she made a great half gasp and her head fell forward. She was dead, sir, dead.'

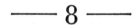

8

'St Mary Mead, you say?' Chief-Inspector Craddock looked up sharply.

The assistant commissioner was a little surprised.

'Yes,' he said, 'St Mary Mead. Why? Does it—'

'Nothing really,' said Dermot Craddock.

'It's quite a small place, I understand,' went on the other. 'Though of course there's a great deal of building development going on there now. Practically all the way from St Mary Mead to Much Benham, I understand. Hellingforth Studios,' he added, 'are on the other side of St Mary Mead, towards Market Basing.' He was still looking slightly inquiring. Dermot Craddock felt that he should perhaps explain.

'I know someone living there,' he said. 'At St Mary Mead. An old lady. A very old lady by now. Perhaps she's dead, I don't know. But if not—'

The assistant commissioner took his subordinate's point, or at any rate thought he did.

'Yes,' he said, 'it would give you an "in" in a way. One needs a bit of local gossip. The whole thing is a curious business.'

'The County have called us in?' Dermot asked.

'Yes. I've got the chief constable's letter here. They don't seem to feel it's necessarily a local affair. The largest house in the neighbourhood, Gossington Hall, was recently sold as a residence for Marina Gregg, the film star, and her husband. They're shooting a film at their new studios, at Hellingforth, in which she is starring. A fête was held in the grounds in aid of St John's Ambulance. The dead woman – her name is Mrs Heather Badcock – was the local secretary of this and had done most of the administrative work for the fête. She seems to have been a competent, sensible person, well liked locally.'

'One of those bossy women?' suggested Craddock.

'Very possibly,' said the assistant commissioner. 'Still in my experience, bossy women seldom get themselves murdered. I can't think why not. When you come to think of it, it's rather a pity. There was a record attendance at the fête, it seems, good weather, everything running to plan. Marina Gregg and her husband held a kind of small private reception in Gossington Hall. About thirty or forty people attended this. The local notables, various people connected with the St John's Ambulance Association, several friends of Marina Gregg herself, and a few people connected with the studios. All very peaceful, nice and happy. But fantastically and improbably, Heather Badcock was poisoned there.'

Dermot Craddock said thoughtfully, 'An odd place to choose.'

'That's the chief constable's point of view. If anyone wanted to poison Heather Badcock, why choose that particular afternoon and circumstances? Hundreds of much simpler ways of doing it. A risky business anyway, you know, to slip a dose of deadly poison into a cocktail in the middle of twenty or thirty people milling about. Somebody ought to have seen something.'

'It definitely was in the drink?'

'Yes, it was definitely in the drink. We have the particulars here. One of those long inexplicable names that doctors delight in, but actually a fairly common prescription in America.'

'In America. I see.'

'Oh, this country too. But these things are handed out much more freely on the other side of the Atlantic. Taken in small doses, beneficial.'

'Supplied on prescription or can it be bought freely?'

'No. You have to have a prescription.'

'Yes, it's odd,' said Dermot. 'Heather Badcock have any connection with these film people?'

'None whatsoever.'

'Any member of her own family at this do?'

'Her husband.'

'Her husband,' said Dermot thoughtfully.

'Yes, one always thinks that way,' agreed his superior officer, 'but the local man – Cornish, I think his name is – doesn't seem to think there's anything in that, although he does report that Badcock seemed ill at ease and nervous, but he agrees that respectable people often are like that when interviewed by the police. They appear to have been quite a devoted couple.'

'In other words, the police there don't think it's their pigeon. Well, it ought to be interesting. I take it I'm going down there, sir?'

'Yes. Better get there as soon as possible, Dermot. Who do you want with you?'

Dermot considered for a moment or two.

'Tiddler, I think,' he said thoughtfully. 'He's a good man and, what's more, he's a film fan. That might come in useful.'

The assistant commissioner nodded. 'Good luck to you,' he said.

II

'Well!' exclaimed Miss Marple, going pink with pleasure and surprise. 'This *is* a surprise. How are you, my dear boy – though you're hardly a boy now. What are you – a Chief-Inspector or this thing they call a Commander?'

Dermot explained his present rank.

'I suppose I need hardly ask what you are doing down here,' said Miss Marple. 'Our local murder is considered worthy of the attention of Scotland Yard.'

'They handed it over to us,' said Dermot, 'and so, naturally, as soon as I got down here I came to headquarters.'

'Do you mean—' Miss Marple fluttered a little.

'Yes, Aunty,' said Dermot disrespectfully. 'I mean you.'

'I'm afraid,' said Miss Marple regretfully, 'I'm very much out of things nowadays. I don't get out much.'

'You get out enough to fall down and be picked up by a woman who's going to be murdered ten days later,' said Dermot Craddock.

Miss Marple made the kind of noise that would once have been written down as 'tut-tut.'

'I don't know where you hear these things,' she said.

'You should know,' said Dermot Craddock. 'You told me yourself that in a village everybody knows everything.'

'And just off the record,' he added, 'did you think she was going to be murdered as soon as you looked at her?'

'Of course not, of course not,' exclaimed Miss Marple. 'What an idea!'

'You didn't see that look in her husband's eye that reminded you of Harry Simpson or David Jones or somebody you've known years ago, and who subsequently pushed his wife off a precipice.'

'No, I did *not*!' said Miss Marple. 'I'm sure Mr Badcock would never do a wicked thing of that kind. At least,' she added thoughtfully, 'I'm nearly sure.'

'But human nature being what it is—' murmured Craddock, wickedly.

'Exactly,' said Miss Marple. She added, 'I dare say, after the first natural grief, he won't miss her very much . . .'

'Why? Did she bully him?'

'Oh no,' said Miss Marple, 'but I don't think that she – well, she wasn't a considerate woman. Kind, yes. Considerate – no. She would be fond of him and look after him when he was ill and see to his meals and be a good housekeeper, but I don't think she would ever – well, that she would ever know what he might be feeling or thinking. That makes rather a lonely life for a man.'

'Ah,' said Dermot, 'and is his life less likely to be lonely in future?'

'I expect he'll marry again,' said Miss Marple. 'Perhaps quite soon. And probably, which is such a pity, a woman of much the same type. I mean he'll marry someone with a stronger personality than his own.'

'Anyone in view?' asked Dermot.

'Not that I know of,' said Miss Marple. She added regretfully, 'But I know so little.'

'Well, what do you *think*?' urged Dermot Craddock. 'You've never been backward in thinking things.'

'I think,' said Miss Marple, unexpectedly, 'that you ought to go and see Mrs Bantry.'

'Mrs Bantry? Who is she? One of the film lot?'

'No,' said Miss Marple, 'she lives in the East Lodge at Gossington. She was at the party that day. She used to own Gossington at one time. She and her husband, Colonel Bantry.'

'She was at the party. And she saw something?'

'I think she must tell you herself what it was she saw. You mayn't think it has any bearing on the matter, but I think it might be – just might be – suggestive. Tell her I sent you to her and – ah yes, perhaps you'd better just mention the Lady of Shalott.'

Dermot Craddock looked at her with his head just slightly on one side.

'The Lady of Shalott,' he said. 'Those are the code words, are they?'

'I don't know that I should put it that way,' said Miss Marple, 'but it will remind her of what I mean.'

Dermot Craddock got up. 'I shall be back,' he warned her.

'That is very nice of you,' said Miss Marple. 'Perhaps if you have time, you would come and have tea with me one day. If you still drink tea,' she added, rather wistfully. 'I know that so many young people nowadays only go out to drinks and things. They think that afternoon tea is a very outmoded affair.'

'I'm not as young as all that,' said Dermot Craddock. 'Yes, I'll come and have tea with you one day. We'll have tea and gossip, and talk about the village. Do you know any of the film stars, by the way, or any of the studio lot?'

'Not a thing,' said Miss Marple, 'except what I hear,' she added.

'Well, you usually hear a good deal,' said Dermot Craddock. 'Goodbye. It's been very nice to see you.'

III

'Oh, how do you do?' said Mrs Bantry, looking slightly taken aback when Dermot Craddock had introduced himself and explained who he was. 'How very exciting to see you. Don't you always have sergeants with you?'

'I've got a sergeant down here, yes,' said Craddock. 'But he's busy.'

'On routine inquiries?' asked Mrs Bantry, hopefully.

'Something of the kind,' said Dermot gravely.

'And Jane Marple sent you to me,' said Mrs Bantry, as she ushered him into her small sitting-room. 'I was just arranging some flowers,' she explained. 'It's one of those days when flowers won't do anything you want them to. They fall out, or stick up where they shouldn't stick up or won't lie down where you want them to lie down. So I'm thankful to have a distraction, and especially such an exciting one. So it really was murder, was it?'

Did you think it was murder?'

'Well, it could have been an accident, I suppose,' said Mrs Bantry. 'Nobody's said anything definite, officially, that is. Just that rather silly piece about no evidence to show by whom or in what way the poison was administered. But, of course, we all talk about it as murder.'

'And about who did it?'

'That's the odd part of it,' said Mrs Bantry. 'We don't. Because I really don't see who *can* have done it.'

'You mean as a matter of definite physical fact you don't see who could have done it?'

'Well, no, not that. I suppose it would have been difficult but not impossible. No, I mean, I don't see who could have *wanted* to do it.'

'Nobody, you think, could have wanted to kill Heather Badcock?'

'Well, frankly,' said Mrs Bantry, 'I can't imagine *anybody* wanting to kill Heather Badcock. I've seen her quite a few times, on local things, you know. Girl Guides and St John's Ambulance, and various parish things. I found her a rather trying sort of woman. Very enthusiastic about everything and a bit given to over-statement, and just a little bit of a gusher. But you don't want to murder people for that. She was the kind of woman who in the old days if you'd seen her approaching the front door, you'd have hurried out to say to your parlourmaid – which was an institution we had in those days and very useful too – and told her to say "Not at home" or "Not at home to visitors," if she had conscientious scruples about the truth.'

'You mean that one might take pains to avoid Mrs Badcock, but one would have no urge to remove her permanently.

'Very well put,' said Mrs Bantry, nodding approval.

'She had no money to speak of,' mused Dermot, 'so nobody stood to gain by her death. Nobody seems to have disliked her to the point of hatred. I don't suppose she was blackmailing anybody?'

'She wouldn't have dreamed of doing such a thing, I'm sure,' said Mrs Bantry. 'She was the conscientious and high-principled kind.'

'And her husband wasn't having an affair with someone else?'

'I shouldn't think so,' said Mrs Bantry. 'I only saw him at the party. He looked like a bit of chewed string. Nice but wet.'

'Doesn't leave much, does it?' said Dermot Craddock. 'One falls back on the assumption that she knew something.'

'Knew something?'

'To the detriment of somebody else.'

Mrs Bantry shook her head again. 'I doubt it,' she said. 'I doubt it very much. She struck me as the kind of woman who if she had known anything about anyone, couldn't have helped talking about it.'

'Well, that washes that out,' said Dermot Craddock, 'so we'll come, if we may, to my reasons for coming to see you. Miss Marple, for whom I have the greatest admiration and respect, told me that I was to say to you the Lady of Shalott.'

'Oh, *that*!' said Mrs Bantry.

'Yes,' said Craddock. '*That!* Whatever it is.'

'People don't read much Tennyson nowadays,' said Mrs Bantry.

'A few echoes come back to me,' said Dermot Craddock. 'She looked out to Camelot, didn't she?'

> '*Out flew the web and floated wide;*
> *The mirror crack'd from side to side:*
> *"The curse has come upon me," cried*
> *The Lady of Shalott.*'

'Exactly. She did,' said Mrs Bantry.

'I beg your pardon. Who did? Did what?'

'Looked like that,' said Mrs Bantry.

'Who looked like what?'

'Marina Gregg.'

'Ah. Marina Gregg. When was this?'

'Didn't Jane Marple tell you?'

'She didn't tell me anything. She sent me to you.'

'That's tiresome of her,' said Mrs Bantry, 'because she can always tell things better than I can. My husband always used to say that I was so abrupt that he didn't know what I was talking about. Anyway, it may have been only my fancy. But when you see anyone looking like that you can't help remembering it.'

'Please tell me,' said Dermot Craddock.

'Well, it was at the party. I call it a party because what can one call things? But it was just a sort of reception up at the top of the stairs where they've made a kind of recess. Marina Gregg was there and her husband. They fetched some of us in. They fetched me, I suppose, because I once owned the house, and they fetched Heather Badcock and her husband because she'd done all the running of the fête, and the arrangements. And we happened to go up the stairs at about the same time, so I was standing there, you see, when I noticed it.'

'Quite. When you noticed what?'

'Well, Mrs Badcock went into a long spiel as people do when they meet celebrities. You know, how wonderful it was, and what a thrill and they'd always hoped to see them. And she went into a long story of how she'd once met her years ago and how exciting it had been. And I thought, in my own mind, you know, what a bore it must be for these poor celebrities to have to say all the right things. And then I noticed that Marina Gregg wasn't saying the right things. She was just staring.'

'Staring – at Mrs Badcock?'

'No – no, it looked as though she'd forgotten Mrs Badcock altogether. I mean, I don't believe she'd even heard what Mrs Badcock was saying. She was just staring with what I call this Lady of Shalott look, as though she'd seen something awful. Something frightening, something that she could hardly believe she saw and couldn't bear to see.'

'The curse has come upon me?' suggested Dermot Craddock, helpfully.

'Yes, just that. That's why I called it the Lady of Shalott look.'

'But what was she looking *at*, Mrs Bantry?'

'Well, I wish I knew,' said Mrs Bantry.

'She was at the top of the stairs, you say?'

'She was looking over Mrs Badcock's head – no, more over one shoulder, I think.'

'Straight at the middle of the staircase?'

'It might have been a little to one side.'

'And there were people coming up the staircase?'

'Oh yes, I should think about five or six people.'

'Was she looking at one of these people in particular?'

'I can't possibly tell,' said Mrs Bantry. 'You see, I wasn't facing that way. I was looking at *her*. My back was to the stairs. I thought perhaps she was looking at one of the pictures.'

'But she must know the pictures quite well if she's living in the house.'

'Yes, yes, of course. No, I suppose she must have been looking at one of the people. I wonder which.'

'We have to try and find out,' said Dermot Craddock. 'Can you remember at all who the people were?'

'Well, I know the mayor was one of them and his wife. There was someone who I think was a reporter, with red hair, because I was introduced to him later, but I can't remember his name. I never hear names. Galbraith – something like that. Then there was a big black man. I don't mean a negro – I just mean very dark, forceful looking. And an actress with him. A bit over-blonde and the minky kind. And old General Barnstaple from Much Benham. He's practically ga-ga now, poor old boy. I don't think *he* could have been anybody's doom. Oh! and the Grices from the farm.'

'Those are all the people you can remember?'

'Well, there may have been others. But you see I wasn't – well, I mean I wasn't noticing particularly. I know that the mayor and General Barnstaple and the Americans did arrive about that time. And there were people taking photographs. One I think was a local man, and there was a girl from London, an arty-looking girl with long hair and a rather large camera.'

'And you think it was one of those people who brought that look to Marina Gregg's face?'

'I didn't really think anything,' said Mrs Bantry with complete frankness. 'I just wondered what on earth made her look like that and then I didn't think of it any more. But afterwards one remembers about these things. But of course,' added Mrs Bantry with honesty, 'I *may* have imagined it. After all, she may have had sudden toothache or a safety pin run into her or a sudden violent colic. The sort of thing where you try to go on as usual and not to show anything, but your face can't help looking awful.'

Dermot Craddock laughed. 'I'm glad to see you're a realist, Mrs Bantry,' he said. 'As you say, it may have been something of that kind. But it's certainly just one interesting little fact that might be a pointer.'

He shook hands and departed to present his official credentials in Much Benham.

614

9

'So locally you've drawn a blank?' said Craddock offering his cigarette case to Frank Cornish.

'Completely,' said Cornish. 'No enemies, no quarrels, on good terms with her husband.'

'No question of another woman or another man?'

The other shook his head. 'Nothing of that kind. No hint of scandal anywhere. She wasn't what you'd call the sexy kind. She was on a lot of committees and things like that and there were some small local rivalries, but nothing beyond that.'

'There wasn't anyone else the husband wanted to marry? No one in the office where he worked?'

'He's in Biddle & Russell, the estate agents and valuers. There's Florrie West with adenoids, and Miss Grundle, who is at least fifty and as plain as a haystack – nothing much there to excite a man. Though for all that I shouldn't be surprised if he *did* marry again soon.'

Craddock looked interested.

'A neighbour,' explained Cornish. 'A widow. When I went back with him from the inquest she'd gone in and was making him tea and looking after him generally. He seemed surprised and grateful. If you ask me, she's made up her mind to marry him, but he doesn't know it yet, poor chap.'

'What sort of a woman is she?'

'Good looking,' admitted the other. 'Not young but handsome in a gipsyish sort of way. High colour. Dark eyes.'

'What's her name?'

'Bain. Mrs Bain. Mary Bain. She's a widow.'

'What'd her husband do?'

'No idea. She's got a son working near here who lives with her. She seems a quiet, respectable woman. All the same, I've a feeling I've seen her before.' He looked at his watch. 'Ten to twelve. I've made an appointment for you at Gossington Hall at twelve o'clock. We'd best be going.'

II

Dermot Craddock's eyes, which always looked gently inattentive, were in actuality making a close mental note of the features of

Gossington Hall. Inspector Cornish had taken him there, had delivered him over to a young man called Hailey Preston, and had then taken a tactful leave. Since then, Dermot Craddock had been gently nodding at intervals as he listened to the flood of talk emanating from Mr Preston. Hailey Preston, he gathered, was a kind of public relations or personal assistant, or private secretary, or more likely, a mixture of all three, to Jason Rudd. He talked. He talked freely and at length without much modulation and managing miraculously not to repeat himself too often. He was a pleasant young man, anxious that his own views, reminiscent of those of Dr Pangloss that all was for the best in the best of all possible worlds, should be shared by anyone in whose company he happened to be. He said several times and in different ways what a terrible shame this had been, how worried everyone had been, how Marina was absolutely prostrated, how Mr Rudd was more upset than he could possibly say, how it absolutely beat anything that a thing like that should happen, didn't it? Possibly there might have been some kind of allergy to some particular kind of substance? He just put that forward as an idea – allergies were extraordinary things. Chief-Inspector Craddock was to count on every possible co-operation that Hellingforth Studios or any of their staff could give. He was to ask any questions he wanted, go anywhere he liked. If they could help in any way they would do so. They all had had the greatest respect for Mrs Badcock and appreciated her strong social sense and the valuable work she had done for the St John's Ambulance Association.

He then started again, not in the same words but using the same motifs. No one could have been more eagerly co-operative. At the same time he endeavoured to convey how very far this was from the cellophane world of studios; and Mr Jason Rudd and Miss Marina Gregg, or any of the people in the house who surely were going to do their utmost to help in any way they possibly could. Then he nodded gently some forty-four times. Dermot Craddock took advantage of the pause to say:

'Thank you very much.'

It was said quietly but with a kind of finality that brought Mr Hailey Preston up with a jerk. He said:

'Well—?' and paused inquiringly.

'You said I might ask questions?'

'Sure. Sure. Fire ahead.'

'Is this where she died?'

'Mrs Badcock?'

'Mrs Badcock. Is this the place?'

'Yes, sure. Right here. At least, well actually I can show you the chair.'

They were standing on the landing recess. Hailey Preston walked a short way along the corridor and pointed out a rather phony-looking oak arm-chair.

'She was sitting right there,' he said. 'She said she didn't feel well. Someone went to get her something and then she just died, right there.'

'I see.'

'I don't know if she'd seen a physician lately. If she'd been warned that she had anything wrong with her heart—'

'She had nothing wrong with her heart,' said Dermot Craddock. 'She was a healthy woman. She died of six times the maximum dose of a substance whose official name I will not try to pronounce but which I understand is generally known as Calmo.'

'I know, I know,' said Hailey Preston. 'I take it myself sometimes.'

'Indeed? That's very interesting. You find it has a good effect?'

'Marvellous. Marvellous. It bucks you up *and* it soothes you down, if you understand what I mean. 'Naturally,' he added, 'you have to take it in the proper dosage.'

'Would there be supplies of this substance in the house?'

He knew the answer to the question, but he put it as though he did not. Hailey Preston's answer was frankness itself.

'Loads of it, I should say. There'll be a bottle of it in most of the bathroom cupboards here.'

'Which doesn't make our task easier.'

'Of course,' said Hailey Preston, 'she might have used the stuff herself and taken a dose, and as I say, had an allergy.'

Craddock looked unconvinced – Hailey Preston sighed and said:

'You're quite definite about the dosage?'

'Oh yes. It was a lethal dose and Mrs Badcock did not take any such things herself. As far as we can make out the only things she ever took were bicarbonate of soda or aspirin.'

Hailey Preston shook his head and said, 'That sure gives us a problem. Yes, it sure does.'

'Where did Mr Rudd and Miss Gregg receive their guests?'

'Right here.' Hailey Preston went to the spot at the top of the stairs.

Chief-Inspector Craddock stood beside him. He looked at the wall opposite him. In the centre was an Italian Madonna and child. A good copy, he presumed, of some well-known picture. The blue-robed Madonna held aloft the infant Jesus and both child and mother were laughing. Little groups of people stood on either side, their eyes upraised to the child. One of the more pleasing Madonnas, Dermot Craddock thought. To the right and left of this picture were two narrow windows. The whole effect was very charming but it seemed to him that there was emphatically nothing there that could cause a woman to look like the Lady of Shalott whose doom had come upon her.

'People, of course, were coming up the stairs?' he asked.

'Yes. They came in driblets, you know. Not too many at once. I shepherded up some, Ella Zielinsky, that's Mr Rudd's secretary, brought some of the others. We wanted to make it all pleasant and informal.'

'Were you here yourself at the time Mrs Badcock came up?'

'I'm ashamed to tell you, Chief-Inspector Craddock, that I just can't remember. I had a list of names, I went out and I shepherded people in. I introduced them, saw to drinks, then I'd go out and come up with the next batch. At the time I didn't know this Mrs Badcock by sight, and she wasn't one of the ones on my list to bring up.'

'What about a Mrs Bantry?'

'Ah yes, she's the former owner of this place, isn't she? I believe she, and Mrs Badcock and her husband, *did* come up about the same time.' He paused. 'And the mayor came just about then. He had a big chain on and a wife with yellow hair, wearing royal blue with frills. I remember all of them. I didn't pour drinks for any of them because I had to go down and bring up the next lot.'

'Who did pour drinks for them?'

'Why, I can't exactly say. There were three or four of us on duty. I know I went down the stairs just as the mayor was coming up.'

'Who else was on the stairs as you went down, if you can remember?'

'Jim Galbraith, one of the newspaper boys who was covering this, three or four others whom I didn't know, There were a couple of photographers, one of the locals, I don't remember his name, and an arty girl from London, who rather specialises in queer angle shots. Her camera was set right up in that corner so that she could get a view of Miss Gregg receiving. Ah, now let me think, I rather fancy that that was when Ardwyck Fenn arrived.'

'And who is Ardwyck Fenn?'

Hailey Preston looked shocked. 'He's a big shot, Chief-Inspector. A very big shot in the Television and Moving Picture world. We didn't even know he was in this country.'

'His turning up was a surprise?'

'I'll say it was,' said Preston. 'Nice of him to come and quite unexpected.'

'Was he an old friend of Miss Gregg's and Mr Rudd's?'

'He was a close friend of Marina's a good many years ago when she was married to her second husband. I don't know how well Jason knew him.'

'Anyway, it was a pleasant surprise when he arrived?'

'Sure it was. We were all delighted.'

Craddock nodded and passed from that to other subjects. He made meticulous inquiries about the drinks, their ingredients, how they were served, who served them, what servants and hired servants were on duty. The answers seemed to be, as Inspector Cornish had already hinted was the case that, although any one of thirty people *could* have poisoned Heather Badcock with the utmost ease, yet at the same time any one of the thirty might have been seen doing so! It was, Craddock reflected, a big chance to take.

'Thank you,' he said at last, 'now I would like, if I may, to speak to Miss Marina Gregg.'

Hailey Preston shook his head.

'I'm sorry,' he said, 'I really am sorry but that's right out of the question.'

Craddock's eyebrows rose.

'Surely!'

'She's prostrated. She's absolutely prostrated. She's got her own physician here looking after her. He wrote out a certificate. I've got it here. I'll show it to you.'

Craddock took it and read it.

'I see,' he said. He asked, 'Does Marina Gregg always have a physician in attendance?'

'They're very high strung, all these actors and actresses. It's a big strain, this life. It's usually considered desirable in the case of the big shots that they should have a physician who understands their constitution and their nerves. Maurice Gilchrist has a very big reputation. He's looked after Miss Gregg for many years now. She's had a great deal of illness, as you may have read, in the last few years. She was hospitalised for a very long time. It's only about a year ago that she got her strength and health back.'

'I see.'

Hailey Preston seemed relieved that Craddock was not making any more protests.

'You'll want to see Mr Rudd?' he suggested. 'He'll be—' he looked at his watch, '—he'll be back from the studios in about ten minutes if that's all right for you.'

'That'll do admirably,' said Craddock. 'In the meantime is Dr Gilchrist actually here in the house?'

'He is.'

'Then I'd like to talk to him.'

'Why, certainly. I'll fetch him right away.'

The young man bustled away. Dermot Craddock stood thoughtfully at the top of the stairs. Of course this frozen look that Mrs Bantry had described might have been entirely Mrs Bantry's imagination. She was, he thought, a woman who would jump to conclusions. At the same timt he thought it quite likely that the conclusion to which she had jumped was a just one. Without going so far as to look like the Lady of Shalott seeing doom coming upon her, Marina Gregg might have seen something that vexed or annoyed her. Something that had caused her to have been negligent to a guest to whom she was talking. Somebody had come up those stairs, perhaps, who could be described as an unexpected guest – an unwelcome guest?

He turned at the sound of footsteps. Hailey Preston was back and with him was Dr Maurice Gilchrist. Dr Gilchrist was not at all as Dermot Craddock had imagined him. He had no suave bedside manner, neither was he theatrical in appearance. He seemed, on the face of it, a blunt, hearty, matter-of-fact man. He was dressed in tweeds, slightly florid tweeds to the English idea. He had a thatch of brown hair and observant, keen dark eyes.

'Doctor Gilchrist? I am Chief-Inspector Dermot Craddock. May I have a word or two with you in private?'

The doctor nodded. He turned along the corridor and went along it almost to the end, then he pushed the door open and invited Craddock to enter.

'No one will disturb us here,' he said.

It was obviously the doctor's own bedroom, a very comfortably appointed one. Dr Gilchrist indicated a chair and then sat down himself.

'I understand,' said Craddock, 'that Miss Marina Gregg, according to you, is unable to be interviewed. What's the matter with her, Doctor?'

Gilchrist shrugged his shoulders very slightly.

'Nerves,' he said. 'If you were to ask her questions now she'd be in a state bordering on hysteria within ten minutes. I can't permit that. If you like to send your police doctor to see me, I'd be willing to give him my views. She was unable to be present at the inquest for the same reason.'

'How long,' asked Craddock, 'is such a state of things likely to continue?'

Dr Gilchrist looked at him and smiled. It was a likeable smile.

'If you want my opinion,' he said, 'a human opinion, that is, not a medical one, any time within the next forty-eight hours, she'll be not only willing, but asking to see you! She'll be wanting to ask questions. She'll be wanting to answer your questions. They're like that!' He leaned forward. 'I'd like to try and make you understand if I can, Chief-Inspector, a little bit what makes these people act the way they do. The motion picture life is a life of continuous strain, and the more successful you are, the greater the strain. You live always, all day, in the public eye. When you're on location, when you're working, it's hard monotonous work with long hours. You're there in the morning, you sit and you wait. You do your small bit, the bit that's being shot over and over again. If you're rehearsing on the stage you'd be rehearsing as likely as not a whole act, or at any rate a part of an act. The thing would be in sequence, it would be more or less human and credible. But when you're shooting a picture everything's taken out of sequence. It's a monotonous, grinding business. It's exhausting. You live in luxury, of course, you have soothing drugs, you have baths and creams and powders and medical attention, you have relaxations and parties and people, but you're always in the public eye. You can't enjoy yourself quietly. You can't really – *ever relax.*'

'I can understand that,' said Dermot. 'Yes, I can understand.'

'And there's another thing,' went on Gilchrist. 'If you adopt this career, and especially if you're any good at it, you are a certain kind of person. You're a person – or so I've found in my experience – with a skin too few – a person who is plagued the whole time with diffidence. A terrible feeling of inadequacy, of apprehension that you can't do what's required of you. People say that actors and actresses are vain. That isn't true. They're not *conceited* about themselves; they're *obsessed* with themselves, yes, but they need reassurance the whole time. They *must* be continually reassured. Ask Jason Rudd. He'll tell you the same. You have to make them feel they can do it, to assure them they can do it, take them over and over again over the same thing encouraging them the whole time until you get the effect you want. But they are always doubtful of themselves. And that makes them, in an ordinary, human, unprofessional word: nervy. Damned nervy! A mass of nerves. And the worse their nerves are the better they are at the job.'

'That's interesting,' said Craddock. 'Very interesting.' He paused, adding: 'Though I don't see quite why you—'

'I'm trying to make you understand Marina Gregg,' said Maurice Gilchrist. 'You've seen her pictures, no doubt.'

'She's a wonderful actress,' said Dermot, 'wonderful. She has a personality, a beauty, a sympathy.'

'Yes,' said Gilchrist, 'she has all those, and she's had to work like the devil to produce the effects that she has produced. In the process her nerves get shot to pieces, and she's not actually a strong woman physically. Not as strong as you need to be. She's got one of those temperaments that swing to and fro between despair and rapture. She can't help it. She's made that way. She's suffered a great deal in her life. A large part of the suffering has been her own fault, but some of it hasn't. None of her marriages has been happy, except, I'd say, this last one. She's married to a man now who loves her dearly and who's loved her for years. She's sheltering in that love and she's happy in it. At least at the moment she's happy in it. One can't say how long all that will last. The trouble with her is that either she thinks that at last she's got to that spot or place or that moment in her life where everything's like a fairy tale come true, that nothing can go wrong, that she'll never be unhappy again; or else she's down in the dumps, a woman whose life is ruined, who's never known love and happiness and who never will again.' He added dryly, 'If she could only stop half-way between the two it'd be wonderful for her; and the world would lose a fine actress.'

He paused, but Dermot Craddock did not speak. He was wondering why Maurice Gilchrist was saying what he did. Why this close detailed analysis of Marina Gregg? Gilchrist was looking at him. It was as though he was urging Dermot to ask one particular question. Dermot wondered very much what the question was that he ought to ask. He said at last slowly, with the air of one feeling his way:

'She's been very much upset by this tragedy happening here?'

'Yes,' said Gilchrist, 'she has.'

'Almost unnaturally so?'

'That depends,' said Dr Gilchrist.

'On what does it depend?'

'On her reason for being so upset.'

'I suppose,' said Dermot, feeling his way, 'that it was a shock, a sudden death happening like that in the midst of a party.'

He saw very little response in the face opposite him. 'Or might it,' he said, 'be something more than that?'

'You can't tell, of course,' said Dr Gilchrist, 'how people are going to react. You can't tell however well you know them. They can always surprise you. Marina might have taken this in her stride. She's a soft-hearted creature. She might say, "Oh, poor, poor woman, how tragic. I wonder how it could have happened.' She could have been sympathetic without really caring. After all deaths do occasionally occur at studio parties. Or she might, if there wasn't anything very interesting going on, choose – choose unconsciously, mind you – to dramatise herself over it. She might decide to throw a scene. Or there might be some quite different reason.'

Dermot decided to take the bull by the horns. 'I wish,' he said, 'you would tell me what you really think?'

'I don't know,' said Dr Gilchrist, 'I can't be sure.' He paused and then said, 'There's professional etiquette, you know. There's the relationship between doctor and patient.'

'She has told you something?'

'I don't think I could go as far as that.'

'Did Marina Gregg know this woman, Heather Badcock? Had she met her before?'

'I don't think she knew her from Adam,' said Dr Gilchrist. 'No. That's not the trouble. If you ask me it's nothing to do with Heather Badcock.'

Dermot said, 'This stuff, this Calmo. Does Marina Gregg ever use it herself?'

'Lives on it, pretty well,' said Dr Gilchrist. 'So does everyone else around here,' he added. 'Ella Zielinsky takes it, Hailey Preston takes it, half the boiling takes it – it's the fashion at this moment. They're all much the same, these things. People get tired of one and they try a new one that comes out and they think it's wonderful, and that it makes all the difference.'

'And does it make all the difference?'

'Well,' said Gilchrist, 'it makes *a* difference. It does its work. It calms you or peps you up, makes you feel you could do things which otherwise you might fancy that you couldn't. I don't prescribe them more than I can help, but they're not dangerous taken properly. They help people who can't help themselves.'

'I wish I knew,' said Dermot Craddock, 'what it is that you are trying to tell me.'

'I'm trying to decide,' said Gilchrist, 'what is my duty. There are two duties. There's the duty of a doctor to his patient. What his patient says to him is confidential and must be kept so. But there's another point of view. You can fancy that there is danger to a patient. You have to take steps to avoid that danger.'

He stopped. Craddock looked at him and waited.

'Yes,' said Dr Gilchrist. 'I think I know what I must do. I must ask you, Chief-Inspector Craddock, to keep what I am telling you confidential. Not from your colleagues, of course. But as far as regards the outer world, particularly people in the house here. Do you agree?'

'I can't bind myself,' said Craddock, 'I don't know what will arise. In general terms, yes, I agree. That is to say, I imagine that any piece of information you gave me I should prefer to keep to myself and to my colleagues.'

'Now listen,' said Gilchrist, 'this mayn't mean anything at all. Women say anything when they're in the state of nerves Marina Gregg is in now. I'm telling you something which she said to me. There may be nothing in it at all.'

'What did she say?' asked Craddock.

'She broke down after this thing happened. She sent for me. I gave her a sedative. I stayed there beside her, holding her hand, telling her to calm down, telling her things were going to be all right. Then, just before she went off into unconsciousness she said, "It was meant for *me*, Doctor." '

Craddock stared. 'She said that, did she? And afterwards – the next day?'

'She never alluded to it again. I raised the point once. She evaded it. She said, 'Oh, you must have made a mistake. I'm sure I never said anything like that. I expect I was half doped at the time." '

'But you think she meant it?'

'She meant it all right,' said Gilchrist. 'That's not to say that it is so,' he added warningly. 'Whether someone meant to poison her or meant to poison Heather Badcock I don't know. You'd probably know better than I would. All I do say is that Marina Gregg definitely thought and believed that that dose was meant for her.'

Craddock was silent for some moments. Then he said, 'Thank you, Doctor Gilchrist. I appreciate what you have told me and I realize your motive. If what Marina Gregg said to you was founded on fact it may mean, may it not, that there is still danger to her?'

'That's the point,' said Gilchrist. 'That's the whole point.'

'Have you any reason to believe that that might be so?'

'No, I haven't.'

'No idea what her reason for thinking so was?'

'No.'

'Thank you.'

Craddock got up. 'Just one thing more, Doctor. Do you know if she said the same thing to her husband?'

Slowly Gilchrist shook his head. 'No,' he said, 'I'm quite sure of that. She didn't tell her husband.'

His eyes met Dermot's for a few moments then he gave a brief nod of his head and said, 'You don't want me any more? All right. I'll go back and have a look at the patient. You shall talk to her as soon as it's possible.'

He left the room and Craddock remained, pursing his lips up and whistling very softly beneath his breath.

—— IO ——

'Jason's back now,' said Hailey Preston. 'Will you come with me, Chief-Inspector, I'll take you to his room.'

The room which Jason Rudd used partly for office and partly for a sitting-room, was on the first floor. It was comfortably but not luxuriously furnished. It was a room which had little personality and no indication of the private tastes or predilection of its user. Jason Rudd rose from the desk at which he was sitting, and came forward to meet Dermot. It was wholly unnecessary, Dermot thought, for the room to have a personality; the user of it had so much. Hailey Preston had been an efficient and voluble gasbag. Gilchrist had force and magnetism. But here was a man whom, as Dermot immediately admitted to himself, it would not be easy to read. In the course of his career, Craddock had met and summed up many people. By now he was fully adept in realizing the potentialities and very often reading the thoughts of most of the people with whom he came in contact. But he felt at once that one would be able to gauge only so much of Jason Rudd's thoughts as Jason Rudd himself permitted. The eyes, deepset and thoughtful, perceived but would not easily reveal. The ugly, rugged head spoke of an excellent intellect. The clown's face could repel you or attract you. Here, thought Dermot Craddock, to himself, is where I sit and listen and take very careful notes.

'Sorry, Chief-Inspector, if you've had to wait for me. I was held up by some small complication over at the Studios. Can I offer you a drink?'

'Not just now, thank you, Mr Rudd.'

The clown's face suddenly crinkled into a kind of ironic amusement.

'Not the house to take a drink in, is that what you're thinking?'

'As a matter of fact it wasn't what I was thinking.'

'No, no I suppose not. Well, Chief-Inspector, what do you want to know? What can I tell you?'

'Mr Preston has answered very adequately all the questions I have put to him.'

'And that has been helpful to you?'

'Not as helpful as I could wish.'

Jason Rudd looked inquiring.

'I've also seen Dr Gilchrist. He informs me that your wife is not yet strong enough to be asked questions.'

'Marina,' said Jason Rudd, 'is very sensitive. She's subject, frankly, to nerve storms. And murder at such close quarters is, as you will admit, likely to produce a nerve storm.'

'It is not a pleasant experience,' Dermot Craddock agreed, dryly.

'In any case I doubt if there is anything my wife could tell you that you could not learn equally well from me. I was standing beside her when the thing happened, and frankly I would say that I am a better observer than my wife.'

'The first question I would like to ask,' said Dermot (and it is a question that you have probably answered already but for all that I would like to ask it again), had you or your wife any previous acquaintance with Heather Badcock?'

Jason Rudd shook his head.

'None whatever. I certainly have never seen the woman before in my life. I had had two letters from her on behalf of the St John's Ambulance Association, but I had not met her personally until about five minutes before her death.'

'But she claimed to have met your wife?'

Jason Rudd nodded.

'Yes, some twelve or fifteen years ago, I gather. In Bermuda. Some big garden party in aid of ambulances, which Marina opened for them, I think, and Mrs Badcock, as soon as she was introduced, burst into some long rigmarole of how although she was in bed with 'flu, she had got up and had managed to come to this affair and had asked for and got my wife's autograph.'

Again the ironical smile crinkled his face.

'That, I may say, is a very common occurrence, Chief-Inspector. Large mobs of people are usually lined up to obtain my wife's autograph and it is a moment that they treasure and remember. Quite understandably, it is an event in their lives. Equally naturally it is not likely that my wife would remember one out of a thousand or so autograph hunters. She had, quite frankly, no recollection of ever having seen Mrs Badcock before.'

'That I can well understand,' said Craddock. 'Now I have been told, Mr Rudd, by an onlooker that your wife was slightly *distrait* during the few moments that Heather Badcock was speaking to her. Would you agree that such was the case?'

'Very possibly,' said Jason Rudd. 'Marina is not particularly strong. She was, of course, used to what I may describe as her public social work, and could carry out her duties in that line almost automatically. But towards the end of a long day she was inclined occasionally to flag. This may have been such a moment. I did not, I may say, observe anything of the kind myself. No, wait a minute, that is not quite true. I do remember that she was a little slow in making her reply to Mrs Badcock. In fact I think I nudged her very gently in the ribs.'

'Something had perhaps distracted her attention?' said Dermot.

'Possibly, but it may have been just a momentary lapse through fatigue.'

Dermot Craddock was silent for a few minutes. He looked out of the window where the view was the somewhat sombre one over the woods surrounding Gossington Hall. He looked at the pictures on the walls, and finally he looked at Jason Rudd. Jason Rudd's face was attentive but nothing more. There was no guide to his feelings. He appeared courteous and completely at ease, but he might, Craddock thought, be actually nothing of the kind. This was a man of very high mental calibre. One would not, Dermot thought, get anything out of him that he was not prepared to say unless one put one's cards on the table. Dermot took his decision. He would do just that.

'Has it occurred to you, Mr Rudd, that the poisoning of Heather Badcock may have been entirely accidental? That the real intended victim was your wife?'

There was a silence. Jason Rudd's face did not change it's expression. Dermot waited. Finally Jason Rudd gave a deep sigh and appeared to relax.

'Yes,' he said quietly, 'you're quite right, Chief-Inspector. I have been sure of it all along.'

'But you have said nothing to that effect, not to Inspector Cornish, not at the inquest?'

'No.'

'Why not, Mr Rudd?'

'I could answer you very adequately by saying that it was merely a belief on my part unsupported by any kind of evidence. The facts that led me to deduce it, were facts equally accessible to the law which was probably better qualified to decide than I was. I knew nothing about Mrs Badcock personally. She might have enemies, someone might have decided to administer a fatal dose to her on this particular occasion, though it would seem a very curious and far-fetched decision. But it might have been chosen conceivably for the reason that at a public occasion of this kind the issues would be more confused, the number of strangers present would be considerable and just for that reason it would be more difficult to bring home to the person in question the commission of such a crime. All that is true, but I am going to be frank with you, Chief-Inspector. That was *not* my reason for keeping silent. I will tell you what that reason was. I didn't want my wife to suspect for one moment that it was she who had narrowly escaped dying by poison.'

'Thank you for your frankness,' said Dermot. 'Not that I quite understand your motive in keeping silent.'

'No? Perhaps it is a little difficult to explain. You would have to know Marina to understand. She is a person who badly needs happiness and security. Her life has been highly successful in the material sense. She has won renown artistically but her personal life has been one of deep unhappiness. Again and again she has thought that she has found happiness and was wildly and unduly elated thereby, and has had her hopes dashed to the ground. She is incapable, Mr Craddock, of taking a rational, prudent view of life. In her previous marriages she has expected, like a child reading a fairy story, to live happily ever afterwards.'

Again the ironic smile changed the ugliness of the clown's face into a strange, sudden sweetness.

'But marriage is not like that, Chief-Inspector. There can be no rapture continued indefinitely. We are fortunate indeed if we can achieve a life of quiet content, affection, and serene and sober happiness.' He added, 'Perhaps you are married, Chief-Inspector?'

Dermot Craddock shook his head.

'I have not so far that good, or bad, fortune,' he murmured.

'In our world, the moving picture world, marriage is a fully occupational hazard. Film stars marry often. Sometimes happily, sometimes disastrously, but seldom permanently. In that respect I should not say that Marina has had any undue cause to complain, but to one of her temperament things of that kind matter very deeply. She imbued herself with the idea that she was unlucky, that nothing would ever go right for her. She has always been looking desperately for the same things, love, happiness, affection, security. She was wildly anxious to have children. According to some medical opinion, the very strength of that anxiety frustrated its object. One very celebrated physician advised the adoption of a child. He said it is often the case that when an intensive desire for maternity is assuaged by having adopted a baby, a child is born naturally shortly afterwards. Marina adopted no less than three children. For a time she got a certain amount of happiness and serenity, but it was not the real thing. You can imagine her delight when eleven years ago she found she was going to have a child. Her pleasure and delight were quite indescribable. She was in good health and the doctors assured her that there was every reason to believe that everything would go well. As you may or may not know, the result was tragedy. The child, a boy, was born mentally deficient, imbecile. The result was disastrous. Marina had a complete breakdown and was severely ill for years, confined to a sanatorium. Though her recovery was slow she did recover. Shortly after that we married and she began once more to take an interest in life and to feel that perhaps she could be happy. It was difficult at first for her to get a worth while contract for a picture. Everyone was inclined to doubt whether her health would stand the strain. I had to battle for that.' Jason Rudd's lips set firmly together. 'Well, the battle was successful. We have started shooting the picture. In the meantime we bought this house and set about altering it. Only about a fortnight ago Marina was saying to me how happy she was, and how she felt at last she was going to be able to settle down to a happy home life, her troubles behind her. I was a little nervous because, as usual, her expectations were too optimistic. But there was no doubt that she was happy. Her nervous symptoms disappeared, there was a calmness and a quietness about her that I had never seen before. Everything was going well until—' he paused. His voice became suddenly bitter. 'Until this happened! That woman had to die – *here*! That in itself was shock enough. I couldn't risk – I was determined not to risk – Marina's knowing that an attempt had been made on *her* life. That would have been a second, perhaps fatal, shock. It might have precipitated another mental collapse.'

'He looked directly at Dermot.

'Do you understand – now?'

'I see your point of view,' said Craddock, 'but forgive me, isn't there one aspect that you are neglecting? You give me your conviction that an attempt was made to poison your wife. Doesn't that danger still remain? If a poisoner does not succeed, isn't it likely that the attempt may be repeated?'

'Naturally I've considered that,' said Jason Rudd, 'but I am confident that, being forewarned so to speak, I can take all reasonable precautions for my wife's safety. I shall watch over her and arrange that others shall watch over her. The great thing, I feel, is that she herself should not know that any danger threatened her.'

'And you think,' said Dermot cautiously, 'that she does *not* know?'

'Of course not. She has no idea.'

'You're sure of that?'

'Certain. Such an idea would never occur to her.'

'But it occurred to you,' Dermot pointed out.

'That's very different,' said Jason Rudd. 'Logically, it was the only solution. But my wife isn't logical, and to begin with she could not possibly imagine that anyone would want to do away with her. Such a possibility would simply not occur to her mind.'

'You may be right,' said Dermot slowly, 'but that leaves us now with several other questions. Again, let me put this bluntly. Whom do you suspect?'

'I can't tell you.'

'Excuse me, Mr Rudd, do you mean by that you can't or that you won't?'

Jason Rudd spoke quickly. 'Can't. Can't every time. It seems to me just as impossible as it would seem to her that anyone would dislike her enough – should have a sufficient grudge against her – to do such a thing. On the other hand, on the sheer, downright evidence of the facts, that is exactly what must have occurred.'

'Will you outline the facts to me as you see them?'

'If you like. The circumstances are quite clear. I poured out two daiquiri cocktails from an already prepared jug. I took them to Marina and to Mrs Babcock. What Mrs Badcock did I do not know. She moved on, I presume, to speak to someone she knew. My wife had her drink in her hand. At that moment the mayor and his wife were approaching. She put down her glass, as yet untouched, and greeted them. Then there were more greetings. An old friend we'd not seen for years, some other locals and one or two people from the studios. During that time the glass containing the cocktail stood on the table which was situated at that time behind us since we had both moved forward a little to the top of the stairs. One or two photographs were taken of my wife talking to the mayor, which we hoped would please the local population, at the special request of the representatives of the local newspaper. While this was being done I brought some fresh drinks to a few of the last arrivals. During that time my wife's glass must have been poisoned. Don't ask me *how* it was done, it cannot have been easy to do. On the other hand, it is startling, if anyone has the nerve to do an action openly and unconcernedly, how little people are likely to notice it! You ask me if I have suspicions; all I can say is that at least one of about twenty people *might* have done it. People, you see, were moving about in little groups, talking, occasionally going off to have a look at the alterations which had been done to the house. There was movement, continual movement. I've thought and I've thought, I've racked my brains but there is nothing, absolutely *nothing* to direct my suspicions to any particular person.'

He paused and gave an exasperated sigh.

'I understand,' said Dermot. 'Go on, please.'

'I dare say you've heard the next part before.'

'I should like to hear it again from you.'

'Well, I had come back towards the head of the stairs. My wife had turned towards the table and was just picking up her glass. There was a slight exclamation from Mrs Badcock. Somebody must have jogged her arm and the glass slipped out of her fingers and was broken on the floor. Marina did the natural hostess's act. Her own skirt had been slightly touched with the liquid. She insisted no harm was done, used her own handkerchief to wipe Mrs Badcock's skirt and insisted on her having her own drink. If I remember she said, "I've had far too much already." So that was that. But I can assure you of this. The fatal dose could not have been added *after* that for Mrs Badcock immediately began to drink from the glass. As you know, four or five minutes later she was dead. I wonder – how I wonder – what the poisoner must have felt when he realized how badly his scheme had failed . . .'

'All this occurred to you at the time?'

'Of course not. At the end I concluded, naturally enough, that this woman had had some kind of a seizure. Perhaps heart, coronary thrombosis, something of that sort. It never occurred to me that *poisoning* was involved. Would it occur to you – would it occur to anybody?'

'Probably not,' said Dermot. 'Well, your account is clear enough and you seem sure of your facts. You say you have no suspicion of any particular person. I can't quite accept that, you know.'

'I assure you it's the truth.'

'Let us approach it from another angle. Who is there who could wish to harm your wife? It all sounds melodramatic if you put it this way, but what enemies has she got?'

Jason Rudd made an expressive gesture.

'Enemies? Enemies It's so hard to define what one means by an enemy. There's plenty of envy and jealousy in the world my wife and I occupy. There are always people who say malicious things, who'll start a whispering campaign, who will do someone they are jealous of a bad turn if the opportunity occurs. But that doesn't mean that any of those people is a murderer, or indeed even a likely murderer. Don't you agree?'

'Yes, I agree. There must be something beyond petty dislikes or envies. Is there anyone whom your wife has injured say, in the past?'

Jason Rudd did not rebut this easily. Instead he frowned.

'Honestly, I don't think so,' he said at last, 'and I may say I've given a lot of thought to that point.'

'Anything in the nature of a love affair, an association with some man?'

'There have of course been affairs of that kind. It may be considered, I suppose, that Marina has occasionally treated some man badly. But there is nothing to cause any lasting ill-will. I'm sure of it.'

'What about women? Any woman who has had a lasting grudge against Miss Gregg?'

'Well,' said Jason Rudd, 'you can never tell with women. I can't think of any particular one offhand.'

'Who'd benefit financially by your wife's death?'

'Her will benefits various people but not to any large extent. I suppose the people who'd benefit, as you put it, financially, would be myself as her husband and from another angle, possibly the star who might replace her in this film. Though, of course, the film might be abandoned altogether. These things are very uncertain.'

'Well, we need not go into all that now,' said Dermot.

'And I have your assurance that Marina will not be told that she is in possible danger?'

'We shall have to go into that matter,' said Dermot. 'I want to impress upon you that you are taking quite a considerable risk there. However, the matter will not arise for some days since your wife is still under medical care. Now there is one more thing I would like you to do. I would like you to write down for me as accurately as you can every single person who was in that recess at the top of the stairs, or whom you saw coming up the stairs at the time of the murder.'

'I'll do my best, but I'm rather doubtful. You'd do far better to consult my secretary, Ella Zielinsky. She has a most accurate memory and also lists of the local people who were there. If you'd like to see her now—'

'I would like to talk to Miss Ella Zielinsky very much,' said Dermot.

—— II ——

Surveying Dermot Craddock unemotionally through her large horn-rimmed spectacles, Ella Zielinsky seemed to him almost too good to be true. With quiet businesslike alacrity she whipped out of a drawer a typewritten sheet and passed it across to him.

'I think I can be fairly sure that there are no omissions,' she said. 'But it is just possible that I may have included one or two names – local names they will be – who were not actually there. That is to say who may have left earlier or who may not have been found and brought up. Actually, I'm pretty sure that it is correct.'

'A very efficient piece of work if I may say so,' said Dermot.

'Thank you.'

'I suppose – I am quite an ignoramus in such things – that you have to attain a high standard of efficiency in your job?'

'One has to have things pretty well taped, yes.'

'What exactly does your job comprise? Are you a kind of liaison officer, so to speak, between the studios and Gossington Hall?'

'No. I've nothing to do with the studios, actually, though of course I naturally take messages from there on the telephone or send them. My job is to look after Miss Gregg's social life, her public and private engagements, and to supervise in some degree the running of the house.'

'You like the job?'

'It's extremely well paid and I find it reasonably interesting. I didn't however bargain for murder,' she added dryly.

'Did it seem very incredible to you?'

'So much so that I am going to ask you if you are really sure it *is* murder?'

'Six times the dose of di-ethyl-mexine etc. etc., could hardly be anything else.'

'It might have been an accident of some kind.'

'And how would you suggest such an accident could have occurred?'

'More easily than you'd imagine, since you don't know the set-up. This house is simply full of drugs of all kinds. I don't mean dope when I say drugs. I mean properly prescribed remedies, but, like most of these things, what they call, I understand, the lethal dose is not very far removed from the therapeutic dose.'

Dermot nodded.

'These theatrical and picture people have the most curious lapses in their intelligence. Sometimes it seems to me that the more of an artistic genius you are, the less common sense you have in everyday life.'

'That may well be.'

'What with all the bottles, cachets, powders, capsules, and little boxes that they carry about with them; what with popping in a tranquilliser here and a tonic there and a pep pill somewhere else, don't you think it would be easy enough that the whole thing might get mixed up?'

'I don't see how it could apply in this case.'

'Well, I think it could. Somebody, one of the guests, may have wanted a sedative, or a reviver, and whipped out his or her little container which they carry around and possibly because they were talking to someone or possibly because they hadn't remembered the dose because they hadn't had one for some time, might have put too much in a glass. Then their mind was distracted and they went off somewhere, and let's say this Mrs What's-her-name comes along, thinks it's her glass, picks it up

634

and drinks it. That's surely a more feasible idea than anything
else?'

'You don't think that all those possibilities haven't been gone
into, do you?'

'No, I suppose not. But there were a lot of people there and a
lot of glasses standing about with drinks in them. It happens
often enough, you know, that you pick up the wrong glass and
drink out of it.'

'Then you don't think that Heather Badcock was deliberately
poisoned? You think that she drank out of somebody else's
glass?'

'I can't imagine anything more likely to happen.'

'In that case,' said Dermot speaking carefully, 'it would have
had to be Marina Gregg's glass. You realize that? Marina handed
her her own glass.'

'Or what she thought was her own glass,' Ella Zielinsky corrected him. 'You haven't talked to Marina yet, have you? She's
extremely vague. She'd pick up any glass that looked as though it
were hers, and drink it. I've seen her do it again and again.'

'She takes Calmo?'

'Oh yes, we all do.'

'You too, Miss Zielinsky?'

'I'm driven to it sometimes,' said Ella Zielinsky. 'These things
are rather imitative, you know.'

'I shall be glad,' said Dermot, 'when I am able to talk to Miss
Gregg. She – er – seems to be prostrated for a very long time.'

'That's just throwing a temperament,' said Ella Zielinsky.
'She dramatises herself a good deal, you know. She'd never take
murder in her stride.'

'As you manage to do, Miss Zielinsky?'

'When everybody about you is in a continual state of agitation,' said Ella dryly, 'it develops in you a desire to go to the
opposite extreme.'

'You learn to take a pride in not turning a hair when some
shocking tragedy occurs?'

She considered. 'It's not a really nice trait, perhaps. But I
think if you didn't develop that sense you'd probably go round
the bend yourself.'

'Was Miss Gregg – is Miss Gregg a difficult person to work
for?'

It was something of a personal question but Dermot Craddock regarded it as a kind of test. If Ella Zielinsky raised her
eyebrows and tacitly demanded what this had to do with the

murder of Mrs Badcock, he would be forced to admit that it had nothing to do with it. But he wondered if Ella Zielinsky might perhaps enjoy telling him what she thought of Marina Gregg.

'She's a great artist. She's got a personal magnetism that comes over on the screen in the most extraordinary way. Because of that one feels it's rather a privilege to work with her. Taken purely personally, of course, she's hell!'

'Ah,' said Dermot.

'She's no kind of moderation, you see. She's up in the air or down in the dumps and everything is always terrifically exaggerated, and she changes her mind and there are an enormous lot of things that one must never mention or allude to because they upset her.'

'Such as?'

'Well, naturally mental breakdown, or sanatoriums for mental cases. I think it is quite to be understood that she should be sensitive about that. And anything to do with children.'

'Children? In what way?'

'Well, it upsets her to see children, or to hear of people being happy with children. If she hears someone is going to have a baby or has just had a baby, it throws her into a state of misery at once. She can never have another child herself, you see, and the only one she did have is batty. I don't know if you knew that?'

'I had heard it, yes. It's all very sad and unfortunate. But after a good many years you'd think she'd forget about it a little.'

'She doesn't. It's an obsession with her. She broods on it.'

'What does Mr Rudd feel about it?'

'Oh, it wasn't his child. It was her last husband's, Isidore Wright's.'

'Ah yes, her last husband. Where is he now?'

'He married again and lives in Florida,' said Ella Zielinsky promptly.

'Would you say that Marina Gregg had made many enemies in her life?'

'Not unduly so. Not more than most, that is to say. There are always rows over other women or other men or over contracts or jealousy – all those things.'

'She wasn't as far as you know afraid of anyone?'

'Marina? *Afraid* of anyone? I don't think so. Why? Why should she be?'

'I don't know,' said Dermot. He picked up the list of names.

23

'Thank you very much, Miss Zielinsky. If there's anything else I want to know I'll come back. May I?'

'Certainly. I'm only too anxious – we're all only too anxious – to do anything we can to help.'

II

'Well, Tom, what have you got for me?'

Detective-Sergeant Tiddler grinned appreciatively. His name was not Tom, it was William, but the combination of Tom Tiddler had always been too much for his colleagues.

'What gold and silver have you picked up for me?' continued Dermot Craddock.

The two were staying at the Blue Boar and Tiddler had just come back from a day spent at the studios.

'The proportion of gold is very small,' said Tiddler. 'Not much gossip. No startling rumours. One or two suggestions of suicide.'

'Why suicide?'

'They thought she might have had a row with her husband and be trying to make him sorry. That line of country. But that she didn't really mean to go as far as doing herself in.'

'I can't see that that's a very hopeful line,' said Dermot.

'No, of course it isn't. They know nothing about it, you see. They don't know anything except what they're busy on. It's all highly technical and there's an atmosphere of "the show must go on," or as I suppose one ought to say the picture must go on, or the shooting must go on. I don't know any of the right terms. All they're concerned about it when Marina Gregg will get back to the set. She's mucked up a picture once or twice before by staging a nervous breakdown.'

'Do they like her on the whole?'

'I should say they consider her the devil of a nuisance but for all that they can't help being fascinated by her when she's in the mood to fascinate them. Her husband's besotted about her, by the way.'

'What do they think of him?'

'They think he's the finest director or producer or whatever it is that there's ever been.'

'No rumours of his being mixed up with some other star or some woman of some kind?'

Tom Tiddler stared. 'No,' he said, 'no.' Not a hint of such a thing. Why, do you think there might be?'

'I wondered,' said Dermot. 'Marina Gregg is convinced that that lethal dose was meant for her.'

'Is she now? Is she right?'

'Almost certainly, I should say,' Dermot replied. 'But that's not the point. The point is that she hasn't told her husband so, only her doctor.'

'Do you think she would have told him if—'

'I just wondered,' said Craddock, 'whether she might have had at the back of her mind an idea that her husband had been responsible. The doctor's manner was a little peculiar. I may have imagined it but I don't think I did.'

'Well, there were no such rumours going about at the studios,' said Tom. 'You hear that sort of thing soon enough.'

'She herself is not embroiled with any other man?'

'No, she seems to be devoted to Rudd.'

'No interesting snippets about her past?'

Tiddler grinned. 'Nothing to what you can read in a film magazine any day of the week.'

'I think I'll have to read a few,' said Dermot, 'to get the atmosphere.'

'The things they say and hint!' said Tiddler.

'I wonder,' said Dermot thoughtfully, 'if my Miss Marple reads film magazines.'

'Is that the old lady who lives in the house by the church?'

'That's right.'

'They say she's sharp,' said Tiddler. 'They say there's nothing goes on here that Miss Marple doesn't hear about. She may not know much about the film people, but she ought to be able to give you the low-down on the Badcocks all right.'

'It's not as simple as it used to be,' said Dermot. 'There's a new social life springing up here. A housing estate, big building development. The Badcocks are fairly new and come from there.'

'I didn't hear much about the locals, of course,' said Tiddler. 'I concentrated on the sex life of film stars and such things.'

'You haven't brought back very much,' grumbled Dermot. 'What about Marina Gregg's past, anything about that?'

'Done a bit of marrying in her time but not more than most. Her first husband didn't like getting the chuck, so they said, but he was a very ordinary sort of bloke. He was a realtor or something like that. What is a realtor, by the way?'

'I think it means in the real estate business.'

'Oh well, anyway, he didn't line up as very glamorous so she got rid of him and married a foreign count or prince. That lasted hardly any time at all but there don't seem to be any bones broken. She just shook him off and teamed up with number three. Film Star Robert Truscott. That was said to be a passionate love match. His wife didn't much like letting go of him, but she had to take it in the end. Big alimony. As far as I can make out everybody's hard up because they've got to pay so much alimony to all their ex-wives.'

'But it went wrong?'

'Yes. She was the broken-hearted one, I gather. But another big romance came along a year or two later. Isidore Somebody – a playwright.'

'It's an exotic life,' said Dermot. 'Well, we'll call it a day now. Tomorrow we've got to get down to a bit of hard work.'

'Such as?'

'Such as checking a list I've got here. Out of twenty-odd names we ought to be able to do *some* elimination and out of what's left we'll have to look for X.'

'Any idea who X is?'

'Not in the least. If it isn't Jason Rudd, that is.' He added with a wry and ironic smile, 'I shall have to go to Miss Marple and get briefed on local matters.'

12

Miss Marple was pursuing her own methods of research.

'It's very kind of you, Mrs Jameson, very kind of you indeed. I can't tell you how grateful I am.'

'Oh, don't mention it, Miss Marple. I'm sure I'm glad to oblige you. I suppose you'll want the latest ones?'

'No, no, not particularly,' said Miss Marple. 'In fact I think I'd rather have some of the older numbers.'

'Well, here you are then,' said Mrs Jameson, 'there's a nice armful and I can assure you we shan't miss them. Keep them as long as you like. Now it's too heavy for you to carry. Jenny, how's your perm doing?'

'She's all right, Mrs Jameson. She's had her rinse and now she's having a good dry-out.'

'In that case, dear, you might just run along with Miss Marple here, and carry these magazines for her. No, really, Miss Marple, it's no trouble at all. Always pleased to do anything we can for you.'

How kind people were, Miss Marple thought, especially when they'd known you practically all their lives. Mrs Jameson, after long years of running a hairdressing parlour, had steeled herself to going as far in the cause of progress as to repaint her sign and call herself 'DIANE. Hair Stylist.' Otherwise the shop remained much as before and catered in much the same way to the needs of its clients. It turned you out with a nice perm: it accepted the task of shaping and cutting for the younger generation and the resultant mess was accepted without too much recrimination. But the bulk of Mrs Jameson's clientele was a bunch of solid, stick in the mud middle-aged ladies who found it extremely hard to get their hair done the way they wanted it anywhere else.

'Well, I never,' said Cherry the next morning, as she prepared to run a virulent Hoover round the lounge as she still called it in her mind. 'What's all this?'

'I am trying,' said Miss Marple, 'to instruct myself a little in the moving picture world.'

She laid aside *Movie News* and picked up *Amongst the Stars*.

'It's really very interesting. It reminds one so much of so many things.'

'Fantastic lives they must lead,' said Cherry.

'Specialised lives,' said Miss Marple. 'Highly specialised. It reminds me very much of the things a friend of mine used to tell me. She was a hospital nurse. The same simplicity of outlook and all the gossip and the rumours. And good-looking doctors causing any amount of havoc.'

'Rather sudden, isn't it, this interest of yours?' said Cherry.

'I'm finding it difficult to knit nowadays,' said Miss Marple. 'Of course the print of these *is* rather small, but I can always use a magnifying glass.'

Cherry looked at her curiously.

'You're always surprising me,' she said. 'The things you take an interest in.'

'I take an interest in everything,' said Miss Marple.

'I mean taking up new subjects at your age.'

Miss Marple shook her head.

'They aren't really new subjects. It's human nature I'm interested in, you know, and human nature is much the same whether it's film stars or hospital nurses or people in St Mary

Mead or,' she added thoughtfully, 'people who live in the Development.'

'Can't see much likeness between me and a film star,' said Cherry laughing, 'more's the pity. I suppose it's Marina Gregg and her husband coming to live at Gossington Hall that set you off on this.'

'That and the very sad event that occurred there,' said Miss Marple.

'Mrs Badcock, you mean? It was bad luck, that.'

'What do you think of in the—' Miss Marple paused with the 'D' hovering on her lips. 'What do you and your friends think about it?' she amended her question.

'It's a queer do,' said Cherry. 'Looks as though it were murder, doesn't it, though of course the police are too cagey to say so outright. Still, that's what it looks like.'

'I don't see what else it could be,' said Miss Marple.

'It couldn't be suicide,' agreed Cherry, 'not with Heather Badcock.'

'Did you know her well?'

'No, not really. Hardly at all. She was a bit of a nosy parker, you know. Always wanting you to join this, join that, turn up for her meetings at so-and-so. Too much energy. Her husband got a bit sick of it sometimes, I think.'

'She doesn't seem to have had any real enemies.'

'People used to get a bit fed up with her sometimes. The point is, I don't see who could have murdered her unless it was her husband. And he's a very meek type. Still, the worm will turn, or so they say. I've always heard that Crippen was ever so nice a man and that man, Haigh, who pickled them all in acid – they said he couldn't have been more charming! So one never knows, does one?'

'Poor Mr Badcock,' said Miss Marple.

'And people say he was upset and nervy at the fête that day – before it happened, I mean – but people always say that kind of thing afterwards. If you ask me, he's looking better now than he's looked for years. Seems to have got a bit more spirit and go in him.'

'Indeed?' said Miss Marple.

'Nobody *really* thinks he did it,' said Cherry. 'Only, if he didn't, who did? I can't help thinking myself it must have been an accident of some kind. Accidents do happen. You think you know all about mushrooms and go out and pick some. One fungus gets in among them and there you are, rolling about in agony and lucky if the doctor gets to you in time.'

'Cocktails and glasses of sherry don't seem to lend themselves to accident,' said Miss Marple.

'Oh, I don't know,' said Cherry. 'A bottle of something or other could have got in by mistake. Somebody I knew took a dose of concentrated DDT once. Horribly ill they were.'

'Accident,' said Miss Marple thoughtfully. 'Yes, it certainly seems the best solution. I must say I can't believe that in the case of Heather Badcock it *could* have been deliberate murder. I won't say it's impossible. Nothing is impossible, but it doesn't seem like it. No, I think the truth lies somewhere here.' She rustled her magazines and picked up another one.

'You mean you're looking for some special story about someone?'

'No,' said Miss Marple. 'I'm just looking for odd mentions of people and a way of life and something – some little something that might help.' She returned to her perusal of the magazines and Cherry removed her vacuum cleaner to the upper floor. Miss Marple's face was pink and interested, and being slightly deaf now, she did not hear the footsteps that came along the garden path towards the drawing-room window. It was only when a slight shadow fell on the page that she looked up. Dermot Craddock was standing smiling at her.

'Doing your homework, I see,' he remarked.

'Inspector Craddock, how very nice to see you. And how kind to spare time to come and see me. Would you like a cup of coffee, or possibly a glass of sherry?'

'A glass of sherry would be splendid,' said Dermot. 'Don't you move,' he added. 'I'll ask for it as I come in.'

He went round by the side door and presently joined Miss Marple.

'Well,' he said, 'is all that bumph giving you ideas?'

'Rather too many ideas,' said Miss Marple. 'I'm not often shocked, you know, but this does shock me a little.'

'What, the private lives of film stars?'

'Oh no,' said Miss Marple, 'not *that*! That all seems to be *most* natural, given the circumstances and the money involved and the opportunities for propinquity. Oh no, that's natural enough. I mean the way they're written about. I'm rather old-fashioned, you know, and I feel that that really shouldn't be allowed.'

'It's news,' said Dermot Craddock, 'and some pretty nasty things can be said in the way of fair comment.'

'I know,' said Miss Marple. 'It makes me sometimes very angry. I expect you think it's silly of me reading all these. But one does so badly want to be *in* things and of course sitting here in the house I can't really know as much about things as I would like to.'

'That's just what I thought,' said Dermot Craddock, 'and that's why I've come to tell you about them.'

'But, my dear boy, excuse me, would your superiors really approve of that?'

'I don't see why not,' said Dermot. 'Here,' he added, 'I have a list. A list of people who were there on that landing during the short time of Heather Badcock's arrival until her death. We've eliminated a lot of people, perhaps precipitately, but I don't think so. We've eliminated the mayor and his wife and Alderman somebody and his wife and a great many of the locals, though we've kept in the husband. If I remember rightly you were always very suspicious of husbands.'

'They are often the obvious suspects,' said Miss Marple, apologetically, 'and the obvious is so often right.'

'I couldn't agree with you more,' said Craddock.

'But which husband, my dear boy, are you referring to?'

'Which one do you think?' asked Dermot. He eyed her sharply.

Miss Marple looked at him.

'Jason Rudd?' she asked.

'Ah!' said Craddock. 'Your mind works just as mine does. I don't think it was Arthur Badcock, because you see, I don't think that Heather Badcock was meant to be killed. I think the intended victim was Marina Gregg.'

'That would seem almost certain, wouldn't it?' said Miss Marple.

'And so,' said Craddock, 'as we both agree on that, the field widens. To tell you who was there on that day, what they saw or said they saw, and where they were or said they were, is only a thing you could have observed for yourself if you'd been there. So my superiors, as you call them, couldn't possibly object to my discussing that with you, could they?'

'That's very nicely put, my dear boy,' said Miss Marple.

'I'll give you a little précis of what I was told and then we'll come to the list.'

He gave a brief résumé of what he had heard, and then he produced his list.

'It must be one of these,' he said. 'My godfather, Sir Henry

Clithering told me that you once had a club here. You called it the Tuesday Night Club. You all dined with each other in turn and then someone would tell a story – a story of some real life happening which had ended in mystery. A mystery of which only the teller of the tale knew the answer. And every time, so my grandfather told me, you guessed right. So I thought I'd come along and see if you'd do a bit of guessing for me this morning.'

'I think that is rather a frivolous way of putting it,' said Miss Marple, reprovingly, 'but there is one question I should like to ask.'

'Yes?'

'What about the children?'

'The children? There's only one. An imbecile child in a sanatorium in America. Is that what you mean?'

'No,' said Miss Marple, 'that's not what I mean. It's very sad of course. One of those tragedies that seem to happen and there's no one to blame for it. No, I meant the children that I've seen mentioned in some article here.' She tapped the papers in front of her. 'Children that Marina Gregg adopted. Two boys, I think, and a girl. In one case a mother with a lot of children and very little money to bring them up in this country, wrote to her, and asked if she couldn't take a child. There was a lot of very silly false sentiment written about that. About the mother's unselfishness and the wonderful home and education and future the child was going to have. I can't find out much about the other two. One I think was a foreign refugee and the other was some American child. Marina Gregg adopted them at different times. I'd like to know what's happened to them.'

Dermot Craddock looked at her curiously. 'It's odd that you should think of that,' he said. 'I did just vaguely wonder about those children myself. But how do you connect them up?'

'Well,' said Miss Marple, 'as far as I can hear or find out, they're not living with her now, are they?'

'I expect they were provided for,' said Craddock. 'In fact, I think that the adoption laws would insist on that. There was probably money settled on them in trust.'

'So when she got – tired of them,' said Miss Marple with a very faint pause before the word 'tired,' 'they were dismissed! After being brought up in luxury with every advantage. Is that it?'

'Probably,' said Craddock. 'I don't know exactly.' He continued to look at her curiously.

'Children feel things, you know,' said Miss Marple, nodding her head. 'They feel things more than the people around them

ever imagine. The sense of hurt, of being rejected, of not belonging. It's a thing that you don't get over just because of advantages. Education is no substitute for it, or comfortable living,
or an assured income, or a start in a profession. It's the sort of
thing that might rankle.'

'Yes. But all the same, isn't it rather far-fetched to think that –
well, what exactly do you think?'

'I haven't got as far as that,' said Miss Marple. 'I just wondered where they were and how old they would be now? Grown
up, I should imagine, from what I've read here.'

'I could find out, I suppose,' said Dermot Craddock slowly.

'Oh, I don't want to bother you in any way, or even to suggest that my little idea's worth while at all.'

'There's no harm,' said Dermot Craddock, 'in having that
checked up on.' He made a note in his little book. 'Now do you
want to look at my little list?'

'I don't really think I should be able to do anything useful
about that. You see, I wouldn't know who the people were.'

'Oh, I could give you a running commentary,' said Craddock.
'Here we are. *Jason Rudd, husband,* (husbands always highly
suspicious). Everyone says that Jason Rudd adored her. That is
suspicious in itself, don't you think?'

'Not necessarily,' said Miss Marple with dignity.

'He's been very active in trying to conceal the fact that his
wife was the object of attack. He hadn't hinted any suspicion of
such a thing to the police. I don't know why he thinks we're such
asses as not to think of it for ourselves. We've considered it from
the first. But anyway, that's his story. He was afraid that knowledge of that fact might get to his wife's ears and that she'd go
into a panic about it.'

'Is she the sort of woman who goes into panics?'

'Yes, she's neurasthenic, throws temperaments, has nervous
breakdowns, gets in states.'

'That might not mean any lack of courage,' Miss Marple objected.

'On the other hand,' said Craddock, 'if she knows quite well
that she was the object of the attack, it's also possible that she
may know who did it.'

'You mean she knows who did it – but does not want to dis-
close the fact?'

'I just say it's a possibility, and if so, one rather wonders why
not? It looks as though the motive, the root of the matter, was
something she didn't want to come to her husband's ear.'

'That is certainly an interesting thought,' said Miss Marple.

'Here are a few more names. The secretary, Ella Zielinsky. An extremely competent and efficient young woman.'

'In love with the husband, do you think?' asked Miss Marple.

'I should think definitely,' answered Craddock, 'but why should you think so?'

'Well, it so often happens,' said Miss Marple. 'And therefore not very fond of poor Marina Gregg, I expect?'

'Therefore possible motive for murder,' said Craddock.

'A lot of secretaries and employees are in love with their employers' husbands,' said Miss Marple, 'but very, very few of them try to poison them.'

'Well, we must allow for exceptions,' said Craddock. 'Then there were two local and one London photographer, and two members of the Press. None of them seem likely but we will follow them up. There was the woman who was formerly married to Marina Gregg's second or third husband. She didn't like it when Marina Gregg took her husband away. Still, that's about eleven or twelve years ago. It seems unlikely that she'd make a visit here at this juncture on purpose to poison Marina because of that. Then there's a man called Adrwyck Fenn. He was once a very close friend of Marina Gregg's. He hasn't seen her for years. He was not known to be in this part of the world and it was a great surprise when he turned up on this occasion.'

'She would be startled then when she saw him?'

'Presumably yes.'

'Startled – and possibly frightened.'

' "*The doom has come upon me,*" ' said Craddock. 'That's the idea. Then there was young Hailey Preston dodging about that day, doing his stuff. Talks a great deal but definitely heard nothing, saw nothing and knew nothing. Almost too anxious to say so. Does anything there ring a bell?'

'Not exactly,' said Miss Marple. 'Plenty of interesting possibilities. But I'd still like to know a little more about the children.'

He looked at her curiously. 'You've got quite a bee in your bonnet about that, haven't you?' he said. 'All right, I'll find out.'

13

'I suppose it couldn't possibly have been the mayor?' said Inspector Cornish wistfully.

He tapped the paper with the list of names on it with his pencil. Dermot Craddock grinned.

'Wishful thinking?' he asked.

'You could certainly call it that,' said Cornish. 'Pompous, canting old hypocrite!' he went on. 'Everybody's got it in for him. Throws his weight about, ultra sanctimonious, *and* neck deep in graft for years past!'

'Can't you ever bring it home to him?'

'No,' said Cornish. 'He's too slick for that. He's always just on the right side of the law.'

'It's tempting, I agree,' said Dermot Craddock, 'but I think you'll have to banish that rosy picture from your mind, Frank.'

'I know, I know,' said Cornish. 'He's a possible, but a wildly improbable. Who else have we got?'

Both men studied the list again. There were still eight names on it.

'We're pretty well agreed,' said Craddock, 'that there's nobody missed out from here?' There was a faint question in his voice. Cornish answered it.

'I think you can be pretty sure that's the lot. After Mrs Bantry came the vicar, and after that the Badcocks. There were then eight people on the stairs. The mayor and his wife, Joshua Grice and wife from Lower Farm. Donald McNeil of the Much Benham *Herald & Argus*. Ardwyck Fenn, USA, Miss Lola Brewster, USA, Moving Picture Star. There you are. In addition there was an arty photographer from London with a camera set up on the angle of the stairs. If, as you suggest, this Mrs Bantry's story of Marina Gregg having a "frozen look" was occasioned by someone she saw on the stairs, you've got to take your pick among that lot. Mayor regretfully out. Grices out – never been away from St Mary Mead I should say. That leaves four. Local journalist unlikely, photographer girl had been there for half an hour already, so why should Marina react so late in the day? What does that leave?'

'Sinister strangers from America,' said Craddock with a faint smile.

'You've said it.'

'They're out best suspects by far, I agree,' said Craddock. 'They turned up unexpectedly. Ardwyck Fenn was an old flame of Marina's whom she had not seen for years. Lola Brewster was once married to Marina Gregg's third husband, who got a divorce from her in order to marry Marina. It was not, I gather, a very amicable divorce.'

'I'd put her down as Suspect Number One,' said Cornish.

'Would you, Frank? After a lapse of about fifteen years or so, and having remarried twice herself since then?'

Cornish said that you never knew with women. Dermot accepted that as a general dictum, but remarked that it seemed odd to him to say the least of it.

'But you agree that it lies between them?'

'Possibly. But I don't like it very much. What about the hired help who were serving the drinks?'

'Discounting the "frozen look" we've heard so much about? Well, we've checked up in a general way. Local catering firm from Market Basing had the job – for the fête, I mean. Actually in the house, there was the butler, Giuseppe, in charge; and two local girls from the studios canteen. I know both of them. Not over bright, but harmless.'

'Pushing it back at me, are you? I'll go and have a word with the reporter chap. He might have seen something helpful. Then to London. Ardwyck Fenn, Lola Brewster – and the photographer girl – what's her name? – Margot Bence. She also might have seen something.'

Cornish nodded. 'Lola Brewster is my best bet,' he said. He looked curiously at Craddock. 'You don't seem as sold on her as I am.'

'I'm thinking of the difficulties,' said Dermot slowly.

'Difficulties?'

'Of putting poison into Marina's glass without anybody seeing her.'

'Well, that's the same for everybody, isn't it? It was a mad thing to do.'

'Agreed that it was a mad thing to do, but it would be a madder thing for someone like Lola Brewster than for anybody else.'

'Why?' asked Cornish.

'Because she was a guest of some importance. She's a somebody, a big name. Everyone would be looking at her.'

'True enough,' Cornish admitted.

'The locals would nudge each other and whisper and stare, and after Marina Gregg and Jason Rudd had greeted her she'd have been passed on for the secretaries to look after. It wouldn't be easy, Frank. However adroit you were, you couldn't be sure *someone* wouldn't see you. That's the snag there, and it's a big snag.'

'As I say, isn't that snag the same for everybody?'

'No,' said Craddock. 'Oh no. Far from it. Take the butler now, Giuseppe. He's busy with the drinks and glasses, with pouring things out, with handling them. He could put a pinch or a tablet or two of Calmo in a glass easily enough.'

'Giuseppe?' Frank Cornish reflected. 'Do you think he did?'

'No reason to believe so,' said Craddock, 'but we might find a reason. A nice solid bit of motive, that is to say. Yes, he could have done it. Or one of the catering staff could have done it – unfortunately they weren't on the spot – a pity.'

'Someone might have managed to get himself or herself deliberately planted in the firm for the purpose.'

'You mean it might have been as premeditated as all that?'

'We don't know anything about it yet,' said Craddock, vexedly. 'We absolutely don't know the first thing about it. Not until we can prise what we want to know out of Marina Gregg, or out of her husband. They *must* know or suspect – but they're not telling. And we don't know yet *why* they're not telling. We've a long way to go.'

He paused and then resumed: 'Discounting the "frozen look" which may have been pure coincidence, there are other people who could have done it fairly easily. The secretary woman, Ella Zielinsky. She was also busy with glasses, with handing things to people. Nobody would be watching *her* with any particular interest. The same applies to that willow wand of a young man – I've forgotten him name. Hailey – Hailey Preston? That's right. There would be a good opportunity for either of them. In fact if either of them *had* wanted to do away with Marina Gregg it would have been far safer to do so on a public occasion.'

'Anyone else?'

'Well, there's always the husband,' said Cornish.

'Back to husbands again,' said Cornish, with a faint smile. 'We thought it was that poor devil, Badcock, before we realized that Marina was the intended victim. Now we've transferred our suspicions to Jason Rudd. He seems devoted enough though, I must say.'

THE MIRROR CRACK'D FROM SIDE TO SIDE

'He has the reputation of being so,' said Craddock, 'but one never knows.'

'If he wanted to get rid of her, wouldn't divorce be much easier?'

'It would be far more usual,' agreed Dermot, 'but there may be a lot of ins and outs to this business that we don't know yet.'

The telephone rang. Cornish took up the receiver.

'What? Yes? Put them through. Yes, he's here.' He listened for a moment then put his hand over the receiver and looked at Dermot. 'Miss Marina Gregg,' he said, 'is feeling very much better. She is quite ready to be interviewed.'

'I'd better hurry along,' said Dermot Craddock, 'before she changes her mind.'

II

At Gossington Hall Dermot Craddock was received by Ella Zielinsky. She was, as usual, brisk and efficient.

'Miss Gregg is waiting for you, Mr Craddock,' she said.

Dermot looked at her with some interest. From the beginning he had found Ella Zielinsky an intriguing personality. He had said to himself, 'A poker face if I ever saw one.' She had answered any questions he had asked with the utmost readiness. She had shown no signs of keeping anything back, but what she really thought or felt or even knew about the business, he still had no idea. There seemed to be no chink in the armour of her bright efficiency. She might know no more than she said she did; she might know a good deal. The only thing he was sure of – and he had to admit to himself that he had no reasons to adduce for that surety – was that she was in love with Jason Rudd. It was, as he said, an occupational disease of secretaries. It probably meant nothing. But the fact did at least suggest a motive and he was sure, quite sure, that she was concealing something. It might be love, it might be hate. It might, quite simply, be guilt. She might have taken her opportunity that afternoon, or she might have deliberately planned what she was going to do. He could see her in the part quite easily, as far as the execution of it went. Her swift but unhurried movements, moving here and there, looking after guests, handing glasses to one or another, taking glasses away, her eyes marking the spot where Marina had put her glass down on the table. And then, perhaps at the very moment when Marina had been greeting the arrivals from the

States, with surprise and joyous cries and everybody's eyes turned towards their meeting, she could have quietly and unobtrusively dropped the fatal dose into that glass. It would require audacity, nerve, swiftness. She would have had all those. Whatever she had done, she would not have looked guilty whilst she was doing it. It would have been a simple, brilliant crime, a crime that could hardly fail to be successful. But chance had ruled otherwise. In the rather crowded floor-space someone had joggled Heather Badcock's arm. Her drink had been spilt, and Marina, with her natural impulsive grace, had quickly proffered her own glass, standing there untouched. And so the wrong woman had died.

A lot of pure theory, and probably hooey at that, said Dermot Craddock to himself at the same time as he was making polite remarks to Ella Zielinsky.

'One thing I wanted to ask you, Miss Zielinsky. The catering was done by a Market Basing firm, I understand?'

'Yes.'

'Why was that particular firm chosen?'

'I really don't know,' said Ella. 'That doesn't lie amongst my duties. I know Mr Rudd thought it would be more tactful to employ somebody local rather than to employ a firm from London. The whole thing was really quite a small affair from our point of view.'

'Quite.' He watched her as she stood frowning a little and looking down. A good forehead, a determined chin, a figure which could look quite voluptuous if it was allowed to do so, a hard mouth, an acquisitive mouth. The eyes? He looked at them in faint surprise. The lids were reddened. He wondered. Had she been crying? It looked like it. And yet he could have sworn she was not the type of young woman to cry. She looked up at him, and as though she read his thoughts, she took out her handkerchief and blew her nose heartily.

'You've got a cold,' he said.

'Not a cold. Hay-fever. It's an allergy of some kind, really. I always get it at this time of year.'

There was a low buzz. There were two phones in the room, one on the table and one on another table in the corner. It was the latter one that was beginning to buzz. Ella Zielinsky went over to it and picked up the receiver.

'Yes,' she said, 'he's here. I'll bring him up at once.' She put the receiver down again. 'Marina's ready for you,' she said.

III

Marina Gregg received Craddock in a room on the first floor, which was obviously her own private sitting-room opening out of her bedroom. After the accounts of her prostration and her nervous state, Dermot Craddock had expected to find a fluttering invalid. But although Marina was half reclining on a sofa her voice was vigorous and her eyes were bright. She had very little make-up on, but in spite of this she did not look her age, and he was struck very forcibly by the subdued radiance of her beauty. It was the exquisite line of cheek and jawbone, the way the hair fell loosely and naturally to frame her face. The long sea-green eyes, the pencilled eyebrows, owing something to art but more to nature, and the warmth and sweetness of her smile, all had a subtle magic. She said:

'Chief-Inspector Craddock? I've been behaving disgracefully. I do apologise. I just let myself go to pieces after this awful thing. I could have snapped out of it but I didn't. I'm ashamed of myself.' The smile came, rueful, sweet, turning up the corners of the mouth. She extended a hand and he took it.

'It was only natural,' he said, 'that you should feel upset.'

'Well, everyone was upset,' said Marina. 'I'd no business to make out it was worse for me than anyone else.'

'Hadn't you?'

She looked at him for a minute and then nodded. 'Yes,' she said, 'you're very perceptive. Yes, I had.' She looked down and with one long forefinger gently stroked the arm of the sofa. It was a gesture he had noticed in one of her films. It was a meaningless gesture, yet it seemed fraught with significance. It had a kind of musing gentleness.

'I'm a coward,' she said, her eyes still cast down. 'Somebody wanted to kill me and I didn't want to die.'

'Why do you think someone wanted to kill you?'

Her eyes opened wide. 'Because it was my glass – *my* drink – that had been tampered with. It was just a mistake that that poor stupid woman got it. That's what's so horrible and so tragic. Besides—'

'Yes, Miss Gregg?'

She seemed a little uncertain about saying more.

'You had other reasons perhaps for believing that you were the intended victim?'

She nodded.

'What reasons, Miss Gregg?'

She paused a minute longer before saying, 'Jason says I must tell you all about it.'

'You've confided in him then?'

'Yes . . . I didn't want to at first – but Dr Gilchrist put it to me that I must. And then I found that he thought so too. He'd thought it all along but – it's rather funny really' – a rueful smile curled her lips again – 'he didn't want to alarm me by telling me. Really!' Marina sat up with a sudden vigorous movement. 'Darling Jinks! Does he think I'm a complete fool?'

'You haven't told me yet, Miss Gregg, why you should think anyone wanted to kill you.'

She was silent for a moment and then with a sudden, brusque gesture, she stretched out for her handbag, opened it, took out a piece of paper and thrust it into his hand. He read it. Typed on it was one line of writing.

'Don't think you'll escape next time.'

Craddock said sharply, 'When did you get this?'

'It was on my dressing-table when I came back from the bath.'

'So someone in the house—'

'Not necessarily. Someone could have climbed up the balcony outside my window and pushed it through there. I think they meant it to frighten me still more, but actually it didn't. I just felt furiously angry and send word to you to come and see me.'

Dermot Craddock smiled. 'Possibly a rather unexpected result for whoever sent it. Is this the first kind of message like that you've had?'

Again Marina hesitated. Then she said, 'No, it isn't.'

'Will you tell me about any others?'

'It was three weeks ago, when we first came here. It came to the studio, not here. It was quite ridiculous. It was just a message. Not typewritten that time. In capital letters. It said, "*Prepare to die.*" ' She laughed. There was perhaps a very faint tinge of hysteria in the laugh. The mirth was genuine enough. 'It was so silly,' she said. 'Of course one often gets crank messages, threats, things like that. I thought it was probably religious you know. Someone who didn't approve of film actresses. I just tore it up and threw it into the waste-paper basket.'

'Did you tell anyone about it, Miss Gregg?'

Marina shook her head. 'No, I never said a word to anyone. As a matter of fact, we were having a bit of worry at the moment about the scene we were shooting. I just couldn't have thought of anything but that at the moment. Anyway, as I say, I thought it was either a silly joke or one of those religious cranks who write and disapprove of play-acting and things like that.'

'And after that, was there another?'

'Yes. On the day of the fête. One of the gardeners brought it to me, I think. He said someone had left a note for me and was there any answer? I thought perhaps it had to do with the arrangements. I just tore it open. It said "Today will be your last day on earth." I just crumpled it up and said, "No answer." Then I called the man back and asked him who gave it to him. He said it was a man with spectacles on a bicycle. Well, I mean, what could you do about that? I thought it was more silliness. I didn't think – I didn't think for a moment, it was a real genuine threat.'

'Where's that note now, Miss Gregg?'

'I've no idea. I was wearing one of those coloured Italian silk coats and I think, as far as I remember, that I crumpled it up and shoved it into the pocket of it. But it's not there now. It probably fell out.'

'And you've no idea who wrote those notes, Miss Gregg? Who inspired them. Not even now?'

Her eyes opened widely. There was a kind of innocent wonder in them that he took note of. He admired it, but he did not believe in it.

'How can I tell? How can I possibly tell?'

'I think you might have quite a good idea, Miss Gregg.'

'I haven't. I assure you I haven't.'

'You're a very famous person,' said Dermot. 'You've had great successes. Successes in your profession, and personal successes, too. Men have fallen in love with you, wanted to marry you, have married you. Women have been jealous and envied you. Men have been in love with you and been rebuffed by you. It's a pretty wide field, I agree, but I should think you must have *some* idea who could have written these notes.'

'It could have been anybody.'

'No, Miss Gregg, it couldn't have been *anybody*. It could possibly have been one of quite a number of people. It could be someone quite humble, a dresser, an electricia, a servant; or it could be someone among the ranks of your friends, or so-called friends. But you must have some idea. Some name, more than one name, perhaps, to suggest.'

The door opened and Jason Rudd came in. Marina turned to him. She swept out an arm appealingly.

'Jinks, darling, Mr Craddock is insisting that I must know who wrote those horrid notes. And I don't. You know I don't. Neither of us know. We haven't got the least idea.'

'Very urgent about that,' thought Craddock. 'Very urgent. Is Marina Gregg afraid of what her husband might say?'

Jason Rudd, his eyes dark with fatigue and the scowl on his face deeper than usual, came over to join them. He took Marina's hand in his.

'I know it sounds unbelievable to you, Inspector,' he said, 'but honestly neither Marina nor I have any idea about this business.'

'So you're in the happy position of having no enemies, is that it?' The irony was manifest in Dermot's voice.

Jason Rudd flushed a little. 'Enemies? That's a very biblical word, Inspector. In that sense, I can assure you I can think of no enemies. People who dislike one, would like to get the better of one, would do a mean turn to one if they could, in malice and uncharitableness, yes. But it's a long step from that to putting an overdose of poison in a drink.'

'Just now, in speaking to your wife, I asked her who could have written or inspired those letters. She said she didn't know. But when we come to the actual action, it narrows it down. *Somebody actually put the poison in that glass.* And that's a fairly limited field, you know.'

'I saw nothing,' said Jason Rudd.

'I certainly didn't,' said Marina. 'Well, I mean – if I had seen anyone putting anything in my glass, I wouldn't have drunk the stuff, would I?'

'I can't help believing you, you know,' said Dermot Craddock gently, 'that you do know a little more than you're telling me.'

'It's not *true*,' said Marina. 'Tell him that that isn't true, Jason!'

'I assure you,' said Jason Rudd, 'that I am completely and absolutely at a loss. The whole thing's fantastic. I might believe it was a joke – a joke that had somehow gone wrong – that had proved dangerous, done by a person who never dreamt that it would be dangerous ...'

There was a slight question in his voice, then he shook his head. 'No. I see that idea doesn't appeal to you.'

'There's one more thing I should like to ask you,' said Dermot Craddock. 'You remember Mr and Mrs Badcock's arrival, of course. They came immediately after the vicar. You greeted them, I understand, Miss Gregg, in the same charming way as you had received all your guests. But I am told by an eye-witness that immediately after greeting them you looked over Mrs Badcock's shoulder and that you saw something which seemed to alarm you. Is that true, and if so, what was it?'

Marina said quickly, 'Of course it isn't true. Alarm me – what should have alarmed me?'

'That's what we want to know,' said Dermot Craddock patiently. 'My witness is very insistent on the point, you know.'

'Who was your witness? What did he or she say they saw?'

'You were looking at the staircase,' said Dermot Craddock. 'There were people coming up that staircase. There was a journalist, there was Mr Grice and his wife, elderly residents in this place, there was Mr Ardwyck Fenn who had just arrived from the States, and there was Miss Lola Brewster. Was it the sight of one of those people that upset you, Miss Gregg?'

'I tell you I wasn't upset.' She almost barked the words.

'And yet your attention wavered from greeting Mrs Badcock. She had said something to you which you left unanswered because you were staring past her at something else.'

Marina Gregg took hold on herself. She spoke quickly and convincingly.

'I can explain that, I really can. If you knew anything about acting you'd be able to understand quite easily. There comes a moment, even when you know a part well – in fact, it usually happens when you *do* know a part well – when you go on with it mechanically. Smiling, making the proper movements and gestures, saying the words with the usual inflexions. But your mind isn't on it. And quite suddenly there's a horrible blank moment when you don't know where you are, where you've got to in the play, what your next lines are! Drying up, that's what we call it. Well, that's what happened to me. I'm not terribly strong, as my husband will tell you. I've had rather a strenuous time, and a good deal of nervous apprehension about this film. I wanted to make a success of this fête and to be nice and pleasant and welcoming to everybody. But one does say the same things over and over again, mechanically, to the people who are always saying the same things to you. You know, how they've always wanted to meet you. How they once saw you outside a theatre in San Francisco – or travelled in a plane with you. Something silly, really, but one has to be nice about it and say things. Well, as I'm telling you, one does that automatically. One doesn't need to think what to say because one's said it so often before. Suddenly, I think, a wave of tiredness came over me. My brain went blank. Then I realized that Mrs Badcock had been telling me a long story which I hadn't really heard at all, and was now looking at me in an eager sort of way and that I hadn't answered her or said any of the proper things. It was just tiredness.'

'Just tiredness,' said Dermot Craddock slowly. 'You insist on that, Miss Gregg?'

'Yes, I do. I can't see why you don't believe me.'

Dermot Craddock turned towards Jason Rudd. 'Mr Rudd,' he said, 'I think you're more likely to understand my meaning than your wife is. I am concerned, very much concerned, for your wife's safety. There has been an attempt on her life, there have been threatening letters. That means, doesn't it, that there is someone who was here on the day of the fête and possibly is still here, someone in very close touch with this house and what goes on in it. That person, whoever it is, may be slightly insane. It's not just a question of threats. Threatened men live long, as they say. The same goes for women. But whoever it was didn't stop at threats. A deliberate attempt was made to poison Miss Gregg. Don't you see in the whole nature of things, that the attempt is bound to be repeated? There's only one way to achieve safety. That is to give me all the clues you possibly can. I don't say that you *know* who that person is, but I think that you must be able to give a guess or to have a vague idea. Won't you tell me the truth? Or if, which is possible, you yourself do not know the truth, won't you urge your wife to do so. It's in the interests of her own safety that I'm asking you.'

Jason Rudd turned his head slowly. 'You hear what Inspector Craddock says, Marina,' he said. 'It's possible, as he says that you may know something that I do not. If so, for God's sake, don't be foolish about it. If you've the least suspicion of *anyone*, tell it to us now.'

'But I haven't.' Her voice rose in a wail. 'You must believe me.'

'Who were you afraid of that day?' asked Dermot.

'I wasn't afraid of anyone.'

'Listen, Miss Gregg, of the people on the stairs or coming up it, there were two friends whom you were surprised to see, whom you had not seen for a long time and whom you did not expect to see that day. Mr Ardwyck Fenn and Miss Brewster. Had you any special emotions when you suddenly saw them coming up the stairs? You didn't know they were coming, did you?'

'No, we'd no idea they were even in England,' said Jason Rudd.

'I was delighted,' said Marina, 'absolutely delighted!'

'Delighted to see Miss Brewster?'

'Well—' she shot him a quick, faintly suspicious glance.

Craddock said, 'Lola Brewster was, I believe, originally married to your third husband Robert Truscott?'

'Yes, that's so.'

He divorced her in order to marry you.'

'Oh, everyone knows about that,' said Marina Gregg impatiently. 'You needn't think it's anything you've found out. There was a bit of a rumpus at the time, but there wasn't any bad feeling about it in the end.'

'Did she make threats against you?'

'Well – in a way, yes. But, oh dear, I wish I could explain. No one takes those sort of threats *seriously*. It was at a party, she'd had a lot of drink. She might have taken a pot-shot at me with a pistol if she'd had one. But luckily she didn't. All that was *years* ago! None of these things last, these emotions! They don't, really they don't. That's true, isn't it, Jason?'

'I'd say it was true enough,' said Jason Rudd, 'and I can assure you, Mr Craddock, that Lola Brewster had no opportunity on the day of the fête of poisoning my wife's drink. I was close beside her most of the time. The idea that Lola would suddenly, after a long period of friendliness, come to England, and arrive at our house all prepared to poison my wife's drink – why the whole idea's absurd!'

'I appreciate your point of view,' said Craddock.

'It's not only that, it's a matter of *fact* as well. She was nowhere near Marina's glass.'

'And your other visitor – Ardwyck Fenn?'

There was, he thought, a very slight pause before Jason Rudd spoke.

'He's a very old friend of ours,' he said. 'We haven't seen him for a good many years now, though we occasionally correspond. He's quite a big figure in American Television.'

'Was he an old friend of yours too?' Dermot Craddock asked Marina.

Her breath came rather quickly as she replied. 'Yes, oh yes. He – he was quite a friend of mine always, but I've rather lost sight of him of late years.' Then with a sudden quick rush of words, she went on, 'If you think that I looked up and saw Ardwyck and was frightened of him, it's nonsense. It's absolute *nonsense*. Why should I be frightened of him, what reason would I have to be frightened of him? We were great friends. I was just very, very pleased when I suddenly saw him. It was a

658

delightful surprise, as I told you. Yes, a delightful surprise.' She raised her head, looking at him, her face vivid and defiant.

'Thank you, Miss Gregg,' said Craddock quietly. 'If you should feel inclined at any moment to take me a little further into your confidence I should strongly advise you to do so.'

— 14 —

Mrs Bantry was on her knees. A good day for hoeing. Nice dry soil. But hoeing wouldn't do everything. Thistles now, and dandelions. She dealt vigorously with these pests.

She rose to her feet, breathless but triumphant, and looked out over the hedge on to the road. She was faintly surprised to see the dark-haired secretary whose name she couldn't remember coming out of the public call box that was situated near the bus stop on the other side of the road.

What was her name now. It began with a B – or was it an R? No, *Zielinsky*, that was it. Mrs Bantry remembered just in time, as Ella crossed the road and came into the drive past the Lodge.

'Good morning, Miss Zielinsky,' she called in a friendly tone.

Ella Zielinsky jumped. It was not so much a jump, as a shy – the shy of a frightened horse. It surprised Mrs Bantry.

'Good morning,' said Ella, and added quickly: 'I came down to telephone. There's something wrong with our line today.'

Mrs Bantry felt more surprise. She wondered why Ella Zielinsky bothered to explain her action. She responded civilly. 'How annoying for you. Do come in and telephone any time you want to.'

'Oh – thank you very much . . .' Ella was interrupted by a fit of sneezing.

'You've got hay-fever,' said Mrs Bantry with immediate diagnosis. 'Try weak bicarbonate of soda and water.'

'Oh, that's all right. I have some very good patent stuff in an atomizer. Thank you all the same.'

She sneezed again as she moved away, walking briskly up the drive.

Mrs Bantry looked after her. Then her eyes returned to her garden. She looked at it in a dissatisfied fashion. Not a weed to be seen anywhere.

'Othello's occupation's gone,' Mrs Bantry murmured to herself confusedly. 'I dare say I'm a nosy old woman but I would like to know if—'

A moment of irresolution and then Mrs Bantry yielded to temptation. She was going to be a nosy old woman and the hell with it! She strode indoors to the telephone, lifted the receiver and dialled. A brisk transatlantic voice spoke.

'Gossington Hall.'

'This is Mrs Bantry, at the East Lodge.'

'Oh, good morning, Mrs Bantry. This is Hailey Preston. I met you on the day of the fête. What can I do for you?'

'I thought perhaps I could do something for you. If your telephone's out of order—'

His astonished voice interrupted her.

'Our telephone out of order? There's been nothing wrong with it. Why did you think so?'

'I must have made a mistake,' said Mrs Bantry. 'I don't always hear very well,' she explained unblushingly.

She put the receiver back, waited a minute, then dialled once more.

'Jane? Dolly here.'

'Yes, Dolly. What is it?'

'Well, it seems rather *odd*. That secretary woman was dialling from the public call box in the road. She took the trouble to explain to me quite unnecessarily that she was doing so because the line at Gossington Hall was out of order. But I've rung up there, and it *isn't* . . .'

She paused, and waited for intelligence to pronounce.

'In-deed,' said Miss Marple thoughtfully. 'Interesting.'

'For what reason, do you think?'

'Well, clearly, she didn't want to be overheard—'

'Exactly.'

'And there might be quite a number of reasons for that.'

'Yes.'

'Interesting,' said Miss Marple again.

II

Nobody could have been more ready to talk than Donald McNeil. He was an amiable red-headed young man. He greeted Dermot Craddock with pleasure and curiosity.

'How are you getting along,' he asked cheerfully, 'got any little special tit-bit for me?'

'Not as yet. Later perhaps.'

'Stalling as usual. You're all the same. Affable oysters! Haven't you come to the stage yet of inviting someone to come and "assist you in your inquiries"?'

'I've come to you,' said Dermot Craddock with a grin.

'Is there a nasty double entendre in that remark. Are you really suspicious that I murdered Heather Badcock and do you think I did it in mistake for Marina Gregg or that I meant to murder Heather Badcock all the time?'

'I haven't suggested anything,' said Craddock.

'No, no, you wouldn't do that, would you? You'd be very correct. All right. Let's go into it. I was there. I had opportunity but had I any motive? Ah, that's what you'd like to know. What was my motive?'

'I haven't been able to find one so far,' said Craddock.

'That's very gratifying. I feel safer.'

'I'm just interested in what you may have seen that day.'

'You've had that already. The local police had that straight away. It's humiliating. There I was on the scene of a murder. I practically *saw* the murder committed, must have done and yet I've no idea who did it. I'm ashamed to confess that the first *I* knew about it was seeing the poor, dear woman sitting on a chair gasping for breath and then pegging out. Of course it made a very good eye-witness account. It was a good scoop for me – and all that. But I'll confess to you that I feel humiliated that I don't know more. I ought to know more. And you can't kid me that the dose was meant for Heather Badcock. She was a nice woman who talked too much, but nobody gets murdered for that – unless of course they give away secrets. But I don't think anybody would ever have told Heather Badcock a secret. She wasn't the kind of woman who'd have been interested in other people's secrets. My view of her is of a woman who invariably talked about *herself*.'

'That seems to be the generally accepted view,' agreed Craddock.

'So we come to the famous Marina Gregg. I'm sure there are lots of wonderful motives for murdering Marina. Envy and jealousy and love tangles – all the stuff of drama. But who did it? Someone with a screw loose, I presume. There! You've had my valuable opinion. Is that what you wanted?'

'Not that alone. I understand that you arrived and came up the stairs about the same time as the vicar and the mayor.'

'Quite correct. But that wasn't the first time I'd arrived. I'd been there earlier.'

'I didn't know that.'

'Yes. I was on a kind of roving commission, you know, going here and there. I had a photographer with me. I'd gone down to take a few local shots of the mayor arriving and throwing a hoopla and putting in a peg for buried treasure, and that kind of thing. Then I went back up again, not so much on the job, as to get a drink or two. The drink was good.'

'I see. Now can you remember who else was on the staircase when you went up?'

'Margot Bence from London was there with her camera.'

'You know her well?'

'Oh I run against her quite often. She's a clever girl, who makes a success of her stuff. She takes all the fashionable things – First Nights, Gala Performances – specialises in photographs from unusual angles. Arty! She was in a corner of the half landing very well placed for taking anyone who came up and for taking the greetings going on at the top. Lola Brewster was just ahead of me on the stairs. Didn't know her at first. She's got a new rust-red hair-do. The very latest Fiji Islander type. Last time I saw her it was lank waves falling round her face and chin in a nice shade of auburn. There was a big dark man with her, American. I don't know who he was but he looked important.'

'Did you look at Marina Gregg herself at all as you were coming up?'

'Yes, of course I did.'

'She didn't look upset at all or as though she'd had a shock or been frightened?'

'It's odd you should say that. I *did* think for a moment or two she was going to faint.'

'I see,' said Craddock thoughtfully. 'Thanks. There's nothing else you'd like to tell me?'

McNeil gave him a wide innocent stare.

'What could there be?'

'I don't trust you,' said Craddock.

'But you seem quite sure I didn't do it. Disappointing. Suppose I turn out to be her first husband. Nobody knows who he was except that he was so insignificant that even his name's been forgotten.'

Dermot grinned.

'Married from your prep school?' he asked. 'Or possibly in rompers! I must hurry. I've got a train to catch.'

III

There was a neatly docketed pile of papers on Craddock's desk at New Scotland Yard. He gave a perfunctory glance through them, then threw a question over his shoulder.

'Where's Lola Brewster staying?'

'At the Savoy, sir. Suite 1800. She's expecting you.'

'And Ardwyck Fenn?'

'He's at the Dorchester. First floor, 190.'

'Good.'

He picked up some cablegrams and read them through again before shoving them into his pocket. He smiled a moment to himself over the last one. 'Don't say I don't do my stuff, Aunt Jane,' he murmured under his breath.

He went out and made his way to the Savoy.

In Lola Brewster's suite Lola went out of her way to welcome him effusively. With the report he had just read in his mind, he studied her carefully. Quite a beauty still, he thought, in a lush kind of way, what you might call a trifle over-blown, perhaps, but they still liked them that way. A completely different type, of course, from Marina Gregg. The amenities over, Lola pushed back her Fiji Islander hair, drew her generous lipsticked mouth into a provocative pout, and flickering blue eyelids over wide brown eyes, said:

'Have you come to ask me a lot more horrible questions? Like that local inspector did.'

'I hope they won't be too horrible, Miss Brewster.'

'Oh, but I'm sure they will be, and I'm sure the whole thing must have been some terrible mistake.'

'Do you really think so?'

'Yes. It's all such nonsense. Do you really mean that someone tried to poison Marina. Who on earth would poison Marina? She's an absolute sweetie, you know. Everybody loves her.'

'Including you?'

'I've always been devoted to Marina.'

'Oh come now, Miss Brewster, wasn't there a little trouble about eleven or twelve years ago?'

'Oh that.' Lola waved it away. 'I was terribly nervy and distraught, and Rob and I had been having the most frightful quarrels. We were neither of us normal at the moment. Marina just fell wildly in love with him and rushed him off his feet, the poor pet.'

'And you minded very much?'

'Well, I thought I did, Inspector. Of course I see now it was one of the best things that ever happened for me. I was really worried about the *children*, you know. Breaking up our home. I'm afraid I'd already realized that Rob and I were incompatible. I expect you know I got married to Eddie Groves as soon as the divorce went through? I think really I'd been in love with him for a long time, but of course I didn't want to break up my marriage, because of the children. It's so important, isn't it, that children should have a *home*?'

'Yet people say that actually you were terribly upset.'

'Oh, people always say things,' said Lola vaguely.

'You said quite a lot, didn't you, Miss Brewster? You went about threatening to shoot Marina Gregg, or so I understand.'

'I've told you one *says* things. One's *supposed* to say things like that. Of course I wouldn't really shoot *anyone*.'

'In spite of taking a pot-shot at Eddie Groves some few years later?'

'Oh, that was because we'd had an argument,' said Lola. 'I lost my temper.'

'I have it on very good authority, Miss Brewster, that you said – and these are your exact words or so I'm told,' (he read from a note-book) – "That bitch needn't think she'll get away with it. If I don't shoot her now I'll wait and get her in some other way. I don't care how long I wait, years if need be, but I'll get even with her in the end." '

'Oh, I'm sure I never said anything of the kind,' Lola laughed.

'I'm sure, Miss Brewster, that you did.'

'People exaggerate so.' A charming smile broke over her face. 'I was just mad at the moment, you know,' she murmured confidentially. 'One says all sorts of things when one's mad with people. But you don't really think I'd wait fourteen years and come across to England, and look up Marina and drop some deadly poison into her cocktail glass within three minutes of seeing her again?'

Dermot Craddock didn't really think so. It seemed to him wildly improbable. He merely said:

'I'm only pointing out to you, Miss Brewster, that there had been threats in the past and that Marina Gregg was certainly startled and frightened to see someone who came up the stairs that day. Naturally one feels that the someone must have been you.'

'But darling Marina was delighted to see me! She kissed me

664

and exclaimed how wonderful it was. Oh really, Inspector, I do think that you're being very, very silly.'

'In fact, you were all one big happy family?'

'Well, that's really much more true than all the things you've been thinking.'

'And you've no ideas that could help us in any way? No ideas who might have killed her?'

'I tell you nobody would have wanted to kill Marina. She's a very silly woman anyway. Always making terrible fusses about her health, and changing her mind and wanting this, that and the other, and when she's got it being dissatisfied with it! I can't think why people are as fond of her as they are. Jason's always been absolutely mad about her. What that man has to put up with! But there it is. Everybody puts up with Marina, puts themselves out for her. Then she gives them a sad, sweet smile and thanks them! And apparently that makes them feel that all the trouble is worth while. I really don't know how she does it. You'd better put the idea that somebody wanted to kill her right out of your head.'

'I should like to,' said Dermot Craddock. 'Unfortunately I can't put it out of my head because, you see, it happened.'

'What do you mean, *it happened*, nobody has killed Marina, have they?'

'No. But the attempt was made.'

'I don't believe it for a moment! I expect whoever it was meant to kill the other woman all the time – the one who *was* killed. I expect someone comes into money when she dies.'

'She hadn't any money, Miss Brewster.'

'Oh well, there was some other reason. Anyway, I shouldn't worry about Marina if I were you. Marina is *always* all right!'

'Is she? She doesn't look a very happy woman to me.'

'Oh, that's because she makes such a song and dance about everything. Unhappy love affairs. Not being able to have any children.'

'She adopted some children, didn't she?' said Dermot with a lively remembrance of Miss Marple's urgent voice.

'I believe she did once. It wasn't a great success I believe. She does these impulsive things and then wishes she hadn't.'

'What happened to the children she adopted?'

'I've no idea. They just sort of vanished after a bit. She got tired of them, I suppose, like everything else.'

'I see,' said Dermot Craddock.

IV

Next – the Dorchester. Suite 190.

'Well, Chief-Inspector —' Ardwyck Fenn looked down at the card in his hand.

'Craddock.'

'What can I do for you?'

'I hope you won't mind if I ask you a few questions.'

'Not at all. It's this business at Much Benham. No – what's the actual name, St Mary Mead?'

'Yes. That's right. Gossington Hall.'

'Can't think what Jason Rudd wanted to buy a place like that for. Plenty of good Georgian houses in England – or even Queen Anne. Gossington Hall is a purely Victorian mansion. What's the attraction in that, I wonder?'

'Oh, there's some attraction – for some people, that is, in Victorian stability.'

'Stability? Well, perhaps you've got something there. Marina, I suppose, had a feeling for stability. It's a thing she never had herself, poor girl, so I suppose that's why she always covets it. Perhaps this place will satisfy her for a bit.'

'You know her well, Mr Fenn?'

Ardwyck Fenn shrugged his shoulders.

'Well? I don't know that I'd say that. I've known her over a long period of years. Known her off and on, that is to say.'

Craddock looked at him appraisingly. A dark man, heavily built, shrewd eyes behind thick glasses, heavy jowl and chin. Ardwyck Fenn went on:

'The idea is, I gather, from what I read in the newspapers, that this Mrs Whatever-her-name-was, was poisoned by mistake. That the dose was intended for Marina. Is that right?'

'Yes. That's it. The dose was in Marina Gregg's cocktail. Mrs Badcock spilt hers and Marina handed over her drink to her.'

'Well, that seems pretty conclusive. I really can't think, though, who would want to poison Marina. Especially as Lynette Brown wasn't there.'

'Lynette Brown?' Craddock looked slightly at sea.

Ardwyck Fenn smiled. 'If Marina breaks this contract, throws up this part – Lynette will get it and it would mean a good deal to Lynette to get it. But for all that, I don't imagine she'd send some emissary along with poison. Much too melodramatic an idea.'

'It seems a little far-fetched,' said Dermot dryly.

666

'Ah, you'd be surprised what women will do when they're ambitious,' said Ardwyck Fenn. 'Mind you, death mayn't have been intended. It may have been just meant to give her a fright – Enough to knock her out but not to finish her.'

Craddock shook his head. 'It wasn't a borderline dose,' he said.

'People make mistakes in doses, quite big ones.'

'Is this really your theory?'

'Oh no, it isn't. It was only a suggestion. I've no theory. I was only an innocent bystander.'

'Was Marina Gregg very surprised to see you?'

'Yes, it was a complete surprise to her.' He laughed amusedly. 'Just couldn't believe her eyes when she saw me coming up the stairs. She gave me a very nice welcome, I must say.'

'You hadn't seen her for a long time?'

'Not for four or five years, I should say.'

'And some years before that there was a time when you and she were very close friends, I believe?'

'Are you insinuating anything in particular by that remark, Inspector Craddock?'

There was very little change in the voice but there was something there that had not been there before. A hint of steel, of menace. Dermot felt suddenly that this man would be a very ruthless opponent.

'It would be as well, I think,' said Ardwyck Fenn, 'that you said exactly what you do mean.'

'I'm quite prepared to do so, Mr Fenn. I have to inquire into the past relations of everyone who was there on that day with Marina Gregg. It seems to have been a matter of common gossip that at the time I have just referred to, you were wildly in love with Marina Gregg.'

Arywyck Fenn shrugged his shoulders.

'One has these infatuations, Inspector. Fortunately, they pass.'

'It is said that she encouraged you and that later she turned you down and that you resented the fact.'

'It is said – it is said! I suppose you read all that in *Confidential*?'

'It has been told me by quite well informed and sensible people.'

Ardwyck Fenn threw back his head, showing the bull-like line of his neck.

'I had a yen for her at one time, yes,' he admitted. 'She was a beautiful and attractive woman and still is. To say that I ever threatened her is going a little far. I'm never pleased to be thwarted, Chief-Inspector, and most people who thwart me tend to be sorry that they have done so. But that principle applies mainly in my business life.'

'You did, I believe, use your influence to have her dropped from a picture that she was making?'

Fenn shrugged his shoulders.

'She was unsuitable for the role. There was conflict between her and the director. I had money in that picture and I had no intention of jeopardising it. It was, I assure you, purely a business transaction.'

'But perhaps Marina Gregg did not think so?'

'Oh, naturally she did not think so. She would always think that anything like that was personal.'

'She actually told certain friends of hers that she was afraid of you, I believe?'

'Did she? How childish. I expect she enjoyed the sensation.'

'You think there was no need for her to be afraid of you?'

'Of course not. Whatever personal disappointment I might have had, I soon put it behind me. I've always gone on the principle that where women are concerned there are as good fish in the sea as ever came out of it.'

'A very satisfactory way to go through life, Mr Fenn.'

'Yes, I think it is.'

'You have a wide knowledge of the moving picture world?'

'I have financial interests in it.'

'And therefore you are bound to know a lot about it?'

'Perhaps.'

'You are a man whose judgment would be worth listening to. Can you suggest to me any person who is likely to have such a deep grudge against Marina Gregg that they would be willing to do away with her?'

'Probably a dozen,' said Ardwyck Fenn, 'that is to say, if they hadn't got to do anything about it personally. If it was a mere matter of pressing a button in a wall, I dare say there'd be a lot of willing fingers.'

'You were there that day. You saw her and talked to her. Do you think that amongst any of the people who were around you in that brief space of time – from when you arrived to the moment when Heather Badcock died – do you think that amongst them you can suggest – only suggest, mind you, I'm asking you for nothing more than a guess – anyone who might poison Marina Gregg?'

'I wouldn't like to say,' said Ardwyck Fenn.

'That means that you have some idea?'

'It means that I have nothing to say on that subject. And that, Chief-Inspector, is all you'll get out of me,'

—— 15 ——

Dermot Craddock looked down at the last name and address he had written down in his note-book. The telephone number had been rung twice for him but there had been no response. He tried it now once more. He shrugged his shoulders, got up and decided to go and see for himself.

Margot Bence's studio was in a cul-de-sac off the Tottenham Court Road. Beyond the name on a plate on the side of a door, there was little to identify it, and certainly no form of advertising. Craddock groped his way to the first floor. There was a large notice here painted in black on a white board. 'Margot Bence, Personality Photographer. Please enter.'

Craddock entered. There was a small waiting-room but nobody in charge of it. He stood there hesitating, then cleared his throat in a loud and theatrical manner. Since that drew no attention he raised his voice.

'Anybody here?'

He heard a flap of slippers behind a velvet curtain, the curtain was pushed aside and a young man with exuberant hair and a pink and white face, peered round it.

'Terribly sorry, my dear,' he said. 'I didn't hear you. I had an absolutely new idea and I was just trying it out.'

He pushed the velvet curtain farther aside and Craddock followed him into an inner room. This proved to be unexpectedly large. It was clearly the working studio. There were cameras, lights, arc-lights, piles of drapery, screens on wheels.

'Such a mess,' said the young man, who was almost as willowy as Hailey Preston. 'But one finds it very hard to work, I think, unless one *does* get into a mess. Now what were you wanting to see us about?'

'I wanted to see Miss Margot Bence.'

'Ah, Margot. Now what a pity. If you'd been half an hour earlier you'd have found her here. She's gone off to produce some photographs of models for *Fashion Dream*. You should have rung up, you know, to make an appointment. Margot's terribly busy these days.'

'I did ring up. There was no reply.'

'Of course,' said the young man. 'We took the receiver off. I remember now. It disturbed us.' He smoothed down a kind of lilac smock that he was wearing. 'Can I do anything for you? Make an appointment? I do a lot of Margot's business arrangements for her. You wanted to arrange for some photography somewhere? Private or business?'

'From that point of view, neither,' said Dermot Craddock. He handed his card to the young man.

'How perfectly rapturous,' said the young man. 'CID! I believe, you know, I've seen pictures of you. Are you one of the Big Four or the Big Five, or is it perhaps the Big Six nowadays? There's so much crime about, they'd have to increase the numbers, wouldn't they? Oh dear, is that disrespectful? I'm afraid it is. I didn't mean to be disrespectful at all. Now, what do you want Margot for – not to arrest her, I hope.'

'I just wanted to ask her one or two questions.'

'She doesn't do indecent photographs or anything like that,' said the young man anxiously. 'I hope nobody's been telling you any stories of that kind because it isn't true. Margot's very artistic. She does a lot of stage work and studio work. But her studies are terribly, terribly pure – almost prudish, I'd say.'

'I can tell you quite simply why I want to speak to Miss Bence,' said Dermot. 'She was recently an eye-witness of a crime that took place near Much Benham, at a village called St Mary Mead.'

'Oh, my dear, of *course*! I know about *that*. Margot came back and told me about it. Hemlock in the cocktails, wasn't it? Something of that kind. So *bleak* it sounded! But all mixed up with St John's Ambulance, which doesn't seem so bleak, does it? But haven't you already asked Margot questions about that – or was it somebody else?'

'One always finds there are more questions, as the case goes on,' said Dermot.

'You mean it develops. Yes, I can quite see that. Murder develops. Yes, like a photograph, isn't it?'

'It's very much like a photograph really,' said Dermot. 'Quite a good comparison of yours.'

'Well, it's very nice of you to say so, I'm sure. Now about Margot. Would you like to get hold of her right away?'

'If you can help me do so, yes.'

'Well, at the moment,' said the young man, consulting his watch, 'at the moment she'll be outside Keats' house at Hampstead Heath. My car's outside. Shall I run you up there?'

'That would be very kind of you, Mr—?'

'Jethroe,' said the young man, 'Johnny Jethroe.'

As they went down the stairs Dermot asked:

'Why Keats' house?'

'Well, you know we don't pose fashion photographs in the studio anymore. We like them to seem natural, blown about by the wind. And if possible some rather unlikely background. You know an Ascot frock against Wandsworth Prison, or a frivolous little suit outside a poet's house.'

Mr Jethroe drove rapidly but skilfully up Tottenham Court Road, through Camden Town and finally to the neighbourhood of Hampstead Heath. On the pavement near Keats' house a pretty little scene was being enacted. A slim girl wearing diaphanous organdie, was standing clutching an immense black hat. On her knees, a little way behind her, a second girl was holding the first girl's skirt well pulled back so that it clung around her knees and legs. In a deep hoarse voice a girl with a camera was directing operations.

'For goodness' sake, Jane, get your *behind* down. It's showing behind her right knee. Get down *flatter*. That's it. No, more to the left. That's right. Now you're masked by the bush. That'll do. Hold it. We'll have one more. Both hands on the back of the hat this time. Head up. Good – now turn round, Elsie. Bend over. More. Bend! *Bend,* you've got to pick up that cigarette case. That's right. That's *heaven!* Got it! Now move over to the left. Same pose, only just turn your head over your shoulder. So.'

'I can't see what you want to go taking photographs of my behind for,' said the girl called Elsie rather sulkily.

'It's a lovely behind, dear. It looks smashing,' said the photographer. 'And when you turn your head your chin comes up like the rising moon over a mountain. I don't think we need bother with any more.'

'Hi – Margot,' said Mr Jethroe.

She turned her head. 'Oh, it's you. What are you doing here?'

'I brought someone along to see you. Chief Detective-Inspector Craddock, CID.'

The girl's eyes turned swiftly on to Dermot. He thought they had a wary, searching look but that, as he well knew, was nothing extraordinary. It was a fairly common reaction to detective-inspectors. She was a thin girl, all elbows and angles, but was an interesting shape for all that. A heavy curtain of black hair fell down on either side of her face. She looked dirty as well as sallow and not particularly prepossessing, to his eyes. But he acknowledged that there was character there. She raised her eyebrows which were slightly raised by art already and remarked:

'And what can I do for you, Detective-Inspector Craddock?'

'How do you do, Miss Bence. I wanted to ask you if you would be so kind as to answer a few questions about that very unfortunate business at Gossington Hall, near Much Benham. You went there, if I remember, to take some photographs.'

The girl nodded. 'Of course. I remember quite well.' She shot him a quick searching look. 'I didn't see you there. Surely it was somebody else. Inspector – Inspector—'

'Inspector Cornish?' said Dermot.

'That's right.'

'We were called in later.'

'You're from Scotland Yard?'

'Yes.'

'You butted in and took over from the local people. Is that it?'

'Well, it isn't quite a question of butting in, you know. It's up to the Chief Constable of the County to decide whether he wants to keep it in his own hands or whether he thinks it'll be better handled by us.'

'What makes him decide?'

'It very often turns on whether the case has a local background or whether it's a more – universal one. Sometimes, perhaps, an international one.'

'And he decided, did he, that this was an international one?'

'Transatlantic, perhaps, would be a better word.'

'They've been hinting that in the papers, haven't they? Hinting that the killer, whoever he was, was out to get Marina Gregg and got some wretched local woman by mistake. Is that true or is it a bit of publicity for their film?'

'I'm afraid there isn't much doubt about it, Miss Bence.'

'What do you want to ask me? Have I got to come to Scotland Yard?'

He shook his head. 'Not unless you like. We'll go back to your studio if you prefer.'

'All right, let's do that. My car's just up the street.'

She walked rapidly along the footpath. Dermot went with her. Jethroe called after them.

'So long, darling, I won't butt in. I'm sure you and the inspector are going to talk big secrets.' He joined the two models on the pavement and began an animated discussion with them.

Margot got into the car, unlocked the door on the other side, and Dermot Craddock got in beside her. She said nothing at all during the drive back to Tottenham Court Road. She turned down the cul-de-sac and at the bottom of it drove through an open doorway.

'Got my own parking place here,' she remarked. 'It's a furniture depository place really, but they rent me a bit of space. Parking a car is one of the big headaches in London, as you probably know only too well, though I don't suppose you deal with traffic, do you?'

'No, that's not one of my troubles.'

'I should think murder would be infinitely preferable,' said Margot Bence.

She led the way back to the studio, motioned him to a chair, offered him a cigarette and sank down on the large pouffe opposite him. From behind the curtain of dark hair she looked at him in a sombre questioning way.

'Shoot stranger,' she said.

'You were taking photographs on the occasion of this death, I understaid.'

'Yes.'

'You'd been engaged professionally?'

'Yes. They wanted someone to do a few specialized shots. I do quite a lot of that stuff. I do some work for film studios sometimes, but this time I was just taking photographs of the fête, and afterwards a few shots of special people being greeted by Marina Gregg and Jason Rudd. Local notabilities or other personalities. That sort of thing.'

'Yes. I understand that. You had your camera on the stairs, I understand?'

'A part of the time, yes. I got a very good angle from there. You get people coming up the stairs below you and you could swivel round and get Marina shaking hands with them. You could get a lot of different angles without having to move much.'

'I know, of course, that you answered some questions at the time as to whether you'd seen anything unusual, anything that might be helpful. They were general questions.'

'Have you got more specialized ones?'

'A little more specialized, I think. You had a good view of Marina Gregg from where you were standing?'

She nodded. 'Excellent.'

'And of Jason Rudd?'

'Occasionally. But he was moving about more. Drinks and things and introducing people to one another. The locals to the celebrities. That kind of thing, I should imagine. I didn't see this Mrs Baddeley—'

'Badcock.'

'Sorry, Badcock. I didn't see her drink the fatal draught or anything like that. In fact I don't think I really know which she was.'

'Do you remember the arrival of the mayor?'

'Oh yes. I remember the mayor all right. He had on his chain and his robes of office. I got one of him coming up the stairs – a close-up – rather a cruel profile, and then I got him shaking hands with Marina.'

'Then you can fix that time at least in your mind. Mrs Badcock and her husband came up the stairs to Marina Gregg immediately in front of him.'

She shook her head. 'Sorry. I still don't remember her.'

'That doesn't matter so much. I presume that you had a pretty good view of Marina Gregg and that you had your eyes on her and were pointing the camera at her fairly often.'

'Quite right. Most of the time. I'd wait till I got just the right moment.'

'Do you know a man called Ardwyck Fenn by sight?'

'Oh yes. I know him well enough. Television network – films, too.'

'Did you take a photograph of him?'

'Yes, I got him coming up with Lola Brewster.'

'That would be just after the mayor?'

She thought a minute then agreed. 'Yes, about then.'

'Did you notice that about that time Marina Gregg seemed to feel suddenly ill. Did you notice any unusual expression on her face?'

Margot Bence leant forward, opened a cigarette box and took out a cigarette. She lit it. Although she had not answered Dermot did not press her. He waited, wondering what it was she was turning over in her mind. She said at last, abruptly:

'Why do you ask me that?'

'Because it's a question to which I am very anxious to have an answer – a reliable answer.'

'Do you think my answer's likely to be reliable?'

'Yes I do, as a matter of fact. You must have the habit of

674

watching people's faces very closely, waiting for certain expressions, certain propitious moments.'

She nodded her head.

'Did you see anything of that kind?'

'Somebody else saw it too, did they?'

'Yes. More than one person, but it's been described rather differently.'

'How did the other people describe it?'

'One person has told me that she was taken faint.'

Margot Bence shook her head slowly.

'Someone else said that she was startled.' He paused a moment then went on, 'and somebody else describes her as having a frozen look on her face.'

'Frozen,' said Margot Bence thoughtfully.

'Do you agree to that last statement?'

'I don't know. Perhaps.'

'It was put rather more fancifully still,' said Dermot. 'In the words of the late poet, Tennyson. "The mirror crack'd from side to side: The doom has come upon me, cried the Lady of Shalott." '

'There wasn't any mirror,' said Margot Bence, 'but if there had been it might have cracked.' She got up abruptly. 'Wait,' she said. 'I'll do something better than describe it to you. I'll show you.'

She pushed aside the curtain at the far end and disappeared for some moments. He could hear her uttering impatient mutterings under her breath.

'What hell it is,' she said as she emerged again, 'one never can find things when one wants them. I've got it now though.'

She came across to him and put a glossy print into his hand. He looked down at it. It was a very good photograph of Marina Gregg. Her hand was clasped in the hand of a woman standing in front of her, and therefore with her back to the camera. But Marina Gregg was not looking at the woman. Her eyes stared not quite into the camera but slightly obliquely to the left. The interesting thing to Dermot Craddock was that the face expressed nothing whatever. There was no fear on it, no pain. The woman portrayed there was staring at *something*, something she saw, and the emotion it aroused in her was so great that she was physically unable to express it by any kind of facial expression. Dermot Craddock had seen such a look once on a man's face, a man who a second later had been shot dead . . .

'Satisfied?' asked Margot Bence.

Craddock gave a deep sigh. 'Yes, thank you. It's hard, you know, to make up one's mind if witnesses are exaggerating, if they are imagining they see things. But that's not so in this case. There *was* something to see and she saw it.' He asked, 'Can I keep this picture?'

'Oh yes, you can have the print. I've got the negative.'

'You didn't send it to the Press?'

Margot Bence shook her head.

'I rather wonder why you didn't. After all, it's rather a dramatic photograph. Some paper might have paid a good price for it.'

'I wouldn't care to do that,' said Margot Bence. 'If you look into somebody's soul by accident, you feel a bit embarrassed about cashing in.'

'Did you know Marina Gregg at all?'

'No.'

'You come from the States, don't you?'

'I was born in England. I was trained in America though. I came over here, oh, about three years ago.'

Dermot Craddock nodded. He had known the answers to his questions. They had been waiting for him among the other lists of information on his office table. The girl seemed straightforward enough. He asked:

'Where did you train?'

'Reingarden Studios. I was with Andrew Quilp for a time. He taught me a lot.'

'Reingarden Studios and Andrew Quilp.' Dermot Craddock was suddenly alert. The names struck a chord of remembrance.

'You lived in Seven Springs, didn't you?'

She looked amused.

'You seem to know a lot about me. Have you been checking up?'

'You're a very well-known photographer, Miss Bence. There have been articles written about you, you know. Why did you come to England?'

She shrugged her shoulders.

'Oh, I like a change. Besides, as I tell you, I was born in England although I went to the States as a child.'

'Quite a young child, I think.'

'Five years old, if you're interested.'

'I am interested. I think, Miss Bence, you could tell me a little more than you have done.'

Her face hardened. She stared at him.

'What do you mean by that?'

Dermot Craddock looked at her and risked it. It wasn't much to go on. Reingarden Studios and Andrew Quilp and the name of one town. But he felt rather as if old Miss Marple were at his shoulder egging him on.

'I think you knew Marina Gregg better than you say.'

She laughed. 'Prove it. You're imagining things.'

'Am I? I don't think I am. And it *could* be proved, you know, with a little time and care. Come now, Miss Bence, hadn't you better admit the truth? Admit that Marina Gregg adopted you as a child and that you lived with her for four years.'

She drew her breath in sharply with a hiss.

'You nosy bastard!' she said.

It startled him a little, it was such a contrast to her former manner. She got up, shaking her black head of hair.

'All right, all right, it's true enough! Yes. Marina Gregg took me over to America with her. My mother had eight kids. She lived in a slum somewhere. She was one of hundreds of people, I suppose, who write to any film acrtess that they happen to see or hear about, spilling a hard luck story, begging her to adopt the child a mother couldn't give advantages to. Oh, it's such a sickening business, all of it.'

'There were three of you,' said Dermot. 'Three children adopted at different times from different places.'

'That's right. Me and Rod and Angus. Angus was older than I was, Rod was practically a baby. We had a wonderful life. Oh, a wonderful life! All the advantages!' Her voice rose mockingly. 'Clothes and cars and a wonderful house to live in and people to look after us, good schooling and teaching, and delicious food. Everything piled on! And she herself, our "Mom." "Mom" in inverted commas, playing her part, crooning over us, being photographed with us! Ah, such a pretty sentimental picture.'

'But she really wanted children,' said Dermot Craddock. 'That was real enough, wasn't it? It wasn't just a publicity stunt.'

'Oh, perhaps. Yes, I think that was true. She wanted children. But she didn't want *us*! Not really. It was just a glorious bit of play-acting. *"My family." "So lovely to have a family of my own."* And Izzy let her do it. He ought to have known better.'

'Izzy was Isidore Wright?'

'Yes, her third husband or her fourth, I forget which. He was a wonderful man really. He understood her, I think, and he was worried sometimes about us. He was kind to us, but he didn't pretend to be a father. He didn't feel like a father. He only cared about his own writing. I've read some of his things since. They're sordid and rather cruel, but they're powerful. I think people will call him a great writer one day.'

'And this went on until when?'

Margot Bence's smile curved suddenly. 'Until she got sick of that particular bit of play-acting. No, that's not quite true . . . She found she was going to have a child of her own.'

'And then?'

She laughed with sudden bitterness. 'Then we'd had it! We weren't wanted any more. We'd done very well as little stopgaps, but she didn't care a damn about us really, not a damn. Oh, she pensioned us off very prettily. With a home and a foster-mother and money for our education and a nice little sum to start us off in the world. Nobody can say that she didn't behave correctly and handsomely. But she'd never wanted *us* – all she wanted was a child of her own.'

'You can't blame her for that,' said Dermot gently.

'I don't blame her for wanting a child of her own, no! But what about us? She took us away from our own parents, from the places where we belonged. My mother sold me for a mess of pottage, if you like, but she didn't sell me for advantage to herself. She sold me because she was a damn' silly woman who thought I'd get "advantages" and "education" and have a wonderful life. She thought she was doing the best for me. Best for me? If she only knew.'

'You're still very bitter, I see.'

'No, I'm not bitter now. I've got over that. I'm bitter because I'm remembering, because I've gone back to those days. We were all pretty bitter.'

'All of you?'

'Well, not Rod. Rod never cared about anything. Besides, he was rather small. But Angus felt like I did, only I think he was more rerevengeful. He said that when he was grown up he would go and kill that baby she was going to have.'

'You knew about the baby?'

'Oh, of course I knew. And everyone knows what happened. She went crazy with rapture about having it and then when it was born it was an idiot! Serve her right. Idiot or no idiot, she didn't want *us* back again.'

'You hate her very much?'

'Why shouldn't I hate her? She did the worst thing to me that anyone can do to anyone else. Let them believe that they're loved and wanted and then show them that it's all a sham.'

'What happened to your two – I'll call them brothers, for the sake of convenience.'

'Oh, we all drifted apart later. Rod's farming somewhere in the Middle West. He's got a happy nature, and always had. Angus? I don't know. I lost sight of him.'

'Did he continue to feel revengeful?'

'I shouldn't think so,' said Margot. 'It's not the sort of thing you can go on feeling. The last time I saw him, he said he was going on the stage. I don't know whether he did.'

'*You*'ve remembered, though,' said Dermot.

'Yes. I've remembered,' said Margot Bence.

'Was Marina Gregg surprised to see you on that day or did she make the arrangements for your photography on purpose to please you?'

'She?' The girl smiled scornfully. 'She knew nothing about the arrangements. I was curious to see her, so I did a bit of lobbying to get the job. As I say I've got some influence with studio people. I wanted to see what she looked like nowadays.' She stroked the surface of the table. 'She didn't even recognise me. What do you think of that? I was with her for four years. From five years old to nine, and she didn't recognise me.'

'Children change,' said Dermot Craddock, 'they change so much that you'd hardly know them. I have a niece I met the other day and I assure you I'd have passed her in the street.'

'Are you saying that to make me feel better? I don't care really. Oh, what the hell, let's be honest. I do care. I did. She had a magic, you know. Marina! A wonderful calamitous magic that took hold of you. You can hate a person and still mind.'

'You didn't tell her who you were?'

She shook her head. 'No, I didn't tell her. That's the last thing I'd do.'

'Did you try and poison her, Miss Bence?'

Her mood changed. She got up and laughed.

'What ridiculous questions you do ask! But I suppose you have to. It's part of your job. No. I can assure you I didn't kill her.'

'That isn't what I asked you, Miss Bence.'

She looked at him, frowning, puzzled.

'Marina Gregg,' he said, 'is still alive.'

'For how long?'

'What do you mean by that?'

'Don't you think it's likely, Inspector, that someone will try again, and this time – this time, perhaps – they'll succeed?'

'Precautions will be taken.'

'Oh, I'm sure they will. The adoring husband will look after her, won't he, and make sure that no harm comes to her?'

He was listening carefully to the mockery in her voice.

'What did you mean when you said you didn't ask me that?' she said, harking back suddenly.

'I asked you if you tried to kill her. You replied that you didn't kill her. That's true enough, but *someone* died, *someone* was killed.'

'You mean I tried to kill Marina and instead I killed Mrs What's-her-name. If you'd like me to make it quite clear, I *didn't* try to poison Marina and I *didn't* poison Mrs Badcock.'

'But you know perhaps who did?'

'I don't know anything, Inspector, I assure you.'

'But you have some idea?'

'Oh, one always has ideas.' She smiled at him, a mocking smile. 'Among so many people it might be, mightn't it, the black-haired robot of a secretary, the elegant Hailey Preston, servants, maids, a masseur, the hairdresser, someone at the studios, so many people – *and one of them mightn't be what he or she pretended to be.*'

Then as he took an unconscious step towards her she shook her head vehemently.

'Relax, Inspector,' she said. 'I'm only teasing you. *Somebody's* out for Marina's blood, but who it is I've no idea. Really. I've no idea at all.'

—— 16 ——

At No. 16 Aubrey Close, young Mrs Baker was talking to her husband. Jim Baker, a big good-looking blond giant of a man, was intent on assembling a model construction unit.

'Neighbours!' said Cherry. She gave a toss of her black curly head. 'Neighbours!' she said again with venom.

She carefully lifted the frying pan from the stove, then neatly shot its contents on to two plates, one rather fuller than the other. She placed the fuller one before her husband.

'Mixed grill,' she announced.

Jim looked up and sniffed appreciatively.

'That's something like,' he said. 'What is today? My birthday?'

'You have to be well nourished,' said Cherry.

She was looking very pretty in a cerise and white striped apron with little frills on it. Jim Baker shifted the component parts of a strato-cruiser to make room for his meal. He grinned at his wife and asked:

'Who says so?'

'My Miss Marple for one!' said Cherry. 'And if it comes to that,' she added, sitting down opposite Jim and pulling her plate towards her, 'I should say *she* could do with a bit more solid nourishment herself. That old cat of a White Knight of hers, gives her nothing but carbohydrates. It's all she can think of! A "nice custard," a "nice bread and butter pudding," a "nice macaroni cheese." Squashy puddings with pink sauce. And gas, gas, gas, all day. Talks her head off, she does.'

'Oh well,' said Jim vaguely, 'it's invalid diet, I suppose.'

'Invalid diet!' said Cherry and snorted. 'Miss Marple isn't an invalid – she's just *old*. Always interfering, too.'

'Who, Miss Marple?'

'No. That Miss Knight. Telling me how to do things! She even tries to tell me how to cook! I know a lot more about cooking than she does.'

'You're tops for cooking, Cherry,' said Jim appreciatively.

'There's something *to* cooking,' said Cherry, 'something you can get your teeth into.'

Jim laughed. 'I'm getting my teeth into this all right. Why did your Miss Marple say that I needed nourishing? Did she think I looked run-down, the other day when I came in to fix that bathroom shelf?'

Cherry laughed. 'I'll tell you what she said to me. She said, "You've got a handsome husband, my dear. A *very* handsome husband." Sounds like one of those period books they read aloud on the telly.'

'I hope you agreed with her?' said Jim with a grin.

'I said you were all right.'

'All right indeed! That's a nice lukewarm way of talking.'

And then she said "You must take care of your husband, my dear. Be sure you *feed* him properly. Men need plently of good meat meals, well cooked." '

'Hear, hear!'

'And she told me to be sure and prepare fresh food for you and not buy ready-made pies and things and slip them in the oven to warm up. Not that I do that often,' added Cherry virtuously.

'You can't do it too seldom for me,' said Jim. 'They don't taste a bit the same.'

'So long as you notice what you eat,' said Cherry, 'and aren't so taken up with those strato-cruisers and things you're always building. And don't tell me you bought that set as a Christmas present for your nephew Michael. You bought it so that you could play with it yourself.'

'He's not quite old enough for it yet,' said Jim apologetically.

'And I suppose you're going on dithering about with it all the evening. What about some music? Did you get that new record you were talking about?'

'Yes, I did. Tchaikovski 1812.'

'That's the loud one with the battle, isn't it?' said Cherry. She made a face. 'Our Mrs Hartwell won't half like that! Neighbours! I'm fed up with neighbours. Always grousing and complaining. I don't know which is the worst. The Hartwells or the Barnabys. The Hartwells start rapping on the wall as early as twenty to eleven sometimes. It's a bit thick! After all even the telly and the BBC go on later than that. Why *shouldn't* we have a bit of music if we like? And always asking us to turn it down low.'

'You can't turn these things down low,' said Jim with authority. 'You don't get the *tone* unless you've got the volume. Everyone knows that. It's absolutely recognised in musical circles. And what about their cat – always coming over into our garden, digging up the beds, just when I've got it nice.'

'I tell you what, Jim. I'm fed up with this place.'

'You didn't mind your neighbours up in Huddersfield,' remarked Jim.

'It wasn't the same there,' said Cherry. 'I mean, you're all independent there. If you're in trouble, somebody'd give you a hand and you'd give a hand to them. But you don't interfere. There's something about a new estate like this that makes people look sideways at their neighbours. Because we're all new I suppose. The amount of back-biting and tale-telling and writing to the council and one thing and another round here beats me! People in real towns are too busy for it.'

'You may have something there, my girl.'

'D'you like it here, Jim?'

'The job's all right. And after all, this is a brand new house. I

wish there was a bit more room in it so that I could spread myself a bit more. It would be fine if I could have a workshop.'

'I thought it was lovely at first,' said Cherry, 'but now I'm not
so sure. The house is all right and I love the blue paint and the
bathroom's nice, but I don't like the people and the *feeling*
round here. Some of the people are nice enough. Did I tell you
that Lily Price and that Harry of hers have broken off? It was a
funny business that day in that house they went to look over.
You know when she more or less fell out of the window. She
said Harry just stood there like a stuck pig.'

'I'm glad she's broken off with him. He's a no-good if I ever
saw one,' said Jim.

'No good marrying a chap just because a baby's on the way,'
said Cherry. 'He didn't want to marry her, you know. He's not
a very nice fellow. Miss Marple said he wasn't,' she added
thoughtfully. 'She spoke to Lily about him. Lily thought she was
crackers.'

'Miss Marple? I didn't know she'd ever seen him?'

'Oh yes, she was round here walking the day she fell down
and Mrs Babcock picked her up and took her into her house.
Do you think Arthur and Mrs Bain will make a match of it?'

Jim frowned as he picked up a bit of strato-cruiser and consulted the instructional diagram.

'I do wish you'd listen when I'm talking,' said Cherry.

'What did you say?'

'Arthur Badcock and Mary Bain.'

For the Lord's sake, Cherry, his wife's only just dead! You
women! I've heard he's in a terrible state of nerves still – jumps
if you speak to him.'

'I wonder why . . . I shouldn't have thought he'd take it that
way, would you?'

'Can you clear off this end of the table a bit?' said Jim, relin-
quishing even a passing interest in the affairs of his neighbours.
'Just so that I can spread some of these pieces out a bit.'

Cherry heaved an exasperated sigh.

'To get any attention round here, you have to be a super jet,
or a turbo prop,' she said bitterly. 'You and your constructional
models!'

She piled the tray with the remains of supper and carried it
over to the sink. She decided not to wash up, a necessity of daily
life she always put off as long as possible. Instead, she piled
everything into the sink haphazard, slipped on a corduroy jacket
and went out of the house, pausing to call over her shoulder:

'I'm just going to slip along to see Gladys Dixon. I want to borrow one of her *Vogue* patterns.'

'All right, old girl.' Jim bent over his model.

Casting a venomous look at her next-door neighbour's front door as she passed, Cherry went round the corner into Blenheim Close and stopped at No. 16. The door was open and Cherry tapped on it and went into the hall calling out:

'Is Gladdy about?'

'Is that you, Cherry?' Mrs Dixon looked out of the kitchen. 'She's upstairs in her room, dressmaking.'

'Right. I'll go up.'

Cherry went upstairs to a small bedroom in which Gladys, a plump girl with a plain face, was kneeling on the floor, her cheeks flushed, and several pins in her mouth, tacking up a paper pattern.'

'Hallo, Cherry. Look, I got a lovely bit of stuff at Harper's sale in Much Benham. I'm going to do that cross-over pattern with frills again, the one I did in Terylene before.'

'That'll be nice,' said Cherry.

Gladys rose to her feet, panting a little.

'Got indigestion now,' she said.

'You oughtn't to do dressmaking right after supper,' said Cherry, 'bending over like that.'

'I suppose I ought to slim a bit,' said Gladys. She sat down on the bed.

'Any news from the studios?' asked Cherry, always avid for film news.

'Nothing much. There's a lot of talk still. Marina Gregg came back on the set yesterday – and she created something frightful.'

'What about?'

'She didn't like the taste of her coffee. You know, they have coffee in the middle of the morning. She took one sip and said there was something wrong with it. Which was nonsense, of course. There couldn't have been. It comes in a jug straight from the canteen. Of course I always put hers in a special china cup, rather posh – different from the others – but it's the same coffee. So there couldn't have been anything wrong with it, could there?'

'Nerves, I suppose,' said Cherry. 'What happened?'

'Oh, nothing. Mr Rudd just calmed everyone down. He's wonderful that way. He took the coffee from her and poured it down the sink.'

'That seems to be rather stupid,' said Cherry slowly.

'Why – what do you mean?'

'Well, if there *was* anything wrong with it – now nobody will ever know.'

'Do you think there really might have been?' asked Gladys looking alarmed.

'Well—' Cherry shrugged her shoulders, '—there was something wrong with her cocktail the day of the fête, wasn't there, so why not the coffee? If at first you don't succeed, try, try, try again.'

Gladys shivered.

'I don't half like it, Cherry,' she said. 'Somebody's got it in for her all right. She's had more letters, you know, threatening her – and there was that bust business the other day.'

'What bust business?'

'A marble bust. On the set. It's a corner of a room in some Austrian palace or other. Funny name like Shotbrown. Pictures and china and marble busts. This one was up on a bracket – suppose it hadn't been pushed back enough. Anyway, a heavy lorry went past out in the road and jarred it off – right on to the chair where Marina sits for her big scene with Count Somebody-or-other. Smashed it to smithereens! Lucky they weren't shooting at the time. Mr Rudd, he said not to say a word about it to her, and he put another chair there, and when she came yesterday and asked why the chair had been changed, he said the other chair was the wrong period, and this gave a better angle for the camera. Bue he didn't half like it – I can tell you that.'

The two girls looked at each other.

'It's exciting in a way,' said Cherry slowly. 'And yet – it isn't . . .'

'I think I'm going to give up working in the canteen at the studios,' said Gladys.

'Why? Nobody wants to poison you or drop marble busts on your head!'

'No. But it's not always the person who's meant to get done in who gets done in. It may be someone else. Like Heather Badcock that day.'

'True enough,' said Cherry.

'You know,' said Gladys, 'I've been thinking. I was up at the Hall that day, helping. I was quite close to them at the time.'

'When Heather died?'

'No, when she spilt the cocktail. All down her dress. A lovely dress it was, too, royal blue nylon taffeta. She'd got it quite new for the occasion. And it was funny.'

'What was funny?'

'I didn't think anything of it at the time. But it does seem funny when I think it over.'

Cherry looked at her expectantly. She accepted the adjective 'funny' in the sense that it was meant. It was not intended humorously.

'For goodness' sake, what was funny?' she demanded.

'I'm almost sure she did it on purpose.'

'Spilt the cocktail on purpose?'

'Yes. And I do think that was funny, don't you?'

'On a brand new dress? I don't believe it.'

'I wonder now,' said Gladys, 'what Arthur Badcock will do with all Heather's clothes. That dress would clean all right. Or I could take out half a breadth, it's a lovely full skirt. Do you think Arthur Badcock would think it very awful of me if I wanted to buy it off him? It would need hardly any attention – and it's lovely stuff.'

'You wouldn't—' Cherry hesitated – 'mind?'

'Mind what?'

'Well – having a dress that a woman had died in – I mean died that way . . .'

Gladys stared at her.

'I hadn't thought of that,' she admitted. She considered for a moment or two. Then she cheered up.

'I can't see that it really matters,' she said. 'After all, every time you buy something second-hand, somebody's usually worn it who has died, haven't they?'

'Yes. But it's not quite the same.'

'I think you're being fanciful,' said Gladys. 'It's a lovely bright shade of blue, and really expensive stuff. About that funny business,' she continued thoughtfully, 'I'll think I'll go up to the hall tomorrow on my way to work and have a word with Mr Giuseppe about it.'

'Is he the Italian butler?'

'Yes. He's awfully handsome. Flashing eyes. He's got a terrible temper. When we go and help there, he chivvies us girls something terrible.' She giggled. 'But none of us really mind. He can be awfully nice sometimes . . . Anyway, I might just tell him about it, and ask him what I ought to do.'

'I don't see that you've got anything to tell,' said Cherry.

'Well – it was funny,' said Gladys, defiantly clinging to her favourite adjective.

'*I* think,' said Cherry, 'that you just want an excuse to go and

686

talk to Mr Giuseppe – and you'd better be careful, my girl.
You know what these wops are like! Affiliation orders all over
the place. Hot-blooded and passionate, that's what these Italians
are.'

Gladys sighed ecstatically.

Cherry looked at her friend's fat slightly spotty face and decided that her warnings were unnecessary. Mr Giuseppe, she
thought, would have better fish to fry elsewhere.

II

'Aha!' said Dr Haydock, 'unravelling, I see.'

He looked from Miss Marple to a pile of fluffy white fleecy
wool.

'You advised me to try unravelling if I couldn't knit,' said
Miss Marple.

'You seem to have been very thorough about it.'

'I made a mistake in the pattern right at the beginning. That
made the whole thing go out of proportion, so I've had to un-
ravel it all. It's a very elaborate pattern, you see.'

'What are elaborate patterns to you? Nothing at all.'

'I ought really, I suppose, with my bad eyesight, to stick to
plain knitting.'

'You'd find that very boring. Well, I'm flattered that you took
my advice.'

'Don't I always take your advice, Doctor Haydock?'

'You do when it suits you,' said Dr Haydock.

'Tell me, Doctor, was it really knitting you had in mind
when you gave me that advice?'

He met the twinkle in her eyes and twinkled back at her.

'How are you getting on with unravelling the murder?' he
asked.

'I'm afraid my faculties aren't quite what they were,' said Miss
Marple shaking her head with a sigh.

'Nonsense,' said Dr Haydock. 'Don't tell me you haven't
formed *some* conclusions.'

'Of course I have formed conclusions. Very definite ones.'

'Such as?' asked Haydock inquiringly.

'If the cocktail glass was tampered with that day – and I don't
see quite how that could have been done—'

'Might have had the stuff ready in an eye-dropper,' suggested
Haydock.

'You are so professional,' said Miss Marple admiringly. 'But even then it seems to me so very peculiar that nobody saw it happen.'

'Murder should not only be done, but be *seen* to be done! Is that it?'

'You know exactly what I mean,' said Miss Marple.

'That was a chance the murderer had to take,' said Haydock.

'Oh quite so. I'm not disputing *that* for a moment. But there were, I have found by inquiry and adding up the persons, at least eighteen to twenty people on the spot. It seems to me that amongst twenty people *somebody* must have seen that action occur.'

Haydock nodded. 'One would think so, certainly. But obviously no one did.'

'I wonder,' said Miss Marple thoughtfully.

'What have you got in mind exactly?'

'Well, there are three possibilities. I'm assuming that at least one person *would* have seen something. One out of twenty. I think it's only reasonable to assume that.'

'I think you're begging the question,' said Haydock, 'and I can see looming ahead one of those terrible exercises in probability where six men have white hats and six have black hats and you have to work it out by mathematics how likely it is that the hats will get mixed up and in what proportion. If you start thinking about things like that you would go round the bend. Let me assure you of that!'

'I wasn't thinking of anything like that,' said Miss Marple. 'I was just thinking of what is likely—'

'Yes,' said Haydock thoughtfully, 'you're very good at that. You always have been.'

'It *is* likely, you know,' said Miss Marple, 'that out of twenty people one at least should be an observant one.'

'I give in,' said Haydock. 'Let's have the three possibilities.'

'I'm afraid I'll have to put them rather sketchily,' said Miss Marple. 'I haven't quite thought it out. Inspector Craddock, and probably Frank Cornish before him, will have questioned everybody who was there so the natural thing would be that whoever saw anything of the kind would have said so at once.'

'Is that one of the possibilities?'

'No, of course it isn't,' said Miss Marple, 'because it hasn't happened. What you have to account for is if one person *did* see something why didn't that person say so?'

'I'm listening.'

688

'Possibility One,' said Miss Marple, her cheeks going pink with animation. 'The person who saw it didn't realize what they had seen. That would mean, of course, that it would have to be a rather stupid person. Someone, let us say, who can use their eyes but not their brain. The sort of person who, if you asked them "Did you see anyone put anything in Marina Gregg's glass?" would answer, "Oh no," but if you said "Did you see anyone put their hand over the top of Marina Gregg's glass" would say "Oh yes, of course I did!"'

Haydock laughed. 'I admit,' he said, 'that one never quite allows for the moron in our midst. All right, I grant you Possibility One. The moron saw it, the moron didn't grasp what the action meant. And the second possibility?'

'This one's very far-fetched, but I do think it *is* just a possibility. It might have been a person whose action in putting something in a glass was natural.'

'Wait, wait, explain that a little more clearly.'

'It seems to me nowadays,' said Miss Marple, 'that people are always adding things to what they eat and drink. In my young days it was considered to be very bad manners to take medicines with one's meals. It was on a par with blowing your nose at the dinner table. It just wasn't *done*. If you *had* to take pills or capsules, or a spoonful of something, you went out of the room to do so. That's not the case now. When staying with my nephew, Raymond, I observed some of his guests seemed to arrive with quite a quantity of little bottles of pills and tablets. They take then with food, or before food, or after food. They keep aspirins and such things in their handbags and take them the whole time – with cups of tea or with their after-dinner coffee. You understand what I mean?'

'Oh yes,' said Dr Haydock, 'I've got your meaning now and it's interesting. You mean that someone—' he stopped. 'Let me have it in your own words.'

'I meant,' said Miss Marple, 'that it would be quite possible, audacious but possible, for someone to pick up that glass which as soon as it was in his hand or her hand, of course, would be assumed to be his or her own drink and to add whatever was added quite *openly*. In that case, you see, people wouldn't think twice of it.'

'He – or she – couldn't be sure of that, though,' Haydock pointed out.

'No,' agreed Miss Marple, 'it would be a gamble, a risk – but it *could* happen. And then,' she went on, 'there's the third possibility.'

'Possibility One, a moron,' said the doctor. 'Possibility Two, a gambler – what's Possibility Three.'

'Somebody saw what happened, and has held their tongue deliberately.'

Haydock frowned. 'For what reason?' he asked. 'Are you suggesting blackmail? If so—'

'If so,' said Miss Marple, 'it's a very dangerous thing to do.'

'Yes, indeed.' He looked sharply at the placid old lady with the white fleecy garment on her lap. 'Is the third possibility the one you consider the most probable one?'

'No,' said Miss Marple, 'I wouldn't go as far as that. I have, at the moment, insufficient grounds. Unless,' she added carefully, 'someone else gets killed.'

'Do you think someone else is going to get killed?'

'I hope not,' said Miss Marple, 'I trust and pray not. But it so often happens, Doctor Haydock. That's the sad and frightening thing. It so often happens.'

—— 17 ——

Ella put down the telephone receiver, smiled to herself and came out of the public telephone box. She was pleased with herself.

'Chief-Inspector God Almighty Craddock!' she said to herself. 'I'm twice as good as he is at the job. Variations on the theme of: "Fly, all is discovered!"'

She pictured to herself with a good deal of pleasure the reactions recently suffered by the person at the other end of the line. That faint menacing whisper coming through the receiver. '*I saw you ...*'

She laughed silently, the corners of her mouth curving up in a feline cruel line. A student of psychology might have watched her with some interest. Never until the last few days had she had this feeling of power. She was hardly aware herself of how much the heady intoxication of it affected her ...

She passed the East Lodge and Mrs Bantry, busy as usual in the garden, waved a hand to her.

'Damn that old woman,' thought Ella. She could feel Mrs Bantry's eyes following her as she walked up the drive.

A phrase came into her head for no particular reason.

The pitcher goes to the well once too often . . .

Nonsense. Nobody could suspect that it was she who had whispered those menacing words . . .

She sneezed.

'Damn this hay-fever,' said Ella Zielinsky.

When she came into her office, Jason Rudd was standing by the window.

He wheeled round.

'I couldn't think where you were.'

'I had to go and speak to the gardener. There were—' she broke off as she caught sight of his face.

She asked sharply: 'What is it?'

His eyes seemed set deeper in his face than ever. All the gaiety of the clown was gone. This was a man under strain. She had seen him under strain before but never looking like this.

She said again, 'What is it?'

He held a sheet of paper out to her. 'It's the analysis of that coffee. The coffee that Marina complained about and wouldn't drink.'

'You sent it to be analysed?' She was startled. 'But you poured it away down the sink. I saw you.'

His wide mouth curled up in a smile. 'I'm pretty good at sleight of hand, Ella,' he said. 'You didn't know that, did you? Yes, I poured most of it away but I kept a little and I took it along to be analysed.'

She looked down at the paper in her hand.

'*Arsenic.*' She sounded incredulous.

'Yes, arsenic.'

'So Marina was right about it tasting bitter?'

'She wasn't right about that. Arsenic has no taste. But her instinct was quite right.'

'And we thought she was just being hysterical!'

'She is hysterical! Who wouldn't be? She has a woman drop dead at her feet practically. She gets threatening notes – one after another – there's not been anything today, has there?'

Ella shook her head.

'Who plants the damned things? Oh well, I suppose it's easy enough – all these open windows. Anyone could slip in.'

'You mean we ought to keep the house barred and locked?

But it's such hot weather. There's a man posted in the grounds, after all.'

'Yes, and I don't want to frighten her more than she's frightened already. Threatening notes don't matter two hoots. But arsenic, Ella, arsenic's different . . .'

'Nobody could tamper with food here in the house.'

'Couldn't they, Ella? Couldn't they?'

'Not without being seen. No unauthorised person—'

He interrupted.

'People will do things for money, Ella.'

'Hardly murder!'

'Even that. And they mightn't realize it *was* murder . . . The servants . . .'

'I'm sure the servants are all right.'

'Giuseppe now. I doubt if I'd trust Giuseppe very far if it came to the question of money . . . He's been with us some time, of course, but—'

'Must you torture yourself like this, Jason?'

He flung himself down in the chair. He leaned forward, his long arms hanging down between his knees.

'What to do?' he said slowly and softly. 'My God, what to do?'

Ella did not speak. She sat there watching him.

'She was happy here,' said Jason. He was speaking more to himself than to Ella. He stared down between his knees at the carpet. If he had looked up, the expression on her face might perhaps have surprised him.

'She was happy,' he said again. 'She hoped to be happy and she *was* happy. She was saying so that day, the day Mrs What's-her-name—'

'Bantry?'

'Yes. The day Mrs Bantry came to tea. She said it was "so peaceful." She said that at last she'd found a place where she could settle down and be happy and feel secure. My goodness, secure!'

'Happy ever after?' Ella's voice held a slight tone of irony. 'Yes, put like that, it sounds just like a fairy story.'

'At any rate she believed it.'

'But you didn't,' said Ella. 'You never thought it *would* be like that?'

Jason Rudd smiled. 'No. I didn't go the whole hog. But I did think that for a while, a year – two years – there might be a period of calm and content. It might have made a new woman of her. It might have given her confidence in herself. She can be happy, you know. When she is happy she's like a child. Just like a child. And now – *this* had to happen to her.'

Ella moved restlessly. 'Things have to happen to all of us,' she said brusquely. 'That's the way life is. You just have to take it. Some of us can, some of us can't. She's the kind that can't.'

She sneezed.

'Your hay-fever bad again?'

'Yes. By the way, Giuseppe's gone to London.'

Jason looked faintly surprised.

'To London? Why?'

'Some kind of family trouble. He's got relations in Soho, and one of them's desperately ill. He went to Marina about it and she said it was all right, so I gave him the day off. He'll be back sometime tonight. You don't mind, do you?'

'No,' said Jason, 'I don't mind . . .'

He got up and walked up and down.

'If I could take her away . . . now . . . at once.'

'Scrap the picture? But just think—'

His voice rose.

'I can't think of anything but Marina. Don't you understand? She's in danger. That's all I can think about.'

She opened her mouth impulsively, then closed it.

She gave another muffled sneeze and rose.

'I'd better get my atomizer.'

She left the room and went to her bedroom, a word echoing in her mind.

Marina . . . Marina . . . Marina . . . Always Marina . . .

Fury rose up in her. She stilled it. She went into the bathroom and picked up the spray she used.

She inserted the nozzle into one nostril and squeezed.

The warning came a second too late . . . Her brain recognised the unfamiliar odour of bitter almonds . . . but not in time to paralyse the squeezing fingers. . . .

18

Frank Cornish replaced the receiver.

'Miss Brewster is out of London for the day,' he announced.

'Is she now?' said Craddock.

'Do you think she—'

'I don't know. I shouldn't think so, but I don't know. Ard-wyck Fenn?'

'Out. I left word for him to ring you. And Margot Bence, Personality Photographer, has got an assignment somewhere in the country. Her pansy partner didn't know where – or said he didn't. And the butler's hooked it to London.'

'I wonder,' said Craddock thoughtfully, 'if the butler has hooked it for good. I always suspect dying relatives. Why was he suddenly anxious to go to London today?'

'He could have put the cyanide in the atomizer easily enough before he left.'

'Anybody could.'

'But I think he's indicated. It could hardly be someone from outside.'

'Oh yes, it could. You'd have to judge your moment. You could leave a car in one of the side drives, wait until everyone is in the dining-room, say, and slip in through a window and up-stairs. The shrubberies come close up to the house.'

'Damn' risky.'

'This murderer doesn't mind taking risks, you know. That's been apparent all along.'

'We've had a man on duty in the grounds.'

'I know. One man wasn't enough. So long as it was a question of these anonymous letters I didn't feel so much urgency. Marina Gregg herself is being well guarded. It never occurred to me that anyone else was in danger. I—'

The telephone rang. Cornish took the call.

'It's the Dorchester. Mr Ardwyck Fenn is on the line.'

He profered the receiver to Craddock who took it.

'Mr Fenn? This is Craddock here.'

'Ah yes. I heard you had rung me. I have been out all day.'

'I am sorry to tell you, Mr Fenn, that Miss Zielinsky died this morning – of cyanide poisoning.'

'Indeed? I am shocked to hear it. An accident? Or not an accident?'

'Not an accident. Prussic acid had been put in an atomizer she was in the habit of using.'

'I see. Yes, I see . . .' There was a short pause. 'And why, may I ask, should you ring me about this distressing occurrence?'

'You knew Miss Zielinsky, Mr Fenn.'

'Certainly I knew her. I have known her for some years. But she was not an intimate friend.'

'We hoped that you could, perhaps, assist us?'

694

'In what way?'

'We wondered if you could suggest any motive for her death. She is a stranger in this country. We know very little about her friends and associates and the circumstances of her life.'

'I would suggest that Jason Rudd is the person to question about that.'

'Naturally. We have done so. But there might be an off-chance that you might know something about her that he does not.'

'I'm afraid that is not so. I know next to nothing about Ella Zielinsky except that she was a most capable young woman, and first-class at her job. About her private life I know nothing at all.'

'So you have no suggestions to make?'

Craddock was ready for the decisive negative, but to his surprise it did not come. Instead there was a pause. He could hear Ardwyck Fenn breathing rather heavily at the other end.

'Are you still there, Chief-Inspector?'

'Yes, Mr Fenn. I'm here.'

'I have decided to tell you something that may be of assistance to you. When you hear what it is, you will realize that I have every reason to keep it to myself. But I judge that in the end that might be unwise. The facts are these. A couple of days ago I received a telephone call. A voice spoke to me in a whisper. It said – I am quoting now – *I saw you . . . I saw you put the tablets in the glass . . . You didn't know there had been an eye-witness, did you? That's all for now – very soon you will be told what you have to do.*'

Craddock uttered an ejaculation of astonishment.

'Surprising, was it not, Mr Craddock? I will assure you categorically that the accusation was entirely unfounded. I did *not* put tablets in anybody's glass. I defy anyone to prove that I did. The suggestion is utterly absurd. But it would seem, would it not, that Miss Zielinsky was embarking on blackmail.'

'You recognised her voice?'

'You cannot recognise a whisper. But it was Ella Zielinsky all right.'

'How do you know?'

'The whisperer sneezed heavily before ringing off. I knew that Miss Zielinsky suffered from hay-fever.'

'And you think – what?'

'I think that Miss Zielinsky got hold of the wrong person at her first attempt. It seems to me possible that she was more successful later. Blackmail can be a dangerous game.'

Craddock pulled himself together.

'I must thank you very much for your statement, Mr Fenn. As a matter of form, I shall have to check upon your movements today.'

'Naturally. My chauffeur will be able to give you precise information.'

Craddock rang off and repeated what Fenn had said. Cornish whistled.

'Either that lets him out completely. Or else—'

'Or else it's a magnificent piece of bluff. It could be. He's the kind of man who has the nerve for it. If there's the least chance that Ella Zielinsky left a record of her suspicions, then this taking of the bull by the horns is a magnificent bluff.'

'And his alibi?'

'We've come across some very good faked alibis in our time,' said Craddock. 'He could afford to pay a good sum for one.'

II

It was past midnight when Giuseppe returned to Gossington. He took a taxi from Much Benham, as the last train on the branch line to St Mary Mead had gone.

He was in very good spirits. He paid off the taxi at the gate, and took a short cut through the shrubbery. He opened the back door with his key. The house was dark and silent. Giuseppe shut and bolted the door. As he turned to the stair which led up to his own comfortable suite of bed and bath, he noticed that there was a draught. A window open somewhere, perhaps. He decided not to bother. He went upstairs smiling and fitted a key into his door. He always kept his suite locked. As he turned the key and pushed the door open, he felt the pressure of a hard round ring in his back. A voice said, 'Put your hands up and don't scream.'

Giuseppe threw his hands up quickly. He was taking no chances. Actually there was no chance to take.

The trigger was pressed – once – twice.

Giuseppe fell forward. . . .

Bianca lifted her head from her pillow.

Was that a shot . . . She was almost sure she had heard a shot . . . She waited some minutes. Then she decided she had been mistaken and lay down again.

19

'It's too dreadful,' said Miss Knight. She put down her parcels and gasped for breath.

'Something has happened?' asked Miss Marple.

'I really don't like to tell you about it, dear. I really don't. It might be a shock to you.'

'If you don't tell me,' said Miss Marple, 'somebody else will.'

'Dear, dear, that's true enough,' said Miss Knight. 'Yes, that's terribly true. Everybody talks too much, they say. And I'm sure there's a lot in that. I never repeat anything myself. Very careful I am.'

'You were saying,' said Miss Marple, 'that something rather terrible had happened?'

'It really quite bowled me over,' said Miss Knight. 'Are you sure you don't feel the draught from that window, dear?'

'I like a little fresh air,' said Miss Marple.

'Ah, but we mustn't catch cold, must we?' said Miss Knight archly. 'I'll tell you what. I'll just pop out and make you a nice egg-nog. We'd like that, wouldn't we?'

'I don't know whether *you* would like it,' said Miss Marple. '*I* should be delighted for you to have it if you would like it.'

'Now, now,' said Miss Knight, shaking her finger, 'so fond of our joke, aren't we?'

'But you were going to tell me something,' said Miss Marple.

'Well, you mustn't worry about it,' said Miss Knight, 'and you mustn't let it make you nervous in any way, because I'm sure it's nothing to do with *us*. But with all these American gangsters and things like that, well I suppose it's nothing to be surprised about.'

'Somebody else has been killed,' said Miss Marple, 'is that it?'

'Oh, that's very sharp of you, dear. I don't know what should put such a thing into your head.'

'As a matter of fact,' said Miss Marple thoughtfully, 'I've been expecting it.'

'Oh really!' exclaimed Miss Knight.

'Somebody always sees something,' said Miss Marple, 'only sometimes it takes a little while for them to realize what it is they have seen. Who is it who's dead?'

'The Italian butler. He was shot last night.'

'I see,' said Miss Marple thoughtfully. 'Yes, very likely, of course, but I should have thought that he'd have realized before now the importance of what he saw—'

'Really!' exclaimed Miss Knight, 'you talk as thought you knew all about it. Why should he have been killed?'

'I expect,' said Miss Marple, thoughtfully, 'that he tried to blackmail somebody.'

'He went to London yesterday, they say.'

'Did he now,' said Miss Marple, 'that's very interesting, and suggestive too, I think.'

Miss Knight departed to the kitchen intent on the concoction of nourishing beverages. Miss Marple remained sitting thoughtfully till disturbed by the loud aggressive humming of the vacuum cleaner, assisted by Cherry's voice singing the latest favourite ditty of the moment, 'I Said to You and You Said to Me.'

Miss Knight popped her head round the kitchen door.

'Not quite so much noise, please, Cherry,' she said. 'You don't want to disturb dear Miss Marple, do you? You mustn't be thoughtless, you know.'

She shut the kitchen door again as Cherry remarked, either to herself or the world at large, 'And who said you could call me Cherry, you old jelly-bag?' The vacuum continued to whine while Cherry sang in a more subdued voice. Miss Marple called in a high clear voice:

'Cherry, come here a minute.'

Cherry switched off the vacuum and opened the drawing-room door.

'I didn't mean to disturb you by singing, Miss Marple.'

'Your singing is much pleasanter than the horrid noise that vacuum makes,' said Miss Marple, 'but I know one has to go with the times. It would be no use on earth asking any of you young people to use the dustpan and brush in the old-fashioned way'.

'What, get down on my knees with a dustpan and brush?' Cherry registered alarm and surprise.

'Quite unheard of, I know,' said Miss Marple. 'Come in and shut the door. I called you because I wanted to talk to you.'

Cherry obeyed and came towards Miss Marple looking inquiringly at her.

'We've not much time,' said Miss Marple. 'That old – Miss Knight I mean – will come in any moment with an egg drink of some kind.'

'Good for you, I expect. It'll pep you up,' said Cherry encouragingly.

'Had you heard,' asked Miss Marple, 'that the butler at Gossington Hall was shot last night?'

'What, the wop?' demanded Cherry.

'Yes. His name is Giuseppe, I understand.'

'No,' said Cherry, 'I hadn't heard *that*. I heard that Mr Rudd's secretary had a heart attack yesterday, and somebody said she was actually dead – but I suspect that was just a rumour. Who told you about the butler?'

'Miss Knight came back and told me.'

'Of course I haven't seen anyone to speak to this morning,' said Cherry, 'not before coming along here. I expect the news has only just got round. Was he bumped off?' she demanded.

'That seems to be assumed,' said Miss Marple, 'whether rightly or wrongly I don't quite know.'

'This is a wonderful place for talk,' said Cherry. 'I wonder if Gladys got to see him or not,' she added thoughtfully.

'Gladys?'

'Oh, a sort of friend of mine. She lives a few doors away. Works in the canteen at the studios.'

'And she talked to you about Giuseppe?'

'Well, there was something that struck her as a bit funny and she was going to ask him what he thought about it. But if you ask me it was just an excuse – she's a bit sweet on him. Of course he's quite handsome and Italians do have a way with them – I told her to be careful about him though. You know what Italians are.'

'He went to London yesterday,' said Miss Marple, 'and only returned in the evening I understand.'

'I wonder if she managed to get to see him before he went?'

'Why did she want to see him, Cherry?'

'It was just something which she felt was a bit funny,' said Cherry.

Miss Marple looked at her inquiringly. She was able to take the word 'funny' at the valuation it usually had for the Gladyses of the neighbourhood.

'She was one of the girls who helped at the party there,' explained Cherry. 'The day of the fête. You know, when Mrs Badcock got hers.'

'Yes?' Miss Marple was looking more alert than ever, much as a fox terrier might look at a waiting rathole.

'And there was something that she saw that struck her as a bit funny.'

'Why didn't she go to the police about it?'

'Well, she didn't really think it meant anything, you see,' explained Cherry. 'Anyway she thought she'd better ask Mr Giuseppe first.'

'What was it that she saw that day?'

'Frankly,' said Cherry, 'what she told me seemed nonsense! I've wondered, perhaps, if she was just putting me off – and what she was going to see Mr Giuseppe about was something quite different.'

'What *did* she say?' Miss Marple was patient and pursuing.

Cherry frowned. 'She was talking about Mrs Badcock and the cocktail and she said she was quite near her at the time. And she said she did it herself.'

'Did what herself?'

'Spilt her cocktail all down her dress, and ruined it.'

'You mean it was clumsiness?'

'No, not clumsiness. Gladys said she did it on *purpose* – that she *meant* to do it. Well, I mean, that doesn't make sense, does it, however you look at it?'

Miss Marple shook her head, perplexed. 'No,' she said. 'Certainly not – no, I can't see any sense in that.'

'She'd got on a new dress too,' said Cherry. 'That's how the subject came up. Gladys wondered whether she'd be able to buy it. Said it ought to clean all right but she didn't like to go and ask Mr Badcock herself. She's very good at dressmaking, Gladys is, and she said it was lovely stuff. Royal blue artificial taffeta; and she said even if the stuff *was* ruined where the cocktail stained it, she could take out a seam – half a breadth say – because it was one of those full skirts.'

Miss Marple considered this dressmaking problem for a moment and then set it aside.

'But you think your friend Gladys might have been keeping something back?'

'Well, I just wondered because I don't see if that's all she saw – Heather Badcock deliberately spilling her cocktail over herself – I don't see that there'd be anything to ask Mr Giuseppe *about*, do you?'

'No, I don't.' said Miss Marple. She sighed. 'But it's always interesting when one doesn't see,' she added. 'If you don't see what a thing means you must be looking at it wrong way round, unless of course you haven't got full information. Which is probably the case here.' She sighed. 'It's a pity she didn't go straight to the police.'

The door opened and Miss Knight bustled in holding a tall tumbler with a delicious pale yellow froth on top.

'Now here you are, dear,' she said, 'a nice little treat. We're going to enjoy this.'

She pulled forward a little table and placed it beside her employer. Then she turned a glance on Cherry. 'The vacuum cleaner,' she said coldly, 'is left in a most difficult position in the hall. I nearly fell over it. *Anyone* might have had an accident.'

'Righty-ho,' said Cherry. 'I'd better get on with things.'

She left the room.

'Really,' said Miss Knight, 'that Mrs Baker! I'm continually having to speak to her about something or other. Leaving vacuum cleaners all over the place and coming in here chattering to you when you want to be quiet.'

'I called her in,' said Miss Marple. 'I wanted to speak to her.'

'Well, I hope you mentioned the way the beds are made,' said Miss Knight. 'I was quite shocked when I came to turn down your bed last night. I had to make it all over again.'

'That was very kind of you,' said Miss Marple.

'Oh, I never grudge being helpful,' said Miss Knight. 'That's why I'm here, isn't it. To make a certain person we know as comfortable and happy as possible. Oh dear, dear,' she added, 'you've pulled out a lot of your knitting again.'

Miss Marple leaned back and closed her eyes. 'I'm going to have a litle rest,' she said. 'Put the glass here – thank you. And please don't come in and disturb me for at least three-quarters of an hour.'

'Indeed I won't, dear,' said Miss Knight. 'And I'll tell that Mrs Baker to be very quiet.'

She bustled out purposefully.

II

The good-looking young American glanced round him in a puzzled way.

The ramifications of the housing estate perplexed him.

He addressed himself politely to an old lady with white hair and pink cheeks who seemed to be the only human being in sight.

'Excuse me, ma'am, but could you tell me where to find Blenheim Close?'

The old lady considered him for a moment. He had just begun to wonder if she was deaf, and had prepared himself to repeat his demand in a louder voice, when she spoke.

'Along here to the right, then turn left, second to the right again, and straight on. What number do you want?'

'No. 16.' He consulted a small piece of paper. 'Gladys Dixon.'

'That's right,' said the old lady. 'But I believe she works at the Hellingforth Studios. In the canteen. You'll find her there if you want her.'

'She didn't turn up this morning,' explained the young man. 'I want to get hold of her to come up to Gossington Hall. We're very short-handed there today.'

'Of course,' said the old lady. 'The butler was shot last night, wasn't he?'

The young man was slightly staggered by this reply.

'I guess news gets round pretty quickly in these parts,' he said.

'It does indeed,' said the old lady. 'Mr Rudd's secretary died of some kind of seizure yesterday, too, I understand.' She shook her head. 'Terrible. Quite terrible. What are we coming to?'

—— 20 ——

A little later in the day yet another visitor found his way to 16 Blenheim Close. Detective-Sergeant William (Tom) Tiddler.

In reply to his sharp knock on the smart yellow painted door, it was opened to him by a girl of about fifteen. She had long straggly fair hair and was wearing tight black pants and an orange sweater.

'Miss Gladys Dixon live here?'

'You want Gladys? You're unlucky. She isn't here.'

'Where is she? Out for the evening?'

'No. She's gone away. Bit of a holiday like.'

'Where's she gone to?'

'That's telling,' said the girl.

Tom Tiddler smiled at her in his most ingratiating manner. 'May I come in? Is your mother at home?'

'Mum's out at work. She won't be in until half past seven. But she can't tell you any more than I can. Gladys has gone off for a holiday.'

'Oh, I see. When did she go?'

'This morning. All of a sudden like. Said she'd got the chance of a free trip.'

'Perhaps you wouldn't mind giving me her address.'

The fair-haired girl shook her head. 'Haven't got an address,' she said. 'Gladys said she'd send us her address as soon as she knew where she was going to stay. As like as not she won't though,' she added. 'Last summer she went to Newquay and never sent us as much as a postcard. She's slack that way and besides, she says, why do mothers have to bother all the time?'

'Did somebody stand her this holiday?'

'Must have,' said the girl. 'She's pretty hard up at the moment. Went to the sales last week.'

'And you've no idea at all who gave her this trip or – er – paid for her going there?'

The fair girl bristled suddenly.

'Now don't you get any wrong ideas. Our Gladys isn't that sort. She and her boy friend may like to go to the same place for holidays in August, but there's nothing wrong about it. She pays for herself. So don't you get ideas, mister.'

Tiddler said meekly that he wouldn't get ideas but he would like the address if Gladys Dixon should send a postcard.

He returned to the station with the result of his various inquiries. From the studios, he had learnt that Gladys Dixon had rung up that day and said she wouldn't be able to come to work for about a week. He had also learned some other things.

'No end of a shemozzle there's been there lately,' he said. 'Marina Gregg's been having hysterics most days. Said some coffee she was given was poisoned. Said it tasted bitter. Awful state of nerves she was in. Her huband took it and threw it down the sink and told her not to make so much fuss.'

'Yes?' said Craddock. It seemed plain there was more to come.

'But word went round as Mr Rudd didn't throw it all away. He kept some and had it analysed and it *was* poison.'

'It sounds to me,' said Craddock, 'very unlikely. I'll have to ask him about that.'

II

Jason Rudd was nervous, irritable.

'Surely, Inspector Craddock,' he said, 'I was only doing what I had a perfect right to do.'

'If you suspected anything was wrong with that coffee, Mr Rudd, it would have been much better if you'd turned it over to us.'

'The truth of it is that I didn't suspect for a moment that anything was wrong with it.'

'In spite of your wife saying that it tasted odd?'

'Oh, that!' A faintly rueful smile came to Rudd's face. 'Ever since the date of the fête everything that my wife has eaten or drunk has tasted odd. What with that and the threatening notes that have been coming—'

'There have been more of them?'

'Two more. One through the window down there. The other one was slipped in the letter-box. Here they are if you would like to see them.'

Craddock looked. They were printed, as the first one had been. One ran:

It won't be long now. Prepare yourself.

The other had a rough drawing of a skull and crossbones and below it was written: *This means you, Marina.*

Craddock's eyebrows rose.

'Very childish,' he said.

'Meaning you discount them as dangerous?'

'Not at all,' said Craddock. 'A murderer's mind usually is childish. You've really no idea at all, Mr Rudd, who sent these?'

'Not the least,' said Jason. 'I can't help feeling it's more like a macabre joke than anything else. It seemed to me perhaps—' he hesitated.

'Yes, Mr Rudd?'

'It could be somebody local, perhaps, who – who had been excited by the poisoning on the day of the fête. Someone perhaps, who has a grudge against the acting profession. There are rural pockets where acting is considered to be one of the devil's weapons.'

'Meaning that you think Miss Gregg is not actually threatened? But what about this business of the coffee?'

'I don't know how you got to hear about that,' said Rudd with some annoyance.

Craddock shook his head.

'Everything's talked about. It always comes to one's ears sooner or later. But you should have come to us. Even when you got the result of the analysis you didn't let us know, did you?'

'No,' said Jason. 'No, I didn't. But I had other things to think about. Poor Ella's death for one thing. And now this business of Giuseppe. Inspector Craddock, when can I get my wife away from here? She's half frantic.'

'I can understand that. But there will be inquests to attend.'

'You do realize that her life is still in danger?'

'I hope not. Every precaution will be taken—'

'Every precaution! I've heard that before, I think . . . I must get her away from here, Craddock. I *must*.'

II

Marina was lying on the chaise-longue in her bedroom, her eyes closed. She looked grey with strain and fatigue.

Her husband stood there for a moment looking at her. Her eyes opened.

'Was that that Craddock man?'

'Yes.'

'What did he come about? Ella?'

'Ella – and Giuseppe.'

Marina frowned.

'Giuseppe? Have they found out who shot him?'

'Not yet.'

'It's all like a nightmare . . . Did he say we could go away?'

'He said – not yet.'

'Why not? We must. Didn't you make him see that I can't go on waiting day after day for someone to kill me. It's fantastic.'

'Every precaution will be taken.'

'They said that before. Did it stop Ella being killed? Or Giuseppe? Don't you see, they'll get me in the end . . . There was something in my coffee that day at the studio. I'm sure there was . . . If only you hadn't poured it away! If we'd kept it, we could have have it analysed or whatever you call it. We'd have known for sure . . .'

'Would it have made you happier to know for sure?'

She stared at him, the pupils of her eyes widely dilated.

'I don't see what you mean. If they'd known for sure that some-one was trying to poison me, they'd have let us leave here, they'd have let us get away.'

'Not necessarily.'

'But I can't go on like this! I can't . . . I can't . . . You must help me, Jason. You must do *something*. I'm frightened. I'm so terribly frightened . . . There's an enemy here. And I don't know who it is . . . It might be anyone – anyone. At the studios – or here in the house. Someone who hates me – but why? . . . Someone who wants me dead . . . But who is it? Who is it? I thought – I was almost sure – it was Ella. But now—'

'You thought it was Ella?' Jason sounded astonished. 'But why?'

'Because she hated me – oh yes, she did. Don't men ever see these things? She was madly in love with you. I don't believe you had the least idea of it. But it can't be Ella, because Ella's dead. Oh, Jinks, Jinks – do help me – get me away from here – let me go somewhere safe . . . safe . . .'

She sprang up and walked rapidly up and down, turning and twisting her hands.

The director in Jason was full of admiration for those passionate, tortured movements. I must remember them, he thought. For Hedda Gabler, perhaps? Then, with a shock, he remembered that it was his wife he was watching.

He went to her and put his arms round her.

'It's all right, Marina – all right. I'll look after you.'

'We must go away from this hateful house – at once. I hate this house – hate it.'

'Listen, we can't go away immediately.'

'Why not? Why *not*?'

'Because,' said Rudd, 'deaths cause complications . . . and there's something else to consider. Will running away do any good?'

'Of course it will. We'll get away from this person who hates me.'

'If there's anyone who hates you that much, they could follow you easily enough.'

'You mean – you mean— I shall *never* get away? I shall never be safe again?'

'Darling – it will be all right. I'll look after you. I'll keep you safe.'

She clung to him.

'Will you, Jinks? Will you see that nothing happens to me?'

She sagged against him, and he laid her down gently on the chaise-longue.

'Oh, I'm a coward,' she murmured, 'a coward . . . If I knew

who it was – and why? ... Get me my pills – the yellow ones – not the brown. I must have something to calm me.'

'Don't take too many, for God's sake, Marina.'

'All right – all right ... Sometimes they don't have any effect any more ...' She looked up in his face.

She smiled, a tender exquisite smile.

'You'll take care of me, Jinks? Swear you'll take care of me ...'

'Always,' said Jason Rudd. 'To the bitter end.'

Her eyes opened wide.

'You looked so – so odd when you said that.'

'Did I? How did I look?'

'I can't explain. Like – like a clown laughing at something terribly sad, that no one else has seen ...'

—— 2 1 ——

It was a tired and depressed Inspector Craddock who came to see Miss Marple the following day.

'Sit down and be comfortable,' she said. 'I can see you've had a very hard time.'

'I don't like to be defeated,' said Inspector Craddock. 'Two murders within twenty-four hours. Ah well, I'm poorer at my job than I thought I was. Give me a nice cup of tea, Aunt Jane, with some thin bread and butter and soothe me with your earliest remembrances of St Mary Mead.'

Miss Marple clicked with her tongue in a sympathetic manner.

'Now it's no good talking like that, my dear boy, and I don't think tea and bread and butter is *at all* what you want. Gentlemen, when they've had a disappointment want something stronger than tea.'

As usual, Miss Marple said the word 'gentlemen' in the way of someone describing a foreign species.

'I should advise a good stiff whisky and soda,' she said.

'Would you really, Aunt Jane? Well, I won't say no.'

'And I shall get it for you myself,' said Miss Marple, rising to her feet.

'Oh no, don't do that. Let me. Or what about Miss What's-her-name?'

'We don't want Miss Knight fussing about here,' said Miss Marple. 'She won't be bringing my tea for another twenty

minutes so that gives us a little peace and quiet. Clever of you
to come to the window and not through the front door. Now we
can have a nice quiet little time by ourselves.'

She went to a corner cupboard, opened it and produced a
bottle, a syphon of soda water and a glass.

'You are full of surprises,' said Dermot Craddock. 'I'd no idea
that's what you kept in your corner cupboard. Are you quite
sure you're not a secret drinker, Aunt Jane?'

'Now, now,' Miss Marple admonished him. 'I have never been
an advocate of teetotalism. A little strong drink is always advisable on the premises in case there is a shock or an accident. Invaluable at such times. Or, of course, if a gentleman should arrive suddenly. There!' said Miss Marple, handing him her
remedy with an air of quiet triumph. 'And you don't need to
joke any more. Just sit quietly there and relax.'

'Wonderful wives there must have been in your young days,'
said Dermot Craddock.

'I'm sure, my dear boy, you would find the young lady of the
type you refer to as a very inadequate helpmeet nowadays. Young
ladies were not encouraged to be intellectual and very few of
them had university degrees or any kind of academic distinction.'

'There are things that are preferable to academic distinctions,'
said Dermot. 'One of them is knowing when a man wants a
whisky and soda and giving it to him.'

Miss Marple smiled at him affectionately.

'Come,' she said, 'tell me all about it. Or as much as you are
allowed to tell me.'

'I think you probably know as much as I do. And very likely
you have something up your sleeve. How about your dog's-body,
your dear Miss Knight? What about her having committed the
crime?'

'Now why should Miss Knight have done such a thing?' demanded Miss Marple surprised.

'Because she's the most unlikely person,' said Dermot. 'It so
often seems to hold good when your produce your answer.'

'Not at all,' said Miss Marple with spirit. 'I have said over and
over again, not only to you, my dear Dermot – if I may call you
so – that it is always the *obvious* person who has done the crime.
One thinks so often of the wife or the husband and so very often
it *is* the wife or the husband.'

'Meaning Jason Rudd?' He shook his head. 'That man adores
Marina Gregg.'

'I was speaking generally,' said Miss Marple, with dignity.

'First we had Mrs Badcock apparently murdered. One asked oneself who could have done such a thing and the first answer would naturally be the husband. So one had to examine that possibility. Then we decide that the real object of the crime was Marina Gregg and there again we have to look for the person most intimately connected with Marina Gregg, starting as I say with the husband. Because there is no doubt about it that husbands do, very frequently, want to make away with their wives, though sometimes, of course, they only *wish* to make away with their wives and do not actually do so. But I agree with you, my dear boy, that Jason Rudd really cares with all his heart for Marina Gregg. It *might* be very clever acting, though I can hardly believe that. And one certainly cannot see a motive of any kind for his doing away with her. If he wanted to marry someone else there could, I should say, be nothing more simple. Divorce, if I may say so, seems second nature to film stars. A practical advantage does not seem to arise either. He is not a poor man by any means. He has his own career, and is, I understand, most successful in it. So we must go farther afield. But it certainly is difficult. Yes, very difficult.'

'Yes,' said Craddock, 'it must hold particular difficulties for you because of course this film world is entirely new to you. You don't know the local scandals and animosities and all the rest of it.'

' I know a little more than you may think,' said Miss Marple. 'I have studied very closely various numbers of *Confidential, Film Life, Film Talk* and *Film Topics*.'

Dermot Craddock laughed. He couldn't help it.

'I must say,' he said, 'it tickles me to see you sitting there and telling me what your course of literature has been.'

'I found it very interesting,' said Miss Marple. 'They're not particularly well written, if I may say so. But it really is disappointing in a way that it is all so much the same as it used to be in my young days. *Modern Society* and *Tit Bits* and all the rest of them. A lot of gossip. A lot of scandal. A great preoccupation with who is in love with who, and all the rest of it. Really, you know, practically exactly the same sort of thing that goes on in St Mary Mead. And in the Development too. Human nature, I mean, is just the same everywhere. One comes back, I think, to the question of who could have been likely to want to kill Marina Gregg, to want to so much that having failed once they sent threatening letters and made repeated attempts to do so. Someone perhaps a little—' very gently she tapped her fore-head.

'Yes,' said Craddock, 'that certainly seems indicated. And of course it doesn't always show.'

'Oh, I know,' agreed Miss Marple, fervently. 'Old Mrs Pike's second boy, Alfred, *seemed* perfectly rational and normal. Al-most painfully prosaic, if you know what I mean, but actually, it seems, he had the most abnormal psychology, or so I under-stand. Really positively dangerous. He seems quite happy and contented, so Mrs Pike told me, now that he is in Fairways Mental Home. They understand him there, and the doctors think him a most interesting case. That of course pleases him very much. Yes, it all ended quite happily, but she had one or two very near escapes.'

Craddock revolved in his mind the possibility of a parallel be-tween someone in Marina Gregg's entourage and Mrs Pike's second son.

'The Italian butler,' continued Miss Marple, 'the one who was killed. He went to London, I understand, on the day of his death. Does anyone know what he did there – if you are allowed to tell me, that is,' she added conscientiously.

'He arrived in London at eleven-thirty in the morning.' said Craddock, 'and what he did in London nobody knows until at a quarter to two he visited his bank and made a deposit of five hundred pounds in cash. I may say that there was no confirma-tion of his story that he went to London to visit an ill relative or a relative who had got into trouble. None of his relatives there had seen him.'

Miss Marple nodded her head appreciatively.

'Five hundred pounds,' she said. 'Yes, that's quite an interest-ing sum, isn't it. I should imagine it would be the first instalment of a good many other sums, wouldn't you?'

'It looks that way,' said Craddock.

'It was probably all the ready money the person he was threatening could raise. He may have pretended to be satisfied with that or he may have accepted it as a down payment and the victim may have promised to raise further sums in the immedi-ate future. It seems to knock out the idea that Marina Gregg's killer could have been someone in humble circumstances who had a private vendetta against her. It would also knock out, I should say, the idea of someone who's obtained work as a studio helper or attendant or a servant or a gardener. Unless' – Miss Marple pointed out – 'such a person may have been the active agent whereas the employing agent may not have been in the neighbourhood. Hence the visit to London.'

'Exactly. We have in London Ardwyck Fenn, Lola Brewster and Margot Bence. All three were present at the party. All three of them could have met Giuseppe at an arranged meeting-place somewhere in London between the hours of eleven and a quarter to two. Ardwyck Fenn was out of his office during those hours, Lola Brewster had left her suite to go shopping, Margot Bence was not in her studio. By the way—'

'Yes?' said Miss Marple, 'have you something to tell me?'

'You asked me,' said Dermot, 'about the children. The children that Mrina Gregg adopted before she knew she could have a child of her own.'

'Yes I did.'

Craddock told her what he had learned.

'Margot Bence,' said Miss Marple softly. 'I had a feeling, you know, that it had something to do with children . . .'

'I can't believe that after all these years—'

'I know, I know. One never can. But do you really, my dear Dermot, know very much about children? Think back to your own childhood. Can't you remember some incident, some happening that caused grief, or a passion quite incommensurate with its real importance? Some sorrow or passionate resentment that has really never been equalled since? There was such a clever book, you know, written by that brilliant writer, Mr Richard Hughes. I forget the name of it but it was about some children who had been through a hurricane. Oh yes – the hurricane in Jamaica. What made a vivid impression on them was their cat rushing madly through the house. It was the only thing they remembered. But the whole of the horror and excitement and fear that they had experienced was bound up in that one incident.'

'It's odd you should say that,' said Craddock thoughtfully.

'Why, has it made you remember something?'

'I was thinking of when my mother died. I was five I think. Five or six. I was having dinner in the nursery, jam roll pudding. I was very fond of jam roll pudding. One of the servants came in and said to my nursery governess, "Isn't it awful? There's been an accident and Mrs Craddock has been killed." . . . Whenever I think of my mother's death, d'you know what I see?'

'What?'

'A plate with jam roll pudding on it, and I'm staring at it. Staring at it and I can see as well now as then, how the jam oozed out of it at one side. I didn't cry or say anything. I remember just sitting there as though I'd been frozen stiff, staring at the pudding. And d'you know, even now if I see in a shop or a restaurant or in anyone's house a portion of jam roll pudding, a whole wave of horror and misery and despair comes over me. Sometimes for a moment I don't remember *why*. Does that seem very crazy to you?'

'No,' said Miss Marple, 'it seems entirely natural. It's very interesting, that. It's given me a sort of idea . . .'

The door opened and Miss Knight appeared bearing the tea tray.

'Dear, dear,' she exclaimed, 'and so we've got a visitor, have we? How very nice. How do you do, Inspector Craddock. I'll just fetch another cup.'

'Don't bother,' Dermot called after her, 'I've had a drink instead.'

Miss Knight popped her head back round the door.

'I wonder – could you just come here a minute, Mr Craddock?'

Dermot joined her in the hall. She went to the dining-room and shut the door.

'You will be careful, won't you,' she said.

'Careful? In what way, Miss Knight?'

'Our old dear in there. You know, she's so interested in everything but it's not very good for her to get excited over murders and nasty things like that. We don't want her to brood and have bad dreams. She's very old and frail, and she really must lead a very sheltered life. She always has, you know. I'm sure all this talk of murders and gangsters and things like that is very, very bad for her.'

Dermot looked at her with faint amusement.

'I don't think,' he said gently, 'that anything that you or I could say about murders is likely unduly to excite or shock Miss Marple. I can assure you, my dear Miss Knight, that Miss Marple can contemplate murder and sudden death and indeed crime of all kinds with the utmost equanimity.'

He went back to the drawing-room, and Miss Knight, clucking a little in an indignant manner, followed him. She talked briskly during tea with an emphasis on political news in the paper and the most cheerful subjects she could think of. When she finally removed the tea tray and shut the door behind her, Miss Marple drew a deep breath.

'At last we've got some peace,' she said. 'I hope I shan't murder that woman some day. Now listen, Dermot, there are some things I want to know?'

'Yes? What are they?'

'I want to go over very carefully exactly what happened on the day of the fête. Mrs Bantry has arrived, and the vicar shortly after her. Then come Mr and Mrs Badcock and on the stairs at that time were the mayor and his wife, this man Ardwyck Fenn, Lola Brewster, a reporter from the *Herald & Argus* of Much Benham, and this photographer girl, Margot Bence. Margot Bence, you said, had her camera at an angle on the stairs, and was taking photographs of the proceedings. Have you seen any of those photographs?'

'Actually I brought one to show you.'

He took from his pocket an unmounted print. Miss Marple looked at it steadfastly. It showed Marina Gregg with Jason Rudd a little behind her to one side, Arthur Badcock, his hand to his face, looking slightly embarrassed, was standing back, whilst his wife had Marina Gregg's hand in hers and was looking up at her and talking. Marina was not looking at Mrs Badcock. She was staring over her head looking, it seemed, full into the camera, or possibly just slightly to the left of it.

'*Very* interesting,' said Miss Marple. 'I've had descriptions, you know, of what this look was on her face. A frozen look. Yes, that describes it quite well. A look of doom. I'm not really so sure about that. It's more a kind of paralysis of feeling rather than apprehension of doom. Don't you think so? I wouldn't say it was actually fear, would you, although fear of course might take you that way. It might paralyse you. But I don't think it was fear. I think rather that it was *shock*. Dermot, my dear boy, I want you to tell me if you've got notes of it, what exactly Heather Badcock said to Marina Gregg on that occasion. I know roughly the gist of it, of course, but how near can you get to the actual *words*. I suppose you had accounts of it from different people.'

Dermot nodded.

'Yes. Let me see. Your friend, Mrs Bantry, then Jason Rudd and I think Arthur Badcock. As you say they varied a little in wording, but the gist of them was the same.'

'I know. It's the variations that I want. I think it might help us.'

'I don't see how,' said Dermot, 'though perhaps you do. Your friend, Mrs Bantry, was probably the most definite on the point.

As far as I remember – wait – I carry a good many of my jottings around with me.'

He took out a small note-book from his pocket, looked through it to refresh his memory.

'I haven't got the exact words here,' he said, 'but I made a rough note. Apparently Mrs Badcock was very cheerful, rather arch, and delighted with herself. She said something like "I can't tell you how wonderful this is for me. You won't remember but years ago in Bermuda – I got up from bed when I had chicken pox and came along to see you and you gave me an autograph and it's one of the proudest days of my life which I have never forgotten."'

'I see,' said Miss Marple, 'she mentioned the place but not the date, did she?'

'Yes.'

'And what did Rudd say?'

'Jason Rudd? He said that Mrs Badcock told his wife that she'd got up from bed when she had the 'flu and had come to meet Marina and that she still had her autograph. It was a shorter account than your friend's but the gist of it was the same.'

'Did he mention the time and place?'

'No. I don't think he did. I think he said roughly that it was some ten or twelve years ago.'

'I see. And what about Mr Badcock?'

'Mr Badcock said that Heather was extremely excited and anxious to meet Miss Gregg, that she was a great fan of Marina Gregg's and that she'd told him that once when she was ill as a girl she managed to get up and meet Miss Gregg and get her autograph. He didn't go into any close particulars, as it was evidently in the days before he was married to his wife. He impressed me as not thinking the incident of much importance.'

'I see,' said Miss Marple. 'Yes, I see . . .'

'And what do you see?' asked Craddock.

'Not quite as much as I'd like to yet,' said Miss Marple, honestly, 'but I have a sort of feeling if I only knew why she'd ruined her new dress—'

'Who – Mrs Badcock?'

'Yes. It seems to me such a very odd thing – such an inexplicable one unless – of course— Dear me, I think I must be *very* stupid!'

Miss Knight opened the door and entered, switching the light on as she did so.

'I think we want a little light in here,' she said brightly.

'Yes,' said Miss Marple, 'you are so right, Miss Knight. That is exactly what we did want. A little light. I think, you know, that at last we've got it.'

The tête-à-tête seemed ended and Craddock rose to his feet.

'There only remains one thing,' he said, 'and that is for you to tell me just what particular memory from your own past is agitating your mind now.'

'Everyone always teases me about that,' said Miss Marple, 'but I must say that I was reminded just for a moment of the Lauriston's parlourmaid.'

'The Lauriston's parlourmaid?' Craddock looked completely mystified.

'She had, of course, to take messages on the telephone,' said Miss Marple, 'and she wasn't very good at it. She used to get the general *sense* right, if you know what I mean, but the way she wrote it down used to make quite nonsense of it sometimes. I suppose really, because her grammar was so bad. The result was that some very unfortunate incidents occurred. I remember one in particular. A Mr Burroughs, I think it was, rang up and said he had been to see Mr Elvaston about the fence being broken down but he said that the fence wasn't his business at all to repair. It was on the other side of the property and he said he would like to know if that was really the case before proceeding further as it would depend on whether he was liable or not and it was important for him to know the proper lie of the land before instructing solicitors. A very obscure message, as you see. It confused rather than enlightened.'

'If you're talking about parlourmaids,' said Miss Knight with a little laugh, 'that must have been a *very* long time ago. I've never even heard of a parlourmaid for many years now.'

'It was a good many years ago,' said Miss Marple, 'but nevertheless human nature was very much the same then as it is now. Mistakes were made for very much the same reasons. Oh dear,' she added, 'I *am* thankful that that girl is safely in Bournemouth.'

'The girl? What girl?' asked Dermot.

'That girl who did dressmaking and went up to see Giuseppe that day. What was her name – Gladys something.'

'Gladys Dixon?'

'Yes, that's the name.'

'She's in *Bournemouth*, do you say? How on earth do you know that?'

'I know,' said Miss Marple, 'because I sent her there.'

'What?' Dermot stared at her. 'You? Why?'

'I went out to see her,' said Miss Marple, 'and I gave her some money and told her to take a holiday and not to write home.'

'Why on earth did you do that?'

'Because I didn't want her to be killed, of course,' said Miss Marple, and blinked at him placidly.

—— 22 ——

'Such a sweet letter from Lady Conway,' Miss Knight said two days later as she deposited Miss Marple's breakfast tray. 'You remember my telling you about her? Just a little, you know—' she tapped her forehead – 'wanders sometimes. And her memory's bad. Can't recognise her relations always and tells them to go away.'

'That might be shrewdness really,' said Miss Marple, 'rather than a loss of memory.'

'Now, now,' said Miss Knight, 'aren't we being naughty to make suggestions like that? She's spending the winter at the Belgrave Hotel at Llandudno. *Such* a nice residential hotel. Splendid grounds and a very nice glassed-in terrace. She's most anxious for me to come and join her there.' She sighed.

Miss Marple sat herself upright in bed.

'But please,' she said, 'if you are wanted – if you are needed there and would like to go—'

'No, no, I couldn't hear of it,' cried Miss Knight. 'Oh no, I never meant anything like that. Why, what would Mr Raymond West say? He explained to me that being here might turn out to be a permanency. I should *never* dream of not fulfilling my obligations. I was only just mentioning the fact in passing, so don't worry, dear,' she added, patting Miss Marple on the shoulder. 'We're not going to be deserted! No, no, indeed we're not! We're going to be looked after and cosseted and made very happy and comfortable always.'

She went out of the room. Miss Marple sat with an air of determination, staring at her tray and failing to eat anything. Finally she picked up the receiver of the telephone and dialled with vigour.

'Dr Haydock?'

'Yes?'

'Jane Marple here.'

'And what's the matter with you? In need of my professional services?'

'No,' said Miss Marple. 'But I want to see you as soon as possible.'

When Dr Haydock came, he found Miss Marple still in bed waiting for him.

'You look the picture of health,' he complained.

'That is why I wanted to see you,' said Miss Marple. 'To tell you that I am perfectly well.'

'An unusual reason for sending for the doctor.'

'I'm quite strong, I'm quite fit, and it's absurd to have anybody living in the house. So long as someone comes every day and does the cleaning and all that I don't see any need at all for having someone living here permanently.'

'I dare say you don't, but I do,' said Dr Haydock.

'It seems to me you're turning into a regular old fuss-budget,' said Miss Marple unkindly.

'And don't call me names!' said Dr Haydock. 'You're a very healthy woman for your age; you were pulled down a bit by bronchitis which isn't good for the elderly. But to stay alone in a house at your age is a risk. Supposing you fall down the stairs one evening or fall out of bed or slip in the bath. There you'd lie and nobody'd know about it.'

'One can imagine anything,' said Miss Marple. 'Miss Knight might fall down the stairs and I'd fall over her rushing out to see what had happened.'

'It's no good your bullying me,' said Dr Haydock. 'You're an old lady and you've got to be looked after in a proper manner. If you don't like this woman you've got, change her and get somebody else.'

'That's not always so easy,' said Miss Marple.

'Find some old servant of yours, someone that you like, and who's lived with you before. I can see this old hen irritates you. She'd irritate me. There must be some old servant somewhere. That nephew of yours is one of the best-selling authors of the day. He'd make it worth her while if you found the right person.'

'Of course dear Raymond would do anything of that kind. He is most generous,' said Miss Marple. 'But it's not so easy to find the right person. Young people have their own lives to live, and so many of my faithful old servants, I am sorry to say, are dead.'

'Well, you're not dead,' said Dr Haydock, 'and you'll live a good deal longer if you take proper care of yourself.'

He rose to his feet.

'Well,' he said. 'No good my stopping here. You look as fit as a fiddle. I shan't waste time taking your blood pressure or feeling your pulse or asking you questions. You're thriving on all this local excitement, even if you can't get about to poke your nose in as much as you'd like to do. Goodbye, I've got to go now and do some real doctoring. Eight to ten cases of German measles, half a dozen whooping coughs, and a suspected scarlet fever as well as my regulars!'

Dr Haydock went out breezily— But Miss Marple was frowning . . . Something that he had said . . . what was it? Patients to see . . . the usual village ailments . . . village ailments? Miss Marple pushed her breakfast tray farther away with a purposeful gesture. Then she rang up Mrs Bantry.

'Dolly? Jane here. I want to ask you something. Now pay attention. Is it true that you told Inspector Craddock that Heather Badcock told Marina Gregg a long pointless story about how she had chicken pox and got up in spite of it to go and meet Marina and get her autograph?'

'That was it more or less.'

'*Chicken pox?*'

'Well, something like that. Mrs Allcock was talking to me about Vodka at the time, so I wasn't really listening closely.'

'You're sure,' Miss Marple took a breath, 'that she didn't say whooping cough?'

'Whooping cough?' Mrs Bantry sounded astounded. 'Of course not. She wouldn't have had to powder her face and do it up for whooping cough.'

'I see –that's what you went by – her special mention of make-up?'

'Well, she laid stress on it – she wasn't the making up kind. But I think you're right, it wasn't chicken pox . . . Nettlerash, perhaps.'

'You only say that,' said Miss Marple coldly, 'because you once had nettlerash yourself and couldn't go to a wedding. You're hopeless, Dolly, quite hopeless.'

She put the receiver down with a bang, cutting off Mrs Bantry's astonished protest of 'Really, Jane.'

Miss Marple made a ladylike noise of vexation like a cat sneezing to indicate profound disgust. Her mind reverted to the problem of her own domestic comfort. Faithful Florence? Could

718

faithful Florence, that grenadier of a former parlourmaid be persuaded to leave her comfortable small house and come back to St Mary Mead to look after her erstwhile mistress? Faithful Florence had always been very devoted to her. But faithful Florence was very attached to her own little house. Miss Marple shook her head vexedly. A gay rat-tat-tat sounded at the door. On Miss Marple's calling 'Come in' Cherry entered.

'Come for your tray,' she said. 'Has anything happened? You're looking rather upset, aren't you?'

'I feel so helpless,' said Miss Marple. 'Old and helpless.'

'Don't worry,' said Cherry, picking up the tray. 'You're very far from helpless. You don't know the things I hear about you in this place! Why practically everybody in the Development knows about you now. All sorts of extraordinary things you've done. *They* don't think of you as the old and helpless kind. It's *she* puts it into your head.'

'She?'

Cherry gave a vigorous nod of her head backwards towards the door behind her.

'Pussy, pussy,' she said. 'Your Miss Knight. Don't you let her get you down.'

'She's very kind,' said Miss Marple, 'really *very* kind,' she added, in the tone of one who convinces herself.

'Care killed the cat, they say,' said Cherry. 'You don't want kindness rubbed into your skin, so to speak, do you?'

'Oh well,' said Miss Marple sighing, 'I suppose we all have our troubles.'

'I should say we do,' said Cherry. 'I oughtn't to complain but I feel sometimes that if I live next door to Mrs Hartwell any longer there's going to be a regrettable incident. Sour-faced old cat, always gossiping and complaining. Jim's pretty fed up too. He had a first-class row with her last night. Just because we had *The Messiah* on a bit loud! You can't object to *The Messiah*, can you? I mean, it's religious.'

'Did she object?'

'She created something terrible,' said Cherry. 'Banged on the wall and shouted and one thing and another.'

'Do you have to have your music tuned in so loud?' asked Miss Marple.

'Jim likes it that way,' said Cherry. 'He says you don't get the tone unless you have full volume.'

'It might,' suggested Miss Marple, 'be a *little* trying for any-one if they *weren't* musical.'

'It's these houses being semi-detached,' said Cherry. 'Thin as anything, the walls. I'm not so keen really on all this new building, when you come to think of it. It looks all very prissy and nice but you can't express your personality without somebody being down on you like a ton of bricks.'

Miss Marple smiled at her.

'You've got a lot of personality to express, Cherry,' she said.

'D'you think so?' Cherry was pleased and she laughed. 'I wonder,' she began. Suddenly she looked embarrassed. She put down the tray and came back to the bed.

'I wonder if you'd think it cheek if I asked you something? I mean – you've only got to say "out of the question" and that's that.'

'Something you want me to do?'

'Not quite. It's those rooms over the kitchen. They're never used nowadays, are they?'

'No.'

'Used to be a gardener and wife there once, so I heard. But that's old stuff. What I wondered – what Jim and I wondered – is if we could have them. Come and live here, I mean.'

Miss Marple stared at her in astonishment.

'But your beautiful new house in the Development?'

'We're both fed up with it. We like gadgets, but you can have gadgets anywhere – get them on H.P. and there would be a nice lot of room here, especially if Jim could have the room over the stables. He'd fix it up like new, and he could have all his construction models there, and wouldn't have to clear them away all the time. And if we had out stereo gram there too, you'd hardly hear it.'

'Are you really serious about this, Cherry?'

'Yes, I am. Jim and I, we've talked about it a lot. Jim could fix things for you any time – you know, plumbing or a bit of carpentry. And I'd look after you every bit as well as your Miss Knight does. I know you think I'm a bit slap-dash – but I'd try and take trouble with the beds and the washing-up – and I'm getting quite a dab hand at cooking. Did Beef Stroganoff last night, it's quite easy, really.'

Miss Marple contemplated her.

Cherry was looking like an eager kitten – vitality and joy of life radiated from her. Miss Marple thought once more of faithful Florence. Faithful Florence would, of course, keep the house far better. (Miss Marple put no faith in Cherry's promise.) But she was at least sixty-five – perhaps more. And would she really want to be uprooted? She might accept that out of her very real devotion for Miss Marple. But did Miss Marple really want sacrifices made for her? Wasn't she already suffering from Miss Knight's conscientious devotion to duty?

Cherry, however inadequate her housework, *wanted* to come. And she had qualities that to Miss Marple at this moment seemed of supreme importance.

Warm-heartedness, vitality, and a deep interest in everything that was going on.

'I don't want, of course,' said Cherry, 'to go behind Miss Knight's back in any way.'

'Never mind about Miss Knight,' said Miss Marple, coming to a decision. 'She'll go off to someone called Lady Conway at a hotel in Llandudno – and enjoy herself thoroughly. We'll have to settle a lot of details, Cherry, and I shall want to talk to your husband – but if you really think you'd be happy . . .'

'It'll suit us down to the ground,' said Cherry. 'And you really can rely on me doing things properly. I'll even use the dustpan and brush if you like.'

Miss Marple laughed at this supreme offer.

Cherry picked up the breakfast tray again.

'I must get cracking. I got here late this morning – hearing about poor Arthur Badcock.'

'Arthur Badcock? What happened to him?'

'Haven't you heard? He's up at the police-station now,' said Cherry. 'They asked him if he'd come and "assist them with their inquiries" and you know what that always means.'

'When did this happen?' demanded Miss Marple.

'This morning,' said Cherry. 'I suppose,' she added, 'that it got out about his once having been married to Marina Gregg.'

'What!' Miss Marple sat up again. 'Arthur Badcock was once married to Marina Gregg?'

'That's the story,' said Cherry. 'Nobody had any idea of it. It was Mr Upshaw put it about. He's been to the States once or twice on business for his firm and so he knows a lot of gossip from over there. It was a long time ago, you know. Really before she'd begun her career. They were only married a year or two and then she won a film award and of course he wasn't good enough for her then, so they had one of these easy American divorces and he just faded out, as you might say. He's the fading out kind, Arthur Badcock. He wouldn't make a fuss. He changed his name and came back to England. It's all ever so long ago. You wouldn't think anything like that mattered nowadays, would you? Still, there it is. It's enough for the police to go on, I suppose.'

'Oh no,' said Miss Marple. 'Oh *no*. This mustn't happen. If I could only think what to do— Now, let me see.' She made a gesture to Cherry. 'Take the tray away, Cherry, and send Miss Knight up to me. I'm going to get up.'

Cherry obeyed. Miss Marple dressed herself with fingers that fumbled slightly. It irritated her when she found excitement of any kind affected her. She was just hooking up her dress when Miss Knight entered.

'Did you want me? Cherry said—'

Miss Marple broke in incisively.

'Get Inch,' she said.

'I beg your pardon,' said Miss Knight, startled.

'Inch,' said Miss Marple, 'get Inch. Telephone for him to come at once.'

'Oh, oh I see. You mean the taxi people. But his name's Roberts, isn't it?'

'To me,' said Miss Marple, 'he is Inch and always will be. But anyway get him. He's to come here at once.'

'You want to go for a little drive?'

'Just get him, can you?' said Miss Marple, 'and hurry, please.'

Miss Knight looked at her doubtfully and proceeded to do as she was told.

'We are feeling all right, dear, aren't we?' she said anxiously.

'We are both feeling very well,' said Miss Marple, 'and I am feeling *particularly* well. Inertia does not suit me, and never has. A practical course of action, that is what I have been wanting for a long time.'

'Has that Mrs Baker been saying something that has upset you?'

'Nothing has upset me,' said Miss Marple, 'I feel particularly well. I am annoyed with myself for being stupid. But really, until I got a hint from Dr Haydock this morning – now I wonder if I remember rightly. Where is that medical book of mine?' She gestured Miss Knight aside and walked firmly down the stairs. She found the book she wanted in a shelf in the drawing-room. Taking it out she looked up the index, murmured 'Page 210,' turned to the page in question, read for a few moments then nodded her head, satisfied.

'Most remarkable,' she said, 'most curious. I don't suppose anybody would ever have thought of it. I didn't myself, until the two things came together, so to speak.'

Then she shook her head, and a little line appeared between her eyes. 'If only there was *someone* . . .'

She went over in her mind the various accounts she had been given of that particular scene . . .

Her eyes widened in thought. There was someone – but would he, she wondered, be any good? One never knew with the vicar. He was quite unpredictable.

Nevertheless she went to the telephone and dialled.

'Good morning, Vicar, this is Miss Marple.'

'Oh yes, Miss Marple – anything I can do for you?'

'I wonder if you could help me on a small point. It concerns the day of the fête when poor Mrs Badcock died. I believe you were standing quite near Miss Gregg when Mr and Mrs Badcock arrived.'

'Yes – yes – I was just before them, I think. Such a tragic day.'

'Yes, indeed. And I believe that Mrs Badcock was recalling to Miss Gregg that they had met before in Bermuda. She had been ill in bed and had got up specially.'

Yes, yes, I do remember.'

'And do you remember if Mrs Badcock mentioned the illness she was suffering from?'

'I think now – let me see – yes, it was measles – at least not real measles – German measles – a much less serious disease. Some people hardly feel ill at all with it. I remember my cousin Caroline . . .'

Miss Marple cut off reminiscences of Cousin Caroline by saying firmly: 'Thank you so much, Vicar,' and replacing the receiver.

There was an awed expression on her face. One of the great mysteries of St Mary Mead was what made the vicar remember certain things – only outstripped by the greater mystery of what the vicar could manage to forget!

'The taxi's here, dear,' said Miss Knight, bustling in. 'It's a very old one, and not too clean I should say. I don't really like you driving in a thing like that. You might pick up some germ or other.'

'Nonsense,' said Miss Marple. Setting her hat firmly on her head and buttoning up her summer coat, she went out to the waiting taxi.

'Good morning, Roberts,' she said.

'Good morning, Miss Marple. You're early this morning. Where do you want to go?'

'Gossington Hall, please,' said Miss Marple.

'I'd better come with you, hadn't I, dear,' said Miss Knight. 'It won't take me a minute just to slip on outdoor shoes.'

'No, thank you,' said Miss Marple, firmly. 'I'm going by myself. Drive on, Inch. I mean Roberts.'

Mr Roberts drove on, merely remarking:

'Ah, Gossington Hall. Great changes there and everywhere nowadays. All that development. Never thought anything like that'd come to St Mary Mead.'

Upon arrival at Gossington Hall Miss Marple rang the bell and asked to see Mr Jason Rudd.

Giuseppe's successor, a rather shaky-looking elderly man, conveyed doubt.

'Mr Rudd,' he said, 'does not see anybody without an appointment, madam. And today especially—'

'I have no appointment,' said Miss Marple, 'but I will wait,' she added.

She stepped briskly past him into the hall and sat down on a hall chair.

'I'm afraid it will be quite impossible this morning, madam.'

'In that case,' said Miss Marple, 'I shall wait until this afternoon.'

Baffled, the new butler retired. Presently a young man came to Miss Marple. He had a pleasant manner and a cheerful, slightly American voice.

'I've seen you before,' said Miss Marple. 'In the Development. You asked me the way to Blenheim Close.'

Hailey Preston smiled good-naturedly. 'I guess you did your best, but you misdirected me badly.'

'Dear me, did I?' said Miss Marple. 'So many Closes, aren't there. Can I see Mr Rudd?'

'Why, now, that's too bad,' said Hailey Preston. 'Mr Rudd's a very busy man and he's – er – fully occupied this morning and really can't be disturbed.'

'I'm sure he's very busy,' said Miss Marple. 'I came here quite prepared to wait.'

'Why, I'd suggest now,' said Hailey Preston, 'that you should tell me what it is you want. I deal with all these things for Mr Rudd, you see. Everyone has to see me first.'

'I'm afraid,' said Miss Marple, 'that I want to see Mr Rudd himself. And,' she added, 'I shall wait here until I do.'

She settled herself more firmly in the large oak chair.

Hailey Preston hesitated, started to speak, finally turned away and went upstairs.

He returned with a large man in tweeds.

'This is Dr Gilchrist, Miss – er—'

'Miss Marple.'

'So you're Miss Marple,' said Dr Gilchrist. He looked at her with a good deal of interest.

Hailey Preston slipped away with celerity.

'I've heard about you,' said Dr Gilchrist. 'From Dr Haydock.'

'Dr Haydock is a very old friend of mine.'

'He certainly is. Now you want to see Mr Jason Rudd? Why?'

'It is necessary that I should,' said Miss Marple.

Dr Gilchrist's eyes appraised her.

'And you're camping here until you do?' he asked.

'Exactly.'

'You would, too,' said Dr Gilchrist. 'In that case I will give you a perfectly good reason why you cannot see Mr Rudd. His wife died last night in her sleep.'

'Dead!' exclaimed Miss Marple. 'How?'

'An overdose of sleeping stuff. We don't want the news to leak out to the Press for a few hours. So I'll ask you to keep this knowledge to yourself for the moment.'

'Of course. Was it an accident?'

'That is definitely my view,' said Gilchrist.

'But it could be suicide.'

'It could – but most unlikely.'

'Or someone could have given it to her?'

Gilchrist shrugged his shoulders.

'A most remote contingency. And a thing,' he added firmly, 'that would be quite impossible to prove.'

'I see,' said Miss Marple. She took a deep breath. 'I'm sorry, but it's more necessary than ever that I should see Mr Rudd.'

Gilchrist looked at her.

'Wait here,' he said.

—— 23 ——

Jason Rudd looked up as Gilchrist entered.

'There's an old dame downstairs,' said the doctor; looks about a hundred. Wants to see you. Won't take no and says she'll wait. She'll wait till this afternoon, I gather, or she'll wait till this evening and she's quite capable, I should say, of spending the night here. She's got something she badly wants to say to you. I'd see her if I were you.'

Jason Rudd looked up from his desk. His face was white and strained.

'Is she mad?'

'No. Not in the least.'

'I don't see why I— Oh, all right – send her up. What does it matter?'

Gilchrist nodded, went out of the room and called to Hailey Preston.

'Mr Rudd can spare you a few minutes now, Miss Marple,' said Hailey Preston, appearing again by her side.

'Thank you. That's very kind of him,' said Miss Marple as she rose to her feet. 'Have you been with Mr Rudd long?' she asked.

'Why, I've worked with Mr Rudd for the last two and a half years. My job is public relations generally.'

'I see.' Miss Marple looked at him thoughtfully. 'You remind me very much,' she said, 'of someone I knew called Gerald French.'

'Indeed? What did Gerald French do?'

'Not very much,' said Miss Marple, 'but he was a very good talker.' She sighed. 'He had had an unfortunate past.'

'You don't say,' said Hailey Preston, slightly ill at ease. 'What kind of a past?'

'I won't repeat it,' said Miss Marple. 'He didn't like it talked about.'

Jason Rudd rose from his desk and looked with some surprise at the slender elderly lady who was advancing towards him.

'You wanted to see me?' he said. 'What can I do for you?'

'I am very sorry about your wife's death,' said Miss Marple. 'I can see it has been a great grief to you and I want you to believe that I should not intrude upon you now or offer you sympathy unless it was absolutely necessary. But there are things that need badly to be cleared up unless an innocent man is going to suffer.'

'An innocent man? I don't understand you.'

'Arthur Badcock,' said Miss Marple. 'He is with the police now, being questioned.'

'Questioned in connexion with my wife's death? But that's absurd, absolutely absurd. He's never been near the place. He didn't even know her.'

'I think he knew her,' said Miss Marple. 'He was married to her once.'

'Arthur *Badcock*? But – he was – he was Heather Badcock's husband. Aren't you perhaps—' he spoke kindly and apologetically – 'making a little mistake?'

'He was married to both of them,' said Miss Marple. 'He was married to your wife when she was very young, before she went into pictures.'

Jason Rudd shook his head.

'My wife was married to a man called Alfred Beadle. He was in real estate. They were not suited and they parted almost immediately.'

'Then Alfred Beadle changed his name to Badcock,' said Miss Marple. 'He's in a real estate firm here. It's odd how some people never seem to like to change their job and want to go on doing the same thing. I expect really that's why Marina Gregg felt that he was no use to her. He couldn't have kept up with her.'

'What you've told me is most surprising.'

'I can assure you that I am not romancing or imagining things. What I am telling you is sober fact. These things get round very quickly in a village, you know, though they take a little longer,' she added, 'in reaching the Hall.'

'Well,' Jason Rudd stalled, uncertain what to say, then he accepted the position, 'and what do you want me to do for you, Miss Marple?' he asked.

'I want, if I may, to stand on the stairs at the spot where you and your wife received guests on the day of the fête.'

He shot a quick doubtful glance at her. Was this, after all, just another sensation-seeker. But Miss Marple's face was grave and composed.

'Why certainly,' he said, 'if you want to do so. Come with me.'

He led her to the staircase head and paused in the hollowed-out bay at the top of it.

'You've made a good many changes in the house since the Bantrys were here,' said Miss Marple. 'I like this. Now, let me see. The tables would be about here, I suppose, and you and your wife would be standing—'

'My wife stood here.' Jason Rudd showed her the place. 'People came up the stairs, she shook hands with them and passed them on to me.'

'She stood here,' said Miss Marple.

She moved over and took her place where Marina Gregg had stood. She remained there quite quietly without moving. Jason Rudd watched her. He was perplexed but interested. She raised her right hand slightly as though shaking, looked down the stairs

727

as though to see people coming up it. Then she looked straight ahead of her. On the wall half-way up the stairs was a large picture, a copy of an Italian Old Master. On either side of it were narrow windows, one giving out on the garden and the other giving on to the end of the stables and the weathercock. But Miss Marple looked at neither of these. Her eyes were fixed on the picture itself.

'Of course you always hear a thing right the first time,' she said. 'Mrs Bantry told me that your wife stared at the picture and her face "froze," as she put it.' She looked at the rich red and blue robes of the Madonna, a Madonna with her head slightly back, laughing up at the Holy Child that she was holding up in her arms. 'Giacomo Bellini's "Laughing Madonna",' she said. 'A religious picture, but also a painting of a happy mother with her child. Isn't that so, Mr Rudd?'

'I would say so, yes.'

'I understand now,' said Miss Marple. 'I understand quite well. The whole thing is really very simple, isn't it?' She looked at Jason Rudd.

'Simple?'

'I think you know how simple it is,' said Miss Marple. There was a peal on the bell below.

'I don't think,' said Jason Rudd, 'I quite understand.' He looked down the stairway. There was a sound of voices.

'I know that voice,' said Miss Marple, 'it's Inspector Craddock's voice, isn't it?'

'Yes, it seems to be Inspector Craddock.'

'He wants to see you, too. Would you mind very much if he joined us?'

'Not at all as far as I am concerned. Whether he will agree—'

'I think he will agree,' said Miss Marple. 'There's really not much time now to be lost, is there? We've got to the moment when we've got to understand just how everything happened.'

'I thought you said it was simple,' said Jason Rudd.

'It was so simple,' said Miss Marple, 'that one just couldn't see it.'

The decayed butler arrived at this moment up the stairs.

'Inspector Craddock is here, sir,' he said.

'Ask him to join us here, please,' said Jason Rudd. The butler disappeared again and a moment or two later Dermot Craddock came up the stairs.

'You!' he said to Miss Marple, 'how did you get here?'

'I came in Inch,' said Miss Marple, producing the usual confused effect that that remark always caused.

From slightly behind her Jason Rudd rapped his forehead interrogatively. Dermot Craddock shook his head.

'I was saying to Mr Rudd,' said Miss Marple, '—has that butler gone away—'

Dermot Craddock cast a look down the stairs.

'Oh yes,' he said, 'he's not listening. Sergeant Tiddler will see to that.'

'Then that is all right,' said Miss Marple. 'We could of course have gone into a room to talk, but I prefer it like this. Here we are on the spot where the thing happened, which makes it so much easier to understand.'

'You are talking,' said Jason Rudd, 'of the day of the fête here, the day when Heather Badcock was poisoned.'

'Yes,' said Miss Marple, 'and I'm saying that it is all very simple if one only looks at it in the proper way. It all began, you see, with Heather Badcock being the kind of person she was. It was inevitable, really, that something of that kind should happen some day to Heather.'

'I don't understand what you mean,' said Jason Rudd, 'I don't understand at all.'

'No, it has to be explained a little. You see, when my friend, Mrs Bantry who was here, described the scene to me, she quoted a poem that was a great favourite in my youth, a poem of dear Lord Tennyson's, "The Lady of Shalott".' She raised her voice a little.

> *'The mirror crack'd from side to side:*
> *"The curse is come upon me," cried*
> *The Lady of Shalott.*

'That's what Mrs Bantry saw, or thought she saw, though actually she misquoted and said doom instead of curse – perhaps a better word in the circumstances. She saw your wife speaking to Heather Badcock and heard Heather Badcock speaking to your wife and she saw this look of doom on your wife's face.'

'Haven't we been over that a great many times?' said Jason Rudd.

'Yes, but we shall have to go over it once more,' said Miss Marple. 'There was that expression on your wife's face and she was looking not at Heather Badcock but at that picture. At a picture of a laughing, happy mother holding up a happy child.

The mistake was that though there *was* doom foreshadowed in Marina Gregg's face, it was not on *her* the doom would come. The doom was to come upon Heather. Heather was doomed from the first moment that she began talking and boasting of an incident in the past.'

'Could you make yourself a little clearer?' said Dermot Craddock.

Miss Marple turned to him.

'Of course I will. This is something that you know nothing about. You couldn't know about it, because nobody has told you what it was Heather Badcock actually said.'

'But they have,' protested Dermot. 'They've told me over and over again. Several people have told me.'

'Yes,' said Miss Marple, 'but you don't know because, you see, Heather Badcock didn't tell it to *you*.'

'She hardly could tell it to me seeing she was dead when I arrived here,' said Dermot.

'Quite so,' said Miss Marple. 'All you know is that she was ill but she got up from bed and came along to a celebration of some kind where she met Marina Gregg and spoke to her and asked for an autograph and was given one.'

'I know,' said Craddock with slight impatience. 'I've heard all that.'

'But you didn't hear the one operative phrase, because no one thought it was important,' said Miss Marple. 'Heather Badcock was ill in bed – with *German measles*.'

'German measles? What on earth has that got to do with it?'

'It's a very slight illness, really,' said Miss Marple. 'It hardly makes you feel ill at all. You have a rash which is easy to cover up with powder, and you have a little fever, but not very much. You feel quite well enough to go out and see people if you want to. And of course in repeating all this the fact that it was German measles didn't strike people particularly. Mrs Bantry, for instance, just said that Heather had been ill in bed and mentioned chicken pox and nettlerash. Mr Rudd here said that it was 'flu, but of course he did that on purpose. But I think myself that what Heather Badcock said to Marina Gregg was that she had had German measles and got up from bed and went off to meet Marina. And that's really the answer to the whole thing, because, you see, German measles is extremely infectious. People catch it very easily. And there's one thing about it which you've got to remember. If a woman contracts it in the first four months of—' Miss Marple spoke the next word with a slight Victorian modesty '—of – er – pregnancy, it may have a terribly serious effect. It may cause an unborn child to be born blind or to be born mentally affected.'

She turned to Jason Rudd.

'I think I am correct in saying, Mr Rudd, that your wife had a child who was born mentally afflicted and that she has never really recovered from the shock. She has always wanted a child and when at last the child came, this was the tragedy that happened. A tragedy she has never forgotten, that she has not allowed herself to forget and which ate into her as a kind of deep sore, an obsession.'

'It's quite true,' said Jason Rudd. 'Marina developed German measles early on in her pregnancy and was told by the doctor that the mental affliction of her child was due to that cause. It was not a case of inherited insanity or anything of that kind. He was trying to be helpful but I don't think it helped her much. She never knew how, or when or from whom she had contracted the disease.'

'Quite so,' said Miss Marple, 'she never knew until one afternoon here when a perfectly strange woman came up those stairs and told her the fact – told her, what was more – with a great deal of pleasure! With an air of being proud of what she'd done! *She* thought she'd been resourceful and brave and shown a lot of spirit in getting up from her bed, covering her face with make-up, and going along to meet the actress on whom she had such a crush and obtaining her autograph. It's a thing she has boasted of all through her life. Heather Badcock meant no harm. She never did mean harm but there is no doubt that people like Heather Badcock (and like my old friend Alison Wilde), are capable of doing a lot of harm because they lack – not kindness, they have kindness – but any real consideration for the way their actions may affect other people. She thought always of what an action meant to *her*, never sparing a thought of what it might mean to somebody else.'

Miss Marple nodded her head gently.

'So she died, you see, for a simple reason out of her own past. You must imagine what that moment meant to Marina Gregg. I think Mr Rudd understands it very well. I think she had nursed all those years a kind of hatred for the unknown person who had been the cause of her tragedy. And here suddenly she meets the person face to face. And a person who is gay, jolly and pleased with herself. It was too much for her. If she had had time to think, to calm down, to be persuaded to relax – but she gave herself no time. Here was this woman who had destroyed her happiness and destroyed the sanity and health of her child. She wanted to punish her. She wanted to kill her. And unfortunately the means were to hand. She carried with her that well-known specific, Calmo. A somewhat dangerous drug because you had to be careful of the exact dosage. It was very easy to do. She put the stuff into her own glass. If by any chance anyone noticed what she was doing they were probably so used to her pepping herself up or soothing herself down in any handy liquid that they'd hardly notice it. It's possible that one person did see her, but I rather doubt it. I think that Miss Zielinsky did no more than guess. Marina Gregg put her glass down on the table and presently she managed to jog Heather Badcock's arm so that Heather Badcock spilt her drink all down her new dress. And that's where the element of puzzle has come into the matter, owing to the fact that people cannot remember to use their pronouns properly.

'It reminds me so much of that parlourmaid I was telling you about,' she added to Dermot. 'I only had the account, you see, of what Gladys Dixon said to Cherry which simply was that she was worried about the ruin of Heather Badcock's dress with the cocktail spilt down it. What seemed so funny, she said, was that she did it on purpose. But the "she" that Gladys referred to was not Heather Badcock, it was Marina Gregg. As Gladys said: She did it on purpose! She jogged Heather's arm. Not by accident but because she *meant* to do so. We do know that she must have been standing very close to Heather because we have heard that she mopped up both Heather's dress and her own before pressing her cocktail on Heather. It was really,' said Miss Marple meditatively, 'a very perfect murder; because, you see, it was committed on the spur of the moment without pausing to think or reflect. She wanted Heather Badcock dead and a few minutes later Heather Badcock *was* dead. She didn't realize, perhaps, the seriousness of what she'd done and certainly not the danger of it until afterwards. But she realized it then. She was afraid, horribly afraid. Afraid that someone had seen her dope her own glass, that someone had seen her deliberately jog Heather's elbow, afraid that someone would accuse her of having poisoned Heather. She could see only one way out. To insist that the murder had been aimed at *her*, that *she* was the prospective victim. She tried that idea first on her doctor. She refused to let him tell her husband because I think she knew that her husband would not be deceived. She did fantastic things. She wrote notes to herself and arranged to find them in extraordinary places and at extraordinary moments. She doctored her own coffee at the studios one day. She did things that could really have been seen through fairly easily if one had happened to be thinking that way. They were seen through by one person.'

She looked at Jason Rudd.

'This is only a theory of yours,' said Jason Rudd.

'You can put it that way if you like,' said Miss Marple, 'but you know quite well, don't you, Mr Rudd, that I'm speaking the truth. You know, because you knew from the first. You knew because you heard that mention of German measles. You knew and you were frantic to protect her. But you didn't realize how much you would have to protect her from. You didn't realize that it was not only a question of hushing up one death, the death of a woman whom you might say quite fairly had brought her death on herself. But there were other deaths – the death of Giuseppe, a blackmailer, it is true, but a human being. And the death of Ella Zielinsky of whom I expect you were fond. You were frantic to protect Marina and also to prevent her from doing more harm. All you wanted was to get her safely away somewhere. You tried to watch her all the time, to make sure that nothing more should happen.'

She paused, and then coming nearer to Jason Rudd, she laid a gentle hand on his arm.

'I am very sorry for you,' she said, 'very sorry. I do realize the agony you've been through. You cared for her so much, didn't you?'

Jason Rudd turned slightly away.

'That,' he said, 'is, I believe, common knowledge.'

'She was such a beautiful creature,' said Miss Marple gently. 'She had such a wonderful gift. She had a great power of love and hate but no stability. That's what's so sad for anyone, to be born with no stability. She couldn't let the past go and she could never see the future as it really was, only as she imagined it to be. She was a great actress and a beautiful and very unhappy woman. What a wonderful Mary, Queen of Scots she was! I shall never forget her.'

Sergeant Tiddler appeared suddenly on the stairs.

'Sir,' he said, 'can I speak to you a moment?'

Craddock turned.

'I'll be back,' he said to Jason Rudd, then he went towards the stairs.

'Remember,' Miss Marple called after him, 'poor Arthur Badcock had nothing to do with this. He came to the fête because he wanted to have a glimpse of the girl he had married long ago. I should say she didn't even recognise him. Did she?' she asked Jason Rudd.

Jason Rudd shook his head.

'I don't think so. She certainly never said anything to me. I don't think,' he added thoughtfully, 'she would recognise him.'

'Probably not,' said Miss Marple. 'Anyway,' she added, 'he's quite innocent of wanting to kill her or anything of that kind. Remember that,' she added to Dermot Craddock as he went down the stairs

'He's not been in any real danger, I can assure you,' said Craddock, 'but of course when we found out that he had actually been Miss Marina Gregg's first husband we naturally had to question him on the point. Don't worry about him, Aunt Jane,' he added in a low murmur, then he hurried down the stairs.

Miss Marple turned to Jason Rudd. He was standing there like a man in a daze, his eyes far away.

'Would you allow me to see her?' said Miss Marple.

He considered her for a moment or two, then he nodded.

'Yes, you can see her. You seem to – understand her very well.'

He turned and Miss Marple followed him. He preceded her into the big bedroom and drew the curtains slightly aside.

Marina Gregg lay in the great white shell of the bed – her eyes closed, her hands folded.

So, Miss Marple thought, might the Lady of Shalott have lain in the boat that carried her down to Camelot. And there, standing musing, was a man with a rugged, ugly face, who might pass as a Lancelot of a later day.

Miss Marple said gently, 'It's very fortunate for her that she – took an overdose. Death was really the only way of escape left to her. Yes – very fortunate she took that overdose – or – *was given it*?'

His eyes met hers, but he did not speak.

He said brokenly, 'She was – so lovely – and she had suffered so much.'

Miss Marple looked back again at the still figure.

She quoted softly the last lines of the poem:

> *'He said: "She has a lovely face;*
> *God in His mercy lend her grace,*
> *The Lady of Shalott." '*

734

AT
BERTRAM'S
HOTEL

In the heart of the West End, there are many quiet pockets, unknown to almost all but taxi drivers who traverse them with expert knowledge, and arrive triumphantly thereby at Park Lane, Berkeley Square or South Audley Street.

If you turn off an unpretentious street from the Park, and turn left and right once or twice, you will find yourself in a quiet street with Bertram's Hotel on the right hand side. Bertram's Hotel has been there a long time. During the war, houses were demolished on the right of it, and a little farther down on the left of it, but Bertram's itself remained unscathed. Naturally it could not escape being, as house agents would say, scratched, bruised and marked, but by the expenditure of only a reasonable amount of money it was restored to its original condition. By 1955 it looked precisely as it had looked in 1939 – dignified, unostentatious, and quietly expensive.

Such was Bertram's, patronised over a long stretch of years by the higher echelons of the clergy, dowager ladies of the aristocracy up from the country, girls on their way home for the holidays from expensive finishing schools. ('So few places where a girl can stay alone in London but of course it is *quite* all right at Bertram's. We have stayed there for *years*.')

There had, of course, been many other hotels on the model of Bertram's. Some still existed, but nearly all had felt the wind of change. They had had necessarily to modernise themselves, to cater for a different clientele. Bertram's, too, had had to change, but it had been done so cleverly that it was not at all apparent at the first casual glance.

Outside the steps that led up to the big swing doors stood what at first sight appeared to be no less than a Field-Marshal. Gold braid and medal ribbons adorned a broad and manly chest. His deportment was perfect. He received you with tender concern as you emerged with rheumatic difficulty from a taxi or a car, guided you carefully up the steps and piloted you through the silently swinging doorway.

Inside, if this was the first time you had visited Bertram's, you felt, almost with alarm, that you had re-entered a vanished

737

world. Time had gone back. You were in Edwardian England once more.

There was, of course, central heating, but it was not apparent. As there had always been, in the big central lounge, there were two magnificent coal fires; beside them big brass coal scuttles shone in the way they used to shine when Edwardian housemaids polished them, and they were filled with exactly the right sized lumps of coal. There was a general appearance of rich red velvet and plushy cosiness. The arm-chairs were not of this time and age. They were well above the level of the floor, so that rheumatic old ladies had not to struggle in an undignified manner in order to get to their feet. The seats of the chairs did not, as in so many modern high-priced arm-chairs, stop half-way between the thigh and the knee, thereby inflicting agony on those suffering from arthritis and sciatica; and they were not all of a pattern. There were straight backs and reclining backs, different widths to accommodate the slender and the obese. People of almost any dimension could find a comfortable chair at Bertram's.

Since it was now the tea hour, the lounge hall was full. Not that the lounge hall was the only place where you could have tea. There was a drawing-room (chintzy), a smoking-room, (by some hidden influence reserved for gentlemen only) where the vast chairs were of fine leather, two writing-rooms, where you could take a special friend and have a cosy little gossip in a quiet corner – and even write a letter if you wanted to. Besides these amenities of the Edwardian age, there were other retreats, not in any way publicised, but known to those who wanted them. There was a double bar, with two bar attendants, an American barman to make the Americans feel at home and to provide them with bourbon, rye, and every kind of cocktail, and an English one to deal with sherries and Pimms No. 1, and to talk knowledgeably about the runners at Ascot and Newbury to the middle-aged men who stayed at Bertram's for the more serious race meetings. There was also, tucked down a passage, in a secretive way, a television room for those who asked for it.

But the big entrance lounge was the favourite place for the afternoon tea drinking. The elderly ladies enjoyed seeing who came in and out, recognising old friends, and commenting unfavourably on how these had aged. There were also American visitors fascinated by seeing the titled English really getting down to their traditional afternoon tea. For afternoon tea was quite a feature of Bertram's.

It was nothing less than splendid. Presiding over the ritual was Henry, a large and magnificent figure, a ripe fifty, avuncular, sympathetic, and with the courtly manners of that long-vanished species: the perfect butler. Slim youths performed the actual work under Henry's austere direction. There were large crested silver trays, and Georgian silver teapots. The china, if not actually Rockingham and Davenport, looked like it. The Blind Earl services were particular favourites. The tea was the best India, Ceylon, Darjeeling, Lapsang, etc. As for eatables, you could ask for anything you liked – and get it!

On this particular day, November the 17th, Lady Selina Hazy, sixty-five, up from Leicestershire, was eating delicious well-buttered muffins with all an elderly lady's relish.

Her absorption with muffins, however, was not so great that she failed to look up sharply every time the inner pair of swing doors opened to admit a newcomer.

So it was that she smiled and nodded to welcome Colonel Luscombe – erect, soldierly, race glasses hanging round his neck. Like the old autocrat that she was, she beckoned imperiously and in a minute or two, Luscombe came over to her.

'Hallo, Selina, what brings you up to Town?'

'Dentist,' said Lady Selina, rather indistinctly, owing to muffin. 'And I thought as I *was* up, I might as well go and see that man in Harley Street about my arthritis. You know whom I mean.'

Although Harley Street contained several hundreds of fashionable practitioners for all and every ailment, Luscombe did know whom she meant.

'Do you any good?' he asked.

'I rather think he did,' said Lady Selina grudgingly. 'Extraordinary fellow. Took me by the neck when I wasn't expecting it, and wrung it like a chicken.' She moved her neck gingerly.

'Hurt you?'

'It must have done, twisting it like that, but really I hadn't time to know.' She continued to move her neck gingerly. 'Feels all right. Can look over my right shoulder for the first time in years.'

She put this to a practical test and exclaimed.

'Why I do believe that's old Jane Marple. Thought she was dead years ago. Looks a hundred.'

Colonel Luscombe threw a glance in the direction of Jane Marple thus resurrected, but without much interest: Bertram's always had a sprinkling of what he called fluffy old pussies.

Lady Selina was continuing.

'Only place in London you can still get muffins. Real muffins.
Do you know when I went to America last year they had something *called* muffins on the breakfast menu. Not real muffins at
all. Kind of teacake with raisins in them. I mean, why call
them muffins?'

She pushed in the last buttery morsel and looked round
vaguely. Henry materialised immediately. Not quickly or
hurriedly. It seemed that, just suddenly, he was there.

'Anything further I can get you, my lady? Cake of any kind?'

'Cake?' Lady Selina thought about it, was doubtful.

'We are serving very good seed cake, my lady. I can recommend it.'

'Seed cake? I haven't eaten seed cake for *years*. It is *real* seed
cake?'

'Oh yes, my lady. The cook has had the receipt for years.
You'll enjoy it, I'm sure.'

Henry gave a glance at one of his retinue, and the lad departed in search of seed cake.

'I suppose you've been at Newbury, Derek?'

'Yes. Darned cold, I didn't wait for the last two races. Disastrous day. That filly of Harry's was no good at all.'

'Didn't think she would be. What about Swanhilda?'

'Finished fourth.' Luscombe rose. 'Got to see about my room.'

He walked across the lounge to the reception desk. As he
went he noted the tables and their occupants. Astonishing
number of people having tea here. Quite like old days. Tea
as a meal had rather gone out of fashion since the war. But
evidently not at Bertram's. Who *were* all these people? Two
Canons and the Dean of Chislehampton. Yes, and another pair
of gaitered legs over in the corner, a Bishop, no less! Mere
Vicars were scarce. 'Have to be at least a Canon to afford
Bertram's,' he thought. The rank and file of the clergy certainly
couldn't, poor devils. As far as that went, he wondered how
on earth people like old Selina Hazy could. She'd only got two-
pence or so a year to bless herself with. And there was old Lady
Berry, and Mrs Posselthwaite from Somerset, and Sybil Kerr –
all poor as church mice.

Still thinking about this he arrived at the desk and was
pleasantly greeted by Miss Gorringe the receptionist. Miss Gorringe was an old friend. She knew every one of the clientele and,
like Royalty, never forgot a face. She looked frumpy but respectable. Frizzled yellowish hair (old-fashioned tongs, it suggested),

black silk dress, a high bosom on which reposed a large gold locket and a cameo brooch.

'Number fourteen,' said Miss Gorringe. 'I think you had fourteen last time, Colonel Luscombe, and liked it. It's quiet.'

'How you always manage to remember these things, I can't imagine, Miss Gorringe.'

'We like to make our old friends comfortable.'

'Takes me back a long way, coming in here. Nothing seems to have changed.'

He broke off as Mr Humfries came out from an inner sanctum to greet him.

Mr Humfries was often taken by the uninitiated to be Mr Bertram in person. Who the actual Mr Bertram was, or indeed, if there ever *had* been a Mr Bertram was now lost in the mists of antiquity. Bertram's had existed since about 1840, but nobody had taken any interest in tracing its past history. It was just there, solid, a fact. When addressed as Mr Bertram, Mr Humfries never corrected the impression. If they wanted him to be Mr Bertram he would be Mr Bertram. Colonel Luscombe knew his name, though he didn't know if Humfries was the manager or the owner. He rather fancied the latter.

Mr Humfries was a man of about fifty. He had very good manners, and the presence of a Junior Minister. He could, at any moment, be all things to all people. He could talk racing shop, cricket, foreign politics, tell anecdotes of Royalty, give Motor Show information, knew the most interesting plays on at present – advise on places Americans ought to see in England however short their stay. He had knowledgeable information about where it would suit persons of all incomes and tastes to dine. With all this, he did not make himself too cheap. He was not on tap all the time. Miss Gorringe had all the same facts at her fingertips and could retail them efficiently. At brief intervals Mr Humfries, like the sun, made his appearance above the horizon and flattered someone by his personal attention.

This time it was Colonel Luscombe who was so honoured. They exchanged a few racing platitudes, but Colonel Luscombe was absorbed by his problem. And here was the man who could give him the answer.

'Tell me, Humfries, how do all these old dears manage to come and stay here?'

'Oh, you've been wondering about that?' Mr Humfries seemed amused. 'Well, the answer's simple. They couldn't afford it. Unless—'

He paused.

'Unless you make special prices for them? Is that it?'

'More or less. They don't know, usually, that they *are* special prices, or if they do realize it, they think it's because they're old customers.'

'And it isn't just that?'

'Well, Colonel Luscombe, I *am* running a hotel. I couldn't afford actually to lose money.'

'But how can that pay you?'

'It's a question of atmosphere . . . Strangers coming to this country (Americans, in particular, because they are the ones who have the money) have their own rather queer ideas of what England is like. I'm not talking, you understand, of the rich business tycoons who are always crossing the Atlantic. They usually go to the Savoy or the Dorchester. They want modern décor, American food, all the things that will make them feel at home. But there are a lot of people who come abroad at rare intervals who expect this country to be – well, I won't go back as far as Dickens, but they've read *Cranford* and Henry James, and they don't want to find this country just the same as their own! So they go back home afterwards and say: "There's a wonderful place in London: Bertram's Hotel, it's called. It's just like stepping back a hundred years. It just *is* old England! And the people who stay there! People you'd never come across anywhere else. Wonderful old Duchesses. They serve all the old English dishes, there's a marvellous old-fashioned beafsteak pudding! You've never tasted anything like it; and great sirloins of beef and saddles of mutton, and an old-fashioned English tea and a wonderful English breakfast. And of course all the usual things as well. And it's wonderfully comfortable. *And* warm. Great log fires.' "

Mr Humfries ceased his impersonation and permitted himself something nearly approaching a grin.

'I see,' said Luscombe thoughtfully. 'These people; decayed aristocrats, impoverished members of the old County families, they are all so much *mise en scène*?'

Mr Humfries nodded agreement.

'I really wonder no one else thought of it. Of course I found Bertram's ready made, so to speak. All it needed was some rather expensive restoration. All the people who come here think it's something that they've discovered for themselves, that no one else knows about.'

'I suppose,' said Luscombe, 'that the restoration *was* quite expensive?'

'Oh yes. The place has got to *look* Edwardian, but it's got to have the modern comforts that we take for granted in these days. Our old dears – if you will forgive me referring to them as that – have got to feel that nothing has changed since the turn of the century, and our travelling clients have got to feel they can have period surroundings, and still have what they are used to having at home, and can't really live without!'

'Bit difficult sometimes?' suggested Luscombe.

'Not really. Take central heating for instance. Americans require – need, I should say – at least ten degrees Fahrenheit higher than English people do. We actually have two quite different sets of bedrooms. The English we put in one lot, the Americans in the other. The rooms all look alike, but they are full of actual differences – electric razors, and showers as well as tubs in some of the bathrooms, and if you want an American breakfast, it's there – cereals and iced orange juice and all – or if you prefer you can have the English breakfast.'

'Eggs and bacon?'

'As you say – but a good deal more than that if you want it. Kippers, kidney and bacon, cold grouse, York ham. Oxford marmalade.'

'I must remember all that tomorrow morning. Don't get that sort of thing any more at home.'

Humfries smiled.

'Most gentlemen only ask for eggs and bacon. They've – well, they've got out of the way of thinking about the things there used to be.'

'Yes, yes . . . I remember when I was a child . . . Sideboards groaning with hot dishes. Yes, it was a luxurious way of life.'

'We endeavour to give people anything they ask for.'

'Including seed cake and muffins – yes, I see. To each accord- to his need – I see . . . Quite Marxian.'

'I beg your pardon?'

'Just a thought, Humfries. Extremes meet.'

Colonel Luscombe turned away, taking the key Miss Gorringe offered him. A page-boy sprang to attention and conducted him to the lift. He saw in passing that Lady Selina Hazy was now sitting with her friend Jane Something or other.

2

'And I suppose you're still living at that dear St Mary Mead?' Lady Selina was asking. 'Such a sweet unspoilt village. I often think about it. Just the same as ever, I suppose?'

'Well, not quite.' Miss Marple reflected on certain aspects of her place of residence. The new Building Estate. The additions to the Village Hall, the altered appearance of the High Street with its up-to-date shop fronts— She sighed. 'One has to accept change, I suppose.'

'Progress,' said Lady Selina vaguely. 'Though it often seems to me that it isn't progress. All these smart plumbing fixtures they have nowadays. Every shade of colour and superb what they call "finish" – but do any of them really *pull*? Or *push*, when they're that kind. Every time you go to a friend's house, you find some kind of a notice in the Loo – "Press sharply and release," "Pull to the *left*," "Release *quickly*." But in the old days, one just pulled up a handle *any* kind of way, and cataracts of water came *at once*— There's the dear Bishop of Medmenham,' Lady Selina broke off to say, as a handsome, elderly cleric passed by. 'Practically quite blind, I believe. But such a splendid *militant* priest.'

A little clerical talk was indulged in, interspersed by Lady Selina's recognition of various friends and acquaintances, many of whom were not the people she thought they were. She and Miss Marple talked a little of 'old days', though Miss Marple's upbringing, of course, had been quite different from Lady Selina's, and their reminiscences were mainly confined to the few years when Lady Selina, a recent widow of severely straitened means, had taken a small house in the village of St Mary Mead during the time her second son had been stationed at an airfield near-by.

'Do you always stay here when you come up, Jane? Odd I haven't seen you here before.'

'Oh no, indeed. I couldn't afford to, and anyway, I hardly ever leave home these days. No, it was a very kind niece of mine who thought it would be a treat for me to have a short visit to London. Joan is a very kind girl – at least perhaps hardly a girl.' Miss Marple reflected with a qualm that Joan must now be close on fifty. 'She is a painter, you know. Quite a well-known painter. Joan West. She had an exhibition not long ago.'

Lady Selina had little interest in painters, or indeed in any-thing artistic. She regarded writers, artists and musicians as a species of clever performing animals; she was prepared to feel indulgent towards them, but to wonder privately why they wanted to do what they did.

'This modern stuff, I suppose,' she said, her eyes wandering. 'There's Cicely Longhurst – dyed her hair again, I see.'

'I'm afraid dear Joan *is* rather modern.'

Here Miss Marple was quite wrong. Joan West had been modern about twenty years ago, but was now regarded by the young *arriviste* artists as completely old-fashioned.

Casting a brief glance at Cicely Longhurst's hair, Miss Marple relapsed into a pleasant remembrance of how kind Joan had been. Joan had actually said to her husband, 'I wish we could do something for poor old Aunt Jane. She never gets away from home. Do you think she'd like to go to Bournemouth for a week or two?'

'Good idea,' said Raymond West. His last book was doing very well indeed, and he felt in a generous mood.

'She enjoyed her trip to the West Indies, I think, though it was a pity she had to get mixed up in a murder case. Quite the wrong thing at her age.'

'That sort of thing seems to happen to her.'

Raymond was very fond of his old aunt and was constantly devising treats for her, and sending her books that he thought might interest her. He was surprised when she often politely declined the treats, and though she always said the books were 'so interesting' he sometimes suspected that she had not read them. But then, of course, her eyes were failing.

In this last he was wrong. Miss Marple had remarkable eye-sight for her age, and was at this moment taking in everything that was going on round her with keen interest and pleasure.

To Joan's proffer of a week or two at one of Bournemouth's best hotels, she had hesitated, murmured, 'It's very, very kind of you, my dear, but I really don't think—'

'But it's *good* for you, Aunt Jane. Good to get away from home sometimes. It gives you new ideas, and new things to think about.'

'Oh yes, you are quite right there, and I *would* like a little visit somewhere for a change. Not, perhaps, Bournemouth.'

Joan was slightly surprised. She had thought Bournemouth would have been Aunt Jane's Mecca.

'Eastbourne? Or Torquay?'

'What I would really like—' Miss Marple hesitated.

'Yes?'

'I dare say you will think it rather silly of me.'

'No, I'm sure I shan't.' (Where *did* the old dear want to go?)

'I would really like to go to Bertram's Hotel – in London.'

'Bertram's Hotel?' The name was vaguely familiar.

Words came from Miss Marple in a rush.

'I stayed there once – when I was fourteen. With my uncle and aunt, Uncle Thomas, that was, he was Canon of Ely. And I've never forgotten it. If I could stay there – a week would be quite enough – two weeks might be too expensive.'

'Oh, that's all right. Of course you shall go. I ought to have thought that you might want to go to London – the shops and everything. We'll fix it up – if Bertram's Hotel still exists. So many hotels have vanished, sometimes bombed in the war and sometimes just given up.'

'No, I happen to know Bertram's Hotel is still going. I had a letter from there – from my American friend Amy McAllister of Boston. She and her husband were staying there.'

'Good, then I'll go ahead and fix it up.' She added gently, 'I'm afraid you may find it's changed a good deal from the days when you knew it. So don't be disappointed.'

But Bertram's Hotel had not changed. It was just as it had always been. Quite miraculously so, in Miss Marple's opinion. In fact, she wondered . . .

It really seemed too good to be true. She knew quite well with her usual clear-eyed common sense, that what she wanted was simply to refurbish her memories of the past in their old original colours. Much of her life had, perforce, to be spent recalling past pleasures. If you could find someone to remember them with, that was indeed happiness. Nowadays that was not easy to do; she had outlived most of her contemporaries. But she still sat and remembered. In a queer way, it made her come to life again – Jane Marple, that pink and white eager young girl . . . Such a silly girl in many ways . . . now who was that very unsuitable young man whose name – oh dear, she couldn't even remember it now! How wise her mother had been to nip that friendship so firmly in the bud. She had come across him years later – and really he was quite dreadful! At the time she had cried herself to sleep for at least a week!

Nowadays, of course – she considered nowadays . . . These poor young things. Some of them had mothers, but never mothers who seemed to be any good – mothers who were quite incapable of protecting their daughters from silly affairs, illegitimate babies, and early and unfortunate marriages. It was all very sad.

Her friend's voice interrupted these meditations.

'Well, I never. Is it – yes, it is – Bess Sedgwick over there! Of all the unlikely places—'

Miss Marple had been listening with only half an ear to Lady Selina's comments on her surroundings. She and Miss Marple moved in entirely different circles, so that Miss Marple had been unable to exchange scandalous titbits about the various friends or acquaintances that Lady Selina recognised or thought she recognised.

But Bess Sedgwick was different. Bess Sedgwick was a name that almost everyone in England knew. For over thirty years now, Bess Sedgwick had been reported by the Press as doing this or that outrageous or extraordinary thing. For a good part of the war she had been a member of the French Resistance, and was said to have six notches on her gun representing dead Germans. She had flown solo across the Atlantic years ago, had ridden on horseback across Europe and fetched up at Lake Van. She had driven racing cars, had once saved two children from a burning house, had several marriages to her credit and dis-credit and was said to be the second best-dressed woman in Europe. It was also said that she had successfully smuggled her-self on board a nuclear submarine on its test voyage.

It was therefore with the most intense interest that Miss Marple sat up and indulged in a frankly avid stare.

Whatever she had expected of Bertram's Hotel, it was not to find Bess Sedgwick there. An expensive night club, or a lorry drivers' pull up – either of those would be quite in keeping with Bess Sedgwick's range of interests. But this highly respectable and old world hostelry seemed strangely alien.

Still there she was – no doubt of it. Hardly a month passed without Bess Sedgwick's face appearing in the fashion maga-zines or the popular Press. Here she was in the flesh, smoking a cigarette in a quite impatient manner and looking in a sur-prised way at the large tea tray in front of her as though she had never seen one before. She had ordered – Miss Marple screwed up her eyes and peered – it was rather far away – yes, *doughnuts*. Very interesting.

As she watched, Bess Sedgwick stubbed out her cigarette in her saucer, lifted a doughnut and took an immense bite. Rich red real strawberry jam gushed out over her chin. Bess threw back her head and laughed, one of the loudest and gayest sounds to have been heard in the lounge of Bertram's Hotel for some time.

Henry was immediately beside her, a small delicate napkin proffered. She took it, scrubbed her chin with the vigour of a schoolboy, exclaiming: 'That's what I call a *real* doughnut. Gorgeous.'

She dropped the napkin on the tray and stood up. As usual every eye was on her. She was used to that. Perhaps she liked it, perhaps she no longer noticed it. She was worth looking at – a striking woman rather than a beautiful one. The palest of platinum hair fell sleek and smooth to her shoulders. The bones of her head and face were exquisite. Her nose was faintly aquiline, her eyes deep set and a real grey in colour. She had the wide mouth of a natural comedian. Her dress was of such simplicity that it puzzled most men. It looked like the coarsest kind of sacking, had no ornamentation of any kind, and no apparent fastening or seams. But women knew better. Even the provincial old dears in Bertram's knew, quite certainly, that it had cost the earth!

Striding across the lounge towards the lift, she passed quite close to Lady Selina and Miss Marple, and she nodded to the former.

'Hallo, Lady Selina. Haven't seen you since Crufts. How are the Borzois?'

'What on earth are you doing here, Bess?'

'Just staying here. I've just driven up from Land's End. Four hours and three quarters. Not bad.'

'You'll kill yourself one of these days. Or someone else.'

'Oh I hope not.'

'But why are you staying *here*?'

Bess Sedgwick threw a swift glance round. She seemed to see the point and acknowledged it with an ironic smile.

'Someone told me I ought to try it. I think they're right. I've just had the most marvellous doughnut.'

'My dear, they have *real* muffins too.'

'Muffins,' said Lady Sedgwick thoughtfully. 'Yes . . . She seemed to concede the point. 'Muffins!'

She nodded and went on towards the lift.

'Extraordinary girl,' said Lady Selina. To her, like to Miss Marple, every woman under sixty was a girl. 'Known her ever since she was a child. Nobody could do anything with her. Ran away with an Irish groom when she was sixteen. They managed to get her back in time – or perhaps not in time. Anyway they bought him off and got her safely married to old Coniston – thirty years older than she was, awful old rip, quite dotty about her. *That* didn't last long. She went off with Johnnie Sedgwick. That *might* have stuck if he hadn't broken his neck steeple-chasing. After that she married Ridgway Becker, an American yacht owner. He divorced her three years ago and I hear she's taken up with some Racing Motor Driver – a Pole or something. I don't know whether she's actually married him or not. After the American divorce she went back to calling herself Sedgwick. She goes about with *the* most extraordinary people. They *say* she takes drugs. . . . I don't know, I'm sure.'

'One wonders if she is happy,' said Miss Marple.

Lady Selina, who had clearly never wondered anything of the kind, looked rather startled.

'She's got packets of money, I suppose,' she said doubtfully. 'Alimony and all that. Of course that isn't everything . . .'

'No, indeed.'

'And she's usually got a man – or several men – in tow.'

'Yes?'

'Of course when some women get to that age, that's all they want . . . But somehow—'

She paused.

'No,' said Miss Marple. '*I* don't think so either.'

There were people who would have smiled in gentle derision at this pronouncement on the part of an old-fashioned old lady who could hardly be expected to be an authority on nympho-mania, and indeed it was not a word that Miss Marple would have used – her own phrase would have been 'always too fond of men.' But Lady Selina accepted her opinion as a confirmation of her own.

'There have been a lot of men in her life,' she pointed out.

'Oh yes, but I should say, wouldn't you, that men were an adventure to her, not a need?'

And would any woman, Miss Marple wondered, come to Bertram's Hotel for an assignation with a man? Bertram's was very definitely not that sort of place. But possibly that could be, to someone of Bess Sedgwick's disposition, the very reason for choosing it.

She sighed, looked up at the handsome grandfather clock decorously ticking in the corner, and rose with the careful effort of the rheumatic to her feet. She walked slowly towards the lift. Lady Selina cast a glance around her and pounced upon an elderly gentleman of military appearance who was reading the *Spectator*.

'How nice to see you again. Er – it is General Arlington, isn't it?'

But with great courtesy the old gentleman declined being General Arlington. Lady Selina apologized, but was not unduly discomposed. She combined short sight with optimism and since the thing she enjoyed most was meeting old friends and acquaintances, she was always making this kind of mistake. Many other people did the same, since the lights were pleasantly dim and heavily shaded. But nobody ever took offence – usually indeed it seemed to give them pleasure.

Miss Marple smiled to herself as she waited for the lift to come down. So like Selina! Always convinced that she knew everybody. She herself could not compete. Her solitary achievement in that line had been the handsome and well-gaitered Bishop of Westchester whom she had addressed affectionately as 'dear Robbie' and who had responded with equal affection and with memories of himself as a child in a Hampshire village calling out lustily 'Be a crocodile now, Aunty Jane. Be a crocodile and eat me.'

The lift came down, the uniformed middle-aged man threw open the door. Rather to Miss Marple's surprise the alighting passenger was Bess Sedgwick whom she had seen go up only a minute or two before.

And then, one foot poised, Bess Sedgwick stopped dead, with a suddenness that surprised Miss Marple and made her own forward step falter. Bess Sedgwick was staring over Miss Marple's shoulder with such concentration that the old lady turned her own head.

The commissionaire had just pushed open the two swing doors of the entrance and was holding them to let two women pass through into the lounge. One of them was a fussy looking middle-aged lady wearing a rather unfortunate flowered violet hat, the other was a tall, simply but smartly dressed, girl of perhaps seventeen or eighteen with long straight flaxen hair.

Bess Sedgwick pulled herself together, wheeled round abruptly and re-entered the lift. As Miss Marple followed her in, she turned to her and apologized.

'I'm so sorry. I nearly ran into you.' She had a warm, friendly voice. 'I just remembered I'd forgotten something – which sounds nonsense but isn't really.'

'Second floor?' said the operator. Miss Marple smiled and

nodded in acknowledgement of the apology, got out and walked slowly along to her room, pleasurably turning over sundry little unimportant problems in her mind as was so often her custom.

For instance what Lady Sedgwick had said wasn't true. She had only just gone up to her room, and it must have been then that she 'remembered she had forgotten something' (if there had been any truth in that statement at all) and had come down to find it. Or had she perhaps come down to meet someone or look for someone? But if so, what she had seen as the lift door opened had startled and upset her, and she had immediately swung round into the lift again and gone up so as *not* to meet whoever it was she had seen.

It must have been the two newcomers. The middle-aged woman and the girl. Mother and daughter? No, Miss Marple thought, *not* mother and daughter.

Even at Bertram's, thought Miss Marple, happily, interesting things could happen ...

3

'Er – is Colonel Luscombe—?'

The woman in the violet hat was at the desk. Miss Gorringe smiled in a welcoming manner and a page, who had been standing at the ready, was immediately dispatched but had no need to fulfil his errand, as Colonel Luscombe himself entered the lounge at that moment and came quickly across to the desk.

'How do you do, Mrs Carpenter.' He shook hands politely, then turned to the girl. 'My dear Elvira.' He took both her hands affectionately in his. 'Well, well, this *is* nice. Splendid – splendid. Come and let's sit down.' He led them to chairs, established them. 'Well, well,' he repeated, 'this is nice.'

The effort he made was somewhat palpable as was his lack of ease. He could hardly go on saying how nice this was. The two ladies were not very helpful. Elvira smiled very sweetly. Mrs Carpenter gave a meaningless little laugh, and smoothed her gloves.

'A good journey, eh?'

'Yes, thank you,' said Elvira.

'No fog. Nothing like that?'

'Oh no.'

'Our flight was five minutes ahead of time,' said Mrs Carpenter.

'Yes, yes. Good, very good.' He took a pull upon himself. 'I hope this place will be all right for you?'

'Oh, I'm sure it's *very* nice,' said Mrs Carpenter warmly, glancing round her. 'Very comfortable.'

'Rather old-fashioned, I'm afraid,' said the Colonel apologetically. 'Rather a lot of old fogies. No – er –dancing, anything like that.'

'No. I suppose not,' agreed Elvira.

She glanced round in an expressionless manner. It certainly seemed impossible to connect Bertram's with dancing.

'Lot of old fogies here, I'm afraid,' said Colonel Luscombe, repeating himself. 'Ought, perhaps, to have taken you somewhere more modern. Not very well up in these things, you see.'

'This is very nice,' said Elvira politely.

'It's only for a couple of nights,' went on Colonel Luscombe. 'I thought we'd go to a show this evening. A musical—' he said the word rather doubtfully, as though not sure he was using the right term. *'Let Down Your Hair Girls.* I hope that will be all right?'

'How delightful,' exclaimed Mrs Carpenter. 'That will be a treat, won't it, Elvira?'

'Lovely,' said Elvira, tonelessly.

'And then supper afterwards? At the Savoy?'

Fresh exclamations from Mrs Carpenter. Colonel Luscombe, stealing a glance at Elvira, cheered up a little. He thought that Elvira was pleased, though quite determined to express nothing more than polite approval in front of Mrs Carpenter. 'And I don't blame her,' he said to himself.

He said to Mrs Carpenter,

'Perhaps you'd like to see your rooms – see they're all right and all that—'

'Oh, I'm sure they will be.'

'Well, if there's anything you don't like about them, we'll make them change it. They know me here very well.'

Miss Gorringe, in charge at the desk, was pleasantly welcoming. Nos. 28 and 29 on the second floor with an adjoining bathroom.

'I'll go up and get things unpacked,' said Mrs Carpenter. 'Perhaps, Elvira, you and Colonel Luscombe would like to have a little gossip.'

Tact, thought Colonel Luscombe. A bit obvious, perhaps, but

anyway it would get rid of her for a bit. Though what he was going to gossip about to Elvira, he really didn't know. A very nice-mannered girl, but he wasn't used to girls. His wife had died in childbirth and the baby, a boy, had been brought up by his wife's family whilst an elder sister had come to keep house for him. His son had married and gone to live in Kenya, and his grandchildren were eleven, five and two and a half and had been entertained on their last visit by football and space science talk, electric trains, and a ride on his foot. Easy! But young girls!

He asked Elvira if she would like a drink. He was about to propose a bitter lemon, ginger ale, or orangeade, but Elvira forestalled him.

'Thank you. I should like a gin and vermouth.'

Colonel Luscombe looked at her rather doubtfully. He supposed girls of – what was she? – sixteen? Seventeen? – did drink gin and vermouth. But he reassured himself that Elvira knew, so to speak, correct Greenwich social time. He ordered a gin and vermouth and a dry sherry.

He cleared his throat and asked:]

'How was Italy?'

'Very nice, thank you.'

'And that place you were at, the Contessa what's-her-name? Not too grim?'

'She is rather strict. But I didn't let that worry me.'

He looked at her, not quite sure whether the reply was not slightly ambiguous.

He said, stammering a little, but with a more natural manner than he had been able to manage before:

'I'm afraid we don't know each other as well as we ought to, seeing I'm your guardian as well as your grandfather. Difficult for me, you know – difficult for a man who's an old buffer like me – to know what a girl wants – at least – I mean to know what a girl ought to have. Schools and then after schools – what they used to call finishing in my day. But now, I suppose it's all more serious. Careers eh? Jobs? All that? We'll have to have a talk about all that sometime. Anything in particular you want to do?'

'I suppose I shall take a secretarial course,' said Elvira without enthusiasm.

'Oh. You want to be a secretary?'

'Not particularly.'

'Oh – well, then—'

'It's just what you start with,' Elvira explained.

Colonel Luscombe had an odd feeling of being relegated to his place.

'These cousins of mine, the Melfords. You think you'll like living with them? If not—'

'Oh I think so. I like Nancy quite well. And Cousin Mildred is rather a dear.'

'That's all right then?'

'Quite, for the present.'

Luscombe did not know what to say to that. Whilst he was considering what next to say, Elvira spoke. Her words were simple and direct.

'Have I any money?'

Again he took his time before answering, studying her thoughtfully. Then he said:

'Yes. You've got quite a lot of money. That is to say, you will have when you are twenty-one.'

'Who has got it now?'

He smiled. 'It's held in trust for you; a certain amount is deducted each year from the income to pay for your maintenance and education.'

'And you are the trustee?'

'One of them. There are three.'

'What happens if I die?'

'Come, come, Elvira, you're not going to die. What nonsense!'

'I hope not – but one never knows, does one? An airliner crashed only last week and everyone was killed.'

'Well, it's not going to happen to you,' said Luscombe firmly.

'You can't really know that,' said Elvira. 'I was just wondering who would get my money if I died?'

'I haven't the least idea,' said the Colonel irritably. 'Why do you ask?'

'It might be interesting,' said Elvira thoughtfully. 'I wondered if it would be worth anyone's while to kill me.'

'Really, Elvira! This is a most unprofitable conversation. I can't understand why your mind dwells on such things.'

'Oh, just ideas. One wants to know what the facts really are.'

'You're not thinking of the *Mafia* – or something like that?'

'Oh no. That would be silly. Who would get my money if I was married?'

'Your husband, I suppose. But really—'

'Are you sure of that?'

'No, I'm not in the least sure. It depends on the wording of the Trust. But you're not married, so why worry?'

Elvira did not reply. She seemed lost in thought. Finally she came out of her trance and asked:

'Do you ever see my mother?'

'Sometimes. Not very often.'

'Where is she now?'

'Oh – abroad.'

'Where abroad?'

'France – Portugal. I don't really know.'

'Does she ever want to see me?'

Her limpid gaze met his. He didn't know what to reply. Was this a moment for truth? Or for vagueness? Or for a good thumping lie? What could you say to a girl who asked a question of such simplicity, when the answer was of great complexity? He said unhappily,

'I don't know.'

Her eyes searched him gravely. Luscombe felt thoroughly ill at ease. He was making a mess of this. The girl must wonder – clearly was wondering. Any girl would.

He said, 'You mustn't think – I mean it's difficult to explain. Your mother is, well, rather different from—' Elvira was nodding energetically.

'I know. I'm always reading about her in the papers. She's something rather special, isn't she? In fact, she's rather a wonderful person.'

'Yes,' agreed the Colonel. 'That's exactly right. She's a wonderful person.' He paused and then went on. 'But a wonderful person is very often—' He stopped and started again – it's not always a happy thing to have a wonderful person for a mother. You can take that from me because it's the truth.'

'You don't like speaking the truth very much, do you? But I think what you've just said *is* the truth.'

They both sat staring towards the big brass-bound swing doors that led to the world outside.

Suddenly the doors were pushed open with violence – a violence quite unusual in Bertram's Hotel – and a young man strode in and went straight across to the desk. He wore a black leather jacket. His vitality was such that Bertram's Hotel took on the atmosphere of a museum by way of contrast. The people were the dust encrusted relics of a past age. He bent towards Miss Gorringe and asked,

'Is Lady Sedgwick staying here?'

755

Miss Gorringe on this occasion had no welcoming smile. Her eyes were flinty. She said,

'Yes.' Then, with definite unwillingness, she stretched out her hand towards the telephone. 'Do you want to—?'

'No,' said the young man. 'I just wanted to leave a note for her.'

He produced it from a pocket of his leather coat and slid it across the mahogany counter.

'I only wanted to be sure this was the right hotel.'

There might have been some slight incredulity in his voice as he looked round him, then turned back towards the entrance. His eyes passed indifferently over the people sitting round him. They passed over Luscombe and Elvira in the same way, and Luscombe felt a sudden unsuspected anger. 'Dammit all,' he thought to himself, 'Elvira's a pretty girl. When I was a young chap I'd have noticed a pretty girl, especially among all these fossils.' But the young man seemed to have no interested eyes to spare for pretty girls. He turned back to the desk and asked, raising his voice slightly as though to call Miss Gorringe's attention,

'What's the telephone number here? 1129 isn't it?'

'No,' said Miss Gorringe, '3925.'

'Regent?'

'No. Mayfair.'

He nodded. Then swiftly he strode across to the door and passed out, swinging the doors to behind him with something of the same explosive quality he had shown on entering.

Everybody seemed to draw a deep breath; to find difficulty in resuming their interrupted conversations.

'Well,' said Colonel Luscombe, rather inadequately, as if at a loss for words. 'Well, really! These young fellows nowadays...'

Elvira was smiling.

'You recognised him, didn't you?' she said. 'You know who he is?' She spoke in a slightly awed voice. She proceeded to enlighten him. 'Ladislaus Malinowski.'

'Oh, that chap.' The name was indeed faintly familiar to Colonel Luscombe. 'Racing driver.'

'Yes. He was world champion two years running. He had a bad crash a year ago. Broke lots of things. But I believe he's driving again now.' She raised her head to listen. 'That's a racing car he's driving now.'

The roar of the engine had penetrated through to Bertram's

Hotel from the street outside. Colonel Luscombe perceived that Ladislaus Malinowski was one of Elvira's heroes. 'Well,' he thought to himself, 'better that than one of those pop singers or crooners or long-haired Beatles or whatever they call themselves.' Luscombe was old-fashioned in his views of young men.

The swing doors opened again. Both Elvira and Colonel Luscombe looked at them expectantly but Bertram's Hotel had reverted to normal. It was merely a white-haired elderly cleric who came in. He stood for a moment looking round him with a slightly puzzled air as of one who fails to understand where he was or how he had come there. Such an experience was no novelty to Canon Pennyfather. It came to him in trains when he did not remember where he had come from, where he was going, or why! It came to him when he was walking along the street, it came to him when he found himself sitting on a committee. It had come to him before now when he was in his cathedral stall, and did not know whether he had already preached his sermon or was about to do so.

'I believe I know that old boy,' said Luscombe, peering at him. 'Who is he now? Stays here fairly often, I believe. Abercrombie? Archdeacon Abercrombie – no, it's not Abercrombie, though he's rather like Abercrombie.'

Elvira glanced round at Canon Pennyfather without interest. Compared with a racing driver he had no appeal at all. She was not interested in ecclesiastics of any kind although, since being in Italy, she admitted to a mild admiration for Cardinals whom she considered as at any rate properly picturesque.

Canon Pennyfather's face cleared and he nodded his head appreciatively. He had recognised where he was. In Bertram's Hotel, of course; where he was going to spend the night on his way to – now where was he on his way to? Chadminster? No, no, he had just *come* from Chadminster. He was going to – of course – to the Congress at Lucerne. He stepped forward, beaming, to the reception desk and was greeted warmly by Miss Gorringe.

'So glad to see you, Canon Pennyfather. How well you are looking.'

'Thank you – thank you – I had a severe cold last week but I've got over it now. You have a room for me. I *did* write?'

Miss Gorringe reassured him.

'Oh yes, Canon Pennyfather, we got your letter. We've reserved No. 19 for you, the room you had last time.'

'Thank you – thank you. For – let me see – I shall want it

for four days. Actually I am going to Lucerne and shall be away for one night, but please keep the room. I shall leave most of my things here and only take a small bag to Switzerland. There won't be any difficulty over that?'

Again Miss Gorringe reassured him.

'Everything's going to be quite all right. You explained very clearly in your letter.'

Other people might not have used the word 'clearly'. 'Fully' would have been better, since he had certainly written at length.

All anxieties set at rest, Canon Pennyfather breathed a sigh of relief and was conveyed, together with his baggage, to Room 19.

In Room 28 Mrs Carpenter had removed her crown of violets from her head and was carefully adjusting her nightdress on the pillow of her bed. She looked up as Elvira entered.

'Ah, there you are, my dear. Would you like me to help you with your unpacking?'

'No, thank you,' said Elvira politely. 'I shan't unpack very much, you know.'

'Which of the bedrooms would you like to have? The bathroom is between them. I told them to put your luggage in the far one. I thought this room might be a little noisy.'

'That was very kind of you,' said Elvira in her expressionless voice.

'You're sure you wouldn't like me to help you?'

'No, thanks, really I wouldn't. I think I might perhaps have a bath.'

'Yes, I think that's a very good idea. Would you like to have the first bath? I'd rather finish putting my things away.'

Elvira nodded. She went into the adjoining bathroom, shut the door behind her and pushed the bolts across. She went into her own room, opened her suitcase and flung a few things on the bed. Then she undressed, put on a dressing-gown, went into the bathroom and turned the taps on. She went back into her own room and sat down on the bed by the telephone. She listened a moment or two in case of interruptions, then lifted the receier.

'This is Room 29. Can you give me Regent 1129 please?'

—— 4 ——

Within the confines of Scotland Yard a conference was in progress. It was by way of being an informal conference. Six or seven men were sitting easily around a table and each of those six men was a man of some importance in his own line. The subject that occupied the attention of these guardians of the law was a subject that had grown terrifically in importance during the last two or three years. It concerned a branch of crime whose success had been overwhelmingly disquieting. Robbery on a big scale was increasing. Bank hold-ups, snatches of payrolls, thefts of consignments of jewels sent through the mail, train robberies. Hardly a month passed but some daring and stupendous coup was attempted and brought off successfully.

Sir Ronald Graves, Assistant Commissioner of Scotland Yard, was presiding at the head of the table. According to his usual custom he did more listening than talking. No formal reports were being presented on this occasion. All that belonged to the ordinary routine of CID work. This was a high level consultation, a general pooling of ideas between men looking at affairs from slightly different points of view. Sir Ronald Graves's eyes went slowly round his little group, then he nodded to a man at the end of the table.

'Well, Father,' he said, 'let's hear a few homely wisecracks from you.'

The man addressed as 'Father' was Chief-Inspector Fred Davy. His retirement lay not long ahead and he appeared to be even more elderly than he was. Hence his nickname of 'Father'. He had a comfortable spreading presence, and such a benign and kindly manner that many criminals had been disagreeably surprised to find him a less genial and gullible man that he had seemed to be.

'Yes, Father, let's hear your views,' said another Chief-Inspector.

'It's big,' said Chief-Inspector Davy with a deep sigh. 'Yes, it's big. Maybe its growing.'

'When you say big, do you mean numerically?'

'Yes, I do.'

Another man, Comstock, with a sharp, foxy face and alert eyes, broke in to say,

'Would you say that was an advantage to them?'

'Yes and no,' said Father. 'It *could* be a disaster. But so far, devil take it, they've got it well under control.'

Superintendent Andrews, a fair, slight, dreamy-looking man, said thoughtfully,

'I've always thought there's a lot more to size than people realize. Take a little one-man business. If that's well run and if it's the right size, it's a sure and certain winner. Branch out, make it bigger, increase personnel, and perhaps you'll get it suddenly to the *wrong* size and down the hill it goes. The same way with a great big chain of stores. An empire in industry. If that's *big* enough it will succeed. If it's *not* big enough it just won't manage it. Everything has got its right size. When it is its right size and well run it's the tops.'

'How big do you think this show is?' Sir Ronald barked.

'Bigger than we thought at first,' said Comstock.

A tough looking man, Inspector McNeill, said,

'It's growing, I'd say. Father's right. Growing all the time.'

'That may be a good thing,' said Davy. 'It may grow a bit *too* fast, and then it'll get out of hand.'

'The question is, Sir Ronald,' said McNeill, 'who we pull in and when?'

'There's a round a dozen or so we could pull in,' said Comstock. 'The Harris lot are mixed up in it, we know that. There's a nice little pocket down Luton way. There's a garage at Epsom, there's a pub near Maidenhead, and there's a farm on the Great North Road.'

'Any of them worth pulling in?'

'I don't think so. Small fry all of them. Links. Just links here and there in the chain. A spot where cars are converted, and turned over quickly; a respectable pub where messages get passed; a second-hand clothes shop where appearance can be altered, a theatrical costumier in the East End, also very useful. They're paid, these people. Quite well paid but they don't really *know* anything!'

The dreamy Superintendent Andrews said again,

'We're up against some good brains. We haven't got near them yet. We know some of their affiliations and that's all. As I say, the Harris crowd are in it and Marks is in on the financial end. The foreign contacts are in touch with Weber but he's only an agent. We've nothing actually *on* any of these people. We know that they all have ways of maintaining contact with each other, and with the different branches of the concern, but we don't know exactly how they do it. We watch them and follow them, and they know we're watching them. *Somewhere* there's a great central exchange. What we want to get at is the planners.'

Comstock said,

'It's like a giant network. I agree that there must be an operational headquarters somewhere. A place where each operation is planned and detailed and dovetailed completely. Somewhere, someone plots it all, and produces a working blueprint of Operation Mailbag or Operation Payroll. Those are the people we're out to get.'

'Possibly they are not even in this country,' said Father quietly.

'No, I dare say that's true. Perhaps they're in an igloo somewhere, or in a tent in Morocco or in a chalet in Switzerland.'

'I don't believe in these master-minds,' said McNeill, shaking his head, 'they sound all right in a story. There's got to *be* a head, of course, but I don't believe in a Master Criminal. I'd say there was a very clever little Board of Directors behind this. Centrally planned, with a Chairman. They've got on to something good, and they're improving their technique all the time. All the same—'

'Yes?' said Sir Ronald encouragingly.

'Even in a right tight little team, there are probably expendables. What I call the Russian Sledge principle. From time to time, if they think we might be getting hot on the scent, they throw off one of them, the one they think they can best afford.'

'Would they dare to do that? Wouldn't it be rather risky?'

'I dare say it could be done in such a way that whoever it was wouldn't even know he *had* been pushed off the sledge. He'd just think he'd fallen off. He'd keep quiet because he'd think it was worth his while to keep quiet. So it would be, of course. They've got plenty of money to play with, and they can afford to be generous. Family looked after, if he's got one, whilst he's in prison. Possibly an escape engineered.'

'There's been too much of that,' said Comstock.

'I think, you know,' said Sir Ronald, 'that it's not much good going over and over our speculations again. We always say much the same thing.'

McNeill laughed.

'What is it you really wanted us for, sir?'

'Well—' Sir Ronald thought a moment, 'we're all agreed on the main things,' he said slowly. 'We're agreed on our main policy, on what we're trying to do. I think it *might* be profitable to have a look around for some of the small things, the things that don't matter much, that are just a bit out of the usual run. It's hard to explain what I mean, but like that business some years ago in the Culver case. An ink stain. Do you remember? An ink stain round a mouse-hole. Now why on earth should a man empty a bottle of ink into a mouse-hole? It didn't seem important. It was hard to get at the answer. But when we did hit on the answer, it led somewhere. That's – roughly – the sort of thing I was thinking about. Odd things. Don't mind saying if you come across something that strikes you as a bit out of the usual. Petty if you like, but irritating, because it doesn't quite fit in. I see Father's nodding his head.'

'Couldn't agree with you more,' said Chief-Inspector Davy. 'Come on, boys, try to come up with something. Even if it's only a man wearing a funny hat.'

There was no immediate response. Everyone looked a little uncertain and doubtful.

'Come on,' said Father. 'I'll stick my neck out first. It's just a funny story, really, but you might as well have it for what it's worth. The London and Metropolitan Bank hold-up. Carmolly Street Branch. Remember it? A whole list of car numbers and car colours and makes. We appealed to people to come forward and they responded – how they responded! About a hundred and fifty pieces of misleading information! Got it sorted out in the end to about seven cars that had been seen in the neighbourhood, any one of which *might* have been concerned in the robbery.'

'Yes,' said Sir Ronald, 'go on.'

'There were one or two we couldn't get tags on. Looked as though the numbers might have been changed. Nothing out of the way in that. It's often done. Most of them got tracked down in the end. I'll just bring up one instance. Morris Oxford, black saloon, number CMG 256, reported by a probation officer. He said it was being driven by Mr Justice Ludgrove.'

He looked round. They were listening to him, but without any manifest interest.

'I know,' he said, 'wrong as usual. Mr Justice Ludgrove is a rather noticeable old boy, ugly as sin for one thing. Well, it wasn't Mr Justice Ludgrove because at that exact time he was actually in Court. He *has* got a Morris Oxford, but its number isn't CMG 256.' He looked round. 'All right. All right. So there's no point in it, you'll say. But do you know what the number *was*? CMG 265. Near enough, eh? Just the sort of mistake one does make when you're trying to remember a car number.'

'I'm sorry,' said Sir Ronald, 'I don't quite see—'

'No,' said Chief-Inspector Davy, 'there's nothing *to* see really, is there? Only – it was very like the actual car number, wasn't it? 265 – 256 CMG. Really rather a coincidence that there should be a Morris Oxford car of the right colour with the number just one digit wrong, and with a man in it closely resembling the owner of the car.'

'Do you mean—?'

'Just one little digit difference. Today's "deliberate mistake." It almost seems like that.'

'Sorry, Davy. I still don't get it.'

'Oh, I don't suppose there's anything *to* get. There's a Morris Oxford car, CMG 265, proceeding along the street two and a half minutes after the bank snatch. In it, the probation officer recognises Mr Justice Ludgrove.'

'Are you suggesting it really *was* Mr Justice Ludgrove? Come now, Davy.'

'No, I'm not suggesting that it was Mr Justice Ludgrove and that he was mixed up in a bank robbery. He was staying at Bertram's Hotel in Pond Street, and he was at the Law Courts at that exact time. All proved up to the hilt. I'm saying the car number and make and the identification by a probation officer who knows old Ludgrove quite well by sight is the kind of coincidence that *ought* to mean something. Apparently it doesn't. Too bad.'

Comstock stirred uneasily.

'There was another case a bit like that in connection with the Jewellery business at Brighton. Some old Admiral or other. I've forgotten his name now. Some woman identified him most positively as having been on the scene.'

'And he wasn't?'

'No, he'd been in London that night. Went up for some naval dinner or other, I think.'

'Staying at his club?'

'No, he was staying at a hotel – I believe it was that one you mentioned just now, Father, Bertram's, isn't it? Quiet place. A lot of old service geezers go there, I believe.'

'Bertram's Hotel,' said Chief-Inspector Davy, thoughtfully.

Miss Marple awoke early because she always woke early. She was appreciative of her bed. Most comfortable.

She pattered across to the window and pulled the curtains, admitting a little pallid London daylight. As yet, however, she did not try to dispense with the electric light. A very nice bedroom they had given her, again quite in the tradition of Bertram's. A rose-flowered wallpaper, a large well-polished mahogany chest of drawers – a dressing-table to correspond. Two upright chairs, one easy chair of a reasonable height from the ground. A connecting door led to a bathroom which was modern but which had a tiled wallpaper of roses and so avoided any suggestion of over-frigid hygiene.

Miss Marple got back into bed, plumped her pillows up, glanced at her clock, half-past seven, picked up the small devotional book that always accompanied her, and read as usual the page and a half allotted to the day. Then she picked up her knitting and began to knit, slowly at first, since her fingers were stiff and rheumatic when she first awoke, but very soon her pace grew faster, and her fingers lost their painful stiffness.

'Another day,' said Miss Marple to herself, greeting the fact with her usual gentle pleasure. Another day – and who knew what it might bring forth?

She relaxed, and abandoning her knitting, let thoughts pass in an idle stream through her head . . . Selina Hazy . . . what a pretty cottage she had had in St Mary Mead's – and now someone had put on that ugly green roof . . . Muffins . . . very wasteful in butter . . . but very good . . . And fancy serving old-fashioned seed cake! She had never expected, not for a moment, that things would be as much like they used to be . . . because, after all, Time didn't stand still . . . And to have made it stand still in this way must really have cost a lot of money . . . Not a bit of plastic in the place! . . . It must pay them, she supposed. The out-of-date returns in due course as the picturesque . . . Look how people wanted old-fashioned roses now, and scorned hybrid teas! . . . None of this place seemed real at all . . . well, why should it? . . . It was fifty – no, nearer sixty years since she had stayed here. And it didn't seem real to her because she was now acclimitised in this present year of Our Lord— Really, the whole thing opened up a very interesting set of problems . . .

The atmosphere and the *people* . . . Miss Marple's fingers pushed her knitting farther away from her.

'Pockets,' she said aloud . . . 'Pockets, I suppose . . . And quite difficult to find . . .'

Would that account for that curious feeling of uneasiness she had had last night? That feeling that something was wrong . . .

All those elderly people – really very much like those she remembered when she had stayed here fifty years ago. They had been natural then – but they weren't very natural now. Elderly people nowadays weren't like elderly people then – they had that worried harried look of domestic anxieties with which they are too tired to cope, or they rushed around to committees and tried to appear bustling and competent, or they dyed their hair gentian blue, or wore wigs, and their hands were not the hands she remembered, tapering, delicate hands – they were harsh from washing up and detergents . . .

And so – well, so these people didn't look real. But the point was that they *were* real. Selina Hazy was real. And that rather handsome old military man in the corner was real – she had met him once, although she did not recall his name – and the Bishop (dear Robbie!) was dead.

Miss Marple glanced at her little clock. It was eight-thirty, Time for her breakfast.

She examined the instructions given by the hotel— Splendid big print so that it wasn't necessary to put one's spectacles on.

Meals could be ordered through the telephone by asking for Room Service, or you could press the bell labelled Chambermaid.

Miss Marple did the latter. Talking to Room Service always flustered her.

The result was excellent. In no time at all there was a tap on the door and a highly satisfactory chambermaid appeared. A real chambermaid looking unreal, wearing a striped lavender print dress and actually a *cap,* a freshly laundered cap. A smiling, rosy, positively *countrified* face. (Where did they *find* these people?)

Miss Marple ordered her breakfast. Tea, poached eggs, fresh rolls. So adept was the chambermaid that she did not even mention cereals or orange juice.

Five minutes later breakfast came. A comfortable tray with a big pot-bellied teapot, creamy-looking milk, a silver hot water jug. Two beautifully poached eggs on toast, poached the proper way, not little round hard bullets shaped in tin cups, a good-sized round of butter stamped with a thistle. Marmalade, honey and strawberry jam. Delicious-looking rolls, not the hard kind with papery interiors – they *smelt* of fresh bread (the most delicious smell in the world!). There were also an apple, a pear and a banana.

Miss Marple inserted a knife gingerly but with confidence. She was not disappointed. Rich deep yellow yolk oozed out, thick and creamy. *Proper* eggs!

Everything piping hot. A *real* breakfast. She could have cooked it herself but she hadn't had to! It was brought to her as if – no, not as though she were a queen – as though she were a middle-aged lady staying in a good but not unduly expensive hotel. In fact – back to 1909. Miss Marple expressed appreciation to the chambermaid who replied smiling,

'Oh, yes, Madam, the Chef is very particular about his breakfasts.'

Miss Marple studied her appraisingly. Bertram's Hotel could certainly produce marvels. A *real* housemaid. She pinched her left arm surreptitiously.

'Have you been here long?' she asked.

'Just over three years, Madam.'

'And before that?'

'I was in a hotel at Eastbourne. Very modern and up-to-date –put I prefer an old-fashioned place like this.'

Miss Marple took a sip of tea. She found herself humming in a vague way – words fitting themselves to a long forgotten song.
   'Oh where have you been all my life . . .'

The chambermaid was looking slightly startled.

'I was just remembering an old song,' twittered Miss Marple apologetically. 'Very popular at one time.'

Again she sang softly. 'Oh where have you been all my life . . .'

'Perhaps you know it?' she asked.

'Well—' The chambermaid looked rather apologetic.

'Too long ago for you,' said Miss Marple. 'Ah well, one gets to remember things – in a place like this.'

'Yes, Madam, a lot of the ladies who stay here feel like that, I think.'

'It's partly why they come, I expect,' said Miss Marple.

The chambermaid went out. She was obviously used to old ladies who twittered and reminisced.

Miss Marple finished her breakfast, and got up in a pleasant leisurely fashion. She had a plan ready made for a delightful morning of shopping. Not too much – to overtire herself. Oxford Street today, perhaps. And tomorrow Knightsbridge. She planned ahead happily.

It was about ten o'clock when she emerged from her room fully equipped: hat, gloves, umbrella – just in case, though it looked fine – handbag – her smartest shopping bag—

The door next but one on the corridor opened sharply and someone looked out. It was Bess Sedgwick. She withdrew back into the room and closed the door sharply.

Miss Marple wondered as she went down the stairs. She preferred the stairs to the lift first thing in the morning. It limbered her up. Her steps grew slower and slower . . . she stopped.

II

As Colonel Luscombe strode along the passage from his room, a door at the top of the stairs opened sharply and Lady Sedgwick spoke to him.

'There you are at last! I've been on the look-out for you – waiting to pounce. Where can we go and talk? That is to say without falling over some old pussy every second.'

'Well, really, Bess, I'm not quite sure – I think on the mezzanine floor there's a sort of writing-room.'

'You'd better come in here. Quick now, before the chambermaid gets peculiar ideas about us.'

Rather unwillingly, Colonel Luscombe stepped across the threshold and had the door shut firmly behind him.

'I'd no idea you would be staying here, Bess, I hadn't the faintest idea of it.'

'I don't suppose you had.'

'I mean – I would never have brought Elvira here. I *have* got Elvira here, you know?'

'Yes, I saw her with you last night.'

'But I really didn't know that you were here. It seemed such an unlikely place for you.'

'I don't see why,' said Bess Sedgwick, coldly. 'It's far and away the most comfortable hotel in London. Why shouldn't I stay here?'

'You must understand that I hadn't any idea of . . . I mean—'

She looked at him and laughed. She was dressed ready to go out in a well cut dark suit and a shirt of bright emerald green.

She looked gay and very much alive. Beside her, Colonel Luscombe looked rather old and faded.

'Darling Derek, don't look so worried. I'm not accusing you of trying to stage a mother and daughter sentimental meeting. It's just one of those things that happen; where people meet each other in unsuspected places. But you *must* get Elvira out of here, Derek. You must get her out of it at once – today.'

'Oh, she's going. I mean, I only brought her here just for a couple of nights. Do a show – that sort of thing. She's going down to the Melfords tomorrow.'

'Poor girl, that'll be boring for her.'

Luscombe looked at her with concern. 'Do you think she will be very bored?'

Bess took pity on him.

'Probably not after duress in Italy. She might even think it wildly thrilling.'

Luscombe took his courage in both hands.

'Look here, Bess, I was startled to find you here, but don't you think it – well, you know, it might be *meant* in a way. I mean that it might be an opportunity – I don't think you really know how – well, how the girl might feel.'

'What are you trying to say, Derek?'

'Well, you *are* her mother, you know.'

'Of course I'm her mother. She's my daughter. And what good has that fact ever been to either of us, or ever will be?'

'You can't be sure. I think – I think she feels it.'

'What gives you that idea?' said Bess Sedgwick sharply.

'Something she said yesterday. She asked where you were, what you were doing.'

Bess Sedgwick walked across the room to the window. She stood there a moment tapping on the pane.

'You're so nice, Derek,' she said. 'You have such nice ideas. But they don't work, my poor angel. That's what you've got to say to yourself. They don't work and they might be dangerous.

'Oh come now, Bess. Dangerous?'

'Yes, yes, yes. Dangerous. *I'm* dangerous. I've always been dangerous.'

'When I think of some of the things you've done,' said Colonel Luscombe.

'That's my own business,' said Bess Sedgwick. 'Running into danger has become a kind of habit with me. No, I wouldn't say habit. More an addiction. Like a drug. Like that nice little dollop of heroin addicts have to have every so often to make life seem bright coloured and worth living. Well, that's all right. That's my funeral – or not – as the case may be. I've never taken drugs – never needed them— Danger has been my drug. But people who live as I do can be a source of harm to others. Now don't be an obstinate old fool, Derek. You keep that girl well away from me. I can do her no good. Only harm. If possible, don't even let her know I was staying in the same hotel. Ring up the Melfords and take her down there *today*. Make some excuse about a sudden emergency—'

Colonel Luscombe hesitated, pulling his moustache.

'I think you're making a mistake, Bess.' He sighed. 'She asked where you were. I told her you were abroad.'

'Well, I shall be in another twelve hours, so that all fits very nicely.'

She came up to him, kissed him on the point of his chin, turned him smartly around as though they were about to play Blind Man's Buff, opened the door, gave him a gentle little propelling shove out of it. As the door shut behind him, Colonel Luscombe noticed an old lady turning the corner from the stairs. She was muttering to herself as she looked into her handbag. 'Dear, dear me. I suppose I must have left it in my room. Oh dear.'

She passed Colonel Luscombe without paying much attention to him apparently, but as he went on down the stairs Miss Marple paused by her room door and directed a piercing glance after him. Then she looked towards Bess Sedgwick's door. 'So that's who she was waiting for,' said Miss Marple to herself. 'I wonder why.'

III

Canon Pennyfather, fortified by breakfast, wandered across the lounge, remembered to leave his key at the desk, pushed his way through the swinging doors, and was neatly inserted into a taxi by the Irish commissionaire who existed for this purpose.

'Where to, sir?'

'Oh dear,' said Canon Pennyfather in sudden dismay. 'Now let me see – where *was* I going?'

The traffic in Pond Street was held up for some minutes whilst Canon Pennyfather and the commissionaire debated this knotty point.

Finally Canon Pennyfather had a brainwave and the taxi was directed to go to the British Museum.

The commissionaire was left on the pavement with a broad grin on his face, and since no other exits seemed to be taking place, he strolled a little way along the façade of the hotel whistling an old tune in a muted manner.

One of the windows on the ground floor of Bertram's was flung up – but the commissionaire did not even turn his head until a voice spoke unexpectedly through the open window.

'So this is where you've landed up, Micky. What on earth brought you to this place?'

He swung round, startled – and stared.

Lady Sedgwick thrust her head through the open window. 'Don't you know me?' she demanded.

A sudden gleam of recognition came across the man's face. 'Why, if it isn't little Bessie now! Fancy that! After all these years. Little Bessie.'

'Nobody but you ever called me Bessie. It's a revolting name. What have you been doing all these years?'

'This and that,' said Micky with some reserve. 'I've not been in the news like you have. I've read of your doings in the paper time and again.'

Bess Sedgwick laughed. 'Anyway. I've worn better than you have,' she said. 'You drink too much. You always did.'

'You've worn well because you've always been in the money.'

'Money wouldn't have done you any good. You'd have drunk even more and gone to the dogs completely. Oh yes, you would! What brought you *here*? That's what I want to know. How did you ever get taken on at this place?'

'I wanted a job. I had these—' his hand flicked over the row of medals.

'Yes, I see.' She was thoughtful. 'All genuine too, aren't they?'

'Sure they're genuine. Why shouldn't they be?'

'Oh I believe you. You always had courage. You've always been a good fighter. Yes, the army suited you. I'm sure of that.'

'The army's all right in time of war, but it's no good in peace time.'

'So you took to this suff. I hadn't the least idea—' she stopped.

'You hadn't the least idea what, Bessie?'

'Nothing. It's queer seeing you again after all these years.'

'*I* haven't forgotten,' said the man. 'I've never forgotten you, little Bessie. Ah! a lovely girl you were! A lovely slip of a girl.'

'A damn' fool of a girl, that's what I was,' said Lady Sedgwick.

'That's true now. You hadn't much sense. If you had, you wouldn't have taken up with me. What hands you had for a horse. Do you remember that mare – what was her name now? – Molly O'Flynn. As, she was a wicked devil that one was.'

'You were the only one that could ride her,' said Lady Sedgwick.

'She'd have had me off if she could! When she found she couldn't, she gave in. Ah, she was a beauty, now. But talking of sitting a horse, there wasn't one lady in those parts better than you. A lovely seat you had, lovely hands. Never any fear in you, not for a minute! And it's been the same ever since, so I judge. Aeroplanes, racing cars.'

Bess Sedgwick laughed.

'I must get on with my letters.'

She drew back from the window.

Micky leaned over the railing. 'I've not forgotten Ballygowlan,' he said with meaning. 'Sometimes I've thought of writing to you—'

Bess Sedgwick's voice came out harshly.

'And what do you mean by that, Mick Gorman?'

'I was just saying as I haven't forgotten – anything. I was just – reminding you like.'

Bess Sedgwick's voice still held its harsh note.

'If you mean what I think you mean, I'll give you a piece of advice. Any trouble from you, and I'd shoot you as easily as I'd shoot a rat. I've shot men before—'

'In foreign parts, maybe—'

'Foreign parts or here – it's all the same to me.'

'Ah, good lord, now, and I believe you would do just that!' His voice held admiration. 'In Ballygowlan—'

'In Ballygowlan,' she cut in, 'they paid you to keep your mouth shut and paid you well. You took the money. You'll get no more from me so don't think it.'

'It would be a nice romantic story for the Sunday papers . . .'

'You heard what I said.'

'Ah,' he laughed, 'I'm not serious. I was just joking. I'd never do anything to hurt my little Bessie. I'll keep my mouth shut.'

'Mind you do,' said Lady Sedgwick.

She shut down the window. Staring down at the desk in front of her she looked at her unfinished letter on the blotting paper. She picked it up, looked at it, crumpled it into a ball and slung it into the waste-paper basket. Then abruptly she got up from her seat and walked out of the room. She did not even cast a glance around her before she went.

The smaller writing-rooms at Bertram's often had an appearance of being empty even when they were not. Two well-appointed desks stood in the windows, there was a table on the right that held a few magazines, on the left were two very high-backed arm-chairs turned towards the fire. These were favourite spots in the afternoon for elderly military or naval gentlemen to ensconce themselves and fall happily asleep until tea-time. Anyone coming in to write a letter did not usually even notice them. The chairs were not so much in demand during the morning.

As it happened, however, they were on this particular morning both occupied. An old lady was in one and a young girl in the other. The young girl rose to her feet. She stood a moment looking uncertainly towards the door through which Lady Sedgwick had passed out, then she moved slowly towards it. Elvira Blake's face was deadly pale.

It was another five minutes before the old lady moved. Then Miss Marple decided that the little rest which she always took after dressing and coming downstairs had lasted quite long enough. It was time to go out and enjoy the pleasures of London. She might walk as far as Piccadilly, and take a No. 9 bus to High Street, Kensington, or she might walk along to Bond Street and take a 25 bus to Marshall & Snelgrove's or she might take a 25 the other way which as far as she remembered would land her up at the Army & Navy Stores. Passing through the swing doors she was still savouring these delights in her mind. The Irish commissionaire, back on duty, made up her mind for her.

'You'll be wanting a taxi, Ma'am,' he said with firmness.

'I don't think I do,' said Miss Marple. 'I think there's a 25 bus I could take quite near here – or a 2 from Park Lane.'

'You'll not be wanting a bus,' said the commissionaire firmly. 'It's very dangerous springing on a bus when you're getting on in life. The way they start and stop and go on again. Jerk you off your feet, they do. No heart at all, these fellows, nowadays. I'll whistle you along a taxi and you'll go to wherever you want to like a queen.'

Miss Marple considered and fell.

'Very well then,' she said, 'perhaps I *had* better have a taxi.'

The commissionaire had no need even to whistle. He merely clicked his thumb and a taxi appeared like magic. Miss Marple was helped into it with every possible care and decided on the spur of the moment to go to Robinson & Cleaver's and look at their splendid offer of real linen sheets. She sat happily in her taxi feeling indeed as the commissionaire had promised her, just like a queen. Her mind was filled with pleasurable antici-pation of linen sheets, linen pillow cases and proper glass- and kitchen-cloths without pictures of bananas, figs or performing dogs and other pictorial distractions to annoy you when you were washing up.

Lady Sedgwick came up to the Reception desk.

'Mr Humfries in his office?'

'Yes, Lady Sedgwick.' Miss Gorringe looked startled.

Lady Sedgwick passed behind the desk, tapped on the door and went in without waiting for any response.

Mr Humfries looked up startled.

'What—?'

'Who engaged that man Michael Gorman?'

Mr Humfries spluttered a little.

'Parfitt left – he had a car accident a month ago. We had to replace him quickly. This man seemed all right. References OK – ex-army – quite good record – Not very bright perhaps – but that's all the better sometimes – you don't know anything against him, do you?'

'Enough not to want him here.'

'If you insist,' Humfries said slowly, 'we'll give him his notice—'

'No,' said Lady Sedgwick slowly. 'No – it's too late for that— Never mind.'

— 6 —

'Elvira.'

'Hallo, Bridget.'

The Hon. Elvira Blake pushed her way through the front door of 180 Onslow Square, which her friend Bridget had rushed down to open for her, having been watching through the window.

'Let's go upstairs,' said Elvira.

'Yes, we'd better. Otherwise we'll get entangled by Mummy.'

The two girls rushed up the stairs, thereby circumventing Bridget's mother, who came out on to the landing from her own bedroom just too late.

'You really are lucky not to have a mother,' said Bridget, rather breathlessly, as she took her friend into her bedroom and shut the door firmly. 'I mean, Mummy's quite a pet and all that, but the *questions* she asks! Morning, noon and night. Where are you going, and who have you met? And are they cousins of somebody else of the same name in Yorkshire? I mean, the *futility* of it all.'

'I suppose they have nothing else to think about,' said Elvira vaguely. 'Look here, Bridget, there's something terribly important I've got to do, and you've got to help me.'

'Well, I will if I can. What is it – a man?'

'No, it isn't, as a matter of fact.' Bridget looked disappointed. 'I've got to get away to Ireland for twenty-four hours or perhaps longer, and you've got to cover up for me.'

'To Ireland? Why?'

'I can't tell you all about it now. There's no time. I've got to meet my guardian, Colonel Luscombe, at Prunier's for lunch at half-past one.'

'What have you done with the Carpenter?'

'Gave her the slip in Debenham's.'

Bridget giggled.

'And after lunch they're taking me down to the Melfords. I'm going to live with them until I'm twenty-one.'

'How ghastly!'

'I expect I shall manage. Cousin Mildred is fearfully easy to deceive. It's arranged I'm to come up for classes and things. There's a place called World of Today. They take you to lectures and to Museums and to Picture Galleries and the House of Lords, and all that. The whole point is that nobody will know whether you're where you ought to be or not! We'll manage lots of things.'

'I expect we will.' Bridget giggled. 'We managed in Italy, didn't we? Old Macaroni thought she was so strict. Little did she know what we got up to when we tried.'

Both girls laughed in the pleasant consciousness of successful wickedness.

'Still, it did need a lot of planning,' said Elvira.

'And some splendid lying,' said Bridget. 'Have you heard from Guido?'

'Oh yes, he wrote me a long letter signed Ginevra as though

774

he was a girl-friend. But I do wish you'd stop talking so much, Bridget. We've got a lot to do and only about an hour and a half to do it in. Now first of all just *listen*. I'm coming up to-morrow for an appointment with the dentist. That's easy, I can put it off by telephone – or you can from here. Then, about midday, you can ring up the Melfords pretending to be your mother and explain that the dentist wants to see me again the next day and so I'm staying over with you here.'

'That ought to go down all right. They'll say how very kind and gush. But supposing you're *not* back the next day?'

'Then you'll have to do some more ringing up.'

Bridget looked doubtful.

'We'll have lots of time to think up something before then,' said Elvira impatiently. 'What's worrying me now is *money*. You haven't got any, I suppose?' Elvira spoke without much hope.

'Only about two pounds.'

'That's no good. I've got to buy my air ticket. I've looked up the flights. It only takes about two hours. A lot depends upon how long it takes me when I get there.'

'Can't you tell me what you're going to do?'

'No, I can't. But it's terribly, terribly important.'

Elvira's voice was so different that Bridget looked at her in some surprise.

'Is anything really the matter, Elvira?'

'Yes, it is.'

'Is it something nobody's got to know about?'

'Yes, that's the sort of thing. It's frightfully, frightfully secret. I've got to find out if something is really true or not. It's a bore about the money. What's maddening is that I'm really quite rich. My guardian told me so. But all they give me is a measly dress allowance. And that seems to go as soon as I get it.'

'Wouldn't your guardian – Colonel Thingummybob lend you some money?'

'That wouldn't do at all. He'd ask a lot of questions and want to know what I wanted it for.'

'Oh dear, I suppose he would. I can't think why everybody wants to ask so many questions. Do you know that if somebody rings me up, Mummy has to ask *who it is*? When it really is *no* business of hers!'

Elvira agreed, but her mind was on another tack.

'Have you ever pawned anything, Bridget?'

'Never. I don't think I'd know how to.'

'It's quite easy, I believe,' said Elvira. 'You go to the sort of jeweller who has three balls over the door, isn't that right?'

'I don't think I've got anything that would be any good taking to a pawnbroker,' said Bridget.

'Hasn't your mother got some jewellery somewhere?'

'I don't think we'd better ask her to help.'

'No, perhaps not— But we could pinch something perhaps.'

'Oh, I don't think we could do that,' said Bridget shocked.

'No? Well, perhaps you're right. But I bet she wouldn't notice. We could get it back before she missed it. *I* know. We'll go to Mr Bollard.'

'Who's Mr Bollard?'

'Oh, he's a sort of family jeweller. I take my watch there always to have it mended. He's known me ever since I was six. Come on, Bridget, we'll go there right away. We'll just have time.'

'We'd better go out the back way,' said Bridget, 'and then Mummy won't ask us where we're going.'

Outside the old established business of Bollard and Whitley in Bond Street the two girls made their final arrangements.

'Are you sure you understand, Bridget?'

'I think so,' said Bridget in a far from happy voice.

'First,' said Elvira, 'we synchronise our watches.'

Bridget brightened up a little. This familiar literary phrase had a heartening effect. They solemnly synchronised their watches, Bridget adjusting hers by one minute.

'Zero hour will be twenty-five past exactly,' said Elvira. 'That will give me plenty of time. Perhaps even more than I need, but it's better that way about.'

'But supposing—?' began Bridget.

'Supposing what?' asked Elvira.

'Well, I mean, supposing I *really* got run over?'

'Of course you won't get run over,' said Elvira. 'You know how nippy you are on your feet, and all London traffic is used to pulling up suddenly. It'll be all right.'

Bridget looked far from convinced.

'You won't let me down, Bridget, will you?'

'All right,' said Bridget, 'I won't let you down.'

'Good,' said Elvira.

Bridget crossed to the other side of Bond Street and Elvira pushed open the doors of Messrs Bollard and Whitley, old established jewellers and watchmakers. Inside there was a beautiful and hushed atmosphere. A frock-coated nobleman came forward and asked Elvira what he could do for her.

'Could I see Mr Bollard?'

'Mr Bollard. What name shall I say?'

'Miss Elvira Blake.'

The nobleman disappeared and Elvira drifted to a counter where, below plate glass, brooches, rings and bracelets showed off their jewelled proportions against suitable shades of velvet. In a very few moments Mr Bollard made his appearance. He was the senior partner of the firm, an elderly man of sixty odd. He greeted Elvira with warm friendliness.

'Ah, Miss Blake, so you are in London. It's a great pleasure to see you. Now what can I do for you?'

Elvira produced a dainty little evening wrist-watch.

'This watch doesn't go properly,' said Elvira. 'Could you do something to it?'

'Oh yes, of course. There's no difficulty about *that*.' Mr Bollard took it from her. 'What address shall I send it to?'

Evira gave the address.

'And there's another thing,' she said. 'My guardian – Colonel Luscombe you know—'

'Yes, yes of course.'

'He asked me what I'd like for a Christmas present,' said Elvira. 'He suggested I should come in here and look at some different things. He said would I like him to come with me, and I said I'd rather come along first – because I always think it's rather embarrassing, don't you? I mean, prices and all that.'

'Well, that's certainly one aspect,' said Mr Bollard, beaming in an avuncular manner. 'Now what had you in mind, Miss Blake? A brooch, bracelet – a ring?'

'I think really brooches are more useful,' said Elvira. 'But I wonder – could I look at a *lot* of things?' She looked up at him appealingly. He smiled sympathetically.

'Of course, of course. No pleasure at all if one has to make up one's mind too quickly, is it?'

The next five or six minutes were spent very agreeably. Nothing was too much trouble for Mr Bollard. He fetched things from one case and another, brooches and bracelets piled up on the piece of velvet spread in front of Elvira. Occasionally she turned aside to look at herself in a mirror, trying the effect of a brooch or a pendant. Finally, rather uncertainly, a pretty little bangle, a small diamond wrist-watch and two brooches were laid aside.

'We'll make a note of these,' said Mr Bollard, 'and then when Colonel Luscombe is in London next, perhaps he'll come in and see what he decides himself he'd like to give you.'

'I think that way will be very nice,' said Elvira. 'Then he'll feel more that he's chosen my present himself, won't he?' Her limpid blue gaze was raised to the jeweller's face. That same blue gaze had registered a moment earlier that the time was now exactly twenty five minutes past the hour.

Outside there was the squealing of brakes and a girl's loud scream. Inevitably the eyes of everyone in the shop turned towards the windows of the shop giving on Bond Street. The movement of Elvira's hand on the counter in front of her and then to the pocket of her neat tailor-made coat and skirt was so rapid and unobtrusive as to be almost unnoticeable, even if anybody had been looking.

'Tcha, tcha,' said Mr Bollard, turning back from where he had been peering out into the street. 'Very nearly an accident. Silly girl! Rushing across the road like that.'

Elvira was already moving towards the door. She looked at her wrist-watch and uttered an exclamation.

'Oh dear, I've been far too long in here. I shall miss my train back to the country. Thank you *so* much, Mr Bollard, and you won't forget which the four things are, will you?'

In another minute she was out of the door. Turning rapidly to the left and then to the left again, she stopped in the arcade of a shoe shop until Bridget, rather breathless, rejoined her.

'Oh,' said Bridget. 'I was terrified. I thought I was going to be killed. And I've torn a hole in my stocking, too.'

'Never mind,' said Elvira and walked her friend rapidly along the street and round yet another corner to the right. 'Come on.'

'Is it – was it – all right?'

Elvira's hand slipped into her pocket and out again, showing the diamond and sapphire bracelet in her palm.

'Oh, Elvira, how you dared!'

'Now, Bridget, you've got to get along to that pawnshop we marked down. Go in and see how much you can get for this. Ask for a hundred.'

'Do you think – supposing they say – I mean – I mean, it might be on a list of stolen things—'

'Don't be silly. How could it be on a list so soon? They haven't even noticed it's gone yet.'

'But Elvira, when they *do* notice it's gone, they'll think – perhaps they'll know – that you must have taken it.'

'They *might* think so – if they discover it soon.'

'Well, then they'll go to the police and—'

She stopped as Elvira shook her head slowly, her pale yellow hair swinging to and fro and a faint enigmatic smile curving up the corners of her mouth.

'They won't go to the police, Bridget. Certainly not if they think *I* took it.'

'Why – you mean—?'

'As I told you, I'm going to have a lot of money when I'm twenty-one. I shall be able to buy lots of jewels from them. *They* won't make a scandal. Go on and get the money quick. Then go to Aer Lingus and book the ticket – I must take a taxi to Prunier's. I'm already ten minutes late. I'll be with you tomorrow morning by half-past ten.'

'Oh Elvira, I wish you wouldn't take such frightful risks,' moaned Bridget.

But Elvira had hailed a taxi.

II

Miss Marple had a very enjoyable time at Robinson & Cleaver's. Besides purchasing expensive but delicious sheets – she loved linen sheets with their texture and their coolness – she also indulged in a purchase of good quality red-bordered glass-cloths. Really the difficulty in getting proper glass-cloths nowadays! Instead, you were offered things that might as well have been ornamental table-cloths, decorated with radishes or lobsters or the *Tour Eiffel* or Trafalgar Square, or else littered with lemons and oranges. Having given her address in St Mary Mead, Miss Marple found a convenient bus which took her to the Army & Navy Stores.

The Army & Navy Stores had been a haunt of Miss Marple's aunt in days long gone. It was not, of course, quite the same nowadays. Miss Marple cast her thoughts back to Aunt Helen seeking out her own special man in the grocery department, settling herself comfortably in a chair, wearing a bonnet and what she always called her 'black poplin' mantle. Then there would ensue a long hour with nobody in a hurry and Aunt Helen thinking of every conceivable grocery that could be purchased and stored up for future use. Christmas was provided for, and there was even a far-off look towards Easter. The young

Jane had fidgeted somewhat, and had been told to go and look at the glass department by way of amusement.

Having finished her purchases, Aunt Helen would then proceed to lengthy inquiries about her chosen shop-assistant's mother, wife, second boy and crippled sister-in-law. Having had a thoroughly pleasant morning, Aunt Helen would say in the playful manner of those times, 'And how would a little girl feel about some luncheon?' Whereupon they went up in the lift to the fourth floor and had luncheon which always finished with a strawberry ice. After that, they bought half a pound of coffee chocolate creams and went to a matinée in a four wheeler.

Of course, the Army & Navy Stores had had a good many face lifts since those days. In fact, it was now quite unrecognisable from the old times. It was gayer and much brighter. Miss Marple, though throwing a kindly and indulgent smile at the past, did not object to the amenities of the present. There was still a restaurant, and there she repaired to order her lunch.

As she was looking carefully down the menu and deciding what to have, she looked across the room and her eyebrows went up a little. How extraordinary coincidence was? Here was a woman she had never seen till the day before, though she had seen plenty of newspaper photographs of her – at race meetings, in Bermuda, or standing by her own plane or car. Yesterday, for the first time, she had seen her in the flesh. And now, as was so often the case, there was the coincidence of running into her again in a most unlikely place. For somehow she did not connect lunch at the Army & Navy Stores with Bess Sedgwick. She would not have been surprised to see Bess Sedgwick emerging from a den in Soho, or stepping out of Covent Garden Opera House in evening dress with a diamond tiara on her head. But somehow, not in the Army & Navy Stores which in Miss Marple's mind was, and always would be, connected with the armed forces, their wives, daughters, aunts and grandmothers. Still, there Bess Sedgwick was, looking as usual very smart, in her dark suit and her emerald shirt, lunching at a table with a man. A young man with a lean hawklike face, wearing a black leather jacket. They were leaning forward talking earnestly together, forking in mouthfuls of food as though they were quite unaware what they were eating.

An assignation, perhaps? Yes, probably an assignation. The man must be fifteen or twenty years younger than she was – but Bess Sedgwick was a magnetically attractive woman.

Miss Marple looked at the young man consideringly and decided that he was what she called a 'handsome fellow'. She also decided that she didn't like him very much. 'Just like Harry Russell,' said Miss Marple to herself, dredging up a prototype as usual from the past. 'Never up to any good. Never did any woman who had anything to do with him any good either.'

'She wouldn't take advice from me,' thought Miss Marple, 'but I could give her some.' However, other people's love affairs were no concern of hers, and Bess Sedgwick, by all accounts, could take care of herself very well when it came to love affairs.

Miss Marple sighed, ate her lunch, and meditated a visit to the stationery department.

Curiosity, or what she preferred herself to call 'taking an interest' in other people's affairs, was undobutedly one of Miss Marpe's characteristics.

Deliberately leaving her gloves on the table, she rose and crossed the floor to the cash desk, taking a route that passed close to Lady Sedgwick's table. Having paid her bill she 'discovered' the absence of her gloves and returned to get them – unfortunately dropping her handbag on the return route. It came open and spilled various oddments. A waitress rushed to assist her in picking them up, and Miss Marple was forced to show a great shakiness and dropped coppers and keys a second time.

She did not get very much by these subterfuges but they were not entirely in vain – and it was interesting that neither of the two objects of her curiosity spared as much as a glance for the dithery old lady who kept dropping things.

As Miss Marple waited for the lift down she memorised such scraps as she had heard.

'What about the weather forecast?'

'OK. No fog.'

'All set for Lucerne?'

'Yes. Plane leaves 9.40.'

That was all she had got the first time. On the way back it had lasted a little longer.

Bess Sedgwick had been speaking angrily.

'What possessed you to come to Bertram's yesterday – you shouldn't have come near the place.'

'It's all right. I asked if you were staying there and everyone knows we're close friends—'

'That's not the point. Bertram's is all right for me— Not for you. You stick out like a sore thumb. Everyone stares at you.'

'Let them!'

'*You really are an idiot. Why – why? What reason did you have? You* had *a reason – I know you ...*'

'*Calm down, Bess.*'

'*You're such a liar!*'

That was all she had been able to hear. She found it interesting.

—— 7 ——

On the evening of 19th November Canon Pennyfather had finished an early dinner at the Athenæum, he had nodded to one or two friends, had had a pleasant acrimonious discussion on some crucial points of the dating of the Dead Sea scrolls and now, glancing at his watch, saw that it was time to leave to catch his plane to Lucerne. As he passed through the hall he was greeted by one more friend: Dr Whittaker, of the SOAS, who said cheerfully:

'How are you, Pennyfather? Haven't seen you for a long time. How did you get on at the Congress? Any points of interest come up?'

'I am sure there will be.'

'Just come back from it, haven't you?'

'No, no, I am on my way there. I'm catching a plane this evening.'

'Oh I see.' Whittaker looked slightly puzzled. 'Somehow or other I thought the Congress was today.'

'No, no. Tomorrow, the 19th.'

Canon Pennyfather passed out through the door while his friend, looking after him, was just saying,

'But my dear chap, *today* is the 19th, isn't it?'

Canon Pennyfather, however, had gone beyond earshot. He picked up a taxi in Pall Mall, and was driven to the air terminal in Kensington. There was quite a fair crowd this evening. Presenting himself at the desk it at last came to his turn. He managed to produce ticket and passport and other necessities for the journey. The girl behind the desk, about to stamp these credentials, paused abruptly.

'I beg your pardon, sir, this seems to be the wrong ticket.'

'The wrong ticket? No, no, that is quite right. Flight one

hundred and – well, I can't really read without my glasses – one hundred and something to Lucerne.'

'It's the date, sir. This is dated Wednesday the 18th.'

'No, no, surely. At least – I mean – today is Wednesday the 18th.'

'I'm sorry, sir. Today is the 19th.'

'The 19th!' The Canon was dismayed. He fished out a small diary, turning the pages eagerly. In the end he had to be convinced. Today *was* the 19th. The plane he had meant to catch had gone yesterday.

'Then that means – that means – dear me, it means the Congress at Lucerne has taken place there *today*.'

He stared in deep dismay across the counter; but there were many others travelling; the Canon and his perplexities were elbowed aside. He stood sadly, holding the useless ticket in his hand. His mind ranged over various possibilities. Perhaps his ticket could be changed? But that would be no use – no indeed – what time was it now? Going on for 9 o'clock? The conference had actually taken place; starting at 10 o'clock this morning. Of course, that was what Whittaker had meant at the Athenæum. He thought Canon Pennyfather had already *been* to the Congress.

'Oh dear, oh dear,' said Canon Pennyfather, to himself. '*What* a muddle I have made of it all!' He wandered sadly and silently into the Cromwell Road, not at its best a very cheerful place.

He walked slowly along the street carrying his bag and revolving perplexities in his mind. When at last he had worked out to his satisfaction the various reasons for which he had made a mistake in the day, he shook his head sadly.

'Now, I suppose,' he said to himself, 'I suppose – let me see, it's after nine o'clock, yes, I suppose I had better have something to eat.'

It was curious, he thought, that he did not feel hungry.

Wandering disconsolately along the Cromwell Road he finally settled upon a small restaurant which served Indian curries. It seemed to him that though he was not quite as hungry as he ought to be, he had better keep his spirits up by having a meal, and after that he must find a hotel and – but no, there was no need to do *that*. He had a hotel! Of course. He was staying at Bertram's; and had reserved his room for four days. What a piece of luck! What a splendid piece of luck! So his room was there, waiting for him. He had only to ask for his key at the desk and – here another reminiscence assailed him. Something heavy in his pocket?

He dipped his hand in and brought out one of those large and solid keys with which hotels try and discourage their vaguer guests from taking them away in their pockets. It had not prevented the Canon from doing so!

'No. 19,' said the Canon, in happy recognition. 'That's right. It's very fortunate that I haven't got to go and find a room in a hotel. They say they're very crowded just now. Yes, Edmunds was saying so at the Athenæum this evening. He had a terrible job finding a room.'

Somewhat pleased with himself and the care he had taken over his travelling arrangements by booking a hotel beforehand, the Canon abandoned his curry, remembered to pay for it, and strode out once more into the Cromwell Road.

It seemed a little tame to go home just like this when he ought to have been dining in Lucerne and talking about all sorts of interesting and fascinating problems. His eye was caught by a cinema. *Walls of Jericho*. It seemed an eminently suitable title. It would be interesting to see if biblical accuracy had been preserved.

He bought himself a seat and stumbled into the darkness. He enjoyed the film, though it seemed to him to have no relationship to the biblical story whatsoever. Even Joshua seemed to have been left out. The walls of Jericho seemed to be a symbolical way of referring to a certain lady's marriage vows. When they had tumbled down several times, the beautiful star met the dour and uncouth hero whom she had secretly loved all along and between them they proposed to build up the walls in a way that would stand the test of time better. It was not a film destined particularly to appeal to an elderly clergyman; but Canon Pennyfather enjoyed it very much. It was not the sort of film he often saw and he felt it was enlarging his knowledge of life. The film ended, the lights went up, the National Anthem was played and Canon Pennyfather stumbled out into the lights of London, slightly consoled for the sad events of earlier in the evening.

It was a fine night and he walked home to Bertram's Hotel after first getting into a bus which took him in the opposite direction. It was midnight when he got in and Bertram's Hotel at midnight usually preserved a decorous appearance of everyone having gone to bed. The lift was on a higher floor so the

Canon walked up the stairs. He came to his room, inserted the key in the lock, threw the door open and entered!

Good gracious, was he seeing things? But who – how – he saw the upraised arm too late . . .

Stars exploded in a kind of Guy Fawkes' display within his head . . .

—— 8 ——

The Irish Mail rushed through the night. Or, more correctly through the darkness of the early morning hours.

At intervals the diesel engine gave its weird banshee warning cry. It was travelling at well over eighty miles an hour. It was on time.

Then, with some suddenness, the pace slackened as the brakes came on. The wheels screamed as they gripped the metals. Slower . . . slower . . . The guard put his head out of the window, noting the red signal ahead as the train came to a final halt. Some of the passengers woke up. Most did not.

One elderly lady, alarmed by the suddenness of the deceleration, opened the door and looked out along the corridor. A little way along one of the doors to the line was open. An elderly cleric with a thatch of thick white hair was climbing up from the permanent way. She presumed he had previously climbed down to the line to investigate.

The morning air was distinctly chilly. Someone at the end of the corridor said: 'Only a signal.' The elderly lady withdrew into her compartment and tried to go to sleep again.

Farther up the line, a man waving a lantern was running towards the train from a signal box. The fireman climbed down from the engine. The guard who had descended from the train came along to join them. The man with the lantern arrived, rather short of breath, and spoke in a series of gasps.

'Bad crash ahead . . . Goods train derailed . . .'

The engine driver looked out of his cab, then climbed down also to join the others.

At the rear of the train, six men who had just climbed up the embankment boarded the train through a door left open for them in the last coach. Six passengers from different coaches met them. With well rehearsed speed, they proceeded to take charge of the postal van, isolating it from the rest of the train. Two men in Balaclava helmets at front and rear of the compartment stood on guard, coshes in hand.

A man in railway uniform went forward along the corridor of the stationary train, uttering explanations to such as demanded them.

'Block on the line ahead. Ten minutes' delay, maybe, not much more . . .' It sounded friendly and reassuring.

By the engine, the driver and the fireman lay neatly gagged and trussed up. The man with the lantern called out:

'Everything OK here.'

The guard lay by the embankment, similarly gagged and tied.

The expert cracksmen in the postal van had done their work. Two more neatly trussed bodies lay on the floor. The special mailbags sailed out to where other men on the embankment awaited them.

In their compartments, passengers grumbled to each other that the railways were not what they used to be.

Then, as they settled themselves to sleep again, there came through the darkness the roar of an exhaust.

'Goodness,' murmured a woman. 'Is that a jet plane?'

'Racing car, I should say.'

The roar died away.

On the Bedhampton Motorway, nine miles away, a steady stream of night lorries was grinding its way north. A big white racing car flashed past them.

Ten minutes later, it turned off the motorway.

The garage on the corner of the B road bore the sign CLOSED. But the big doors swung open and the white car was driven straight in, the doors closing again behind it. Three men worked at lightning speed. A fresh set of number plates were attached. The driver changed his coat and cap. He had worn white sheepskin before. Now he wore black leather. He drove out again. Three minutes after his departure, an old Morris Oxford, driven by a clergyman, chugged out on to the road and proceeded to take a route through various turning and twisting country lanes.

A station wagon, driven along a country road, slowed up as it came upon an old Morris Oxford stationary by the hedge, with an elderly man standing over it.

The driver of the station wagon put out a head.

'Having trouble? Can I help?'

'Very good of you. It's my lights.'

The two drivers approached each other – listened. 'All clear.' Various expensive American-style cases were transferred from the Morris Oxford to the station wagon.

A mile or two farther on, the station wagon turned off on what looked like a rough track but which presently turned out to be the back way to a large and opulent mansion. In what had been a stableyard, a big white Mercedes car was standing. The driver of the station wagon opened its boot with a key, transferred the cases to the boot, and drove away again in the station wagon.

In a near-by farmyard a cock crowed noisily.

9

Elvira Blake looked up at the sky, noted that it was a fine morning and went into a telephone box. She dialled Bridget's number in Onslow Square. Satisfied by the response, she said,

'Hallo? Bridget?'

'Oh Elvira, is that you?' Bridget's voice sounded agitated.

'Yes. Has everything been all right?'

'Oh no. It's been *awful*. Your cousin, Mrs Melford, rang up Mummy yesterday afternoon.'

'What, about me?'

'Yes. I thought I'd done it so well when I rang her up at lunch-time. But it seems she got worried about your teeth. Thought there might be something really wrong with them. Abscesses or something. So she rang up the dentist herself and found, of course, that you'd never been there at all. So then she rang up Mummy and unfortunately Mummy was right there by the telephone. So I couldn't get there first. And naturally Mummy said *she* didn't know anything about it, and that you certainly weren't staying *here*. I didn't know *what* to do.'

'What *did* you do?'

'Pretended I knew nothing about it. I did say that I thought you'd said something about going to see some friends at Wimbledon.'

'Why Wimbledon?'

'It was the first place came into my head.'

Elvira sighed. 'Oh well, I suppose I'll have to cook up something. An old governess, perhaps, who lives at Wimbledon. All this fussing does make things so *complicated*. I hope Cousin Mildred doesn't make a real fool of herself and ring up the police or something like that?'

'Are you going down there now?'

'Not till this evening. I've got a lot to do first.'

'You got to Ireland. Was it – all right?'

'I found out what I wanted to know.'

'You sound – sort of grim.'

'I'm feeling grim.'

'Can't I help you, Elvira? Do anything?'

'Nobody can help me really . . . It's a thing I have to do myself. I hoped something wasn't true, but it *is* true. I don't know quite what to do about it.'

'Are you in danger, Elvira?'

'Don't be melodramatic, Bridget. I'll have to be careful that's all. I'll have to be very careful.'

'Then you *are* in danger.'

Elvira said after a moment's pause, 'I expect I'm just imagining things, that's all.'

'Elvira, what are you going to do about that bracelet?'

'Oh, that's all right. I've arranged to get some money from someone, so I can go and – what's the word? – redeem it. Then just take it back to Bollards.'

'D'you think they'll be all right about it? – No, Mummy, it's just the laundry. They say we never sent that sheet. Yes, Mummy, yes, I'll tell the manageress. All right then.'

At the other end of the line Elvira grinned and put down the receiver. She opened her purse, sorted through her money, counted out the coins she needed and arranged them in front of her and proceeded to put through a call. When she got the number she wanted she put in the necessary coins, pressed Button A and spoke in a small rather breathless voice.

'Hallo, Cousin Mildred. Yes, it's me . . . I'm terribly sorry . . . Yes, I know . . . well I was going to . . . yes it was dear old Maddy, you know our old Mademoiselle . . . yes I wrote a postcard, then I forgot to post it. It's still in my pocket now . . . well, you see she was ill and there was no one to look after her and so I just stopped to see she was all right. Yes, I *was* going to Bridget's but this changed things . . . I don't understand about the message you got. Someone must have jumbled it up . . . Yes, I'll explain it all to you when I get back . . . yes, this afternoon. No, I shall just wait and see the nurse who's coming to look after old Maddy – well, not really a nurse. You know one of those – er – practical aid nurses or something like that. No, she would hate to go to hospital . . . But I *am* sorry, Cousin Mildred, I really am very, very sorry.' She put down the receiver and sighed in an exasperated manner. 'If only,' she murmured to herself, 'one didn't have to tell so many lies to everybody.'

She came out of the telephone box, noting as she did so the big newspaper placards – BIG TRAIN ROBBERY. IRISH MAIL ATTACKED BY BANDITS.

II

Mr Bollard was serving a customer when the shop door opened. He looked up to see the Honourable Elvira Blake entering.

'No,' she said to an assistant who came forward to her. 'I'd rather wait until Mr Bollard is free.'

Presently Mr Bollard's customer's business was concluded and Elvira moved into the vacant place.

'Good morning, Mr Bollard,' she said.

'I'm afraid your watch isn't done quite as soon as this, Miss Elvira,' said Mr Bollard.

'Oh, it's not the watch,' said Elvira. 'I've come to apologise. A dreadful thing happened.' She opened her bag and took out a small box. From it she extracted the sapphire and diamond bracelet. 'You will remember when I came in with my watch to be repaired that I was looking at things for a Christmas present and there was an accident outside in the street. Somebody was run over I think, or nearly run over. I suppose I must have had the bracelet in my hand and put it into the pocket of my suit without thinking, although I only found it this morning. So I rushed along *at once* to bring it back. I'm so terribly sorry, Mr Bollard, I don't know how I came to do such an idiotic thing.'

'Why, that's quite all right, Miss Elvira,' said Mr Bollard, slowly.

'I suppose you thought someone had stolen it,' said Elvira.

Her limpid blue eyes met his.

'We *had* discovered its loss,' said Mr Bollard. 'Thank you very much, Miss Elvira, for bringing it back so promptly.'

'I felt simply awful about it when I found it,' said Elvira.

'Well, thank you very much, Mr Bollard, for being so nice about it.'

'A lot of strange mistakes do occur,' said Mr Bollard. He smiled at her in an avuncular manner. 'We won't think of it any more. But don't do it again, though.' He laughed with the air of one making a genial little joke.

'Oh no,' said Elvira, 'I shall be terribly careful in future.' She smiled at him, turned and left the shop.

'Now I wonder,' said Mr Bollard to himself, 'I really do wonder . . .'

One of his partners, who had been standing near, moved nearer to him.

'So she *did* take it?' he said.

'Yes. She took it all right,' said Mr Bollard.

'But she brought it back,' his partner pointed out.

'She brought it back,' agreed Mr Bollard. 'I didn't actually expect that.'

'You mean you didn't expect her to bring it back?'

'No, not if it was she who'd taken it.'

'Do you think her story is true?' his partner inquired curiously. 'I mean, that she slipped it into her pocket by accident?'

'I suppose it's possible,' said Bollard, thoughtfully.

'Or it *could* be kleptomania, I suppose.'

'Or it could be kleptomania,' agreed Bollard. 'It's more likely that she took it on purpose . . . But if so, why did she bring it back so soon? It's curious—'

'Just as well we didn't notify the police. I admit *I* wanted to.'

'I know, I know. You haven't got as much experience as I have. In this case, it was definitely better not.' He added softly to himself, 'The thing's interesting, though. Quite interesting. I wonder how old she is? Seventeen or eighteen I suppose. She might have got herself in a jam of some kind.'

'I thought you said she was rolling in money.'

'You may be an heiress and rolling in money,' said Bollard, 'but at seventeen you can't always get your hands on it. The funny thing is, you know, they keep heiresses much shorter of cash than they keep the more impecunious. It's not always a good idea. Well, I don't suppose we shall ever know the truth of it.'

He put the bracelet back in its place in the display case and shut down the lid.

The offices of Egerton, Forbes & Willborough were in Blooms-
bury, in one of those imposing and dignified squares which
have as yet not felt the wind of change. Their brass plate was
suitably worn down to illegibility. The firm had been going
for over a hundred years and a good proportion of the landed
gentry of England were their clients. There was no Forbes in
the firm any more and no Willborough. Instead there were
Atkinsons, father and son, and a Welsh Lloyd and a Scottish
MacAllister. There was, however, still an Egerton, descendant
of the original Egerton. This particular Egerton was a man of
fifty-two and he was adviser to several families which had in
their day been advised by his grandfather, his uncle, and his
father.

At this moment he was sitting behind a large mahogany
desk in his handsome room on the first floor, speaking kindly
but firmly to a dejected looking client. Richard Egerton was
a handsome man, tall, dark with a touch of grey at the temples
and very shrewd grey eyes. His advice was always good advice,
but he seldom minced his words.

'Quite frankly you haven't got a leg to stand upon, Freddie,'
he was saying. 'Not with those letters you've written.'

'You don't think—' Freddie murmured dejectedly.

'No, I don't,' said Egerton. 'The only hope is to settle out
of court. It might even be held that you've rendered yourself
liable to criminal prosecution.'

'Oh look here, Richard, that's carrying things a bit far.'

There was a small discreet buzz on Egerton's desk. He picked
up the telephone receiver with a frown.

'I thought I said I wasn't to be disturbed.'

There was a murmur at the other end. Egerton said, 'Oh.
Yes— Yes, I see. Ask her to wait, will you.'

He replaced the receiver and turned once more to his unhappy looking client.

'Look here, Freddie,' he said, 'I know the law and you don't.
You're in a nasty jam. I'll do my best to get you out of it, but
it's going to cost you a bit. I doubt if they'd settle for less than
twelve thousand.'

'Twelve thousand!' The unfortunate Freddie was aghast.
'Oh, I say! I haven't got it, Richard.'

'Well, you'll have to raise it then. There are always ways and means. If she'll settle for twelve thousand, you'll be lucky, and if you fight the case it'll cost you a lot more.'

'You lawyers!' said Freddie. 'Sharks, all of you!'

He rose to his feet. 'Well,' he said, 'do your bloody best for me, Richard old boy.'

He took his departure, shaking his head sadly. Richard Egerton put Freddie and his affairs out of his mind, and thought about his next client. He said softly to himself, 'The Honourable Elvira Blake. I wonder what she's like . . .' He lifted the receiver. 'Lord Frederick's gone. Send up Miss Blake, will you.'

As he waited he made little calculations on his desk pad. How many years since—? She must be fifteen – seventeen – perhaps even more than that. Time went so fast. 'Coniston's daugher,' he thought, 'and Bess's daughter. I wonder which of them she takes after?'

The door opened, the clerk announced Miss Elvira Blake and the girl walked into the room. Egerton rose from his chair and came towards her. In appearance, he thought, she did not resemble either of her parents. Tall, slim, very fair, Bess's colouring but none of Bess's vitality, with an old-fashioned air about her; though that was difficult to be sure of, since the fashion in dress happened at the moment to be ruffles and baby bodices.

'Well, well,' he said, as he shook hands with her. 'This is a surprise. Last time I saw you, you were eleven years old. Come and sit here.' He pulled forward a chair and she sat down.

'I suppose,' said Elvira, a little uncertainly, 'that I ought to have written first. Written and made an appointment. Something like that, but I really made up my mind very suddenly and it seemed an opportunity, since I was in London.'

'And what are you doing in London?'

'Having my teeth seen to.'

'Beastly things, teeth,' said Egerton. 'Give us trouble from the cradle to the grave. But I am grateful for the teeth, if it gives me an opportunity of seeing you. Let me see now; you've been in Italy, haven't you, finishing your education there at one of these places all girls go to nowadays?'

'Yes,' said Elvira, 'the Contessa Martinelli. But I've left there now for good. I'm living with the Melfords in Kent until I make up my mind if there's anything I'd like to do.'

'Well, I hope you'll find something satisfactory. You're not thinking of a university or anything like that?'

'No,' said Elvira, 'I don't think I'd be clever enough for that.' She paused before saying, 'I suppose *you'd* have to agree to anything if I did want to do it?'

Egerton's keen eyes focused sharply.

'I am one of your guardians, and a trustee under your father's will, yes,' he said. 'Therefore, you have a perfect right to approach me at any time.'

Elvira said 'Thank you' politely. Egerton asked:

'Is there anything worrying you?'

'No. Not really. But you see, I don't *know* anything. Nobody's ever told me things. One doesn't always like to ask.'

He looked at her attentively.

'You mean things about yourself?'

'Yes,' said Elvira. 'It's kind of you to understand. Uncle Derek—' she hesitated.

'Derek Luscombe, you mean?'

'Yes. I've always called him uncle.'

'I see.'

'He's very kind,' said Elvira, 'but he's not the sort of person who ever tells you anything. He just arranges things, and looks a little worried in case they mightn't be what I'd like. Of course he listens to a lot of people – women, I mean – who tell him things. Like Contessa Martinelli. He arranges for me to go to schools or to finishing places.'

'And they haven't been where you wanted to go?'

'No, I didn't mean that. They've been quite all right. I mean they've been more or less where everyone else goes.'

'I see.'

'But I don't know anything about *myself*. I mean what money I've got, and how much, and what I could do with it if I wanted.'

'In fact,' said Egerton, with his attractive smile, 'you want to talk business. Is that it? Well, I think you're quite right. Let's see. How old are you? Sixteen – seventeen?'

'I'm nearly twenty.'

'Oh dear. I'd no idea.'

'You see,' explained Elvira, 'I feel all the time that I'm being shielded and sheltered. It's nice in a way, but it can get very irritating.'

'It's an attitude that's gone out of date,' agreed Egerton, 'but I can quite see that it would appeal to Derek Luscombe.'

'He's a dear,' said Elvira, 'but very difficult, somehow, to talk to seriously.'

'Yes, I can see that that might be so. Well, how much *do* you know about yourself, Elvira? About your family circumstances?'

'I know that my father died when I was five and that my mother had run away from him with someone when I was about two, I don't remember her at all. I barely remember my father. He was very old and had his leg up on a chair. He used to swear. I was rather scared of him. After he died I lived first with an aunt or a cousin or something of my father's, until *she* died, and then I lived with Uncle Derek and his sister. But then she died and I went to Italy. Uncle Derek has arranged for me, now, to live with the Melfords, who are his cousins, and very kind and nice and have two daughters about my age.'

'You're happy there?'

'I don't know yet. I've barely got there. They're all very dull. I really wanted to know how much money I've got.'

'So it's financial information you really want?'

'Yes,' said Elvira. 'I've got *some* money, I know. Is it a lot?'

Egerton was serious now.

'Yes,' he said. 'You've got a lot of money. Your father was a very rich man. You were his only child. When he died, the title and the estate went to a cousin. He didn't like the cousin, so he left all his personal property, which was considerable, to his daughter – to you, Elvira. You're a very rich woman, or will be, when you are twenty-one.'

'You mean I am not rich *now*?'

'Yes,' said Egerton, 'you're rich now, but the money is not yours to dispose of until you are twenty-one or marry. Until that time it is in the hands of your trustees. Luscombe, myself and another.' He smiled at her. 'We haven't embezzled it or anything like that. It's still there. In fact, we've increased your capital consideraby by investments.'

'How much will I have?'

'At the age of twenty-one or upon your marriage, you will come into a sum which at a rough estimate would amount to six or seven hundred thousand pounds.'

'That *is* a lot,' said Elvira, impressed.

'Yes, it is a lot. Probably it is because it is such a lot that nobody has ever talked to you about it much.'

He watched her as she reflected upon this. Quite an interesting girl, he thought. Looked an unbelievably milk-and-water Miss, but she was more than that. A good deal more. He said, with a faintly ironic smile:

'Does that satisfy you?'

23

She gave him a sudden smile.

'It ought to, oughtn't it?'

'Rather better than winning the pools,' he suggested.

She nodded, but her mind was elsewhere. Then she came out abruptly with a question.

'Who gets it if I die?'

'As things stand now, it would go to your next of kin.'

'I mean – I couldn't make a will now, could I? Not until I was twenty-one. That's what someone told me.'

'They were quite right.'

'That's really rather annoying. If I was married and died I suppose my husband would get the money?'

'Yes.'

'And if I wasn't married my mother would be my next of kin and get it. I really seem to have very few relations – I don't even know my mother. What is she like?'

'She's a very remarkable woman,' said Egerton shortly. 'Everybody would agree to that.'

'Didn't she ever *want* to see me?'

'She may have done . . . I think it's very possible that she did. But having made – in certain ways – rather a mess of her own life, she may have thought that it was better for you that you should be brought up quite apart from her.'

'Do you actually *know* that she thinks that?'

'No. I don't really know anything about it.'

Elvira got up.

'Thank you,' she said. 'It's very kind of you to tell me all this.'

'I think perhaps you ought to have been told more about things before,' said Egerton.

'It's rather humiliating *not* to know things,' said Elvira. 'Uncle Derek, of course, thinks I'm just a *child*.'

'Well, he's not a very young man himself. He and I, you know, are well advanced in years. You must make allowances for us when we look at things from the point of view of our advanced age.'

Elvira stood looking at him for a moment or two.

'But *you* don't think I'm really a child, do you?' she said shrewdly, and added, 'I expect you know rather more about girls than Uncle Derek does. He just lived with his sister.' Then she stretched out her hand and said, very prettily, 'Thank you so much. I hope I haven't interrupted some important work you had to do,' and went out.

Egerton stood looking at the door that had closed behind her. He pursed up his lips, whistled a moment, shook his head and sat down again, picked up a pen and tapped thoughtfully on his desk. He drew some papers towards him, then thrust them back and picked up his telephone.

'Miss Cordell, get me Colonel Luscombe, will you? Try his club first. And then the Shropshire address.'

He put back the receiver. Again he drew his papers towards him and started reading them but his mind was not on what he was doing. Presently his buzzer went.

'Colonel Luscombe is on the wire now, Mr Egerton.'

'Right. Put him through. Hallo, Derek. Richard Egerton here. How are you? I've just been having a visit from someone you know. A visit from your ward.'

'From Elvira?' Derek Luscombe sounded very surprised.

'Yes.'

'But why – what on earth – what did she come to you for? Not in any trouble?'

'No, I wouldn't say so. On the contrary, she seemed rather – well, pleased with herself. She wanted to know all about her financial position.'

'You didn't tell her, I hope?' said Colonel Luscombe, in alarm.

'Why not? What's the point of secrecy?

'Well, I can't help feeling it's a little unwise for a girl to know that she is going to come into such a large amount of money.'

'Somebody else will tell her that, if we don't. She's got to be prepared, you know. Money is a responsibility.'

'Yes, but she's so much of a child still.'

'Are you sure of that?'

'What do you mean? Of course she's a child.'

'I wouldn't describe her as such. Who's the boy-friend?'

'I beg your pardon.'

'I said who's the boy-friend? There *is* a boy-friend in the offing, isn't there?'

'No, indeed. Nothing of the sort. What on earth makes you think that?'

'Nothing that she actually said. But I've got some experience, you know. I think you'll find there *is* a boy-friend.'

'Well, I can assure you you're quite wrong. I mean, she's been most carefully brought up, she's been at very strict schools, she's been in a very select finishing establishment in Italy. I should know if there was anything of that kind going on. I dare say she's met one or two pleasant young fellows and all that, but I'm sure there's been nothing of the kind you suggest.'

'Well, my diagnosis is a boy-friend – and probably an undesirable one.'

But why, Richard, why? What do *you* know about young girls?'

'Quite a lot,' said Egerton dryly. 'I've had three clients in the last year, two of whom were made wards of court and the third one managed to bully her parents into agreeing to an almost certainly disastrous marriage. Girls don't get looked after the way they used to be. Conditions are such that it's very difficult to look after them at all—'

'But I assure you Elvira has been most carefully looked after.'

'The ingenuity of the young female of the species is beyond anything you could conjecture! You keep an eye on her, Derek. Make a few inquiries as to what she's been up to.'

'Nonsense. She's just a sweet simple girl.'

'What you don't know about sweet simple girls would fill an album! Her mother ran away and caused a scandal – remember? – when she was younger than Elvira is today. As for old Coniston, he was one of the worst rips in England.'

'You upset me, Richard. You upset me very much.'

'You might as well be warned. What I didn't quite like was one of her other questions. Why is she so anxious to know who'd inherit her money if she dies?'

'It's queer your saying that, because she asked me that same question.'

'Did she now? Why should her mind run on early death? She asked me about her mother, by the way.'

Colonel Luscombe's voice sounded worried as he said: 'I wish Bess would get in touch with the girl.'

'Have you been talking to her on the subject – to Bess, I mean?'

'Well, yes . . . Yes I did. I ran across her by chance. We were staying in the same hotel, as a matter of fact. I urged Bess to make some arrangements to see the girl.'

'What did she say?' asked Egerton curiously.

'Refused point blank. She more or less said that she wasn't a safe person for the girl to know.'

'Looked at from one point of view I don't suppose she is,' said Egerton. 'She's mixed up with that racing fellow, isn't she?'

'I've heard rumours.'

'Yes, I've heard them too. I don't know if there's much in

it really. There might be, I suppose. That could be why she feels as she does. Bess's friends are strong meat from time to time! But what a woman she is, eh Derek? What a woman.'

'Always been her own worst enemy,' said Derek Luscombe, gruffly.

'A really nice conventional remark,' said Egerton. 'Well, sorry I bothered you, Derek, but keep a look-out for undesirables in the background. Don't say you haven't been warned.'

He replaced the receiver and drew the pages on his desk towards him once more. This time he was able to put his whole attention on what he was doing.

—— I I ——

Mrs McCrae, Canon Pennyfather's housekeeper, had ordered a Dover sole for the evening of his return. The advantages attached to a good Dover sole were manifold. It need not be introduced to the grill or frying pan until the Canon was safely in the house. It could be kept until the next day if necessary. Canon Pennyfather was fond of Dover sole; and, if a telephone call or telegram arrived saying that the Canon would after all be elsewhere on this particular evening, Mrs McCrae was fond of a good Dover sole herself. All therefore was in good trim for the Canon's return. The Dover sole would be followed by pancakes. The sole sat on the kitchen table, the batter for the pancakes was ready in a bowl. All was in readiness. The brass shone, the silver sparkled, not a minuscule of dust showed anywhere. There was only one thing lacking. The Canon himself.

The Canon was scheduled to return on the train arriving at 6.30 from London.

At 7 o'clock he had not returned. No doubt the train was late. At 7.30 he still had not returned. Mrs McCrae gave a sigh of vexation. She suspected that this was going to be another of these things. Eight o'clock came and no Canon. Mrs McCrae gave a long, exasperated sigh. Soon, no doubt, she would get a telephone call, though it was quite within the bounds of possibility that there would not be even a telephone call. He might have written to her. No doubt he had written, but he had probably omitted to post the letter.

'Dear, dear!' said Mrs McCrae.

At 9 o'clock she made herself three pancakes with the pancake batter. The sole she put carefully away in the Frigidaire. 'I wonder where the good man's got to now,' she said to herself. She knew by experience that he might be anywhere. The odds were that he would discover his mistake in time to telegraph her or telephone her before she retired to bed. 'I shall sit up until 11 o'clock but no longer,' said Mrs McCrae. Ten-thirty was her bed-time, and extension to eleven she considered her duty, but if at eleven there was nothing, no word from the Canon, then Mrs McCrae would duly lock up the house and betake herself to bed.

It cannot be said that she was worried. This sort of thing had happened before. There was nothing to be done but wait for news of some kind. The possibilities were numerous. Canon Pennyfather might have got on the wrong train and failed to discover his mistake until he was at Land's End or John o' Groats, or he might still be in London having made some mistake in the date, and was therefore convinced he was not returning until tomorrow. He might have met a friend or friends at this foreign conference he was going to and been induced to stay out there perhaps over the week-end. He would have meant to let her know but had entirely forgotten to do so. So, as has been already said, she was not worried. The day after tomorrow his old friend, Archdeacon Simmons, was coming to stay. That was the sort of thing the Canon *did* remember, so no doubt he himself or a telegram from him would arrive tomorrow and at latest he would be home on the day after, or there would be a letter.

The morning of the day after, however, arrived without a word from him. For the first time Mrs McCrae began to be uneasy. Between 9 a.m. and 1 p.m. she eyed the telephone in a doubtful manner. Mrs McCrae had had her own fixed views about the telephone. She used it and recognised its convenience but she was not fond of the telephone. Some of her household shopping was done by telephone, though she much preferred to do it in person owing to a fixed belief that if you did not see what you were being given, a shopkeeper was sure to try and cheat you. Still, telephones were useful for domestic matters. She occasionally, though rarely, telephoned her friends or relations in the near neighbourhood. To make a call of any distance, or a London call, upset her severely. It was a shameful waste of money. Nevertheless, she began to meditate facing that problem.

Finally, when yet another day dawned without any news of him she decided to act. She knew where the Canon was staying in London. Bertram's Hotel. A nice old-fashioned place. It might be as well, perhaps, if she rang up and made certain inquiries. They would probably know where the Canon was. It was not an ordinary hotel. She would ask to be put through to Miss Gorringe. Miss Gorringe was always efficient and thoughtful. The Canon might, of course, return by the twelve-thirty. If so he would be here any minute now.

But the minutes passed and there was no Cannon. Mrs McCrae took a deep breath, nerved herself and asked for a call to London. She waited, biting her lips and holding the receiver clamped firmly to her ear.

'Bertram's Hotel, at your service,' said a voice.

'I would like, if you please, to speak to Miss Gorringe,' said Mrs McCrae.

'Just a moment. What name shall I say?'

'It's Canon Pennyfather's housekeeper. Mrs McCrae.'

'Just a moment please.'

Presently the calm and efficient voice of Miss Gorringe came through.

'Miss Gorringe here. Did you say Canon Pennyfather's housekeeper?'

'That's right. Mrs McCrae.'

'Oh yes. Of course. What can I do for you, Mrs McCrae?'

'Is Canon Pennyfather staying at the hotel still?'

'I'm glad you've rung up,' said Miss Gorringe. 'We have been rather worried as to what exactly to do.'

'Do you mean something's happened to Canon Pennyfather? Has he had an accident?'

'No, no, nothing of that kind. But we expected him back from Lucerne on Friday or Saturday.'

'Eh – that'd be right.'

'But he didn't arrive. Well, of course that wasn't really surprising. He had booked his room on – booked it, that is, until yesterday. He didn't come back yesterday or send any word and his things are still here. The major part of his baggage. We hadn't been quite sure what to do about it. Of course,' Miss Gorringe went on hastily, 'we know the Canon is, well – somewhat forgetful sometimes.'

'You may well say that!'

'It makes it a little difficult for us. We are so fully booked

up. His room is actually booked for another guest.' She added:'
'You have no idea where he is?'

With bitterness Mrs McCrae said,

'The man might be anywhere!' She pulled herself together.

'Well, thank you, Miss Gorringe.'

'Anything I can do—' Miss Gorringe suggested helpfully.

'I dare say I'll hear soon enough,' said Mrs McCrae. She thanked Miss Gorringe again and rang off.

She sat by the telephone, looking upset. She did not fear for the Canon's personal safety. If he had had an accident she would by now have been notified. She felt sure of that. On the whole the Canon was not what one would call accident prone. He was what Mrs McCrae called to herself 'one of the scatty ones', and the scatty ones seemed always to be looked after by a special providence. Whilst taking no care or thought, they could still survive even a Panda crossing. No, she did not visualise Canon Pennyfather as lying groaning in a hospital. He was *somewhere,* no doubt innocently and happily prattling with some friend or other. Maybe he was abroad still. The difficulty was that Archdeacon Simmons would expect to find a host to receive him. She couldn't put Archdeacon Simmons off because she didn't know where he was. It was all very difficult, but it had, like most difficulties, its bright spot. Its bright spot was Archdeacon Simmons. Archdeacon Simmons would know what to do. She would place the matter in his hands.

Archdeacon Simmons was a complete contrast to her employer. He knew where he was going, and what he was doing, and was always cheerfully sure of knowing the right thing to be done and doing it. A confident cleric. Archdeacon Simmons, when he arrived, to be met by Mrs McCrae's explanations, apologies and perturbation, was a tower of strength. He, too, was not alarmed.

'Now don't you worry, Mrs McCrae,' he said in his genial fashion, as he sat down to the meal she had prepared for his arrival. 'We'll hunt the absent-minded fellow down. Ever heard that story about Chesterton? G. K. Chesterton, you know, the writer. Wired to his wife when he'd gone on a lecture tour "Am at Crewe Station. Where ought I to be?" '

He laughed. Mrs McCrae smiled dutifully. She did not think it was very funny because it was so exactly the sort of thing that Canon Pennyfather might have done.

'Ah,' said Archdeacon Simmons, with appreciation, 'one of

your excellent veal cutlets! You're a marvellous cook, Mrs McCrae. I hope my old friend appreciates you.'

Veal cutlets having been succeeded by some small castle puddings with a blackberry sauce which Mrs McCrae had remembered was one of the Archdeacon's favourite sweets, the good man applied himself in earnest to the tracking down of his missing friend. He addressed himself to the telephone with vigour and a complete disregard for expense, which made Mrs McCrae purse her lips anxiously, although not really disapproving, because definitely her master had got to be tracked down.

Having first dutifully tried the Canon's sister who took little notice of her brother's goings and comings and as usual had not the faintest idea where he was or might be, the Archdeacon spread his net farther afield. He addressed himself once more to Bertram's Hotel and got details as precisely as possible. The Canon had definitely left there on the early evening of the 19th. He had with him a small BEA handbag, but his other luggage had remained behind in his room, which he had duly retained. He had mentioned that he was going to a conference of some kind at Lucerne. He had not gone direct to the airport from the hotel. The commissionaire, who knew him well by sight, had put him into a taxi and had directed it, as told by the Canon, to the Athenæum Club. That was the last time that anyone at Bertram's Hotel had seen Canon Pennyfather. Oh yes, a small detail – he had omitted to leave his key behind but had taken it with him. It was not the first time that that had happened.

Archdeacon Simmons paused for a few minutes' consideration before the next call. He could ring up the air station in London. That would no doubt take some time. There might be a short cut. He rang up Dr Weissgarten, a learned Hebrew scholar who was almost certain to have been at the conference.

Dr Weissgarten was at his home. As soon as he heard who was speaking to him he launched out into a torrent of verbiage consisting mostly of disparaging criticism of two papers that had been read at the conference in Lucerne.

'Most unsound, that fellow Hogarov,' he said, 'most unsound. How he gets away with it I don't know! Fellow isn't a scholar at all. Do you know what he actually said?'

The Archdeacon sighed and had to be firm with him. Otherwise there was a good chance that the rest of the evening would be spent in listening to criticism of fellow scholars at the

Lucerne Conference. With some reluctance Dr Weissgarten was pinned down to more personal matters.

'Pennyfather?' he said, 'Pennyfather? He ought to have been there. Can't think why he wasn't there. Said he was going. Told me so only a week before when I saw him in the Athenæum.'

'You mean he wasn't at the conference at all?'

'That's what I've just said. He *ought* to have been there.'

'Do you know *why* he wasn't there? Did he send an excuse?'

'How should I know? He certainly talked about being there. Yes, now I remember. He was expected. Several people remarked on his absence. Thought he might have had a chill or something. Very treacherous weather.' He was about to revert to his criticisms of his fellow scholars but Archdeacon Simmons rang off.

He had got a fact but it was a fact that for the first time awoke in him an uneasy feeling. Canon Pennyfather had not been at Lucerne Conference. He had meant to go to that conference. It seemed very extraordinary to the Archdeacon that he had not been there. He might, of course, have taken the wrong plane, though on the whole BEA were pretty careful of you and shepherded you away from such possibilities. Could Canon Pennyfather have forgotten the actual day that he was going to the conference? It was always possible, he supposed. But if so where had he gone instead?

He addressed himself now to the air terminal. It involved a great deal of patient waiting and being transferred from department to department. In the end he got a definite fact. Canon Pennyfather had booked as a passenger on the 21.40 plane to Lucerne on the 18th but he had not been on the plane.

'We're getting on,' said Archdeacon Simmons to Mrs McCrae, who was hovering in the background. 'Now, let me see. Who shall I try next?'

'All this telephoning will cost a fearful lot of money,' said Mrs McCrae.

'I'm afraid so. I'm afraid so,' said Archdeacon Simmons. 'But we've got to get on his track, you know. He's not a very young man.'

'Oh, sir, you don't think there's anything could really have happened to him?'

'Well I hope not . . . I don't think so, because I think you'd have heard if so. He – er – always had his name and address on him, didn't he?'

'Oh yes, sir, he had cards on him. He'd have letters too, and all sorts of things in his wallet.'

'Well, I don't think he's in a hospital then,' said the Archdeacon. 'Let me see. When he left the hotel he took a taxi to the Athenæum. I'll ring them up next.'

Here he got some definite information. Canon Pennyfather, who was well known there, had dined there at seven thirty on the evening of the 19th. It was then that the Archdeacon was struck by something he had overlooked until then. The aeroplane ticket had been for the 18th but the Canon had left Bertram's Hotel by taxi to the Athenæum, having mentioned he was going to the Lucerne Conference, on the 19th. Light began to break. 'Silly old ass,' thought Archdeacon Simmons to himself, but careful not to say it aloud in front of Mrs McCrae. 'Got his dates wrong. The conference was on the 19th. I'm sure of it. He must have thought that he was leaving on the 18th. He was one day wrong.'

He went over the next bit carefully. The Canon would have gone to the Athenæum, he would have dined, he would have gone on to Kensington Air Station. There, no doubt, it would have been pointed out to him that his ticket was for the day before and he would then have realized that the conference he was going to attend was now over.

'That's what happened,' said Archdeacon Simmons,' depend upon it.' He explained it to Mrs McCrae, who agreed that it was likely enough. 'Then what would he do?'

'Go back to his hotel,' said Mrs McCrae.

'He wouldn't have come straight down here – gone straight to the station, I mean.'

'Not if his luggage was at the hotel. At any rate, he would have called there for his luggage.'

'True enough,' said Simmons. 'All right. We'll think of it like this. He left the airport with his little bag and he went back to the hotel, or started for the hotel at all events. He might have had dinner perhaps – no, he'd dined at the Athenæum. All right, he went back to the hotel. *But* he never arrived there.' He paused a moment or two and then said doubtfully, 'Or did he? Nobody seems to have seen him there. So what happened to him on the way?'

'He could have met someone,' said Mrs McCrae, doubtfully.

'Yes. Of course that's perfectly possible. Some old friend he hadn't seen for a long time . . . He could have gone off with a friend to the friend's hotel or the friend's house, but he wouldn't have stayed there three days, would he? He wouldn't have forgotten for three whole days that his luggage was at the hotel. He'd have rung up about it, he'd have called for it, or in a supreme fit of absent-mindedness he might have come straight home. Three days' silence. That's what's so inexplicable.'

'If he had an accident—'

'Yes, Mrs McCrae, of course that's possible. We can try the hospitals. You say he had plenty of papers on him to identify him? Hm – I think there's only one thing for it.'

Mrs McCrae looked at him apprehensively.

'I think, you know,' said the Archdeacon gently, 'that we've got to go to the police.'

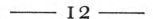

12

Miss Marple had found no difficulty in enjoying her stay in London. She did a lot of things that she had not had the time to do in her hitherto brief visits to the capital. It has to be regretfully noted that she did not avail herself of the wide cultural activities that would have been possible to her. She visited no picture galleries and no museums. The idea of patronising a dress show of any kind would not even have occurred to her. What she did visit were the glass and china departments of the large stores, and the household linen departments, and she also availed herself of some marked down lines in furnishing fabrics. Having spent what she considered a reasonable sum upon these household investments, she indulged in various excursions of her own. She went to places and shops she remembered from her young days, sometimes merely with the curiosity of seeing whether they were still there. It was not a pursuit that she had ever had time for before, and she enjoyed it very much. After a nice little nap after lunch, she would go out, and, avoiding the attentions of the commissionaire if possible, because he was so firmly imbued with the idea that a lady of her age and frailty should always go in a taxi, she walked towards a bus stop, or tube station. She had bought a small guide to buses and their routes – and an Underground Transport Map; and she would plan her excursion carefully. One afternoon she could be seen walking happily and nostalgically round Evelyn Gardens or Onslow Square murmuring softly, 'Yes, that was Mrs Van Dylan's house. Of course it looks *quite* different now. They seem to have remodelled it. Dear me, I see it's got four bells. Four flats, I suppose. Such a nice old-fashioned square this always was.'

Rather shamefacedly she paid a visit to Madame Tussaud's, a well-remembered delight of her childhood. In Westbourne Grove she looked in vain for Bradley's. Aunt Helen had always gone to Bradley's about her sealskin jacket.

Window shopping in the general sense did not interest Miss Marple, but she had a splendid time rounding up knitting patterns, new varieties of knitting wool, and such-like delights. She made a special expedition to Richmond to see the house that had been occupied by Great-Uncle Thomas, the retired admiral. The handsome terrace was still there but here again each house seemed to be turned into flats. Much more painful was the house in Lowndes Square where a distant cousin, Lady Merridew, had lived in some style. Here a vast skyscraper building of modernistic design appeared to have arisen. Miss Marple shook her head sadly and said firmly to herself, 'There must *be* progress I suppose. If Cousin Ethel knew, she'd turn in her grave, I'm sure.'

It was on one particularly mild and pleasant afternoon that Miss Marple embarked on a bus that took her over Battersea Bridge. She was going to combine the double pleasure of taking a sentimental look at Princes Terrace Mansions where an old governess of hers had once lived, and visiting Battersea Park. The first part of her quest was abortive. Miss Ledbury's former home had vanished without trace and had been replaced by a great deal of gleaming concrete. Miss Marple turned into Battersea Park. She had always been a good walker but had to admit that nowadays her walking powers were not what they were. Half a mile was quite enough to tire her. She could manage, she thought, to cross the Park and go out over Chelsea Bridge and find herself once more on a convenient bus route, but her steps grew gradually slower and slower, and she was pleased to come upon a tea enclosure situated on the edge of the lake.

Teas were still being served there in spite of the autumn chill. There were not many people today, a certain amount of mothers and prams, and a few pairs of young lovers. Miss Marple collected a tray with tea and two sponge cakes. She carried her tray carefully to a table and sat down. The tea was just what she needed. Hot, strong and very reviving. Revived, she looked round her, and her eyes stopping suddenly at a particular table, she sat up very straight in her chair. Really, a very strange coincidence, very strange indeed! First the Army & Navy Stores and now here. Very unusual places those particular two people chose! But no! She was wrong. Miss Marple took a second and stronger pair of glasses from her bag. Yes, she had been mistaken. There was a certain similarity, of course. That long straight blonde hair; but this was not Bess Sedgwick. It was someone years younger. Of course! It was the daughter! The young girl who had come into Bertram's with Lady Selina Hazy's friend, Colonel Luscombe. But the man was the same man who had been lunching with Lady Sedgwick in the Army & Navy Stores. No doubt about it, the same handsome, hawk-like look, the same leanness, the same predatory toughness and – yes, the same strong virile attraction.

'Bad!' said Miss Marple. 'Bad all through! Cruel! Unscrupulous. I don't *like* seeing this. First the mother, now the daughter. What does it mean?'

It meant no good. Miss Marpe was sure of that. Miss Marple seldom gave anyone the benefit of the doubt; she invariably thought the worst, and nine times out of ten, so she insisted, she was right in so doing. Both these meetings, she was sure, were more or less secret meetings. She observed now the way these two bent forward over the table until their heads nearly touched; and the earnestness with which they talked. The girl's face – Miss Marple took off her spectacles, rubbed the lenses carefully, then put them on again. Yes, this girl was in love. Desperately in love, as only the young can be in love. But what were her guardians about to let her run about London and have these clandestine assignments in Battersea Park? A nicely brought up, well-behaved girl like that. *Too* nicely brought up, no doubt! Her people probably believed her to be in some quite other spot. She had to tell lies.

On her way out Miss Marple passed the table where they were sitting, slowing down as much as she could without its being too obvious. Unfortunately, their voices were so low that she could not hear what they said. The man was speaking, the girl was listening, half pleased, half afraid. 'Planning to run away together, perhaps?' thought Miss Marple. 'She's still under age.'

Miss Marple passed through the small gate in the fence that led to the side-walk of the park. There were cars parked along there and presently she stopped beside one particular car. Miss

Marple was not particularly knowledgeable over cars but such cars as this one did not come her way very often, so she had noted and remembered it. She had acquired a little information about cars of this style from an enthusiastic great-nephew. It was a racing car. Some foreign make – she couldn't remember the name now. Not only that, she had seen this car or one exactly like it, seen it only yesterday in a side street close to Bertram's Hotel. She had noticed it not only because of its size and its powerful and unusual appearance but because the number had awakened some vague memory, some trace of association in her memory. FAN 2266. It had made her think of her cousin Fanny Godfrey. Poor Fanny who stuttered, who had said 'I have got t-t-t-t-wo s-s-s-potz . . .'

She walked along and looked at the number of this car. Yes, she was quite right. FAN 2266. It was the same car. Miss Marple, her footsteps growing more painful every moment, arrived deep in thought at the other side of Chelsea Bridge and by then was so exhausted that she hailed the first taxi she saw with decision. She was worried by the feeling that there was something she ought to do about things. But what things and what to do about them? It was all so indefinite. She fixed her eyes absently on some news-boards.

'Sensational developments in train robbery,' they ran. 'Engine driver's story,' said another one. Really! Miss Marple thought to herself, every day there seemed to be a bank hold-up or a train robbery or a wage pay snatch.

Crime seemed to have got above itself.

Vaguely reminiscent of a large bumble bee, Chief-Inspector Fred Davy wandered around the confines of the Criminal Investigation Department, humming to himself. It was a well-known idiosyncrasy of his, and caused no particular notice except to give rise to the remark that 'Father was on the prowl again.'

His prowling led him at last to the room where Inspector Campbell was sitting behind a desk with a bored expression. Inspector Campbell was an ambitious young man and he found much of his occupation tedious in the extreme. Nevertheless, he coped with the duties appointed to him and achieved a very fair measure of success in so doing. The powers that be approved of him, thought he should do well and doled out from time to time a few words of encouraging commendation.

'Good morning, sir,' said Inspector Campbell, respectfully, when Father entered his domain. Naturally he called Chief-Inspector Davy 'Father' behind his back as everyone else did; but he was not yet of sufficient seniority to do such a thing to his face.

'Anything I can do for you, sir?' he inquired.

'La, la, boom, boom,' hummed the Chief-Inspector, slightly off key. 'Why must they call me Mary when my name's Miss Gibbs?' After this rather unexpected resurrection of a by-gone musical comedy, he drew up a chair and sat down.

'Busy?' he asked.

'Moderately so.'

'Got some disappearance case or other on, haven't you, to do with some hotel or other. What's the name of it now? Bertram's. Is that it?'

'Yes, that's right, sir. Bertram's Hotel.'

'Contravening the licensing hours? Call girls?'

'Oh no, sir,' said Inspector Campbell, slightly shocked at hearing Bertram's Hotel being referred to in such a connection. 'Very nice, quiet, old-fashioned place.'

'Is it now?' said Father. 'Yes, is it now? Well, that's interesting, really.'

Inspector Campbell wondered why it was interesting. He did not like to ask, as tempers in the upper hierarchy were notoriously short since the mail train robbery which had been a spectacular success for the criminals. He looked at Father's large, heavy, bovine face and wondered as he had once or twice wondered before, how Chief-Inspector Davy had reached his present rank and why he was so highly thought of in the department. 'All right in his day, I suppose,' thought Inspector Campbell, but there are plenty of go-ahead chaps about who could do with some promotion, once the deadwood is cleared away.' But the deadwood had begun another song. partly hummed, with an occasional word or two here and there.

'*Tell me, gentle stranger, are there any more at home like you?*' intoned Father and then in a sudden falsetto, '*A few, kind sir, and nicer girls you never knew.* No, let's see, I've got the sexes mixed up. *Floradora.* That was a good show, too.'

'I believe I've heard of it, sir,' said Inspector Campbell.

'Your mother sang you to sleep in the cradle with it, I expect,' said Chief-Inspector Davy. 'Now then, what's been going on at Bertram's Hotel? Who has disappeared and how and why?'

'A Canon Pennyfather, sir. Elderly clergyman.'

'Dull case, eh?'

Inspector Campbell smiled.

'Yes, sir, it *is* rather dull in a way.'

'What did he look like?'

'Canon Pennyfather?'

'Yes – you've got a description, I suppose?'

'Of course.' Campbell shuffled papers and read: 'Height 5ft. 8. Large thatch of white hair – stoops...'

'And he disappeared from Bertram's Hotel – when?'

'About a week ago – November 19th.'

'And they've just reported it. Took their time about it, didn't they?'

'Well, I think there was a general idea that he'd turn up.'

'Any idea what's behind it?' asked Father. 'Has a decent God-fearing man suddenly gone off with one of the church-wardens' wives? Or does he do a bit of secret drinking, or has he embezzled the church funds? Or is he the sort of absent-minded old chap who goes in for this sort of thing?'

'Well, from all I can hear, sir, I should say the latter. He's done it before.'

'What – disappeared from a respectable West End hotel?'

'No, not exactly that, but he's not always returned home when he was expected. Occasionally he's turned up to stay with friends on a day when they haven't asked him, or not turned up on the date when they *had* asked him. That sort of thing.'

'Yes,' said Father. 'Yes. Well, that sounds very nice and natural and according to plan, doesn't it? When exactly did you say he disappeared?'

'Thursday. November 19th. He was supposed to be attending a congress at—' He bent down and studied some papers on his desk. '—Oh yes, Lucerne. Society of Biblical Historical Studies. That's the English translation of it. I think it's actually a German society.'

'And it was held at Lucerne? The old boy – I suppose he *is* an old boy?'

'Sixty-three, sir, I understand.'

'The old boy didn't turn up, is that it?'

Inspector Campbell drew his papers towards him and gave Father the ascertainable facts in so far as they had been ascertained.

'Doesn't sound as if he'd gone off with a choirboy,' observed Chief-Inspector Davy.

'I expect he'll turn up all right,' said Campbell, 'but we're looking into it, of course. Are you – er –particularly interested in the case, sir?' He could hardly restrain his curiosity on this point.

'No,' said Davy thoughtfully. 'No, I'm not interested in the *case*. I don't see anything to be interesed about in it.'

There was a pause, a pause which clearly contained the words 'Well, then?' with a question mark after it from Inspector Campbell, which he was too well trained to utter in audible tones.

'What I'm *really* interested in,' said Father, 'is the date. And Bertram's Hotel, of course.'

'It's always been very well conducted, sir. No trouble there.'

'That's very nice, I'm sure,' said Father. He added thoughtfully, 'I'd rather like to have a look at the place.'

'Of course, sir,' said Inspector Campbell. 'Any time you like. I was thinking of going round there myself.'

'I might as well come along with you,' said Father. 'Not to butt in, nothing like that. But I'd just rather like to have a look at the place, and this disappearing Archdeacon of yours, or whatever he is, makes rather a good excuse. No need to call me "sir" when we're there – you throw your weight about. I'll be your stooge.'

Inspector Campbell became interested.

'Do you think there's something that might tie in there, sir, something that might tie in with something else?'

'There's no reason to believe so, so far,' said Father. 'But you know how it is. One gets – I don't know what to call them – whims, do you think? Bertram's Hotel, somehow, sounds almost too good to be true.'

He resumed his impersonation of a bumble bee with a rendering of 'Let's All Go Down the Strand.'

The two detective officers went off together, Campbell looking smart in a lounge suit, (he had an excellent figure), and Chief-Inspector Davy carrying with him a tweedy air of being up from the country. They fitted in quite well. Only the astute eye of Miss Gorringe, as she raised it from her ledgers, singled them out and appreciated them for what they were. Since she had reported the disappearance of Canon Pennyfather herself and had already had a word with a lesser personage in the police force, she had been expecting something of this kind. A faint murmur to the earnest-looking girl assistant whom she kept handy in the background enabled the latter to come forward and deal with any ordinary inquiries or services while Miss Gorringe gently shifted herself a little farther along the counter and looked up at the two men. Inspector Campbell laid down his card on the desk in front of her and she nodded. Looking past him to the large tweed-coated figure behind him, she noted that he had turned slightly sideways, and was observing the lounge and its occupants with an apparently naïve pleasure at beholding such a well bred, upper-class world in action.

'Would you like to come into the office?' said Miss Gorringe. 'We can talk better there perhaps.'

'Yes, I think that would be best.'

'Nice place you've got here,' said the large, fat, bovine-looking man, turning his head back towards her. 'Comfortable,' he added, looking approvingly at the large fire. 'Good old-fashioned comfort.'

Miss Gorringe smiled with an air of pleasure.

'Yes indeed. We pride ourselves on making our visitors comfortable,' she said. She turned to her assistant. 'Will you carry on, Alice? There is the ledger. Lady Jocelyn will be arriving quite soon. She is sure to want to change her room as soon as she sees it but you must explain to her we are really full up. If necessary, you can show her number 340 on the third floor and offer her that instead. It's not a very pleasant room and I'm sure she will be content with her present one as soon as she sees that.'

'Yes, Miss Gorringe. I'll do just that, Miss Gorringe.'

'And remind Colonel Mortimer that his field glasses are here. He asked me to keep them for him this morning. Don't let him go off without them.'

'No, Miss Gorringe.'

These duties accomplished, Miss Gorringe looked at the two men, came out from behind the desk and walked along to a plain mahogany door with no legend on it. Miss Gorringe opened it and they went into a small, rather sad-looking office. All three sat down.

'The missing man is Canon Pennyfather, I understand,' said Inspector Campbell. He looked at his notes. 'I've got Sergeant

Wadell's report. Perhaps you'll tell me in your own words just what occurred.'

'I don't think that Canon Pennyfather has really disappeared in the sense in which one would usually use that word,' said Miss Gorringe. 'I think, you know, that he's just met someone somewhere, some old friend or something like that, and has perhaps gone off with him to some scholarly meeting or reunion or something of that kind, on the Continent— He is so very vague.'

'You've known him for a long time?'

'Oh yes, he's been coming here to stay for – let me see – oh five or six years at least, I should think.'

'You've been here some time yourself, ma'am,' said Chief-Inspector Davy, suddenly putting in a word.

'I have been here, let me think, fourteen years,' said Miss Gorringe.

'It's a nice place,' repeated Davy again. 'And Canon Penny-father usually stayed here when he was in London? Is that right?'

'Yes. He always came to us. He wrote well beforehand to retain his room. He was much less vague on paper than he was in real life. He asked for a room from the 17th to the 21st. During that time he expected to be away for one or two nights, and he explained that he wished to keep his room on while he was away. He quite often did that.'

'When did you begin to get worried about him?' asked Campbell.

'Well, I didn't really. Of course it was awkward. You see, his room was let on from the 23rd and when I realized – I didn't at first – that he hadn't come back from Lugano—'

'I've got Lucerne here in my notes,' said Campbell.

'Yes, yes, I think it *was* Lucerne. Some Archæological Congress or other. Anyway, when I realized he hadn't come back here and that his baggage was still here waiting in his room, it made things rather awkward. You see, we are very booked up at this time of year and I had someone else coming into his room. The Honourable Mrs Saunders, who lives at Lyme Regis. She always has that room. And then his housekeeper rang up. She was worried.'

'The housekeeper's name is Mrs McCrae, so I understand from Archdeacon Simmons. Do you know her?'

'Not personally, no, but I have spoken to her on the telephone once or twice. She is, I think, a very reliable woman and has been with Canon Pennyfather for some years. She was worried naturally. I believe she and Archdeacon Simmons got in touch with near friends and relations but they knew nothing of Canon Pennyfather's movements. And since he was expecting the Archdeacon to stay with him it certainly seemed very odd – in fact it still does – that the Canon should not have returned home.'

'Is this Canon usually as absent-minded as that?' asked Father.

Miss Gorringe ignored him. This large man, presumably the accompanying sergeant, seemed to her to be pushing himself forward a little too much.

'And now I understand,' continued Miss Gorringe, in an annoyed voice, 'and now I understand from Archdeacon Simmons that the Canon never even went to this conference in Lucerne.'

'Did he send any message to say he wouldn't go?'

'I don't think so – not from here. No telegram or anything like that. I really know nothing about Lucerne – I am really only concerned with *our* side of the matter. It has got into the evening papers, I see – that fact that he is missing, I mean. They haven't mentioned he was staying *here*. I hope they won't. We don't want the Press here, our visitors wouldn't like that at all. If you can keep them off us, Inspector Campbell, we should be very grateful. I mean it's not as if he had disappeared from *here*.'

'His luggage is still here?'

'Yes. In the baggage room. If he didn't go to Lucerne, have you considered the possibility of his being run over? Something like that?'

'Nothing like that has happened to him.'

'It really does seem very, very curious,' said Miss Gorringe, a faint flicker of interest appearing in her manner, to replace the annoyance. 'I mean, it does make one wonder where he *could* have gone and why?'

Father looked at her comprehendingly.

'Of course,' he said. 'You've only been thinking of it from the hotel angle. Very natural.'

'I understand,' said Inspector Campbell, referring once more to his notes, 'that Canon Pennyfather left here about six-thirty on the evening of Thursday the 19th. He had with him a small overnight bag and he left here in a taxi, directing the commissionaire to tell the driver to drive to the Athenæum Club.'

Miss Gorringe nodded her head.

'Yes, he dined at the Athenæum Club – Archdeacon Simmons told me that *that* was the place he was last seen.'

There was a firmness in Miss Gorringe's voice as she transferred the responsibility of seeing the Canon last from Bertram's Hotel to the Athenæum Club.

'Well, it's nice to get the facts straight,' said Father in a gentle rumbling voice. 'We've got 'em straight now. He went off with his little blue BOAC bag or whatever he'd got with him – it *was* a blue BOAC bag, yes? He went off and he didn't come back, and that's that.'

'So you see, really I cannot help you,' said Miss Gorringe, showing a disposition to rise to her feet and get back to work.

'It doesn't *seem* as if you could help us,' said Father, 'but someone else might be able to,' he added.

'Someone else?'

'Why, yes,' said Father. 'One of the staff perhaps.'

'I don't think anyone knows *anything*; or they would certainly have reported it to me.'

'Well, perhaps they might. Perhaps they mightn't. What I mean is, they'd have told you if they'd distinctly *known* anything. But I was thinking more of something he might have *said*.'

'What sort of thing?' said Miss Gorringe, looking perplexed.

'Oh, just some chance word that might give one a clue. Something like "I'm going to see an old friend tonight that I haven't seen since we met in Arizona." Something like that. Or "I'm going to stay next week with a niece of mine for her daughter's confirmation." With absent-minded people, you know, clues like that are a great help. They show what was in the person's mind. It may be that after his dinner at the Athenæum, he gets into a taxi and thinks "Now where am I going?" and having got – say – the confirmation in his mind – thinks he's going off there.'

'Well, I see what you mean,' said Miss Gorringe doubtfully. 'It seems a little unlikely.'

'Oh, one never knows one's luck,' said Father cheerfully. 'There are the various guests here. I suppose Canon Pennyfather knew some of them since he came here fairly often.'

'Oh yes,' said Miss Gorringe. 'Let me see now. I've seen him talking to – yes, Lady Selina Hazy. Then there was the Bishop of Norwich. They're old friends, I believe. They were at Oxford together. And Mrs Jameson and her daughters. They come from the same part of the world. Oh yes, quite a lot of people.'

'You see,' said Father, 'he might have talked to one of *them*. He might have just mentioned some little thing that would give us a clue. Is there anyone staying here now that the Canon knew fairly well?'

Miss Gorringe frowned in thought.

'Well, I think General Radley is here still. And there's an old lady who came up from the country – who used to stay here as a girl, so she told me. Let me see, I can't remember her name at the moment, but I can find it for you. Oh yes, Miss Marple, that's her name. I believe she knew him.'

'Well, we could make a start with those two. And there'd be a chambermaid, I suppose.'

'Oh yes,' said Miss Gorringe. 'But she has been interviewed already by Sergeant Wadell.'

'I know. But not perhaps from this angle. What about the waiter who attended on his table. Or the head waiter?'

'There's Henry, of course,' said Miss Gorringe.

'Who's Henry?' asked Father.

Miss Gorringe looked almost shocked. It was to her impossible that anyone should not know Henry.

'Henry has been here for more years than I can say,' she said. 'You must have noticed him serving teas as you came in.'

'Kind of personality,' said Davy. 'I remember noticing him.'

'I don't know what we should do without Henry,' said Miss Gorringe with feeling. 'He really is wonderful. He sets the tone of the place, you know.'

'Perhaps he might like to serve some tea to me,' said Chief-Inspector Davy. 'Muffins, I saw he'd got there. I'd like a good muffin again.'

'Certainly if you like,' said Miss Gorringe, rather coldly. 'Shall I order two teas to be served to you in the lounge?' she added, turning to Inspector Campbell.

'That would—' the inspector began, when suddenly the door opened and Mr Humfries appeared in his Olympian manner.

He looked slightly taken aback, then looked inquiringly at Miss Gorringe. Miss Gorringe explained.

'These are two gentlemen from Scotland Yard, Mr Humfries,' she said.

'Detective-Inspector Campbell,' said Campbell.

'Oh yes. Yes, of course,' said Mr Humfries. 'The matter of Canon Pennyfather, I suppose? Most extraordinary business. I hope nothing's happened to him, poor chap.'

'So do I,' said Miss Gorringe. 'Such a dear old man.'

'One of the old school,' said Mr Humfries approvingly.

'You seem to have quite a lot of the old school here,' observed Chief-Inspector Davy.

'I suppose we do, I suppose we do,' said Mr Humfries. 'Yes, in many ways we are quite a survival.'

'We have our regulars you know,' said Miss Gorringe. She spoke proudly. 'The same people come back year after year. We have a lot of Americans. People from Boston, and Washington. Very quiet, nice people.'

'They like our English atmosphere,' said Mr Humfries, showing his very white teeth in a smile.

Father looked at him thoughtfully. Inspector Campbell said, 'You're quite sure that no message came here from the Canon? I mean it might have been taken by someone who forgot to write it down or to pass it on.'

'Telephone messages are always taken down *most* carefully,' said Miss Gorringe with ice in her voice. 'I cannot conceive it possible that a message would not have been passed on to me or to the appropriate person on duty.'

She glared at him.

Inspector Campbell looked momentarily taken aback.

'We've really answered all these questions before, you know,' said Mr Humfries, also with a touch of ice in his voice. 'We gave all the information at our disposal to your sergeant – I can't remember his name for the moment.'

Father stirred a little and said, in a kind of homely way,

'Well you see, things have begun to look rather more serious. It looks like a bit more than absent-mindedness. That's why, I think, it would be a good thing if we could have a word or two with those two people you mentioned – General Radley and Miss Marple.'

'You want me to – to arrange an interview with them?' Mr Humfries looked rather unhappy. 'General Radley's very deaf.'

'I don't think it will be necessary to make it too formal,' said Chief-Inspector Davy. 'We don't want to worry people. You can leave it quite safely to us. Just point out those two you mentioned. There is just a chance, you know, that Canon Pennyfather *might* have mentioned some plan of his, or some person he was going to meet at Lucerne or who was going with him to Lucerne. Anyway, it's worth trying.'

Mr Humfries looked somewhat relieved.

'Nothing more we can do for you?' he asked. 'I'm sure you

understand that we wish to help you in every way, only you do understand how we feel about any Press publicity.'

'Quite,' said Inspector Campbell.

'And I'll just have a word with the chambermaid,' said Father.

'Certainly, if you like. I doubt very much whether she can tell you anything.'

'Probably not. But there might be some detail – some remark the Canon made about a letter or an appointment. One never knows.'

Mr Humfries glanced at his watch.

'She'll be on duty at six,' he said. 'Second floor. Perhaps, in the meantime, you'd care for tea?'

'Suits me,' said Father promptly.

They left the office together.

Miss Gorringe said, 'General Radley will be in the smoking-room. The first room down that passage on the left. He'll be in front of the fire there with *The Times*. I think,' she added discreetly, 'he might be asleep. You're sure you don't want me to—'

'No, no, I'll see to it,' said Father. 'And what about the other one – the old lady?'

'She's sitting over there, by the fireplace,' said Miss Gorringe.

'The one with white fluffy hair and the knitting?' said Father, taking a look. 'Might almost be on the stage, mightn't she? Everybody's universal great-aunt.'

'Great-aunts aren't much like that nowadays,' said Miss Gorringe, 'nor grandmothers nor great-grandmothers, if it comes to that. We had the Marchioness of Barlowe in yesterday. She's a great-grandmother. Honestly, I didn't know her when she came in. Just back from Paris. Her face a mask of pink and white and her hair platinum blonde and I suppose an entirely false figure, but it looked wonderful.'

'Ah,' said Father, 'I prefer the old-fashioned kind myself. Well, thank you, ma'am.' He turned to Campbell. 'I'll look after it, shall I, sir? I know you've got an important appointment.'

'That's right,' said Campbell, taking his cue. 'I don't suppose anything much will come of it, but it's worth trying.'

Mr Humfries disappeared into his inner sanctum, saying as he did so:

'Miss Gorringe – just a moment, please.'

Miss Gorringe followed him in and shut the door behind her.

Humfries was walking up and down. He demanded sharply,

'What do they want to see Rose for? Wadell asked all the necessary questions.'

'I suppose it's just routine,' said Miss Gorringe, doubtfully.

'You'd better have a word with her first.'

Miss Gorringe looked a little startled.

'But surely Inspector Campbell—'

'Oh, I'm not worried about Campbell. It's the other one. Do you know who he is?'

'I don't think he gave his name. Sergeant of some kind, I suppose. He looks rather a yokel.'

'Yokel my foot,' said Mr Humfries, abandoning his elegance. 'That's Chief-Inspector Davy, an old fox if there ever was one. They think a lot of him at the Yard. I'd like to know what *he's* doing here, nosing about and playing the genial hick. I don't like it at all.'

'You can't think—'

'I don't know what to think. But I tell you I don't like it. Did he ask to see anyone else besides Rose?'

'I think he's going to have a word with Henry.'

Mr Humfries laughed. Miss Gorringe laughed too.

'We needn't worry about Henry.'

'No, indeed.'

'And the visitors who knew Canon Pennyfather?'

Mr Humfries laughed again.

'I wish him joy of old Radley. He'll have to shout the place down and then he won't get anything worth having. He's welcome to Radley and that funny old hen, Miss Marple. All the same, I don't much like his poking his nose in . . .'

—— 14 ——

'You know,' said Chief-Inspector Davy thoughtfully, 'I don't much like that chap Humfries.'

'Think there's something wrong with him?' asked Campbell.

'Well—' Father sounded apologetic, 'you know the sort of feeling one gets. Smarmy sort of chap. I wonder if he's the owner or only the manager.'

'I could ask him.' Campbell took a step back towards the desk.

'No, don't ask him,' said Father. 'Just find out – quietly.'

Campbell looked at him curiously.

'What's on your mind, sir?'

'Nothing in particular,' said Father. 'I just think I'd like to have a good deal more information about this place. I'd like to know who is behind it, what its financial status is. All that sort of thing.'

Campbell shook his head.

'I should have said if there was one place in London that was absolutely above suspicion—'

'I know, I know,' said Father. 'And what a useful thing it is to have that reputation!'

Campbell shook his head and left. Father went down the passage to the smoking-room. General Radley was just waking up. *The Times* had slipped from his knees and disintegrated slightly. Father picked it up and reassembled the sheets and handed it to him.

'Thank ye, sir. Very kind,' said General Radley gruffly.

'General Radley?'

'Yes.'

'You'll excuse me,' said Father, raising his voice, 'but I want to speak to you about Canon Pennyfather.'

'Eh – what's that?' The General approached, a hand to his ear.

'Canon Pennyfather,' bellowed Father.

'My father? Dead years ago.'

'Canon *Penny*-father.'

'Oh. What about him? Saw him the other day. He was staying here.'

'There was an address he was going to give me. Said he'd leave it with you.'

This was rather more difficult to get over but he succeeded in the end.

'Never gave me any address. Must have mixed me up with somebody else. Muddle-headed old fool. Always was. Scholarly sort of chap, you know. They're always absent-minded.'

Father persevered for a little longer but soon decided that conversation with General Radley was practically impossible and almost certainly unprofitable. He went and sat down in the lounge at a table adjacent to that of Miss Jane Marple.

'Tea, sir?'

Father looked up. He was impressed, as everyone was impressed by Henry's personality. Though such a large and portly man he had appeared, as it were, like some vast travesty of Ariel who could materialize and vanish at will. Father ordered tea.

'Did I see you've got muffins here?' he asked.

Henry smiled benignly.

'Yes, sir. Very good indeed our muffins are, if I may say so. Everyone enjoys them. Shall I order you muffins, sir? Indian or China tea?'

'Indian,' said Father. 'Or Ceylon if you've got it.'

'Certainly we have Ceylon, sir.'

Henry made the faintest gesture with a finger and the pale young man who was his minion departed in search of Ceylon tea and muffins. Henry moved graciously elsewhere.

'You're *Someone*, you are,' thought Father. 'I wonder where they got hold of you and what they pay you. A packet, I bet, *and* you'd be worth it.' He watched Henry bending in a fatherly manner over an elderly lady. He wondered what Henry thought, if he thought anything, about Father. Father considered that he fitted into Bertram's Hotel reasonably well. He might have been a prosperous gentleman farmer or he might have been a peer of the realm with a resemblance to a bookmaker. Father knew two peers who were very like that. On the whole, he thought, he passed muster, but he also thought it possible that he had not deceived Henry. 'Yes, you're *Someone* you are,' Father thought again.

Tea came and the muffins. Father bit deeply. Butter ran down his chin. He wiped it off with a large handkerchief. He drank two cups of tea with plenty of sugar. Then he leaned forward and spoke to the lady sitting in the chair next to him.

'Excuse me,' he said, 'but aren't you Miss Jane Marple?'

Miss Marple transferred her gaze from her knitting to Chief Detective-Inspector Davy.

'Yes,' she said, 'I am Miss Marple.'

'I hope you don't mind my speaking to you. As a matter of fact I am a police officer.'

'Indeed? Nothing seriously wrong here, I hope?'

Father hastened to reassure her in his best paternal fashion.

'Now, don't you worry, Miss Marple,' he said. 'It's not the sort of thing you mean at all. No burglary or anything like that. Just a little difficulty about an absent-minded clergyman, that's all. I think he's a friend of yours. Canon Pennyfather.'

'Oh, Canon Pennyfather. He was here only the other day. Yes, I've known him slightly for many years. As you say, he *is* very absent-minded.' She added, with some interest, 'What has he done now?'

'Well, as you might say in a manner of speaking, he's lost himself.'

'Oh dear,' said Miss Marple. 'Where ought he to be?'

'Back home in his Cathedral Close,' said Father, 'but he isn't.'

'He told *me*,' said Miss Marple, 'he was going to a conference at Lucerne. Something to do with the Dead Sea scrolls, I believe. He's a great Hebrew and Aramaic scholar, you know.'

'Yes,' said Father. 'You're quite right. That's where he – well, that's where he was supposed to be going.'

'Do you mean he didn't turn up there?'

'No,' said Father, 'he didn't turn up.'

'Oh, well,' said Miss Marple, 'I expect he got his dates wrong.'

'Very likely, very likely.'

'I'm afraid,' said Miss Marple, 'that that's not the first time that that's happened. I went to have tea with him in Chadminster once. He was actually absent from home. His housekeeper told me then how very absent-minded he was.'

'He didn't say anything to you when he was staying here that might give us a clue, I suppose?' asked Father, speaking in an easy and confidential way. 'You know the sort of thing I mean, any old friend he'd met or any plans he'd made apart from this Lucerne Conference?'

'Oh no. He just mentioned the Lucerne Conference. I think he said it was on the 19th. Is that right?'

'That was the date of the Lucerne Conference, yes.'

'I didn't notice the date particularly. I mean –' like most old ladies, Miss Marple here became slightly involved – 'I *thought* he said the 19th and he *might* have said the 19th, but at the same time he might have *meant* the 19th and it might really have been the 20th. I mean, he may have thought the 20th *was* the 19th or he may have thought the 19th was the 20th.'

'Well—' said Father, slightly dazed.

'I'm putting it badly,' said Miss Marple, 'but I mean people like Canon Pennyfather, if they say they're going somewhere on a Thursday, one is quite prepared to find that they didn't mean Thursday, it may be Wednesday or Friday they really mean. Usually they find out in time but sometimes they just don't. I thought at the time that something like that must have happened.'

Father looked slightly puzzled.

'You speak as though you knew already, Miss Marple, that Canon Pennyfather hadn't gone to Lucerne.'

'I knew he wasn't in Lucerne on *Thursday*,' said Miss Marple.

'He was here all day – or most of the day. That's why I thought, of course, that though he may have said Thursday to me, it was really Friday he meant. He certainly left here on Thursday evening carrying his BEA bag.'

'Quite so.'

'I took it he was going off to the airport then,' said Miss Marple. 'That's why I was so surprised to see he was back again.'

'I beg your pardon, what do you mean by "back again"?'

'Well, that he was back here again, I mean.'

'Now, let's get this quite clear,' said Father, careful to speak in an agreeable and reminiscent voice, and not as though it was really important. 'You saw the old idio – you saw the Canon, that is to say, leave as you thought for the airport with his over-night bag, fairly early in the evening. Is that right?'

'Yes. About half-past six, I would say, or quarter to seven.'

'But you say he came *back*.'

'Perhaps he missed the plane. That would account for it.'

'*When* did he come back?'

'Well, I don't really know. I didn't see him come back.'

'Oh,' said Father, taken aback. 'I thought you said you *did* see him.'

'Oh,' I did see him *later*,' said Miss Marple, 'I meant I didn't see him actually come into the hotel.'

'You saw him later? When?'

Miss Marple thought.

'Let me see. It was about 3 a.m. I couldn't sleep very well. Something woke me up. Some sound. There are so many queer noises in London. I looked at my little clock, it was ten minutes past three. For some reason – I'm not quite sure what – I felt uneasy. Footsteps, perhaps, outside my door. Living in the country, if one hears footsteps in the middle of the night it makes one nervous. So I just opened my door and looked out. There was Canon Pennyfather leaving his room – it's next door to mine – and going off down the stairs wearing his overcoat.'

'He came out of his room wearing his overcoat and went down the stairs at 3 a.m. in the morning?'

'Yes,' said Miss Marple, and added: 'I thought it odd at the time.'

Father looked at her for some moments.

'Miss Marple,' he said, 'why haven't you told anyone this before?'

'Nobody asked me,' said Miss Marple simply.

Father drew a deep breath.

'No,' he said. 'No, I suppose nobody would ask you. It's as simple as that.'

He relapsed into silence again.

'You think something has happened to him, don't you?' asked Miss Marple.

'It's over a week now,' said Father. 'He didn't have a stroke and fall down in the street. He's not in a hospital as a result of an accident. So where *is* he? His disappearance has been reported in the Press, but nobody's come forward with any information yet.'

'They may not have seen it. *I* didn't.'

'It looks – it really looks—' Father was following out his own line of thought – 'as though he *meant* to disappear. Leaving this place like that in the middle of the night. You're quite sure about it, aren't you?' he demanded sharply. 'You didn't dream it?'

'I am absolutely sure,' said Miss Marple with finality.

Father heaved himself to his feet.

'I'd better go and see that chambermaid,' he said.

Father found Rose Sheldon on duty and ran an approving eye over her pleasant person.

'I'm sorry to bother you,' he said. 'I know you've seen our sergeant already. But it's about that missing gentleman, Canon Pennyfather.'

'Oh yes, sir, a very nice gentleman. He often stays here.'

'Absent-minded,' said Father.

Rose Sheldon permitted a discreet smile to appear on her respectful mask of a face.

'Now let me see.' Father pretended to consult some notes. 'The last time you saw Canon Pennyfather – was—'

'On the Thursday morning, sir. Thursday the 19th. He told me that he would not be back that night and possibly not the next either. He was going, I think, to Geneva. Somewhere in Switzerland, anyway. He gave me two shirts he wanted washed and I said they would be ready for him on the morning of the following day.'

'And that's the last you saw of him, eh?'

'Yes, sir. You see, I'm not on duty in the afternoons. I come back again at 6 o'clock. By then he must have left or at any rate he was downstairs. Not in his room. He had left two suitcases behind.'

'That's right,' said Father. The contents of the suitcases had been examined, but had given no useful lead. He went on: 'Did you call him the next morning?'

'Call him? No, sir, he was away.'

'What did you do ordinarily – take him early tea? Breakfast?'

'Early tea, sir. He breakfasted downstairs always.'

'So you didn't go into his room at all the next day?'

'Oh yes, sir.' Rose sounded shocked. 'I went into his room as usual. I took his shirts in for one thing. And of course I dusted the room. We dust all the rooms every day.'

'Had the bed been slept in?'

She stared at him. 'The bed, sir? Oh no.'

'Was it rumpled – creased in any way?'

She shook her head.

'What about the bathroom?'

'There was a damp hand towel, sir, that had been used, I presume that would be the evening before. He may have washed his hands last thing before going off.'

'And there was nothing to show that he had come back into the room – perhaps quite late – after midnight?'

She stared at him with an air of bewilderment. Father opened his mouth, then shut it again. Either she knew nothing about the Canon's return or she was a highly accomplished actress.

'What about his clothes – suits. Were they packed up in his suitcases?'

'No, sir, they were hanging up in the cupboards. He was keeping his room on, you see, sir.'

'Who did pack them up?'

'Miss Gorringe gave orders, sir. When the room was wanted for the new lady coming in.'

A straightforward coherent account. But if that old lady was correct in stating that she saw Canon Pennyfather leaving his room at 3 a.m. on Friday morning, then he must have come back to that room sometime. Nobody had seen him enter the hotel. Had he, for some reason, deliberately avoided being seen? He had left no traces in the room. He hadn't even lain down on the bed. Had Miss Marple dreamed the whole thing? At her age it was possible enough. An idea struck him.

'What about his airport bag?'

'I beg your pardon, sir?'

'A small bag, dark blue – a BEA or BOAC bag – you must have seen it?'

'Oh that – yes, sir. But of course he'd take that with him abroad.'

'But he didn't *go* abroad. He never went to Switzerland after all. So he must have left it behind. Or else he came back and left it here with his other luggage.'

'Yes – yes – I think – I'm not quite sure – I believe he did.'

Quite unsolicited, the thought raced into Father's mind:] *They didn't brief you on that, did they?*

Rose Sheldon had been calm and competent up till now. But that question had rattled her. She hadn't known the right answer to it. *But she ought to have known.*

The Canon had taken his bag to the airport, had been turned away from the airport. If he had come back to Bertram's, the bag would have been with him. *But Miss Marple had made no mention of it when she had described the Canon leaving his room and going down the stairs.*

Presumably it was left in the bedroom, but it had not been put in the baggage room with the suitcases. Why not? *Because the Canon was supposed to have gone to Switzerland?*

He thanked Rose genially and went downstairs again.

Canon Pennyfather! Something of an enigma, Canon Pennyfather. Talked a lot about going to Switzerland, muddled up things so that he didn't go to Switzerland, came back to his hotel so secretly that nobody saw him, left it again in the early hours of the morning. (To go where? To do what?)

Could absent-mindedness account for all this?

If not, then what was Canon Pennyfather up to? And more important, where was he?

From the staircase, Father cast a jaundiced eye over the occupants of the lounge, and wondered whether *anyone* was what they seemed to be. He had got to that stage! Elderly people, middle-aged people (nobody very young), nice old-fashioned people, nearly all well-to-do, all highly respectable. Service people, lawyers, clergymen; American husband and wife near the door, a French family near the fireplace. Nobody flashy, nobody out of place; most of them enjoying an old-fashioned English afternoon tea. Could there really be anything seriously wrong with a place that served old-fashioned afternoon teas?

The Frenchman made a remark to his wife that fitted in appositively enough.

'*Le Five O'clock*,' he was saying. '*C'est bien Anglais ça, n'est-ce pas?*' He looked round him with approval.

'Le Five o'clock,' thought Davy as he passed through the swing doors to the street. 'That chap doesn't know that "le Five o'clock" is as dead as the Dodo!'

Outside, various vast American wardrobe cases and suitcases were being loaded on to a taxi. It seemed that Mr and Mrs Elmer Cabot were on their way to the Hotel Vendôme, Paris.

Beside him on the kerb, Mrs Elmer Cabot was expressing her views to her husband.

'The Pendleburys were quite right about this place, Elmer. Is just *is* old England. So beautifully Edwardian. I just feel Edward the Seventh could walk right in any moment and sit down there for his afternoon tea. I mean to come back here next year – I really do.'

'If we've got a million dollars or so to spare,' said her husband dryly.

'Now, Elmer, it wasn't as bad as all *that*.'

The baggage was loaded, the tall commissionaire helped them in, murmuring 'Thank you, sir' as Mr Cabot made the expected gesture. The taxi drove off. The commissionaire transferred his attention to Father.

'Taxi, sir?'

Father looked up at him.

Over six feet. Good-looking chap. A bit run to seed. Ex-army. Lots of medals – genuine, probably. A bit shifty? Drinks too much.

Aloud he said: 'Ex-army man?'

'Yes, sir. Irish Guards.'

'Military Medal, I see. Where did you get that?'

'Burma.'

'What's your name?'

'Michael Gorman. Sergeant.'

'Good job here?'

'It's a peaceful spot.'

'Wouldn't you prefer the Hilton?'

'I would not. I like it here. Nice people come here, and quite a lot of racing gentlemen – for Ascot and Newbury. I've had good tips from them now and again.'

'Ah, so you're an Irishman and a gambler, is that it?'

'Och! now, what would life be like without a gamble?'

'Peaceful and dull,' said Chief-Inspector Davy, 'like mine.'

'Indeed, sir?'

'Can you guess what my profession is?' asked Father.

The Irishman grinned.

'No offence to you, sir, but if I may guess I'd say you were a cop.'

'Right first time,' said Chief-Inspector Davy. 'You remember Canon Pennyfather?'

'Canon Pennyfather now, I don't seem to mind the name—'

'Elderly clergyman.'

Michael Gorman laughed.

'Ah now, clergymen are as thick as peas in a pod in there.'

'This one disappeared from here.'

'Oh, *that* one!' The commissionaire seemed slightly taken aback.

'Did you know him?'

'I wouldn't remember him if it hadn't been for people asking me questions about him. All I know is, I put him into a taxi and he went to the Athenæum Club. That's the last I saw of him. Somebody told me he'd gone to Switzerland, but I hear he never got there. Lost himself, it seems.'

'You didn't see him later that day?'

'Later – No, indeed.'

'What time do you go off duty?'

'Eleven-thirty.'

Chief-Inspector Davy nodded, refused a taxi and moved slowly away along Pond Street. A car roared past him close to the kerb, and pulled up outside Bertram's Hotel, with a scream of brakes. Chief-Inspector Davy turned his head soberly and noted the number plate. FAN 2266. There was something reminiscent about that number, though he couldn't for the moment place it.

Slowly he retraced his steps. He had barely reached the entrance before the driver of the car, who had gone through the doors a moment or two before, came out again. He and the car matched each other. It was a racing model, white with long gleaming lines. The young man had the same eager greyhound look with a handsome face and a body with not a superfluous inch of flesh on it.

The commissionaire held the car door open, the young man jumped in, tossed a coin to the commissionaire and drove off with a burst of powerful engine.

'You know who *he* is?' said Michael Gorman to Father.

'A dangerous driver, anyway.'

'Ladislaus Malinowski. Won the Grand Prix two years ago –

828

world champion he was. Had a bad smash last year. They say he's all right again now.'

'Don't tell me *he's* staying at Bertram's. Highly unsuitable.' Michael Gorman grinned.

'He's not staying here, no. But a friend of his is—' He winked.

A porter in a striped apron came out with more American luxury travel equipment.

Father stood absent-mindedly watching them being ensconced in a Daimler Hire Car whilst he tried to remember what he knew about Ladislaus Malinowski. A reckless fellow – said to be tied up with some well known woman – what was her name now? Still staring at a smart wardrobe case, he was just turning away when he changed his mind and re-entered the hotel again.

He went to the desk and asked Miss Gorringe for the hotel register. Miss Gorringe was busy with departing Americans, and pushed the book along the counter towards him. He turned the pages. Lady Selina Hazy, Little Cottage, Merryfield, Hants. Mr and Mrs Hennessey King, Elderberries, Essex. Sir John Woodstock, 5 Beaumont Crescent, Cheltenham. Lady Sedgwick, Hurstings House, Northumberland. Mr and Mrs Elmer Cabot, Connecticut. General Radley, 14, The Green, Chichester. Mr and Mrs Woolmer Pickington, Marble Head, Connecticut. La Comtesse de Beauville, Les Sapins, St Germain en Laye. Miss Jane Marple, St Mary Mead, Much Benham. Colonel Luscombe, Little Green, Suffolk. Mrs Carpenter, The Hon. Elvira Blake. Canon Pennyfather, The Close Chadminster. Mrs Holding, Miss Holding, Miss Audrey Holding, The Manor House, Carmanton. Mr and Mrs Rysville, Valley Forge, Pennsylvania. The Duke of Barnstable, Doone Castle, N. Devon . . . A cross section of the kind of people who stayed at Bertram's Hotel. They formed, he thought, a kind of pattern . . .

As he shut the book, a name on an earlier page caught his eye. Sir William Ludgrove.

Mr Justice Ludgrove who had been recognized by a probation officer near the scene of a bank robbery. Mr Justice Ludgrove – Canon Pennyfather – both patrons of Bertram's Hotel . . .

'I hope you enjoyed your tea, sir?' It was Henry, standing at his elbow. He spoke courteously, and with the slight anxiety of the perfect host.

'The best tea I've had for years,' said Chief-Inspector Davy.

He remembered he hadn't paid for it. He attempted to do so, but Henry raised a deprecating hand.

'Oh no, sir. I was given to understand that your tea was on the house. Mr Humfries' orders.'

Henry moved away. Father was left uncertain whether he ought to have offered Henry a tip or not. It was galling to think that Henry knew the answer to the social problem much better than he did!

As he moved away along the street, he stopped suddenly. He took out his note-book and put down a name and an address – no time to lose. He went into a telephone box. He was going to stick out his neck. Come hell or high water, he was going all out on a hunch.

—— 16 ——

It was the wardrobe that worried Canon Pennyfather. It worried him before he was quite awake. Then he forgot it and he fell asleep again. But when his eyes opened once more, there the wardrobe still was in the wrong place. He was lying on his left side facing the window and the wardrobe ought to have been there between him and the window on the left wall. But it wasn't. It was on the right. It worried him. It worried him so much that it made him feel tired. He was conscious of his head aching badly, and on top of that, to have the wardrobe in the wrong place . . . At this point once more his eyes closed.

There was rather more light in the room the next time he woke. It was not daylight yet. Only the faint light of dawn. 'Dear me,' said Canon Pennyfather to himself, suddenly solving the problem of the wardrobe. 'How stupid I am! Of course, I'm not at home.'

He moved gingerly. No, this wasn't his own bed. He was away from home. He was – where was he? Oh, of course. He'd gone to London, hadn't he? He was in Bertram's Hotel and – but no, he *wasn't* in Bertram's Hotel. In Bertram's Hotel his bed was facing the window. So that was wrong, too.

'Dear me, where can I be?' said Canon Pennyfather.

Then he remembered that he was going to Lucerne. 'Of course,' he said to himself, 'I'm in Lucerne.' He began thinking about the paper he was going to read. He didn't think about it long. Thinking about his paper seemed to make his head ache so he went to sleep again.

The next time he woke his head was a great deal clearer. Also there was a good deal more light in the room. He was not at home, he was not at Bertram's Hotel and he was fairly sure that he was not in Lucerne. This wasn't a hotel bedroom at all. He studied it fairly closely. It was an entirely strange room with very little furniture in it. A kind of cupboard (what he'd taken for a wardrobe) and a window with flowered curtains through which the light came. A chair and a table and a chest of drawers. Really, that was about all.

'Dear me,' said Canon Pennyfather, 'this is *most* odd. Where am I?'

He was thinking of getting up to investigate but when he sat up in bed his headache began again so he lay down.

'I must have been ill,' decided Canon Pennyfather. 'Yes, definitely I must have been ill.' He thought a minute or two and then said to himself, 'As a matter of fact, I think perhaps I'm still ill. Influenza, perhaps?' Influenza, people often said, came on very suddenly. Perhaps – perhaps it had come on at dinner at the Athenæum. Yes, that was right. He remembered that he had dined at the Athenæum.

There were sounds of moving about in the house. Perhaps they'd taken him to a nursing home. But no, he didn't think this was a nursing home. With the increased light it showed it-self as a rather shabby and ill-furnished small bedroom. Sounds of movement went on. From downstairs a voice called out, 'Goodbye, ducks. Sausage and mash this evening.'

Canon Pennyfather considered this. Sausage and mash. The words had a faintly agreeable quality.

'I believe,' he said to himself, 'I'm *hungry*.'

The door opened. A middle-aged woman came in, went across to the curtains, pulled them back a little and turned towards the bed.

'Ah, you're awake now,' she said. 'And how are you feeling?'

'Really,' said Canon Pennyfather, rather feebly, 'I'm not quite sure.'

'Ah, I expect not. You've been quite bad, you know. Some-thing hit you a nasty crack, so the doctor said. These motorists! Not even stopping after they'd knocked you down.'

'Have I had an accident?' said Canon Pennyfather. 'A motor accident?'

'That's right,' said the woman. 'Found you by the side of the road when we come home. Thought you was drunk at first.' She chuckled pleasantly at the reminiscence. 'Then my husband

said he'd better take a look. It may have been an accident, he
said. There wasn't no smell of drink or anything. No blood or
anything neither. Anyway, there you was, out like a log. So my
husband said "we can't leave him here lying like that" and he
carried you in here. See?'

'Ah,' said Canon Pennyfather, faintly, somewhat overcome
by all these revelations. 'A good Samaritan.'

'And he saw you were a clergyman so my husband said "it's
all quite respectable". Then he said he'd better not call the
police because being a clergyman and all that you mightn't like
it. That's if you was drunk, in spite of there being no smell of
drink. So then we hit upon getting Dr Stokes to come and have
a look at you. We still call him Dr Stokes although he's been
struck off. A very nice man he is, embittered a bit, of course, by
being struck off. It was only his kind heart really, helping a lot
of girls who were no better than they should be. Anyway, he's
a good enough doctor and we got him to come and take a look
at you. He says you've come to no real harm, says it's mild concussion. All we'd got to do was to keep you lying flat and quiet
in a dark room. "Mind you," he said, "I'm not giving an
opinion or anything like that. This is unofficial. I've no right to
prescribe or to say anything. By rights I dare say you ought to
report it to the police, but if you don't want to, why should
you?" Give the poor old geezer a chance, that's what he said.
Excuse me if I'm speaking disrespectful. He's a rough and ready
speaker, the doctor is. Now what about a drop of soup or some
hot bread and milk?'

'Either,' said Canon Pennyfather faintly, 'would be very welcome.'

He relapsed on to his pillows. An accident? So *that* was it.
An accident, and he couldn't remember a thing about it! A
few minutes later the good woman returned bearing a tray with
a steaming bowl on it.

'You'll feel better after this,' she said. 'I'd like to have put a
drop of whisky or a drop of brandy in it but the doctor said you
wasn't to have nothing like that.'

'Certainly not,' said Canon Pennyfather, 'not with concussion.
No. It would have been unadvisable.'

'I'll put another pillow behind your back, shall I, ducks?
There, is that all right?'

Canon Pennyfather was a little startled by being addressed as
'ducks'. He told himself that it was kindly meant.

'Upsydaisy,' said the woman, 'there we are.'

'Yes, but where are we?' said Canon Pennyfather. 'I mean, where am I? Where is this place?'

'Milton St John,' said the woman. 'Didn't you know?'

'Milton St John?' said Canon Pennyfather. He shook his head. 'I never heard the name before.'

'Oh well, it's not much of a place. Only a village.'

'You have been very kind,' said Canon Pennyfather. 'May I ask your name?'

'Mrs Wheeling. Emma Wheeling.'

'You are most kind,' said Canon Pennyfather again. 'But this accident now. I simply cannot remember—'

'You put yourself outside that, luv, and you'll feel better and up to remembering things.'

'Milton St John,' said Canon Pennyfather to himself, in a tone of wonder. 'The name means nothing to me *at all*. How very extraordinary!'

—— 17 ——

Sir Ronald Graves drew a cat upon his blotting pad. He looked at the large portly figure of Chief-Inspector Davy sitting opposite him and drew a bulldog.

'Ladislaus Malinowski?' he said. 'Could be. Got any evidence?'

'No. He'd fit the bill, would he?'

'A daredevil. No nerves. Won the World Championship. Bad crash about a year ago. Bad reputation with women. Sources of income doubtful. Spends money here and abroad very freely. Always going to and fro to the Continent. Have you got some idea that he's the man behind these big organized robberies and hold-ups?'

'I don't think he's the planner. But I think he's in with them.'

'Why?'

'For one thing, he runs a Mercedes-Otto car. Racing model. A car answering to that description was seen near Bedhampton on the morning of the mail robbery. Different number plates – but we're used to that. And it's the same stunt – unlike, but not too unlike. FAN 2299 instead of 2266. There aren't so many Mercedes-Otto models of that type about. Lady Sedgwick has one and young Lord Merrivale.'

'You don't think Malinowski runs the show?'

'No – I think there are better brains than his at the top. But he's in it. I've looked back over the files. Take the hold-up at the Midland and West London. Three vans happened – just happened – to block a certain street. A Mercedes-Otto that was on the scene got clear away owing to that block.'

'It was stopped later.'

'Yes. And given a clear bill of health. Especially as the people who'd reported it weren't sure of the correct number. It was reported as FAM 3366 – Malinowski's registration number is FAN 2266 – It's all the same picture.'

'And you persist in tying it up with Bertram's Hotel. They dug up some stuff about Bertram's for you—'

Father tapped his pocket.

'Got it here. Properly registered company. Balance – paid up capitals – directors – etcetera, etcetera, etcetera. Doesn't mean a thing! These financial shows are all the same – just a lot of snakes swallowing each other! Companies, and holding companies – makes your brain reel!'

'Come now, Father. That's just a way they have in the City. Has to do with taxation—'

'What I want is the real dope. If you'll give me a chit, sir, I'd like to go and see some top-brass.'

The A.C. stared at him.

'And what exactly do you mean by top brass?'

Father mentioned a name.

The A.C. looked upset. 'I don't know about that. I hardly think we dare approach *him*.'

'It might be very helpful.'

There was a pause. The two men looked at each other. Father looked bovine, placid, and patient. The A.C. gave in.

'You're a stubborn old devil, Fred,' he said. 'Have it your own way. Go and worry the top brains behind the international financiers of Europe.'

'*He'll* know,' said Chief-Inspector Davy. 'He'll *know*. And if he doesn't, he can find out by pressing one buzzer on his desk or making one telephone call.'

'I don't know that he'll be pleased.'

'Probably not,' said Father, 'but it won't take much of his time. I've got to have authority behind me, though.'

'You're really serious about this place, Bertram's, aren't you? But what have you got to go on? It's well run, has a good respectable clientele – no trouble with the licensing laws.'

'I know – I know. No drinks, no drugs, no gambling, no accommodation for criminals. All pure as the driven snow. No beatniks, no thugs, no juvenile delinquents. Just sober Victorian-Edwardian old ladies, county families, visiting travellers from Boston and the more respectable parts of the USA. All the same, a respectable Canon of the church is seen to leave it at 3 a.m. in the morning in a somewhat surreptitious manner—'

'Who saw that?'

'An old lady.'

'How did she manage to see him? Why wasn't she in bed and asleep?'

'Old ladies are like that, sir.'

'You're not talking of – what's his name – Canon Penny-father?'

'That's right, sir. His disappearance was reported and Campbell has been looking into it.'

'Funny coincidence – his name's just come up in connection with the mail robbery at Bedhampton.'

'Indeed? In what way, sir?'

'Another old lady – or middle-aged anyway. When the train was stopped by that signal that had been tampered with, a good many people woke up and looked out into the corridor. This woman, who lives in Chadminster and knows Canon Penny-father by sight, says she saw him entering the train by one of the doors. She thought he'd got out to see what was wrong and was getting in again. We were going to follow it up because of his disappearance being reported—'

'Let's see – the train was stopped at 5.30 a.m. Canon Penny-father left Bertram's Hotel not long after 3 a.m. Yes, it could be done. If he were driven there – say – in a racing car . . .'

'So we're back again to Ladislaus Malinowski!'

The A.C. looked at his blotting pad doodles. 'What a bulldog you are, Fred,' he said.

Half an hour later Chief-Inspector Davy was entering a quiet and rather shabby office.

The large man behind the desk rose and put forward a hand.

'Chief-Inspector Davy? Do sit down,' he said. 'Do you care for a cigar?'

Chief-Inspector Davy shook his head.

'I must apologize,' he said, in his deep countryman's voice, 'for wasing your valuable time.'

Mr Robinson smiled. He was a fat man and very well dressed. He had a yellow face, his eyes were dark and sad looking and

835

his mouth was large and generous. He frequently smiled to display over-large teeth. 'The better to eat you with,' though Chief-Inspector Davy irrelevantly. His English was perfect and without accent but he was not an Englishman. Father wondered, as many others had wondered before him, what nationality Mr Robinson really was.

'Well, what can I do for you?'

'I'd like to know,' said Chief-Inspector Davy, 'who owns Bertram's Hotel!'

The expression on Mr Robinson's face did not change. He showed no surprise at hearing the name nor did he show recognition. He said thoughtfully,

'You want to know who owns Bertram's Hotel. That, I think, is in Pond Street, off Piccadilly.'

'Quite right, sir.'

'I have occasionally stayed there myself. A quiet place. Well run.'

'Yes,' said Father, 'particularly well run.'

'And you want to know who owns it? Surely that is easy to ascertain?'

There was a faint irony behind his smile.

'Through the usual channels, you mean? Oh yes.' Father took a small piece of paper from his pocket and read out three or four names and addresses.

'I see,' said Robinson, 'someone has taken quite a lot of trouble. Interesting. And you come to me?'

'If anyone knows, you would, sir.'

'Actually I do not know. But it is true that I have ways of obtaining information. One has –' he shrugged his very large, fat shoulders – 'one has contacts.'

'Yes, sir,' said Father with an impassive face.

Mr Robinson looked at him, then he picked up the telephone on his desk.

'Sonia? Get me Carlos.' He waited a minute or two then spoke again. 'Carlos?' He spoke rapidly half a dozen sentences in a foreign language. It was not a language that Father could even recognise.

Father could converse in good British French. He had a smattering of Italian and he could make a guess at plain travellers' German. He knew the sounds of Spanish, Russian and Arabic, though he could not understand them. This language was none of those. At a faint guess he hazarded it might be Turkish or

Persian or Armenian, but even of that he was by no means sure. Mr Robinson replaced the receiver.

'I do not think,' he said genially, 'that we shall have long to wait. I am interested, you know. Very much interested. I have occasionally wondered myself—'

Father looked inquiring.

'About Bertram's Hotel,' said Mr Robinson. 'Financially, you know. One wonders how it can pay. However, it has never been any of my business. And one appreciates –' He shrugged his shoulders, – 'a comfortable hostelry with an unusually talented personnel and staff . . . Yes, I have wondered.' He looked at Father. 'You know how and why?'

'Not yet,' said Father, 'but I mean to.'

'There are several possibilities,' said Mr Robinson, thoughtfully. 'It is like music, you know. Only so many notes to the octave, yet one can combine them in – what is it – several million different ways? A musician told me once that you do not get the same tune twice. Most interesting.'

There was a slight buzz on his desk and he picked up the receiver once more.

'Yes? Yes, you have been very prompt. I am pleased. I see. Oh! Amsterdam, yes . . . Ah . . . Thank you . . . Yes. You will spell that? Good.'

He wrote rapidly on a pad at his elbow.

'I hope this will be useful to you,' he said, as he tore off the sheet and passed it across the table to Father, who read the name out loud. 'Wilhelm Hoffman.'

'Nationality Swiss,' said Mr Robinson. 'Though not, I would say, born in Switzerland. Has a good deal of influence in Banking circles and though keeping strictly on the right side of the law, he has been behind a great many – questionable deals. He operates solely on the Continent, not in this country.'

'Oh.'

'But he has a brother,' said Mr Robinson. 'Robert Hoffman. Living in London – a diamond merchant – most respectable business – His wife is Dutch – He also has offices in Amsterdam – Your people may know about him. As I say, he deals mainly in diamonds, but he is a very rich man, and he owns a lot of property, not usually in his own name. Yes, he is behind quite a lot of enterprises. He and his brother are the real owners of Bertram's Hotel.'

'Thank you, sir.' Chief-Inspector Davy rose to his feet. 'I needn't tell you that I'm much obliged to you. It's wonderful,' he added, allowing himself to show more enthusiasm than was normal.

'That I should know?' inquired Mr Robinson, giving one of his larger smiles. 'But that is one of my specialities. Information. I like to know. That is why you came to me, is it not?'

'Well,' said Chief-Inspector Davy, 'we do know about you. The Home Office. The Special Branch and all the rest of it.' He added almost naïvely, 'It took a bit of nerve on my part to approach you.'

Again Mr Robinson smiled.

'I find you an interesting personality, Chief-Inspector Davy,' he said. 'I wish you success in whatever you are undertaking.'

'Thank you, sir. I think I shall need it. By the way, these two brothers, would you say they were violent men?'

'Certainly not,' said Mr Robinson. 'It would be quite against their policy. The brothers Hoffman do not apply violence in business matters. They have other methods that serve them better. Year by year, I would say, they get steadily richer, or so my information from Swiss Banking circles tells me.'

'It's a useful place, Switzerland,' said Chief-Inspector Davy.

'Yes, indeed. What we should all do without it I do not know! So much rectitude. Such a fine business sense! Yes, we business men must all be very grateful to Switzerland. I myself,' he added, 'have also a high opinion of Amsterdam.' He looked hard at Davy, then smiled again, and the Chief-Inspector left.

When he got back to headquarters again, he found a note awaiting him.

Canon Pennyfather has turned up – safe if not sound. Apparently was knocked down by a car at Milton St John and has concussion.

—— 18 ——

Canon Pennyfather looked at Chief-Inspector Davy and Inspector Campbell, and Chief-Inspector Davy and Inspector Campbell looked at him. Canon Pennyfather was at home again. Sitting in the big arm-chair in his library, a pillow behind his head and his feet up on a pouffe, with a rug over his knees to emphasize his invalid status.

'I'm afraid,' he was saying politely, 'that I simply cannot remember anything at all.'

'You can't remember the accident when the car hit you?'

'I'm really afraid not.'

'Then how did you know a car hit you?' demanded Inspector Campbell acutely.

'The woman there, Mrs – Mrs – was her name Wheeling? – told me about it.'

'And how did she know?'

Canon Pennyfather looked puzzled.

'Dear me, you are quite right. She couldn't have known, could she? I suppose she thought it was what must have happened.'

'And you really cannot remember *anything*? How did you come to be in Milton St John?'

'I've no idea,' said Canon Pennyfather. 'Even the name is quite unfamiliar to me.'

Inspector Campbell's exasperation was mounting, but Chief-Inspector Davy said in his soothing, homely voice,

'Just tell us again the last thing you do remember, sir.'

Canon Pennyfather turned to him with relief. The inspector's dry scepticism had made him uncomfortable.

'I was going to Lucerne to a congress. I took a taxi to the airport – at least to Kensington Air Station.'

'Yes. And then?'

'That's all. I can't remember any more. The next thing I remember is the wardrobe.'

'What wardrobe?' demanded Inspector Campbell.

'It was in the wrong place.'

Inspector Campbell was tempted to go into this question of a wardrobe in the wrong place. Chief-Inspector Davy cut in.

'Do you remember arriving at the air station, sir?'

'I suppose so,' said Canon Pennyfather, with the air of one who has a great deal of doubt on the matter.

'And you duly flew to Lucerne.'

'Did I? I don't remember anything about it if so.'

'Do you remember arriving back at Bertram's Hotel that night?'

'No.'

'You do remember Bertram's Hotel?'

'Of course. I was staying there. Very comfortable. I kept my room on.'

'Do you remember travelling in a train?'

'A train? No, I can't recall a train.'

'There was a hold-up. The train was robbed. Surely, Canon Pennyfather, you can remember *that*.'

'I ought to, oughtn't I?' said Canon Pennyfather. 'But somehow—' he spoke apologetically, '—I don't.' He looked from one to the other of the officers with a bland gentle smile.

'Then your story is that you remember nothing after going in a taxi to the air station until you woke up in the Wheelings' cottage at Milton St John.'

'There is nothing unusual in that,' the Canon assured him. 'It happens quite often in cases of concussion.'

'What did you think had happened to you when you woke up?'

'I had such a headache I really couldn't think. Then of course I began to wonder where I was and Mrs Wheeling explained and brought me some excellent soup. She called me "love" and "dearie", and "ducks",' said the Canon with slight distaste, 'but she was very kind. Very kind indeed.'

'She ought to have reported the accident to the police. Then you would have been taken to hospital and properly looked after,' said Campbell.

'She looked after me very well,' the Canon protested, with spirit, 'and I understand that with concussion there is very little you *can* do except keep the patient quiet.'

'If you should remember anything more, Canon Pennyfather—'

The Canon interrupted him.

'Four whole days I seem to have lost out of my life,' he said. 'Very curious. Really very curious indeed. I wonder so much where I was and what I was doing. The doctor tells me it may all come back to me. On the other hand it may not. Possibly I shall never know what happened to me during those days.' His eyelids flickered. 'You'll excuse me. I think I am rather tired.'

'That's quite enough now,' said Mrs McCrae, who had been hovering by the door, ready to intervene if she thought it necessary. She advanced upon them. 'Doctor says he wasn't to be worried,' she said firmly.

The policemen rose and moved towards the door. Mrs McCrae shepherded them out into the hall rather in the manner of a conscientious sheepdog. The Canon murmured something and Chief-Inspector Davy who was the last to pass through the door wheeled round at once.

'What was that?' he asked, but the Canon's eyes were now closed.

'What did you think he said?' said Campbell as they left the house after refusing Mrs McCrae's lukewarm offer of refreshment.

Father said thoughtfully,

'I thought he said "the walls of Jericho".'

'What could he mean by that?'

'It sounds biblical,' said Father.

'Do you think we'll ever know,' asked Campbell, 'how that old boy got from the Cromwell Road to Milton St John?'

'It doesn't seem as if we shall get much help from him,' agreed Davy.

'That woman who says she saw him on the train after the hold-up. Can she possibly be right? Can he be mixed up in some way with these robberies? It seems impossible. He's such a thoroughly respectable old boy. Can't very well suspect a Canon of Chadminster Cathedral of being mixed up with a train robbery, can one?'

'No,' said Father thoughtfully, 'no. No more than one can imagine Mr Justice Ludgrove being mixed up with a bank hold-up.'

Inspector Campbell looked at his superior officer curiously.

The expedition to Chadminster concluded with a short and unprofitable interview with Dr Stokes.

Dr Stokes was aggressive, unco-operative and rude.

'I've known the Wheelings quite a while. They're by way of being neighbours of mine. They'd picked some old chap up off the road. Didn't know whether he was dead drunk, or ill. Asked me in to have a look. I told them he wasn't drunk – that it was concussion—'

'And you treated him for that.'

'Not at all. I didn't treat him, or prescribe for him or attend him. I'm not a doctor – I was once, but I'm not now – I told them what they ought to do was ring up the police. Whether they did or not I don't know. Not my business. They're a bit dumb, both of them – but kindly folk.'

'You didn't think of ringing up the police yourself?'

'No, I did not. I'm not a doctor. Nothing to do with me. As a human being I told them not to pour whisky down his throat and to keep him quiet and flat until the police came.'

He glared at them and, reluctantly, they had to leave it at that.

19

Mr Hoffman was a big solid-looking man. He gave the appearance of being carved out of wood – preferably teak.

His face was so expressionless as to give rise to surmise – could such a man be capable of thinking – of feeling emotion? It seemed impossible.

His manner was highly correct.

He rose, bowed, and held out a wedge-like hand.

'Chief-Inspector Davy? It is some years since I had the pleasure – you may not even remember—'

'Oh yes I do, Mr Hoffman. The Aaronberg Diamond Case. You were a witness for the Crown – a most excellent witness, let me say. The Defence was quite unable to shake you.'

'I am not easily shaken,' said Mr Hoffman gravely.

He did not look a man who would easily be shaken.

'What can I do for you?' he went on. 'No trouble, I hope – I always want to agree well with the police. I have the greatest admiration for your superb police force.'

'Oh! there is no trouble. It is just that we wanted you to confirm a little information.'

'I shall be delighted to help you in any way I can. As I say, I have the highest opinion of your London Police Force. You have such a splendid class of men. So full of integrity, so fair, so just.'

'You'll make me embarrassed,' said Father.

'I am at your service. What is it that you want to know?'

'I was just going to ask you to give me a little dope about Bertram's Hotel.'

Mr Hoffman's face did not change. It was possible that his entire attitude became for a moment or two even more static than it had been before – that was all.

'Bertram's Hotel?' he said. His voice was inquiring, slightly puzzled. It might have been that he had never heard of Bertram's Hotel or that he could not quite remember whether he knew Bertram's Hotel or not.

'You have a connection with it, have you not, Mr Hoffman?'

Mr Hoffman moved his shoulders.

'There are so many things,' he said. 'One cannot remember them all. So much business – so much – it keeps me very busy.'

'You have your fingers in a lot of pies, I know that.'

'Yes,' Mr Hoffman smiled a wooden smile. 'I pull out many plums, that is what you think? And so you believe I have a connection with this – Bertram's Hotel?'

'I shouldn't have said a connection. As a matter of fact, you own it, don't you?' said Father genially.

This time, Mr Hoffman definitely did stiffen.

'Now who told you *that*, I wonder?' he said softly.

'Well, it's true, isn't it?' said Chief-Inspector Davy, cheerfully. 'Very nice place to own, I should say. In fact, you must be quite proud of it.'

'Oh yes,' said Hoffman. 'For the moment – I could not quite remember – you see—' he smiled deprecatingly, '—I own quite a lot of property in London. It is a good investment – property. If something comes on the market in what I think is a good position, and there is a chance of snapping it up cheap, I invest.'

'And was Bertram's Hotel going cheap?'

'As a running concern, it had gone down the hill,' said Mr Hoffman, shaking his head.

'Well, it's on its feet now,' said Father. 'I was in there just the other day. I was very much struck with the atmosphere there. Nice old-fashioned clinetele, comfortable, old-fashioned premises, nothing rackety about it, a lot of luxury without looking luxurious.'

'I know very little about it personally,' explained Mr Hoffman. 'It is just one of my investments – but I believe it is doing well.'

'Yes, you seem to have a first-class fellow running it. What is his name? Humfries? Yes, Humfries.'

'An excellent man,' said Mr Hoffman. 'I leave everything to him. I look at the balance sheet once a year to see that all is well.'

'The place was thick with titles,' said Father. 'Rich travelling Americans, too.' He shook his head thoughtfully. 'Wonderful combination.'

'You say you were in there the other day?' Mr Hoffman inquired. 'Not – not officially, I hope?'

'Nothing serious. Just trying to clear up a little mystery.'

'A mystery? In Bertram's Hotel?'

'So it seems. The Case of the Disappearing Clergyman, you might label it.'

'That is a joke,' Mr Hoffman said. 'That is your Sherlock Holmes language.'

'This clergyman walked out of the place one evening and was never seen again.'

'Peculiar,' said Mr Hoffman, 'but such things happen. I remember many, many years ago now, a great sensation. Colonel – now let me think of his name – Colonel Fergusson I think, one of the equerries of Queen Mary. He walked out of his club one night and he, too, was never seen again.'

'Of course,' said Father, with a sigh, 'a lot of these disappearances are voluntary.'

'You know more about that than I do, my dear Chief-Inspector,' said Mr Hoffman. He added, 'I hope they gave you every assistance at Bertram's Hotel?'

'They couldn't have been nicer,' Father assured him. 'That Miss Gorringe, she has been with you some time, I believe?'

'Possibly. I really know so very little about it. I take no *personal* interest, you understand. In fact—' he smiled disarmingly, '—I was surprised that you even knew it belonged to me.'

It was not quite a question; but once more there was a slight uneasiness in his eyes. Father noted it without seeming to.

'The ramifications that go on in the City are like a gigantic jigsaw,' he said. 'It would make my head ache if I had to deal with that side of things. I gather that a company – Mayfair Holding Trust or some name like that – is the registered owner. They're owned by another company and so on and so on. The real truth of the matter is that it belongs to *you*. Simple as that. I'm right, aren't I?'

'I and my fellow directors are what I dare say you'd call behind it, yes,' admitted Mr Hoffman rather reluctantly.

'Your fellow directors. And who might they be? Yourself and, I believe, a brother of yours?'

'My brother Wilhelm is associated with me in this venture. You must understand that Bertram's is only a part of a chain of various hotels, offices, clubs and other London properties.'

'Any other directors?'

'Lord Pomfret, Abel Isaacstein.' Hoffman's voice was suddenly edged. 'Do you really need to know all these things? Just because you are looking into the Case of the Disappearing Clergyman?'

Father shook his head and looked apologetic.

'I suppose it's really curiosity. Looking for my disappearing clergyman was what took me to Bertram's, but then I got – well, interested if you understand what I mean. One thing leads to another sometimes, doesn't it?'

'I suppose that could be so, yes. And now?' he smiled, 'your curiosity is satisfied?'

'Nothing like coming to the horse's mouth when you want information, is there?' said Father, genially. He rose to his feet. 'There's only one thing I'd really like to know – and I don't suppose you'll tell me that.'

'Yes, Chief-Inspector?' Hoffman's voice was wary.

'Where do Bertram's get hold of their staff? Wonderful!' That fellow what's-his-name – Henry. The one that looks like an Archduke or an Archbishop, I'm not sure which. Anyway, he serves you tea and muffins – most wonderful muffins! An unforgettable experience.'

'You like muffins with much butter, yes?' Mr Hoffman's eyes rested for a moment on the rotundity of Father's figure with disapprobation.

'I expect you can see I do,' said Father. 'Well, I mustn't be keeping you. I expect you're pretty busy taking over take-over bids, or something like that.'

'Ah. It amuses you to pretend to be ignorant of all these things. No, I am not busy. I do not let business absorb me too much. My tastes are simple. I live simply, with leisure, with growing of roses, and my family to whom I am devoted.'

'Sounds ideal,' said Father. 'Wish I could live like that.'

Mr Hoffman smiled and rose ponderously to shake hands with him.

'I hope you will find your disappearing clergyman very soon.'

'Oh! that's all right. I'm sorry I didn't make myself clear. He's found – disappointing case, really. Had a car accident and got concussion – simple as that.'

Father went to the door, then turned and asked:

'By the way, is Lady Sedgwick a director of your company?'

'Lady Sedgwick?' Hoffman took a moment or two. 'No. Why should she be?'

'Oh well, one hears things— Just a shareholder?'

'I – yes.'

'Well, goodbye, Mr Hoffman. Thanks very much.'

Father went back to the Yard and straight to the A.C.

'The two Hoffman brothers are the ones behind Bertram's Hotel – financially.'

'What? Those scoundrels?' demanded Sir Ronald.

'Yes.'

'They've kept it very dark.'

845

'Yes – and Robert Hoffman didn't half like our finding it out. It was a shock to him.'

'What did he say?'

'Oh, we kept it all very formal and polite, He tried, not too obviously, to learn how I had found out about it.'

'And you didn't oblige him with that information, I suppose.

'I certainly did not.'

'What excuse did you give for going to see him?'

'I didn't give any,' said Father.

'Didn't he think that a bit odd?'

'I expect he did. On the whole I thought that was a good way to play it, sir.'

'If the Hoffmans are behind all this, it accounts for a lot. They're never concerned in anything crooked themselves – oh no! *They* don't organise crime – they finance it though!'

'Wilhelm deals with the banking side from Switzerland. He was behind those foreign currency rackets just after the war – we knew it – but we couldn't prove it. Those two brothers control a great deal of money and they use it for backing all kinds of enterprises – some legitimate – some not. But they're careful – they know every trick of the trade. Robert's diamond broking is straightforward enough – but it makes a suggestive picture – diamonds – banking interests, and property – clubs, cultural foundations, office buildings, restaurants, hotels – all apparently owned by somebody else.'

'Do you think Hoffman is the planner of these organised robberies?'

'No, I think those two deal only with finance. No. you'll have to look elsewhere for your planner. Somewhere there's a first-class brain at work.'

20

The fog had come down over London suddenly that evening. Chief-Inspector Davy pulled up his coat collar and turned into Pond Street. Walking slowly like a man who was thinking of something else, he did not look particularly purposeful but anyone who knew him well would realize that his mind was wholly alert. He was prowling as a cat prowls before the moment comes for it to pounce on its prey.

Pond Street was quiet tonight. There were few cars about. The fog had been patchy to begin with, had almost cleared, then had deepened again. The noise of the traffic from Park Lane was muted to the level of a suburban side road. Most of the buses had given up. Only from time to time individual cars went on their way with determined optimism. Chief-Inspector Davy turned up a cul-de-sac, went to the end of it and came back again. He turned again, aimlessly as it seemed, first one way, then the other, but he was not aimless. Actually his cat prowl was taking him in a circle round one particular building. Bertram's Hotel. He was appraising carefully just what lay to the east of it, to the west of it, to the north of it and to the south of it. He examined the cars that were parked by the pavement, he examined the cars that were in the cul-de-sac. He examined a mews with special care. One car in particular interested him and he stopped. He pursed up his lips and said softly, 'So you're here again, you beauty.' He checked the number and nodded to himself. 'FAN 2266 tonight, are you?' He bent down and ran his fingers over the number plate delicately, then nodded approval. 'Good job they made of it,' he said under his breath.

He went on, came out at the other end of the mews, turned right and right again and came out in Pond Street once more, fifty yards from the entrance of Bertram's Hotel. Once again he paused, admiring the handsome lines of yet another racing car.

'You're a beauty, too,' said Chief-Inspector Davy. 'Your number plate's the same as the last time I saw you. I rather fancy your number plate always *is* the same. And that should mean—' he broke off '—or should it?' he muttered. He looked up towards what could have been the sky. 'Fog's getting thicker,' he said to himself.

Outside the door to Bertram's, the Irish Commissionaire was standing swinging his arms backwards and forwards with some violence to keep himself warm. Chief-Inspector Davy said good evening to him.

'Good evening, sir. Nasty night.'

'Yes. I shouldn't think anyone would want to go out tonight who hadn't got to.'

The swing doors were pushed open and a middle-aged lady came out and paused uncertainly on the step.

'Want a taxi, ma'am?'

'Oh dear. I meant to walk.'

'I wouldn't if I were you, ma'am. It's very nasty, this fog. Even in a taxi it won't be too easy.'

'Do you think you could find me a taxi?' said the lady doubtfully.

'I'll do my best. You go inside now, and keep warm and I'll come in and tell you if I've got one.' His voice changed, modulated to a persuasive tone. 'Unless you *have* to, ma'am, I wouldn't go out tonight at all.'

'Oh dear. Perhaps you're right. But I'm expected at some friends in Chelsea. I don't know. It might be very difficult getting back here. What do you think?'

Michael Gorman took charge.

'If I were you, ma'am,' he said firmly, 'I'd go in and telephone to your friends. It's not nice for a lady like you to be out on a foggy night like this.'

'Well – really – yes, well, perhaps you're right.'

She went back in again.

'I have to look after them,' said Micky Gorman turning in an explanatory manner to Father. 'That kind would get her bag snatched, she would. Going out this time of night in a fog and wandering about Chelsea or West Kensington or wherever she's trying to go.'

'I suppose you've had a good deal of experience of dealing with elderly ladies?' said Davy.

'Ah yes, indeed. This place is a home from home to them, bless their ageing hearts. How about you, sir? Were you wanting a taxi?'

'Don't suppose you could get me one if I did,' said Father. 'There don't seem to be many about in this. And I don't blame them.'

'Ah, now, I might lay my hand on one for you. There's a place round the corner where there's usually a taxi driver got his cab parked, having a warm up and a drop of something to keep the cold out.'

'A taxi's no good to me,' said Father with a sigh.

He jerked his thumb towards Bertram's Hotel.

'I've got to go inside. I've got a job to do.'

'Indeed now? Would it be still the missing Canon?'

'Not exactly. He's been found.'

'Found?' The man stared at him. 'Found where?'

'Wandering about with concussion after an accident.'

'Ah, that's just what one might expect of him. Crossed the road without looking, I expect.'

'That seems to be the idea,' said Father.

He nodded, and pushed through the doors into the hotel. There were not very many people in the lounge this evening. He saw Miss Marple sitting in a chair near the fire and Miss Marple saw him. She made, however, no sign of recognition. He went towards the desk. Miss Gorringe, as usual, was behind her books. She was, he thought, faintly discomposed to see him. It was a very slight reaction, but he noted the fact.

'You remember me, Miss Gorringe,' he said. 'I came here the other day.'

'Yes, of course I remember you, Chief-Inspector. Is there anything more you want to know? Do you want to see Mr Humfries?'

'No thank you. I don't think that'll be necessary. I'd just like one more look at your register if I may.'

'Of course.' She pushed it along to him.

He opened it and looked slowly down the pages. To Miss Gorringe he gave the appearance of a man looking for one particular entry. In actuality this was not the case. Father had an accomplishment which he had learnt early in life and had developed into a highly skilled art. He could remember names and addresses with a perfect and photographic memory. That memory would remain with him for twenty-four or even forty-eight hours. He shook his head as he shut the book and returned it to her.

'Canon Pennyfather hasn't been in, I suppose?' he said in a light voice.

'Canon Pennyfather?'

'You know he's turned up again?'

'No indeed. Nobody has told *me*. Where?'

'Some place in the country. Car accident it seems. Wasn't reported to us. Some good Samaritan just picked him up and looked after him.'

'Oh! I am pleased. Yes, I really am very pleased. I was worried about him.'

'So were his friends,' said Father. 'Actually I was looking to see if one of them might be staying here now. Archdeacon – Archdeacon – I can't remember his name now, but I'd know it if I saw it.'

'Tomlinson?' said Miss Gorringe helpfully. 'He is due next week. From Salisbury.'

'No, not Tomlinson. Well, it doesn't matter.' He turned away.

It was quiet in the lounge tonight.

An ascetic looking middle-aged man was reading through a badly typed thesis, occasionally writing a comment in the margin in such small crabbed handwriting as to be almost illegible. Every time he did this, he smiled in vinegary satisfaction.

There were one or two married couples of long standing who had little need to talk to each other. Occasionally two or three people were gathered together in the name of the weather conditions, discussing anxiously how they or their families were going to get where they wanted to be.

'—I rang up and begged Susan not to come by car . . . it means the M1 and always so dangerous in fog—'

'They say it's clearer in the Midlands . . .'

Chief-Inspector Davy noted them as he passed. Without haste, and with no seeming purpose, he arrived at his objective.

Miss Marple was sitting near the fire and observing his approach.

'So you're still here, Miss Marple. I'm glad.'

'I go tomorrow,' said Miss Marple.

That fact had, somehow, been implicit in her attitude. She had sat, not relaxed, but upright, as one sits in an airport lounge, or a railway waiting-room. Her luggage, he was sure, would be packed, only toilet things and night wear to be added.

'It is the end of my fortnight's holiday,' she explained.

'You've enjoyed it, I hope?'

Miss Marple did not answer at once.

'In a way – yes . . .' She stopped.

'And in another way, no?'

'It's difficult to explain what I mean—'

'Aren't you, perhaps, a little too near the fire? Rather hot, here. Wouldn't you like to move – into that corner perhaps.'

Miss Marple looked at the corner indicated, then she looked at Chief-Inspector Davy.

'I think you are quite right,' she said.

He gave her a hand up, carried her handbag and her book for her and established her in the quiet corner he had indicated.

'All right?'

'Quite all right.'

'You know why I suggested it?'

'You thought – very kindly – that it was too hot for me by the fire. Besides,' she added, 'our conversation cannot be overheard here.'

'Have you got something you want to tell me, Miss Marple?'

'Now why should you think that?'

'You looked as though you had,' said Davy.

'I'm sorry I showed it so plainly,' said Miss Marple. 'I didn't mean to.'

'Well, what about it?'

'I don't know if I ought to do so. I would like you to believe, Inspector, that I am not really fond of interfering, I am against interference. Though often well meant, it can cause a great deal of harm.'

'It's like that, is it? I see. Yes, it's quite a problem for you.'

'Sometimes one sees people doing things that seem to one unwise – even dangerous. But has one any right to interfere? Usually not, I think.'

'Is this Canon Pennyfather you're talking about?'

'Canon Pennyfather?' Miss Marple sounded very surprised. 'Oh no. Oh dear me no, nothing whatever to do with him. It concerns – a girl.'

'A girl, indeed? And you thought I could help?'

'I don't know,' said Miss Marple. 'I simply don't know. But I'm worried, very worried.'

Father did not press her. He sat there looking large and comfortable and rather stupid. He let her take her time. She had been willing to do her best to help him, and he was quite prepared to do anything he could to help her. He was not, perhaps, particularly interested. On the other hand, one never knew.

'One reads in the papers,' said Miss Marple in a low clear voice, 'accounts of proceedings in court, of young people, children or girls "in need of care and protection". It's just a sort of legal phrase, I suppose, but it could mean something real.'

'This girl you mentioned, you feel she is in need of care and protection?'

'Yes. Yes I do.'

'Alone in the world?'

'Oh no,' said Miss Marple. 'Very much not so, if I may put it that way. She is to all outward appearances very heavily protected and very well cared for.'

'Sounds interesting,' said Father.

'She was staying in this hotel,' said Miss Marple, 'with a Mrs Carpenter, I think. I looked in the register to see the name. The girl's name is Elvira Blake.'

Father looked up with a quick air of interest.

'She was a lovely girl. Very young, very much as I say, sheltered and protected. Her guardian was a Colonel Luscombe, a very nice man. Quite charming. Elderly of course, and I am afraid terribly innocent.'

'The guardian or the girl?'

'I meant the guardian,' said Miss Marple. 'I don't know about the girl. But I do think she is in danger. I came across her quite by chance in Battersea Park. She was sitting at a refreshment place there with a young man.'

'Oh, that's it, is it?' said Father. 'Undesirable, I suppose. Beatnik – spiv – thug—'

'A very handsome man,' said Miss Marple. 'Not so very young. Thirty-odd, the kind of man that I should say is very attractive to women, but his face is a bad face. Cruel, hawk-like, predatory.'

'He mayn't be as bad as he looks,' said Father soothingly.

'If anything he is worse than he looks,' said Miss Marple. I am convinced of it. He drives a large racing car.'

Father looked up quickly.

'Racing car?'

'Yes. Once or twice I've seen it standing near this hotel.'

'You don't remember the number, do you?'

'Yes, indeed I do. FAN 2266. I had a cousin who stuttered,' Miss Marple explained. 'That's how I remember it.'

Father looked puzzled.

'Do you know who he is?' demanded Miss Marple.

'As a matter of fact I do,' said Father slowly. 'Half French, half Polish. Very well known racing driver, he was world champion three years ago. His name is Ladislaus Malinowski. You're quite right in some of your views about him. He has a bad reputation where women are concerned. That is to say, he is not a suitable friend for a young girl. But it's not easy to do anything about that sort of thing. I suppose she is meeting him on the sly, is that it?'

'Almost certainly,' said Miss Marple.

'Did you approach her guardian?'

'I don't know him,' said Miss Marple. 'I've only just been introduced to him once by a mutual friend. I don't like the idea of going to him in a tale-bearing way. I wondered if perhaps in some way *you* could do something about it.'

'I can try,' said Father. 'By the way, I thought you might like to know that your friend, Canon Pennyfather, has turned up all right.'

'Indeed!' Miss Marple looked animated. 'Where?'

'A place called Milton St John.'

'How very odd. What was he doing there? Did he know?'

'*Apparently*—' Chief-Inspector Davy stressed the word. '—He had had an accident.'

'What kind of an accident?'

'Knocked down by a car – concussed – or else, of course, he might have been conked on the head.'

'Oh! I see.' Miss Marple considered the point. 'Doesn't he know himself?'

'He *says*—' again the Chief-Inspector stressed the word, '—that he does not know anything.'

'Very remarkable.'

'Isn't it? The last thing he remembers is driving in a taxi to Kensington Air Station.'

Miss Marple shook her head perplexedly.

'I know it does happen that way in concussion,' she murmured. 'Didn't he say anything – useful?'

'He murmured something about the Walls of Jericho.'

'Joshua?' hazarded Miss Marple, 'or Archæology – excavations? – or I remember, long ago, a play – by Mr Sutro, I think.'

'And all this week north of the Thames, Gaumont Cinemas – *The Walls of Jericho,* featuring Olga Radbourne and Bart Levinne,' said Father.

Miss Marple looked at him suspiciously.

'He could have gone to that film in the Cromwell Road. He could have come out about eleven and come back here – though if so, someone ough to have seen him – it would be well before midnight—'

'Took the wrong bus,' Miss Marple suggested. 'Something like that—'

'Say he got back here *after* midnight,' Father said, '—he *could* have walked up to his room without anyone seeing him— But if so, what happened then – and why did he go out again three hours later?'

Miss Marple groped for a word.

'The only idea that occurs to me is – oh!'

She jumped as a report sounded from the street outside.

'Car backfiring,' said Father soothingly.

'I'm sorry to be so jumpy – I am nervous tonight – that feeling one has—'

'That something's going to happen? I don't think you need worry.'

'I have never liked fog.'

'I wanted to tell you,' said Chief-Inspector Davy, 'that you've given me a lot of help. The things you've noticed here – just little things – they've added up.'

'So there *was* something wrong with this place?'

'There was and is everything wrong with it.'

Miss Marple sighed.

'It seemed wonderful at first – unchanged you know – like stepping back into the past – to the part of the past that one had loved and enjoyed.'

She paused.

'But of course, it wasn't really like that. I learned (what I suppose I really knew already) that one can never go back, that one should not ever try to go back – that the essence of life is going forward. Life is really a One Way Street, isn't it?'

'Something of the sort,' agreed Father.

'I remember,' said Miss Marple, diverging from her main topic in a characteristic way, 'I remember being in Paris with my mother and my grandmother, and we went to have tea at the Elysée Hotel. And my grandmother looked round, and she said suddenly, "Clara, I do believe I am the only woman here in a *bonnet*!" And she was, too! When she got home she packed up all her bonnets, and her beaded mantles too – and sent them off—'

'To the Jumble Sale?' inquired Father, sympathetically.

'Oh no. Nobody would have wanted them at a jumble sale. She sent them to a theatrical Repertory Company, They appreciated them very much. But let me see—' Miss Marple recovered her direction. '—Where was I?'

'Summing up this place.'

'Yes. It seemed all right – but it wasn't. It was mixed up – real people and people who weren't real. One couldn't always tell them apart.'

'What do you mean by not real?'

'There were retired military men, but there were also what seemed to be military men but who had never been in the army. And clergymen who weren't clergymen. And admirals and sea captains who've never been in the navy. My friend, Selina Hazy – it amused me at first how she was always so anxious to recognise people she knew (quite natural, of course) and how often she was mistaken and they weren't the people she thought they were. But it happened too often. And so – I began to wonder. Even Rose, the chambermaid – so nice – but I began to think that perhaps *she* wasn't real, either.'

854

'If it interests you to know, she's an ex-actress. A good one. Gets a better salary here than she ever drew on the stage.'

'But – why?'

'Mainly, as part of the décor. Perhaps there's more than that to it.'

'I'm glad to be leaving here,' said Miss Marple. She gave a little shiver. 'Before anything happens.'

Chief-Inspector Davy looked at her curiously.

'What do you expect to happen?' he asked.

'Evil of some kind,' said Miss Marple.

'Evil is rather a big word—'

'You think it is too melodramatic? But I have some experience – I seem to have been – so often – in contact with murder.'

'Murder?' Chief-Inspector Davy shook his head. 'I'm not suspecting murder. Just a nice cosy round up of some remarkably clever criminals—'

'That's not the same thing. Murder – the wish to do murder – is something quite different. It – how shall I say – it defies God.'

He looked at her and shook his head gently and reassuringly.

'There won't be any murders,' he said.

A sharp report, louder than the former one, came from outside. It was followed by a scream and another report.

Chief-Inspector Davy was on his feet, moving with a speed surprising in such a bulky man. In a few seconds he was through the swing doors and out in the street.

II

The screaming – a woman's – was piercing the mist with a note of terror. Chief-Inspector Davy raced down Pond Street in the direction of the screams. He could dimly visualise a woman's figure backed against a railing. In a dozen strides he had reached her. She wore a long pale fur coat, and her shining blonde hair hung down each side of her face. He thought for a moment that he knew who she was, then he realized that this was only a slip of a girl. Sprawled on the pavement at her feet was the body of a man in uniform. Chief-Inspector Davy recognised him. It was Michael Gorman.

As Davy came up to the girl, she clutched at him, shivering all over, stammering out broken phrases.

'Someone tried to kill me . . . Someone . . . they shot at me . . .

If it hadn't been for *him*—' she pointed down at the motionless figure at her feet. 'He pushed me back and got in front of me – and then the second shot came . . . and he fell . . . He saved my life. I think he's hurt – badly hurt . . .'

Chief-Inspector Davy went down on one knee. His torch came out. The tall Irish commissionaire had fallen like a soldier. The left hand side of his tunic showed a wet patch that was growing wetter as the blood oozed out into the cloth. Davy rolled up an eyelid, touched a wrist. He rose to his feet again.

'He's had it all right,' he said.

The girl gave a sharp cry. 'Do you mean he's *dead*? Oh no, no! He can't be *dead*.'

'Who was it shot at you?'

'I don't know . . . I'd left my car just round the corner and was feeling my way along by the railings – I was going to Bertram's Hotel. And then suddenly there was a shot – and a bullet went past my cheek and then – he – the porter from Bertram's – came running down the street towards me, and shoved me behind him, and then another shot came . . . I think – I think whoever it was must have been hiding in that area there.'

Chief-Inspector Davy looked where she pointed. At this end of Bertram's Hotel there was an old-fashioned area below the level of the street, with a gate and some steps down to it. Since it gave only on some store-rooms it was not much used, But a man could have hidden there easily enough.

'You didn't see him?'

'Not properly. He rushed past me like a shadow. It was all thick fog.'

Davy nodded.

The girl began to sob hysterically.

'But who could possibly want to kill me? Why should anyone want to kill me? That's the second time. I don't understand . . . why . . .'

One arm round the girl, Chief-Inspector Davy fumbled in his pocket with the other hand.

The shrill notes of a police whistle penetrated the mist.

III

In the lounge of Bertram's Hotel, Miss Gorringe had looked up sharply from the desk.

One or two of the visitors had looked up also. The older and deafer did not look up.

Henry, about to lower a glass of old brandy to a table, stopped poised with it still in his hand.

Miss Marple sat forward, clutching the arms of her chair. A retired admiral said decisively,

'Accident! Cars collided in the fog, I expect.'

The swing doors from the street were pushed open. Through them came what seemed like an outsize policeman, looking a good deal larger than life.

He was supporting a girl in a pale fur coat. She seemed hardly able to walk. The policeman looked round for help with some embarrassment.

Miss Gorringe came out from behind the desk, prepared to cope. But at that moment the lift came down. A tall figure emerged, and the girl shook herself free from the policeman's support, and ran frantically across the lounge.

'Mother,' she cried. 'Oh *Mother, Mother* . . .' and threw herself, sobbing, into Bess Sedgwick's arms.

21

Chief-Inspector Davy settled himself back in his chair and looked at the two women sitting opposite him. It was past midnight. Police officials had come and gone. There had been doctors, fingerprint men, an ambulance to remove the body; and now everything had narrowed to this one room dedicated for the purposes of the Law by Bertram's Hotel. Chief-Inspector Davy sat one side of the table. Bess Sedgwick and Elvira sat the other side. Against the wall a policeman sat unobtrusively writing. Detective-Sergeant Wadell sat near the door.

Father looked thoughtfully at the two women facing him. Mother and daughter. There was, he noted, a strong superficial likeness between them. He could understand how for one moment in the fog he had taken Elvira Blake for Bess Sedgwick. But now, looking at them, he was more struck by the points of difference than the points of resemblance. They were not really alike save in colouring, yet the impression persisted that here he had a positive and a negative version of the same personality. Everything about Bess Sedgwick was positive. Her vitality, her

energy, her magnetic attraction. He admired Lady Sedgwick.
He always had admired her. He had admired her courage and
had always been excited over her exploits; had said, reading
his Sunday papers: 'She'll never get away with *that*,' and invariably she had got away with it! He had not thought it possible
that she would reach journey's end and she had reached
journey's end. He admired particularly the indestructible
quality of her. She had had one air crash, several car crashes,
had been thrown badly twice from her horse, but at the end of
it here she was. Vibrant, alive, a personality one could not
ignore for a moment. He took off his hat to her mentally. Some
day, of course, she would come a cropper. You could only bear
a charmed life for so long. His eyes went from mother to
daughter. He wondered. He wondered very much.

In Elvira Blake, he thought, everything had been driven inward. Bess Sedgwick had got through life by imposing her will
on it. Elvira, he guessed, had a different way of getting through
life. She submitted, he thought. She obeyed. She smiled in com-
pliance and behind that, he thought, she slipped away through
your fingers. 'Sly,' he said to himself, appraising that fact.
'That's the only way she can manage, I expect. She can never
brazen things out or impose herself. That's why, I expect, the
people who've looked after her have never had the least idea of
what she might be up to.'

He wondered what she had been doing slipping along the
street to Bertram's Hotel on a late foggy evening. He was going
to ask her presently. He thought it highly probable that the
answer he would get would not be the true one. 'That's the
way,' he thought, 'that the poor child defends herself.' Had she
come here to meet her mother or to find her mother? It was
perfectly possible, but he didn't think so. Not for a moment.
Instead he thought of the big sports car tucked away round the
corner – the car with the number plate FAN 2266. Ladislaus
Malinowski must be somewhere in the neighbourhood since
his car was there.

'Well,' said Father, addressing Elvira in his most kindly and
father-like manner, 'well, and how are you feeling now?'

'I'm quite all right,' said Elvira.

'Good. I'd like you to answer a few questions if you feel up
to it; because, you see, time is usually the essence of these things.
You were shot at twice and a man was killed. We want as many
clues as we can get to the person who killed him.'

'I'll tell you everything I can, but it all came so suddenly.

And you can't *see* anything in a fog. I've no idea myself who it could have been – or even what he looked like. That's what was so frightening.'

'You said this was the second time somebody had tried to kill you. Does that mean there was an attempt on your life before?'

'Did I say that? I can't remember.' Her eyes moved uneasily. 'I don't think I said that.'

'Oh, but you did, you know,' said Father.

'I expect I was just being – being hysterical.'

'No,' said Father, 'I don't think you were. I think you meant just what you said.'

'I might have been imagining things,' said Elvira. Her eyes shifted again.

Bess Sedgwick moved. She said quietly:

'You'd better tell him, Elvira.'

Elvira shot a quick, uneasy look at her mother.

'You needn't worry,' said Father, reassuringly. 'We know quite well in the police force that girls don't tell their mothers or their guardians everything. We don't take those things too seriously, but we've got to *know* about them, because, you see, it all helps.'

Bess Sedgwick said,

'Was it in Italy?'

'Yes,' said Elvira.

'Father said: 'That's where you've been at school, isn't it, or to a finishing place or whatever they call it nowadays?'

'Yes. I was at Contessa Martinelli's. There were about eighteen or twenty of us.'

'And you thought that somebody tried to kill you. How was that?'

'Well, a big box of chocolates and sweets and things came for me. There was a card with it written in Italian in a flowery hand. The sort of thing they say, you know, "To the bellissima Signorina." Something like that. And my friends and I – well – we laughed about it a bit, and wondered who'd sent it.'

'Did it come by post?'

'No. No, it couldn't have come by post. It was just there in my room. Someone must have put it there.'

'I see. Bribed one of the servants, I suppose. I am to take it that you didn't let the Contessa whoever-it-was in on this?'

A faint smile appeared on Elvira's face. 'No. No. We certainly didn't. Anyway we opened the box and they were lovely choc-olates. Different kinds, you know, but there were some violet creams. That's the sort of chocolate that has a crystallized violet on top. My favourite. So of course I ate one or two of those first. And then afterwards, in the night, I felt terribly ill. I didn't think it was the chocolates, I just thought it was something perhaps that I'd eaten at dinner.'

'Anybody else ill?'

'No. Only me. Well, I was very sick and all that, but I felt all right by the end of the next day. Then a day or two later I ate another of the same chocolates, and the same thing happened. So I talked to Bridget about it. Bridget was my special friend. And we looked at the chocolates, and we found that the violet creams had got a sort of hole in the bottom that had been filled up again, so we thought that someone had put some poison in and they'd only put it in the violet creams so that I would be the one who ate them.'

'Nobody else was ill?'

'No.'

'So presumably nobody else ate the violet creams?'

'No. I don't think they could have. You see, it was my present and they knew I liked the violet ones, so they'd leave them for me.'

'The chap took a risk, whoever he was,' said Father. 'The whole place might have been poisoned.'

'It's absurd,' said Lady Sedgwick sharply. 'Utterly absurd! I never heard of anything so crude.'

Chief-Inspector Davy made a slight gesture with his hand. 'Please,' he said, then he went on to Elvira: 'Now I find that very interesting, Miss Blake. And you still didn't tell the Contessa?'

'Oh no, we didn't. She'd have made a terrible fuss.'

'What did you do with the chocolates?'

'We threw them away,' said Elvira. 'They were lovely chocolates,' she added, with a tone of slight grief.

'You didn't try and find out who sent them?'

Elvira looked embarrassed.

'Well, you see, I thought it might have been Guido.'

'Yes?' said Chief-Inspector Davy, cheerfully. 'And who is Guido?'

'Oh, Guido . . .' Elvira paused. She looked at her mother.

'Don't be stupid,' said Bess Sedgwick. 'Tell Chief-Inspector Davy about Guido, whoever he is. Every girl of your age has a Guido in her life. You met him out there, I suppose?'

'Yes. When we were taken to the opera. He spoke to me there. He was nice. Very attractive. I used to see him sometimes when we went to classes. He used to pass me notes.'

'And I suppose,' said Bess Sedgwick, 'that you told a lot of lies, and made plans with some friends and you managed to get out and meet him? Is that it?'

Elvira looked relieved by this short cut to confession.

'Yes. Bridget and I sometimes went out together. Sometimes Guido managed to—'

'What was Guido's other name?'

'I don't know,' said Elvira. 'He never told me.'

Chief-Inspector Davy smiled at her.

'You mean you're not going to tell? Never mind. I dare say we'll be able to find out quite all right without your help, if it should really matter. But why should you think that this young man, who was presumably fond of you, should want to kill you?'

'Oh, because he used to threaten things like that. I mean, we used to have rows now and then. He'd bring some of his friends with him, and I'd pretend to like them better than him, and then he'd get very, very wild and angry. He said I'd better be careful what I did. I couldn't give him up just like that! That if I wasn't faithful to him he'd kill me! I just thought he was being melodramatic and theatrical.' Elvira smiled suddenly and unexpectedly. 'But it was all rather fun. I didn't think it was *real* or *serious*.'

'Well,' said Chief-Inspector Davy, 'I don't think it *does* seem very likely that a young man such as you describe would really poison chocolates and send them to you.'

'Well, I don't think so really either,' said Elvira, 'but it must have been him because I can't see that there's anyone else. It worried me. And then, when I came back here, I got a note—' She stopped.

'What sort of note?'

'It just came in an envelope and was printed. It said, "*Be on your guard. Somebody wants to kill you*".'

Chief-Inspector Davy's eyebrows went up.

'Indeed? Very curious. Yes, very curious. And it worried you. You were frightened?'

'Yes. I began to – to wonder who could possibly want me out of the way. That's why I tried to find out if I was really very rich.'

'Go on.'

'And the other day in London something else happened. I

was in the tube and there were a lot of people on the platform. I thought someone tried to push me on to the line.'

'My dear child!' said Bess Sedgwick. 'Don't romance.'

Again Father made that slight gesture of his hand.

'Yes,' said Elvira apologetically. 'I expect I *have* been imagining it all but – I don't know – I mean, after what happened this evening it seems, doesn't it, as though it might all be true?' She turned suddenly to Bess Sedgwick, speaking with urgency, '*Mother! You* might know. *Does* anyone want to kill me? *Could* there be anyone? Have I got an enemy?'

'Of course you've not got an enemy,' said Bess Sedgwick, impatiently. 'Don't be an idiot. Nobody wants to kill you. Why should they?'

'Then who shot at me tonight?'

'In that fog,' said Bess Sedgwick, 'you might have been mistaken for someone else. That's possible, don't you think?' she said, turning to Father.

'Yes, I think it might be quite possible,' said Chief-Inspector Davy.

Bess Sedgwick was looking at him very intently. He almost fancied the motion of her lips saying 'later.'

'Well,' he said cheerfully, 'we'd better get down to some more facts now. Where had you come from tonight? What were you doing walking along Pond Street on such a foggy evening.'

'I came up for an Art class at the Tate this morning. Then I went to lunch with my friend Bridget. She lives in Onslow Square. We went to a film and when we came out, there was this fog – quite thick and getting worse, and I thought perhaps I'd better not drive home.'

'You drive a car, do you?'

'Yes. I took my driving test last summer. Only, I'm not a very good driver and I hate driving in fog. So Bridget's mother said I could stay the night, so I rang up Cousin Mildred – that's where I live in Kent—'

Father nodded.

'– and I said I was going to stay up over-night. She said that was very wise.'

'And what happened next?' asked Father.

'And then the fog seemed lighter suddenly. You know how patchy fogs are. So I said I would drive down to Kent after all. I said goodbye to Bridget and started off. But then it began to come down again. I didn't like it very much. I ran into a very thick patch of it and I lost my way and I didn't know where I was. Then after a bit I realized I was at Hyde Park Corner and I thought "I really *can't* go down to Kent in this." At first, I thought I'd go back to Bridget's but then I remembered how I'd lost my way already. And then I realized that I was quite close to this nice hotel where Uncle Derek took me, when I came back from Italy, and I thought, "I'll go there and I'm sure they can find me a room." That was fairly easy, I found a place to leave the car and then I walked back up the street towards the hotel.'

'Did you meet anyone or did you hear anyone walking near you?'

'It's funny you saying that, because I did think I heard some-one walking behind me. Of course, there must be lots of people walking about in London. Only in a fog like this, it gives you a nervous feeling. I waited and listened but I didn't hear any footsteps and I thought I'd imagined them. I was quite close to the hotel by then.'

'And then?'

'And then quite suddenly there was a shot. As I told you, it seemed to go right past my ear. The commissionaire man who stands outside the hotel came running down towards me and he pushed me behind him and then – then – the other shot came . . . He – he fell down and I screamed.' She was shaking now. Her mother spoke to her.

'Steady, girl,' said Bess in a low, firm voice. 'Steady now.' It was the voice Bess Sedgwick used for her horses and it was quite as efficacious when used on her daughter. Elvira blinked at her, drew herself up a little, and became calm again.

'Good girl,' said Bess.

'And then *you* came,' said Elvira to Father. 'You blew your whistle, you told the policeman to take me into the hotel. And as soon as I got in, I saw – I saw Mother.' She turned and looked at Bess Sedgwick.

'And that brings us more or less up to date,' said Father. He shifted his bulk a little in the chair.

'Do you know a man called Ladislaus Malinowski?' he asked. His tone was even, casual, without any direct inflection. He did not look at the girl, but he was aware, since his ears were functioning at full attention, of a quick little gasp she gave. His eyes were not on the daughter but on the mother.

'No,' said Elvira, having waited just a shade too long to say it. 'No, I don't.'

'Oh,' said Father. 'I thought you might. I thought he might have been here this evening.'

'Oh? Why should he be here?'

'Well, his car is here,' said Father. 'That's why I thought he might be.'

'I don't know him,' said Elvira.

'My mistake,' said Father. 'You do, of course?' he turned his head towards Bess Sedgwick.

'Naturally,' said Bess Sedgwick. 'Known him for many years.' She added, smiling slightly, 'He's a madman, you know. Drives like an angel or a devil – he'll break his neck one of these days. Had a bad smash eighteen months ago.'

'Yes, I remember reading about it,' said Father. 'Not racing again yet, is he?'

'No, not yet. Perhaps he never will.'

'Do you think I could go to bed now?' asked Elvira, plaintively. 'I'm – really terribly tired.'

'Of course. You must be,' said Father. 'You've told us all you can remember?'

'Oh. Yes.'

'I'll go up with you,' said Bess.

Mother and daughter went out together.

'*She* knows him all right,' said Father.

'Do you really think so?' asked Sergeant Wadell.

'I know it. She had tea with him in Battersea Park only a day or two ago.'

'How did you find that out?'

'Old lady told me – distressed. Didn't think he was a nice friend for a young girl. He isn't of course.'

'Especially if he and the mother—' Wadell broke off delicately. 'It's pretty general gossip—'

'Yes. May be true, may not. Probably *is*.'

'In that case which one is he really after?'

Father ignored that point. He said:

'I want him picked up. I want him badly. His car's here – just round the corner.'

'Do you think he might be actually staying in this hotel?'

'Don't think so. It wouldn't fit into the picture. He's not supposed to be here. *If* he came here, he came to meet the girl. She definitely came to meet him, I'd say.'

The door opened and Bess Sedgwick reappeared.

'I came back,' she said, 'because I wanted to speak to you.'

She looked from him to the other two men.

864

'I wonder if I could speak to you alone? I've given you all the information I have, such as it is; but I would like a word or two with you in private.'

'I don't see any reason why not,' said Chief-Inspector Davy. He motioned with his head, and the young detective-constable took his note-book and went out. Wadell went with him. 'Well?' said Chief-Inspector Davy.

Lady Sedgwick sat down again opposite him.

'That silly story about poisoned chocolates,' she said. 'It's nonsense. Absolutely ridiculous. I don't believe anything of the kind ever happened.'

'You don't, eh?'

'Do you?'

Father shook his head doubtfully. 'You think your daughter cooked it up?'

'Yes. But why?'

'Well, if you don't know why,' said Chief-Inspector Davy, 'how should I know? She's your daughter. Presumably you know her better than I do.'

'I don't know her at all,' said Bess Sedgwick bitterly. 'I've not seen her or had anything to do with her since she was two years old, when I ran away from my husband.'

'Oh yes. I know all that. I find it curious. You see, Lady Sedgwick, courts usually give the mother, even if she is a guilty party in a divorce, custody of a young child if she asks for it. Presumably then you didn't ask for it? You didn't want it.'

'I thought it – better not.'

'Why?'

'I didn't think it was – safe for her.'

'On moral grounds?'

'No. Not on moral grounds. Plenty of adultery nowadays. Children have to learn about it, have to grow up with it. No. It's just that *I* am not really a safe person to be with. The life I'd lead wouldn't be a safe life. You can't help the way you're born. I was born to live dangerously. I'm not law-abiding or conventional. I thought it would be better for Elvira, happier, to have a proper English conventional bringing-up. Shielded, looked after . . .'

'But minus a mother's love?'

'I thought if she learned to love me it might bring sorrow to her. Oh, you mayn't believe me, but that's what I felt.'

'I see. Do you still think you were right?'

865

'No,' said Bess. 'I don't. I think now I may have been entirely wrong.'

'*Does* your daughter know Ladislaus Malinowski?'

'I'm sure she doesn't. She said so. You heard her.'

'I heard her, yes.'

'Well, then?'

'She was afraid, you know, when she was sitting here. In our profession we get to know fear when we meet up with it. She was afraid – why? Chocolates or no chocolates, her life has been attempted. That tube story may be true enough—'

'It was ridiculous. Like a thriller—'

'Perhaps. But that sort of thing does happen. Lady Sedgwick. Oftener than you'd think. Can you give me any idea who might want to kill your daughter?'

'Nobody – nobody at all!'

She spoke vehemently.

Chief-Inspector Davy sighed and shook his head.

—— 22 ——

Chief-Inspector Davy waited patiently until Mrs Melford had finished talking. It had been a singularly unprofitable interview. Cousin Mildred had been incoherent, unbelieving and generally feather-headed. Or that was Father's private view. Accounts of Elvira's sweet manners, nice nature, troubles with her teeth, odd excuses told through the telephone, had led on to serious doubts whether Elvira's friend Bridget was really a suitable friend for her. All these matters had been presented to the Chief-Inspector in a kind of general hasty pudding. Mrs Melford knew nothing, had heard nothing, had seen nothing and had apparently deduced very little.

A short telephone call to Elvira's guardian, Colonel Luscombe, had been even more unproductive, though fortunately less wordy. 'More Chinese monkeys,' he muttered to his sergeant as he put down the receiver. 'See no evil, hear no evil, speak no evil.

'The trouble is that everyone who's had anything to do with this girl has been far too nice – if you get my meaning. Too many nice people who don't know anything about evil. Not like my old lady.'

'The Bertram's Hotel one?'

'Yes, that's the one. She's had a long life of experience in noticing evil, fancying evil, suspecting evil and going forth to do battle with evil. Let's see what we can get out of girl friend Bridget.'

The difficulties in this interview were represented first, last, and most of the time by Bridget's mamma. To talk to Bridget without the assistance of her mother took all Chief-Inspector Davy's adroitness and cajolery. He was, it must be admitted, ably seconded by Bridget. After a certain amount of stereotyped questions and answers and expressions of horror on the part of Bridget's mother at hearing of Elvira's narrow escape from death, Bridget said, 'You know it's time for that committee meeting, Mum. You said it was very important.'

'Oh dear, dear,' said Bridget's mother.

'You know they'll get into a frightful mess without you, Mummy.'

'Oh they will, they certainly will. But perhaps I ought—'

'Now that's quite all right, Madam,' said Chief-Inspector Davy, putting on his kindly old father look. 'You don't want to worry. Just you get off. I've finished all the important things. You've told me really everything I wanted to know. I've just one or two routine inquiries about people in Italy which I think your daughter, Miss Bridget, might be able to help me with.'

'Well, if you think you could manage, Bridget—'

'Oh, I can manage, Mummy,' said Bridget.

Finally, with a great deal of fuss, Bridget's mother went off to her committee.

'Oh dear,' said Bridget, sighing, as she came back after closing the front door. 'Really! I do think mothers are *difficult.*'

'So they tell me,' said Chief-Inspector Davy. 'A lot of young ladies I come across have a lot of trouble with their mothers.'

'I'd have thought you'd put it the other way round,' said Bridget.

'Oh I do, I do,' said Davy. 'But that's not how the young ladies see it. Now you can tell me a little more.'

'I couldn't really speak frankly in front of Mummy,' explained Bridget. 'But I do feel, of course, that it is really important that you should know as much as possible about all this. I do know Elvira was terribly worried about something and *afraid.* She wouldn't exactly admit she was in danger, but she was.'

867

'I thought that might have been so. Of course I didn't like to ask you too much in front of your mother.'

'Oh no,' said Bridget, 'we don't want *Mummy* to hear about it. She gets in such a frightful state about things and she'd go and *tell* everyone. I mean, if Elvira doesn't want things like this to be known . . .'

'First of all,' said Chief-Inspector Davy, 'I want to know about a box of chocolates in Italy. I gather there was some idea that a box was sent to her which might have been poisoned.'

Bridget's eyes opened wide. 'Poisoned,' she said. 'Oh no. I don't think so. At least . . .'

'There was something?'

'Oh yes. A box of chocolates came and Elvira did eat a lot of them and she was rather sick that night. Quite ill.'

'But she didn't suspect poison?'

'No. At least – oh yes, she did say that someone was trying to poison one of us and we looked at the chocolates to see, you know, if anything had been injected into them.'

'And had it?'

'No, it hadn't,' said Bridget. 'At least, not as far as we could see.'

'But perhaps your friend, Miss Elvira, might still have thought so?'

'Well, she might – but she didn't *say* any more.'

'But you think she was afraid of someone?'

'I didn't think so at the time or notice anything. It was only here, later.'

'What about this man, Guido?'

Bridget giggled.

'He had a terrific crush on Elvira,' she said.

'And you and your friend used to meet him places?'

'Well, I don't mind telling *you*,' said Bridget. 'After all you're the police. It isn't important to you, that sort of thing, and I expect you understand. Countess Martinelli was frightfully strict – or thought she was. And of course we had all sorts of dodges and things. We all stood in with each other. You know.'

'And told the right lies, I suppose?'

'Well, I'm afraid so,' said Bridget. 'But what can one do when anyone is so suspicious?'

'So you did meet Guido and all that. And used he to threaten Elvira?'

'Oh, not seriously, I don't think.'

'Then perhaps there was someone else she used to meet?'

'Oh – that – well, I don't know.'

'Please tell me, Miss Bridget. It might be – vital, you know.'

'Yes. Yes I can see that. Well there was *someone*. I don't know who it was, but there was someone else – she really minded about. She was deadly serious. I mean it was a really *important* thing.'

'She used to meet him?'

'I think so. I mean she'd *say* she was meeting Guido but it wasn't always Guido. It was this other man.'

'Any idea who it was?'

'No.' Bridget sounded a little uncertain.

'It wouldn't be a racing motorist called Ladislaus Malinowski?'

Bridget gaped at him.

'So you *know*?'

'Am I right?'

'Yes – I think so. She'd got a photograph of him torn out of a paper. She kept it under her stockings.'

'That might have been just a pin-up hero, mightn't it?'

'Well it *might*, of course, but I don't think it was.'

'Did she meet him here in this country, do you know?'

'I don't know. You see I don't know really what she's been doing since she came back from Italy.'

'She came up to London to the dentist,' Davy prompted her. 'Or so she said. Instead she came to you. She rang up Mrs Melford with some story about an old governess.'

A faint giggle came from Bridget.

'That wasn't true, was it?' said the Chief-Inspector, smiling. 'Where did she really go?'

Bridget hesitated and then said, 'She went to Ireland.'

'She went to Ireland, did she? Why?'

'She wouldn't tell me. She said there was something she had to find out.'

'Do you know where she went in Ireland?'

'Not exactly. She mentioned a name. Bally something. Ballygowlan, I think it was.'

'I see. You're sure she went to Ireland?'

'I saw her off at Kensington Airport. She went by Aer Lingus.'

'She came back when?'

'The following day.'

'Also by air?'

'Yes.'

'You're quite sure, are you, that she came back by air?'

'Well – I suppose she did!'

'Had she taken a return ticket?'

'No. No, she didn't. I remember.'

'She might have come back another way, mightn't she?'

'Yes, I suppose so.'

'She might have come back for instance by the Irish Mail?'

'She didn't say she had.'

'But she didn't *say* she'd come by air, did she?'

'No,' Bridget agreed. 'But why should she come back by boat and train instead of by air?'

'Well, if she had found out what she wanted to know and had had nowhere to stay, she might think it would be easier to come back by the Night Mail.'

'Why, I suppose she *might*.'

Davy smiled faintly.

'I don't suppose you young ladies,' he said, 'think of going anywhere except in terms of flying, do you, nowadays?'

'I suppose we don't really,' agreed Bridget.

'Anyway, she came back to England. Then what happened? Did she come to you or ring you up?'

'She rang up.'

'What time of day?'

'Oh, in the morning some time. Yes, it must have been about eleven or twelve o'clock, I think.'

'And she said, what?'

'Well, she just asked if everything was all right.'

'And was it?'

'No, it wasn't, because, you see, Mrs Melford had rung up and Mummy had answered the phone and things had been very difficult and I hadn't known what to say. So Elvira said she would not come to Onslow Square, but that she'd ring up her cousin Mildred and try to fix up some story or other.'

'And that's all you can remember?'

'That's all,' said Bridget, making certain reservations. She thought of Mr Bollard and the bracelet. That was certainly a thing she was not going to tell Chief-Inspector Davy. Father knew quite well that something was being kept from him. He could only hope that it was not something pertinent to his inquiry. He asked again:

'You think your friend was really frightened of someone or something?'

'Yes I do.'

'Did she mention it to you or did you mention it to her?'

'Oh, I asked her outright. At first she said no and then she admitted that she *was* frightened. And I know she was,' went on Bridget violently. 'She was in danger. She was quite sure of it. But I don't know why or how or anything about it.'

'Your surety on this point relates to that particular morning, does it, the morning she had come back from Ireland?'

'Yes. Yes, that's when I was so sure about it.'

'On the morning when she *might* have come back on the Irish Mail?'

'I don't think it's very likely that she did. Why don't you ask her?'

'I probably shall do in the end. But I don't want to call attention to that point. Not at the moment. It might just possibly make things more dangerous for her.'

Bridget opened round eyes.

'What do you mean?'

'You may not remember it, Miss Bridget, but that was the night, or rather the early morning, of the Irish Mail robbery.'

'Do you mean that Elvira was in *that* and never told me a thing about it?'

'I agree it's unlikely,' said Father. 'But it just occurred to me that she might have seen something or someone, or some incident might have occurred connected with the Irish Mail. She might have seen someone she knew, for instance, and that might have put her in danger.'

'Oh!' said Bridget. She thought it over. 'You mean – someone she knew was mixed up in the robbery.'

Chief-Inspector Davy got up.

'I think that's all,' he said. 'Sure there's nothing more you can tell me? Nowhere where your friend went that day? Or the day before?'

Again visions of Mr Bollard and the Bond Street shop rose before Bridget's eyes.

'No,' she said.

'I think there is something you haven't told me,' said Chief-Inspector Davy.

Bridget grasped thankfully at a straw.

'Oh, I forgot,' she said. 'Yes. I mean she did go to some lawyers. Lawyers who were trustees, to find out something.'

'Oh, she went to some lawyers who were her trustees. I don't suppose you know their name?'

'Their name was Egerton – Forbes Egerton and Something,' said Bridget. 'Lots of names. I think that's more or less right.'

'I see. And she wanted to find out something, did she?'

'She wanted to know how much money she'd got,' said Bridget.

Inspector Davy's eyebrows rose.

'Indeed!' he said. 'Interesting. Why didn't she know herself?'

'Oh, because people never told her anything about money,' said Bridget. 'They seem to think it's bad for you to know actually how much money you have.'

'And she wanted to know badly, did she?'

'Yes,' said Bridget. 'I think she thought it was important.'

'Well, thank you,' said Chief-Inspector Davy. 'You've helped me a good deal.'

—— 23 ——

Richard Egerton looked again at the official card in front of him, then up into the Chief-Inspector's face.

'Curious business,' he said.

'Yes, sir,' said Chief-Inspector Davy, 'a very curious business.'

'Bertram's Hotel,' said Egerton, 'in the fog. Yes, it was a bad fog last night. I suppose you get a lot of that sort of thing in fogs, don't you? Snatch and grab – handbags – that sort of thing?'

'It wasn't quite like that,' said Father. 'Nobody attempted to snatch anything from Miss Blake.'

'Where did the shot come from?'

'Owing to the fog we can't be sure. She wasn't sure herself. But we think – it seems the best idea – that the man may have been standing in the area.'

'He shot at her twice, you say?'

'Yes. The first shot missed. The commissionaire rushed along from where he was standing outside the hotel door and shoved her behind him just before the second shot.'

'So that he got hit instead, eh?'

'Yes.'

'Quite a brave chap.'

'Yes. He was brave,' said the Chief-Inspector. 'His military record was very good. An Irishman.'

'What's his name?'

'Gorman. Michael Gorman.'

'Michael Gorman.' Egerton frowned for a minute. 'No,' he said. 'For a moment I thought the name meant something.'

'It's a very common name, of course. Anyway, he saved the girl's life.'

'And why exactly have you come to me, Chief-Inspector?'

'I hoped for a little information. We always like full information, you know, about the victim of a murderous assault.'

'Oh, naturally, naturally. But really, I've only seen Elvira twice since she was a child.'

'You saw her when she came to call upon you about a week ago, didn't you?'

'Yes, that's quite right. What exactly do you want to know? If it's anything about her personally, who her friends were or about boy-friends, or lovers' quarrels – all that sort of thing – you'd do better to go to one of the women. There's a Mrs Carpenter who brought her back from Italy, I believe, and there's Mrs Melford with whom she lives in Sussex.'

'I've seen Mrs Melford.'

'Oh.'

'No good. Absolutely no good at all, sir. And I don't so much want to know about the girl personally – after all, I've seen her for myself and I've heard what she can tell me – or rather what she's willing to tell me—'

At a quick movement of Egerton's eyebrows he saw that the other had appreciated the point of the word 'willing.'

'I've been told that she was worried, upset, afraid about something, and convinced that her life was in danger. Was that your impression when she came to see you?'

'No,' said Egerton, slowly, 'no, I wouldn't go as far as that; though she did say one or two things that struck me as curious.'

'Such as?'

'Well, she wanted to know who would benefit if she were to die suddenly.'

'Ah, said Chief-Inspectod Davy, 'so she had that possibility in her mind, did she? That she might die suddenly. Interesting.'

'She'd got something in her head but I didn't know what it was. She also wanted to know how much money she had – or would have when she was twenty-one. That, perhaps, is more understandable.'

'It's a lot of money I believe.'

'It's a very large fortune, Chief-Inspector.'

'Why do you think she wanted to know?'

'About the money?'

'Yes, and about who would inherit it?'

'I don't know,' said Egerton. 'I don't know at all. She also brought up the subject of marriage—'

'Did you form the impression that there was a man in the case?'

'I've no evidence – but – yes, I did think just that. I felt sure there was a boy-friend somewhere in the offing. There usually is! Luscombe – that's Colonel Luscombe, her guardian, doesn't seem to know anything about a boy-friend. But then dear old Derek Luscombe wouldn't. He was quite upset when I suggested that there was such a thing in the background and probably an unsuitable one at that.'

'He is unsuitable,' said Chief-Inspector Davy.

'Oh. Then you know who he is?'

'I can have a very good guess at it. Ladislaus Malinowski.'

'The racing motorist? Really! A handsome daredevil. Women fall for him easily. I wonder how he came across Elvira. I don't see very well where their orbits would meet except – yes, I believe he was in Rome a couple of months ago. Possible she met him there.'

'Very possibly. Or she could have met him through her mother?'

'What, through Bess? I wouldn't say that was at all likely.'

Davy coughed.

'Lady Sedgwick and Malinowski are said to be close friends, sir.'

'Oh yes, yes, I know that's the gossip. May be true, may not. They are close friends – thrown together constantly by their way of life. Bess has had her affairs, of course; though, mind you, she's not the nymphomaniac type. People are ready enough to say that about a woman, but it's not true in Bess's case. Anyway, as far as I know, Bess and her daughter are practically not even acquainted with each other.'

'That's what Lady Sedgwick told me. And you agree?'

Egerton nodded.

'What other relatives has Miss Blake got?'

'For all intents and purposes, none. Her mother's two brothers were killed in the war – and she was old Coniston's only child. Mrs Melford, though the girl calls her "Cousin Mildred," is actually a cousin of Colonel Luscombe's. Luscombe's done his best for the girl in his conscientious old-fashioned way – but it's difficult . . . for a man.'

'Miss Blake brought up the subject of marriage, you say?

There's no possibility, I suppose, that she may actually already *be* married—'

'She's well under age – she'd have to have the assent of her guardian and trustees.'

'Technically, yes. But they don't always wait for that,' said Father.

'I know. Most regrettable. One has to go through all the machinery of making them Wards of Court, and all the rest of it. And even that has its difficulties.'

'And once they're married, they're married,' said Father. 'I suppose, if she *were* married, and died suddenly, her husband would inherit?'

'This idea of marriage is most unlikely. She has been most carefully looked after and . . .' He stopped, reacting to Chief-Inspector' Davy's cynical smile.

However carefully Elvira had been looked after, she seemed to have succeeded in making the acquaintance of the highly unsuitable Ladislaus Malinowski.

He said dubiously, 'Her mother bolted, it's true.'

'Her mother bolted, yes – that's what she would do – but Miss Blake's a different type. She's just as set on getting her own way, but she'd go about it differently.'

'You don't really think—'

'I don't think anything – *yet*,' said Chief-Inspector Davy.

—— 24 ——

Ladislaus Malinowski looked from one to the other of the two police officers and flung back his head and laughed.

'It is very amusing!' he said. 'You look solemn as owls. It is ridiculous that you should ask me to come here and wish to ask me questions. You have nothing against me, nothing.'

'We think you may be able to assist us in our inquiries, Mr Malinowski.' Chief-Inspector Davy spoke with official smoothness. 'You own a car, Mercedes-Otto, registration number FAN 2266.'

'Is there any reason why I should not own such a car?'

'No reason at all, sir. There's just a little uncertainty as to the correct number. Your car was on a motor road, M7, and the registration plate on that occasion was a different one.'

'Nonsense. It must have been some other car.'

'There aren't so many of that make. We have checked up on those there are.'

'You believe everything, I suppose, that your traffic police tell you! It is laughable! Where was all this?'

'The place where the police stopped you and asked to see your licence is not very far from Bedhampton. It was on the night of the Irish Mail robbery.'

'You really do amuse me,' said Ladislaus Malinowski.

'You have a revolver?'

'Certainly, I have a revolver and an automatic pistol. I have proper licences for them.'

'Quite so. They are both still in your possession?'

'Certainly.'

'I have already warned you, Mr Malinowski.'

'The famous policeman's warning! Anything you say will be taken down and used against you at your trial.'

'That's not quite the wording,' said Father mildly. 'Used, yes. Against, no. You don't want to qualify that statement of yours?'

'No, I do not.'

'And you are sure you don't want your solicitor here?'

'I do not like solicitors.'

'Some people don't. Where are those firearms now?'

'I think you know very well where they are, Chief-Inspector. The small pistol is in the pocket of my car, the Mercedes-Otto whose registered number is, as I have said, FAN 2266. The revolver is in a drawer in my flat.'

'You're quite right about the one in the drawer in your flat,' said Father, 'but the other – the pistol – is not in your car.'

'Yes, it is. It is in the left hand pocket.'

Father shook his head. 'It may have been once. It isn't now. Is this it, Mr Malinowski?'

He passed a small automatic pistol across the table. Ladislaus Malinowski, with an air of great surprise, picked it up.

'Ah-ha, yes. That is it. So it was *you* who took it from my car?'

'No,' said Father, 'we didn't take it from your car. It was not in your car. We found it somewhere else.'

'Where did you find it?'

'We found it,' said Father, 'in an area in Pond Street which – as you no doubt know – is a street near Park Lane. It could have been dropped by a man walking down that street – or running perhaps.'

Ladislaus Malinowski shrugged his shoulders. 'That is nothing to do with me – I did not put it there. It was in my car a day or two ago. One does not continually look to see if a thing is still where one has put it. One assumes it will be.'

'Do you know, Mr Malinowski, that this is the pistol which was used to shoot Michael Gorman on the night of November 26th?'

'Michael Gorman? I do not know a Michael Gorman.'

'The commissionaire from Bertram's Hotel.'

'Ah yes, the one who was shot. I read about it. And you say *my* pistol shot him? Nonsense!'

'It's not nonsense. The ballistic experts have examined it. You know enough of firearms to be aware that their evidence is reliable.'

'You are trying to frame me. I know what you police do!'

'I think you know the police of this country better than that, Mr Malinowski.'

'Are you suggesting that I shot Michael Gorman?'

'So far we are only asking for a statement. No charge has been made.'

'But this is what you think – that I shot that ridiculous dressed-up military figure. Why should I? I didn't owe him money, I had no grudge against him.'

'It was a young lady who was shot at. Gorman ran to protect her and received the second bullet in his chest.'

'A young lady?'

'A young lady whom I think you know. Miss Elvira Blake.'

'Do you say someone tried to shoot Elvira with *my* pistol?' He sounded incredulous.

'It could be that you had a disagreement.'

'You mean that I quarrelled with Elvira and shot her? What madness! Why should I shoot the girl I am going to marry?'

'Is that part of your statement? That you are going to marry Miss Elvira Blake?'

Just for a moment or two Ladislaus hesitated. Then he said, shrugging his shoulders,

'She is still very young. It remains to be discussed.'

'Perhaps she had promised to marry you, and then – she changed her mind. There was *someone* she was afraid of. Was it you, Mr Malinowski?'

'Why should *I* want her to die? I am in love with her and want to marry her or if I do not want to marry her I need not marry her. It is as simple as that. So why should I kill her?'

'There aren't many people close enough to her to want to kill her.' Davy waited a moment and then said, almost casually: 'There's her mother, of course.'

'What!' Malinowski sprang up. '*Bess?* Bess kill her own daughter? You are mad! Why should Bess kill Elvira?'

'Possibly because, as next of kin, she might inherit an enormous fortune.'

'Bess? You mean Bess would kill for money? She has plenty of money from her American husband. Enough, anyway.'

'Enough is not the same as a great fortune,' said Father. 'People do do murder for a large fortune, mothers have been known to kill their children, and children have killed their mothers.'

'I tell you, you are mad!'

'You say that you may be going to marry Miss Blake. Perhaps you have already married her? If so, then *you* would be the one to inherit a vast fortune.'

'What more crazy, stupid things can you say! No, I am not married to Elvira. She is a pretty girl. I like her, and she is in love with me. Yes, I admit it. I met her in Italy. We had fun – but that is all. No more, do you understand?'

'Indeed? Just now, Mr Malinowski, you said quite definitely that she was the girl you were going to marry.'

'Oh that.'

'Yes – that. Was it true?'

'I said it because – it sounded more respectable that way. You are so – prudish in this country—'

'That seems to me an unlikely explanation.'

'You do not understand anything at all. The mother and I – we are lovers – I did not wish to say so – so I suggest instead that the daughter and I – we are engaged to be married. That sounds very English and proper.'

'It sounds to me even more far-fetched. You're rather badly in need of money, aren't you, Mr Malinowski?'

'My dear Chief-Inspector, I am always in need of money. It is very sad.'

'And yet a few months ago I understand you were flinging money about in a very carefree way.'

'Ah. I had had a lucky flutter. I am a gambler. I admit it.'

'I find that quite easy to believe. Where did you have this "flutter"?'

'That I do not tell. You can hardly expect it.'

'I don't expect it.'

'Is that all you have to ask me?'

'For the moment, yes. You have identified the pistol as yours. That will be very helpful.'

'I don't understand – I can't conceive—' he broke off and stretched out his hand. 'Give it me please.'

'I'm afraid we'll have to keep it for the present, so I'll write you out a receipt for it.'

He did so and handed it to Malinowski.

The latter went out slamming the door.

'Temperamental chap,' said Father.

'You didn't press him on the matter of the false number plate and Bedhampton?'

'No. I wanted him rattled. But not too badly rattled. We'll give him one thing to worry about at a time— And he *is* worried.'

'The Old Man wanted to see you, sir, as soon as you were through.'

Chief-Inspector Davy nodded and made his way to Sir Ronald's room.

'Ah! Father. Making progress?'

'Yes. Getting along nicely – quite a lot of fish in the net. Small fry mostly. But we're closing in on the big fellows. Everything's in train—'

'Good show, Fred,' said the A.C.

—— 25 ——

Miss Marple got out of her train at Paddington and saw the burly figure of Chief-Inspector Davy standing on the platform waiting for her.

He said, 'Very good of you, Miss Marple,' put his hand under her elbow and piloted her through the barrier to where a car was waiting. The driver opened the door, Miss Marple got in, Chief-Inspector Davy followed her and the car drove off.

'Where are you taking me, Chief-Inspector Davy?'

'To Bertram's Hotel.'

'Dear me, Bertram's Hotel again. Why?'

'The official reply is: because the police think you can assist them in their inquiries.'

'That sounds familiar, but surely rather sinister? So often the prelude to an arrest, is it not?'

'I am not going to arrest you, Miss Marple.' Father smiled. 'You have an alibi.'

Miss Marple digested this in silence. Then she said, 'I see.'

'They drove to Bertram's Hotel in silence. Miss Gorringe looked up from the desk as they entered, but Chief-Inspector Davy piloted Miss Marple straight to the lift.

'Second floor.'

The lift ascended, stopped, and Father led the way along the corridor.

As he opened the door of No. 18 Miss Marple said, 'This is the same room I had when I was staying here before.'

'Yes,' said Father.

Miss Marple sat down in the arm-chair.

'A very comfortable room,' she observed, looking round with a slight sigh.

'They certainly know what comfort is here,' Father agreed.

'You look tired, Chief-Inspector,' said Miss Marple unexpectedly.

'I've had to get around a bit. As a matter of fact I've just got back from Ireland.'

'Indeed. From Ballygowlan?'

'Now how the devil did *you* know about Ballygowlan? I'm sorry – I beg your pardon.'

Miss Marple smiled forgiveness.

'I suppose Michael Gorman happened to tell you he came from there – was that it?'

'No, not exactly,' said Miss Marple.

'Then how, if you'll excuse me asking you, *did* you know?'

'Oh dear,' said Miss Marple, 'it's really very embarrassing. It was just something I – happened to overhear.'

'Oh, I see.'

'I wasn't eavesdropping. It was in a public room – at least technically a public room. Quite frankly, I enjoy listening to people talking. One does. Especially when one is old and doesn't get about very much. I mean, if people are talking near you, you listen.'

'Well, that seems to me quite natural,' said Father.

'Up to a point, yes,' said Miss Marple. 'If people do not choose to lower their voices, one must assume that they are prepared to be overheard. But of course matters may develop. The situation sometimes arises when you realize that though it *is* a public room, other people talking do not realize that there is anyone else in it. And then one has to decide what to do about it. Get up and cough, or just stay quite quiet and hope they won't realize you've been there. Either way is embarrassing.'

Chief-Inspector Davy glanced at his watch.

'Look here,' he said, 'I want to hear more about this – but I've got Canon Pennyfather arriving at any moment. I must go and collect him. You don't mind?'

Miss Marple said she didn't mind. Chief-Inspector Davy left the room.

II

Canon Pennyfather came through the swing doors into the hall of Bertram's Hotel. He frowned slightly, wondering what it was that seemed a little different about Bertram's today. Perhaps it had been painted or done up in some way? He shook his head. That was not it, but there was *something*. It did not occur to him that it was the difference between a six foot seven commissionaire with blue eyes and dark hair and a five foot seven commissionaire with sloping shoulders, freckles and a sandy thatch of hair bulging out under his commissionaire's cap. He just knew something was different. In his usual vague way he wandered up to the desk. Miss Gorringe was there and greeted him.

'Canon Pennyfather. How nice to see you. Have you come to fetch your baggage? It's all ready for you. If you'd only let us know we could have sent it to you to any address you like.'

'Thank you,' said Canon Pennyfather, 'thank you very much. You're always most kind, Miss Gorringe. But as I had to come up to London anyway today I thought I might as well call for it.'

'We were so worried about you,' said Miss Gorringe. 'Being missing, you know. Nobody able to find you. You had a car accident, I hear?'

'Yes,' said Canon Pennyfather. 'Yes. People drive much too fast nowadays. Most dangerous. Not that I can remember much about it. It affected my head. Concussion, the doctor says. Oh well, as one is getting on in life, one's memory—' he shook his head sadly. 'And how are you, Miss Gorringe?'

'Oh, I'm very well,' said Miss Gorringe.

At that moment it struck Canon Pennyfather that Miss Gorringe also was different. He peered at her, trying to analyse where the difference lay. Her hair? That was the same as usual. Perhaps even a little frizzier. Black dress, large locket, cameo brooch. All there as usual. But there was a difference. Was she perhaps a little thinner? Or was it – yes, surely, she looked *worried*. It was not often that Canon Pennyfather noticed whether people looked worried, he was not the kind of man who noticed emotion in the faces of others, but it struck him today, perhaps because Miss Gorringe had so invariably presented exactly the same countenance to guests for so many years.

'You've not been ill, I hope?' he asked solicitously. 'You look a little thinner.'

'Well, we've had a good deal of worry, Canon Pennyfather.'

'Indeed. Indeed. I'm sorry to hear it. Not due to my disappearance, I hope?'

'Oh no,' said Miss Gorringe. 'We were worried, of course, about that, but as soon as we heard that you were all right—' She broke off and said, 'No. No – it's this – well, perhaps you haven't read about it in the papers. Gorman, our outside porter, got killed.'

'Oh yes,' said Canon Pennyfather. 'I remember now. I did see it mentioned in the paper – that you had had a murder here.'

Miss Gorringe shuddered at this blunt mention of the word murder. The shudder went all up her black dress.

'Terrible,' she said, 'terrible. Such a thing has *never* happened at Bertram's. I mean, we're not the sort of hotel where murders happen.'

'No, no, indeed,' said Canon Pennyfather quickly. 'I'm sure you're not. I mean it would never have occurred to me that anything like that could happen *here*.'

'Of course it wasn't *inside* the hotel,' said Miss Gorringe, cheering up a little at this aspect of the affair struck her. 'It was outside in the street.'

'So really nothing to do with you at all,' said the Canon, helpfully.

That apparently was not quite the right thing to say.

'But it was connected with Bertram's. We had to have the police here questioning people, since it was our commissionaire who was shot.'

'So that's a new man you have outside. D'you know, I thought somehow things looked a little strange.'

'Yes, I don't know that he's very satisfactory. I mean, not quite the style we're used to here. But of course we had to get someone quickly.'

'I remember all about it now,' said Canon Pennyfather, assembling some rather dim memories of what he had read in the paper a week ago. 'But I thought it was a *girl* who was shot.'

'You mean Lady Sedgwick's daughter? I expect you remember seeing her here with her guardian, Colonel Luscombe. Apparently she was attacked by someone in the fog. I expect they wanted to snatch her bag. Anyway they fired a shot at her and then Gorman, who of course had been a soldier and was a man with a lot of presence of mind, rushed down, got in front of her and got himself shot, poor fellow.'

'Very sad, very sad,' said the Canon, shaking his head.

'It makes everything terribly difficult,' complained Miss Gorringe. 'I mean, the police constantly in and out. I suppose that's to be expected, but we don't *like* it here, though I must say Chief-Inspector Davy and Sergeant Wadell are very respectable looking. Plain clothes, and very good style, not the sort with boots and macintoshes like one sees on films. Almost like one of *us.*'

'Er – yes,' said Canon Pennyfather.

'Did you have to go to hospital?' inquired Miss Gorringe.

'No,' said the Canon, 'some very nice people, really good Samaritans – a market gardener, I believe – picked me up and his wife nursed me back to health. I'm most grateful, most grateful. It is refreshing to find that there is still human kindness in the world. Don't you think so?'

Miss Gorringe said she thought it was very refreshing. 'After all one reads about the increase in crime,' she added, 'all those dreadful young men and girls holding up banks and robbing trains and ambushing people.' She looked up and said, 'There's Chief-Inspector Davy coming down the stairs now. I think he wants to speak to you.'

'I don't know why he should want to speak to me,' said Canon Pennyfather, puzzled. 'He's already been to see me, you know,' he said, 'At Chadminster. He was very disappointed, I think, that I couldn't tell him anything useful.'

'You couldn't?'

The Canon shook his head sorrowfully.

'I couldn't remember. The accident took place somewhere near a place called Bedhampton and really I don't understand *what* I can have been doing there. The Chief-Inspector kept asking me why I was there and I couldn't tell him. Very odd, isn't it? He seemed to think I'd been driving a car from somewhere near a railway station to a vicarage.'

'That sounds very possible,' said Miss Gorringe.

'It doesn't seem possible at all,' said Canon Pennyfather. 'I mean, why should I be driving about in a part of the world that I don't really know?'

Chief-Inspector Davy had come up to them.

'So here you are, Canon Pennyfather,' he said. 'Feeling quite yourself again?'

'Oh, I feel quite well now,' said the Canon, 'but rather inclined to have headaches still. And I've been told not to do too much. But I still don't seem to remember what I ought to remember and the doctor says it may never come back.'

'Oh well,' said Chief-Inspector Davy, 'we mustn't give up hope.' He led the Canon away from the desk. 'There's a little experiment I want you to try,' he said. 'You don't mind helping me, do you?'

III

When Chief-Inspector Davy opened the door of Number 18 Miss Marple was still sitting in the arm-chair by the window.

'A good many people in the street today,' she observed. 'More than usual.'

'Oh well – this is a way through to Berkeley Square and Shepherd's Market.'

'I didn't mean only passers-by. Men doing things – road repairs, a telephone repair van – a meat trolley – a couple of private cars—'

'And what – may I ask – do you deduce from that?'

'I didn't say that I deduced anything.'

Father gave her a look. Then he said,

'I want you to help me.'

'O course. That is why I am here. What do you want me to do?'

'I want you to do exactly what you did on the night of November 19th. You were asleep – you woke up – possibly awakened by some unusual noise. You switched on the light, looked at the time, got out of bed, opened the door and looked out. Can you repeat those actions?'

'Certainly,' said Miss Marple. She got up and went across to the bed.

'Just a moment.'

Chief-Inspector Davy went and tapped on the connecting walls of the next room.

'You'll have to do that louder,' said Miss Marple. 'This place is very well built.'

The Chief-Inspector redoubled the force of his knuckles.

'I told Canon Pennyfather to count ten,' he said, looking at his watch. 'Now then, off you go.'

Miss Marple touched the electric lamp, looked at an imaginary clock, got up, walked to the door, opened it and looked out. To her right, just leaving his room, walking to the top of the stairs, was Canon Pennyfather. He arrived at the top of the stairs and started down them. Miss Marple gave a slight catch of her breath. She turned back.

'Well?' said Chief-Inspector Davy.

'The man I saw that night can't have been Canon Pennyfather,' said Miss Marple. 'Not if that's Canon Pennyfather now.'

'I thought you said—'

'I know. He looked like Canon Pennyfather. His hair and his clothes and everything. But he didn't walk the same way. I think – I think he must have been a younger man. I'm sorry, very sorry, to have misled you, but it wasn't Canon Pennyfather that I saw that night. I'm quite sure of it.'

'You really are quite sure this time, Miss Marple.'

'Yes,' said Miss Marple. 'I'm sorry,' she added again, 'to have misled you.'

'You were very nearly right. Canon Pennyfather did come back to the hotel that night. Nobody saw him come in – but that wasn't remarkable. He came in after midnight. He came up the stairs, he opened the door of his room next door and he went in. What he saw or what happened next we don't know, because he can't or won't tell us. If there was only some way we could jog his memory . . .'

'There's that German word of course,' said Miss Marple, thoughtfully.

'What German word?'

'Dear me, I've forgotten it now, but—'

There was a knock at the door.

'May I come in?' said Canon Pennyfather. He entered. 'Was it satisfactory?'

'Most satisfactory,' said Father. 'I was just telling Miss Marple – you know Miss Marple?'

'Oh yes,' said Canon Pennyfather, really slightly uncertain as to whether he did or not.

'I was just telling Miss Marple how we have traced your movements. You came back to the hotel that night after midnight. You came upstairs and you opened the door of your room and went in—' He paused.

Miss Marple gave an exclamation.

'I remember now,' she said, 'what that German word is. *Doppelganger!*'

Canon Pennyfather uttered an exclamation. 'But of course,' he said, '*of course!* How could I have forgotten? You're quite right, you know. After that film, *The Walls of Jericho* I came back here and I came upstairs and I opened my room and I saw – extraordinary, I distinctly saw *myself* sitting in a chair facing me. As you say, dear lady, a *doppelganger*. How very remarkable! And then – let me see—' He raised his eyes, trying to think.

'And then,' said Father, 'startled out of their lives to see you, when they thought you were safely in Lucerne, somebody hit you on the head.'

—— 26 ——

Canon Pennyfather had been sent on his way in a taxi to the British Museum. Miss Marple had been ensconced in the lounge by the Chief-Inspector. Would she mind waiting for him there for about ten minutes? Miss Marple had not minded. She welcomed the opportunity to sit and look around her and think.

Bertram's Hotel. So many memories . . . The past fused itself with the present. A French phrase came back to her, *Plus ça change, plus c'est la même chose.* She reversed the wording. *Plus c'est la même chose, plus ça change.* Both true, she thought.

She felt sad – for Bertram's Hotel and for herself. She wondered what Chief-Inspector Davy wanted of her next. She sensed in him the excitement of purpose. He was a man whose plans were at last coming to fruition. It was Chief-Inspector Davy's D-Day.

The life of Bertram's went on as usual. No, Miss Marple decided, *not* as usual. There was a difference, though she could not have defined where the difference lay. An underlying uneasiness, perhaps?

The doors swung open once more and this time the big

bovine-looking countryman came through them and across to where Miss Marple sat.

'All set?' he inquired genially.

'Where are you taking me now?'

'We're going to pay a call on Lady Sedgwick.'

'Is she staying here?'

'Yes. With her daughter.'

Miss Marple rose to her feet. She cast a glance round her and murmured: 'Poor Bertram's.'

'What do you mean – poor Bertram's?'

'I think you know quite well what I mean.'

'Well – looking at it from your point of view, perhaps I do.'

'It is always sad when a work of art has to be destroyed.'

'You call this place a work of art?'

'Certainly I do. So do you.'

'I see what you mean,' admitted Father.

'It is like when you get ground elder really badly in a border. There's nothing else you can do about it – except dig the whole thing up.'

'I don't know much about gardens. But change the metaphor to dry rot and I'd agree.'

They went up in the lift and along a passage to where Lady Sedgwick and her daughter had a corner suite.

Chief-Inspector Davy knocked on the door, a voice said Come in, and he entered with Miss Marple behind him.

Bess Sedgwick was sitting in a high-backed chair near the window. She had a book on her knee which she was not reading.

'So it's you again, Chief-Inspector.' Her eyes went past him towards Miss Marple and she looked slightly surprised.

'This is Miss Marple,' explained Chief-Inspector Davy. 'Miss Marple – Lady Sedgwick.'

'I've met you before,' said Bess Sedgwick. 'Yo were with Selina Hazy the other day, weren't you? Do sit down,' she added. Then she turned towards Chief-Inspector Davy again. 'Have you any news of the man who shot at Elvira?'

'Not actually what you'd call *news*.'

'I doubt if you ever will have. In a fog like that, predatory creatures come out and prowl around looking for women walking alone.'

'True up to a point,' said Father. 'How is your daughter?'

'Oh, Elvira is quite all right again.'

'You've got her here with you?'

'Yes. I rang up Colonel Luscombe – her guardian. He was

delighted that I was willing to take charge.' She gave a sudden laugh. 'Dear old boy. He's always been urging a mother-and-daughter reunion act!'

'He may be right at that,' said Father.

'Oh no, he isn't. Just at the moment, yes, I think it is the best thing.' She turned her head to look out of the window and spoke in a changed voice. 'I hear you've arrested a friend of mine – Ladislaus Malinowski. On what charge?'

'Not *arrested*,' Chief-Inspector Davy corrected her. 'He's just assisting us with our inquiries.'

'I've sent my solicitor to look after him.'

'Very wise,' said Father approvingly. 'Anyone who's having a little difficulty with the police is very wise to have a solicitor. Otherwise they may so easily say the wrong thing.'

'Even if completely innocent?'

'Possibly it's even more necessary in that case,' said Father.

'You're quite a cynic, aren't you? What are you questioning him about, may I ask? Or mayn't I?'

'For one thing we'd like to know just exactly what his movements were on the night when Michael Gorman died.'

Bess Sedgwick sat up sharply in her chair.

'Have you got some ridiculous idea that *Ladislaus* fired those shots at Elvira? They didn't even know each other.'

'He could have done it. His car was just round the corner.'

'Rubbish,' said Lady Sedgwick robustly.

'How much did that shooting business the other night upset you, Lady Sedgwick?'

She looked faintly surprised.

'Naturally I was upset when my daughter had a narrow escape of her life. What do you expect?'

'I didn't mean that. I mean how much did the death of Michael Gorman upset you?'

'I was very sorry about it. He was a brave man.'

'Is that all?'

'What more would you expect me to say?'

'You knew him, didn't you?'

'Of course. He worked here.'

'You knew him a little better than that, though, didn't you?'

'What do you mean?'

'Come, Lady Sedgwick. He was your husband, wasn't he?'

She did not answer for a moment or two, though she displayed no signs of agitation or surprise.

'You know a good deal, don't you, Chief-Inspector?' She

sighed and sat back in her chair. 'I hadn't seen him for – let me see – a great many years. Twenty – more than twenty. And then I looked out of a window one day, and suddenly recognised Micky.'

'And he recognised you?'

'Quite surprising that we did recognise each other,' said Bess Sedgwick. 'We were only together for about a week. Then my family caught up with us, paid Micky off, and took me home in disgrace.'

She sighed.

'I was very young when I ran away with him. I knew very little. Just a fool of a girl with a head full of romantic notions. He was a hero to me, mainly because of the way he rode a horse. He didn't know what fear was. And he was handsome and gay with an Irishman's tongue! I suppose really *I* ran away with *him*! I doubt if he'd have thought of it himself! But I was wild and headstrong and madly in love!' She shook her head. 'It didn't last long . . . The first twenty-four hours were enough to disillusion me. He drank and he was coarse and brutal. When my family turned up and took me back with them, I was thankful. I never wanted to see him or hear of him again.'

'Did your family know that you were married to him?'

'No.'

'You didn't tell them?'

'I didn't think I *was* married.'

'How did that come about?'

'We were married in Ballygowlan, but when my people turned up, Micky came to me and told me the marriage had been a fake. He and his friends had cooked it up between them, he said. By that time it seemed to me quite a natural thing for him to have done. Whether he wanted the money that was being offered to him, or whether he was afraid he'd committed a breach of the law by marrying me when I wasn't of age, I don't know. Anyway, I didn't doubt for a moment that what he said was true – not then.'

'And later?'

She seemed lost in her thoughts. 'It wasn't until – oh, quite a number of years afterwards, when I knew a little more of life, and of legal matters, that it suddenly occurred to me that probably I was married to Micky Gorman after all!'

'In actual fact, then, when you married Lord Coniston, you committed bigamy.'

'And when I married Johnnie Sedgwick, and again when I

married my American husband, Ridgeway Becker.' She looked at Chief-Inspector Davy and laughed with what seemed like genuine amusement.

'So much bigamy,' she said. 'It really does seem very ridiculous.'

'Did you never think of getting a divorce?'

She shrugged her shoulders. 'It all seemed like a silly dream. Why rake it up? I'd told Johnnie, of course.' Her voice softened and mellowed as she said his name.

'And what did he say?'

'He didn't care. Neither Johnnie nor I were ever very law-abiding.'

'Bigamy carries certain penalties, Lady Sedgwick.'

She looked at him and laughed.

'Who was ever going to worry about something that had happened in Ireland years ago? The whole thing was over and done with. Micky had taken his money and gone off. Oh don't you understand? It seemed just a silly little incident. An incident I wanted to forget. I put it aside with the things – the very many things – that don't matter in life.'

'And then,' said Father, in a tranquil voice, 'one day in November, Michael Gorman turned up again and blackmailed you?'

'Nonsense! Who said he blackmailed me?'

Slowly Father's eyes went round to the old lady sitting quietly, very upright, in her chair.

'You.' Bess Sedgwick stared at Miss Marple. 'What can *you* know about it?'

Her voice was more curious than accusing.

'The arm-chairs in this hotel have very high backs,' said Miss Marple. 'Very comfortable they are. I was sitting in one in front of the fire in the writing-room. Just resting before I went out one morning. You came in to write a letter. I suppose you didn't realize there was anyone else in the room. And so – I heard your conversation with this man Gorman.'

'You listened?'

'Naturally,' said Miss Marple. Why not? It was a public room. When you threw up the window and called to the man outside, I had no idea that it was going to be a private conversation.'

Bess stared at her for a moment, then she nodded her head slowly.

'Fair enough,' she said. 'Yes, I see. But all the same you misunderstood what you heard. Micky didn't blackmail me. He might have thought of it – but I warned him off before he could try!' Her lips curled up again in that wide generous smile that made her face so attractive. 'I frightened him off.'

'Yes,' agreed Miss Marple. 'I think you probably did. You threatened to shoot him. You handled it – if you won't think it impertinent of me to say so – very well indeed.'

Bess Sedgwick's eyebrows rose in some amusement.

'But I wasn't the only person to hear you,' Miss Marple went on.

'Good gracious! Was the whole hotel listening?'

'The other arm-chair was also occupied.'

'By whom?'

Miss Marple closed her lips. She looked at Chief-Inspector Davy, and it was almost a pleading glance. 'If it *must* be done, *you* do it,' the glance said, 'but I can't . . .'

'Your daughter was in the other chair,' said Chief-Inspector Davy.

'Oh, no!' The cry came out sharply. 'Oh, *no*. Not Elvira! I see – yes, I see. She must have thought—'

'She thought seriously enough of what she had overheard to go to Ireland and search for the truth. It wasn't difficult to discover.'

Again Bess Sedgwick said softly: 'Oh no . . .' And then: 'Poor child! . . . Even now, she's never asked me a thing. She's kept it all to herself. Bottled it up inside herself. If she'd only told me I could have explained it all to her – showed her how it didn't matter.'

'She mightn't have agreed with you there,' said Chief-Inspector Davy. 'It's a funny thing, you know,' he went on, in a reminiscent, almost gossipy manner, looking like an old farmer discussing his stock and his land, 'I've learnt after a great many years' trial and error – I've learnt to distrust a pattern when it's simple. Simple patterns are often too good to be true. The pattern of this murder the other night was like that. Girl says someone shot at her and missed. The commissionaire came running to save her, and copped it with a second bullet. That may be all true enough. That may be the way the girl saw it. But actually behind the appearances, things might be rather different.

'You said pretty vehemently just now, Lady Sedgwick, that there could be no reason for Ladislaus Malinowski to attempt your daughter's life. Well, I'll agree with you. I don' think there was. He's the sort of young man who might have a row with a woman, pull out a knife and stick it into her. But I don't think he'd hide in an area, and wait cold-bloodedly to shoot her. But supposing he wanted to shoot *someone else*. Screams and shots – but what actually has happened is that *Michael Gorman* is dead. Suppose that was actually what was *meant* to happen. Malinowski plans it very carefully He chooses a foggy night, hides in the area and waits until your daughter comes up the street. He knows she's coming because he has managed to arrange it that way. He fires a shot. It's not meant to hit the girl. He's careful not to let the bullet go anywhere near her, but *she* thinks it's aimed at her all right. She screams. The porter from the hotel, hearing the shot and the scream, comes rushing down the street *and then Malinowski shoots the person he's come to shoot. Michael Gorman.'*

'I don't believe a word of it! Why on earth should Ladislaus want to shoot Micky Gorman?'

'A little matter of blackmail, perhaps,' said Father.

'Do you mean that Micky was blackmailing *Ladislaus*? What about?'

'Perhaps,' said Father, about the things that go on at Bertram's Hotel. Michael Gorman might have found out quite a lot about that.'

'Things that go on at Bertram's Hotel? What *do* you mean?'

'It's been a good racket,' said Father. 'Well planned, beautifully executed. But nothing lasts for ever. Miss Marple here asked me the other day what was wrong with this place. Well, I'll answer that question now. Bertram's Hotel is to all intents and purposes the headquarters of one of the best and biggest crime syndicates that's been known for years.'

—— 27 ——

There was silence for about a minute and a half. Then Miss Marple spoke.

'How *very* interesting,' she said conversationally.

Bess Sedgwick turned on her. 'You don't seem surprised, Miss Marple.'

'I'm not. Not really. There were so many curious things that didn't seem quite to fit in. It was all too good to be true – if you know what I mean. What they call in theatrical circles, a beautiful performance. But it *was* a performance – not real.

'And there were a lot of little things, people claiming a friend or an acquaintance – and turning out to be wrong.'

'These things happen,' said Chief-Inspector Davy, 'but they happened too often. Is that right, Miss Marple?'

'Yes,' agreed Miss Marple. 'People like Selina Hazy do make that kind of mistake. But there were so many other people doing it too. One couldn't help *noticing* it.'

'She notices a lot,' said Chief-Inspector Davy, speaking to Bess Sedgwick as though Miss Marple was his pet performing dog.

Bess Sedgwick turned on him sharply.

'What did you mean when you said this place was the head-quarters of a Crime Syndicate? I should have said that Bertram's Hotel was the most respectable place in the world.'

'Naturally,' said Father. 'It would have to be. A lot of money, time, and thought has been spent on making it just what it is. The genuine and the phony are mixed up very cleverly. You've got a superb actor manager running the show in Henry. You've got that chap, Humfries, wonderfully plausible. He hasn't got a record in this country but he's been mixed up in some rather curious hotel dealings abroad. There are some very good character actors playing various parts here. I'll admit, if you like, that I can't help feeling a good deal of admiration for the whole set-up. It has cost this country a mint of money. It's given the CID and the provincial police force constant headaches. Every time we seemed to be getting somewhere, and put our finger on some particular incident – it turned out to be the kind of incident that had nothing to do with anything else. But we've gone on working on it, a piece there, a piece here. A garage where stacks of number plates were kept, transferable at a moment's notice to certain cars. A firm of furniture vans, a butcher's van, a grocer's van, even one or two phony postal vans. A racing driver with a racing car covering incredible distances in incredibly few minutes, and at the other end of the scale an old clergyman jogging along in his old Morris Oxford. A cottage with a market gardener in it who lends first aid if necessary and who is in touch with a useful doctor. I needn't go into it all. The ramifications seem unending. That's one half of it. The foreign visitors who come to Bertram's are the other half. Mostly from America, or from the Dominions. Rich people above suspicion, coming here with a lot of luxury luggage, leaving here with a good lot of luxury baggage which looks the same but isn't. Rich tourists arriving in France and not worried unduly by the Customs because the customs don't worry tourists when they're bringing money into the country. Not the same tourists too many times. The pitcher mustn't go to the well too often. None of it's going to be easy to prove or to tie up, but it will all tie up in the end. We've made a beginning. The Cabots, for instance—'

'What about the Cabots?' asked Bess sharply.

'You remember them? Very nice Americans. Very nice indeed. They stayed here last year and they've been here again this year. They wouldn't have come a third time. Nobody ever comes here more than twice on the same racket. Yes, we arrested them when they arrived at Calais. Very well made job, that wardrobe case they had with them. It had over three hundred thousand pounds neatly stashed. Proceeds of the Bedhampton train robbery. Of course, that's only a drop in the ocean.

'Bertram's Hotel, let me tell you, is the headquarters of the whole thing! Half the staff are in on it. Some of the guests are in on it. Some of the guests are who they say they are – some are not. The real Cabots, for instance, are in Yucatan just now. Then there was the identification racket. Take Mr Justice Ludgrove. A familiar face, bulbous nose and a wart. Quite easy to impersonate. Canon Pennyfather. A mild country clergyman, with a great white thatch of hair and notable absent-minded behaviour. His mannerisms, his way of peering over his spectacles – all very easily imitated by a good character actor.'

'But what was the use of all that?' asked Bess.

'Are you really asking me? Isn't it obvious? Mr Justice Ludgrove is seen near the scene of a bank hold-up. Someone recognises him, mentions it. We go into it. It's all a mistake. He was somewhere else at the time. But it wasn't for a while that we realized that these were all what is sometimes called "deliberate mistakes". Nobody's bothered about the man who had looked so like him. And doesn't look particularly like him really. He takes off his make-up and stops acting his part. The whole thing brings about confusion. At one time we had a High Court judge, an Archdeacon, an Admiral, a Major-General, all seen near the scene of a crime.

'After the Bedhampton train robbery at least four vehicles were concerned before the loot arrived in London. A racing car driven by Malinowski took part in it, a false Metal Box lorry, an old-fashioned Daimler with an admiral in it, and an old clergyman with a thatch of white hair in a Morris Oxford. The whole thing was a splendid operation, beautifully planned.

'And then one day the gang had a bit of bad luck. That muddle-headed old ecclesiastic, Canon Pennyfather, went off to catch his plane on the wrong day, they turned him away from the air station, he wandered out into Cromwell Road, went to a film, arrived back here after midnight, came up to his room of which he had the key in his pocket, opened the door, and walked in to get the shock of his life when he saw what appeared to be *himself* sitting in a chair facing him! The last thing the gang expected was to see the real Canon Pennyfather, supposed to be safely in Lucerne, walk in! His double was just getting ready to start off to play his part at Bedhampton when in walked the real man. They didn't know what to do but there was a quick reflex action from one member of the party. Humfries, I suspect. He hit the old man on the head, and he went down unconscious. Somebody, I think, was angry over that. Very angry. However, they examined the old boy, decided he was only knocked out, and would probably come round later and they went on with their plans. The false Canon Pennyfather left his room, went out of the hotel, and drove to the scene of activities where he was to play his part in the relay race. What they did with the real Canon Pennyfather I don't know. I can only guess. I presume he too was moved later that night, driven down in a car, taken to the market gardener's cottage which was at a spot not too far from where the train was to be held up and where a doctor could attend to him. Then, if reports came through about Canon Pennyfather having been seen in that neighbourhood, it would all fit in. It must have been an anxious moment for all concerned until he regained consciousness and they found that at least three days had been knocked out of his remembrance.'

'Would they have killed him otherwise?' asked Miss Marple.

'No,' said Father. 'I don't think they would have killed him. Someone wouldn't have let that happen. It has seemed very clear all along that whoever ran this show had an objection to murder.'

'It sounds fantastic,' said Bess Sedgwick. 'Utterly fantastic! And I don't believe you have any evidence whatever to link Ladislaus Malinowski with this rigmarole.'

'I've got plenty of evidence against Ladislaus Malinowski,' said Father. 'He's careless, you know. He hung around here when he shouldn't have. On the first occasion he came to establish connection with your daughter. They had a code arranged.'

'Nonsense. She told you herself that she didn't know him.'

'She may have told me that but it wasn't true. She's in love with him. She wants the fellow to marry her.'

'I don't believe it!'

'You're not in a position to know,' Chief-Inspector Davy pointed out. 'Malinowski isn't the sort of person who tells all his secrets and your daughter you don't know at all. You admitted as much. You were angry, weren't you, when you found out Malinowski had come to Bertram's Hotel.'

'Why should I be angry?'

'*Because you're the brains of the show,*' said Father. 'You and Henry. The financial side was run by the Hoffman brothers. They made all the arrangements with the continental banks and accounts and that sort of thing, but the boss of the syndicate, the brains that run it, and plan it, are your brains, Lady Sedgwick.'

Bess looked at him and laughed. 'I never heard anything so ridiculous!' she said.

'Oh no, it's not ridiculous at all. You've got brains, courage and daring. You've tried most things; you thought you'd turn your hand to crime. Plenty of excitement in it, plenty of risk. It wasn't the money that attracted you, I'd say, it was the fun of the whole thing. But you wouldn't stand for murder, or for undue violence. There were no killings, no brutal assaults, only nice quiet scientific taps on the head if necessary. You're a very interesting woman, you know. One of the few really interesting great criminals.'

There was silence for some minutes. Then Bess Sedgwick rose to her feet.

'I think you must be mad.' She put her hand out to the telephone.

'Going to ring up your solicitor? Quite the right thing to do before you say too much.'

With a sharp gesture she slammed the receiver back on the hook.

'On second thoughts I hate solicitors . . . All right. Have it your own way. Yes, I ran this show. You're quite correct when you say it was fun. I loved every minute of it. It was fun scooping money from banks, trains and post offices and so-called security vans! It was fun planning and deciding; glorious fun and I'm glad I had it. The pitcher goes to the well once too often? That's what you said just now, wasn't it? I suppose it's true. Well, I've had a good run for my money! But you're wrong about Ladislaus Malinowski shooting Michael Gorman! He didn't. *I* did.' She laughed a sudden high, excited laugh. 'Never mind what it was he did, what he threatened . . . I told him I'd shoot him – Miss Marple heard me – and I *did* shoot him. I did very much what you suggested Ladislaus did. I hid in that area. When

Elvira passed, I fired one shot wild, and when she screamed and Micky came running down the street, I'd got him where I wanted him, and I let him have it! I've got keys to all the hotel entrances, of course. I just slipped in through the area door and up to my room. It never occurred to me you'd trace the pistol to Ladislaus – or would even suspect him. I'd pinched it from his car without his knowledge. But not, I can assure you, with any idea of throwing suspicion on *him*.'

She swept round on Miss Marple. 'You're a witness to what I've said, remember. *I killed Gorman.*'

'Or perhaps you are saying so because you're in love with Malinowski,' suggested Davy.

'I'm not.' Her retort came sharply. 'I'm his good friend, that's all. Oh yes, we've been lovers in a casual kind of way, but I'm not in love with him. In all my life, I've only loved one person – John Sedgwick.' Her voice changed and softened as she pronounced the name.

'But Ladislaus is my friend. I don't want him railroaded for something he didn't do. *I killed Michael Gorman.* I've said so, and Miss Marple has heard me . . . And now, dear Chief-Inspector Davy—' Her voice rose excitedly, and her laughter rang out – '*Catch me if you can.*'

With a sweep of her arm, she smashed the window with the heavy telephone set, and before Father could get to his feet, she was out of the window and edging her way rapidly along the narrow parapet. With surprising quickness in spite of his bulk, Davy had moved to the other window and flung up the sash. At the same time he blew the whistle he had taken from his pocket.

Miss Marple, getting to her feet with rather more difficulty a moment or two later, joined him. Together they stared out along the façade of Bertram's Hotel.

'She'll fall. She's climbing up a drainpipe,' Miss Marple exclaimed. 'But why *up*?'

'Going to the roof. It's her only chance and she knows it. Good God, look at her. Climbs like a cat. She looks like a fly on the side of the wall. The risks she's taking!'

Miss Marple murmured, her eyes half closing, 'She'll fall. She can't do it . . .'

The woman they were watching disappeared from sight. Father drew back a little into the room.

Miss Marple asked,

'Don't you want to go and—?'

Father shook his head. 'What good am I with my bulk? I've

got my men posted ready for something like this. They know what to do. In a few minutes we shall know . . . I wouldn't put it past her to beat the lot of them! She's a woman in a thousand, you know.' He sighed. 'One of the wild ones. Oh, we've some of them in every generation. You can't tame them, you can't bring them into the community and make them live in law and order. They go their own way. If they're saints they go and tend lepers or something, or get themselves martyred in jungles. If they're bad lots they commit the atrocities that you don't like hearing about. And sometimes – they're just wild! They'd have been all right, I suppose, born in another age when it was everyone's hand for himself, everyone fighting to keep life in their veins. Hazards at every turn, danger all round them, and they themselves perforce dangerous to others. That world would have suited them; they'd have been at home in it. This one doesn't.'

'Did you know what she was going to do?'

'Not really. That's one of her gifts. The unexpected. She must have thought this out, you know. She knew what was coming. So she sat looking at us – keeping the ball rolling – and thinking. Thinking and planning hard. I expect – ah—' He broke off as there came the sudden roar of a car's exhaust, the screaming of wheels, and the sound of a big racing engine. He leaned out. 'She's made it, she's got to her car.'

There was more screaming as the car came round the corner on two wheels, a great roar, and the beautiful white monster came tearing up the street.

'She'll kill someone,' said Father, 'she'll kill a lot of people . . . even if she doesn't kill herself.'

'I wonder,' said Miss Marple.

'She's a good driver, of course. A damn' good driver. Whoof, that was a near one!'

They heard the roar of the car racing away with the horn blaring, heard it grow fainter. Heard cries, shouts, the sound of brakes, cars hooting and pulling up and finally a great scream of tyres and a roaring exhaust and—

'She's crashed,' said Father.

He stood there very quietly waiting with the patience that was characteristic of his whole big patient form. Miss Marple stood silent beside him. Then, like a relay race, word came down along the street. A man on the pavement opposite looked up at Chief-Inspector Davy and made rapid signs with his hands.

'She's had it,' said Father heavily. 'Dead!' Went about ninety miles an hour into the park railings. No other casualties bar a few slight collisions. Magnificent driving. Yes, she's dead.' He turned back into the room and said heavily, 'Well, she told her story first. You heard her.'

'Yes,' said Miss Marple. 'I heard her.' There was a pause. 'It wasn't true, of course,' said Miss Marple quietly.

Father looked at her. 'You didn't believe her, eh?'

'Did you?'

'No,' said Father. 'No, it wasn't the right story. She thought it out so that it would meet the case exactly, but it wasn't true. She didn't shoot Michael Gorman. D'you happen to know who did?'

'Of course I know,' said Miss Marple. 'The girl.'

'Ah! When did you begin to think that?'

'I always wondered,' said Miss Marple.

'So did I,' said Father. 'She was full of fear that night. And the lies she told were poor lies. But I couldn't see a motive at first.'

'That puzzled me,' said Miss Marple. 'She had found out her mother's marriage was bigamous, but would a girl do murder for that? Not nowadays! I suppose – there was a money side to it?'

'Yes, it was money,' said Chief-Inspector Davy. 'Her father left her a colossal fortune. When she found out that her mother was married to Michael Gorman she realized that the marriage to Coniston hadn't been legal. She thought that meant that the money wouldn't come to her because, though she was his daughter, she wasn't legitimate. She was wrong, you know. We had a case something like that before. Depends on the terms of a will. Coniston left it quite clearly to her, naming her by name. She'd get it all right, but she didn't know that. And she wasn't going to let go of the cash.'

'Why did she need it so badly?'

Chief-Inspector Davy said grimly, 'To buy Ladislaus Malinowski. He would have married her for her money. He wouldn't have married her without it. She wasn't a fool, that girl. She knew that. But she wanted him on any terms. She was desperately in love with him.'

'I know,' said Miss Marple. She explained: 'I saw her face that day in Battersea Park . . .'

'She knew that with the money she'd get him, and without the money she'd lose him,' said Father. 'And so she planned a cold-blooded murder. She didn't hide in the area, of course. There was nobody in the area. She just stood by the railings and fired a shot and screamed, and when Michael Gorman came racing down the street from the hotel, she shot him at close quarters. Then she went on screaming. She was a cool hand. She'd no idea of incriminating young Ladislaus. She pinched his pistol because it was the only way she could get hold of one easily; and she never dreamed that he would be suspected of the crime, or that he would be anywhere in the neighbourhood that night. She thought it would be put down to some thug taking advantage of the fog. Yes, she was a cool hand. But she was afraid that night – afterwards! And her mother was afraid for her . . .'

'And now – what will you do?'

'I know she did it,' said Father, 'but I've no evidence. Maybe she'll have beginner's luck . . . Even the law seems to go on the principle now of allowing a dog to have one bite – translated into human terms. An experienced counsel could make great play with the sob stuff – so young a girl, unfortunate upbringing – and she's beautiful, you know.'

'Yes,' said Miss Marple. 'The children of Lucifer are often beautiful— And as we know, they flourish like the green bay tree.'

'But, as I tell you, it probably won't even come to that – there's no evidence – take yourself – you'll be called as a witness – a witness to what her mother said – to her mother's confession of the crime.'

'I know,' said Miss Marple. 'She impressed it on me, didn't she? She chose death for herself, at the price of her daughter going free. She forced it on me as a dying request . . .'

The connecting door to the bedroom opened. Elvira Blake came through. She was wearing a straight shift dress of pale blue. Her fair hair fell down each side of her face. She looked from one to the other of them. She said,

'I heard a car and a crash and people shouting . . . Has there been an accident?'

'I'm sorry to tell you, Miss Blake,' said Chief-Inspector Davy formally, 'that your mother is dead.'

Elvira gave a little gasp. 'Oh no,' she said. It was a faint uncertain protest.

'Before she made her escape,' said Chief-Inspector Davy, 'because it *was* an escape – she confessed to the murder of Michael Gorman.'

'You mean – she said – that it was *she—*'

'Yes,' said Father. 'That is what she *said*. Have you anything to add?'

Elvira looked for a long time at him. Very fainly she shook her head.

'No,' she said, 'I haven't anything to add.'

Then she turned and went out of the room.

'Well,' said Miss Marple. 'Are you going to let her get away with it?'

There was a pause, then Father brought down his fist with a crash on the table.

'No,' he roared— 'No, by God I'm not!'

Miss Marple nodded her head slowly and gravely.

'May God have mercy on her soul,' she said.